Masterpieces of Murder

MASTERPIECES OF MURDER

including

The Murder of Roger Ackroyd

And Then There Were None

Witness for the Prosecution

Death on the Nile

By AGATHA CHRISTIE

DODD, MEAD & COMPANY · NEW YORK

THE MURDER OF ROGER ACKROYD
Copyright, 1926, by Dodd, Mead & Company, Inc.
Copyright renewed, 1954, by Agatha Christie Mallowan

AND THEN THERE WERE NONE
Copyright, 1939, 1940, by Agatha Christie Mallowan
Copyright renewed, 1969, by Agatha Christie Mallowan

WITNESS FOR THE PROSECUTION
Copyright, 1924, by Agatha Christie
Copyright renewed, 1952, by Agatha Christie Mallowan

DEATH ON THE NILE
Copyright, 1937, by Agatha Christie Mallowan
Copyright renewed, 1969, by Agatha Christie Mallowan

Printed in the United States of America

Library of Congress Cataloging in Publication Data

Christie, Agatha Miller, Dame, 1891–1976.
    MASTERPIECES OF MURDER.

    CONTENTS: THE MURDER OF ROGER ACKROYD.
—AND THEN THERE WERE NONE.—WITNESS FOR
THE PROSECUTION.—DEATH ON THE NILE.
    1. Detective and mystery stories, English.
I. Title.
  PZ3.C4637Mas4 [PR6005.H66]   823'.9'12 76-44421
  ISBN 0-396-07412-X

Contents

The Murder of
Roger Ackroyd

CHAPTER 1

MRS. FERRARS died on the night of the 16th-17th September—a Thursday. I was sent for at eight o'clock on the morning of Friday the 17th. There was nothing to be done. She had been dead some hours.

It was just a few minutes after nine when I reached home once more. I opened the front door with my latchkey, and purposely delayed a few moments in the hall, hanging up my hat and the light overcoat that I had deemed a wise precaution against the chill of an early autumn morning. To tell the truth, I was considerably upset and worried. I am not going to pretend that at that moment I foresaw the events of the next few weeks. I emphatically did not do so. But my instinct told me that there were stirring times ahead.

From the dining-room on my left there came the rattle of tea-cups and the short, dry cough of my sister Caroline.

"Is that you, James?" she called.

An unnecessary question, since who else could it be? To tell the truth, it was precisely my sister Caroline who was the cause of my few minutes' delay. The motto of the mongoose family, so Mr. Kipling tells us, is: "Go and find out." If Caroline ever adopts a crest, I should certainly suggest a mongoose rampant. One might omit the first part of the motto. Caroline can do any amount of finding out by sitting placidly at home. I don't know how she manages it, but there it is. I suspect that the servants and the tradesmen constitute her Intelligence Corps. When she goes out, it is not to gather in information, but to spread it. At that, too, she is amazingly expert.

It was really this last named trait of hers which was causing me these pangs of indecision. Whatever I told Caroline now concerning the demise of Mrs. Ferrars would be common knowledge all over the village within the space of an hour and a half. As a professional man,

I naturally aim at discretion. Therefore I have got into the habit of continually withholding all information possible from my sister. She usually finds out just the same, but I have the moral satisfaction of knowing that I am in no way to blame.

Mrs. Ferrars's husband died just over a year ago, and Caroline has constantly asserted, without the least foundation for the assertion, that his wife poisoned him.

She scorns my invariable rejoinder that Mr. Ferrars died of acute gastritis, helped on by habitual over-indulgence in alcoholic beverages. The symptoms of gastritis and arsenical poisoning are not, I agree, unlike, but Caroline bases her accusation on quite different lines.

"You've only got to look at her," I have heard her say.

Mrs. Ferrars, though not in her first youth, was a very attractive woman, and her clothes, though simple, always seemed to fit her very well, but all the same, lots of women buy their clothes in Paris and have not, on that account, necessarily poisoned their husbands.

As I stood hesitating in the hall, with all this passing through my mind, Caroline's voice came again, with a sharper note in it.

"What on earth are you doing out there, James? Why don't you come and get your breakfast?"

"Just coming, my dear," I said hastily. "I've been hanging up my overcoat."

"You could have hung up half a dozen overcoats in this time."

She was quite right. I could have.

I walked into the dining-room, gave Caroline the accustomed peck on the cheek, and sat down to eggs and bacon. The bacon was rather cold.

"You've had an early call," remarked Caroline.

"Yes," I said. "King's Paddock. Mrs. Ferrars."

"I know," said my sister.

"How did you know?"

"Annie told me."

Annie is the house parlormaid. A nice girl, but an inveterate talker.

There was a pause. I continued to eat eggs and bacon. My sister's nose, which is long and thin, quivered a little at the tip, as it always does when she is interested or excited over anything.

"Well?" she demanded.

"A bad business. Nothing to be done. Must have died in her sleep."

"I know," said my sister again.

This time I was annoyed.

"You can't know," I snapped. "I didn't know myself until I got there, and I haven't mentioned it to a soul yet. If that girl Annie knows, she must be a clairvoyant."

"It wasn't Annie who told me. It was the milkman. He had it from the Ferrars' cook."

As I say, there is no need for Caroline to go out to get information. She sits at home, and it comes to her.

My sister continued:

"What did she die of? Heart failure?"

"Didn't the milkman tell you that?" I inquired sarcastically.

Sarcasm is wasted on Caroline. She takes it seriously and answers accordingly.

"He didn't know," she explained.

After all, Caroline was bound to hear sooner or later. She might as well hear from me.

"She died of an overdose of veronal. She's been taking it lately for sleeplessness. Must have taken too much."

"Nonsense," said Caroline immediately. "She took it on purpose. Don't tell me!"

It is odd how, when you have a secret belief of your own which you do not wish to acknowledge, the voicing of it by some one else will rouse you to a fury of denial. I burst immediately into indignant speech.

"There you go again," I said. "Rushing along without rhyme or reason. Why on earth should Mrs. Ferrars wish to commit suicide? A widow, fairly young still, very well off, good health, and nothing to do but enjoy life. It's absurd."

"Not at all. Even you must have noticed how different she has been looking lately. It's been coming on for the last six months. She's looked positively hag-ridden. And you have just admitted that she hasn't been able to sleep."

"What is your diagnosis?" I demanded coldly. "An unfortunate love affair, I suppose?"

My sister shook her head.

"*Remorse,*" she said, with great gusto.

"Remorse?"

"Yes. You never would believe me when I told you she poisoned her husband. I'm more than ever convinced of it now."

"I don't think you're very logical," I objected. "Surely if a woman committed a crime like murder, she'd be sufficiently cold-blooded to enjoy the fruits of it without any weak-minded sentimentality such as repentance."

Caroline shook her head.

"There probably are women like that—but Mrs. Ferrars wasn't one of them. She was a mass of nerves. An overmastering impulse drove her on to get rid of her husband because she was the sort of person who simply can't endure suffering of any kind, and there's no doubt that the wife of a man like Ashley Ferrars must have had to suffer a good deal——"

I nodded.

"And ever since she's been haunted by what she did. I can't help feeling sorry for her."

I don't think Caroline ever felt sorry for Mrs. Ferrars whilst she was alive. Now that she has gone where (presumably) Paris frocks can no longer be worn, Caroline is prepared to indulge in the softer emotions of pity and comprehension.

I told her firmly that her whole idea was nonsense. I was all the more firm because I secretly agreed with some part, at least, of what she had said. But it is all wrong that Caroline should arrive at the truth simply by a kind of inspired guesswork. I wasn't going to encourage that sort of thing. She will go round the village airing her views, and every one will think that she is doing so on medical data supplied by me. Life is very trying.

"Nonsense," said Caroline, in reply to my strictures. "You'll see. Ten to one she's left a letter confessing everything."

"She didn't leave a letter of any kind," I said sharply, and not seeing where the admission was going to land me.

"Oh!" said Caroline. "So you *did* inquire about that, did you? I believe, James, that in your heart of hearts, you think very much as I do. You're a precious old humbug."

"One always has to take the possibility of suicide into consideration," I said repressively.

"Will there be an inquest?"

"There may be. It all depends. If I am able to declare myself absolutely satisfied that the overdose was taken accidentally, an inquest might be dispensed with."

"And are you absolutely satisfied?" asked my sister shrewdly.

I did not answer, but got up from table.

CHAPTER 2

BEFORE I proceed further with what I said to Caroline and what Caroline said to me, it might be as well to give some idea of what I should describe as our local geography. Our village, King's Abbot, is, I imagine, very much like any other village. Our big town is Cranchester, nine miles away. We have a large railway station, a small post office, and two rival "General Stores." Able-bodied men are apt to leave the place early in life, but we are rich in unmarried ladies and retired military officers. Our hobbies and recreations can be summed up in the one word, "gossip."

There are only two houses of any importance in King's Abbot. One is King's Paddock, left to Mrs. Ferrars by her late husband. The other, Fernly Park, is owned by Roger Ackroyd. Ackroyd has always interested me by being a man more impossibly like a country squire than any country squire could really be. He reminds one of the red-faced sportsmen who always appeared early in the first act of an old-fashioned musical comedy, the setting being the village green. They usually sang a song about going up to London. Nowadays we have revues, and the country squire has died out of musical fashion.

Of course, Ackroyd is not really a country squire. He is an immensely successful manufacturer of (I think) wagon wheels. He is a man of nearly fifty years of age, rubicund of face and genial of manner. He is hand and glove with the vicar, subscribes liberally to parish funds (though rumor has it that he is extremely mean in personal expenditure), encourages cricket matches, Lads' Clubs, and Disabled Soldiers' Institutes. He is, in fact, the life and soul of our peaceful village of King's Abbot.

Now when Roger Ackroyd was a lad of twenty-one, he fell in love with, and married, a beautiful woman some five or six years his senior. Her name was Paton, and she was a widow with one child. The history of the marriage was short and painful. To put it bluntly, Mrs. Ackroyd was a dipsomaniac. She succeeded in drinking herself into her grave four years after her marriage.

In the years that followed, Ackroyd showed no disposition to make a second matrimonial adventure. His wife's child by her first marriage was only seven years old when his mother died. He is now twenty-five. Ackroyd has always regarded him as his own son, and has brought him up accordingly, but he has been a wild lad and a continual source of worry and trouble to his stepfather. Nevertheless we are all very fond of Ralph Paton in King's Abbot. He is such a good-looking youngster for one thing.

As I said before, we are ready enough to gossip in our village. Everybody noticed from the first that Ackroyd and Mrs. Ferrars got on very well together. After her husband's death, the intimacy became more marked. They were always seen about together, and it was freely conjectured that at the end of her period of mourning, Mrs. Ferrars would become Mrs. Roger Ackroyd. It was felt, indeed, that there was a certain fitness in the thing. Roger Ackroyd's wife had admittedly died of drink. Ashley Ferrars had been a drunkard for many years before his death. It was only fitting that these two victims of alcoholic excess should make up to each other for all that they had previously endured at the hands of their former spouses.

The Ferrars only came to live here just over a year ago, but a halo of gossip has surrounded Ackroyd for many years past. All the time that Ralph Paton was growing up to manhood, a series of lady housekeepers presided over Ackroyd's establishment, and each in turn was regarded with lively suspicion by Caroline and her cronies. It is not too much to say that for at least fifteen years the whole village has confidently expected Ackroyd to marry one of his housekeepers. The last of them, a redoubtable lady called Miss Russell, has reigned undisputed for five years, twice as long as any of her predecessors. It is felt that but for the advent of Mrs. Ferrars, Ackroyd could hardly have escaped. That—and one other factor—the unexpected arrival of a widowed sister-in-law with her daughter from Canada. Mrs. Cecil Ackroyd, widow of Ackroyd's ne'er-do-well younger brother, has taken up her residence at Fernly Park, and has succeeded, according to Caroline, in putting Miss Russell in her proper place.

I don't know exactly what a "proper place" constitutes—it sounds chilly and unpleasant—but I know that Miss Russell goes about with pinched lips, and what I can only describe as an acid smile, and that she professes the utmost sympathy for "poor Mrs. Ackroyd—dependent on the charity of her husband's brother. The bread of charity is so bitter, is it not? *I* should be quite miserable if I did not work for my living."

I don't know what Mrs. Cecil Ackroyd thought of the Ferrars

affair when it came on the tapis. It was clearly to her advantage that Ackroyd should remain unmarried. She was always very charming—not to say gushing—to Mrs. Ferrars when they met. Caroline says that proves less than nothing.

Such have been our preoccupations in King's Abbot for the last few years. We have discussed Ackroyd and his affairs from every standpoint. Mrs. Ferrars has fitted into her place in the scheme.

Now there has been a rearrangement of the kaleidoscope. From a mild discussion of probable wedding presents, we have been jerked into the midst of tragedy.

Revolving these and sundry other matters in my mind, I went mechanically on my round. I had no cases of special interest to attend, which was, perhaps, as well, for my thoughts returned again and again to the mystery of Mrs. Ferrars's death. Had she taken her own life? Surely, if she had done so, she would have left some word behind to say what she contemplated doing. Women, in my experience, if they once reach the determination to commit suicide, usually wish to reveal the state of mind that led to the fatal action. They covet the limelight.

When had I last seen her? Not for over a week. Her manner then had been normal enough considering—well—considering everything.

Then I suddenly remembered that I had seen her, though not to speak to, only yesterday. She had been walking with Ralph Paton, and I had been surprised because I had had no idea that he was likely to be in King's Abbot. I thought, indeed, that he had quarreled finally with his stepfather. Nothing had been seen of him down here for nearly six months. They had been walking along, side by side, their heads close together, and she had been talking very earnestly.

I think I can safely say that it was at this moment that a foreboding of the future first swept over me. Nothing tangible as yet—but a vague premonition of the way things were setting. That earnest *tête-à-tête* between Ralph Paton and Mrs. Ferrars the day before struck me disagreeably.

I was still thinking of it when I came face to face with Roger Ackroyd.

"Sheppard!" he exclaimed. "Just the man I wanted to get hold of. This is a terrible business."

"You've heard then?"

He nodded. He had felt the blow keenly, I could see. His big red cheeks seemed to have fallen in, and he looked a positive wreck of his usual jolly, healthy self.

"It's worse than you know," he said quietly. "Look here, Sheppard, I've got to talk to you. Can you come back with me now?"

"Hardly. I've got three patients to see still, and I must be back by twelve to see my surgery patients."

"Then this afternoon—no, better still, dine to-night. At seven-thirty? Will that suit you?"

"Yes—I can manage that all right. What's wrong? Is it Ralph?"

I hardly knew why I said that—except, perhaps, that it had so often been Ralph.

Ackroyd stared blankly at me as though he hardly understood. I began to realize that there must be something very wrong indeed somewhere. I had never seen Ackroyd so upset before.

"Ralph?" he said vaguely. "Oh! no, it's not Ralph. Ralph's in London—— Damn! Here's old Miss Ganett coming. I don't want to have to talk to her about this ghastly business. See you to-night, Sheppard. Seven-thirty."

I nodded, and he hurried away, leaving me wondering. Ralph in London? But he had certainly been in King's Abbot the preceding afternoon. He must have gone back to town last night or early this morning, and yet Ackroyd's manner had conveyed quite a different impression. He had spoken as though Ralph had not been near the place for months.

I had no time to puzzle the matter out further. Miss Ganett was upon me, thirsting for information. Miss Ganett has all the characteristics of my sister Caroline, but she lacks that unerring aim in jumping to conclusions which lends a touch of greatness to Caroline's maneuvers. Miss Ganett was breathless and interrogatory.

Wasn't it sad about poor dear Mrs. Ferrars? A lot of people were saying she had been a confirmed drug-taker for years. So wicked the way people went about saying things. And yet, the worst of it was, there was usually a grain of truth somewhere in these wild statements. No smoke without fire! They were saying too that Mr. Ackroyd had found out about it, and had broken off the engagement —because there *was* an engagement. She, Miss Ganett, had proof positive of that. Of course *I* must know all about it—doctors always did— but they never tell?

And all this with a sharp beady eye on me to see how I reacted to these suggestions. Fortunately long association with Caroline has led me to preserve an impassive countenance, and to be ready with small non-committal remarks.

On this occasion I congratulated Miss Ganett on not joining in ill-natured gossip. Rather a neat counterattack, I thought. It left her in difficulties, and before she could pull herself together, I had passed on.

I went home thoughtful, to find several patients waiting for me in the surgery.

I had dismissed the last of them, as I thought, and was just contemplating a few minutes in the garden before lunch when I perceived one more patient waiting for me. She rose and came towards me as I stood somewhat surprised.

I don't know why I should have been, except that there is a suggestion of cast iron about Miss Russell, a something that is above the ills of the flesh.

Ackroyd's housekeeper is a tall woman, handsome but forbidding in appearance. She has a stern eye, and lips that shut tightly, and I feel that if I were an under housemaid or a kitchenmaid I should run for my life whenever I heard her coming.

"Good morning, Dr. Sheppard," said Miss Russell. "I should be much obliged if you would take a look at my knee."

I took a look, but, truth to tell, I was very little wiser when I had done so. Miss Russell's account of vague pains was so unconvincing that with a woman of less integrity of character I should have suspected a trumped-up tale. It did cross my mind for one moment that Miss Russell might have deliberately invented this affection of the knee in order to pump me on the subject of Mrs. Ferrars's death, but I soon saw that there, at least, I had misjudged her. She made a brief reference to the tragedy, nothing more. Yet she certainly seemed disposed to linger and chat.

"Well, thank you very much for this bottle of liniment, doctor," she said at last. "Not that I believe it will do the least good."

I didn't think it would either, but I protested in duty bound. After all, it couldn't do any harm, and one must stick up for the tools of one's trade.

"I don't believe in all these drugs," said Miss Russell, her eyes sweeping over my array of bottles disparagingly. "Drugs do a lot of harm. Look at the cocaine habit."

"Well, as far as that goes——"

"It's very prevalent in high society."

I'm sure Miss Russell knows far more about high society than I do. I didn't attempt to argue with her.

"Just tell me this, doctor," said Miss Russell. "Suppose you are really a slave of the drug habit. Is there any cure?"

One cannot answer a question like that offhand. I gave her a short lecture on the subject, and she listened with close attention. I still suspected her of seeking information about Mrs. Ferrars.

"Now, veronal, for instance——" I proceeded.

But, strangely enough, she didn't seem interested in veronal. Instead she changed the subject, and asked me if it was true that there were certain poisons so rare as to baffle detection.

"Ah!" I said. "You've been reading detective stories."

She admitted that she had.

"The essence of a detective story," I said, "is to have a rare poison —if possible something from South America, that nobody has ever heard of—something that one obscure tribe of savages uses to poison their arrows with. Death is instantaneous, and Western science is powerless to detect it. That is the kind of thing you mean?".

"Yes. Is there really such a thing?"

I shook my head regretfully.

"I'm afraid there isn't. There's *curare,* of course."

I told her a good deal about curare, but she seemed to have lost interest once more. She asked me if I had any in my poison cupboard, and when I replied in the negative I fancy I fell in her estimation.

She said she must be getting back, and I saw her out at the surgery door just as the luncheon gong went.

I should never have suspected Miss Russell of a fondness for detective stories. It pleases me very much to think of her stepping out of the housekeeper's room to rebuke a delinquent housemaid, and then returning to a comfortable perusal of *The Mystery of the Seventh Death,* or something of the kind.

CHAPTER 3

THE MAN WHO GREW VEGETABLE MARROWS

I TOLD Caroline at lunch time that I should be dining at Fernly. She expressed no objection—on the contrary——

"Excellent," she said. "You'll hear all about it. By the way, what is the trouble with Ralph?"

"With Ralph?" I said, surprised; "there isn't any."

"Then why is he staying at the Three Boars instead of at Fernly Park?"

I did not for a minute question Caroline's statement that Ralph Paton was staying at the local inn. That Caroline said so was enough for me.

"Ackroyd told me he was in London," I said. In the surprise of the moment I departed from my valuable rule of never parting with information.

"Oh!" said Caroline. I could see her nose twitching as she worked on this.

"He arrived at the Three Boars yesterday morning," she said. "And he's still there. Last night he was out with a girl."

That did not surprise me in the least. Ralph, I should say, is out with a girl most nights of his life. But I did rather wonder that he chose to indulge in the pastime in King's Abbot instead of in the gay metropolis.

"One of the barmaids?" I asked.

"No. That's just it. He went out to meet her. I don't know who she is."

(Bitter for Caroline to have to admit such a thing.)

"But I can guess," continued my indefatigable sister.

I waited patiently.

"His cousin."

"Flora Ackroyd?" I exclaimed in surprise.

Flora Ackroyd is, of course, no relation whatever really to Ralph Paton, but Ralph has been looked upon for so long as practically Ackroyd's own son, that cousinship is taken for granted.

"Flora Ackroyd," said my sister.

"But why not go to Fernly if he wanted to see her?"

"Secretly engaged," said Caroline, with immense enjoyment. "Old Ackroyd won't hear of it, and they have to meet this way."

I saw a good many flaws in Caroline's theory, but I forbore to point them out to her. An innocent remark about our new neighbor created a diversion.

The house next door, The Larches, has recently been taken by a stranger. To Caroline's extreme annoyance, she has not been able to find out anything about him, except that he is a foreigner. The Intelligence Corps has proved a broken reed. Presumably the man has milk and vegetables and joints of meat and occasional whitings just like everybody else, but none of the people who make it their business to supply these things seem to have acquired any information. His name, apparently, is Mr. Porrott—a name which conveys an odd feeling of unreality. The one thing we do know about him is that he is interested in the growing of vegetable marrows.

But that is certainly not the sort of information that Caroline is after. She wants to know where he comes from, what he does, whether he is married, what his wife was, or is, like, whether he has children, what his mother's maiden name was—and so on. Somebody very like Caroline must have invented the questions on passports, I think.

"My dear Caroline," I said. "There's no doubt at all about what the man's profession has been. He's a retired hairdresser. Look at that mustache of his."

Caroline dissented. She said that if the man was a hairdresser, he would have wavy hair—not straight. All hairdressers did.

I cited several hairdressers personally known to me who had straight hair, but Caroline refused to be convinced.

"I can't make him out at all," she said in an aggrieved voice. "I borrowed some garden tools the other day, and he was most polite, but I couldn't get anything out of him. I asked him point blank at last whether he was a Frenchman, and he said he wasn't—and somehow I didn't like to ask him any more."

I began to be more interested in our mysterious neighbor. A man who is capable of shutting up Caroline and sending her, like the Queen of Sheba, empty away must be something of a personality.

"I believe," said Caroline, "that he's got one of those new vacuum cleaners——"

I saw a meditated loan and the opportunity of further questioning gleaming from her eye. I seized the chance to escape into the garden. I am rather fond of gardening. I was busily exterminating dandelion roots when a shout of warning sounded from close by and a heavy body whizzed by my ear and fell at my feet with a repellant squelch. It was a vegetable marrow!

I looked up angrily. Over the wall, to my left, there appeared a face. An egg-shaped head, partially covered with suspiciously black hair, two immense mustaches, and a pair of watchful eyes. It was our mysterious neighbor, Mr. Porrott.

He broke at once into fluent apologies.

"I demand of you a thousand pardons, monsieur. I am without defense. For some months now I cultivate the marrows. This morning suddenly I enrage myself with these marrows. I send them to promenade themselves—alas! not only mentally but physically. I seize the biggest. I hurl him over the wall. Monsieur, I am ashamed. I prostrate myself."

Before such profuse apologies, my anger was forced to melt. After all, the wretched vegetable hadn't hit me. But I sincerely hoped that throwing large vegetables over walls was not our new friend's hobby. Such a habit could hardly endear him to us as a neighbor.

The strange little man seemed to read my thoughts.

"Ah! no," he exclaimed. "Do not disquiet yourself. It is not with me a habit. But can you figure to yourself, monsieur, that a man may work towards a certain object, may labor and toil to attain a certain kind of leisure and occupation, and then find that, after all, he yearns for the old busy days, and the old occupations that he thought himself so glad to leave?"

"Yes," I said slowly. "I fancy that that is a common enough occurrence. I myself am perhaps an instance. A year ago I came into a legacy—enough to enable me to realize a dream. I have always wanted to travel, to see the world. Well, that was a year ago, as I said, and—I am still here."

My little neighbor nodded.

"The chains of habit. We work to attain an object, and the object gained, we find that what we miss is the daily toil. And mark you, monsieur, my work was interesting work. The most interesting work there is in the world."

"Yes?" I said encouragingly. For the moment the spirit of Caroline was strong within me.

"The study of human nature, monsieur!"

"Just so," I said kindly.

Clearly a retired hairdresser. Who knows the secrets of human nature better than a hairdresser?

"Also, I had a friend—a friend who for many years never left my side. Occasionally of an imbecility to make one afraid, nevertheless he was very dear to me. Figure to yourself that I miss even his stupidity. His _naïveté,_ his honest outlook, the pleasure of delighting and surprising him by my superior gifts—all these I miss more than I can tell you."

"He died?" I asked sympathetically.

"Not so. He lives and flourishes—but on the other side of the world. He is now in the Argentine."

"In the Argentine," I said enviously.

I have always wanted to go to South America. I sighed, and then looked up to find Mr. Porrott eyeing me sympathetically. He seemed an understanding little man.

"You will go there, yes?" he asked.

I shook my head with a sigh.

"I could have gone," I said, "a year ago. But I was foolish—and worse than foolish—greedy. I risked the substance for the shadow."

"I comprehend," said Mr. Porrott. "You speculated?"

I nodded mournfully, but in spite of myself I felt secretly entertained. This ridiculous little man was so portentously solemn.

"Not the Porcupine Oilfields?" he asked suddenly.

I stared.

"I thought of them, as a matter of fact, but in the end I plumped for gold mine in Western Australia."

My neighbor was regarding me with a strange expression which I could not fathom.

"It is Fate," he said at last.

"What is Fate?" I asked irritably.

"That I should live next to a man who seriously considers Porcupine Oilfields, and also West Australian Gold Mines. Tell me, have you also a penchant for auburn hair?"

I stared at him open-mouthed, and he burst out laughing.

"No, no, it is not the insanity that I suffer from. Make your mind easy. It was a foolish question that I put to you there, for, see you, my friend of whom I spoke was a young man, a man who thought all women good, and most of them beautiful. But you are a man of middle age, a doctor, a man who knows the folly and the vanity of most things in this life of ours. Well, well, we are neighbors. I beg of you to accept and present to your excellent sister my best marrow."

He stooped, and with a flourish produced an immense specimen of the tribe, which I duly accepted in the spirit in which it was offered.

"Indeed," said the little man cheerfully, "this has not been a wasted morning. I have made the acquaintance of a man who in some ways resembles my far-off friend. By the way, I should like to ask you a question. You doubtless know every one in this tiny village. Who is the young man with the very dark hair and eyes, and the handsome face. He walks with his head flung back, and an easy smile on his lips?"

The description left me in no doubt.

"That must be Captain Ralph Paton," I said slowly.

"I have not seen him about here before?"

"No, he has not been here for some time. But he is the son—

adopted son, rather—of Mr. Ackroyd of Fernly Park."

My neighbor made a slight gesture of impatience.

"Of course, I should have guessed. Mr. Ackroyd spoke of him many times."

"You know Mr. Ackroyd?" I said, slightly surprised.

"Mr. Ackroyd knew me in London—when I was at work there. I have asked him to say nothing of my profession down here."

"I see," I said, rather amused by this patent snobbery, as I thought it.

But the little man went on with an almost grandiloquent smirk.

"One prefers to remain incognito. I am not anxious for notoriety. I have not even troubled to correct the local version of my name."

"Indeed," I said, not knowing quite what to say.

"Captain Ralph Paton," mused Mr. Porrott. "And so he is engaged to Mr. Ackroyd's niece, the charming Miss Flora."

"Who told you so?" I asked, very much surprised.

"Mr. Ackroyd. About a week ago. He is very pleased about it—has long desired that such a thing should come to pass, or so I understood from him. I even believe that he brought some pressure to bear upon the young man. That is never wise. A young man should marry to please himself—not to please a stepfather from whom he has expectations."

My ideas were completely upset. I could not see Ackroyd taking a hairdresser into his confidence, and discussing the marriage of his niece and stepson with him. Ackroyd extends a genial patronage to the lower orders, but he has a very great sense of his own dignity. I began to think that Porrott couldn't be a hairdresser after all.

To hide my confusion, I said the first thing that came into my head.

"What made you notice Ralph Paton? His good looks?"

"No, not that alone—though he is unusually good-looking for an Englishman—what your lady novelists would call a Greek god. No, there was something about that young man that I did not understand."

He said the last sentence in a musing tone of voice which made an indefinable impression upon me. It was as though he was summing up the boy by the light of some inner knowledge that I did not share. It was that impression that was left with me, for at that moment my sister's voice called me from the house.

I went in. Caroline had her hat on, and had evidently just come in from the village. She began without preamble.

"I met Mr. Ackroyd."

"Yes?" I said.

"I stopped him, of course, but he seemed in a great hurry, and anxious to get away."

I have no doubt but that that was the case. He would feel towards Caroline much as he had felt towards Miss Ganett earlier in the day —perhaps more so. Caroline is less easy to shake off.

"I asked him at once about Ralph. He was absolutely astonished. Had no idea the boy was down here. He actually said he thought I must have made a mistake. I! A mistake!"

"Ridiculous," I said. "He ought to have known you better."

"Then he went on to tell me that Ralph and Flora are engaged."

"I know that too," I interrupted, with modest pride.

"Who told you?"

"Our new neighbor."

Caroline visibly wavered for a second or two, much as a roulette ball might coyly hover between two numbers. Then she declined the tempting red herring.

"I told Mr. Ackroyd that Ralph was staying at the Three Boars."

"Caroline," I said, "do you never reflect that you might do a lot of harm with this habit of yours of repeating everything indiscriminately?"

"Nonsense," said my sister. "People ought to know things. I consider it my duty to tell them. Mr. Ackroyd was very grateful to me."

"Well?" I said, for there was clearly more to come.

"I think he went straight off to the Three Boars, but if so he didn't find Ralph there."

"No?"

"No. Because as I was coming back through the wood——"

"Coming back through the wood?" I interrupted.

Caroline had the grace to blush.

"It was such a lovely day," she exclaimed. "I thought I would make a little round. The woods with their autumnal tints are so perfect at this time of year."

Caroline does not care a hang for woods at any time of year. Normally she regards them as places where you get your feet damp, and where all kinds of unpleasant things may drop on your head. No, it was good sound mongoose instinct which took her to our local wood. It is the only place adjacent to the village of King's Abbot where you can talk with a young woman unseen by the whole of the village. It adjoins the Park of Fernly.

"Well," I said, "go on."

"As I say, I was just coming back through the wood when I heard voices."

Caroline paused.

"Yes?"

"One was Ralph Paton's—I knew it at once. The other was a girl's. Of course I didn't mean to listen——"

"Of course not," I interjected, with patent sarcasm—which was, however, wasted on Caroline.

"But I simply couldn't help overhearing. The girl said something—I didn't quite catch what it was, and Ralph answered. He sounded very angry. 'My dear girl,' he said. 'Don't you realize that it is quite on the cards the old man will cut me off with a shilling? He's been pretty fed up with me for the last few years. A little more would do it. And we need the dibs, my dear. I shall be a very rich man when the old fellow pops off. He's mean as they make 'em, but he's rolling in money really. I don't want him to go altering his will. You leave it to me, and don't worry.' Those were his exact words. I remember them perfectly. Unfortunately, just then I stepped on a dry twig or something, and they lowered their voices and moved away. I couldn't, of course, go rushing after them, so wasn't able to see who the girl was."

"That must have been most vexing," I said. "I suppose, though, you hurried on to the Three Boars, felt faint, and went into the bar for a glass of brandy, and so were able to see if both the barmaids were on duty?"

"It wasn't a barmaid," said Caroline unhesitatingly. "In fact, I'm almost sure that it was Flora Ackroyd, only——"

"Only it doesn't seem to make sense," I agreed.

"But if it wasn't Flora, who could it have been?"

Rapidly my sister ran over a list of maidens living in the neighborhood, with profuse reasons for and against.

When she paused for breath, I murmured something about a patient, and slipped out.

I proposed to make my way to the Three Boars. It seemed likely that Ralph Paton would have returned there by now.

I knew Ralph very well—better, perhaps, than any one else in King's Abbot, for I had known his mother before him, and therefore I understood much in him that puzzled others. He was, to a certain extent, the victim of heredity. He had not inherited his mother's fatal propensity for drink, but nevertheless he had in him a strain of weakness. As my new friend of this morning had declared, he was extraordinarily handsome. Just on six feet, perfectly proportioned, with the easy grace of an athlete, he was dark, like his mother, with a handsome, sunburnt face always ready to break into a smile. Ralph Paton was of those born to charm easily and without effort. He was self-indulgent and extravagant, with no veneration for anything on earth, but he was lovable nevertheless, and his friends were all devoted to him.

Could I do anything with the boy? I thought I could.

On inquiry at the Three Boars I found that Captain Paton had just come in. I went up to his room and entered unannounced.

For a moment, remembering what I had heard and seen, I was doubtful of my reception, but I need have had no misgivings.

"Why, it's Sheppard! Glad to see you."

He came forward to meet me, hand outstretched, a sunny smile lighting up his face.

"The one person I am glad to see in this infernal place."

I raised my eyebrows.

"What's the place been doing?"

He gave a vexed laugh.

"It's a long story. Things haven't been going well with me, doctor. But have a drink, won't you?"

"Thanks," I said, "I will."

He pressed the bell, then, coming back, threw himself into a chair.

"Not to mince matters," he said gloomily, "I'm in the devil of a mess. In fact, I haven't the least idea what to do next."

"What's the matter?" I asked sympathetically.

"It's my confounded stepfather."

"What has he done?"

"It isn't what he's done yet, but what he's likely to do."

The bell was answered, and Ralph ordered the drinks. When the man had gone again, he sat hunched in the arm-chair, frowning to himself.

"Is it really—serious?" I asked.

He nodded.

"I'm fairly up against it this time," he said soberly.

The unusual ring of gravity in his voice told me that he spoke the truth. It took a good deal to make Ralph grave.

"In fact," he continued, "I can't see my way ahead. . . . I'm damned if I can."

"If I could help——" I suggested diffidently.

But he shook his head very decidedly.

"Good of you, doctor. But I can't let you in on this. I've got to play a lone hand."

He was silent a minute and then repeated in a slightly different tone of voice:—

"Yes—I've got to play a lone hand. . . ."

CHAPTER 4

DINNER AT FERNLY

IT WAS just a few minutes before half-past seven when I rang the front door bell of Fernly Park. The door was opened with admirable promptitude by Parker, the butler.

The night was such a fine one that I had preferred to come on foot. I stepped into the big square hall and Parker relieved me of my overcoat. Just then Ackroyd's secretary, a pleasant young fellow by the name of Raymond, passed through the hall on his way to Ackroyd's study, his hands full of papers.

"Good-evening, doctor. Coming to dine? Or is this a professional call?"

The last was in allusion to my black bag, which I had laid down on the oak chest.

I explained that I expected a summons to a confinement case at any moment, and so had come out prepared for an emergency call. Raymond nodded, and went on his way, calling over his shoulder:—

"Go into the drawing-room. You know the way. The ladies will be down in a minute. I must just take these papers to Mr. Ackroyd, and I'll tell him you're here."

On Raymond's appearance Parker had withdrawn, so I was alone in the hall. I settled my tie, glanced in a large mirror which hung there, and crossed to the door directly facing me, which was, as I knew, the door of the drawing-room.

I noticed, just as I was turning the handle, a sound from within— the shutting down of a window, I took it to be. I noted it, I may say, quite mechanically, without attaching any importance to it at the time.

I opened the door and walked in. As I did so, I almost collided with Miss Russell, who was just coming out. We both apologized.

For the first time I found myself appraising the housekeeper and thinking what a handsome woman she must once have been—indeed, as far as that goes, still was. Her dark hair was unstreaked with gray, and when she had a color, as she had at this minute, the stern quality of her looks was not so apparent.

Quite subconsciously I wondered whether she had been out, for she was breathing hard, as though she had been running.

"I'm afraid I'm a few minutes early," I said.

"Oh! I don't think so. It's gone half-past seven, Dr. Sheppard." She paused a minute before saying, "I—didn't know you were expected to dinner to-night. Mr. Ackroyd didn't mention it."

I received a vague impression that my dining there displeased her in some way, but I couldn't imagine why.

"How's the knee?" I inquired.

"Much the same, thank you, doctor. I must be going now. Mrs. Ackroyd will be down in a moment. I—I only came in here to see if the flowers were all right."

She passed quickly out of the room. I strolled to the window, wondering at her evident desire to justify her presence in the room. As I did so, I saw what, of course, I might have known all the time had I troubled to give my mind to it, namely, that the windows were long French ones opening on the terrace. The sound I had heard, therefore, could not have been that of a window being shut down.

Quite idly, and more to distract my mind from painful thoughts than for any other reason, I amused myself by trying to guess what could have caused the sound in question.

Coals on the fire? No, that was not the kind of noise at all. A drawer of the bureau pushed in? No, not that.

Then my eye was caught by what, I believe, is called a silver table, the lid of which lifts, and through the glass of which you can see the contents. I crossed over to it, studying the things. There were one or two pieces of old silver, a baby shoe belonging to King Charles the First, some Chinese jade figures, and quite a number of African implements and curios. Wanting to examine one of the jade figures more closely, I lifted the lid. It slipped through my fingers and fell.

At once I recognized the sound I had heard. It was this same table lid being shut down gently and carefully. I repeated the action once or twice for my own satisfaction. Then I lifted the lid to scrutinize the contents more closely.

I was still bending over the open silver table when Flora Ackroyd came into the room.

Quite a lot of people do not like Flora Ackroyd, but nobody can help admiring her. And to her friends she can be very charming. The first thing that strikes you about her is her extraordinary fairness. She has the real Scandinavian pale gold hair. Her eyes are blue—blue as the waters of a Norwegian fiord, and her skin is cream and roses. She has square, boyish shoulders and slight hips. And to a jaded medical man it is very refreshing to come across such perfect health.

A simple straightforward English girl—I may be old-fashioned, but I think the genuine article takes a lot of beating.

Flora joined me by the silver table, and expressed heretical doubts as to King Charles I ever having worn the baby shoe.

"And anyway," continued Miss Flora, "all this making a fuss about things because some one wore or used them seems to me all nonsense. They're not wearing or using them now. The pen that George Eliot wrote *The Mill on the Floss* with—that sort of thing— well, it's only just a pen after all. If you're really keen on George Eliot, why not get *The Mill on the Floss* in a cheap edition and read it."

"I suppose you never read such old out-of-date stuff, Miss Flora?"

"You're wrong, Dr. Sheppard. I love *The Mill on the Floss*."

I was rather pleased to hear it. The things young women read nowadays and profess to enjoy positively frighten me.

"You haven't congratulated me yet, Dr. Sheppard," said Flora. "Haven't you heard?"

She held out her left hand. On the third finger of it was an exquisitely set single pearl.

"I'm going to marry Ralph, you know," she went on. "Uncle is very pleased. It keeps me in the family, you see."

I took both her hands in mine.

"My dear," I said, "I hope you'll be very happy."

"We've been engaged for about a month," continued Flora in her cool voice, "but it was only announced yesterday. Uncle is going to do up Cross-stones, and give it to us to live in, and we're going to pretend to farm. Really, we shall hunt all the winter, town for the season, and then go yachting. I love the sea. And, of course, I shall take a great interest in the parish affairs, and attend all the Mothers' Meetings."

Just then Mrs. Ackroyd rustled in, full of apologies for being late.

I am sorry to say I detest Mrs. Ackroyd. She is all chains and teeth and bones. A most unpleasant woman. She has small pale flinty blue eyes, and however gushing her words may be, those eyes of hers always remain coldly speculative.

I went across to her, leaving Flora by the window. She gave me a handful of assorted knuckles and rings to squeeze, and began talking volubly.

Had I heard about Flora's engagement? So suitable in every way. The dear young things had fallen in love at first sight. Such a perfect pair, he so dark and she so fair.

"I can't tell you, my dear Dr. Sheppard, the relief to a mother's heart."

Mrs. Ackroyd sighed—a tribute to her mother's heart, whilst her eyes remained shrewdly observant of me.

"I was wondering. You are such an old friend of dear Roger's. We know how much he trusts to your judgment. So difficult for me—in my position, as poor Cecil's widow. But there are so many tiresome things—settlements, you know—all that. I fully believe that Roger intends to make settlements upon dear Flora, but, as you know, he is just a *leetle* peculiar about money. Very usual, I've heard, amongst men who are captains of industry. I wondered, you know, if you could just *sound* him on the subject? Flora is so fond of you. We feel you are quite an old friend, although we have only really known you just over two years."

Mrs. Ackroyd's eloquence was cut short as the drawing-room door opened once more. I was pleased at the interruption. I hate interfering in other people's affairs, and I had not the least intention of tackling Ackroyd on the subject of Flora's settlements. In another moment I should have been forced to tell Mrs. Ackroyd as much.

"You know Major Blunt, don't you, doctor?"

"Yes, indeed," I said.

A lot of people know Hector Blunt—at least by repute. He has shot more wild animals in unlikely places than any man living, I suppose. When you mention him, people say: "Blunt—you don't mean the big game man, do you?"

His friendship with Ackroyd has always puzzled me a little. The two men are so totally dissimilar. Hector Blunt is perhaps five years Ackroyd's junior. They made friends early in life, and though their ways have diverged, the friendship still holds. About once in two years Blunt spends a fortnight at Fernly, and an immense animal's head, with an amazing number of horns which fixes you with a glazed stare as soon as you come inside the front door, is a permanent reminder of the friendship.

Blunt had entered the room now with his own peculiar, deliberate, yet soft-footed tread. He is a man of medium height, sturdily and rather stockily built. His face is almost mahogany-colored, and is peculiarly expressionless. He has gray eyes that give the impression of always watching something that is happening very far away. He talks little, and what he does say is said jerkily, as though the words were forced out of him unwillingly.

He said now: "How are you, Sheppard?" in his usual abrupt fashion, and then stood squarely in front of the fireplace looking over our heads as though he saw something very interesting happening in Timbuktu.

"Major Blunt," said Flora, "I wish you'd tell me about these African things. I'm sure you know what they all are."

I have heard Hector Blunt described as a woman hater, but I noticed that he joined Flora at the silver table with what might be described as alacrity. They bent over it together.

I was afraid Mrs. Ackroyd would begin talking about settlements again, so I made a few hurried remarks about the new sweet pea. I knew there was a new sweet pea because the *Daily Mail* had told me so that morning. Mrs. Ackroyd knows nothing about horticulture, but she is the kind of woman who likes to appear well-informed about the topics of the day, and she, too, reads the *Daily Mail*. We were able to converse quite intelligently until Ackroyd and his secretary joined us, and immediately afterwards Parker announced dinner.

My place at table was between Mrs. Ackroyd and Flora. Blunt was on Mrs. Ackroyd's other side, and Geoffrey Raymond next to him.

Dinner was not a cheerful affair. Ackroyd was visibly preoccupied. He looked wretched, and ate next to nothing. Mrs. Ackroyd, Raymond, and I kept the conversation going. Flora seemed affected by her uncle's depression, and Blunt relapsed into his usual taciturnity.

Immediately after dinner Ackroyd slipped his arm through mine and led me off to his study.

"Once we've had coffee, we shan't be disturbed again," he explained. "I told Raymond to see to it that we shouldn't be interrupted."

I studied him quietly without appearing to do so. He was clearly under the influence of some strong excitement. For a minute or two he paced up and down the room, then, as Parker entered with the coffee tray, he sank into an arm-chair in front of the fire.

The study was a comfortable apartment. Book-shelves lined one wall of it. The chairs were big and covered in dark blue leather. A large desk stood by the window and was covered with papers neatly docketed and filed. On a round table were various magazines and sporting papers.

"I've had a return of that pain after food lately," remarked Ackroyd casually, as he helped himself to coffee. "You must give me some more of those tablets of yours."

It struck me that he was anxious to convey the impression that our conference was a medical one. I played up accordingly.

"I thought as much. I brought some up with me."

"Good man. Hand them over now."

"They're in my bag in the hall. I'll get them."

Ackroyd arrested me.

"Don't you trouble. Parker will get them. Bring in the doctor's bag, will you, Parker?"

"Very good, sir."

Parker withdrew. As I was about to speak, Ackroyd threw up his hand.

"Not yet. Wait. Don't you see I'm in such a state of nerves that I can hardly contain myself?"

I saw that plainly enough. And I was very uneasy. All sorts of forebodings assailed me.

Ackroyd spoke again almost immediately.

"Make certain that window's closed, will you?" he asked.

Somewhat surprised, I got up and went to it. It was not a French window, but one of the ordinary sash type. The heavy blue velvet curtains were drawn in front of it, but the window itself was open at the top.

Parker reëntered the room with my bag while I was still at the window.

"That's all right," I said, emerging again into the room.

"You've put the latch across?"

"Yes, yes. What's the matter with you, Ackroyd?"

The door had just closed behind Parker, or I would not have put the question.

Ackroyd waited just a minute before replying.

"I'm in hell," he said slowly, after a minute. "No, don't bother with those damned tablets. I only said that for Parker. Servants are so curious. Come here and sit down. The door's closed too, isn't it?"

"Yes. Nobody can overhear; don't be uneasy."

"Sheppard, nobody knows what I've gone through in the last twenty-four hours. If a man's house ever fell in ruins about him, mine has about me. This business of Ralph's is the last straw. But we won't talk about that now. It's the other—the other——! I don't know what to do about it. And I've got to make up my mind soon."

"What's the trouble?"

Ackroyd remained silent for a minute or two. He seemed curiously averse to begin. When he did speak, the question he asked came as a complete surprise. It was the last thing I expected.

"Sheppard, you attended Ashley Ferrars in his last illness, didn't you?"

"Yes, I did."

He seemed to find even greater difficulty in framing his next question.

"Did you never suspect—did it ever enter your head—that—well, that he might have been poisoned?"

I was silent for a minute or two. Then I made up my mind what to say. Roger Ackroyd was not Caroline.

"I'll tell you the truth," I said. "At the time I had no suspicion whatever, but since—well, it was mere idle talk on my sister's part that first put the idea into my head. Since then I haven't been able to get it out again. But, mind you, I've no foundation whatever for that suspicion."

"He *was* poisoned," said Ackroyd.

He spoke in a dull heavy voice.

"Who by?" I asked sharply.

"His wife."

"How do you know that?"

"She told me so herself."

"When?"

"Yesterday! My God! yesterday! It seems ten years ago."

I waited a minute, and then he went on.

"You understand, Sheppard, I'm telling you this in confidence. It's to go no further. I want your advice—I can't carry the whole weight by myself. As I said just now, I don't know what to do."

"Can you tell me the whole story?" I said. "I'm still in the dark. How did Mrs. Ferrars come to make this confession to you?"

"It's like this. Three months ago I asked Mrs. Ferrars to marry me. She refused. I asked her again and she consented, but she refused to allow me to make the engagement public until her year of mourning was up. Yesterday I called upon her, pointed out that a year and three weeks had now elapsed since her husband's death, and that there could be no further objection to making the engagement public property. I had noticed that she had been very strange in her manner for some days. Now, suddenly, without the least warning, she broke down completely. She—she told me everything. Her hatred of her brute of a husband, her growing love for me, and the—the dreadful means she had taken. Poison! My God! It was murder in cold blood."

I saw the repulsion, the horror, in Ackroyd's face. So Mrs. Ferrars must have seen it. Ackroyd is not the type of the great lover who can forgive all for love's sake. He is fundamentally a good citizen. All that was sound and wholesome and law-abiding in him must have turned from her utterly in that moment of revelation.

"Yes," he went on, in a low, monotonous voice, "she confessed everything. It seems that there is one person who has known all along —who has been blackmailing her for huge sums. It was the strain of that that drove her nearly mad."

"Who was the man?"

Suddenly before my eyes there arose the picture of Ralph Paton and Mrs. Ferrars side by side. Their heads so close together. I felt a momentary throb of anxiety. Supposing—oh! but surely that was impossible. I remembered the frankness of Ralph's greeting that very afternoon. Absurd!

"She wouldn't tell me his name," said Ackroyd slowly. "As a matter of fact, she didn't actually say that it was a man. But of course——"

"Of course," I agreed. "It must have been a man. And you've no suspicion at all?"

For answer Ackroyd groaned and dropped his head into his hands.

"It can't be," he said. "I'm mad even to think of such a thing. No, I won't even admit to you the wild suspicion that crossed my mind. I'll tell you this much, though. Something she said made me think that the person in question might be actually among my household— but that can't be so. I must have misunderstood her."

"What did you say to her?" I asked.

"What could I say? She saw, of course, the awful shock it had been to me. And then there was the question, what was my duty in the matter? She had made me, you see, an accessory after the fact. She saw all that, I think, quicker than I did. I was stunned, you know. She asked me for twenty-four hours—made me promise to do nothing till the end of that time. And she steadfastly refused to give me the name of the scoundrel who had been blackmailing her. I suppose she was afraid that I might go straight off and hammer him, and then the fat would have been in the fire as far as she was concerned. She told me that I should hear from her before twenty-four hours had passed. My God! I swear to you, Sheppard, that it never entered my head what she meant to do. Suicide! And I drove her to it."

"No, no," I said. "Don't take an exaggerated view of things. The responsibility for her death doesn't lie at your door."

"The question is, what am I to do now? The poor lady is dead. Why rake up past trouble?"

"I rather agree with you," I said.

"But there's another point. How am I to get hold of that scoundrel who drove her to death as surely as if he'd killed her. He knew of the first crime, and he fastened on to it like some obscene vulture. She's paid the penalty. Is he to go scot-free?"

"I see," I said slowly. "You want to hunt him down? It will mean a lot of publicity, you know."

"Yes, I've thought of that. I've zigzagged to and fro in my mind."

"I agree with you that the villain ought to be punished, but the cost has got to be reckoned."

Ackroyd rose and walked up and down. Presently he sank into the chair again.

"Look here, Sheppard, suppose we leave it like this. If no word comes from her, we'll let the dead things lie."

"What do you mean by word coming from her?" I asked curiously.

"I have the strongest impression that somewhere or somehow she must have left a message for me—before she went. I can't argue about it, but there it is."

I shook my head.

"She left no letter or word of any kind. I asked."

"Sheppard, I'm convinced that she did. And more, I've a feeling that by deliberately choosing death, she wanted the whole thing to come out, if only to be revenged on the man who drove her to desperation. I believe that if I could have seen her then, she would have told me his name and bid me go for him for all I was worth."

He looked at me.

"You don't believe in impressions?"

"Oh, yes, I do, in a sense. If, as you put it, word should come from her——"

I broke off. The door opened noiselessly and Parker entered with a salver on which were some letters.

"The evening post, sir," he said, handing the salver to Ackroyd.

Then he collected the coffee cups and withdrew.

My attention, diverted for a moment, came back to Ackroyd. He was staring like a man turned to stone at a long blue envelope. The other letters he had let drop to the floor.

"*Her writing,*" he said in a whisper. "She must have gone out and posted it last night, just before—before——"

He ripped open the envelope and drew out a thick enclosure. Then he looked up sharply.

"You're sure you shut the window?" he said.

"Quite sure," I said, surprised. "Why?"

"All this evening I've had a queer feeling of being watched, spied upon. What's that——?"

He turned sharply. So did I. We both had the impression of hearing the latch of the door give ever so slightly. I went across to it and opened it. There was no one there.

"Nerves," murmured Ackroyd to himself.

He unfolded the thick sheets of paper, and read aloud in a low voice.

"*My dear, my very dear Roger,—A life calls for a life. I see that—I saw it in your face this afternoon. So I am taking the only road open to me. I leave to you the punishment of the person who has made my life a hell upon earth for the last year. I would not tell you the name this afternoon, but I propose to write it to you now. I have no children or near relations to be spared, so do not fear publicity. If you can, Roger, my very dear Roger, forgive me the wrong I meant to do you, since when the time came, I could not do it after all. . . .*"

Ackroyd, his finger on the sheet to turn it over, paused.

"Sheppard, forgive me, but I must read this alone," he said unsteadily. "It was meant for my eyes, and my eyes only."

He put the letter in the envelope and laid it on the table.

"Later, when I am alone."

"No," I cried impulsively, "read it now."

Ackroyd stared at me in some surprise.

"I beg your pardon," I said, reddening. "I do not mean read it aloud to me. But read it through whilst I am still here."

Ackroyd shook his head.

"No, I'd rather wait."

But for some reason, obscure to myself, I continued to urge him. "At least, read the name of the man," I said.

Now Ackroyd is essentially pig-headed. The more you urge him to do a thing, the more determined he is not to do it. All my arguments were in vain.

The letter had been brought in at twenty minutes to nine. It was just on ten minutes to nine when I left him, the letter still unread. I hesitated with my hand on the door handle, looking back and wondering if there was anything I had left undone. I could think of nothing. With a shake of the head I passed out and closed the door behind me.

I was startled by seeing the figure of Parker close at hand. He looked embarrassed, and it occurred to me that he might have been listening at the door.

What a fat, smug, oily face the man had, and surely there was something decidedly shifty in his eye.

"Mr. Ackroyd particularly does not want to be disturbed," I said coldly. "He told me to tell you so."

"Quite so, sir. I—I fancied I heard the bell ring."

This was such a palpable untruth that I did not trouble to reply. Preceding me to the hall, Parker helped me on with my overcoat, and I stepped out into the night. The moon was overcast and everything seemed very dark and still. The village church clock chimed nine o'clock as I passed through the lodge gates. I turned to the left towards the village, and almost cannoned into a man coming in the opposite direction.

"This the way to Fernly Park, mister?" asked the stranger in a hoarse voice.

I looked at him. He was wearing a hat pulled down over his eyes, and his coat collar turned up. I could see little or nothing of his face, but he seemed a young fellow. The voice was rough and uneducated.

"These are the lodge gates here," I said.

"Thank you, mister." He paused, and then added, quite unnecessarily, "I'm a stranger in these parts, you see."

He went on, passing through the gates as I turned to look after him.

The odd thing was that his voice reminded me of some one's voice that I knew, but whose it was I could not think.

Ten minutes later I was at home once more. Caroline was full of curiosity to know why I had returned so early. I had to make up a slightly fictitious account of the evening in order to satisfy her, and I had an uneasy feeling that she saw through the transparent device.

At ten o'clock I rose, yawned, and suggested bed. Caroline acquiesced.

It was Friday night, and on Friday night I wind the clocks. I did it as usual, whilst Caroline satisfied herself that the servants had locked up the kitchen properly.

It was a quarter past ten as we went up the stairs. I had just reached the top when the telephone rang in the hall below.

"Mrs. Bates," said Caroline immediately.

"I'm afraid so," I said ruefully.

I ran down the stairs and took up the receiver.

"What?" I said. "*What?* Certainly, I'll come at once."

I ran upstairs, caught up my bag, and stuffed a few extra dressings into it.

"Parker telephoning," I shouted to Caroline, "from Fernly. They've just found Roger Ackroyd murdered."

CHAPTER 5

MURDER

I GOT out the car in next to no time, and drove rapidly to Fernly. Jumping out, I pulled the bell impatiently. There was some delay in answering, and I rang again.

Then I heard the rattle of the chain and Parker, his impassivity of countenance quite unmoved, stood in the open doorway.

I pushed past him into the hall.

"Where is he?" I demanded sharply.

"I beg your pardon, sir?"

"Your master. Mr. Ackroyd. Don't stand there staring at me, man. Have you notified the police?"

"The police, sir? Did you say the police?" Parker stared at me as though I were a ghost.

"What's the matter with you, Parker? If, as you say, your master has been murdered——"

A gasp broke from Parker.

"The master? Murdered? Impossible, sir!"

It was my turn to stare.

"Didn't you telephone to me, not five minutes ago, and tell me that Mr. Ackroyd had been found murdered?"

"Me, sir? Oh! no indeed, sir. I wouldn't dream of doing such a thing."

"Do you mean to say it's all a hoax? That there's nothing the matter with Mr. Ackroyd?"

"Excuse me, sir, did the person telephoning use my name?"

"I'll give you the exact words I heard. *'Is that Dr. Sheppard? Parker, the butler at Fernly, speaking. Will you please come at once, sir. Mr. Ackroyd has been murdered.'*"

Parker and I stared at each other blankly.

"A very wicked joke to play, sir," he said at last, in a shocked tone. "Fancy saying a thing like that."

"Where is Mr. Ackroyd?" I asked suddenly.

"Still in the study, I fancy, sir. The ladies have gone to bed, and Major Blunt and Mr. Raymond are in the billiard room."

"I think I'll just look in and see him for a minute," I said. "I know he didn't want to be disturbed again, but this odd practical joke has made me uneasy. I'd just like to satisfy myself that he's all right."

"Quite so, sir. It makes me feel quite uneasy myself. If you don't object to my accompanying you as far as the door, sir——?"

"Not at all," I said. "Come along."

I passed through the door on the right, Parker on my heels, traversed the little lobby where a small flight of stairs led upstairs to Ackroyd's bedroom, and tapped on the study door.

There was no answer. I turned the handle, but the door was locked.

"Allow me, sir," said Parker.

Very nimbly, for a man of his build, he dropped on one knee and applied his eye to the keyhole.

"Key is in the lock all right, sir," he said, rising. "On the inside. Mr. Ackroyd must have locked himself in and possibly just dropped off to sleep."

I bent down and verified Parker's statement.

"It seems all right," I said, "but, all the same, Parker, I'm going to wake your master up. I shouldn't be satisfied to go home without hearing from his own lips that he's quite all right."

So saying, I rattled the handle and called out, "Ackroyd, Ackroyd, just a minute."

But still there was no answer. I glanced over my shoulder.

"I don't want to alarm the household," I said hesitatingly.

Parker went across and shut the door from the big hall through which we had come.

"I think that will be all right now, sir. The billiard room is at the other side of the house, and so are the kitchen quarters and the ladies' bedrooms."

I nodded comprehendingly. Then I banged once more frantically on the door, and stooping down, fairly bawled through the keyhole:—

"Ackroyd, Ackroyd! It's Sheppard. Let me in."

And still—silence. Not a sign of life from within the locked room. Parker and I glanced at each other.

"Look here, Parker," I said, "I'm going to break this door in—or rather, we are. I'll take the responsibility."

"If you say so, sir," said Parker, rather doubtfully.

"I do say so. I'm seriously alarmed about Mr. Ackroyd."

I looked round the small lobby and picked up a heavy oak chair. Parker and I held it between us and advanced to the assault. Once, twice, and three times we hurled it against the lock. At the third blow it gave, and we staggered into the room.

Ackroyd was sitting as I had left him in the arm-chair before the fire. His head had fallen sideways, and clearly visible, just below the collar of his coat, was a shining piece of twisted metalwork.

Parker and I advanced till we stood over the recumbent figure. I heard the butler draw in his breath with a sharp hiss.

"Stabbed from be'ind," he murmured. " 'Orrible!"

He wiped his moist brow with his handkerchief, then stretched out a hand gingerly towards the hilt of the dagger.

"You mustn't touch that," I said sharply. "Go at once to the telephone and ring up the police station. Inform them of what has happened. Then tell Mr. Raymond and Major Blunt."

"Very good, sir."

Parker hurried away, still wiping his perspiring brow.

I did what little had to be done. I was careful not to disturb the position of the body, and not to handle the dagger at all. No object was to be attained by moving it. Ackroyd had clearly been dead some little time.

Then I heard young Raymond's voice, horror-stricken and incredulous, outside.

"What do you say? Oh! impossible! Where's the doctor?"

He appeared impetuously in the doorway, then stopped dead, his face very white. A hand put him aside, and Hector Blunt came past him into the room.

"My God!" said Raymond from behind him; "it's true, then."

Blunt came straight on till he reached the chair. He bent over the body, and I thought that, like Parker, he was going to lay hold of the dagger hilt. I drew him back with one hand.

"Nothing must be moved," I explained. "The police must see him exactly as he is now."

Blunt nodded in instant comprehension. His face was expressionless as ever, but I thought I detected signs of emotion beneath the stolid mask. Geoffrey Raymond had joined us now, and stood peering over Blunt's shoulder at the body.

"This is terrible," he said in a low voice.

He had regained his composure, but as he took off the pince-nez he habitually wore and polished them I observed that his hand was shaking.

"Robbery, I suppose," he said. "How did the fellow get in? Through the window? Has anything been taken?"

He went towards the desk.

"You think it's burglary?" I said slowly.

"What else could it be? There's no question of suicide, I suppose?"

"No man could stab himself in such a way," I said confidently. "It's murder right enough. But with what motive?"

"Roger hadn't an enemy in the world," said Blunt quietly. "Must have been burglars. But what was the thief after? Nothing seems to be disarranged."

He looked round the room. Raymond was still sorting the papers on the desk.

"There seems nothing missing, and none of the drawers show signs of having been tampered with," the secretary observed at last. "It's very mysterious."

Blunt made a slight motion with his head.

"There are some letters on the floor here," he said.

I looked down. Three or four letters still lay where Ackroyd had dropped them earlier in the evening.

But the blue envelope containing Mrs. Ferrars's letter had disappeared. I half opened my mouth to speak, but at that moment the sound of a bell pealed through the house. There was a confused murmur of voices in the hall, and then Parker appeared with our local inspector and a police constable.

"Good-evening, gentlemen," said the inspector. "I'm terribly sorry for this! A good kind gentleman like Mr. Ackroyd. The butler says it is murder. No possibility of accident or suicide, doctor?"

"None whatever," I said.

"Ah! A bad business."

He came and stood over the body.

"Been moved at all?" he asked sharply.

"Beyond making certain that life was extinct—an easy matter—I have not disturbed the body in any way."

"Ah! And everything points to the murderer having got clear away —for the moment, that is. Now then, let me hear all about it. Who found the body?"

I explained the circumstances carefully.

"A telephone message, you say? From the butler?"

"A message that I never sent," declared Parker earnestly. "I've not been near the telephone the whole evening. The others can bear me out that I haven't."

"Very odd, that. Did it sound like Parker's voice, doctor?"

"Well—I can't say I noticed. I took it for granted, you see."

"Naturally. Well, you got up here, broke in the door, and found poor Mr. Ackroyd like this. How long should you say he had been dead, doctor?"

"Half an hour at least—perhaps longer," I said.

"The door was locked on the inside, you say? What about the window?"

"I myself closed and bolted it earlier in the evening at Mr. Ackroyd's request."

The inspector strode across to it and threw back the curtains.

"Well, it's open now anyway," he remarked.

True enough, the window was open, the lower sash being raised to its fullest extent.

The inspector produced a pocket torch and flashed it along the sill outside.

"This is the way he went all right," he remarked, *"and* got in. See here."

In the light of the powerful torch, several clearly defined footmarks could be seen. They seemed to be those of shoes with rubber studs in the soles. One particularly clear one pointed inwards, another, slightly overlapping it, pointed outwards.

"Plain as a pikestaff," said the inspector. "Any valuables missing?"

Geoffrey Raymond shook his head.

"Not so that we can discover. Mr. Ackroyd never kept anything of particular value in this room."

"H'm," said the inspector. "Man found an open window. Climbed in, saw Mr. Ackroyd sitting there—maybe he'd fallen asleep. Man stabbed him from behind, then lost his nerve and made off. But he's left his tracks pretty clearly. We ought to get hold of *him* without much difficulty. No suspicious strangers been hanging about anywhere?"

"Oh!" I said suddenly.

"What is it, doctor?"

"I met a man this evening—just as I was turning out of the gate. He asked me the way to Fernly Park."

"What time would that be?"

"Just nine o'clock. I heard it chime the hour as I was turning out of the gate."

"Can you describe him?"

I did so to the best of my ability.

The inspector turned to the butler.

"Any one answering that description come to the front door?"

"No, sir. No one has been to the house at all this evening."

"What about the back?"

"I don't think so, sir, but I'll make inquiries."

He moved towards the door, but the inspector held up a large hand.

"No, thanks. I'll do my own inquiring. But first of all I want to fix the time a little more clearly. When was Mr. Ackroyd last seen alive?"

"Probably by me," I said, "when I left at—let me see—about ten minutes to nine. He told me that he didn't wish to be disturbed, and I repeated the order to Parker."

"Just so, sir," said Parker respectfully.

"Mr. Ackroyd was certainly alive at half-past nine," put in Raymond, "for I heard his voice in here talking."

"Who was he talking to?"

"That I don't know. Of course, at the time I took it for granted that it was Dr. Sheppard who was with him. I wanted to ask him a question about some papers I was engaged upon, but when I heard the voices I remembered that he had said he wanted to talk to Dr. Sheppard without being disturbed, and I went away again. But now it seems that the doctor had already left?"

I nodded.

"I was at home by a quarter past nine," I said. "I didn't go out again until I received the telephone call."

"Who could have been with him at half-past nine?" queried the inspector. "It wasn't you, Mr.—er——"

"Major Blunt," I said.

"Major Hector Blunt?" asked the inspector, a respectful tone creeping into his voice.

Blunt merely jerked his head affirmatively.

"I think we've seen you down here before, sir," said the inspector. "I didn't recognize you for the moment, but you were staying with Mr. Ackroyd a year ago last May."

"June," corrected Blunt.

"Just so, June it was. Now, as I was saying, it wasn't you with Mr. Ackroyd at nine-thirty this evening?"

Blunt shook his head.

"Never saw him after dinner," he volunteered.

The inspector turned once more to Raymond.

"You didn't overhear any of the conversation going on, did you, sir?"

"I did catch just a fragment of it," said the secretary, "and, supposing as I did that it was Dr. Sheppard who was with Mr. Ackroyd, that fragment struck me as distinctly odd. As far as I can remember, the exact words were these. Mr. Ackroyd was speaking. 'The calls on my purse have been so frequent of late'—that is what he was saying—'of late, that I fear it is impossible for me to accede to your request. . . .' I went away again at once, of course, so did not hear any more. But I rather wondered because Dr. Sheppard——"

"——Does not ask for loans for himself or subscriptions for others," I finished.

"A demand for money," said the inspector musingly. "It may be that here we have a very important clew." He turned to the butler. "You say, Parker, that nobody was admitted by the front door this evening?"

"That's what I say, sir."

"Then it seems almost certain that Mr. Ackroyd himself must have admitted this stranger. But I don't quite see——"

The inspector went into a kind of day-dream for some minutes.

"One thing's clear," he said at length, rousing himself from his absorption. "Mr. Ackroyd was alive and well at nine-thirty. That is the last moment at which he is known to have been alive."

Parker gave vent to an apologetic cough which brought the inspector's eyes on him at once.

"Well?" he said sharply.

"If you'll excuse me, sir, Miss Flora saw him after that."

"Miss Flora?"

"Yes, sir. About a quarter to ten that would be. It was after that that she told me Mr. Ackroyd wasn't to be disturbed again to-night."

"Did he send her to you with that message?"

"Not exactly, sir. I was bringing a tray with soda and whisky when Miss Flora, who was just coming out of this room, stopped me and said her uncle didn't want to be disturbed."

The inspector looked at the butler with rather closer attention than he had bestowed on him up to now.

"You'd already been told that Mr. Ackroyd didn't want to be disturbed, hadn't you?"

Parker began to stammer. His hands shook.

"Yes, sir. Yes, sir. Quite so, sir."

"And yet you were proposing to do so?"

"I'd forgotten, sir. At least I mean, I always bring the whisky and soda about that time, sir, and ask if there's anything more, and I thought—well, I was doing as usual without thinking."

It was at this moment that it began to dawn upon me that Parker was most suspiciously flustered. The man was shaking and twitching all over.

"H'm," said the inspector. "I must see Miss Ackroyd at once. For the moment we'll leave this room exactly as it is. I can return here after I've heard what Miss Ackroyd has to tell me. I shall just take the precaution of shutting and bolting the window."

This precaution accomplished, he led the way into the hall and we followed him. He paused a moment, as he glanced up at the little staircase, then spoke over his shoulder to the constable.

"Jones, you'd better stay here. Don't let any one go into that room."

Parker interposed deferentially.

"If you'll excuse me, sir. If you were to lock the door into the main hall, nobody could gain access to this part. That staircase leads only to Mr. Ackroyd's bedroom and bathroom. There is no communication with the other part of the house. There once was a door through, but Mr. Ackroyd had it blocked up. He liked to feel that his suite was entirely private."

To make things clear and explain the position, I have appended a rough sketch of the right-hand wing of the house. The small staircase leads, as Parker explained, to a big bedroom (made by two being knocked into one) and an adjoining bathroom and lavatory.

The inspector took in the position at a glance. We went through

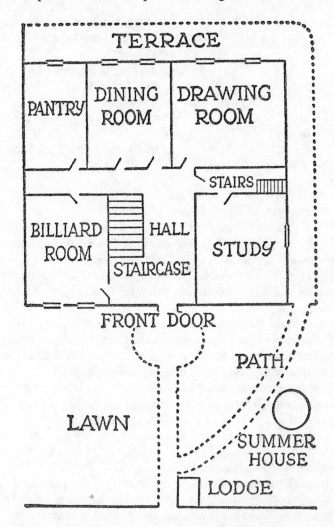

into the large hall and he locked the door behind him, slipping the key into his pocket. Then he gave the constable some low-voiced instructions, and the latter prepared to depart.

"We must get busy on those shoe tracks," explained the inspector.

"But first of all, I must have a word with Miss Ackroyd. She was the last person to see her uncle alive. Does she know yet?"

Raymond shook his head.

"Well, no need to tell her for another five minutes. She can answer my questions better without being upset by knowing the truth about her uncle. Tell her there's been a burglary, and ask her if she would mind dressing and coming down to answer a few questions."

It was Raymond who went upstairs on this errand.

"Miss Ackroyd will be down in a minute," he said, when he returned. "I told her just what you suggested."

In less than five minutes Flora descended the staircase. She was wrapped in a pale pink silk kimono. She looked anxious and excited.

The inspector stepped forward.

"Good-evening, Miss Ackroyd," he said civilly. "We're afraid there's been an attempt at robbery, and we want you to help us. What's this room—the billiard room? Come in here and sit down."

Flora sat down composedly on the wide divan which ran the length of the wall, and looked up at the inspector.

"I don't quite understand. What has been stolen? What do you want me to tell you?"

"It's just this, Miss Ackroyd. Parker here says you came out of your uncle's study at about a quarter to ten. Is that right?"

"Quite right. I had been to say good-night to him."

"And the time is correct?"

"Well, it must have been about then. I can't say exactly. It might have been later."

"Was your uncle alone, or was there any one with him?"

"He was alone. Dr. Sheppard had gone."

"Did you happen to notice whether the window was open or shut?"

Flora shook her head.

"I can't say. The curtains were drawn."

"Exactly. And your uncle seemed quite as usual?"

"I think so."

"Do you mind telling us exactly what passed between you?"

Flora paused a minute, as though to collect her recollections.

"I went in and said, 'Good-night, uncle, I'm going to bed now. I'm tired to-night.' He gave a sort of grunt, and—I went over and kissed him, and he said something about my looking nice in the frock I had on, and then he told me to run away as he was busy. So I went."

"Did he ask specially not to be disturbed?"

"Oh! yes, I forgot. He said: 'Tell Parker I don't want anything more to-night, and that he's not to disturb me.' I met Parker just outside the door and gave him uncle's message."

"Just so," said the inspector.

"Won't you tell me what it is that has been stolen?"

"We're not quite—certain," said the inspector hesitatingly.

A wide look of alarm came into the girl's eyes. She started up.

"What is it? You're hiding something from me?"

Moving in his usual unobtrusive manner, Hector Blunt came between her and the inspector. She half stretched out her hand, and he took it in both of his, patting it as though she were a very small child, and she turned to him as though something in his stolid, rocklike demeanor promised comfort and safety.

"It's bad news, Flora," he said quietly. "Bad news for all of us. Your Uncle Roger——"

"Yes?"

"It will be a shock to you. Bound to be. Poor Roger's dead."

Flora drew away from him, her eyes dilating with horror.

"When?" she whispered. "When?"

"Very soon after you left him, I'm afraid," said Blunt gravely.

Flora raised her hand to her throat, gave a little cry, and I hurried to catch her as she fell. She had fainted, and Blunt and I carried her upstairs and laid her on her bed. Then I got him to wake Mrs. Ackroyd and tell her the news. Flora soon revived, and I brought her mother to her, telling her what to do for the girl. Then I hurried downstairs again.

CHAPTER 6

THE TUNISIAN DAGGER

I MET the inspector just coming from the door which led into the kitchen quarters.

"How's the young lady, doctor?"

"Coming round nicely. Her mother's with her."

"That's good. I've been questioning the servants. They all declare that no one has been to the back door to-night. Your description of that stranger was rather vague. Can't you give us something more definite to go upon?"

"I'm afraid not," I said regretfully. "It was a dark night, you see, and the fellow had his coat collar well pulled up and his hat squashed down over his eyes."

"H'm," said the inspector. "Looked as though he wanted to conceal his face. Sure it was no one you know?"

I replied in the negative, but not as decidedly as I might have done. I remembered my impression that the stranger's voice was not unfamiliar to me. I explained this rather haltingly to the inspector.

"It was a rough, uneducated voice, you say?"

I agreed, but it occurred to me that the roughness had been of an almost exaggerated quality. If, as the inspector thought, the man had wished to hide his face, he might equally well have tried to disguise his voice.

"Do you mind coming into the study with me again, doctor? There are one or two things I want to ask you."

I acquiesced. Inspector Davis unlocked the door of the lobby, we passed through, and he locked the door again behind him.

"We don't want to be disturbed," he said grimly. "And we don't want any eavesdropping either. What's all this about blackmail?"

"Blackmail!" I exclaimed, very much startled.

"Is it an effort of Parker's imagination? Or is there something in it?"

"If Parker heard anything about blackmail," I said slowly, "he must have been listening outside this door with his ear glued against the keyhole."

Davis nodded.

"Nothing more likely. You see, I've been instituting a few inquiries as to what Parker has been doing with himself this evening. To tell the truth, I didn't like his manner. The man knows something. When I began to question him, he got the wind up, and plumped out some garbled story of blackmail."

I took an instant decision.

"I'm rather glad you've brought the matter up," I said. "I've been trying to decide whether to make a clean breast of things or not. I'd already practically decided to tell you everything, but I was going to wait for a favorable opportunity. You might as well have it now."

And then and there I narrated the whole events of the evening as I have set them down here. The inspector listened keenly, occasionally interjecting a question.

"Most extraordinary story I ever heard," he said, when I had finished. "And you say that letter has completely disappeared? It looks bad—it looks very bad indeed. It gives us what we've been looking for—a motive for the murder."

I nodded.

"I realize that."

"You say that Mr. Ackroyd hinted at a suspicion he had that some member of his household was involved? Household's rather an elastic term."

"You don't think that Parker himself might be the man we're after?" I suggested.

"It looks very like it. He was obviously listening at the door when you came out. Then Miss Ackroyd came across him later bent on entering the study. Say he tried again when she was safely out of the way. He stabbed Ackroyd, locked the door on the inside, opened the window, and got out that way, and went round to a side door which he had previously left open. How's that?"

"There's only one thing against it," I said slowly. "If Ackroyd went on reading that letter as soon as I left, as he intended to do, I don't see him continuing to sit on here and turn things over in his mind for another hour. He'd have had Parker in at once, accused him then and there, and there would have been a fine old uproar. Remember, Ackroyd was a man of choleric temper."

"Mightn't have had time to go on with the letter just then," suggested the inspector. "We know some one was with him at half-past nine. If that visitor turned up as soon as you left, and after he went, Miss Ackroyd came in to say good-night—well, he wouldn't be able to go on with the letter until close upon ten o'clock."

"And the telephone call?"

"Parker sent that all right—perhaps before he thought of the locked door and open window. Then he changed his mind—or got in a panic—and decided to deny all knowledge of it. That was it, depend upon it."

"Ye-es," I said rather doubtfully.

"Anyway, we can find out the truth about the telephone call from the exchange. If it was put through from here, I don't see how any one else but Parker could have sent it. Depend upon it, he's our man. But keep it dark—we don't want to alarm him just yet, till we've got all the evidence. I'll see to it he doesn't give us the slip. To all appearances we'll be concentrating on your mysterious stranger."

THE MURDER OF ROGER ACKROYD

He rose from where he had been sitting astride the chair belonging to the desk, and crossed over to the still form in the arm-chair.

"The weapon ought to give us a clew," he remarked, looking up. "It's something quite unique—a curio, I should think, by the look of it."

He bent down, surveying the handle attentively, and I heard him give a grunt of satisfaction. Then, very gingerly, he pressed his hands down below the hilt and drew the blade out from the wound. Still carrying it so as not to touch the handle, he placed it in a wide china mug which adorned the mantelpiece.

"Yes," he said, nodding at it. "Quite a work of art. There can't be many of them about."

It was indeed a beautiful object. A narrow, tapering blade, and a hilt of elaborately intertwined metals of curious and careful workmanship. He touched the blade gingerly with his finger, testing its sharpness, and made an appreciative grimace.

"Lord, what an edge," he exclaimed. "A child could drive that into a man—as easy as cutting butter. A dangerous sort of toy to have about."

"May I examine the body properly now?" I asked.

He nodded.

"Go ahead."

I made a thorough examination.

"Well?" said the inspector, when I had finished.

"I'll spare you the technical language," I said. "We'll keep that for the inquest. The blow was delivered by a right-handed man standing behind him, and death must have been instantaneous. By the expression on the dead man's face, I should say that the blow was quite unexpected. He probably died without knowing who his assailant was."

"Butlers can creep about as soft-footed as cats," said Inspector Davis. "There's not going to be much mystery about this crime. Take a look at the hilt of that dagger."

I took the look.

"I dare say they're not apparent to you, but *I* can see them clearly enough." He lowered his voice. *"Fingerprints!"*

He stood off a few steps to judge of his effect.

"Yes," I said mildly. "I guessed that."

I do not see why I should be supposed to be totally devoid of intelligence. After all, I read detective stories, and the newspapers, and am a man of quite average ability. If there had been toe marks on the dagger handle, now, that would have been quite a different thing. I would then have registered any amount of surprise and awe.

I think the inspector was annoyed with me for declining to get thrilled. He picked up the china mug and invited me to accompany him to the billiard room.

"I want to see if Mr. Raymond can tell us anything about this dagger," he explained.

Locking the outer door behind us again, we made our way to the billiard room, where we found Geoffrey Raymond. The inspector held up his exhibit.

"Ever seen this before, Mr. Raymond?"

"Why—I believe—I'm almost sure that is a curio given to Mr. Ackroyd by Major Blunt. It comes from Morocco—no, Tunis. So the crime was committed with that? What an extraordinary thing. It seems almost impossible, and yet there could hardly be two daggers the same. May I fetch Major Blunt?"

Without waiting for an answer, he hurried off.

"Nice young fellow that," said the inspector. "Something honest and ingenuous about him."

I agreed. In the two years that Geoffrey Raymond has been secretary to Ackroyd, I have never seen him ruffled or out of temper. And he has been, I know, a most efficient secretary.

In a minute or two Raymond returned, accompanied by Blunt.

"I was right," said Raymond excitedly. "It *is* the Tunisian dagger."

"Major Blunt hasn't looked at it yet," objected the inspector.

"Saw it the moment I came into the study," said the quiet man.

"You recognized it then?"

Blunt nodded.

"You said nothing about it," said the inspector suspiciously.

"Wrong moment," said Blunt. "Lot of harm done by blurting out things at the wrong time."

He returned the inspector's stare placidly enough.

The latter grunted at last and turned away. He brought the dagger over to Blunt.

"You're quite sure about it, sir. You identify it positively?"

"Absolutely. No doubt whatever."

"Where was this—er—curio usually kept? Can you tell me that, sir?"

It was the secretary who answered.

"In the silver table in the drawing-room."

"What?" I exclaimed.

The others looked at me.

"Yes, doctor?" said the inspector encouragingly.

"It's nothing."

"Yes, doctor?" said the inspector again, still more encouragingly.

"It's so trivial," I explained apologetically. "Only that when I arrived last night for dinner I heard the lid of the silver table being shut down in the drawing-room."

I saw profound skepticism and a trace of suspicion on the inspector's countenance.

"How did you know it was the silver table lid?"

I was forced to explain in detail—a long, tedious explanation which I would infinitely rather not have had to make.

The inspector heard me to the end.

"Was the dagger in its place when you were looking over the contents?" he asked.

"I don't know," I said. "I can't say I remember noticing it—but, of course, it may have been there all the time."

"We'd better get hold of the housekeeper," remarked the inspector, and pulled the bell.

A few minutes later Miss Russell, summoned by Parker, entered the room.

"I don't think I went near the silver table," she said, when the inspector had posed his question. "I was looking to see that all the flowers were fresh. Oh! yes, I remember now. The silver table was open—which it had no business to be, and I shut the lid down as I passed."

She looked at him aggressively.

"I see," said the inspector. "Can you tell me if this dagger was in its place then?"

Miss Russell looked at the weapon composedly.

"I can't say, I'm sure," she replied. "I didn't stop to look. I knew the family would be down any minute, and I wanted to get away."

"Thank you," said the inspector.

There was just a trace of hesitation in his manner, as though he would have liked to question her further, but Miss Russell clearly accepted the words as a dismissal, and glided from the room.

"Rather a Tartar, I should fancy, eh?" said the inspector, looking after her. "Let me see. This silver table is in front of one of the windows, I think you said, doctor?"

Raymond answered for me.

"Yes, the left-hand window."

"And the window was open?"

"They were both ajar."

"Well, I don't think we need go into the question much further. Somebody—I'll just say somebody—could get that dagger any time he liked, and exactly when he got it doesn't matter in the least. I'll be coming up in the morning with the chief constable, Mr. Raymond. Until then, I'll keep the key of that door. I want Colonel Melrose to see everything exactly as it is. I happen to know that he's dining out the other side of the county, and, I believe, staying the night. . . ."

We watched the inspector take up the jar.

"I shall have to pack this carefully," he observed. "It's going to be an important piece of evidence in more ways than one."

A few minutes later as I came out of the billiard room with Raymond, the latter gave a low chuckle of amusement.

I felt the pressure of his hand on my arm, and followed the direction of his eyes. Inspector Davis seemed to be inviting Parker's opinion of a small pocket diary.

"A little obvious," murmured my companion. "So Parker is the suspect, is he? Shall we oblige Inspector Davis with a set of our fingerprints also?"

He took two cards from the card tray, wiped them with his silk handkerchief, then handed one to me and took the other himself. Then, with a grin, he handed them to the police inspector.

"Souvenirs," he said. "No. 1, Dr. Sheppard; No. 2, my humble self. One from Major Blunt will be forthcoming in the morning."

Youth is very buoyant. Even the brutal murder of his friend and employer could not dim Geoffrey Raymond's spirits for long. Perhaps that is as it should be. I do not know. I have lost the quality of resilience long since myself.

It was very late when I got back, and I hoped that Caroline would have gone to bed. I might have known better.

She had hot cocoa waiting for me, and whilst I drank it, she extracted the whole history of the evening from me. I said nothing of the blackmailing business, but contented myself with giving her the facts of the murder.

"The police suspect Parker," I said, as I rose to my feet and prepared to ascend to bed. "There seems a fairly clear case against him."

"Parker!" said my sister. "Fiddlesticks! That inspector must be a perfect fool. Parker indeed! Don't tell me."

With which obscure pronouncement we went up to bed.

CHAPTER 7

I LEARN MY NEIGHBOR'S PROFESSION

ON THE following morning I hurried unforgivably over my round. My excuse can be that I had no very serious cases to attend. On my return Caroline came into the hall to greet me.

"Flora Ackroyd is here," she announced in an excited whisper.

"What?"

I concealed my surprise as best I could.

"She's very anxious to see you. She's been here half an hour."

Caroline led the way into our small sitting-room, and I followed.

Flora was sitting on the sofa by the window. She was in black and she sat nervously twisting her hands together. I was shocked by the sight of her face. All the color had faded away from it. But when she spoke her manner was as composed and resolute as possible.

"Dr. Sheppard, I have come to ask you to help me."

"Of course he'll help you, my dear," said Caroline.

I don't think Flora really wished Caroline to be present at the interview. She would, I am sure, have infinitely preferred to speak to me privately. But she also wanted to waste no time, so she made the best of it.

"I want you to come to The Larches with me."

"The Larches?" I queried, surprised.

"To see that funny little man?" exclaimed Caroline.

"Yes. You know who he is, don't you?"

"We fancied," I said, "that he might be a retired hairdresser."

Flora's blue eyes opened very wide.

"Why, he's Hercule Poirot! You know who I mean—the private detective. They say he's done the most wonderful things—just like detectives do in books. A year ago he retired and came to live down here. Uncle knew who he was, but he promised not to tell any one, because M. Poirot wanted to live quietly without being bothered by people."

"So that's who he is," I said slowly.

"You've heard of him, of course?"

"I'm rather an old fogey, as Caroline tells me," I said, "but I *have* just heard of him."

"Extraordinary!" commented Caroline.

I don't know what she was referring to—possibly her own failure to discover the truth.

"You want to go and see him?" I asked slowly. "Now why?"

"To get him to investigate this murder, of course," said Caroline sharply. "Don't be so stupid, James."

I was not really being stupid. Caroline does not always understand what I am driving at.

"You haven't got confidence in Inspector Davis?" I went on.

"Of course she hasn't," said Caroline. "I haven't either."

Any one would have thought it was Caroline's uncle who had been murdered.

"And how do you know he would take up the case?" I asked. "Remember he has retired from active work."

"That's just it," said Flora simply. "I've got to persuade him."

"You are sure you are doing wisely?" I asked gravely.

"Of course she is," said Caroline. "I'll go with her myself if she likes."

"I'd rather the doctor came with me if you don't mind, Miss Sheppard," said Flora.

She knows the value of being direct on certain occasions. Any hints would certainly have been wasted on Caroline.

"You see," she explained, following directness with tact, "Dr. Sheppard being the doctor, and having found the body, he would be able to give all the details to M. Poirot."

"Yes," said Caroline grudgingly, "I see that."

I took a turn or two up and down the room.

"Flora," I said gravely, "be guided by me. I advise you not to drag this detective into the case."

Flora sprang to her feet. The color rushed into her cheeks.

"I know why you say that," she cried. "But it's exactly for that reason I'm so anxious to go. You're afraid! But I'm not. I know Ralph better than you do."

"Ralph," said Caroline. "What has Ralph got to do with it?"

Neither of us heeded her.

"Ralph may be weak," continued Flora. "He may have done

foolish things in the past—wicked things even—but he wouldn't murder any one."

"No, no," I exclaimed. "I never thought it of him."

"Then why did you go to the Three Boars last night?" demanded Flora, "on your way home—after uncle's body was found?"

I was momentarily silenced. I had hoped that that visit of mine would remain unnoticed.

"How did you know about that?" I countered.

"I went there this morning," said Flora. "I heard from the servants that Ralph was staying there—"

I interrupted her.

"You had no idea that he was in King's Abbot?"

"No. I was astounded. I couldn't understand it. I went there and asked for him. They told me, what I suppose they told you last night, that he went out at about nine o'clock yesterday evening—and—and never came back."

Her eyes met mine defiantly, and as though answering something in my look, she burst out:—

"Well, why shouldn't he? He might have gone—anywhere. He may even have gone back to London."

"Leaving his luggage behind?" I asked gently.

Flora stamped her foot.

"I don't care. There must be a simple explanation."

"And that's why you want to go to Hercule Poirot? Isn't it better to leave things as they are? The police don't suspect Ralph in the least, remember. They're working on quite another tack."

"But that's just *it*," cried the girl. "They *do* suspect him. A man from Cranchester turned up this morning—Inspector Raglan, a horrid, weaselly little man. I found he had been to the Three Boars this morning before me. They told me all about his having been there, and the questions he had asked. He must think Ralph did it."

"That's a change of mind from last night, if so," I said slowly. "He doesn't believe in Davis's theory that it was Parker then?"

"Parker indeed," said my sister, and snorted.

Flora came forward and laid her hand on my arm.

"Oh! Dr. Sheppard, let us go at once to this M. Poirot. He will find out the truth."

"My dear Flora," I said gently, laying my hand on hers. "Are you quite sure it is the truth we want?"

She looked at me, nodding her head gravely.

"You're not sure," she said. "I am. I know Ralph better than you do."

"Of course he didn't do it," said Caroline, who had been keeping silent with great difficulty. "Ralph may be extravagant, but he's a dear boy, and has the nicest manners."

I wanted to tell Caroline that large numbers of murderers have had nice manners, but the presence of Flora restrained me. Since the girl was determined, I was forced to give in to her and we started at once, getting away before my sister was able to fire off any more pronouncements beginning with her favorite words, "Of course."

An old woman with an immense Breton cap opened the door of The Larches to us. M. Poirot was at home, it seemed.

We were ushered into a little sitting-room arranged with formal precision, and there, after the lapse of a minute or so, my friend of yesterday came to us.

"Monsieur le docteur," he said, smiling. "Mademoiselle."

He bowed to Flora.

"Perhaps," I began, "you have heard of the tragedy which occurred last night."

His face grew grave.

"But certainly I have heard. It is horrible. I offer mademoiselle all my sympathy. In what way can I serve you?"

"Miss Ackroyd," I said, "wants you to—to——"

"To find the murderer," said Flora in a clear voice.

"I see," said the little man. "But the police will do that, will they not?"

"They might make a mistake," said Flora. "They are on their way to make a mistake now, I think. Please, M. Poirot, won't you help us? If—if it is a question of money——"

Poirot held up his hand.

"Not that, I beg of you, mademoiselle. Not that I do not care for money." His eyes showed a momentary twinkle. "Money, it means much to me and always has done. No, if I go into this, you must understand one thing clearly. *I shall go through with it to the end*. The good dog, he does not leave the scent, remember! You may wish that, after all, you had left it to the local police."

"I want the truth," said Flora, looking him straight in the eyes.

"All the truth?"

"All the truth."

"Then I accept," said the little man quietly. "And I hope you will not regret those words. Now, tell me all the circumstances."

"Dr. Sheppard had better tell you," said Flora. "He knows more than I do."

Thus enjoined, I plunged into a careful narrative, embodying all the facts I have previously set down. Poirot listened carefully, inserting a question here and there, but for the most part sitting in silence, his eyes on the ceiling.

I brought my story to a close with the departure of the inspector and myself from Fernly Park the previous night.

"And now," said Flora, as I finished, "tell him all about Ralph."

I hesitated, but her imperious glance drove me on.

"You went to this inn—this Three Boars—last night on your way home?" asked Poirot, as I brought my tale to a close. "Now exactly why was that?"

I paused a moment to choose my words carefully.

"I thought some one ought to inform the young man of his stepfather's death. It occurred to me after I had left Fernly that possibly no one but myself and Mr. Ackroyd were aware that he was staying in the village."

Poirot nodded.

"Quite so. That was your only motive in going there, eh?"

"That was my only motive," I said stiffly.

"It was not to—shall we say—reassure yourself about *ce jeune homme?*"

"Reassure myself?"

"I think, M. le docteur, that you know very well what I mean, though you pretend not to do so. I suggest that it would have been a relief to you if you had found that Captain Paton had been at home all the evening."

"Not at all," I said sharply.

The little detective shook his head at me gravely.

"You have not the trust in me of Miss Flora," he said. "But no matter. What we have to look at is this—Captain Paton is missing, under circumstances which call for an explanation. I will not hide from you that the matter looks grave. Still, it may admit of a perfectly simple explanation."

"That's just what I keep saying," cried Flora eagerly.

Poirot touched no more upon that theme. Instead he suggested an immediate visit to the local police. He thought it better for Flora to return home, and for me to be the one to accompany him there and introduce him to the officer in charge of the case.

We carried out this plan forthwith. We found Inspector Davis outside the police station looking very glum indeed. With him was Colonel Melrose, the Chief Constable, and another man whom, from Flora's description of "weaselly," I had no difficulty in recognizing as Inspector Raglan from Cranchester.

I know Melrose fairly well, and I introduced Poirot to him and explained the situation. The chief constable was clearly vexed, and Inspector Raglan looked as black as thunder. Davis, however, seemed slightly exhilarated by the sight of his superior officer's annoyance.

"The case is going to be plain as a pikestaff," said Raglan. "Not the least need for amateurs to come butting in. You'd think any fool would have seen the way things were last night, and then we shouldn't have lost twelve hours."

He directed a vengeful glance at poor Davis, who received it with perfect stolidity.

"Mr. Ackroyd's family must, of course, do what they see fit," said Colonel Melrose. "But we cannot have the official investigation hampered in any way. I know M. Poirot's great reputation, of course," he added courteously.

"The police can't advertise themselves, worse luck," said Raglan.

It was Poirot who saved the situation.

"It is true that I have retired from the world," he said. "I never intended to take up a case again. Above all things, I have a horror of publicity. I must beg, that in the case of my being able to contribute something to the solution of the mystery, my name may not be mentioned."

Inspector Raglan's face lightened a little.

"I've heard of some very remarkable successes of yours," observed the colonel, thawing.

"I have had much experience," said Poirot quietly. "But most of my successes have been obtained by the aid of the police. I admire enormously your English police. If Inspector Raglan permits me to assist him, I shall be both honored and flattered."

The inspector's countenance became still more gracious.

Colonel Melrose drew me aside.

"From all I hear, this little fellow's done some really remarkable things," he murmured. "We're naturally anxious not to have to call in Scotland Yard. Raglan seems very sure of himself, but I'm not quite certain that I agree with him. You see, I—er—know the parties concerned better than he does. This fellow doesn't seem out after kudos, does he? Would work in with us unobtrusively, eh?"

"To the greater glory of Inspector Raglan," I said solemnly.

"Well, well," said Colonel Melrose breezily in a louder voice, "we must put you wise to the latest developments, M. Poirot."

"I thank you," said Poirot. "My friend, Dr. Sheppard, said something of the butler being suspected?"

"That's all bunkum," said Raglan instantly. "These high-class servants get in such a funk that they act suspiciously for nothing at all."

"The fingerprints?" I hinted.

"Nothing like Parker's." He gave a faint smile, and added: "And yours and Mr. Raymond's don't fit either, doctor."

"What about those of Captain Ralph Paton?" asked Poirot quietly.

I felt a secret admiration for the way he took the bull by the horns. I saw a look of respect creep into the inspector's eye.

"I see you don't let the grass grow under your feet, Mr. Poirot. It will be a pleasure to work with you, I'm sure. We're going to take that young gentleman's fingerprints as soon as we can lay hands upon him."

"I can't help thinking you're mistaken, inspector," said Colonel Melrose warmly. "I've known Ralph Paton from a boy upward. He'd never stoop to murder."

"Maybe not," said the inspector tonelessly.

"What have you got against him?" I asked.

"Went out just on nine o'clock last night. Was seen in neighborhood of Fernly Park somewhere about nine-thirty. Not been seen since. Believed to be in serious money difficulties. I've got a pair of his shoes here—shoes with rubber studs in them. He had two pairs, almost exactly alike. I'm going up now to compare them with those footmarks. The constable is up there seeing that no one tampers with them."

"We'll go at once," said Colonel Melrose. "You and M. Poirot will accompany us, will you not?"

We assented, and all drove up in the colonel's car. The inspector was anxious to get at once to the footmarks, and asked to be put down at the lodge. About half-way up the drive, on the right, a path branched off which led round to the terrace and the window of Ackroyd's study.

"Would you like to go with the inspector, M. Poirot?" asked the chief constable, "or would you prefer to examine the study?"

Poirot chose the latter alternative. Parker opened the door to us. His manner was smug and deferential, and he seemed to have recovered from his panic of the night before.

Colonel Melrose took a key from his pocket, and unlocking the door which led into the lobby, he ushered us through into the study.

"Except for the removal of the body, M. Poirot, this room is exactly as it was last night."

"And the body was found—where?"

As precisely as possible, I described Ackroyd's position. The armchair still stood in front of the fire.

Poirot went and sat down in it.

"The blue letter you speak of, where was it when you left the room?"

"Mr. Ackroyd had laid it down on this little table at his right hand."

Poirot nodded.

"Except for that, everything was in its place?"

"Yes, I think so."

"Colonel Melrose, would you be so extremely obliging as to sit down in this chair a minute. I thank you. Now, M. le docteur, will you kindly indicate to me the exact position of the dagger?"

I did so, whilst the little man stood in the doorway.

"The hilt of the dagger was plainly visible from the door then. Both you and Parker could see it at once?"

"Yes."

Poirot went next to the window.

"The electric light was on, of course, when you discovered the body?" he asked over his shoulder.

I assented, and joined him where he was studying the marks on the window-sill.

"The rubber studs are the same pattern as those in Captain Paton's shoes," he said quietly.

Then he came back once more to the middle of the room. His eye traveled round, searching everything in the room with a quick, trained glance.

"Are you a man of good observation, Dr. Sheppard?" he asked at last.

"I think so," I said, surprised.

"There was a fire in the grate, I see. When you broke the door down and found Mr. Ackroyd dead, how was the fire? Was it low?"

I gave a vexed laugh.

"I—I really can't say. I didn't notice. Perhaps Mr. Raymond or Major Blunt——"

The little man opposite me shook his head with a faint smile.

"One must always proceed with method. I made an error of judgment in asking you that question. To each man his own knowledge. You could tell me the details of the patient's appearance—nothing there would escape you. If I wanted information about the papers on that desk, Mr. Raymond would have noticed anything there was to see. To find out about the fire, I must ask the man whose business it is to observe such things. You permit——"

He moved swiftly to the fireplace and rang the bell.

After a lapse of a minute or two Parker appeared.

"The bell rang, sir," he said hesitatingly.

"Come in, Parker," said Colonel Melrose. "This gentleman wants to ask you something."

Parker transferred a respectful attention to Poirot.

"Parker," said the little man, "when you broke down the door with Dr. Sheppard last night, and found your master dead, what was the state of the fire?"

Parker replied without a pause.

"It had burned very low, sir. It was almost out."

"Ah!" said Poirot. The exclamation sounded almost triumphant. He went on:—

"Look round you, my good Parker. Is this room exactly as it was then?"

The butler's eye swept round. It came to rest on the windows.

"The curtains were drawn, sir, and the electric light was on."

Poirot nodded approval.

"Anything else?"

"Yes, sir, this chair was drawn out a little more."

He indicated a big grandfather chair to the left of the door between it and the window. I append a plan of the room with the chair in question marked with an X.

"Just show me," said Poirot.

The butler drew the chair in question out a good two feet from the wall, turning it so that the seat faced the door.

"*Voilà ce qui est curieux,*" murmured Poirot. "No one would want to sit in a chair in such a position, I fancy. Now who pushed it back into place again, I wonder? Did you, my friend?"

"No, sir," said Parker. "I was too upset with seeing the master and all."

Poirot looked across at me.

"Did you, doctor?"

I shook my head.

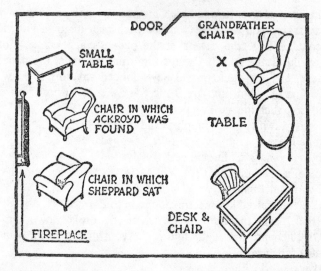

"It was back in position when I arrived with the police, sir," put in Parker. "I'm sure of that."

"Curious," said Poirot again.

"Raymond or Blunt must have pushed it back," I suggested. "Surely it isn't important?"

"It is completely unimportant," said Poirot. "That is why it is so interesting," he added softly.

"Excuse me a minute," said Colonel Melrose. He left the room with Parker.

"Do you think Parker is speaking the truth?" I asked.

"About the chair, yes. Otherwise I do not know. You will find, M. le docteur, if you have much to do with cases of this kind, that they all resemble each other in one thing."

"What is that?" I asked curiously.

"Every one concerned in them has something to hide."

"Have I?" I asked, smiling.

Poirot looked at me attentively.

"I think you have," he said quietly.

"But——"

"Have you told me everything known to you about this young man Paton?" He smiled as I grew red. "Oh! do not fear. I will not press you. I shall learn it in good time."

"I wish you'd tell me something of your methods," I said hastily, to cover my confusion. "The point about the fire, for instance?"

"Oh! that was very simple. You leave Mr. Ackroyd at—ten minutes to nine, was it not?"

"Yes, exactly, I should say."

"The window is then closed and bolted and the door unlocked. At a quarter past ten when the body is discovered, the door is locked and the window is open. Who opened it? Clearly only Mr. Ackroyd himself could have done so, and for one of two reasons. Either because the room became unbearably hot (but since the fire was nearly out and there was a sharp drop in temperature last night, that cannot be the reason), or because he admitted some one that way. And if he admitted some one that way, it must have been some one well known to him, since he had previously shown himself uneasy on the subject of that same window."

"It sounds very simple," I said.

"Everything is simple, if you arrange the facts methodically. We are concerned now with the personality of the person who was with him at nine-thirty last night. Everything goes to show that that was the individual admitted by the window, and though Mr. Ackroyd was seen alive later by Miss Flora, we cannot approach a solution of the mystery until we know who that visitor was. The window may have been left open after his departure and so afforded entrance to the murderer, or the same person may have returned a second time. Ah! here is the colonel who returns."

Colonel Melrose entered with an animated manner.

"That telephone call has been traced at last," he said. "It did not come from here. It was put through to Dr. Sheppard at 10.15 last night from a public call office at King's Abbot station. And at 10.23 the night mail leaves for Liverpool."

CHAPTER 8

INSPECTOR RAGLAN IS CONFIDENT

WE LOOKED at each other.

"You'll have inquiries made at the station, of course?" I said.

"Naturally, but I'm not over-sanguine as to the result. You know what that station is like."

I did. King's Abbot is a mere village, but its station happens to be an important junction. Most of the big expresses stop there, and trains are shunted, re-sorted, and made up. It has two or three public telephone boxes. At that time of night three local trains come in close upon each other, to catch the connection with the express for the north which comes in at 10.19 and leaves at 10.23. The whole place is in a bustle, and the chances of one particular person being noticed telephoning or getting into the express are very small indeed.

"But why telephone at all?" demanded Melrose. "That is what I find so extraordinary. There seems no rhyme or reason in the thing."

Poirot carefully straightened a china ornament on one of the book-cases.

"Be sure there was a reason," he said over his shoulder.

"But what reason could it be?"

"When we know that, we shall know everything. This case is very curious and very interesting."

There was something almost indescribable in the way he said those last words. I felt that he was looking at the case from some peculiar angle of his own, and what he saw I could not tell.

He went to the window and stood there, looking out.

"You say it was nine o'clock, Dr. Sheppard, when you met this stranger outside the gate?"

He asked the question without turning round.

"Yes," I replied. "I heard the church clock chime the hour."

"How long would it take him to reach the house—to reach this window, for instance?"

"Five minutes at the outside. Two or three minutes only if he took the path at the right of the drive and came straight here."

"But to do that he would have to know the way. How can I explain myself?—it would mean that he had been here before—that he knew his surroundings."

"That is true," replied Colonel Melrose.

"We could find out, doubtless, if Mr. Ackroyd had received any strangers during the past week?"

"Young Raymond could tell us that," I said.

"Or Parker," suggested Colonel Melrose.

"*Ou tous les deux,*" suggested Poirot, smiling.

Colonel Melrose went in search of Raymond, and I rang the bell once more for Parker.

Colonel Melrose returned almost immediately, accompanied by the young secretary, whom he introduced to Poirot. Geoffrey Raymond was fresh and debonair as ever. He seemed surprised and delighted to make Poirot's acquaintance.

"No idea you'd been living among us incognito, M. Poirot," he said. "It will be a great privilege to watch you at work—— Hallo, what's this?"

Poirot had been standing just to the left of the door. Now he moved aside suddenly, and I saw that while my back was turned he must have swiftly drawn out the arm-chair till it stood in the position Parker had indicated.

"Want me to sit in the chair whilst you take a blood test?" asked Raymond good-humoredly. "What's the idea?"

"M. Raymond, this chair was pulled out—so—last night when Mr. Ackroyd was found killed. Some one moved it back again into place. Did you do so?"

The secretary's reply came without a second's hesitation.

"No, indeed I didn't. I don't even remember that it was in that position, but it must have been if you say so. Anyway, somebody else must have moved it back to its proper place. Have they destroyed a clew in doing so? Too bad!"

"It is of no consequence," said the detective. "Of no consequence whatever. What I really want to ask you is this, M. Raymond: Did any stranger come to see Mr. Ackroyd during this past week?"

The secretary reflected for a minute or two, knitting his brows, and during the pause Parker appeared in answer to the bell.

"No," said Raymond at last. "I can't remember any one. Can you, Parker?"

"I beg your pardon, sir?"

"Any stranger coming to see Mr. Ackroyd this week?"

The butler reflected for a minute or two.

"There was the young man who came on Wednesday, sir," he said at last. "From Curtis and Troute, I understood he was."

Raymond moved this aside with an impatient hand.

"Oh! yes, I remember, but that is not the kind of stranger this gentleman means." He turned to Poirot. "Mr. Ackroyd had some idea of purchasing a dictaphone," he explained. "It would have enabled us to get through a lot more work in a limited time. The firm in question sent down their representative, but nothing came of it. Mr. Ackroyd did not make up his mind to purchase."

Poirot turned to the butler.

"Can you describe this young man to me, my good Parker?"

"He was fair-haired, sir, and short. Very neatly dressed in a blue serge suit. A very presentable young man, sir, for his station in life."

Poirot turned to me.

"The man you met outside the gate, doctor, was tall, was he not?"

"Yes," I said. "Somewhere about six feet, I should say."

"There is nothing in that, then," declared the Belgian. "I thank you, Parker."

The butler spoke to Raymond.

"Mr. Hammond has just arrived, sir," he said. "He is anxious to knew if he can be of any service, and he would be glad to have a word with you."

"I'll come at once," said the young man. He hurried out. Poirot looked inquiringly at the chief constable.

"The family solicitor, M. Poirot," said the latter.

"It is a busy time for this young M. Raymond," murmured M. Poirot. "He has the air efficient, that one."

"I believe Mr. Ackroyd considered him a most able secretary."

"He has been here—how long?"

"Just on two years, I fancy."

"His duties he fulfills punctiliously. Of that I am sure. In what manner does he amuse himself? Does he go in for *le sport?*"

"Private secretaries haven't much time for that sort of thing," said Colonel Melrose, smiling. "Raymond plays golf, I believe. And tennis in the summer time."

"He does not attend the courses—I should say the running of the horses?"

"Race meetings? No, I don't think he's interested in racing."

Poirot nodded and seemed to lose interest. He glanced slowly round the study.

"I have seen, I think, all that there is to be seen here."

I, too, looked round.

"If those walls could speak," I murmured.

Poirot shook his head.

"A tongue is not enough," he said. "They would have to have also eyes and ears. But do not be too sure that these dead things"—he touched the top of the bookcase as he spoke—"are always dumb. To me they speak sometimes—chairs, tables—they have their message!"

He turned away towards the door.

"What message?" I cried. "What have they said to you to-day?"

He looked over his shoulder and raised one eyebrow quizzically.

"An opened window," he said. "A locked door. A chair that apparently moved itself. To all three I say, 'Why?' and I find no answer."

He shook his head, puffed out his chest, and stood blinking at us. He looked ridiculously full of his own importance. It crossed my mind to wonder whether he was really any good as a detective. Had his big reputation been built up on a series of lucky chances?

I think the same thought must have occurred to Colonel Melrose, for he frowned.

"Anything more you want to see, M. Poirot?" he inquired brusquely.

"You would perhaps be so kind as to show me the silver table from which the weapon was taken? After that, I will trespass on your kindness no longer."

We went to the drawing-room, but on the way the constable waylaid the colonel, and after a muttered conversation the latter excused himself and left us together. I showed Poirot the silver table, and after raising the lid once or twice and letting it fall, he pushed open the window and stepped out on the terrace. I followed him.

Inspector Raglan had just turned the corner of the house, and was coming towards us. His face looked grim and satisfied.

"So there you are, M. Poirot," he said. "Well, this isn't going to be much of a case. I'm sorry, too. A nice enough young fellow gone wrong."

Poirot's face fell, and he spoke very mildly.

"I'm afraid I shall not be able to be of much aid to you, then?"

"Next time, perhaps," said the inspector soothingly. "Though we don't have murders every day in this quiet little corner of the world."

Poirot's gaze took on an admiring quality.

"You have been of a marvelous promptness," he observed. "How exactly did you go to work, if I may ask?"

"Certainly," said the inspector. "To begin with—method. That's what I always say—method!"

"Ah!" cried the other. "That, too, is my watchword. Method, order, and the little gray cells."

"The cells?" said the inspector, staring.

"The little gray cells of the brain," explained the Belgian.

"Oh, of course; well, we all use them, I suppose."

"In a greater or lesser degree," murmured Poirot. "And there are, too, differences in quality. Then there is the psychology of a crime. One must study that."

"Ah!" said the inspector, "you've been bitten with all this psycho-analysis stuff? Now, I'm a plain man——"

"Mrs. Raglan would not agree, I am sure, to that," said Poirot, making him a little bow.

Inspector Raglan, a little taken aback, bowed.

"You don't understand," he said, grinning broadly. "Lord, what a lot of difference language makes. I'm telling you how I set to work. First of all, method. Mr. Ackroyd was last seen alive at a quarter to ten by his niece, Miss Flora Ackroyd. That's fact number one, isn't it?"

"If you say so."

"Well, it is. At half-past ten, the doctor here says that Mr. Ackroyd has been dead at least half an hour. You stick to that, doctor?"

"Certainly," I said. "Half an hour or longer."

"Very good. That gives us exactly a quarter of an hour in which the crime must have been committed. I make a list of every one in the house, and work through it, setting down opposite their names where they were and what they were doing between the hour of 9.45 and 10 p.m."

He handed a sheet of paper to Poirot. I read it over his shoulder. It ran as follows, written in a neat script:—

Major Blunt.—In billiard room with Mr. Raymond.
    (Latter confirms.)
Mr. Raymond.—Billiard room. (See above.)
Mrs. Ackroyd.—9.45 watching billiard match. Went up to bed 9.55.
    (Raymond and Blunt watched her up staircase.)
Miss Ackroyd.—Went straight from her uncle's room upstairs.
    (Confirmed by Parker, also housemaid, Elsie Dale.)
Servants:—
    Parker.—Went straight to butler's pantry. (Confirmed by house-keeper, Miss Russell, who came down to speak to him about something at 9.47, and remained at least ten minutes.)
    Miss Russell.—As above. Spoke to housemaid, Elsie Dale, upstairs at 9.45.
    Ursula Bourne (parlormaid).—In her own room until 9.55. Then in Servants' Hall.
    Mrs. Cooper (cook).—In Servants' Hall.
    Gladys Jones (second housemaid).—In Servants' Hall.

Elsie Dale.—Upstairs in bedroom. Seen there by Miss Russell and Miss Flora Ackroyd.
Mary Thripp (kitchenmaid).—Servants' Hall.

"The cook has been here seven years, the parlormaid eighteen months, and Parker just over a year. The others are new. Except for something fishy about Parker, they all seem quite all right."

"A very complete list," said Poirot, handing it back to him. "I am quite sure that Parker did not do the murder," he added gravely.

"So is my sister," I struck in. "And she's usually right." Nobody paid any attention to my interpolation.

"That disposes pretty effectually of the household," continued the inspector. "Now we come to a very grave point. The woman at the lodge—Mary Black—was pulling the curtains last night when she saw Ralph Paton turn in at the gate and go up towards the house."

"She is sure of that?" I asked sharply.

"Quite sure. She knows him well by sight. He went past very quickly and turned off by the path to the right, which is a short cut to the terrace."

"And what time was that?" asked Poirot, who had sat with an immovable face.

"Exactly twenty-five minutes past nine," said the inspector gravely.

There was a silence. Then the inspector spoke again.

"It's all clear enough. It fits in without a flaw. At twenty-five minutes past nine, Captain Paton is seen passing the lodge; at nine-thirty or thereabouts, Mr. Geoffrey Raymond hears some one in here asking for money and Mr. Ackroyd refusing. What happens next? Captain Paton leaves the same way—through the window. He walks along the terrace, angry and baffled. He comes to the open drawing-room window. Say it's now a quarter to ten. Miss Flora Ackroyd is saying good-night to her uncle. Major Blunt, Mr. Raymond, and Mrs. Ackroyd are in the billiard room. The drawing-room is empty. He steals in, takes the dagger from the silver table, and returns to the study window. He slips off his shoes, climbs in, and—well, I don't need to go into details. Then he slips out again and goes off. Hadn't the nerve to go back to the inn. He makes for the station, rings up from there——"

"Why?" said Poirot softly.

I jumped at the interruption. The little man was leaning forward. His eyes shone with a queer green light.

For a moment Inspector Raglan was taken aback by the question.

"It's difficult to say exactly why he did that," he said at last. "But murderers do funny things. You'd know that if you were in the police force. The cleverest of them make stupid mistakes sometimes. But come along and I'll show you those footprints."

We followed him round the corner of the terrace to the study window. At a word from Raglan a police constable produced the shoes which had been obtained from the local inn.

The inspector laid them over the marks.

"They're the same," he said confidently. "That is to say, they're not the same pair that actually made these prints. He went away in those. This is a pair just like them, but older—see how the studs are worn down."

"Surely a great many people wear shoes with rubber studs in them?" asked Poirot.

"That's so, of course," said the inspector. "I shouldn't put so much stress on the footmarks if it wasn't for everything else."

"A very foolish young man, Captain Ralph Paton," said Poirot thoughtfully. "To leave so much evidence of his presence."

"Ah! well," said the inspector, "it was a dry, fine night, you know. He left no prints on the terrace or on the graveled path. But, unluckily for him, a spring must have welled up just lately at the end of the path from the drive. See here."

A small graveled path joined the terrace a few feet away. In one spot, a few yards from its termination, the ground was wet and boggy. Crossing this wet place there were again the marks of footsteps, and amongst them the shoes with rubber studs.

Poirot followed the path on a little way, the inspector by his side.

"You noticed the women's footprints?" he said suddenly.

The inspector laughed.

"Naturally. But several different women have walked this way—and men as well. It's a regular short cut to the house, you see. It would be impossible to sort out all the footsteps. After all, it's the ones on the window-sill that are really important."

Poirot nodded.

"It's no good going farther," said the inspector, as we came in view of the drive. "It's all graveled again here, and hard as it can be."

Again Poirot nodded, but his eyes were fixed on a small garden house—a kind of superior summer-house. It was a little to the left of the path ahead of us, and a graveled walk ran up to it.

Poirot lingered about until the inspector had gone back towards the house. Then he looked at me.

"You must have indeed been sent from the good God to replace my friend Hastings," he said, with a twinkle. "I observe that you do not quit my side. How say you, Dr. Sheppard, shall we investigate that summer-house? It interests me."

He went up to the door and opened it. Inside, the place was almost dark. There were one or two rustic seats, a croquet set, and some folded deck-chairs.

I was startled to observe my new friend. He had dropped to his hands and knees and was crawling about the floor. Every now and then he shook his head as though not satisfied. Finally, he sat back on his heels.

"Nothing," he murmured. "Well, perhaps it was not to be expected. But it would have meant so much——"

He broke off, stiffening all over. Then he stretched out his hand to one of the rustic chairs. He detached something from one side of it.

"What is it?" I cried. "What have you found?"

He smiled, unclosing his hand so that I should see what lay in the palm of it. A scrap of stiff white cambric.

I took it from him, looked at it curiously, and then handed it back.

"What do you make of it, eh, my friend?" he asked, eyeing me keenly.

"A scrap torn from a handkerchief," I suggested, shrugging my shoulders.

He made another dart and picked up a small quill—a goose quill by the look of it.

"And that?" he cried triumphantly. "What do you make of that?"

I only stared.

He slipped the quill into his pocket, and looked again at the scrap of white stuff.

"A fragment of a handkerchief?" he mused. "Perhaps you are right. But remember this—*a good laundry does not starch a handkerchief.*"

He nodded at me triumphantly, then he put away the scrap carefully in his pocket-book.

CHAPTER 9

THE GOLDFISH POND

WE WALKED back to the house together. There was no sign of the inspector. Poirot paused on the terrace and stood with his back to the house, slowly turning his head from side to side.

"*Une belle propriété,*" he said at last appreciatively. "Who inherits it?"

His words gave me almost a shock. It is an odd thing, but until that moment the question of inheritance had never come into my head. Poirot watched me keenly.

"It is a new idea to you, that," he said at last. "You had not thought of it before—eh?"

"No," I said truthfully. "I wish I had."

He looked at me again curiously.

"I wonder just what you mean by that," he said thoughtfully. "Ah! no," as I was about to speak. "*Inutile!* You would not tell me your real thought."

"Every one has something to hide," I quoted, smiling.

"Exactly."

"You still believe that?"

"More than ever, my friend. But it is not easy to hide things from Hercule Poirot. He has a knack of finding out."

He descended the steps of the Dutch garden as he spoke.

"Let us walk a little," he said over his shoulder. "The air is pleasant to-day."

I followed him. He led me down a path to the left enclosed in yew hedges. A walk led down the middle, bordered on each side with formal flower beds, and at the end was a round paved recess with a seat and a pond of goldfish. Instead of pursuing the path to the end, Poirot took another which wound up the side of a wooded slope. In one spot the trees had been cleared away, and a seat had been put. Sitting there one had a splendid view over the countryside, and one looked right down on the paved recess and the goldfish pond.

"England is very beautiful," said Poirot, his eyes straying over the prospect. Then he smiled. "And so are English girls," he said in a lower tone. "Hush, my friend, and look at the pretty picture below us."

It was then that I saw Flora. She was moving along the path we had just left and she was humming a little snatch of song. Her step was more dancing than walking, and in spite of her black dress, there was nothing but joy in her whole attitude. She gave a sudden pirouette on her toes, and her black draperies swung out. At the same time she flung her head back and laughed outright.

As she did so a man stepped out from the trees. It was Hector Blunt.

The girl started. Her expression changed a little.

"How you startled me—I didn't see you."

Blunt said nothing, but stood looking at her for a minute or two in silence.

"What I like about you," said Flora, with a touch of malice, "is your cheery conversation."

I fancy that at that Blunt reddened under his tan. His voice, when he spoke, sounded different—it had a curious sort of humility in it.

"Never was much of a fellow for talking. Not even when I was young."

"That was a very long time ago, I suppose," said Flora gravely.

I caught the undercurrent of laughter in her voice, but I don't think Blunt did.

"Yes," he said simply, "it was."

"How does it feel to be Methuselah?" asked Flora.

This time the laughter was more apparent, but Blunt was following out an idea of his own.

"Remember the Johnny who sold his soul to the devil? In return for being made young again? There's an opera about it."

"Faust, you mean?"

"That's the beggar. Rum story. Some of us would do it if we could."

"Any one would think you were creaking at the joints to hear you talk," cried Flora, half vexed, half amused.

Blunt said nothing for a minute or two. Then he looked away from Flora into the middle distance and observed to an adjacent tree trunk that it was about time he got back to Africa.

"Are you going on another expedition—shooting things?"

"Expect so. Usually do, you know—shoot things, I mean."

"You shot that head in the hall, didn't you?"

Blunt nodded. Then he jerked out, going rather red, as he did so:—

"Care for some decent skins any time? If so, I could get 'em for you."

"Oh! please do," cried Flora. "Will you really? You won't forget?"

"I shan't forget," said Hector Blunt.

He added, in a sudden burst of communicativeness:—

"Time I went. I'm no good in this sort of life. Haven't got the manners for it. I'm a rough fellow, no use in society. Never remember the things one's expected to say. Yes, time I went."

"But you're not going at once," cried Flora. "Not—not while we're in all this trouble. Oh! please. If you go——"

She turned away a little.

"You want me to stay?" asked Blunt.

He spoke deliberately but quite simply.

"We all——"

"I meant you personally," said Blunt, with directness.

Flora turned slowly back again and met his eyes.

"I want you to stay," she said, "if—if that makes any difference."

"It makes all the difference," said Blunt.

There was a moment's silence. They sat down on the stone seat by the goldfish pond. It seemed as though neither of them knew quite what to say next.

"It—it's such a lovely morning," said Flora at last. "You know, I can't help feeling happy, in spite—in spite of everything. That's awful, I suppose?"

"Quite natural," said Blunt. "Never saw your uncle until two years ago, did you? Can't be expected to grieve very much. Much better to have no humbug about it."

"There's something awfully consoling about you," said Flora. "You make things so simple."

"Things are simple as a rule," said the big game hunter.

"Not always," said Flora.

Her voice had lowered itself, and I saw Blunt turn and look at her, bringing his eyes back from (apparently) the coast of Africa to do so. He evidently put his own construction on her change of tone, for he said, after a minute or two, in rather an abrupt manner:—

"I say, you know, you mustn't worry. About that young chap, I mean. Inspector's an ass. Everybody knows—utterly absurd to think he could have done it. Man from outside. Burglar chap. That's the only possible solution."

Flora turned to look at him.

"You really think so?"

"Don't you?" said Blunt quickly.

"I—oh, yes, of course."

Another silence, and then Flora burst out:—

"I'm—I'll tell you why I felt so happy this morning. However heartless you think me, I'd rather tell you. It's because the lawyer has been—Mr. Hammond. He told us about the will. Uncle Roger has left me twenty thousand pounds. Think of it—twenty thousand beautiful pounds."

Blunt looked surprised.

"Does it mean so much to you?"

"Mean much to me? Why, it's everything. Freedom—life—no more scheming and scraping and lying——"

"Lying?" said Blunt, sharply interrupting.

Flora seemed taken aback for a minute.

"You know what I mean," she said uncertainly. "Pretending to be thankful for all the nasty castoff things rich relations give you. Last year's coats and skirts and hats."

"Don't know much about ladies' clothes; should have said you were always very well turned out."

"It's cost me something, though," said Flora in a low voice. "Don't let's talk of horrid things. I'm so happy I'm free. Free to do what I like. Free not to——"

She stopped suddenly.

"Not to what?" asked Blunt quickly.

"I forget now. Nothing important."

Blunt had a stick in his hand, and he thrust it into the pond, poking at something.

"What are you doing, Major Blunt?"

"There's something bright down there. Wondered what it was—looks like a gold brooch. Now I've stirred up the mud and it's gone."

"Perhaps it's a crown," suggested Flora. "Like the one Mélisande saw in the water."

"Mélisande," said Blunt reflectively—"she's in an opera, isn't she?"

"Yes, you seem to know a lot about operas."

"People take me sometimes," said Blunt sadly. "Funny idea of pleasure—worse racket than the natives make with their tom-toms."

Flora laughed.

"I remember Mélisande," continued Blunt, "married an old chap old enough to be her father."

He threw a small piece of flint into the goldfish pond. Then, with a change of manner, he turned to Flora.

"Miss Ackroyd, can I do anything? About Paton, I mean. I know how dreadfully anxious you must be."

"Thank you," said Flora in a cold voice. "There is really nothing to be done. Ralph will be all right. I've got hold of the most wonderful detective in the world, and he's going to find out all about it."

For some time I had felt uneasy as to our position. We were not exactly eavesdropping, since the two in the garden below had only to lift their heads to see us. Nevertheless, I should have drawn attention to our presence before now, had not my companion put a warning pressure on my arm. Clearly he wished me to remain silent.

But now he rose briskly to his feet, clearing his throat.

"I demand pardon," he cried. "I cannot allow mademoiselle thus extravagantly to compliment me, and not draw attention to my presence. They say the listener hears no good of himself, but that is not the case this time. To spare my blushes, I must join you and apologize."

He hurried down the path with me close behind him, and joined the others by the pond.

"This is M. Hercule Poirot," said Flora. "I expect you've heard of him."

Poirot bowed.

"I know Major Blunt by reputation," he said politely. "I am glad to have encountered you, monsieur. I am in need of some information that you can give me."

Blunt looked at him inquiringly.

"When did you last see M. Ackroyd alive?"

"At dinner."

"And you neither saw nor heard anything of him after that?"

"Didn't see him. Heard his voice."

"How was that?"

"I strolled out on the terrace——"

"Pardon me, what time was this?"

"About half-past nine. I was walking up and down smoking in front of the drawing-room window. I heard Ackroyd talking in his study——"

Poirot stooped and removed a microscopic weed.

"Surely you couldn't hear voices in the study from that part of the terrace," he murmured.

He was not looking at Blunt, but I was, and to my intense surprise, I saw the latter flush.

"Went as far as the corner," he explained unwillingly.

"Ah! indeed?" said Poirot.

In the mildest manner he conveyed an impression that more was wanted.

"Thought I saw—a woman disappearing into the bushes. Just a gleam of white, you know. Must have been mistaken. It was while I was standing at the corner of the terrace that I heard Ackroyd's voice speaking to that secretary of his."

"Speaking to Mr. Geoffrey Raymond?"

"Yes—that's what I supposed at the time. Seems I was wrong."

"Mr. Ackroyd didn't address him by name?"

"Oh, no."

"Then, if I may ask, why did you think——?"

Blunt explained laboriously.

"Took it for granted that it *would* be Raymond, because he had said just before I came out that he was taking some papers to Ackroyd. Never thought of it being anybody else."

"Can you remember what the words you heard were?"

"Afraid I can't. Something quite ordinary and unimportant. Only caught a scrap of it. I was thinking of something else at the time."

"It is of no importance," murmured Poirot. "Did you move a chair back against the wall when you went into the study after the body was discovered?"

"Chair? No—why should I?"

Poirot shrugged his shoulders but did not answer. He turned to Flora.

"There is one thing I should like to know from you, mademoiselle. When you were examining the things in the silver table with Dr. Sheppard, was the dagger in its place, or was it not?"

Flora's chin shot up.

"Inspector Raglan has been asking me that," she said resentfully. "I've told him, and I'll tell you. I'm perfectly certain the dagger was *not* there. He thinks it was and that Ralph sneaked it later in the evening. And—and he doesn't believe me. He thinks I'm saying it to—to shield Ralph."

"And aren't you?" I asked gravely.

Flora stamped her foot.

"You, too, Dr. Sheppard! Oh! it's too bad."

Poirot tactfully made a diversion.

"It is true what I heard you say, Major Blunt. There is something that glitters in this pond. Let us see if I can reach it."

He knelt down by the pond, baring his arm to the elbow, and lowered it in very slowly, so as not to disturb the bottom of the pond. But in spite of all his precautions the mud eddied and swirled, and he was forced to draw his arm out again empty-handed.

He gazed ruefully at the mud upon his arm. I offered him my handkerchief, which he accepted with fervent protestations of thanks. Blunt looked at his watch.

"Nearly lunch time," he said. "We'd better be getting back to the house."

"You will lunch with us, M. Poirot?" asked Flora. "I should like you to meet my mother. She is—very fond of Ralph."

The little man bowed.

"I shall be delighted, mademoiselle."

"And you will stay, too, won't you, Dr. Sheppard?"

I hesitated.

"Oh, do!"

I wanted to, so I accepted the invitation without further ceremony.

We set out towards the house, Flora and Blunt walking ahead.

"What hair," said Poirot to me in a low tone, nodding towards Flora. "The real gold! They will make a pretty couple. She and the dark, handsome Captain Paton. Will they not?"

I looked at him inquiringly, but he began to fuss about a few microscopic drops of water on his coat sleeve. The man reminded me in some ways of a cat. His green eyes and his finicking habits.

"And all for nothing, too," I said sympathetically. "I wonder what it was in the pond?"

"Would you like to see?" asked Poirot.

I stared at him. He nodded.

"My good friend," he said gently and reproachfully, "Hercule Poirot does not run the risk of disarranging his costume without being sure of attaining his object. To do so would be ridiculous and absurd. I am never ridiculous."

"But you brought your hand out empty," I objected.

"There are times when it is necessary to have discretion. Do you tell your patients everything—everything, doctor? I think not. Nor do you tell your excellent sister everything either, is it not so? Before showing my empty hand, I dropped what it contained into my other hand. You shall see what that was."

He held out his left hand, palm open. On it lay a little circlet of gold. A woman's wedding ring.

I took it from him.

"Look inside," commanded Poirot.

I did so. Inside was an inscription in fine writing:—

From R., March 13th.

I looked at Poirot, but he was busy inspecting his appearance in a tiny pocket glass. He paid particular attention to his mustaches, and none at all to me. I saw that he did not intend to be communicative.

CHAPTER 10

THE PARLORMAID

WE FOUND Mrs. Ackroyd in the hall. With her was a small dried-up little man, with an aggressive chin and sharp gray eyes, and "lawyer" written all over him.

"Mr. Hammond is staying to lunch with us," said Mrs. Ackroyd. "You know Major Blunt, Mr. Hammond? And dear Dr. Sheppard— also a close friend of poor Roger's. And, let me see——"

She paused, surveying Hercule Poirot in some perplexity.

"This is M. Poirot, mother," said Flora. "I told you about him this morning."

"Oh! yes," said Mrs. Ackroyd vaguely. "Of course, my dear, of course. He is to find Ralph, is he not?"

"He is to find out who killed uncle," said Flora.

"Oh! my dear," cried her mother. "Please! My poor nerves. I am a wreck this morning, a positive wreck. Such a dreadful thing to happen. I can't help feeling that it must have been an accident of some kind. Roger was so fond of handling queer curios. His hand must have slipped, or something."

This theory was received in polite silence. I saw Poirot edge up to the lawyer, and speak to him in a confidential undertone. They moved aside into the embrasure of the window. I joined them—then hesitated.

"Perhaps I'm intruding," I said.

"Not at all," cried Poirot heartily. "You and I, M. le docteur, we investigate this affair side by side. Without you I should be lost. I desire a little information from the good Mr. Hammond."

"You are acting on behalf of Captain Ralph Paton, I understand," said the lawyer cautiously.

Poirot shook his head.

"Not so. I am acting in the interests of justice. Miss Ackroyd has asked me to investigate the death of her uncle."

Mr. Hammond seemed slightly taken aback.

"I cannot seriously believe that Captain Paton can be concerned in this crime," he said, "however strong the circumstantial evidence against him may be. The mere fact that he was hard·pressed for money——"

"Was he hard pressed for money?" interpolated Poirot quickly.

The lawyer shrugged his shoulders.

"It was a chronic condition with Ralph Paton," he said dryly. "Money went through his hands like water. He was always applying to his stepfather."

"Had he done so of late? During the last year, for instance?"

"I cannot say. Mr. Ackroyd did not mention the fact to me."

"I comprehend. Mr. Hammond, I take it that you are acquainted with the provisions of Mr. Ackroyd's will?"

"Certainly. That is my principal business here to-day."

"Then, seeing that I am acting for Miss Ackroyd, you will not object to telling me the terms of that will?"

"They are quite simple. Shorn of legal phraseology, and after paying certain legacies and bequests——"

"Such as——?" interrupted Poirot.

Mr. Hammond seemed a little surprised.

"A thousand pounds to his housekeeper, Miss Russell; fifty pounds to the cook, Emma Cooper; five hundred pounds to his secretary, Mr. Geoffrey Raymond. Then to various hospitals——"

Poirot held up his hand.

"Ah! the charitable bequests, they interest me not."

"Quite so. The income on ten thousand pounds' worth of shares to be paid to Mrs. Cecil Ackroyd during her lifetime. Miss Flora Ackroyd inherits twenty thousand pounds outright. The residue— including this property, and the shares in Ackroyd and Son—to his adopted son, Ralph Paton."

"Mr. Ackroyd possessed a large fortune?"

"A very large fortune. Captain Paton will be an exceedingly wealthy young man."

There was a silence. Poirot and the lawyer looked at each other.

"Mr. Hammond," came Mrs. Ackroyd's voice plaintively from the fireplace.

The lawyer answered the summons. Poirot took my arm and drew me right into the window.

"Regard the irises," he remarked in rather a loud voice. "Magnificent, are they not? A straight and pleasing effect."

At the same time I felt the pressure of his hand on my arm, and he added in a low tone:—

"Do you really wish to aid me? To take part in this investigation?"

"Yes, indeed," I said eagerly. "There's nothing I should like better. You don't know what a dull old fogey's life I lead. Never anything out of the ordinary."

"Good, we will be colleagues then. In a minute or two I fancy Major Blunt will join us. He is not happy with the good mamma. Now there are some things I want to know—but I do not wish to seem to want to know them. You comprehend? So it will be your part to ask the questions."

"What questions do you want me to ask?" I asked apprehensively.

"I want you to introduce the name of Mrs. Ferrars."

"Yes?"

"Speak of her in a natural fashion. Ask him if he was down here when her husband died. You understand the kind of thing I mean. And while he replies, watch his face without seeming to watch it. *C'est compris?*"

There was no time for more, for at that minute, as Poirot had prophesied, Blunt left the others in his abrupt fashion and came over to us.

I suggested strolling on the terrace, and he acquiesced. Poirot stayed behind.

I stopped to examine a late rose.

"How things change in the course of a day or so," I observed. "I was up here last Wednesday, I remember, walking up and down this same terrace. Ackroyd was with me—full of spirits. And now—three days later—Ackroyd's dead, poor fellow, Mrs. Ferrars's dead—you knew her, didn't you? But of course you did."

Blunt nodded his head.

"Had you seen her since you'd been down this time?"

"Went with Ackroyd to call. Last Tuesday, think it was. Fascinating woman—but something queer about her. Deep—one would never know what she was up to."

I looked into his steady gray eyes. Nothing there surely. I went on:—

"I suppose you'd met her before."

"Last time I was here—she and her husband had just come here to live." He paused a minute and then added: "Rum thing, she had changed a lot between then and now."

"How—changed?" I asked.

"Looked ten years older."

"Were you down here when her husband died?" I asked, trying to make the question sound as casual as possible.

"No. From all I heard it would be a good riddance. Uncharitable, perhaps, but the truth."

I agreed.

"Ashley Ferrars was by no means a pattern husband," I said cautiously.

"Blackguard, I thought," said Blunt.

"No," I said, "only a man with more money than was good for him."

"Oh! money! All the troubles in the world can be put down to money—or the lack of it."

"Which has been your particular trouble?" I asked.

"I've enough for what I want. I'm one of the lucky ones."

"Indeed."

"I'm not too flush just now, as a matter of fact. Came into a legacy a year ago, and like a fool let myself be persuaded into putting it into some wild-cat scheme."

I sympathized, and narrated my own similar trouble.

Then the gong pealed out, and we all went in to lunch. Poirot drew me back a little.

"*Eh! bien?*"

"He's all right," I said. "I'm sure of it."

"Nothing—disturbing?"

"He had a legacy just a year ago," I said. "But why not? Why shouldn't he? I'll swear the man is perfectly square and aboveboard."

"Without doubt, without doubt," said Poirot soothingly. "Do not upset yourself."

He spoke as though to a fractious child.

We all trooped into the dining-room. It seemed incredible that less than twenty-four hours had passed since I last sat at that table.

Afterwards, Mrs. Ackroyd took me aside and sat down with me on a sofa.

"I can't help feeling a little hurt," she murmured, producing a handkerchief of the kind obviously not meant to be cried into. "Hurt, I mean, by Roger's lack of confidence in me. That twenty thousand pounds ought to have been left to *me*—not to Flora. A mother could be trusted to safeguard the interests of her child. A lack of trust, I call it."

"You forget, Mrs. Ackroyd," I said, "Flora was Ackroyd's own niece, a blood relation. It would have been different had you been his sister instead of his sister-in-law."

"As poor Cecil's widow, I think my feelings ought to have been considered," said the lady, touching her eyelashes gingerly with the handkerchief. "But Roger was always most peculiar—not to say *mean* —about money matters. It has been a most difficult position for both Flora and myself. He did not even give the poor child an allowance. He would pay her bills, you know, and even that with a good deal of reluctance and asking what she wanted all those fal-lals for—so like a man—but—now I've forgotten what it was I was going to say! Oh, yes, not a penny we could call our own, you know. Flora resented it—yes, I must say she resented it—very strongly. Though devoted to her uncle, of course. But any girl would have resented it. Yes, I must say Roger had very strange ideas about money. He wouldn't even buy new face towels, though I told him the old ones were in holes. And then," proceeded Mrs. Ackroyd, with a sudden leap highly characteristic of her conversation, "to leave all that money—a thousand pounds—fancy, a thousand pounds!—to that woman."

"What woman?"

"That Russell woman. Something very queer about her, and so I've always said. But Roger wouldn't hear a word against her. Said she was a woman of great force of character, and that he admired and respected her. He was always going on about her rectitude and independence and moral worth. *I* think there's something fishy about her. She was certainly doing her best to marry Roger. But I soon put a stop to that. She's always hated me. Naturally. *I* saw through her."

I began to wonder if there was any chance of stemming Mrs. Ackroyd's eloquence, and getting away.

Mr. Hammond provided the necessary diversion by coming up to say good-by. I seized my chance and rose also.

"About the inquest," I said. "Where would you prefer it to be held. Here, or at the Three Boars?"

Mrs. Ackroyd stared at me with a dropped jaw.

"The inquest?" she asked, the picture of consternation. "But surely there won't have to be an inquest?"

Mr. Hammond gave a dry little cough and murmured, "Inevitable. Under the circumstances," in two short little barks.

"But surely Dr. Sheppard can arrange——"

"There are limits to my powers of arrangement," I said dryly.

"If his death was an accident——"

"He was murdered, Mrs. Ackroyd," I said brutally.

She gave a little cry.

"No theory of accident will hold water for a minute."

Mrs. Ackroyd looked at me in distress. I had no patience with what I thought was her silly fear of unpleasantness.

"If there's an inquest, I—I shan't have to answer questions and all that, shall I?" she asked.

"I don't know what will be necessary," I answered. "I imagine Mr. Raymond will take the brunt of it off you. He knows all the circumstances, and can give formal evidence of identification."

The lawyer assented with a little bow.

"I really don't think there is anything to dread, Mrs. Ackroyd," he said. "You will be spared all unpleasantness. Now, as to the question of money, have you all you need for the present? I mean," he added, as she looked at him inquiringly, "ready money. Cash, you know. If not, I can arrange to let you have whatever you require."

"That ought to be all right," said Raymond, who was standing by. "Mr. Ackroyd cashed a cheque for a hundred pounds yesterday."

"A hundred pounds?"

"Yes. For wages and other expenses due to-day. At the moment it is still intact."

"Where is this money? In his desk?"

"No, he always kept his cash in his bedroom. In an old collar-box, to be accurate. Funny idea, wasn't it?"

"I think," said the lawyer, "we ought to make sure the money is there before I leave."

"Certainly," agreed the secretary. "I'll take you up now. . . . Oh! I forgot. The door's locked."

Inquiry from Parker elicited the information that Inspector Raglan was in the housekeeper's room asking a few supplementary questions. A few minutes later the inspector joined the party in the hall, bringing the key with him. He unlocked the door and we passed into the lobby and up the small staircase. At the top of the stairs the door into

Ackroyd's bedroom stood open. Inside the room it was dark, the curtains were drawn, and the bed was turned down just as it had been last night. The inspector drew the curtains, letting in the sunlight, and Geoffrey Raymond went to the top drawer of a rosewood bureau.

"He kept his money like that, in an unlocked drawer. Just fancy," commented the inspector.

The secretary flushed a little.

"Mr. Ackroyd had perfect faith in the honesty of all the servants," he said hotly.

"Oh! quite so," said the inspector hastily.

Raymond opened the drawer, took out a round leather collar-box from the back of it, and opening it, drew out a thick wallet.

"Here is the money," he said, taking out a fat roll of notes. "You will find the hundred intact, I know, for Mr. Ackroyd put it in the collar-box in my presence last night when he was dressing for dinner, and of course it has not been touched since."

Mr. Hammond took the roll from him and counted it. He looked up sharply.

"A hundred pounds, you said. But there is only sixty here."

Raymond stared at him.

"Impossible," he cried, springing forward. Taking the notes from the other's hand, he counted them aloud.

Mr. Hammond had been right. The total amounted to sixty pounds.

"But—I can't understand it," cried the secretary, bewildered.

Poirot asked a question.

"You saw Mr. Ackroyd put this money away last night when he was dressing for dinner? You are sure he had not paid away any of it already?"

"I'm sure he hadn't. He even said, 'I don't want to take a hundred pounds down to dinner with me. Too bulgy.'"

"Then the affair is very simple," remarked Poirot. "Either he paid out that forty pounds sometime last evening, or else it has been stolen."

"That's the matter in a nutshell," agreed the inspector. He turned to Mrs. Ackroyd. "Which of the servants would come in here yesterday evening?"

"I suppose the housemaid would turn down the bed."

"Who is she? What do you know about her?"

"She's not been here very long," said Mrs. Ackroyd. "But she's a nice ordinary country girl."

"I think we ought to clear this matter up," said the inspector. "If

Mr. Ackroyd paid that money away himself, it may have a bearing on the mystery of the crime. The other servants all right, as far as you know?"

"Oh, I think so."

"Not missed anything before?"

"No."

"None of them leaving, or anything like that?"

"The parlormaid is leaving."

"When?"

"She gave notice yesterday, I believe."

"To you?"

"Oh, no. *I* have nothing to do with the servants. Miss Russell attends to the household matters."

The inspector remained lost in thought for a minute or two. Then he nodded his head and remarked, "I think I'd better have a word with Miss Russell, and I'll see the girl Dale as well."

Poirot and I accompanied him to the housekeeper's room. Miss Russell received us with her usual sang-froid.

Elsie Dale had been at Fernly five months. A nice girl, quick at her duties, and most respectable. Good references. The last girl in the world to take anything not belonging to her.

What about the parlormaid?

"She, too, was a most superior girl. Very quiet and ladylike. An excellent worker."

"Then why is she leaving?" asked the inspector.

Miss Russell pursed up her lips.

"It was none of my doing. I understand Mr. Ackroyd found fault with her yesterday afternoon. It was her duty to do the study, and she disarranged some of the papers on his desk, I believe. He was very annoyed about it, and she gave notice. At least, that is what I understood from her, but perhaps you'd like to see her yourselves?"

The inspector assented. I had already noticed the girl when she was waiting on us at lunch. A tall girl, with a lot of brown hair rolled tightly away at the back of her neck, and very steady gray eyes. She came in answer to the housekeeper's summons, and stood very straight with those same gray eyes fixed on us.

"You are Ursula Bourne?" asked the inspector.

"Yes, sir."

"I understand you are leaving?"

"Yes, sir."

"Why is that?"

"I disarranged some papers on Mr. Ackroyd's desk. He was very angry about it, and I said I had better leave. He told me to go as soon as possible."

"Were you in Mr. Ackroyd's bedroom at all last night? Tidying up or anything?"

"No, sir. That is Elsie's work. I never went near that part of the house."

"I must tell you, my girl, that a large sum of money is missing from Mr. Ackroyd's room."

At last I saw her roused. A wave of color swept over her face.

"I know nothing about any money. If you think I took it, and that that is why Mr. Ackroyd dismissed me, you are wrong."

"I'm not accusing you of taking it, my girl," said the inspector. "Don't flare up so."

The girl looked at him coldly.

"You can search my things if you like," she said disdainfully. "But you won't find anything."

Poirot suddenly interposed.

"It was yesterday afternoon that Mr. Ackroyd dismissed you—or you dismissed yourself, was it not?" he asked.

The girl nodded.

"How long did the interview last?"

"The interview?"

"Yes, the interview between you and Mr. Ackroyd in the study?"

"I—I don't know."

"Twenty minutes? Half an hour?"

"Something like that."

"Not longer?"

"Not longer than half an hour, certainly."

"Thank you, mademoiselle."

I looked curiously at him. He was rearranging a few objects on the table, setting them straight with precise fingers. His eyes were shining.

"That'll do," said the inspector.

Ursula Bourne disappeared. The inspector turned to Miss Russell.

"How long has she been here? Have you got a copy of the reference you had with her?"

Without answering the first question, Miss Russell moved to an adjacent bureau, opened one of the drawers, and took out a handful of letters clipped together with a patent fastener. She selected one and handed it to the inspector.

"H'm," said he. "Reads all right. Mrs. Richard Folliott, Marby Grange, Marby. Who's this woman?"

"Quite good county people," said Miss Russell.

"Well," said the inspector, handing it back, "let's have a look at the other one, Elsie Dale."

Elsie Dale was a big fair girl, with a pleasant but slightly stupid face. She answered our questions readily enough, and showed much distress and concern at the loss of the money.

"I don't think there's anything wrong with her," observed the inspector, after he had dismissed her.

"What about Parker?"

Miss Russell pursed her lips together and made no reply.

"I've a feeling there's something wrong about that man," the inspector continued thoughtfully. "The trouble is that I don't quite see when he got his opportunity. He'd be busy with his duties immediately after dinner, and he's got a pretty good alibi all through the evening. I know, for I've been devoting particular attention to it. Well, thank you very much, Miss Russell. We'll leave things as they are for the present. It's highly probable Mr. Ackroyd paid that money away himself."

The housekeeper bade us a dry good-afternoon, and we took our leave.

I left the house with Poirot.

"I wonder," I said, breaking the silence, "what the papers the girl disarranged could have been for Ackroyd to have got into such a state about them? I wonder if there is any clew there to the mystery?"

"The secretary said there were no papers of particular importance on the desk," said Poirot quietly.

"Yes, but——" I paused.

"It strikes you as odd that Ackroyd should have flown into a rage about so trivial a matter?"

"Yes, it does rather."

"But was it a trivial matter?"

"Of course," I admitted, "we don't know what those papers may have been. But Raymond certainly said——"

"Leave M. Raymond out of it for a minute. What did you think of that girl?"

"Which girl? The parlormaid?"

"Yes, the parlormaid. Ursula Bourne."

"She seemed a nice girl," I said hesitatingly.

Poirot repeated my words, but whereas I had laid a slight stress on the fourth word, he put it on the second.

"She *seemed* a nice girl—yes."

Then, after a minute's silence, he took something from his pocket and handed it to me.

"See, my friend, I will show you something. Look there."

The paper he had handed me was that compiled by the inspector and given by him to Poirot that morning. Following the pointing finger, I saw a small cross marked in pencil opposite the name Ursula Bourne.

"You may not have noticed it at the time, my good friend, but there was one person on this list whose alibi had no kind of confirmation. Ursula Bourne."

"You don't think——"

"Dr. Sheppard, I dare to think anything. Ursula Bourne may have killed Mr. Ackroyd, but I confess I can see no motive for her doing so. Can you?"

He looked at me very hard—so hard that I felt uncomfortable.

"Can you?" he repeated.

"No motive whatsoever," I said firmly.

His gaze relaxed. He frowned and murmured to himself:—

"Since the blackmailer was a man, it follows that she cannot be the blackmailer, then——"

I coughed.

"As far as that goes——" I began doubtfully.

He spun round on me.

"What? What are you going to say?"

"Nothing. Nothing. Only that, strictly speaking, Mrs. Ferrars in her letter mentioned a *person*—she didn't actually specify a man. But we took it for granted, Ackroyd and I, that it *was* a man."

Poirot did not seem to be listening to me. He was muttering to himself again.

"But then it is possible after all—yes, certainly it is possible—but then—ah! I must rearrange my ideas. Method, order; never have I needed them more. Everything must fit in—in its appointed place—otherwise I am on the wrong tack."

He broke off, and whirled round upon me again.

"Where is Marby?"

"It's on the other side of Cranchester."

"How far away?"

"Oh!—fourteen miles, perhaps."

"Would it be possible for you to go there? To-morrow, say?"

"To-morrow? Let me see, that's Sunday. Yes, I could arrange it. What do you want me to do there?"

"See this Mrs. Folliott. Find out all you can about Ursula Bourne."

"Very well. But—I don't much care for the job."

"It is not the time to make difficulties. A man's life may hang on this."

"Poor Ralph," I said with a sigh. "You believe him to be innocent, though?"

Poirot looked at me very gravely.

"Do you want to know the truth?"

"Of course."

"Then you shall have it. My friend, everything points to the assumption that he is guilty."

"What!" I exclaimed.

Poirot nodded.

"Yes, that stupid inspector—for he is stupid—has everything pointing his way. I seek for the truth—and the truth leads me every time to Ralph Paton. Motive, opportunity, means. But I will leave no stone unturned. I promised Mademoiselle Flora. And she was very sure, that little one. But very sure indeed."

CHAPTER 11

POIROT PAYS A CALL

I was slightly nervous when I rang the bell at Marby Grange the following afternoon. I wondered very much what Poirot expected to find out. He had entrusted the job to me. Why? Was it because, as in the case of questioning Major Blunt, he wished to remain in the background? The wish, intelligible in the first case, seemed to me quite meaningless here.

My meditations were interrupted by the advent of a smart parlormaid.

Yes, Mrs. Folliott was at home. I was ushered into a big drawingroom, and looked round me curiously as I waited for the mistress of the house. A large bare room, some good bits of old china, and some beautiful etchings, shabby covers and curtains. A lady's room in every sense of the term.

I turned from the inspection of a Bartolozzi on the wall as Mrs. Folliott came into the room. She was a tall woman, with untidy brown hair, and a very winning smile.

"Dr. Sheppard," she said hesitatingly.

"That is my name," I replied. "I must apologize for calling upon you like this, but I wanted some information about a parlormaid previously employed by you, Ursula Bourne."

With the utterance of the name the smile vanished from her face, and all the cordiality froze out of her manner. She looked uncomfortable and ill at ease.

"Ursula Bourne?" she said hesitatingly.

"Yes," I said. "Perhaps you don't remember the name?"

"Oh, yes, of course. I—I remember perfectly."

"She left you just over a year ago, I understand?"

"Yes. Yes, she did. That is quite right."

"And you were satisfied with her whilst she was with you? How long was she with you, by the way?"

"Oh! a year or two—I can't remember exactly how long. She—she is very capable. I'm sure you will find her quite satisfactory. I didn't know she was leaving Fernly. I hadn't the least idea of it."

"Can you tell me anything about her?" I asked.

"Anything about her?"

"Yes, where she comes from, who her people are—that sort of thing?"

Mrs. Folliott's face wore more than ever its frozen look.

"I don't know at all."

"Who was she with before she came to you?"

"I'm afraid I don't remember."

There was a spark of anger now underlying her nervousness. She flung up her head in a gesture that was vaguely familiar.

"Is it really necessary to ask all these questions?"

"Not at all," I said, with an air of surprise and a tinge of apology in my manner. "I had no idea you would mind answering them. I am very sorry."

Her anger left her and she became confused again.

"Oh! I don't mind answering them. I assure you I don't. Why should I? It—it just seemed a little odd, you know. That's all. A little odd."

One advantage of being a medical practitioner is that you can usually tell when people are lying to you. I should have known from Mrs. Folliott's manner, if from nothing else, that she did mind answering my questions—minded intensely. She was thoroughly uncomfortable and upset, and there was plainly some mystery in the background. I judged her to be a woman quite unused to deception of any kind, and consequently rendered acutely uneasy when forced to practice it. A child could have seen through her.

But it was also clear that she had no intention of telling me anything further. Whatever the mystery centering around Ursula Bourne might be, I was not going to learn it through Mrs. Folliott.

Defeated, I apologized once more for disturbing her, took my hat and departed.

I went to see a couple of patients and arrived home about six o'clock. Caroline was sitting beside the wreck of tea things. She had that look of suppressed exultation on her face which I know only too well. It is a sure sign with her, of either the getting or the giving of information. I wondered which it had been.

"I've had a very interesting afternoon," began Caroline as I dropped into my own particular easy chair, and stretched out my feet to the inviting blaze in the fireplace.

"Have you?" I asked. "Miss Ganett drop in to tea?"

Miss Ganett is one of the chief of our newsmongers.

"Guess again," said Caroline with intense complacency.

I guessed several times, working slowly through all the members of Caroline's Intelligence Corps. My sister received each guess with a triumphant shake of the head. In the end she volunteered the information herself.

"M. Poirot!" she said. "Now what do you think of that?"

I thought a good many things of it, but I was careful not to say them to Caroline.

"Why did he come?" I asked.

"To see me, of course. He said that knowing my brother so well, he hoped he might be permitted to make the acquaintance of his charming sister—your charming sister, I've got mixed up, but you know what I mean."

"What did he talk about?" I asked.

"He told me a lot about himself and his cases. You know that Prince Paul of Mauretania—the one who's just married a dancer?"

"Yes?"

"I saw a most intriguing paragraph about her in Society Snippets the other day, hinting that she was really a Russian Grand Duchess—

one of the Czar's daughters who managed to escape from the Bolsheviks. Well, it seems that M. Poirot solved a baffling murder mystery that threatened to involve them both. Prince Paul was beside himself with gratitude."

"Did he give him an emerald tie pin the size of a plover's egg?" I inquired sarcastically.

"He didn't mention it. Why?"

"Nothing," I said. "I thought it was always done. It is in detective fiction anyway. The super detective always has his rooms littered with rubies and pearls and emeralds from grateful Royal clients."

"It's very interesting to hear about these things from the inside," said my sister complacently.

It would be—to Caroline. I could not but admire the ingenuity of M. Hercule Poirot, who had selected unerringly the case of all others that would most appeal to an elderly maiden lady living in a small village.

"Did he tell you if the dancer was really a Grand Duchess?" I inquired.

"He was not at liberty to speak," said Caroline importantly.

I wondered how far Poirot had strained the truth in talking to Caroline—probably not at all. He had conveyed his innuendoes by means of his eyebrows and his shoulders.

"And after all this," I remarked, "I suppose you were ready to eat out of his hand."

"Don't be coarse, James. I don't know where you get these vulgar expressions from."

"Probably from my only link with the outside world—my patients. Unfortunately my practice does not lie amongst Royal princes and interesting Russian émigrés."

Caroline pushed her spectacles up and looked at me.

"You seem very grumpy, James. It must be your liver. A blue pill, I think, to-night."

To see me in my own home, you would never imagine that I was a doctor of medicine. Caroline does the home prescribing both for herself and me.

"Damn my liver," I said irritably. "Did you talk about the murder at all?"

"Well, naturally, James. What else is there to talk about locally? I was able to set M. Poirot right upon several points. He was very grateful to me. He said I had the makings of a born detective in me—and a wonderful psychological insight into human nature."

Caroline was exactly like a cat that is full to overflowing with rich cream. She was positively purring.

"He talked a lot about the little gray cells of the brain, and of their functions. His own, he says, are of the first quality."

"He would say so," I remarked bitterly. "Modesty is certainly not his middle name."

"I wish you would not be so horribly American, James. He thought it very important that Ralph should be found as soon as possible, and induced to come forward and give an account of himself. He says that his disappearance will produce a very unfortunate impression at the inquest."

"And what did you say to that?"

"I agreed with him," said Caroline importantly. "And I was able to tell him the way people were already talking about it."

"Caroline," I said sharply, "did you tell M. Poirot what you overheard in the wood that day?"

"I did," said Caroline complacently.

I got up and began to walk about.

"You realize what you're doing, I hope," I jerked out. "You're putting a halter round Ralph Paton's neck as surely as you're sitting in that chair."

"Not at all," said Caroline, quite unruffled. "I was surprised *you* hadn't told him."

"I took very good care not to," I said. "I'm fond of that boy."

"So am I. That's why I say you're talking nonsense. I don't believe Ralph did it, and so the truth can't hurt him, and we ought to give M. Poirot all the help we can. Why, think, very likely Ralph was out with that identical girl on the night of the murder, and if so, he's got a perfect alibi."

"If he's got a perfect alibi," I retorted, "why doesn't he come forward and say so?"

"Might get the girl into trouble," said Caroline sapiently. "But if M. Poirot gets hold of her, and puts it to her as her duty, she'll come forward of her own accord and clear Ralph."

"You seem to have invented a romantic fairy story of your own," I said. "You read too many trashy novels, Caroline. I've always told you so."

I dropped into my chair again.

"Did Poirot ask you any more questions?" I inquired.

"Only about the patients you had that morning."

"The patients?" I demanded, unbelievingly.

"Yes, your surgery patients. How many and who they were?"

"Do you mean to say you were able to tell him that?" I demanded. Caroline is really amazing.

"Why not?" asked my sister triumphantly. "I can see the path up to the surgery door perfectly from this window. And I've got an excellent memory, James. Much better than yours, let me tell you."

"I'm sure you have," I murmured mechanically.

My sister went on, checking the names on her fingers.

"There was old Mrs. Bennett, and that boy from the farm with the bad finger, Dolly Grice to have a needle out of her finger; that American steward off the liner. Let me see—that's four. Yes, and old George Evans with his ulcer. And lastly——"

She paused significantly.

"Well?"

Caroline brought out her climax triumphantly. She hissed in the most approved style—aided by the fortunate number of s's at her disposal.

"*Miss Russell!*"

She sat back in her chair and looked at me meaningly, and when Caroline looks at you meaningly, it is impossible to miss it.

"I don't know what you mean," I said, quite untruthfully. "Why shouldn't Miss Russell consult me about her bad knee?"

"Bad knee," said Caroline. "Fiddlesticks! No more bad knee than you and I. She was after something else."

"What?" I asked.

Caroline had to admit that she didn't know.

"But depend upon it, that was what he was trying to get at, M. Poirot, I mean. There's something fishy about that woman, and he knows it."

"Precisely the remark Mrs. Ackroyd made to me yesterday," I said. "That there was something fishy about Miss Russell."

"Ah!" said Caroline darkly, "Mrs. Ackroyd! There's another!"

"Another what?"

Caroline refused to explain her remarks. She merely nodded her head several times, rolled up her knitting, and went upstairs to don the high mauve silk blouse and the gold locket which she calls dressing for dinner.

I stayed there staring into the fire and thinking over Caroline's words. Had Poirot really come to gain information about Miss Russell, or was it only Caroline's tortuous mind that interpreted everything according to her own ideas?

There had certainly been nothing in Miss Russell's manner that morning to arouse suspicion. At least——

I remembered her persistent conversation on the subject of drug-taking and from that she had led the conversation to poisons and poisoning. But there was nothing in that. Ackroyd had not been poisoned. Still, it was odd. . . .

I heard Caroline's voice, rather acid in note, calling from the top of the stairs.

"James, you will be late for dinner."

I put some coal on the fire and went upstairs obediently.

It is well at any price to have peace in the home.

CHAPTER 12

ROUND THE TABLE

A JOINT inquest was held on Monday.

I do not propose to give the proceedings in detail. To do so would only be to go over the same ground again and again. By arrangement with the police, very little was allowed to come out. I gave evidence as to the cause of Ackroyd's death and the probable time. The absence of Ralph Paton was commented on by the coroner, but not unduly stressed.

Afterwards, Poirot and I had a few words with Inspector Raglan. The inspector was very grave.

"It looks bad, Mr. Poirot," he said. "I'm trying to judge the thing fair and square. I'm a local man, and I've seen Captain Paton many times in Cranchester. I'm not wanting him to be the guilty one—but it's bad whichever way you look at it. If he's innocent, why doesn't he come forward? We've got evidence against him, but it's just possible that that evidence could be explained away. Then why doesn't he give an explanation?"

A lot more lay behind the inspector's words than I knew at the time. Ralph's description had been wired to every port and railway station in England. The police everywhere were on the alert. His rooms in town were watched, and any houses he had been known to be in the habit of frequenting. With such a *cordon* it seemed impossible that Ralph should be able to evade detection. He had no luggage, and, as far as any one knew, no money.

"I can't find any one who saw him at the station that night," continued the inspector. "And yet he's well known down here, and you'd think somebody would have noticed him. There's no news from Liverpool either."

"You think he went to Liverpool?" queried Poirot.

"Well, it's on the cards. That telephone message from the station, just three minutes before the Liverpool express left—there ought to be something in that."

"Unless it was deliberately intended to throw you off the scent. That might just possibly be the point of the telephone message."

"That's an idea," said the inspector eagerly. "Do you really think that's the explanation of the telephone call?"

"My friend," said Poirot gravely, "I do not know. But I will tell you this: I believe that when we find the explanation of that telephone call we shall find the explanation of the murder."

"You said something like that before, I remember," I observed, looking at him curiously.

Poirot nodded.

"I always come back to it," he said seriously.

"It seems to me utterly irrelevant," I declared.

"I wouldn't say that," demurred the inspector. "But I must confess I think Mr. Poirot here harps on it a little too much. We've better clews than that. The fingerprints on the dagger, for instance."

Poirot became suddenly very foreign in manner, as he often did when excited over anything.

"M. l'Inspecteur," he said, "beware of the blind—the blind—*comment dire?*—the little street that has no end to it."

Inspector Raglan stared, but I was quicker.

"You mean a blind alley?" I said.

"That is it—the blind street that leads nowhere. So it may be with those fingerprints—they may lead you nowhere."

"I don't see how that can well be," said the police officer. "I suppose you're hinting that they're faked? I've read of such things being done, though I can't say I've ever come across it in my experience. But fake or true—they're bound to lead *somewhere*."

Poirot merely shrugged his shoulders, flinging out his arms wide.

The inspector then showed us various enlarged photographs of the fingerprints, and proceeded to become technical on the subject of loops and whorls.

"Come now," he said at last, annoyed by Poirot's detached manner, "you've got to admit that those prints were made by some one who was in the house that night."

"*Bien entendu,*" said Poirot, nodding his head.

"Well, I've taken the prints of every member of the household, every one, mind you, from the old lady down to the kitchenmaid."

I don't think Mrs. Ackroyd would enjoy being referred to as the old lady. She must spend a considerable amount on cosmetics.

"Every one's," repeated the inspector fussily.

"Including mine," I said dryly.

"Very well. None of them correspond. That leaves us two alternatives. Ralph Paton, or the mysterious stranger the doctor here tells us about. When we get hold of those two——"

"Much valuable time may have been lost," broke in Poirot.

"I don't quite get you, Mr. Poirot?"

"You have taken the prints of every one in the house, you say," murmured Poirot. "Is that the exact truth you are telling me there, M. l'Inspecteur?"

"Certainly."

"Without overlooking any one?"

"Without overlooking any one."

"The quick or the dead?"

For a moment the inspector looked bewildered at what he took to be a religious observation. Then he reacted slowly.

"You mean——"

"The dead, M. l'Inspecteur."

The inspector still took a minute or two to understand.

"I am suggesting," said Poirot placidly, "that the fingerprints on the dagger handle are those of Mr. Ackroyd himself. It is an easy matter to verify. His body is still available."

"But why? What would be the point of it. You're surely not suggesting suicide, Mr. Poirot?"

"Ah! no. My theory is that the murderer wore gloves or wrapped something round his hand. After the blow was struck, he picked up the victim's hand and closed it round the dagger handle."

"But why?"

Poirot shrugged his shoulders again.

"To make a confusing case even more confusing."

"Well," said the inspector, "I'll look into it. What gave you the idea in the first place?"

"When you were so kind as to show me the dagger and draw attention to the fingerprints. I know very little of loops and whorls—see, I confess my ignorance frankly. But it did occur to me that the position of the prints was somewhat awkward. Not so would I have held a dagger in order to strike. Naturally, with the right hand brought up over the shoulder backwards, it would have been difficult to put it in exactly the right position."

Inspector Raglan stared at the little man. Poirot, with an air of great unconcern, flecked a speck of dust from his coat sleeve.

"Well," said the inspector, "it's an idea. I'll look into it all right, but don't you be disappointed if nothing comes of it."

He endeavored to make his tone kindly and patronizing. Poirot watched him go off. Then he turned to me with twinkling eyes.

"Another time," he observed, "I must be more careful of his *amour propre*. And now that we are left to our own devices, what do you think, my good friend, of a little reunion of the family?"

The "little reunion," as Poirot called it, took place about half an hour later. We sat round the table in the dining-room at Fernly—Poirot at the head of the table, like the chairman of some ghastly board meeting. The servants were not present, so we were six in all. Mrs. Ackroyd, Flora, Major Blunt, young Raymond, Poirot, and myself.

When every one was assembled, Poirot rose and bowed.

"Messieurs, mesdames, I have called you together for a certain purpose." He paused. "To begin with, I want to make a very special plea to mademoiselle."

"To me?" said Flora.

"Mademoiselle, you are engaged to Captain Ralph Paton. If any one is in his confidence, you are. I beg you, most earnestly, if you know of his whereabouts, to persuade him to come forward. One little minute"—as Flora raised her head to speak—"say nothing till you have well reflected. Mademoiselle, his position grows daily more dangerous. If he had come forward at once, no matter how damning the facts, he might have had a chance of explaining them away. But this silence—this flight—what can it mean? Surely only one thing, knowledge of guilt. Mademoiselle, if you really believe in his innocence, persuade him to come forward before it is too late."

Flora's face had gone very white.

"Too late!" she repeated, very low.

Poirot leaned forward, looking at her.

"See now, mademoiselle," he said very gently, "it is Papa Poirot who asks you this. The old Papa Poirot who has much knowledge and much experience. I would not seek to entrap you, mademoiselle. Will you not trust me—and tell me where Ralph Paton is hiding?"

The girl rose, and stood facing him.

"M. Poirot," she said in a clear voice, "I swear to you—swear solemnly—that I have no idea where Ralph is, and that I have neither seen him nor heard from him either on the day of—of the murder, or since."

She sat down again. Poirot gazed at her in silence for a minute or two, then he brought his hand down on the table with a sharp rap.

"*Bien!* That is that," he said. His face hardened. "Now I appeal to these others who sit round this table, Mrs. Ackroyd, Major Blunt, Dr. Sheppard, Mr. Raymond. You are all friends and intimates of the missing man. If you know where Ralph Paton is hiding, speak out."

There was a long silence. Poirot looked to each in turn.

"I beg of you," he said in a low voice, "speak out."

But still there was silence, broken at last by Mrs. Ackroyd.

"I must say," she observed in a plaintive voice, "that Ralph's absence is most peculiar—most peculiar indeed. Not to come forward at such a time. It looks, you know, as though there were something *behind* it. I can't help thinking, Flora dear, that it was a very fortunate thing your engagement was never formally announced."

"Mother!" cried Flora angrily.

"Providence," declared Mrs. Ackroyd. "I have a devout belief in Providence—a divinity that shapes our ends, as Shakespeare's beautiful line runs."

"Surely you don't make the Almighty directly responsible for thick ankles, Mrs. Ackroyd, do you?" asked Geoffrey Raymond, his irresponsible laugh ringing out.

His idea was, I think, to loosen the tension, but Mrs. Ackroyd threw him a glance of reproach and took out her handkerchief.

"Flora has been saved a terrible amount of notoriety and unpleasantness. Not for a moment that I think dear Ralph had anything to do with poor Roger's death. I *don't* think so. But then I have a trusting heart—I always have had, ever since a child. I am loath to believe the worst of any one. But, of course, one must remember that Ralph was in several air raids as a young boy. The results are apparent long after, sometimes, they say. People are not responsible for their actions in the least. They lose control, you know, without being able to help it."

"Mother," cried Flora, "you don't think Ralph did it?"

"Come, Mrs. Ackroyd," said Blunt.

"I don't know what to think," said Mrs. Ackroyd tearfully. "It's all very upsetting. What would happen to the estate, I wonder, if Ralph were found guilty?"

Raymond pushed his chair away from the table violently. Major Blunt remained very quiet, looking thoughtfully at her. "Like shellshock, you know," said Mrs. Ackroyd obstinately, "and I dare say Roger kept him very short of money—with the best intentions, of course. I can see you are all against me, but I do think it is very odd that Ralph has not come forward, and I must say I am thankful Flora's engagement was never announced formally."

"It will be to-morrow," said Flora in a clear voice.

"Flora!" cried her mother, aghast.

Flora had turned to the secretary.

"Will you send the announcement to the *Morning Post* and the *Times,* please, Mr. Raymond."

"If you are sure that it is wise, Miss Ackroyd," he replied gravely.

She turned impulsively to Blunt.

"You understand," she said. "What else can I do? As things are, I must stand by Ralph. Don't you see that I must?"

She looked very searchingly at him, and after a long pause he nodded abruptly.

Mrs. Ackroyd burst out into shrill protests. Flora remained unmoved. Then Raymond spoke.

"I appreciate your motives, Miss Ackroyd. But don't you think you're being rather precipitate? Wait a day or two."

"To-morrow," said Flora, in a clear voice. "It's no good, mother, going on like this. Whatever else I am, I'm not disloyal to my friends."

"M. Poirot," Mrs. Ackroyd appealed tearfully, "can't you say anything at all?"

"Nothing to be said," interpolated Blunt. "She's doing the right thing. I'll stand by her through thick and thin."

Flora held out her hand to him.

"Thank you, Major Blunt," she said.

"Mademoiselle," said Poirot, "will you let an old man congratulate you on your courage and your loyalty? And will you not misunderstand me if I ask you—ask you most solemnly—to postpone the announcement you speak of for at least two days more?"

Flora hesitated.

"I asked it in Ralph Paton's interests as much as in yours, mademoiselle. You frown. You do not see how that can be. But I assure you that it is so. *Pas de blagues*. You put the case into my hands—you must not hamper me now."

Flora paused a few minutes before replying.

"I do not like it," she said at last, "but I will do what you say."

She sat down again at the table.

"And now, messieurs et mesdames," said Poirot rapidly, "I will continue with what I was about to say. Understand this, I mean to arrive at the truth. The truth, however ugly in itself, is always curious and beautiful to the seeker after it. I am much aged, my powers may not be what they were." Here he clearly expected a contradiction. "In all probability this is the last case I shall ever investigate. But Hercule Poirot does not end with a failure. Messieurs et mesdames, I tell you, I mean to *know*. And I shall know—in spite of you all."

He brought out the last words provocatively, hurling them in our face as it were. I think we all flinched back a little, excepting Geoffrey Raymond, who remained good humored and imperturbable as usual.

"How do you mean—in spite of us all?" he asked, with slightly raised eyebrows.

"But—just that, monsieur. Every one of you in this room is concealing something from me." He raised his hand as a faint murmur of protest arose. "Yes, yes, I know what I am saying. It may be something unimportant—trivial—which is supposed to have no bearing on the case, but there it is. *Each one of you has something to hide*. Come, now, am I right?"

His glance, challenging and accusing, swept round the table. And every pair of eyes dropped before his. Yes, mine as well.

"I am answered," said Poirot, with a curious laugh. He got up from his seat. "I appeal to you all. Tell me the truth—the whole truth." There was a silence. "Will no one speak?"

He gave the same short laugh again.

"*C'est dommage*," he said, and went out.

CHAPTER 13

THE GOOSE QUILL

THAT EVENING, at Poirot's request, I went over to his house after dinner. Caroline saw me depart with visible reluctance. I think she would have liked to have accompanied me.

Poirot greeted me hospitably. He had placed a bottle of Irish whisky (which I detest) on a small table, with a soda water siphon and a glass. He himself was engaged in brewing hot chocolate. It was a favorite beverage of his, I discovered later.

He inquired politely after my sister, whom he declared to be a most interesting woman.

"I'm afraid you've been giving her a swelled head," I said dryly. "What about Sunday afternoon?"

He laughed and twinkled.

"I always like to employ the expert," he remarked obscurely, but he refused to explain the remark.

"You got all the local gossip anyway," I remarked. "True, and untrue."

"And a great deal of valuable information," he added quietly.

"Such as——?"

He shook his head.

"Why not have told me the truth?" he countered. "In a place like this, all Ralph Paton's doings were bound to be known. If your sister had not happened to pass through the wood that day somebody else would have done so."

"I suppose they would," I said grumpily. "What about this interest of yours in my patients?"

Again he twinkled.

"Only one of them, doctor. Only one of them."

"The last?" I hazarded.

"I find Miss Russell a study of the most interesting," he said evasively.

"Do you agree with my sister and Mrs. Ackroyd that there is something fishy about her?" I asked.

"Eh? What do you say—fishy?"

I explained to the best of my ability.

"And they say that, do they?"

"Didn't my sister convey as much to you yesterday afternoon?"

"*C'est possible.*"

"For no reason whatever," I declared.

"*Les femmes,*" generalized Poirot. "They are marvelous! They invent haphazard—and by miracle they are right. Not that it is that, really. Women observe subconsciously a thousand little details, without knowing that they are doing so. Their subconscious mind adds these little things together—and they call the result intuition. Me, I am very skilled in psychology. I know these things."

He swelled his chest out importantly, looking so ridiculous, that I found it difficult not to burst out laughing. Then he took a small sip of his chocolate, and carefully wiped his mustache.

"I wish you'd tell me," I burst out, "what you really think of it all?"

He put down his cup.

"You wish that?"

"I do."

"You have seen what I have seen. Should not our ideas be the same?"

"I'm afraid you're laughing at me," I said stiffly. "Of course, I've no experience of matters of this kind."

Poirot smiled at me indulgently.

"You are like the little child who wants to know the way the engine works. You wish to see the affair, not as the family doctor sees it, but with the eye of a detective who knows and cares for no one—to whom they are all strangers and all equally liable to suspicion."

"You put it very well," I said.

"So I give you then, a little lecture. The first thing is to get a clear history of what happened that evening—always bearing in mind that the person who speaks may be lying."

I raised my eyebrows.

"Rather a suspicious attitude."

"But necessary—I assure you, necessary. Now first—Dr. Sheppard leaves the house at ten minutes to nine. How do I know that?"

"Because I told you so."

"But you might not be speaking the truth—or the watch you went by might be wrong. But Parker also says that you left the house at ten minutes to nine. So we accept that statement and pass on. At nine o'clock you run into a man—and here we come to what we will call the Romance of the Mysterious Stranger—just outside the Park gates. How do I know that that is so?"

"I told you so," I began again, but Poirot interrupted me with a gesture of impatience.

"Ah! but it is that you are a little stupid to-night, my friend. *You* know that it is so—but how am *I* to know? *Eh bien*, I am able to tell you that the Mysterious Stranger was not a hallucination on your part, because the maid of a Miss Ganett met him a few minutes before you did, and of her too he inquired the way to Fernly Park. We accept his presence, therefore, and we can be fairly sure of two things about him—that he was a stranger to the neighborhood, and that whatever his object in going to Fernly, there was no great secrecy about it, since he twice asked the way there."

"Yes," I said, "I see that."

"Now I have made it my business to find out more about this man. He had a drink at the Three Boars, I learn, and the barmaid there says that he spoke with an American accent and mentioned having just come over from the States. Did it strike you that he had an American accent?"

"Yes, I think he had," I said, after a minute or two, during which I cast my mind back; "but a very slight one."

"*Précisément.* There is also this which, you will remember, I picked up in the summer-house?"

He held out to me the little quill. I looked at it curiously. Then a memory of something I had read stirred in me.

Poirot, who had been watching my face, nodded.

"Yes, heroin 'snow.' Drug-takers carry it like this, and sniff it up the nose."

"Diamorphine hydrochloride," I murmured mechanically.

"This method of taking the drug is very common on the other side. Another proof, if we wanted one, that the man came from Canada or the States."

"What first attracted your attention to that summer-house?" I asked curiously.

"My friend the inspector took it for granted that any one using that path did so as a short cut to the house, but as soon as I saw the summer-house, I realized that the same path would be taken by any one using the summer-house as a rendezvous. Now it seems fairly certain that the stranger came neither to the front nor to the back door. Then did some one from the house go out and meet him? If so, what could be a more convenient place than that little summer-house? I searched it with the hope that I might find some clew inside. I found two, the scrap of cambric and the quill."

"And the scrap of cambric?" I asked curiously. "What about that?"

Poirot raised his eyebrows.

"You do not use your little gray cells," he remarked dryly. "The scrap of starched cambric should be obvious."

"Not very obvious to me." I changed the subject. "Anyway," I said, "this man went to the summer-house to meet somebody. Who was that somebody?"

"Exactly the question," said Poirot. "You will remember that Mrs. Ackroyd and her daughter came over from Canada to live here?"

"Is that what you meant to-day when you accused them of hiding the truth?"

"Perhaps. Now another point. What did you think of the parlor-maid's story?"

"What story?"

"The story of her dismissal. Does it take half an hour to dismiss a servant? Was the story of those important papers a likely one? And remember, though she says she was in her bedroom from nine-thirty until ten o'clock, there is no one to confirm her statement."

"You bewilder me," I said.

"To me it grows clearer. But tell me now your own ideas and theories."

I drew a piece of paper from my pocket.

"I just scribbled down a few suggestions," I said apologetically.

"But excellent—you have method. Let us hear them."

I read out in a somewhat embarrassed voice.

"To begin with, one must look at the thing logically——"

"Just what my poor Hastings used to say," interrupted Poirot, "but alas! he never did so."

"*Point No.* 1.—Mr. Ackroyd was heard talking to some one at half-past nine.

"*Point No.* 2.—At some time during the evening Ralph Paton must have come in through the window, as evidenced by the prints of his shoes.

"*Point No.* 3.—Mr. Ackroyd was nervous that evening, and would only have admitted some one he knew.

"*Point No.* 4.—The person with Mr. Ackroyd at nine-thirty was asking for money. We know Ralph Paton was in a scrape.

"*These four points go to show that the person with Mr. Ackroyd* at nine-thirty was Ralph Paton. But we know that Mr. Ackroyd was alive at a quarter to ten, therefore it was not Ralph who killed him. Ralph left the window open. Afterwards the murderer came in that way."

"And who was the murderer?" inquired Poirot.

"The American stranger. He may have been in league with Parker, and possibly in Parker we have the man who blackmailed Mrs. Ferrars. If so, Parker may have heard enough to realize the game was up, have told his accomplice so, and the latter did the crime with the dagger which Parker gave him."

"It is a theory that," admitted Poirot. "Decidedly you have cells of a kind. But it leaves a good deal unaccounted for."

"Such as——?"

"The telephone call, the pushed-out chair——"

"Do you really think the latter important?" I interrupted.

"Perhaps not," admitted my friend. "It may have been pulled out by accident, and Raymond or Blunt may have shoved it into place unconsciously under the stress of emotion. Then there is the missing forty pounds."

"Given by Ackroyd to Ralph," I suggested. "He may have reconsidered his first refusal."

"That still leaves one thing unexplained."

"What?"

"Why was Blunt so certain in his own mind that it was Raymond with Mr. Ackroyd at nine-thirty?"

"He explained that," I said.

"You think so? I will not press the point. Tell me instead, what were Ralph Paton's reasons for disappearing?"

"That's rather more difficult," I said slowly. "I shall have to speak as a medical man. Ralph's nerves must have gone phut! If he suddenly found out that his uncle had been murdered within a few minutes of his leaving him—after, perhaps, a rather stormy interview—well, he might get the wind up and clear right out. Men have been known to do that—act guiltily when they're perfectly innocent."

"Yes, that is true," said Poirot. "But we must not lose sight of one thing."

"I know what you're going to say," I remarked: "motive. Ralph Paton inherits a great fortune by his uncle's death."

"That is one motive," agreed Poirot.

"One?"

"Mais oui. Do you realize that there are three separate motives

staring us in the face? Somebody certainly stole the blue envelope
and its contents. That is one motive. Blackmail! Ralph Paton may
have been the man who blackmailed Mrs. Ferrars. Remember, as far
as Hammond knew, Ralph Paton had not applied to his stepfather for
help of late. That looks as though he were being supplied with money
elsewhere. Then there is the fact that he was in some—how do you
say—scrape?—which he feared might get to his stepfather's ears. And
finally there is the one you have just mentioned."

"Dear me," I said, rather taken aback. "The case does seem black
against him."

"Does it?" said Poirot. "That is where we disagree, you and I.
Three motives—it is almost too much. I am inclined to believe that,
after all, Ralph Paton is innocent."

CHAPTER 14

MRS. ACKROYD

AFTER THE evening talk I have just chronicled, the affair seemed to
me to enter on a different phase. The whole thing can be divided into
two parts, each clear and distinct from the other. Part I. ranges from
Ackroyd's death on the Friday evening to the following Monday night.
It is the straight-forward narrative of what occurred, as presented to
Hercule Poirot. I was at Poirot's elbow the whole time. I saw what he
saw. I tried my best to read his mind. As I know now, I failed in this
latter task. Though Poirot showed me all his discoveries—as, for instance, the gold wedding ring—he held back the vital and yet logical
impressions that he formed. As I came to know later, this secrecy
was characteristic of him. He would throw out hints and suggestions,
but beyond that he would not go.

As I say, up till the Monday evening, my narrative might have been
that of Poirot himself. I played Watson to his Sherlock. But after
Monday our ways diverged. Poirot was busy on his own account. I
got to hear of what he was doing, because, in King's Abbot, you get
to hear of everything, but he did not take me into his confidence beforehand. And I, too, had my own preoccupations.

On looking back, the thing that strikes me most is the piecemeal
character of this period. Every one had a hand in the elucidation of

the mystery. It was rather like a jig-saw puzzle to which every one contributed their own little piece of knowledge or discovery. But their task ended there. To Poirot alone belongs the renown of fitting those pieces into their correct place.

Some of the incidents seemed at the time irrelevant and unmeaning. There was, for instance, the question of the black boots. But that comes later. . . . To take things strictly in chronological order, I must begin with the summons from Mrs. Ackroyd.

She sent for me early on Tuesday morning, and since the summons sounded an urgent one, I hastened there, expecting to find her *in extremis.*

The lady was in bed. So much did she concede to the etiquette of the situation. She gave me her bony hand, and indicated a chair drawn up to the bedside.

"Well, Mrs. Ackroyd," I said, "and what's the matter with you?"

I spoke with that kind of spurious geniality which seems to be expected of general practitioners.

"I'm prostrated," said Mrs. Ackroyd in a faint voice. "Absolutely prostrated. It's the shock of poor Roger's death. They say these things often aren't felt at the *time,* you know. It's the reaction afterwards."

It is a pity that a doctor is precluded by his profession from being able sometimes to say what he really thinks.

I would have given anything to be able to answer "Bunkum!"

Instead, I suggested a tonic. Mrs. Ackroyd accepted the tonic. One move in the game seemed now to be concluded. Not for a moment did I imagine that I had been sent for because of the shock occasioned by Ackroyd's death. But Mrs. Ackroyd is totally incapable of pursuing a straight-forward course on any subject. She always approaches her object by tortuous means. I wondered very much why it was she had sent for me.

"And then that scene—yesterday," continued my patient.

She paused as though expecting me to take up a cue.

"What scene?"

"Doctor, how can you? Have you forgotten? That dreadful little Frenchman—or Belgian—or whatever he is. Bullying us all like he did. It has quite upset me. Coming on top of Roger's death."

"I'm very sorry, Mrs. Ackroyd," I said.

"I don't know what he meant—shouting at us like he did. I should hope I know my duty too well to *dream* of concealing anything. I have given the police *every* assistance in my power."

Mrs. Ackroyd paused, and I said, "Quite so." I was beginning to have a glimmering of what all the trouble was about.

"No one can say that I have failed in my duty," continued Mrs. Ackroyd. "I am sure Inspector Raglan is perfectly satisfied. Why should this little upstart of a foreigner make a fuss? A most ridiculous-looking creature he is too—just like a comic Frenchman in a revue. I can't think why Flora insisted on bringing him into the case. She never said a word to me about it. Just went off and did it on her own. Flora is too independent. I am a woman of the world and her mother. She should have come to me for advice first."

I listened to all this in silence.

"What does he think? That's what I want to know. Does he actually imagine I'm hiding something? He—he—positively *accused* me yesterday."

I shrugged my shoulders.

"It is surely of no consequence, Mrs. Ackroyd," I said. "Since you are not concealing anything, any remarks he may have made do not apply to you."

Mrs. Ackroyd went off at a tangent, after her usual fashion.

"Servants are so tiresome," she said. "They gossip, and talk amongst themselves. And then it gets round—and all the time there's probably nothing in it at all."

"Have the servants been talking?" I asked. "What about?"

Mrs. Ackroyd cast a very shrewd glance at me. It quite threw me off my balance.

"I was sure *you'd* know, doctor, if any one did. You were with M. Poirot all the time, weren't you?"

"I was."

"Then of course you know. It was that girl, Ursula Bourne, wasn't it? Naturally—she's leaving. She *would* want to make all the trouble she could. Spiteful, that's what they are. They're all alike. Now, you being there, doctor, you must know exactly what she did say? I'm most anxious that no wrong impression should get about. After all, you don't repeat every little detail to the police, do you? There are family matters sometimes—nothing to do with the question of the murder. But if the girl was spiteful, she may have made out all sorts of things."

I was shrewd enough to see that a very real anxiety lay behind these outpourings. Poirot had been justified in his premises. Of the six people round the table yesterday, Mrs. Ackroyd at least had had something to hide. It was for me to discover what that something might be.

"If I were you, Mrs. Ackroyd," I said brusquely, "I should make a clean breast of things."

She gave a little scream.

"Oh! doctor, how can you be so abrupt. It sounds as though—as though—— And I can explain everything so simply."

"Then why not do so," I suggested.

Mrs. Ackroyd took out a frilled handkerchief, and became tearful.

"I thought, doctor, that you might put it to M. Poirot—explain it, you know—because it's so difficult for a foreigner to see our point of view. And you don't know—nobody could know—what I've had to contend with. A martyrdom—a long martyrdom. That's what my life has been. I don't like to speak ill of the dead—but there it is. Not the smallest bill, but it had all to be gone over—just as though Roger had had a few miserly hundreds a year instead of being (as Mr. Hammond told me yesterday) one of the wealthiest men in these parts."

Mrs. Ackroyd paused to dab her eyes with the frilled handkerchief.

"Yes," I said encouragingly. "You were talking about bills?"

"Those dreadful bills. And some I didn't like to show Roger at all. They were things a man wouldn't understand. He would have said the things weren't necessary. And of course they mounted up, you know, and they kept coming in——"

She looked at me appealingly, as though asking me to condole with her on this striking peculiarity.

"It's a habit they have," I agreed.

"And the tone altered—became quite abusive. I assure you, doctor, I was becoming a nervous wreck. I couldn't sleep at nights. And a dreadful fluttering round the heart. And then I got a letter from a Scotch gentleman—as a matter of fact there were two letters—both Scotch gentlemen. Mr. Bruce MacPherson was one, and the other was Colin MacDonald. Quite a coincidence."

"Hardly that," I said dryly. "They are usually Scotch gentlemen, but I suspect a foreign strain in their ancestry."

"Ten pounds to ten thousand on note of hand alone," murmured Mrs. Ackroyd reminiscently. "I wrote to one of them, but it seemed there were difficulties."

She paused.

I gathered that we were just coming to delicate ground. I have never known any one more difficult to bring to the point.

"You see," murmured Mrs. Ackroyd, "it's all a question of expectations, isn't it? Testamentary expectations. And though, of course, I expected that Roger would provide for me, I didn't *know*. I thought that if only I could glance over a copy of his will—not in any sense of vulgar prying—but just so that I could make my own arrangements."

She glanced sideways at me. The position was now very delicate indeed. Fortunately words, ingeniously used, will serve to mask the ugliness of naked facts.

"I could only tell this to you, dear Dr. Sheppard," said Mrs. Ackroyd rapidly. "I can trust you not to misjudge me, and to represent the matter in the right light to M. Poirot. It was on Friday afternoon——"

She came to a stop and swallowed uncertainly.

"Yes," I repeated encouragingly. "On Friday afternoon. Well?"

"Every one was out, or so I thought. And I went into Roger's study—I had some real reason for going there—I mean, there was nothing underhand about it. And as I saw all the papers heaped on the desk, it just came to me, like a flash: 'I wonder if Roger keeps his will in one of the drawers of the desk.' I'm so impulsive, always was, from a child. I do things on the spur of the moment. He'd left his keys—very careless of him—in the lock of the top drawer."

"I see," I said helpfully. "So you searched the desk. Did you find the will?"

Mrs. Ackroyd gave a little scream, and I realized that I had not been sufficiently diplomatic.

"How dreadful it sounds. But it wasn't at all like that really."

"Of course it wasn't," I said hastily. "You must forgive my unfortunate way of putting things."

"You see, men are so peculiar. In dear Roger's place, I should not have objected to revealing the provisions of my will. But men are so secretive. One is forced to adopt little subterfuges in self-defence."

"And the result of the little subterfuge?" I asked.

"That's just what I'm telling you. As I got to the bottom drawer, Bourne came in. Most awkward. Of course I shut the drawer and stood up, and I called her attention to a few specks of dust on the surface. But I didn't like the way she looked—quite respectful in manner, but a very nasty light in her eyes. Almost contemptuous, if you know what I mean. I never have liked that girl very much. She's a good servant, and she says M'am, and doesn't object to wearing caps and aprons (which I declare to you a lot of them do nowadays), and she can say 'Not at home' without scruples if she has to answer the door instead of Parker, and she doesn't have those peculiar gurgling noises inside which so many parlormaids seem to have when they wait at table—— Let me see, where was I?"

"You were saying, that in spite of several valuable qualities, you never liked Bourne."

"No more I do. She's—odd. There's something different about her from the others. Too well educated, that's my opinion. You can't tell who are ladies and who aren't nowadays."

"And what happened next?" I asked.

"Nothing. At least, Roger came in. And I thought he was out for a walk. And he said: 'What's all this?' and I said, 'Nothing. I just came in to fetch *Punch.*' And I took *Punch* and went out with it. Bourne stayed behind. I heard her asking Roger if she could speak to him for a minute. I went straight up to my room, to lie down. I was very upset."

There was a pause.

"You will explain to M. Poirot, won't you? You can see for yourself what a trivial matter the whole thing was. But, of course, when he was so stern about concealing things, I thought of this at once. Bourne may have made some extraordinary story out of it, but you can explain, can't you?"

"That is all?" I said. "You have told me everything?"

"Ye-es," said Mrs. Ackroyd. "Oh! yes," she added firmly.

But I had noted the momentary hesitation, and I knew that there was still something she was keeping back. It was nothing less than a flash of sheer genius that prompted me to ask the question I did.

"Mrs. Ackroyd," I said, "was it you who left the silver table open?"

I had my answer in the blush of guilt that even rouge and powder could not conceal.

"How did you know?" she whispered.

"It was you, then?"

"Yes—I—you see—there were one or two pieces of old silver—very interesting. I had been reading up the subject and there was an illustration of quite a small piece which had fetched an immense sum at Christy's. It looked to me just the same as the one in the silver table. I thought I would take it up to London with me when I went—and—and have it valued. Then if it really was a valuable piece, just think what a charming surprise it would have been for Roger?"

I refrained from comments, accepting Mrs. Ackroyd's story on its merits. I even forbore to ask her why it was necessary to abstract what she wanted in such a surreptitious manner.

"Why did you leave the lid open?" I asked. "Did you forget?"

"I was startled," said Mrs. Ackroyd. "I heard footsteps coming along the terrace outside. I hastened out of the room and just got up the stairs before Parker opened the front door to you."

"That must have been Miss Russell," I said thoughtfully. Mrs. Ackroyd had revealed to me one fact that was extremely interesting. Whether her designs upon Ackroyd's silver had been strictly honorable I neither knew nor cared. What did interest me was the fact that Miss Russell must have entered the drawing-room by the window, and that I had not been wrong when I judged her to be out of breath with running. Where had she been? I thought of the summer-house and the scrap of cambric.

"I wonder if Miss Russell has her handkerchiefs starched!" I exclaimed on the spur of the moment.

Mrs. Ackroyd's start recalled me to myself, and I rose.

"You think you can explain to M. Poirot?" she asked anxiously.

"Oh, certainly. Absolutely."

I got away at last, after being forced to listen to more justifications of her conduct.

The parlormaid was in the hall, and it was she who helped me on with my overcoat. I observed her more closely than I had done heretofore. It was clear that she had been crying.

"How is it," I asked, "that you told us that Mr. Ackroyd sent for you on Friday to his study? I hear now that it was *you* who asked to speak to *him?*"

For a minute the girl's eyes dropped before mine.

Then she spoke.

"I meant to leave in any case," she said uncertainly.

I said no more. She opened the front door for me. Just as I was passing out, she said suddenly in a low voice:—

"Excuse me, sir, is there any news of Captain Paton?"

I shook my head, looking at her inquiringly.

"He ought to come back," she said. "Indeed—indeed he ought to come back."

She was looking at me with appealing eyes.

"Does no one know where he is?" she asked.

"Do you?" I said sharply.

She shook her head.

"No, indeed. I know nothing. But any one who was a friend to him would tell him this: he ought to come back."

I lingered, thinking that perhaps the girl would say more. Her next question surprised me.

"When do they think the murder was done? Just before ten o'clock?"

"That is the idea," I said. "Between a quarter to ten and the hour."

"Not earlier? Not before a quarter to ten?"

I looked at her attentively. She was so clearly eager for a reply in the affirmative.

"That's out of the question," I said. "Miss Ackroyd saw her uncle alive at a quarter to ten."

She turned away, and her whole figure seemed to droop.

"A handsome girl," I said to myself as I drove off. "An exceedingly handsome girl."

Caroline was at home. She had had a visit from Poirot and was very pleased and important about it.

"I am helping him with the case," she explained.

I felt rather uneasy. Caroline is bad enough as it is. What will she be like with her detective instincts encouraged?

"Are you going round the neighborhood looking for Ralph Paton's mysterious girl?" I inquired.

"I might do that on my own account," said Caroline. "No, this is a special thing M. Poirot wants me to find out for him."

"What is it?" I asked.

"He wants to know whether Ralph Paton's boots were black or brown," said Caroline with tremendous solemnity.

I stared at her. I see now that I was unbelievably stupid about these boots. I failed altogether to grasp the point.

"They were brown shoes," I said. "I saw them."

"Not shoes, James, boots. M. Poirot wants to know whether a pair of boots Ralph had with him at the hotel were brown or black. A lot hangs on it."

Call me dense if you like. I didn't see.

"And how are you going to find out?" I asked.

Caroline said there would be no difficulty about that. Our Annie's dearest friend was Miss Ganett's maid, Clara. And Clara was walking out with the Boots at the Three Boars. The whole thing was simplicity itself, and by the aid of Miss Ganett, who coöperated loyally, at once giving Clara leave of absence, the matter was rushed through at express speed.

It was when we were sitting down to lunch that Caroline remarked, with would-be unconcern:—

"About those boots of Ralph Paton's."

"Well," I said, "what about them?"

"M. Poirot thought they were probably brown. He was wrong. They're black."

And Caroline nodded her head several times. She evidently felt that she had scored a point over Poirot.

I did not answer. I was puzzling over what the color of a pair of Ralph Paton's boots had to do with the case.

CHAPTER 15

GEOFFREY RAYMOND

I was to have a further proof that day of the success of Poirot's tactics. That challenge of his had been a subtle touch born of his knowledge of human nature. A mixture of fear and guilt had wrung the truth from Mrs. Ackroyd. She was the first to react.

That afternoon when I returned from seeing my patients, Caroline told me that Geoffrey Raymond had just left.

"Did he want to see me?" I asked, as I hung up my coat in the hall.

Caroline was hovering by my elbow.

"It was M. Poirot he wanted to see," she said. "He'd just come from The Larches. M. Poirot was out. Mr. Raymond thought that he might be here, or that you might know where he was."

"I haven't the least idea."

"I tried to make him wait," said Caroline, "but he said he would call back at The Larches in half an hour, and went away down the village. A great pity, because M. Poirot came in practically the minute after he left."

"Came in here?"

"No, to his own house."

"How do you know?"

"The side window," said Caroline briefly.

It seemed to me that we had now exhausted the topic. Caroline thought otherwise.

"Aren't you going across?"

"Across where?"

"To The Larches, of course."

"My dear Caroline," I said, "what for?"

"Mr. Raymond wanted to see him very particularly," said Caroline. "You might hear what it's all about."

I raised my eyebrows.

"Curiosity is not my besetting sin," I remarked coldly. "I can exist comfortably without knowing exactly what my neighbors are doing and thinking."

"Stuff and nonsense, James," said my sister. "You want to know just as much as I do. You're not so honest, that's all. You always have to pretend."

"Really, Caroline," I said, and retired into my surgery.

Ten minutes later Caroline tapped at the door and entered. In her hand she held what seemed to be a pot of jam.

"I wonder, James," she said, "if you would mind taking this pot of medlar jelly across to M. Poirot? I promised it to him. He has never tasted any home-made medlar jelly."

"Why can't Annie go?" I asked coldly.

"She's doing some mending. I can't spare her."

Caroline and I looked at each other.

"Very well," I said, rising. "But if I take the beastly thing, I shall just leave it at the door. You understand that?"

My sister raised her eyebrows.

"Naturally," she said. "Who suggested you should do anything else?"

The honors were with Caroline.

"If you *do* happen to see M. Poirot," she said, as I opened the front door, "you might tell him about the boots."

It was a most subtle parting shot. I wanted dreadfully to understand the enigma of the boots. When the old lady with the Breton cap opened the door to me, I found myself asking if M. Poirot was in, quite automatically.

Poirot sprang up to meet me, with every appearance of pleasure.

"Sit down, my good friend," he said. "The big chair? This small one? The room is not too hot, no?"

I thought it was stifling, but refrained from saying so. The windows were closed, and a large fire burned in the grate.

"The English people, they have a mania for the fresh air," declared Poirot. "The big air, it is all very well outside, where it belongs. Why admit it to the house? But let us not discuss such banalities. You have something for me, yes?"

"Two things," I said. "First—this—from my sister."

I handed over the pot of medlar jelly.

"How kind of Mademoiselle Caroline. She has remembered her promise. And the second thing?"

"Information—of a kind."

And I told him of my interview with Mrs. Ackroyd. He listened with interest, but not much excitement.

"It clears the ground," he said thoughtfully. "And it has a certain value as confirming the evidence of the housekeeper. She said, you remember, that she found the silver table lid open and closed it down in passing."

"What about her statement that she went into the drawing-room to see if the flowers were fresh?"

"Ah! we never took that very seriously, did we, my friend? It was patently an excuse, trumped up in a hurry, by a woman who felt it urgent to explain her presence—which, by the way, you would probably never have thought of questioning. I considered it possible that her agitation might arise from the fact that she had been tampering with the silver table, but I think now that we must look for another cause."

"Yes," I said. "Whom did she go out to meet? And why?"

"You think she went to meet some one?"

"I do."

Poirot nodded.

"So do I," he said thoughtfully.

There was a pause.

"By the way," I said, "I've got a message for you from my sister. Ralph Paton's boots were black, not brown."

I was watching him closely as I gave the message, and I fancied that I saw a momentary flicker of discomposure. If so, it passed almost immediately.

"She is absolutely positive they are not brown?"

"Absolutely."

"Ah!" said Poirot regretfully. "That is a pity."

And he seemed quite crestfallen.

He entered into no explanations, but at once started a new subject of conversation.

"The housekeeper, Miss Russell, who came to consult you on that Friday morning—is it indiscreet to ask what passed at the interview— apart from the medical details, I mean?"

"Not at all," I said. "When the professional part of the conversation was over, we talked for a few minutes about poisons, and the ease or difficulty of detecting them, and about drug-taking and drug-takers."

"With special reference to cocaine?" asked Poirot.

"How did you know?" I asked, somewhat surprised.

For answer, the little man rose and crossed the room to where newspapers were filed. He brought me a copy of the *Daily Budget,* dated Friday, 16th September, and showed me an article dealing with the smuggling of cocaine. It was a somewhat lurid article, written with an eye to picturesque effect.

"That is what put cocaine into her head, my friend," he said.

I would have catechized him further, for I did not quite understand his meaning, but at that moment the door opened and Geoffrey Raymond was announced.

He came in fresh and debonair as ever, and greeted us both.

"How are you, doctor? M. Poirot, this is the second time I've been here this morning. I was anxious to catch you."

"Perhaps I'd better be off," I suggested rather awkwardly.

"Not on my account, doctor. No, it's just this," he went on, seating himself at a wave of invitation from Poirot, "I've got a confession to make."

"En verité?" said Poirot, with an air of polite interest.

"Oh, it's of no consequence, really. But, as a matter of fact, my conscience has been pricking me ever since yesterday afternoon. You accused us all of keeping back something, M. Poirot. I plead guilty. I've had something up my sleeve."

"And what is that, M. Raymond?"

"As I say, it's nothing of consequence—just this. I was in debt—badly, and that legacy came in the nick of time. Five hundred pounds puts me on my feet again with a little to spare."

He smiled at us both with that engaging frankness that made him such a likable youngster.

"You know how it is. Suspicious looking policeman—don't like to admit you were hard up for money—think it will look bad to them. But I was a fool, really, because Blunt and I were in the billiard room from a quarter to ten onwards, so I've got a watertight alibi and nothing to fear. Still, when you thundered out that stuff about concealing things, I felt a nasty prick of conscience, and I thought I'd like to get it off my mind."

He got up again and stood smiling at us.

"You are a very wise young man," said Poirot, nodding at him with approval. "See you, when I know that any one is hiding things from me, I suspect that the thing hidden may be something very bad indeed. You have done well."

"I'm glad I'm cleared from suspicion," laughed Raymond. "I'll be off now."

"So that is that," I remarked, as the door closed behind the young secretary.

"Yes," agreed Poirot. "A mere bagatelle—but if he had not been in the billiard room—who knows? After all, many crimes have been committed for the sake of less than five hundred pounds. It all depends on what sum is sufficient to break a man. A question of the relativity, is it not so? Have you reflected, my friend, that many people in that house stood to benefit by Mr. Ackroyd's death? Mrs. Ackroyd, Miss Flora, young Mr. Raymond, the housekeeper, Miss Russell. Only one, in fact, does not, Major Blunt."

His tone in uttering that name was so peculiar that I looked up, puzzled.

"I don't quite understand you," I said.

"Two of the people I accused have given me the truth."

"You think Major Blunt has something to conceal also?"

"As for that," remarked Poirot nonchalantly, "there is a saying, is there not, that Englishmen conceal only one thing—their love? And Major Blunt, I should say, is not good at concealments."

"Sometimes," I said, "I wonder if we haven't rather jumped to conclusions on one point."

"What is that?"

"We've assumed that the blackmailer of Mrs. Ferrars is necessarily the murderer of Mr. Ackroyd. Mightn't we be mistaken?"

Poirot nodded energetically.

"Very good. Very good indeed. I wondered if that idea would come to you. Of course it is possible. But we must remember one point. The letter disappeared. Still, that, as you say, may not necessarily mean that the murderer took it. When you first found the body, Parker may have abstracted the letter unnoticed by you."

"Parker?"

"Yes, Parker. I always come back to Parker—not as the murderer —no, he did not commit the murder; but who is more suitable than he as the mysterious scoundrel who terrorized Mrs. Ferrars? He may have got his information about Mr. Ferrars's death from one of the King's Paddock servants. At any rate, he is more likely to have come upon it than a casual guest such as Blunt, for instance."

"Parker might have taken the letter," I admitted. "It wasn't till later that I noticed it was gone."

"How much later? After Blunt and Raymond were in the room, or before?"

"I can't remember," I said slowly. "I think it was before—no, afterwards. Yes, I'm almost sure it was afterwards."

"That widens the field to three," said Poirot thoughtfully. "But Parker is the most likely. It is in my mind to try a little experiment with Parker. How say you, my friend, will you accompany me to Fernly?"

I acquiesced, and we set out at once. Poirot asked to see Miss Ackroyd, and presently Flora came to us.

"Mademoiselle Flora," said Poirot, "I have to confide in you a little secret. I am not yet satisfied of the innocence of Parker. I propose to make a little experiment with your assistance. I want to reconstruct some of his actions on that night. But we must think of something to tell him—ah! I have it. I wish to satisfy myself as to whether voices in the little lobby could have been heard outside on the terrace. Now, ring for Parker, if you will be so good."

I did so, and presently the butler appeared, suave as ever.

"You rang, sir?"

"Yes, my good Parker. I have in mind a little experiment. I have placed Major Blunt on the terrace outside the study window. I want to see if any one there could have heard the voices of Miss Ackroyd and yourself in the lobby that night. I want to enact that little scene over again. Perhaps you would fetch the tray or whatever it was you were carrying?"

Parker vanished, and we repaired to the lobby outside the study door. Presently we heard a chink in the outer hall, and Parker appeared in the doorway carrying a tray with a siphon, a decanter of whisky, and two glasses on it.

"One moment," cried Poirot, raising his hand and seemingly very excited. "We must have everything in order. Just as it occurred. It is a little method of mine."

"A foreign custom, sir," said Parker. "Reconstruction of the crime they call it, do they not?"

He was quite imperturbable as he stood there politely waiting on Poirot's orders.

"Ah! he knows something, the good Parker," cried Poirot. "He has read of those things. Now, I beg you, let us have everything of the most exact. You came from the outer hall—so. Mademoiselle was —where?"

"Here," said Flora, taking up her stand just outside the study door.

"Quite right, sir," said Parker.

"I had just closed the door," continued Flora.

"Yes, miss," agreed Parker. "Your hand was still on the handle as it is now."

"Then *allez,*" said Poirot. "Play me the little comedy."

Flora stood with her hand on the door handle, and Parker came stepping through the door from the hall, bearing the tray.

He stopped just inside the door. Flora spoke.

"Oh! Parker. Mr. Ackroyd doesn't want to be disturbed again to-night."

"Is that right?" she added in an undertone.

"To the best of my recollection, Miss Flora," said Parker, "but I fancy you used the word evening instead of night." Then, raising his voice in a somewhat theatrical fashion: "Very good, miss. Shall I lock up as usual?"

"Yes, please."

Parker retired through the door, Flora followed him, and started to ascend the main staircase.

"Is that enough?" she asked over her shoulder.

"Admirable," declared the little man, rubbing his hands. "By the way, Parker, are you sure there were two glasses on the tray that evening? Who was the second one for?"

"I always bring two glasses, sir," said Parker. "Is there anything further?"

"Nothing. I thank you."

Parker withdrew, dignified to the last.

Poirot stood in the middle of the hall frowning. Flora came down and joined us.

"Has your experiment been successful?" she asked. "I don't quite understand, you know——"

Poirot smiled admiringly at her.

"It is not necessary that you should," he said. "But tell me, were there indeed two glasses on Parker's tray that night?"

Flora wrinkled her brows a minute.

"I really can't remember," she said. "I think there were. Is—is that the object of your experiment?"

Poirot took her hand and patted it.

"Put it this way," he said. "I am always interested to see if people will speak the truth."

"And did Parker speak the truth?"

"I rather think he did," said Poirot thoughtfully.

A few minutes later saw us retracing our steps to the village.

"What was the point of that question about the glasses?" I asked curiously.

Poirot shrugged his shoulders.

"One must say something," he remarked. "That particular question did as well as any other."

I stared at him.

"At any rate, my friend," he said more seriously, "I know now something I wanted to know. Let us leave it at that."

CHAPTER 16

AN EVENING AT MAH JONG

THAT NIGHT we had a little Mah Jong party. This kind of simple entertainment is very popular in King's Abbot. The guests arrive in goloshes and waterproofs after dinner. They partake of coffee and later of cake, sandwiches, and tea.

On this particular night our guests were Miss Ganett and Colonel Carter, who lives near the church. A good deal of gossip is handed round at these evenings, sometimes seriously interfering with the game in progress. We used to play bridge—chatty bridge of the worst description. We find Mah Jong much more peaceful. The irritated demand as to why on earth your partner did not lead a certain card is entirely done away with, and though we still express criticisms frankly, there is not the same acrimonious spirit.

"Very cold evening, eh, Sheppard?" said Colonel Carter, standing with his back to the fire. Caroline had taken Miss Ganett to her own room, and was there assisting her to disentangle herself from her many wraps. "Reminds me of the Afghan passes."

"Indeed?" I said politely.

"Very mysterious business this about poor Ackroyd," continued the colonel, accepting a cup of coffee. "A deuce of a lot behind it—

that's what I say. Between you and me, Sheppard, I've heard the word blackmail mentioned!"

The colonel gave me the look which might be tabulated "one man of the world to another."

"A woman in it, no doubt," he said. "Depend upon it, a woman in it."

Caroline and Miss Ganett joined us at this minute. Miss Ganett drank coffee whilst Caroline got out the Mah Jong box and poured out the tiles upon the table.

"Washing the tiles," said the colonel facetiously. "That's right—washing the tiles, as we used to say in the Shanghai Club."

It is the private opinion of both Caroline and myself that Colonel Carter has never been in the Shanghai Club in his life. More, that he has never been farther east than India, where he juggled with tins of bully beef and plum and apple jam during the Great War. But the colonel is determinedly military, and in King's Abbot we permit people to indulge their little idiosyncrasies freely.

"Shall we begin?" said Caroline.

We sat round the table. For some five minutes there was complete silence, owing to the fact that there is tremendous secret competition amongst us as to who can build their wall quickest.

"Go on, James," said Caroline at last. "You're East Wind."

I discarded a tile. A round or two proceeded, broken by the monotonous remarks of "Three Bamboos," "Two Circles," "Pung," and frequently from Miss Ganett "Unpung," owing to that lady's habit of too hastily claiming tiles to which she had no right.

"I saw Flora Ackroyd this morning," said Miss Ganett. "Pung—no—Unpung. I made a mistake."

"Four Circles," said Caroline. "Where did you see her?"

"She didn't see *me*," said Miss Ganett, with that tremendous significance only to be met with in small villages.

"Ah!" said Caroline interestedly. "Chow."

"I believe," said Miss Ganett, temporarily diverted, "that it's the right thing nowadays to say 'Chee' not 'Chow.'"

"Nonsense," said Caroline. "I have always said *'Chow.'*"

"In the Shanghai Club," said Colonel Carter, "they say *'Chow.'*" Miss Ganett retired, crushed.

"What were you saying about Flora Ackroyd?" asked Caroline, after a moment or two devoted to the game. "Was she with any one?"

"Very much so," said Miss Ganett.

The eyes of the two ladies met, and seemed to exchange information.

"Really," said Caroline interestedly. "Is that it? Well, it doesn't surprise me in the least."

"We're waiting for you to discard, Miss Caroline," said the colonel. He sometimes affects the pose of the bluff male, intent on the game and indifferent to gossip. But nobody is deceived.

"If you ask me," said Miss Ganett. ("Was that a Bamboo you discarded, dear? Oh! no, I see now—it was a Circle.) As I was saying, if you ask me, Flora's been exceedingly lucky. Exceedingly lucky she's been."

"How's that, Miss Ganett?" asked the colonel. "I'll Pung that Green Dragon. How do you make out that Miss Flora's been lucky? Very charming girl and all that, I know."

"I mayn't know very much about crime," said Miss Ganett, with the air of one who knows everything there is to know, "but I can tell you one thing. The first question that's always asked is 'Who last saw the deceased alive?' And the person who did is regarded with suspicion. Now, Flora Ackroyd last saw her uncle alive. It might have looked very nasty for her—very nasty indeed. It's my opinion—and I give it for what it's worth, that Ralph Paton is staying away on her account, to draw suspicion away from her."

"Come, now," I protested mildly, "you surely can't suggest that a young girl like Flora Ackroyd is capable of stabbing her uncle in cold blood?"

"Well, I don't know," said Miss Ganett. "I've just been reading a book from the library about the underworld of Paris, and it says that some of the worst women criminals are young girls with the faces of angels."

"That's in France," said Caroline instantly.

"Just so," said the colonel. "Now, I'll tell you a very curious thing —a story that was going round the Bazaars in India. . . ."

The colonel's story was one of interminable length, and of curiously little interest. A thing that happened in India many years ago cannot compare for a moment with an event that took place in King's Abbot the day before yesterday.

It was Caroline who brought the colonel's story to a close by fortunately going Mah Jong. After the slight unpleasantness always occasioned by my corrections of Caroline's somewhat faulty arithmetic, we started a new hand.

"East Wind passes," said Caroline. "I've got an idea of my own about Ralph Paton. Three Characters. But I'm keeping it to myself for the present."

"Are you, dear?" said Miss Ganett. "Chow—I mean Pung."

"Yes," said Caroline firmly.

"Was it all right about the boots?" asked Miss Ganett. "Their being black, I mean?"

"Quite all right," said Caroline.

"What was the point, do you think?" asked Miss Ganett.

Caroline pursed up her lips, and shook her head with an air of knowing all about it.

"Pung," said Miss Ganett. "No—Unpung. I suppose that now the doctor's in with M. Poirot he knows all the secrets?"

"Far from it," I said.

"James is so modest," said Caroline. "Ah! a concealed Kong."

The colonel gave vent to a whistle. For the moment gossip was forgotten.

"Your own wind, too," he said. "*And* you've got two Pungs of Dragons. We must be careful. Miss Caroline's out for a big hand."

We played for some minutes with no irrelevant conversation.

"This M. Poirot now," said Colonel Carter, "is he really such a great detective?"

"The greatest the world has ever known," said Caroline solemnly. "He had to come here incognito to avoid publicity."

"Chow," said Miss Ganett. "Quite wonderful for our little village, I'm sure. By the way, Clara—my maid, you know—is great friends with Elsie, the housemaid at Fernly, and what do you think Elsie told her? That there's been a lot of money stolen, and it's her opinion—Elsie's—I mean, that the parlormaid had something to do with it. She's leaving at the month, and she's crying a good deal at night. If you ask me, the girl is very likely in league with a *gang*. She's always been a queer girl—she's not friends with any of the girls round here. She goes off by herself on her days out—very unnatural, I call it, and most suspicious. I asked her once to come to our Girls' Friendly Evenings, but she refused, and then I asked her a few questions about her home and her family—all that sort of thing—and I'm bound to say I considered her manner most impertinent. Outwardly very respectful—but she shut me up in the most barefaced way."

Miss Ganett stopped for breath, and the colonel, who was totally uninterested in the servant question, remarked that in the Shanghai Club brisk play was the invariable rule.

We had a round of brisk play.

"That Miss Russell," said Caroline. "She came here pretending to consult James on Friday morning. It's my opinion she wanted to see where the poisons were kept. Five Characters."

"Chow," said Miss Ganett. "What an extraordinary idea. I wonder if you can be right."

"Talking of poisons," said the colonel. "Eh—what? Haven't I discarded? Oh! Eight Bamboos."

"Mah Jong!" said Miss Ganett.

Caroline was very much annoyed.

"One Red Dragon," she said regretfully, "and I should have had a hand of three doubles."

"I've had two Red Dragons all the time," I mentioned.

"So exactly like you, James," said Caroline reproachfully. "You've no conception of the spirit of the game."

I myself thought I had played rather cleverly. I should have had to pay Caroline an enormous amount if she had gone Mah Jong. Miss Ganett's Mah Jong was of the poorest variety possible, as Caroline did not fail to point out to her.

East Wind passed, and we started a new hand in silence.

"What I was going to tell you just now was this," said Caroline.

"Yes?" said Miss Ganett encouragingly.

"My idea about Ralph Paton, I mean."

"Yes, dear," said Miss Ganett, still more encouragingly. "Chow!"

"It's a sign of weakness to Chow so early," said Caroline severely. "You should go for a big hand."

"I know," said Miss Ganett. "You were saying—about Ralph Paton, you know?"

"Yes. Well, I've a pretty shrewd idea where he is."

We all stopped to stare at her.

"This is very interesting, Miss Caroline," said Colonel Carter. "All your own idea, eh?"

"Well, not exactly. I'll tell you about it. You know that big map of the county we have in the hall?"

We all said Yes.

"As M. Poirot was going out the other day, he stopped and looked at it, and he made some remark—I can't remember exactly what it was. Something about Cranchester being the only big town anywhere near us—which is true, of course. But after he had gone—it came to me suddenly."

"What came to you?"

"His meaning. Of course Ralph is in Cranchester."

It was at that moment that I knocked down the rack that held my pieces. My sister immediately reproved me for clumsiness, but half-heartedly. She was intent on her theory.

"Cranchester, Miss Caroline?" said Colonel Carter. "Surely not Cranchester! It's so near."

"That's exactly it," cried Caroline triumphantly. "It seems quite clear by now that he didn't get away from here by train. He must simply have walked into Cranchester. And I believe he's there still. No one would dream of his being so near at hand."

I pointed out several objections to the theory, but when once Caroline has got something firmly into her head, nothing dislodges it.

"And you think M. Poirot has the same idea," said Miss Ganett thoughtfully. "It's a curious coincidence, but I was out for a walk this afternoon on the Cranchester road, and he passed me in a car coming from that direction."

We all looked at each other.

"Why, dear me," said Miss Ganett suddenly, "I'm Mah Jong all the time, and I never noticed it."

Caroline's attention was distracted from her own inventive exercises. She pointed out to Miss Ganett that a hand consisting of mixed suits and too many Chows was hardly worth going Mah Jong on. Miss Ganett listened imperturbably and collected her counters.

"Yes, dear, I know what you mean," she said. "But it rather depends on what kind of a hand you have to start with, doesn't it?"

"You'll never get the big hands if you don't go for them," urged Caroline.

"Well, we must all play our own way, mustn't we?" said Miss Ganett. She looked down at her counters. "After all, I'm up, so far."

Caroline, who was considerably down, said nothing.

East Wind passed, and we set to once more. Annie brought in the tea things. Caroline and Miss Ganett were both slightly ruffled as is often the case during one of these festive evenings.

"If you would only play a leetle quicker, dear," said Caroline, as Miss Ganett hesitated over her discard. "The Chinese put down the tiles so quickly it sounds like little birds pattering."

For some few minutes we played like the Chinese.

"You haven't contributed much to the sum of information, Sheppard," said Colonel Carter genially. "You're a sly dog. Hand in glove with the great detective, and not a hint as to the way things are going."

THE MURDER OF ROGER ACKROYD

...

"James is an extraordinary creature," said Caroline. "He can *not* bring himself to part with information."

She looked at me with some disfavor.

"I assure you," I said, "that I don't know anything. Poirot keeps his own counsel."

"Wise man," said the colonel with a chuckle. "He doesn't give himself away. But they're wonderful fellows, these foreign detectives. Up to all sorts of dodges, I believe."

"Pung," said Miss Ganett, in a tone of quiet triumph. "And Mah Jong."

The situation became more strained. It was annoyance at Miss Ganett's going Mah Jong for the third time running which prompted Caroline to say to me as we built a fresh wall:—

"You are too tiresome, James. You sit there like a dead head, and say nothing at all!"

"But, my dear," I protested, "I have really nothing to say—that is, of the kind you mean."

"Nonsense," said Caroline, as she sorted her hand. "You *must* know something interesting."

I did not answer for a moment. I was overwhelmed and intoxicated. I had read of there being such a thing as the Perfect Winning—going Mah Jong on one's original hand. I had never hoped to hold the hand myself.

With suppressed triumph I laid my hand face upwards on the table.

"As they say in the Shanghai Club," I remarked, "Tin-ho—the Perfect Winning!"

The colonel's eyes nearly bulged out of his head.

"Upon my soul," he said. "What an extraordinary thing. I never saw that happen before!"

It was then that I went on, goaded by Caroline's gibes, and rendered reckless by my triumph.

"And as to anything interesting," I said. "What about a gold wedding ring with a date and 'From R.' inside?"

I pass over the scene that followed. I was made to say exactly where this treasure was found. I was made to reveal the date.

"March 13th," said Caroline. "Just six months ago. Ah!"

Out of the babble of excited suggestions and suppositions three theories were evolved:—

1. That of Colonel Carter: that Ralph was secretly married to Flora. The first or most simple solution.

2. That of Miss Ganett: that Roger Ackroyd had been secretly married to Mrs. Ferrars.

3. That of my sister: that Roger Ackroyd had married his housekeeper, Miss Russell.

A fourth or super-theory was propounded by Caroline later as we went up to bed.

"Mark my words," she said suddenly, "I shouldn't be at all surprised if Geoffrey Raymond and Flora weren't married."

"Surely it would be 'From G.,' not 'From R.' then," I suggested.

"You never know. Some girls call men by their surnames. And you heard what Miss Ganett said this evening—about Flora's carryings on."

Strictly speaking, I had not heard Miss Ganett say anything of the kind, but I respected Caroline's knowledge of innuendoes.

"How about Hector Blunt," I hinted. "If it's anybody——"

"Nonsense," said Caroline. "I dare say he admires her—may even be in love with her. But depend upon it a girl isn't going to fall in love with a man old enough to be her father when there's a good-looking young secretary about. She may encourage Major Blunt just as a blind. Girls are very artful. But there's one thing I *do* tell you, James Sheppard. Flora Ackroyd does not care a penny piece for Ralph Paton, and never has. You can take it from me."

I took it from her meekly.

CHAPTER 17

PARKER

IT OCCURRED to me the next morning that under the exhilaration produced by Tin-ho, or the Perfect Winning, I might have been slightly indiscreet. True, Poirot had not asked me to keep the discovery of the ring to myself. On the other hand, he had said nothing about it whilst at Fernly, and as far as I knew, I was the only person aware that it had been found. I felt distinctly guilty. The fact was by now spreading through King's Abbot like wildfire. I was expecting wholesale reproaches from Poirot any minute.

The joint funeral of Mrs. Ferrars and Roger Ackroyd was fixed for eleven o'clock. It was a melancholy and impressive ceremony. All the party from Fernly were there.

After it was over, Poirot, who had also been present, took me by the arm, and invited me to accompany him back to The Larches. He was looking very grave, and I feared that my indiscretion of the night before had got round to his ears. But it soon transpired that his thoughts were occupied by something of a totally different nature.

"See you," he said. "We must act. With your help I propose to examine a witness. We will question him, we will put such fear into him that the truth is bound to come out."

"What witness are you talking of?" I asked, very much surprised.

"Parker!" said Poirot. "I asked him to be at my house this morning at twelve o'clock. He should await us there at this very minute."

"What do you think," I ventured, glancing sideways at his face.

"I know this—that I am not satisfied."

"You think that it was he who blackmailed Mrs. Ferrars?"

"Either that, or——"

"Well?" I said, after waiting a minute or two.

"My friend, I will say this to you—I hope it was he."

The gravity of his manner, and something indefinable that tinged it, reduced me to silence.

On arrival at The Larches, we were informed that Parker was already there awaiting our return. As we entered the room, the butler rose respectfully.

"Good-morning, Parker," said Poirot pleasantly. "One instant, I pray of you."

He removed his overcoat and gloves.

"Allow me, sir," said Parker, and sprang forward to assist him. He deposited the articles neatly on a chair by the door. Poirot watched him with approval.

"Thank you, my good Parker," he said. "Take a seat, will you not? What I have to say may take some time."

Parker seated himself with an apologetic bend of the head.

"Now what do you think I asked you to come here for this morning—eh?"

Parker coughed.

"I understood, sir, that you wished to ask me a few questions about my late master—private like."

"*Précisément,*" said Poirot, beaming. "Have you made many experiments in blackmail?"

"Sir!"

The butler sprang to his feet.

"Do not excite yourself," said Poirot placidly. "Do not play the farce of the honest, injured man. You know all there is to know about the blackmail, is it not so?"

"Sir, I—I've never—never been——"

"Insulted," suggested Poirot, "in such a way before. Then why, my excellent Parker, were you so anxious to overhear the conversation in Mr. Ackroyd's study the other evening, after you had caught the word blackmail?"

"I wasn't—I——"

"Who was your last master?" rapped out Poirot suddenly.

"My last master?"

"Yes, the master you were with before you came to Mr. Ackroyd."

"A Major Ellerby, sir——"

Poirot took the words out of his mouth.

"Just so, Major Ellerby. Major Ellerby was addicted to drugs, was he not? You traveled about with him. When he was in Bermuda there was some trouble—a man was killed. Major Ellerby was partly responsible. It was hushed up. But you knew about it. How much did Major Ellerby pay you to keep your mouth shut?"

Parker was staring at him open-mouthed. The man had gone to pieces, his cheeks shook flabbily.

"You see, me, I have made inquiries," said Poirot pleasantly. "It is as I say. You got a good sum then as blackmail, and Major Ellerby went on paying you until he died. Now I want to hear about your latest experiment."

Parker still stared.

"It is useless to deny. Hercule Poirot *knows*. It is so, what I have said about Major Ellerby, is it not?"

As though against his will, Parker nodded reluctantly once. His face was ashen pale.

"But I never hurt a hair of Mr. Ackroyd's head," he moaned. "Honest to God, sir, I didn't. I've been afraid of this coming all the time. And I tell you I didn't—I didn't kill him."

His voice rose almost to a scream.

"I am inclined to believe you, my friend," said Poirot. "You have not the nerve—the courage. But I must have the truth."

"I'll tell you anything, sir, anything you want to know. It's true that I tried to listen that night. A word or two I heard made me curious. And Mr. Ackroyd's wanting not to be disturbed, and shutting himself up with the doctor the way he did. It's God's own truth what I told the police. I heard the word blackmail, sir, and well——"

He paused.

"You thought there might be something in it for you?" suggested Poirot smoothly.

"Well—well, yes, I did, sir. I thought that if Mr. Ackroyd was being blackmailed, why shouldn't I have a share of the pickings?"

A very curious expression passed over Poirot's face. He leaned forward.

"Had you any reason to suppose before that night that Mr. Ackroyd was being blackmailed?"

"No, indeed, sir. It was a great surprise to me. Such a regular gentleman in all his habits."

"How much did you overhear?"

"Not very much, sir. There seemed what I might call a spite against me. Of course I had to attend to my duties in the pantry. And when I did creep along once or twice to the study it was no use. The first time Dr. Sheppard came out and almost caught me in the act, and another time Mr. Raymond passed me in the big hall and went that way, so I knew it was no use; and when I went with the tray, Miss Flora headed me off."

Poirot stared for a long time at the man, as if to test his sincerity. Parker returned his gaze earnestly.

"I hope you believe me, sir. I've been afraid all along the police would rake up that old business with Major Ellerby and be suspicious of me in consequence."

"*Eh bien*," said Poirot at last. "I am disposed to believe you. But there is one thing I must request of you—to show me your bank-book. You have a bank-book, I presume?"

"Yes, sir, as a matter of fact, I have it with me now."

With no sign of confusion, he produced it from his pocket. Poirot took the slim, green-covered book and perused the entries.

"Ah! I perceive you have purchased £500 of National Savings Certificates this year?"

"Yes, sir. I have already over a thousand pounds saved—the result of my connection with—er—my late master, Major Ellerby. And I have had quite a little flutter on some horses this year—very successful. If you remember, sir, a rank outsider won the Jubilee. I was fortunate enough to back it—£20."

Poirot handed him back the book.

"I will wish you good-morning. I believe that you have told me the truth. If you have not—so much the worse for you, my friend."

When Parker had departed, Poirot picked up his overcoat once more.

"Going out again?" I asked.

"Yes, we will pay a little visit to the good M. Hammond."

"You believe Parker's story?"

"It is credible enough on the face of it. It seems clear that—unless he is a very good actor indeed—he genuinely believes it was Ackroyd himself who was the victim of blackmail. If so, he knows nothing at all about the Mrs. Ferrars business."

"Then in that case—who——"

"*Précisément!* Who? But our visit to M. Hammond will accomplish one purpose. It will either clear Parker completely or else——"

"Well?"

"I fall into the bad habit of leaving my sentences unfinished this morning," said Poirot apologetically. "You must bear with me."

"By the way," I said, rather sheepishly, "I've got a confession to make. I'm afraid I have inadvertently let out something about that ring."

"What ring?"

"The ring you found in the goldfish pond."

"Ah! yes," said Poirot, smiling broadly.

"I hope you're not annoyed? It was very careless of me."

"But not at all, my good friend, not at all. I laid no commands upon you. You were at liberty to speak of it if you so wished. She was interested, your sister?"

"She was indeed. It created a sensation. All sorts of theories are flying about."

"Ah! And yet it is so simple. The true explanation leapt to the eye, did it not?"

"Did it?" I said dryly.

Poirot laughed.

"The wise man does not commit himself," he observed. "Is not that so? But here we are at M. Hammond's."

The lawyer was in his office, and we were ushered in without any delay. He rose and greeted us in his dry, precise manner.

Poirot came at once to the point.

"Monsieur, I desire from you certain information, that is, if you will be so good as to give it to me. You acted, I understand, for the late Mrs. Ferrars of King's Paddock?"

I noticed the swift gleam of surprise which showed in the lawyer's eyes, before his professional reserve came down once more like a mask over his face.

"Certainly. All her affairs passed through our hands."

"Very good. Now, before I ask you to tell me anything, I should like you to listen to the story Dr. Sheppard will relate to you. You have no objection, have you, my friend, to repeating the conversation you had with Mr. Ackroyd last Friday night?"

"Not in the least," I said, and straightway began the recital of that strange evening.

Hammond listened with close attention.

"That is all," I said, when I had finished.

"Blackmail," said the lawyer thoughtfully.

"You are surprised?" asked Poirot.

The lawyer took off his pince-nez and polished them with his handkerchief.

"No," he replied, "I can hardly say that I am surprised. I have suspected something of the kind for some time."

"That brings us," said Poirot, "to the information for which I am asking. If any one can give us an idea of the actual sums paid, you are the man, monsieur."

"I see no object in withholding the information," said Hammond, after a moment or two. "During the past year, Mrs. Ferrars has sold out certain securities, and the money for them was paid into her account and not reinvested. As her income was a large one, and she lived very quietly after her husband's death, it seems certain that these sums of money were paid away for some special purpose. I once sounded her on the subject, and she said that she was obliged to support several of her husband's poor relations. I let the matter drop, of course. Until now, I have always imagined that the money was paid to some woman who had had a claim on Ashley Ferrars. I never dreamed that Mrs. Ferrars herself was involved."

"And the amount?" asked Poirot.

"In all, I should say the various sums totaled at least twenty thousand pounds."

"Twenty thousand pounds!" I exclaimed. "In one year!"

"Mrs. Ferrars was a very wealthy woman," said Poirot dryly. "And the penalty for murder is not a pleasant one."

"Is there anything else that I can tell you?" inquired Mr. Hammond.

"I thank you, no," said Poirot, rising. "All my excuses for having deranged you."

"Not at all, not at all."

"The word derange," I remarked, when we were outside again, "is applicable to mental disorder only."

"Ah!" cried Poirot, "never will my English be quite perfect. A curious language. I should then have said disarranged, *n'est ce pas?*"

"Disturbed is the word you had in mind."

"I thank you, my friend. The word exact, you are zealous for it. *Eh bien,* what about our friend Parker now? With twenty thousand pounds in hand, would he have continued being a butler? *Je ne pense pas.* It is, of course, possible that he banked the money under another name, but I am disposed to believe he spoke the truth to us. If he is a scoundrel, he is a scoundrel on a mean scale. He has not the big ideas. That leaves us as a possibility, Raymond, or—well—Major Blunt."

"Surely not Raymond," I objected. "Since we know that he was desperately hard up for a matter of five hundred pounds."

"That is what he says, yes."

"And as to Hector Blunt——"

"I will tell you something as to the good Major Blunt," interrupted Poirot. "It is my business to make inquiries. I make them. *Eh bien*—that legacy of which he speaks, I have discovered that the amount of it was close upon twenty thousand pounds. What do you think of that?"

I was so taken aback that I could hardly speak.

"It's impossible," I said at last. "A well-known man like Hector Blunt."

Poirot shrugged his shoulders.

"Who knows? At least he is a man with big ideas. I confess that I hardly see him as a blackmailer, but there is another possibility that you have not even considered."

"What is that?"

"The fire, my friend. Ackroyd himself may have destroyed that letter, blue envelope and all, after you left him."

"I hardly think that likely," I said slowly. "And yet—of course, it may be so. He might have changed his mind."

We had just arrived at my house, and on the spur of the moment I invited Poirot to come in and take pot luck.

I thought Caroline would be pleased with me, but it is hard to satisfy one's women folk. It appears that we were eating chops for lunch

—the kitchen staff being regaled on tripe and onions. And two chops set before three people are productive of embarrassment.

But Caroline is seldom daunted for long. With magnificent mendacity, she explained to Poirot that although James laughed at her for doing so, she adhered strictly to a vegetarian diet. She descanted ecstatically on the delights of nut cutlets (which I am quite sure she has never tasted) and ate a Welsh rarebit with gusto and frequent cutting remarks as to the dangers of "flesh" foods.

Afterwards, when we were sitting in front of the fire and smoking, Caroline attacked Poirot directly.

"Not found Ralph Paton yet?" she asked.

"Where should I find him, mademoiselle?"

"I thought, perhaps, you'd found him in Cranchester," said Caroline, with intense meaning in her tone.

Poirot looked merely bewildered.

"In Cranchester? But why in Cranchester?"

I enlightened him with a touch of malice.

"One of our ample staff of private detectives happened to see you in a car on the Cranchester road yesterday," I explained.

Poirot's bewilderment vanished. He laughed heartily.

"Ah, that! A simple visit to the dentist, *c'est tout*. My tooth, it aches. I go there. My tooth, it is at once better. I think to return quickly. The dentist, he says No. Better to have it out. I argue. He insists. He has his way! That particular tooth, it will never ache again."

Caroline collapsed rather like a pricked balloon.

We fell to discussing Ralph Paton.

"A weak nature," I insisted. "But not a vicious one."

"Ah!" said Poirot. "But weakness, where does it end?"

"Exactly," said Caroline. "Take James here—weak as water, if I weren't about to look after him."

"My dear Caroline," I said irritably, "can't you talk without dragging in personalities?"

"You *are* weak, James," said Caroline, quite unmoved. "I'm eight years older than you are—oh! I don't mind M. Poirot knowing that——"

"I should never have guessed it, mademoiselle," said Poirot, with a gallant little bow.

"Eight years older. But I've always considered it my duty to look after you. With a bad bringing up, Heaven knows what mischief you might have got into by now."

"I might have married a beautiful adventuress," I murmured, gazing at the ceiling, and blowing smoke rings.

"Adventuress!" said Caroline, with a snort. "If we're talking of adventuresses——"

She left the sentence unfinished.

"Well?" I said, with some curiosity.

"Nothing. But I can think of some one not a hundred miles away." Then she turned to Poirot suddenly.

"James sticks to it that you believe some one in the house committed the murder. All I can say is, you're wrong."

"I should not like to be wrong," said Poirot. "It is not—how do you say—my *metier?*"

"I've got the facts pretty clearly," continued Caroline, taking no notice of Poirot's remark, "from James and others. As far as I can see, of the people in the house, only two *could* have had the chance of doing it. Ralph Paton and Flora Ackroyd."

"My dear Caroline——"

"Now, James, don't interrupt me. I know what I'm talking about. Parker met her *outside* the door, didn't he? He didn't hear her uncle saying good-night to her. She could have killed him then and there."

"Caroline."

"I'm not saying she *did,* James. I'm saying she *could* have done. As a matter of fact, though Flora is like all these young girls nowadays, with no veneration for their betters and thinking they know best on every subject under the sun, I don't for a minute believe she'd kill even a chicken. But there it is. Mr. Raymond and Major Blunt have alibis. Mrs. Ackroyd's got an alibi. Even that Russell woman seems to have one—and a good job for her it is she has. Who is left? Only Ralph and Flora! And say what you will, I don't believe Ralph Paton is a murderer. A boy we've known all our lives."

Poirot was silent for a minute, watching the curling smoke rise from his cigarette. When at last he spoke, it was in a gentle far-away voice that produced a curious impression. It was totally unlike his usual manner.

"Let us take a man—a very ordinary man. A man with no idea of murder in his heart. There is in him somewhere a strain of weakness —deep down. It has so far never been called into play. Perhaps it never will be—and if so he will go to his grave honored and respected by every one. But let us suppose that something occurs. He is in difficulties—or perhaps not that even. He may stumble by accident on a secret—a secret involving life or death to some one. And his first impulse will be to speak out—to do his duty as an honest citizen. And then the strain of weakness tells. Here is a chance of money—a great amount of money. He wants money—he desires it—and it is so easy. He has to do nothing for it—just keep silence. That is the beginning. The desire for money grows. He must have more—and more! He is intoxicated by the gold mine which has opened at his feet. He becomes greedy. And in his greed he overreaches himself. One can press a man as far as one likes—but with a woman one must not press too far. For a woman has at heart a great desire to speak the truth. How many husbands who have deceived their wives go comfortably to their graves, carrying their secret with them! How many wives who have deceived their husbands wreck their lives by throwing the fact in those same husbands' teeth! They have been pressed too far. In a reckless moment (which they will afterwards regret, *bien entendu*) they fling safety to the winds and turn at bay, proclaiming the truth with great momentary satisfaction to themselves. So it was, I think, in this case. The strain was too great. And so there came your proverb, the death of the goose that laid the golden eggs. But that is not the end. Exposure faced the man of whom we are speaking. And he is not the same man he was—say, a year ago. His moral fiber is blunted. He is desperate. He is fighting a losing battle, and he is prepared to take any means that come to his hand, for exposure means ruin to him. And so—the dagger strikes!"

He was silent for a moment. It was as though he had laid a spell upon the room. I cannot try to describe the impression his words produced. There was something in the merciless analysis, and the ruthless power of vision which struck fear into both of us.

"Afterwards," he went on softly, "the danger removed, he will be himself again, normal, kindly. But if the need again arises, then once more he will strike."

Caroline roused herself at last.

"You are speaking of Ralph Paton," she said. "You may be right, you may not, but you have no business to condemn a man unheard."

The telephone bell rang sharply. I went out into the hall, and took off the receiver.

"What?" I said. "Yes. Dr. Sheppard speaking."

I listened for a minute or two, then replied briefly. Replacing the receiver, I went back into the drawing-room.

"Poirot," I said, "they have detained a man at Liverpool. His name is Charles Kent, and he is believed to be the stranger who visited Fernly that night. They want me to go to Liverpool at once and identify him."

CHAPTER 18

CHARLES KENT

HALF AN hour later saw Poirot, myself, and Inspector Raglan in the train on the way to Liverpool. The inspector was clearly very excited.

"We may get a line on the blackmailing part of the business, if on nothing else," he declared jubilantly. "He's a rough customer, this fellow, by what I heard over the phone. Takes dope, too. We ought to find it easy to get what we want out of him. If there was the shadow of a motive, nothing's more likely than that he killed Mr. Ackroyd. But in that case, why is young Paton keeping out of the way? The whole thing's a muddle—that's what it is. By the way, M. Poirot, you were quite right about those fingerprints. They were Mr. Ackroyd's own. I had rather the same idea myself, but I dismissed it as hardly feasible."

I smiled to myself. Inspector Raglan was so very plainly saving his face.

"As regards this man," said Poirot, "he is not yet arrested, eh?"

"No, detained under suspicion."

"And what account does he give of himself?"

"Precious little," said the inspector, with a grin. "He's a wary bird, I gather. A lot of abuse, but very little more."

On arrival at Liverpool I was surprised to find that Poirot was welcome with acclamation. Superintendent Hayes, who met us, had worked with Poirot over some case long ago, and had evidently an exaggerated opinion of his powers.

"Now we've got M. Poirot here we shan't be long," he said cheerfully. "I thought you'd retired, moosior?"

"So I had, my good Hayes, so I had. But how tedious is retirement! You cannot imagine to yourself the monotony with which day comes after day."

"Very likely. So you've come to have a look at our own particular find? Is this Dr. Sheppard? Think you'll be able to identify him, sir?"

"I'm not very sure," I said doubtfully.

"How did you get hold of him?" inquired Poirot.

"Description was circulated, as you know. In the press and privately. Not much to go on, I admit. This fellow has an American accent all right, and he doesn't deny that he was near King's Abbot that night. Just asks what the hell it is to do with us, and that he'll see us in — before he answers any questions."

"Is it permitted that I, too, see him?" asked Poirot.

The superintendent closed one eye knowingly.

"Very glad to have you, sir. You've got permission to do anything you please. Inspector Japp of Scotland Yard was asking after you the other day. Said he'd heard you were connected unofficially with this case. Where's Captain Paton hiding, sir, can you tell me that?"

"I doubt if it would be wise at the present juncture," said Poirot primly, and I bit my lips to prevent a smile.

The little man really did it very well.

After some further parley, we were taken to interview the prisoner.

He was a young fellow, I should say not more than twenty-two or three. Tall, thin, with slightly shaking hands, and the evidences of considerable physical strength somewhat run to seed. His hair was dark, but his eyes were blue and shifty, seldom meeting a glance squarely. I had all along cherished the illusion that there was something familiar about the figure I had met that night, but if this were indeed he, I was completely mistaken. He did not remind me in the least of any one I knew.

"Now then, Kent," said the superintendent, "stand up. Here are some visitors come to see you. Recognize any of them."

Kent glared at us sullenly, but did not reply. I saw his glance waver over the three of us, and come back to rest on me.

"Well, sir," said the superintendent to me, "what do you say?"

"The height's the same," I said, "and as far as general appearance goes it might well be the man in question. Beyond that, I couldn't go."

"What the hell's the meaning of all this?" asked Kent. "What have you got against me? Come on, out with it! What am I supposed to have done?"

I nodded my head.

"It's the man," I said. "I recognize the voice."

"Recognize my voice, do you? Where do you think you heard it before?"

"On Friday evening last, outside the gates of Fernly Park. You asked me the way there."

"I did, did I?"

"Do you admit it?" asked the inspector.

"I don't admit anything. Not till I know what you've got on me."

"Have you not read the papers in the last few days?" asked Poirot, speaking for the first time.

The man's eyes narrowed.

"So that's it, is it? I saw an old gent had been croaked at Fernly. Trying to make out I did the job, are you?"

"You were there that night," said Poirot quietly.

"How do you know, mister?"

"By this." Poirot took something from his pocket and held it out. It was the goose quill we had found in the summer-house.

At the sight of it the man's face changed. He half held out his hand.

"Snow," said Poirot thoughtfully. "No, my friend, it is empty. It lay where you dropped it in the summer-house that night."

Charles Kent looked at him uncertainly.

"You seem to know a hell of a lot about everything, you little foreign cock duck. Perhaps you remember this: the papers say that the old gent was croaked between a quarter to ten and ten o'clock?"

"That is so," agreed Poirot.

"Yes, but is it really so? That's what I'm getting at."

"This gentleman will tell you," said Poirot.

He indicated Inspector Raglan. The latter hesitated, glanced at Superintendent Hayes, then at Poirot, and finally, as though receiving sanction, he said:—

"That's right. Between a quarter to ten and ten o'clock."

"Then you've nothing to keep me here for," said Kent. "I was away from Fernly Park by twenty-five minutes past nine. You can ask at the Dog and Whistle. That's a saloon about a mile out of Fernly on the road to Cranchester. I kicked up a bit of a row there, I remember. As near as nothing to quarter to ten, it was. How about that?"

Inspector Raglan wrote down something in his note-book.

"Well?" demanded Kent.

"Inquiries will be made," said the inspector. "If you've spoken the truth, you won't have anything to complain about. What were you doing at Fernly Park anyway?"

"Went there to meet some one."

"Who?"

"That's none of your business."

"You'd better keep a civil tongue in your head, my man," the superintendent warned him.

"To hell with a civil tongue. I went there on my own business, and that's all there is to it. If I was clear away before the murder was done, that's all that concerns the cops."

"Your name, it is Charles Kent," said Poirot. "Where were you born?"

The man stared at him, then he grinned.

"I'm a full-blown Britisher all right," he said.

"Yes," said Poirot meditatively, "I think you are. I fancy you were born in Kent."

The man stared.

"Why's that? Because of my name? What's that to do with it? Is a man whose name is Kent bound to be born in that particular county?"

"Under certain circumstances, I can imagine he might be," said Poirot very deliberately. "Under certain circumstances, you comprehend."

There was so much meaning in his voice as to surprise the two police officers. As for Charles Kent, he flushed a brick red, and for a moment I thought he was going to spring at Poirot. He thought better of it, however, and turned away with a kind of laugh.

Poirot nodded as though satisfied, and made his way out through the door. He was joined presently by the two officers.

"We'll verify that statement," remarked Raglan. "I don't think he's lying, though. But he's got to come clear with a statement as to what he was doing at Fernly. It looks to me as though we'd got our blackmailer all right. On the other hand, granted his story's correct, he couldn't have had anything to do with the actual murder. He'd got ten pounds on him when he was arrested—rather a large sum. I fancy that forty pounds went to him—the numbers of the notes didn't correspond, but of course he'd have changed them first thing. Mr. Ackroyd must have given him the money, and he made off with it as fast as possible. What was that about Kent being his birthplace? What's that got to do with it?"

"Nothing whatever," said Poirot mildly. "A little idea of mine, that was all. Me, I am famous for my little ideas."

"Are you really?" said Raglan, studying him with a puzzled expression.

The superintendent went into a roar of laughter.

"Many's the time I've heard Inspector Japp say that. M. Poirot and his little ideas! Too fanciful for me, he'd say, but always something in them."

"You mock yourself at me," said Poirot, smiling; "but never mind. The old ones they laugh last sometimes, when the young, clever ones do not laugh at all."

And nodding his head at them in a sage manner, he walked out into the street.

He and I lunched together at an hotel. I know now that the whole thing lay clearly unravelled before him. He had got the last thread he needed to lead him to the truth.

But at the time I had no suspicion of the fact. I overestimated his general self-confidence, and I took it for granted that the things which puzzled me must be equally puzzling to him.

My chief puzzle was what the man Charles Kent could have been doing at Fernly. Again and again I put the question to myself and could get no satisfactory reply. At last I ventured a tentative query to Poirot. His reply was immediate.

"*Mon ami,* I do not think; I know."

"Really?" I said incredulously.

"Yes, indeed. I suppose now that to you it would not make sense if I said that he went to Fernly that night because he was born in Kent?"

I stared at him.

"It certainly doesn't seem to make sense to me," I said dryly.

"Ah!" said Poirot pityingly. "Well, no matter. I have still my little idea."

CHAPTER 19

FLORA ACKROYD

As I was returning from my round the following morning, I was hailed by Inspector Raglan. I pulled up, and the inspector mounted on the step.

"Good-morning, Dr. Sheppard," he said. "Well, that alibi is all right enough."

"Charles Kent's?"

"Charles Kent's. The barmaid at the Dog and Whistle, Sally Jones, she remembers him perfectly. Picked out his photograph from among five others. It was just a quarter to ten when he came into the bar, and the Dog and Whistle is well over a mile from Fernly Park. The girl mentions that he had a lot of money on him—she saw him take a handful of notes out of his pocket. Rather surprised her, it did, seeing the class of fellow he was, with a pair of boots clean dropping off him. That's where that forty pounds went right enough."

"The man still refuses to give an account of his visit to Fernly?"

"Obstinate as a mule he is. I had a chat with Hayes at Liverpool over the wire this morning."

"Hercule Poirot says he knows the reason the man went there that night," I observed.

"Does he?" cried the inspector eagerly.

"Yes," I said maliciously. "He says he went there because he was born in Kent."

I felt a distinct pleasure in passing on my own discomfiture.

Raglan stared at me for a moment or two uncomprehendingly. Then a grin overspread his weaselly countenance and he tapped his forehead significantly.

"Bit gone here," he said. "I've thought so for some time. Poor old chap, so that's why he had to give up and come down here. In the family, very likely. He's got a nephew who's quite off his crumpet."

"Poirot has?" I said, very surprised.

"Yes. Hasn't he ever mentioned him to you? Quite docile, I believe, and all that, but mad as a hatter, poor lad."

"Who told you that?"

Again a grin showed itself on Inspector Raglan's face.

"Your sister, Miss Sheppard, she told me all about it."

Really, Caroline is amazing. She never rests until she knows the last details of everybody's family secrets. Unfortunately, I have never been able to instill into her the decency of keeping them to herself.

"Jump in, inspector," I said, opening the door of the car. "We'll go up to The Larches together, and acquaint our Belgian friend with the latest news."

"Might as well, I suppose. After all, even if he is a bit balmy, it was a useful tip he gave me about those fingerprints. He's got a bee in his bonnet about the man Kent, but who knows—there may be something useful behind it."

Poirot received us with his usual smiling courtesy.

He listened to the information we had brought him, nodding his head now and then.

"Seems quite O.K., doesn't it?" said the inspector rather gloomily.

"A chap can't be murdering some one in one place when he's drinking in the bar in another place a mile away."

"Are you going to release him?"

"Don't see what else we can do. We can't very well hold him for obtaining money on false pretences. Can't prove a ruddy thing."

The inspector tossed a match into the grate in a disgruntled fashion. Poirot retrieved it and put it neatly in a little receptacle designed for the purpose. His action was purely mechanical. I could see that his thoughts were on something very different.

"If I were you," he said at last, "I should not release the man Charles Kent yet."

"What do you mean?"

Raglan stared at him.

"What I say. I should not release him yet."

"You don't think he can have had anything to do with the murder, do you?"

"I think probably not—but one cannot be certain yet."

"But haven't I just told you——"

Poirot raised a hand protestingly.

"*Mais oui, mais oui.* I heard. I am not deaf—nor stupid, thank the good God! But see you, you approach the matter from the wrong—the wrong—premises, is not that the word?"

The inspector stared at him heavily.

"I don't see how you make that out. Look here, we know Mr. Ackroyd was alive at a quarter to ten. You admit that, don't you?"

Poirot looked at him for a moment, then shook his head with a quick smile.

"I admit nothing that is not—*proved!*"

"Well, we've got proof enough of that. We've got Miss Flora Ackroyd's evidence."

"That she said good-night to her uncle? But me—I do not always believe what a young lady tells me—no, not even when she is charming and beautiful."

"But hang it all, man, Parker saw her coming out of the door."

"No." Poirot's voice rang out with sudden sharpness. "That is just what he did not see. I satisfied myself of that by a little experiment the other day—you remember, doctor? Parker saw her *outside* the door, with her hand on the handle. He did not see her come out of the room."

"But—where else could she have been?"

"Perhaps on the stairs."

"The stairs?"

"That is my little idea—yes."

"But those stairs only lead to Mr. Ackroyd's bedroom."

"Precisely."

And still the inspector stared.

"You think she'd been up to her uncle's bedroom? Well, why not? Why should she lie about it?"

"Ah! that is just the question. It depends on what she was doing there, does it not?"

"You mean—the money? Hang it all, you don't suggest that it was Miss Ackroyd who took that forty pounds?"

"I suggest nothing," said Poirot. "But I will remind you of this. Life was not very easy for that mother and daughter. There were bills —there was constant trouble over small sums of money. Roger Ackroyd was a peculiar man over money matters. The girl might be at her wit's end for a comparatively small sum. Figure to yourself then what happens. She has taken the money, she descends the little staircase. When she is half-way down she hears the chink of glass from the hall. She has not a doubt of what it is—Parker coming to the study. At all costs she must not be found on the stairs—Parker will not forget it, he will think it odd. If the money is missed, Parker is sure to remember having seen her come down those stairs. She has just time to rush down to the study door—with her hand on the handle to show that she has just come out, when Parker appears in the doorway. She says the first thing that comes into her head, a repetition of Roger Ackroyd's orders earlier in the evening, and then goes upstairs to her own room."

"Yes, but later," persisted the inspector, "she must have realized the vital importance of speaking the truth? Why, the whole case hinges on it!"

"Afterwards," said Poirot dryly, "it was a little difficult for Mademoiselle Flora. She is told simply that the police are here and that there has been a robbery. Naturally she jumps to the conclusion that the theft of the money has been discovered. Her one idea is to stick to her story. When she learns that her uncle is dead she is panic-stricken. Young women do not faint nowadays, monsieur, without considerable provocation. *Eh bien!* there it is. She is bound to stick to her story, or else confess everything. And a young and pretty girl does not like to admit that she is a thief—especially before those whose esteem she is anxious to retain."

Raglan brought his fist down with a thump on the table.

"I'll not believe it," he said. "It's—it's not credible. And you—you've known this all along?"

"The possibility has been in my mind from the first," admitted Poirot. "I was always convinced that Mademoiselle Flora was hiding something from us. To satisfy myself, I made the little experiment I told you of. Dr. Sheppard accompanied me."

"A test for Parker, you said it was," I remarked bitterly.

"Mon ami," said Poirot apologetically, "as I told you at the time, one must say something."

The inspector rose.

"There's only one thing for it," he declared. "We must tackle the young lady right away. You'll come up to Fernly with me, M. Poirot?"

"Certainly. Dr. Sheppard will drive us up in his car."

I acquiesced willingly.

On inquiry for Miss Ackroyd, we were shown into the billiard room. Flora and Major Hector Blunt were sitting on the long window seat.

"Good-morning, Miss Ackroyd," said the inspector. "Can we have a word or two alone with you?"

Blunt got up at once and moved to the door.

"What is it?" asked Flora nervously. "Don't go, Major Blunt. He can stay, can't he?" she asked, turning to the inspector.

"That's as you like," said the inspector dryly. "There's a question or two it's my duty to put to you, miss, but I'd prefer to do so privately, and I dare say you'd prefer it also."

Flora looked keenly at him. I saw her face grow whiter. Then she turned and spoke to Blunt.

"I want you to stay—please—yes, I mean it. Whatever the inspector has to say to me, I'd rather you heard it."

Raglan shrugged his shoulders.

"Well, if you will have it so, that's all there is to it. Now, Miss Ackroyd, M. Poirot here has made a certain suggestion to me. He suggests that you weren't in the study at all last Friday night, that you never saw Mr. Ackroyd to say good-night to him, that instead of being in the study you were on the stairs leading down from your uncle's bedroom when you heard Parker coming across the hall."

Flora's gaze shifted to Poirot. He nodded back at her.

"Mademoiselle, the other day, when we sat round the table, I implored you to be frank with me. What one does not tell to Papa

Poirot he finds out. It was that, was it not? See, I will make it easy for you. You took the money, did you not?"

"The money," said Blunt sharply.

There was a silence which lasted for at least a minute.

Then Flora drew herself up and spoke.

"M. Poirot is right. I took that money. I stole. I am a thief—yes, a common, vulgar little thief. Now you know! I am glad it has come out. It's been a nightmare, these last few days!" She sat down suddenly and buried her face in her hands. She spoke huskily through her fingers. "You don't know what my life has been since I came here. Wanting things, scheming for them, lying, cheating, running up bills, promising to pay—oh! I hate myself when I think of it all! That's what brought us together, Ralph and I. We were both weak! I understood him, and I was sorry—because I'm the same underneath. We're not strong enough to stand alone, either of us. We're weak, miserable, despicable things."

She looked at Blunt and suddenly stamped her foot.

"Why do you look at me like that—as though you couldn't believe? I may be a thief—but at any rate I'm real now. I'm not lying any more. I'm not pretending to be the kind of girl you like, young and innocent and simple. I don't care if you never want to see me again. I hate myself, despise myself—but you've got to believe one thing, if speaking the truth would have made things better for Ralph, I would have spoken out. But I've seen all along that it wouldn't be better for Ralph—it makes the case against him blacker than ever. I was not doing him any harm by sticking to my lie."

"Ralph," said Blunt. "I see—always Ralph."

"You don't understand," said Flora hopelessly. "You never will."

She turned to the inspector.

"I admit everything; I was at my wit's end for money. I never saw my uncle that evening after he left the dinner-table. As to the money, you can take what steps you please. Nothing could be worse than it is now!"

Suddenly she broke down again, hid her face in her hands, and rushed from the room.

"Well," said the inspector in a flat tone, "so that's that."

He seemed rather at a loss what to do next.

Blunt came forward.

"Inspector Raglan," he said quietly, "that money was given to me by Mr. Ackroyd for a special purpose. Miss Ackroyd never touched it. When she says she did, she is lying with the idea of shielding Captain Paton. The truth is as I said, and I am prepared to go into the witness box and swear to it."

He made a kind of jerky bow, then turning abruptly, he left the room.

Poirot was after him in a flash. He caught the other up in the hall.

"Monsieur—a moment, I beg of you, if you will be so good."

"Well, sir?"

Blunt was obviously impatient. He stood frowning down on Poirot.

"It is this," said Poirot rapidly: "I am not deceived by your little fantasy. No, indeed. It was truly Miss Flora who took the money. All the same it is well imagined what you say—it pleases me. It is very good what you have done there. You are a man quick to think and to act."

"I'm not in the least anxious for your opinion, thank you," said Blunt coldly.

He made once more as though to pass on, but Poirot, not at all offended, laid a detaining hand on his arm.

"Ah! but you are to listen to me. I have more to say. The other day I spoke of concealments. Very well, all along have I seen what you are concealing. Mademoiselle Flora, you love her with all your heart. From the first moment you saw her, is it not so? Oh! let us not mind saying these things—why must one in England think it necessary to mention love as though it were some disgraceful secret? You love Mademoiselle Flora. You seek to conceal that fact from all the world. That is very good—that is as it should be. But take the advice of Hercule Poirot—do not conceal it from mademoiselle herself."

Blunt had shown several signs of restlessness whilst Poirot was speaking, but the closing words seemed to rivet his attention.

"What d'you mean by that?" he said sharply.

"You think that she loves the Capitaine Ralph Paton—but I, Hercule Poirot, tell you that that is not so. Mademoiselle Flora accepted Captain Paton to please her uncle, and because she saw in the marriage a way of escape from her life here which was becoming frankly insupportable to her. She liked him, and there was much sympathy and understanding between them. But love—no! It is not Captain Paton Mademoiselle Flora loves."

"What the devil do you mean?" asked Blunt.

I saw the dark flush under his tan.

"You have been blind, monsieur. Blind! She is loyal, the little one. Ralph Paton is under a cloud, she is bound in honor to stick by him."

I felt it was time I put in a word to help on the good work.

"My sister told me the other night," I said encouragingly, "that Flora had never cared a penny piece for Ralph Paton, and never would. My sister is always right about these things."

Blunt ignored my well-meant efforts. He spoke to Poirot.

"D'you really think——" he began, and stopped.

He is one of those inarticulate men who find it hard to put things into words.

Poirot knows no such disability.

"If you doubt me, ask her yourself, monsieur. But perhaps you no longer care to—the affair of the money——"

Blunt gave a sound like an angry laugh.

"Think I'd hold that against her? Roger was always a queer chap about money. She got in a mess and didn't dare tell him. Poor kid. Poor lonely kid."

Poirot looked thoughtfully at the side door.

"Mademoiselle Flora went into the garden, I think," he murmured.

"I've been every kind of a fool," said Blunt abruptly. "Rum conversation we've been having. Like one of those Danish plays. But you're a sound fellow, M. Poirot. Thank you."

He took Poirot's hand and gave it a grip which caused the other to wince in anguish. Then he strode to the side door and passed out into the garden.

"Not every kind of a fool," murmured Poirot, tenderly nursing the injured member. "Only one kind—the fool in love."

CHAPTER 20

MISS RUSSELL

INSPECTOR RAGLAN had received a bad jolt. He was not deceived by Blunt's valiant lie any more than we had been. Our way back to the village was punctuated by his complaints.

"This alters everything, this does. I don't know whether you've realized it, Monsieur Poirot?"

"I think so, yes, I think so," said Poirot. "You see, me, I have been familiar with the idea for some time."

Inspector Raglan, who had only had the idea presented to him a short half-hour ago, looked at Poirot unhappily, and went on with his discoveries.

"Those alibis now. Worthless! Absolutely worthless. Got to start again. Find out what every one was doing from nine-thirty onwards. Nine-thirty—that's the time we've got to hang on to. You were quite right about the man Kent—we don't release *him* yet awhile. Let me see now—nine-forty-five at the Dog and Whistle. He might have got there in a quarter of an hour if he ran. It's just possible that it was *his* voice Mr. Raymond heard talking to Mr. Ackroyd—asking for money which Mr. Ackroyd refused. But one thing's clear—it wasn't he who sent the telephone message. The station is half a mile in the other direction—over a mile and a half from the Dog and Whistle, and he was at the Dog and Whistle until about ten minutes past ten. Dang that telephone call! We always come up against it."

"We do indeed," agreed Poirot. "It is curious."

"It's just possible that if Captain Paton climbed into his uncle's room and found him there murdered, *he* may have sent it. Got the wind up, thought he'd be accused, and cleared out. That's possible, isn't it?"

"Why should he have telephoned?"

"May have had doubts if the old man was really dead. Thought he'd get the doctor up there as soon as possible, but didn't want to give himself away. Yes, I say now, how's that for a theory? Something in that, I should say."

The inspector swelled his chest out importantly. He was so plainly delighted with himself that any words of ours would have been quite superfluous.

We arrived back at my house at this minute, and I hurried in to my surgery patients, who had all been waiting a considerable time, leaving Poirot to walk to the police station with the inspector.

Having dismissed the last patient, I strolled into the little room at the back of the house which I call my workshop—I am rather proud of the home-made wireless set I turned out. Caroline hates my workroom. I keep my tools there, and Annie is not allowed to wreak havoc with a dustpan and brush. I was just adjusting the interior of an alarm clock which had been denounced as wholly unreliable by the household, when the door opened and Caroline put her head in.

"Oh! there you are, James," she said, with deep disapproval. "M. Poirot wants to see you."

"Well," I said, rather irritably, for her sudden entrance had startled me and I had let go of a piece of delicate mechanism, "if he wants to see me, he can come in here."

"In here?" said Caroline.

"That's what I said—in here."

Caroline gave a sniff of disapproval and retired. She returned in a moment or two, ushering in Poirot, and then retired again, shutting the door with a bang.

"Aha! my friend," said Poirot, coming forward and rubbing his hands. "You have not got rid of me so easily, you see!"

"Finished with the inspector?" I asked.

"For the moment, yes. And you, you have seen all the patients?"

"Yes."

Poirot sat down and looked at me, tilting his egg-shaped head on one side, with the air of one who savors a very delicious joke.

"You are in error," he said at last. "You have still one patient to see."

"Not you?" I exclaimed in surprise.

"Ah, not me, *bien entendu*. Me, I have the health magnificent. No, to tell you the truth, it is a little *complot* of mine. There is some one I wish to see, you understand—and at the same time it is not necessary that the whole village should intrigue itself about the matter—which is what would happen if the lady were seen to come to my house—for it is a lady. But to you she has already come as a patient before."

"Miss Russell!" I exclaimed.

"*Précisément*. I wish much to speak with her, so I send her the little note and make the appointment in your surgery. You are not annoyed with me?"

"On the contrary," I said. "That is, presuming I am allowed to be present at the interview?"

"But naturally! In your own surgery!"

"You know," I said, throwing down the pincers I was holding, "it's extraordinarily intriguing, the whole thing. Every new development that arises is like the shake you give to a kaleidoscope—the thing changes entirely in aspect. Now, why are you so anxious to see Miss Russell?"

Poirot raised his eyebrows.

"Surely it is obvious?" he murmured.

"There you go again," I grumbled. "According to you everything is obvious. But you leave me walking about in a fog."

Poirot shook his head genially at me.

"You mock yourself at me. Take the matter of Mademoiselle Flora. The inspector was surprised—but you—you were not."

"I never dreamed of her being the thief," I expostulated.

"That—perhaps no. But I was watching your face and you were not—like Inspector Raglan—startled and incredulous."

I thought for a minute or two.

"Perhaps you are right," I said at last. "All along I've felt that Flora was keeping back something—so the truth, when it came, was subconsciously expected. It upset Inspector Raglan very much indeed, poor man."

"Ah! *pour ça, oui!* The poor man must rearrange all his ideas. I profited by his state of mental chaos to induce him to grant me a little favor."

"What was that?"

Poirot took a sheet of notepaper from his pocket. Some words were written on it, and he read them aloud.

"The police have, for some days been seeking for Captain Ralph Paton, the stepson of Mr. Ackroyd of Fernly Park, whose death occurred under such tragic circumstances last Friday. Captain Paton has been found at Liverpool, where he was on the point of embarking for America."

He folded up the piece of paper again.

"That, my friend, will be in the newspapers to-morrow morning."

I stared at him, dumbfounded.

"But—but it isn't true! He's not at Liverpool!"

Poirot beamed on me.

"You have the intelligence so quick! No, he has not been found at Liverpool. Inspector Raglan was very loath to let me send this paragraph to the press, especially as I could not take him into my confidence. But I assured him most solemnly that very interesting results would follow its appearance in print, so he gave in, after stipulating that he was, on no account, to bear the responsibility."

I stared at Poirot. He smiled back at me.

"It beats me," I said at last, "what you expect to get out of that."

"You should employ your little gray cells," said Poirot gravely.

He rose and came across to the bench.

"It is that you have really the love of the machinery," he said, after inspecting the débris of my labors.

Every man has his hobby. I immediately drew Poirot's attention to my home-made wireless. Finding him sympathetic, I showed him one or two little inventions of my own—trifling things, but useful in the house.

"Decidedly," said Poirot, "you should be an inventor by trade, not a doctor. But I hear the bell—that is your patient. Let us go into the surgery."

Once before I had been struck by the remnants of beauty in the housekeeper's face. This morning I was struck anew. Very simply dressed in black, tall, upright and independent as ever, with her big dark eyes and an unwonted flush of color in her usually pale cheeks, I realized that as a girl she must have been startlingly handsome.

"Good-morning, mademoiselle," said Poirot. "Will you be seated? Dr. Sheppard is so kind as to permit me the use of his surgery for a little conversation I am anxious to have with you."

Miss Russell sat down with her usual composure. If she felt any inward agitation, it did not display itself in any outward manifestation.

"It seems a queer way of doing things, if you'll allow me to say so," she remarked.

"Miss Russell—I have news to give you."

"Indeed!"

"Charles Kent has been arrested at Liverpool."

Not a muscle of her face moved. She merely opened her eyes a trifle wider, and asked, with a tinge of defiance:

"Well, what of it?"

But at that moment it came to me—the resemblance that had haunted me all along, something familiar in the defiance of Charles Kent's manner. The two voices, one rough and coarse, the other painfully ladylike—were strangely the same in timbre. It was of Miss Russell that I had been reminded that night outside the gates of Fernly Park.

I looked at Poirot, full of my discovery, and he gave me an imperceptible nod.

In answer to Miss Russell's question, he threw out his hands in a thoroughly French gesture.

"I thought you might be interested, that is all," he said mildly.

"Well, I'm not particularly," said Miss Russell. "Who is this Charles Kent anyway?"

"He is a man, mademoiselle, who was at Fernly on the night of the murder."

"Really?"

"Fortunately for him, he has an alibi. At a quarter to ten he was at a public-house a mile from here."

"Lucky for him," commented Miss Russell.

"But we still do not know what he was doing at Fernly—who it was he went to meet, for instance."

"I'm afraid I can't help you at all," said the housekeeper politely. "Nothing came to *my* ears. If that is all——"

She made a tentative movement as though to rise. Poirot stopped her.

"It is not quite all," he said smoothly. "This morning fresh developments have arisen. It seems now that Mr. Ackroyd was murdered, not at a quarter to ten, but *before*. Between ten minutes to nine, when Dr. Sheppard left, and a quarter to ten."

I saw the color drain from the housekeeper's face, leaving it dead white. She leaned forward, her figure swaying.

"But Miss Ackroyd said—Miss Ackroyd said——"

"Miss Ackroyd has admitted that she was lying. She was never in the study at all that evening."

"Then——?"

"Then it would seem that in this Charles Kent we have the man we are looking for. He came to Fernly, can give no account of what he was doing there——"

"I can tell you what he was doing there. He never touched a hair of old Ackroyd's head—he never went near the study. He didn't do it, I tell you."

She was leaning forward. That iron self-control was broken through at last. Terror and desperation were in her face.

"M. Poirot! M. Poirot! Oh, do believe me."

Poirot got up and came to her. He patted her reassuringly on the shoulder.

"But yes—but yes, I will believe. I had to make you speak, you know."

For an instant suspicion flared up in her.

"Is what you said true?"

"That Charles Kent is suspected of the crime? Yes, that is true. You alone can save him, by telling the reason for his being at Fernly."

"He came to see me." She spoke in a low, hurried voice. "I went out to meet him——"

"In the summer-house, yes, I know."

"How do you know?"

"Mademoiselle, it is the business of Hercule Poirot to know things. I know that you went out earlier in the evening, that you left a message in the summer-house to say what time you would be there."

"Yes, I did. I had heard from him—saying he was coming. I dared not let him come to the house. I wrote to the address he gave me and said I would meet him in the summer-house, and described it to him so that he would be able to find it. Then I was afraid he might not wait there patiently, and I ran out and left a piece of paper to say I would be there about ten minutes past nine. I didn't want the servants to see me, so I slipped out through the drawing-room window. As I came back, I met Dr. Sheppard, and I fancied that he would think it queer. I was out of breath, for I had been running. I had no idea that he was expected to dinner that night."

She paused.

"Go on," said Poirot. "You went out to meet him at ten minutes past nine. What did you say to each other?"

"It's difficult. You see——"

"Mademoiselle," said Poirot, interrupting her, "in this matter I must have the whole truth. What you tell us need never go beyond these four walls. Dr. Sheppard will be discreet, and so shall I. See, I will help you. This Charles Kent, he is your son, is he not?"

She nodded. The color had flamed into her cheeks.

"No one has ever known. It was long ago—long ago—down in Kent. I was not married. . . ."

"So you took the name of the county as a surname for him. I understand."

"I got work. I managed to pay for his board and lodging. I never told him that I was his mother. But he turned out badly, he drank, then took to drugs. I managed to pay his passage out to Canada. I didn't hear of him for a year or two. Then, somehow or other, he found out that I was his mother. He wrote asking me for money. Finally, I heard from him back in this country again. He was coming to see me at Fernly, he said. I dared not let him come to the house. I have always been considered so—so very respectable. If any one got an inkling—it would have been all up with my post as housekeeper. So I wrote to him in the way I have just told you."

"And in the morning you came to see Dr. Sheppard?"

"Yes. I wondered if something could be done. He was not a bad boy—before he took to drugs."

"I see," said Poirot. "Now let us go on with the story. He came that night to the summer-house?"

"Yes, he was waiting for me when I got there. He was very rough and abusive. I had brought with me all the money I had, and I gave it to him. We talked a little, and then he went away."

"What time was that?"

"It must have been between twenty and twenty-five minutes past nine. It was not yet half-past when I got back to the house."

"Which way did he go?"

"Straight out the same way he came, by the path that joined the drive just inside the lodge gates."

Poirot nodded.

"And you, what did you do?"

"I went back to the house. Major Blunt was walking up and down the terrace smoking, so I made a detour to get round to the side door. It was then just on half-past nine, as I tell you."

Poirot nodded again. He made a note or two in a microscopic note-book.

"I think that is all," he said thoughtfully.

"Ought I——" she hesitated. "Ought I to tell all this to Inspector Raglan?"

"It may come to that. But let us not be in a hurry. Let us proceed slowly, with due order and method. Charles Kent is not yet formally charged with murder. Circumstances may arise which will render your story unnecessary."

Miss Russell rose.

"Thank you very much, M. Poirot," she said. "You have been very kind—very kind indeed. You—you do believe me, don't you? That Charles had nothing to do with this wicked murder!"

"There seems no doubt that the man who was talking to Mr. Ackroyd in the library at nine-thirty could not possibly have been your son. Be of good courage, mademoiselle. All will yet be well."

Miss Russell departed. Poirot and I were left together.

"So that's that," I said. "Every time we come back to Ralph Paton. How did you manage to spot Miss Russell as the person Charles Kent came to meet? Did you notice the resemblance?"

"I had connected her with the unknown man long before we actually came face to face with him. As soon as we found that quill. The quill suggested dope, and I remembered your account of Miss Russell's visit to you. Then I found the article on cocaine in that morning's paper. It all seemed very clear. She had heard from some one that morning—some one addicted to drugs, she read the article in the paper, and she came to you to ask a few tentative questions. She mentioned cocaine, since the article in question was on cocaine. Then, when you seemed too interested, she switched hurriedly to the subject of detective stories and untraceable poisons. I suspected a son or a brother, or some other undesirable male relation. Ah! but I must go. It is the time of the lunch."

"Stay and lunch with us," I suggested.

Poirot shook his head. A faint twinkle came into his eye.

"Not again to-day. I should not like to force Mademoiselle Caroline to adopt a vegetarian diet two days in succession."

It occurred to me that there was not much which escaped Hercule Poirot.

CHAPTER 21

THE PARAGRAPH IN THE PAPER

CAROLINE, of course, had not failed to see Miss Russell come to the surgery door. I had anticipated this, and had ready an elaborate account of the lady's bad knee. But Caroline was not in a cross-questioning mood. Her point of view was that she knew what Miss Russell had really come for and that *I* didn't.

"Pumping you, James," said Caroline. "Pumping you in the most shameless manner, I've not a doubt. It's no good interrupting. I dare say you hadn't the least idea she was doing it even. Men *are* so simple. She knows that you are in M. Poirot's confidence, and she wants to find out things. Do you know what I think, James?"

"I couldn't begin to imagine. You think so many extraordinary things."

"It's no good being sarcastic. I think Miss Russell knows more about Mr. Ackroyd's death than she is prepared to admit."

Caroline leaned back triumphantly in her chair.

"Do you really think so?" I said absently.

"You are very dull to-day, James. No animation about you. It's that liver of yours."

Our conversation then dealt with purely personal matters.

The paragraph inspired by Poirot duly appeared in our daily paper the next morning. I was in the dark as to its purpose, but its effect on Caroline was immense.

She began by stating, most untruly, that she had said as much all along. I raised my eyebrows, but did not argue. Caroline, however, must have felt a prick of conscience, for she went on:—

"I mayn't have actually mentioned Liverpool, but I knew he'd try to get away to America. That's what Crippen did."

"Without much success," I reminded her.

"Poor boy, and so they've caught him. I consider, James, that it's your duty to see that he isn't hung."

"What do you expect me to do?"

"Why, you're a medical man, aren't you? You've known him from a boy upwards. Not mentally responsible. That's the line to take, clearly. I read only the other day that they're very happy in Broadmoor—it's quite like a high-class club."

But Caroline's words had reminded me of something.

"I never knew that Poirot had an imbecile nephew?" I said curiously.

"Didn't you? Oh, he told me all about it. Poor lad. It's a great grief to all the family. They've kept him at home so far, but it's getting to such a pitch that they're afraid he'll have to go into some kind of institution."

"I suppose you know pretty well everything there is to know about Poirot's family by this time," I said, exasperated.

"Pretty well," said Caroline complacently. "It's a great relief to people to be able to tell all their troubles to some one."

"It might be," I said, "if they were ever allowed to do so spontaneously. Whether they enjoy having confidences screwed out of them by force is another matter."

Caroline merely looked at me with the air of a Christian martyr enjoying martyrdom.

"You are so self-contained, James," she said. "You hate speaking out, or parting with any information yourself, and you think everybody else must be just like you. I should hope that I never screw confidences out of anybody. For instance, if M. Poirot comes in this afternoon, as he said he might do, I shall not dream of asking him who it was arrived at his house early this morning."

"Early this morning?" I queried.

"Very early," said Caroline. "Before the milk came. I just happened to be looking out of the window—the blind was flapping. It was a man. He came in a closed car, and he was all muffled up. I couldn't get a glimpse of his face. But I will tell you *my* idea, and you'll see that I'm right."

"What's your idea?"

Caroline dropped her voice mysteriously.

"A Home Office expert," she breathed.

"A Home Office expert," I said, amazed. "My dear Caroline!"

"Mark my words, James, you'll see that I'm right. That Russell woman was here that morning after your poisons. Roger Ackroyd might easily have been poisoned in his food that night."

I laughed out loud.

"Nonsense," I cried. "He was stabbed in the neck. You know that as well as I do."

"After death, James," said Caroline; "to make a false clew."

"My good woman," I said, "I examined the body, and I know what I'm talking about. That wound wasn't inflicted after death—it was the cause of death, and you need make no mistake about it."

Caroline merely continued to look omniscient, which so annoyed me that I went on:—

"Perhaps you will tell me, Caroline, if I have a medical degree or if I have not?"

"You have the medical degree, I dare say, James—at least, I mean I know you have. But you've no imagination whatever."

"Having endowed you with a treble portion, there was none left over for me," I said dryly.

I was amused to notice Caroline's maneuvers that afternoon when Poirot duly arrived. My sister, without asking a direct question, skirted the subject of the mysterious guest in every way imaginable. By the twinkle in Poirot's eyes, I saw that he realized her object. He remained blandly impervious, and blocked her bowling so successfully that she herself was at a loss how to proceed.

Having, I suspect, quietly enjoyed the little game, he rose to his feet and suggested a walk.

"It is that I need to reduce the figure a little," he explained. "You will come with me, doctor? And perhaps later Miss Caroline will give us some tea."

"Delighted," said Caroline. "Won't your—er—guest come in also?"

"You are too kind," said Poirot. "But no, my friend reposes himself. Soon you must make his acquaintance."

"Quite an old friend of yours, so somebody told me," said Caroline, making one last valiant effort.

"Did they?" murmured Poirot. "Well, we must start."

Our tramp took us in the direction of Fernly. I had guessed beforehand that it might do so. I was beginning to understand Poirot's methods. Every little irrelevancy had a bearing upon the whole.

"I have a commission for you, my friend," he said at last. "Tonight, at my house, I desire to have a little conference. You will attend, will you not?"

"Certainly," I said.

"Good. I need also all those in the house—that is to say: Mrs. Ackroyd, Mademoiselle Flora, Major Blunt, M. Raymond. I want you to be my ambassador. This little reunion is fixed for nine o'clock. You will ask them—yes?"

"With pleasure; but why not ask them yourself?"

"Because they will then put the questions: Why? What for? They will demand what my idea is. And, as you know, my friend, I much dislike to have to explain my little ideas until the time comes."

I smiled a little.

"My friend Hastings, he of whom I told you, used to say of me that I was the human oyster. But he was unjust. Of facts, I keep nothing to myself. But to every one his own interpretation of them."

"When do you want me to do this?"

"Now, if you will. We are close to the house."

"Aren't you coming in?"

"No, me, I will promenade myself in the grounds. I will rejoin you by the lodge gates in a quarter of an hour's time."

I nodded, and set off on my task. The only member of the family at home proved to be Mrs. Ackroyd, who was sipping an early cup of tea. She received me very graciously.

"So grateful to you, doctor," she murmured, "for clearing up that little matter with M. Poirot. But life is one trouble after another. You have heard about Flora, of course?"

"What exactly?" I asked cautiously.

"This new engagement. Flora and Hector Blunt. Of course not such a good match as Ralph would have been. But after all, happiness comes first. What dear Flora needs is an older man—some one steady and reliable, and then Hector is really a very distinguished man in his way. You saw the news of Ralph's arrest in the paper this morning?"

"Yes," I said, "I did."

"Horrible." Mrs. Ackroyd closed her eyes and shuddered. "Geoffrey Raymond was in a terrible way. Rang up Liverpool. But they wouldn't tell him anything at the police station there. In fact, they said they hadn't arrested Ralph at all. Mr. Raymond insists that it's all a mistake—a—what do they call it?—*canard* of the newspaper's. I've forbidden it to be mentioned before the servants. Such a terrible disgrace. Fancy if Flora had actually been married to him."

Mrs. Ackroyd shut her eyes in anguish. I began to wonder how soon I should be able to deliver Poirot's invitation.

Before I had time to speak, Mrs. Ackroyd was off again.

"You were here yesterday, weren't you, with that dreadful Inspector Raglan? Brute of a man—he terrified Flora into saying she took that money from poor Roger's room. And the matter was so simple, really. The dear child wanted to borrow a few pounds, didn't like to disturb her uncle since he'd given strict orders against it, but knowing where he kept his notes she went there and took what she needed."

"Is that Flora's account of the matter?" I asked.

"My dear doctor, you know what girls are nowadays. So easily acted on by suggestion. You, of course, know all about hypnosis and that sort of thing. The inspector shouts at her, says the word 'steal' over and over again, until the poor child gets an inhibition—or is it a complex?—I always mix up those two words—and actually thinks herself that she has stolen the money. I saw at once how it was. But I can't be too thankful for the whole misunderstanding in one way—it seems to have brought those two together—Hector and Flora, I mean. And I assure you that I have been very much worried about Flora in the past: why, at one time I actually thought there was going to be some kind of understanding between her and young Raymond. Just think of it!" Mrs. Ackroyd's voice rose in shrill horror. "A private secretary—with practically no means of his own."

"It would have been a severe blow to you," I said. "Now, Mrs. Ackroyd, I've got a message for you from M. Hercule Poirot."

"For me?"

Mrs. Ackroyd looked quite alarmed.

I hastened to reassure her, and I explained what Poirot wanted.

"Certainly," said Mrs. Ackroyd rather doubtfully, "I suppose we must come if M. Poirot says so. But what is it all about? I like to know beforehand."

I assured the lady truthfully that I myself did not know any more than she did.

"Very well," said Mrs. Ackroyd at last, rather grudgingly, "I will tell the others, and we will be there at nine o'clock."

Thereupon I took my leave, and joined Poirot at the agreed meeting-place.

"I've been longer than a quarter of an hour, I'm afraid," I remarked. "But once that good lady starts talking it's a matter of the utmost difficulty to get a word in edgeways."

"It is of no matter," said Poirot. "Me, I have been well amused. This park is magnificent."

We set off homewards. When we arrived, to our great surprise Caroline, who had evidently been watching for us, herself opened the door.

She put her fingers to her lips. Her face was full of importance and excitement.

"Ursula Bourne," she said, "the parlormaid from Fernly. She's here! I've put her in the dining-room. She's in a terrible way, poor thing. Says she must see M. Poirot at once. I've done all I could. Taken her a cup of hot tea. It really goes to one's heart to see any one in such a state."

"In the dining-room?" asked Poirot.

"This way," I said, and flung open the door.

Ursula Bourne was sitting by the table. Her arms were spread out in front of her, and she had evidently just lifted her head from where it had been buried. Her eyes were red with weeping.

"Ursula Bourne," I murmured.

But Poirot went past me with outstretched hands.

"No," he said, "that is not quite right, I think. It is not Ursula Bourne, is it, my child—but Ursula Paton? Mrs. Ralph Paton."

CHAPTER 22

URSULA'S STORY

FOR A MOMENT or two the girl looked mutely at Poirot. Then, her reserve breaking down completely, she nodded her head once, and burst into an outburst of sobs.

Caroline pushed past me, and putting her arm round the girl, patted her on the shoulder.

"There, there, my dear," she said soothingly, "it will be all right. You'll see—everything will be all right."

Buried under curiosity and scandal-mongering there is a lot of kindness in Caroline. For the moment, even the interest of Poirot's revelation was lost in the sight of the girl's distress.

Presently Ursula sat up and wiped her eyes.

"This is very weak and silly of me," she said.

"No, no, my child," said Poirot kindly. "We can all realize the strain of this last week."

"It must have been a terrible ordeal," I said.

"And then to find that you knew," continued Ursula. "How did you know? Was it Ralph who told you?"

Poirot shook his head.

"You know what brought me to you to-night," went on the girl. *"This——"*

She held out a crumpled piece of newspaper, and I recognized the paragraph that Poirot had had inserted.

"It says that Ralph has been arrested. So everything is useless. I need not pretend any longer."

"Newspaper paragraphs are not always true, mademoiselle," murmured Poirot, having the grace to look ashamed of himself. "All the same, I think you will do well to make a clean breast of things. The truth is what we need now."

The girl hesitated, looking at him doubtfully.

"You do not trust me," said Poirot gently. "Yet all the same you came here to find me, did you not? Why was that?"

"Because I don't believe that Ralph did it," said the girl in a very low voice. "And I think that you are clever, and will find out the truth. And also——"

"Yes?"

"I think you are kind."

Poirot nodded his head several times.

"It is very good that—yes, it is very good. Listen, I do in verity believe that this husband of yours is innocent—but the affair marches badly. If I am to save him, I must know all there is to know—even if it should seem to make the case against him blacker than before."

"How well you understand," said Ursula.

"So you will tell me the whole story, will you not? From the beginning."

"You're not going to send *me* away, I hope," said Caroline, settling herself comfortably in an arm-chair. "What I want to know," she continued, "is why this child was masquerading as a parlor-maid?"

"Masquerading?" I queried.

"That's what I said. Why did you do it, child? For a wager?"

"For a living," said Ursula dryly.

And encouraged, she began the story which I reproduce here in my own words.

Ursula Bourne, it seemed, was one of a family of seven—impoverished Irish gentlefolk. On the death of her father, most of the girls were cast out into the world to earn their own living. Ursula's eldest sister was married to Captain Folliott. It was she whom I had seen that Sunday, and the cause of her embarrassment was clear enough now. Determined to earn her living and not attracted to the idea of being a nursery governess—the one profession open to an untrained girl, Ursula preferred the job of parlormaid. She scorned to label herself a "lady parlormaid." She would be the real thing, her reference being supplied by her sister. At Fernly, despite an aloofness which, as has been seen, caused some comment, she was a success at her job—quick, competent, and thorough.

"I enjoyed the work," she explained. "And I had plenty of time to myself."

And then came her meeting with Ralph Paton, and the love affair which culminated in a secret marriage. Ralph had persuaded her into that, somewhat against her will. He had declared that his stepfather would not hear of his marrying a penniless girl. Better to be married secretly, and break the news to him at some later and more favorable minute.

And so the deed was done, and Ursula Bourne became Ursula Paton. Ralph had declared that he meant to pay off his debts, find a job, and then, when he was in a position to support her, and independent of his adopted father, they would break the news to him.

But to people like Ralph Paton, turning over a new leaf is easier in theory than in practice. He hoped that his stepfather, whilst still in ignorance of the marriage, might be persuaded to pay his debts and put him on his feet again. But the revelation of the amount of Ralph's liabilities merely enraged Roger Ackroyd, and he refused to do anything at all. Some months passed, and then Ralph was bidden once more to Fernly. Roger Ackroyd did not beat about the bush. It was the desire of his heart that Ralph should marry Flora, and he put the matter plainly before the young man.

And here it was that the innate weakness of Ralph Paton showed itself. As always, he grasped at the easy, the immediate solution. As far as I could make out, neither Flora nor Ralph made any pretence of love. It was, on both sides, a business arrangement. Roger Ackroyd dictated his wishes—they agreed to them. Flora accepted a chance of liberty, money, and an enlarged horizon; Ralph, of course, was playing a different game. But he was in a very awkward hole financially. He seized at the chance. His debts would be paid. He could start again with a clean sheet. His was not a nature to envisage the future, but I gather that he saw vaguely the engagement with Flora being broken off after a decent interval had elapsed. Both Flora and he stipulated that it should be kept a secret for the present. He was anxious to conceal it from Ursula. He felt instinctively that her nature, strong and resolute, with an inherent distaste for duplicity, was not one to welcome such a course.

Then came the crucial moment when Roger Ackroyd, always high-handed, decided to announce the engagement. He said no word of his intention to Ralph—only to Flora, and Flora, apathetic, raised no objection. On Ursula, the news fell like a bombshell. Summoned by her, Ralph came hurriedly down from town. They met in the wood, where part of their conversation was overheard by my sister. Ralph implored her to keep silent for a little while longer, Ursula was equally determined to have done with concealments. She would tell Mr. Ackroyd the truth without any further delay. Husband and wife parted acrimoniously.

Ursula, steadfast in her purpose, sought an interview with Roger Ackroyd that very afternoon, and revealed the truth to him. Their interview was a stormy one—it might have been even more stormy had not Roger Ackroyd been already obsessed with his own troubles. It was bad enough, however. Ackroyd was not the kind of man to forgive the deceit that had been practiced upon him. His rancor was mainly directed to Ralph, but Ursula came in for her share, since he regarded her as a girl who had deliberately tried to "entrap" the adopted son of a very wealthy man. Unforgivable things were said on both sides.

That same evening Ursula met Ralph by appointment in the small summer-house, stealing out from the house by the side door in order to do so. Their interview was made up of reproaches on both sides. Ralph charged Ursula with having irretrievably ruined his prospects by her ill-timed revelation. Ursula reproached Ralph with his duplicity.

They parted at last. A little over half an hour later came the discovery of Roger Ackroyd's body. Since that night Ursula had neither seen nor heard from Ralph.

As the story unfolded itself, I realized more and more what a damning series of facts it was. Alive, Ackroyd could hardly have failed to alter his will—I knew him well enough to realize that to do so would be his first thought. His death came in the nick of time for Ralph and Ursula Paton. Small wonder the girl had held her tongue, and played her part so consistently.

My meditations were interrupted. It was Poirot's voice speaking, and I knew from the gravity of his tone that he, too, was fully alive to the implications of the position.

"Mademoiselle, I must ask you one question, and you must answer it truthfully, for on it everything may hang: What time was it when you parted from Captain Ralph Paton in the summer-house? Now, take a little minute so that your answer may be very exact."

The girl gave a half laugh, bitter enough in all conscience.

"Do you think I haven't gone over that again and again in my own mind? It was just half-past nine when I went out to meet him. Major Blunt was walking up and down the terrace, so I had to go round through the bushes to avoid him. It must have been about twenty-seven minutes to ten when I reached the summer-house. Ralph was waiting for me. I was with him ten minutes—not longer, for it was just a quarter to ten when I got back to the house."

I saw now the insistence of her question the other day. If only Ackroyd could have been proved to have been killed before a quarter to ten, and not after.

I saw the reflection of that thought in Poirot's next question.

"Who left the summer-house first?"

"I did."

"Leaving Ralph Paton in the summer-house?"

"Yes—but you don't think——"

"Mademoiselle, it is of no importance what I think. What did you do when you got back to the house?"

"I went up to my room."

"And stayed there until when?"

"Until about ten o'clock."

"Is there any one who can prove that?"

"Prove? That I was in my room, you mean? Oh! no. But surely—oh! I see, they might think—they might think——"

I saw the dawning horror in her eyes.

Poirot finished the sentence for her.

"That it was *you* who entered by the window and stabbed Mr. Ackroyd as he sat in his chair? Yes, they might think just that."

"Nobody but a fool would think any such thing," said Caroline indignantly.

She patted Ursula on the shoulder.

The girl had her face hidden in her hands.

"Horrible," she was murmuring. "Horrible."

Caroline gave her a friendly shake.

"Don't worry, my dear," she said. "M. Poirot doesn't think that really. As for that husband of yours, I don't think much of him, and I tell you so candidly. Running away and leaving you to face the music."

But Ursula shook her head energetically.

"Oh, no," she cried. "It wasn't like that at all. Ralph would not run away on his own account. I see now. If he heard of his stepfather's murder, he might think himself that I had done it."

"He wouldn't think any such thing," said Caroline.

"I was so cruel to him that night—so hard and bitter. I wouldn't listen to what he was trying to say—wouldn't believe that he really cared. I just stood there telling him what I thought of him, and saying the coldest, cruelest things that came into my mind—trying my best to hurt him."

"Do him no harm," said Caroline. "Never worry about what you say to a man. They're so conceited that they never believe you mean it if it's unflattering."

Ursula went on, nervously twisting and untwisting her hands.

"When the murder was discovered and he didn't come forward, I was terribly upset. Just for a moment I wondered—but then I knew he couldn't—he couldn't. . . . But I wished he would come forward and say openly that he'd had nothing to do with it. I knew that he was very fond of Dr. Sheppard, and I fancied that perhaps Dr. Sheppard might know where he was hiding."

She turned to me.

"That's why I said what I did to you that day. I thought, if you knew where he was, you might pass on the message to him."

"I?" I exclaimed.

"Why should James know where he was?" demanded Caroline sharply.

"It was very unlikely, I know," admitted Ursula, "but Ralph had often spoken of Dr. Sheppard, and I knew that he would be likely to consider him as his best friend in King's Abbot."

"My dear child," I said, "I have not the least idea where Ralph Paton is at the present moment."

"That is true enough," said Poirot.

"But——" Ursula held out the newspaper cutting in a puzzled fashion.

"Ah! that," said Poirot, slightly embarrassed; "a *bagatelle,* mademoiselle. A *rien du tout*. Not for a moment do I believe that Ralph Paton has been arrested."

"But then——" began the girl slowly.

Poirot went on quickly:—

"There is one thing I should like to know—did Captain Paton wear shoes or boots that night?"

Ursula shook her head.

"I can't remember."

"A pity! But how should you? Now, madame," he smiled at her, his head on one side, his forefinger wagging eloquently, "no questions. And do not torment yourself. Be of good courage, and place your faith in Hercule Poirot."

CHAPTER 23

POIROT'S LITTLE REUNION

"AND NOW," said Caroline, rising, "that child is coming upstairs to lie down. Don't you worry, my dear. M. Poirot will do everything he can for you—be sure of that."

"I ought to go back to Fernly," said Ursula uncertainly.

But Caroline silenced her protests with a firm hand.

"Nonsense. You're in my hands for the time being. You'll stay here for the present, anyway—eh, M. Poirot?"

"It will be the best plan," agreed the little Belgian. "This evening I shall want mademoiselle—I beg her pardon, madame—to attend my little reunion. Nine o'clock at my house. It is most necessary that she should be there."

Caroline nodded, and went with Ursula out of the room. The door shut behind them. Poirot dropped down into a chair again.

"So far, so good," he said. "Things are straightening themselves out."

"They're getting to look blacker and blacker against Ralph Paton," I observed gloomily.

Poirot nodded.

"Yes, that is so. But it was to be expected, was it not?"

I looked at him, slightly puzzled by the remark. He was leaning back in the chair, his eyes half closed, the tips of his fingers just touching each other. Suddenly he sighed and shook his head.

"What is it?" I asked.

"It is that there are moments when a great longing for my friend Hastings comes over me. That is the friend of whom I spoke to you—the one who resides now in the Argentine. Always, when I have had a big case, he has been by my side. And he has helped me—yes, often he has helped me. For he had a knack, that one, of stumbling over the truth unawares—without noticing it himself, *bien entendu*. At times he has said something particularly foolish, and behold that foolish remark has revealed the truth to me! And then, too, it was his practice to keep a written record of the cases that proved interesting."

I gave a slight embarrassed cough.

"As far as that goes," I began, and then stopped.

Poirot sat upright in his chair. His eyes sparkled.

"But yes? What is it that you would say?"

"Well, as a matter of fact, I've read some of Captain Hastings's narratives, and I thought, why not try my hand at something of the same kind? Seemed a pity not to—unique opportunity—probably the only time I'll be mixed up with anything of this kind."

I felt myself getting hotter and hotter, and more and more incoherent, as I floundered through the above speech.

Poirot sprang from his chair. I had a moment's terror that he was going to embrace me French fashion, but mercifully he refrained.

"But this is magnificent—you have then written down your impressions of the case as you went along?"

I nodded.

"*Epatant!*" cried Poirot. "Let me see them—this instant."

I was not quite prepared for such a sudden demand. I racked my brains to remember certain details.

"I hope you won't mind," I stammered. "I may have been a little—er—*personal* now and then."

"Oh! I comprehend perfectly; you have referred to me as comic—as, perhaps, ridiculous now and then? It matters not at all. Hastings, he also was not always polite. Me, I have the mind above such trivialities."

Still somewhat doubtful, I rummaged in the drawers of my desk and produced an untidy pile of manuscript which I handed over to him. With an eye on possible publication in the future, I had divided the work into chapters, and the night before I had brought it up to date with an account of Miss Russell's visit. Poirot had therefore twenty chapters.

I left him with them.

I was obliged to go out to a case at some distance away, and it was past eight o'clock when I got back, to be greeted with a plate of hot dinner on a tray, and the announcement that Poirot and my sister had supped together at half-past seven, and that the former had then gone to my workshop to finish his reading of the manuscript.

"I hope, James," said my sister, "that you've been careful in what you say about me in it?"

My jaw dropped. I had not been careful at all.

"Not that it matters very much," said Caroline, reading my expression correctly. "M. Poirot will know what to think. He understands me much better than you do."

I went into the workshop. Poirot was sitting by the window. The manuscript lay neatly piled on a chair beside him. He laid his hand on it and spoke.

"*Eh bien,*" he said, "I congratulate you—on your modesty!"

"Oh!" I said, rather taken aback.

"And on your reticence," he added.

I said "Oh!" again.

"Not so did Hastings write," continued my friend. "On every page, many, many times was the word 'I.' What *he* thought—what *he* did. But you—you have kept your personality in the background; only once or twice does it obtrude—in scenes of home life, shall we say?"

I blushed a little before the twinkle in his eye.

"What do you really think of the stuff?" I asked nervously.

"You want my candid opinion?"

"Yes."

Poirot laid his jesting manner aside.

"A very meticulous and accurate account," he said kindly. "You have recorded all the facts faithfully and exactly—though you have shown yourself becomingly reticent as to your own share in them."

"And it has helped you?"

"Yes. I may say that it has helped me considerably. Come, we must go over to my house and set the stage for my little performance."

Caroline was in the hall. I think she hoped that she might be invited to accompany us. Poirot dealt with the situation tactfully.

"I should much like to have had you present, mademoiselle," he said regretfully, "but at this juncture it would not be wise. See you, all these people to-night are suspects. Amongst them, I shall find the person who killed Mr. Ackroyd."

"You really believe that?" I said incredulously.

"I see that you do not," said Poirot dryly. "Not yet do you appreciate Hercule Poirot at his true worth."

At that minute Ursula came down the staircase.

"You are ready, my child?" said Poirot. "That is good. We will go to my house together. Mademoiselle Caroline, believe me, I do everything possible to render you service. Good-evening."

We went out, leaving Caroline, rather like a dog who has been refused a walk, standing on the front door step gazing after us.

The sitting-room at The Larches had been got ready. On the table were various *sirops* and glasses. Also a plate of biscuits. Several chairs had been brought in from the other room.

Poirot ran to and fro rearranging things. Pulling out a chair here, altering the position of a lamp there, occasionally stooping to straighten one of the mats that covered the floor. He was specially fussy over the lighting. The lamps were arranged in such a way as to throw a clear light on the side of the room where the chairs were grouped, at the same time leaving the other end of the room, where I presumed Poirot himself would sit, in a dim twilight.

Ursula and I watched him. Presently a bell was heard.

"They arrive," said Poirot. "Good, all is in readiness."

The door opened and the party from Fernly filed in. Poirot went forward and greeted Mrs. Ackroyd and Flora.

"It is most good of you to come," he said. "And Major Blunt and Mr. Raymond."

The secretary was debonair as ever.

"What's the great idea?" he said, laughing. "Some scientific machine? Do we have bands round our wrists which register guilty heart-beats? There is such an invention, isn't there?"

"I have read of it, yes," admitted Poirot. "But me, I am old-fashioned. I use the old methods. I work only with the little gray cells. Now let us begin—but first I have an announcement to make to you all."

He took Ursula's hand and drew her forward.

"This lady is Mrs. Ralph Paton. She was married to Captain Paton last March."

A little shriek burst from Mrs. Ackroyd.

"Ralph! Married! Last March! Oh! but it's absurd. How could he be?"

She stared at Ursula as though she had never seen her before.

"Married to Bourne?" she said. "Really, M. Poirot, I don't believe you."

Ursula flushed and began to speak, but Flora forestalled her.

Going quickly to the other girl's side, she passed her hand through her arm.

"You must not mind our being surprised," she said. "You see, we had no idea of such a thing. You and Ralph have kept your secret very well. I am—very glad about it."

"You are very kind, Miss Ackroyd," said Ursula in a low voice, "and you have every right to be exceedingly angry. Ralph behaved very badly—especially to you."

"You needn't worry about that," said Flora, giving her arm a consoling little pat. "Ralph was in a corner and took the only way out. I should probably have done the same in his place. I do think he might have trusted me with the secret, though. I wouldn't have let him down."

Poirot rapped gently on a table and cleared his throat significantly.

"The board meeting's going to begin," said Flora. "M. Poirot hints that we mustn't talk. But just tell me one thing. Where is Ralph? You must know if any one does."

"But I don't," cried Ursula, almost in a wail. "That's just it, I don't."

"Isn't he detained at Liverpool?" asked Raymond. "It said so in the paper."

"He is not at Liverpool," said Poirot shortly.

"In fact," I remarked, "no one knows where he is."

"Excepting Hercule Poirot, eh?" said Raymond.

Poirot replied seriously to the other's banter.

"Me, I know everything. Remember that."

Geoffrey Raymond lifted his eyebrows.

"Everything?" He whistled. "Whew! that's a tall order."

"Do you mean to say you can really guess where Ralph Paton is hiding?" I asked incredulously.

"You call it guessing. I call it knowing, my friend."

"In Cranchester?" I hazarded.

"No," replied Poirot gravely, "not in Cranchester."

He said no more, but at a gesture from him the assembled party took their seats. As they did so, the door opened once more and two other people came in and sat down near the door. They were Parker and the housekeeper.

"The number is complete," said Poirot. "Every one is here."

There was a ring of satisfaction in his tone. And with the sound of it I saw a ripple of something like uneasiness pass over all those faces grouped at the other end of the room. There was a suggestion in all this as of a trap—a trap that had closed.

Poirot read from a list in an important manner.

"Mrs. Ackroyd, Miss Flora Ackroyd, Major Blunt, Mr. Geoffrey Raymond, Mrs. Ralph Paton, John Parker, Elizabeth Russell."

He laid the paper down on the table.

"What's the meaning of all this?" began Raymond.

"The list I have just read," said Poirot, "is a list of suspected persons. Every one of you present had the opportunity to kill Mr. Ackroyd——"

With a cry Mrs. Ackroyd sprang up, her throat working.

"I don't like it," she wailed. "I don't like it. I would much prefer to go home."

"You cannot go home, madame," said Poirot sternly, "until you have heard what I have to say."

He paused a moment, then cleared his throat.

"I will start at the beginning. When Miss Ackroyd asked me to investigate the case, I went up to Fernly Park with the good Dr. Sheppard. I walked with him along the terrace, where I was shown the footprints on the window-sill. From there Inspector Raglan took me along the path which leads to the drive. My eye was caught by a little summer-house, and I searched it thoroughly. I found two things—a scrap of starched cambric and an empty goose quill. The scrap of cambric immediately suggested to me a maid's apron. When Inspector Raglan showed me his list of the people in the house, I noticed at once that one of the maids—Ursula Bourne, the parlormaid—had no real alibi. According to her own story, she was in her bedroom from nine-thirty until ten. But supposing that instead she was in the summer-house? If so, she must have gone there to meet some one. Now we know from Dr. Sheppard that some one from outside *did* come to the house that night—the stranger whom he met just by the gate. At a first glance it would seem that our problem was solved, and that the stranger went to the summer-house to meet Ursula

Bourne. It was fairly certain that he *did* go to the summer-house because of the goose quill. That suggested at once to my mind a taker
of drugs—and one who had acquired the habit on the other side of the
Atlantic where sniffing 'snow' is more common than in this country.
The man whom Dr. Sheppard met had an American accent, which
fitted in with that supposition.

"But I was held up by one point. *The times did not fit*. Ursula
Bourne could certainly not have gone to the summer-house before
nine-thirty, whereas the man must have got there by a few minutes
past nine. I could, of course, assume that he waited there for half an
hour. The only alternative supposition was that there had been two
separate meetings in the summer-house that night. *Eh bien,* as soon
as I went into that alternative I found several significant facts. I discovered that Miss Russell, the housekeeper, had visited Dr. Sheppard
that morning, and had displayed a good deal of interest in cures for
victims of the drug habit. Taking that in conjunction with the goose
quill, I assumed that the man in question came to Fernly to meet the
housekeeper, and not Ursula Bourne. Who, then, did Ursula Bourne
come to the rendezvous to meet? I was not long in doubt. First I
found a ring—a wedding ring—with 'From R.' and a date inside it.
Then I learnt that Ralph Paton had been seen coming up the path
which led to the summer-house at twenty-five minutes past nine, and
I also heard of a certain conversation which had taken place in the
wood near the village that very afternoon—a conversation between
Ralph Paton and some unknown girl. So I had my facts succeeding
each other in a neat and orderly manner. A secret marriage, an engagement announced on the day of the tragedy, the stormy interview
in the wood, and the meeting arranged for the summer-house that
night.

"Incidentally this proved to me one thing, that both Ralph Paton
and Ursula Bourne (or Paton) had the strongest motives for wishing
Mr. Ackroyd out of the way. And it also made one other point unexpectedly clear. It could not have been Ralph Paton who was with Mr.
Ackroyd in the study at nine-thirty.

"So we come to another and most interesting aspect of the crime.
Who was it in the room with Mr. Ackroyd at nine-thirty? Not
Ralph Paton, who was in the summer-house with his wife. Not
Charles Kent, who had already left. Who, then? I posed my cleverest
—my most audacious question: *Was any one with him?*"

Poirot leaned forward and shot the last words triumphantly at us, drawing back afterwards with the air of one who has made a decided hit.

Raymond, however, did not seem impressed, and lodged a mild protest.

"I don't know if you're trying to make me out a liar, M. Poirot, but the matter does not rest on my evidence alone—except perhaps as to the exact words used. Remember, Major Blunt also heard Mr. Ackroyd talking to some one. He was on the terrace outside, and couldn't catch the words clearly, but he distinctly heard the voices."

Poirot nodded.

"I have not forgotten," he said quietly. "But Major Blunt was under the impression that it was *you* to whom Mr. Ackroyd was speaking."

For a moment Raymond seemed taken aback. Then he recovered himself.

"Blunt knows now that he was mistaken," he said.

"Exactly," agreed the other man.

"Yet there must have been some reason for his thinking so," mused Poirot. "Oh! no," he held up his hand in protest, "I know the reason you will give—but it is not enough. We must seek elsewhere. I will put it this way. From the beginning of the case I have been struck by one thing—the nature of those words which Mr. Raymond overheard. It has been amazing to me that no one has commented on them—has seen anything odd about them."

He paused a minute, and then quoted softly:—

"'. . . *The calls on my purse have been so frequent of late that I fear it is impossible for me to accede to your request.*' Does nothing strike you as odd about that?"

"I don't think so," said Raymond. "He has frequently dictated letters to me, using almost exactly those same words."

"Exactly," cried Poirot. "That is what I seek to arrive at. Would any man use such a phrase in *talking* to another? Impossible that that should be part of a real conversation. Now, if he had been dictating a letter——"

"You mean he was reading a letter aloud," said Raymond slowly. "Even so, he must have been reading to some one."

"But why? We have no evidence that there was any one else in the room. No other voice but Mr. Ackroyd's was heard, remember."

"Surely a man wouldn't read letters of that type aloud to himself—not unless he was—well—going balmy."

"You have all forgotten one thing," said Poirot softly: "the stranger who called at the house the preceding Wednesday."

They all stared at him.

"But yes," said Poirot, nodding encouragingly, "on Wednesday. The young man was not of himself important. But the firm he represented interested me very much."

"The Dictaphone Company," gasped Raymond. "I see it now. A dictaphone. That's what you think?"

Poirot nodded.

"Mr. Ackroyd had promised to invest in a dictaphone, you remember. Me, I had the curiosity to inquire of the company in question. Their reply is that Mr. Ackroyd *did* purchase a dictaphone from their representative. Why he concealed the matter from you, I do not know."

"He must have meant to surprise me with it," murmured Raymond. "He had quite a childish love of surprising people. Meant to keep it up his sleeve for a day or so. Probably was playing with it like a new toy. Yes, it fits in. You're quite right—no one would use quite those words in casual conversation."

"It explains, too," said Poirot, "why Major Blunt thought it was you who were in the study. Such scraps as came to him were fragments of dictation, and so his subconscious mind deduced that you were with him. His conscious mind was occupied with something quite different—the white figure he had caught a glimpse of. He fancied it was Miss Ackroyd. Really, of course, it was Ursula Bourne's white apron he saw as she was stealing down to the summer-house."

Raymond had recovered from his first surprise.

"All the same," he remarked, "this discovery of yours, brilliant though it is (I'm quite sure I should never have thought of it), leaves the essential position unchanged. Mr. Ackroyd was alive at nine-thirty, since he was speaking into the dictaphone. It seems clear that the man Charles Kent was really off the premises by then. As to Ralph Paton——?"

He hesitated, glancing at Ursula.

Her color flared up, but she answered steadily enough.

"Ralph and I parted just before a quarter to ten. He never went near the house, I am sure of that. He had no intention of doing so. The last thing on earth he wanted was to face his stepfather. He would have funked it badly."

"It isn't that I doubt your story for a moment," explained Raymond. "I've always been quite sure Captain Paton was innocent. But one has to think of a court of law—and the questions that would be asked. He is in a most unfortunate position, but if he were to come forward——"

Poirot interrupted.

"That is your advice, yes? That he should come forward?"

"Certainly. If you know where he is——"

"I perceive that you do not believe that I do know. And yet I have told you just now that I know everything. The truth of the telephone call, of the footprints on the window-sill, of the hiding-place of Ralph Paton——"

"Where is he?" said Blunt sharply.

"Not very far away," said Poirot, smiling.

"In Cranchester?" I asked.

Poirot turned towards me.

"Always you ask me that. The idea of Cranchester it is with you an *idée fixe*. No, he is not in Cranchester. He is—*there!*"

He pointed a dramatic forefinger. Every one's head turned.

Ralph Paton was standing in the doorway.

CHAPTER 24

RALPH PATON'S STORY

IT WAS a very uncomfortable minute for *me*. I hardly took in what happened next, but there were exclamations and cries of surprise! When I was sufficiently master of myself to be able to realize what was going on, Ralph Paton was standing by his wife, her hand in his, and he was smiling across the room at me.

Poirot, too, was smiling, and at the same time shaking an eloquent finger at me.

"Have I not told you at least thirty-six times that it is useless to conceal things from Hercule Poirot?" he demanded. "That in such a case he finds out?"

He turned to the others.

"One day, you remember, we held a little séance about a table—just the six of us. I accused the other five persons present of concealing something from me. Four of them gave up their secret. Dr.

Sheppard did not give up his. But all along I have had my suspicions. Dr. Sheppard went to the Three Boars that night hoping to find Ralph. He did not find him there; but supposing, I said to myself, that he met him in the street on his way home? Dr. Sheppard was a friend of Captain Paton's, and he had come straight from the scene of the crime. He must know that things looked very black against him. Perhaps he knew more than the general public did——"

"I did," I said ruefully. "I suppose I might as well make a clean breast of things now. I went to see Ralph that afternoon. At first he refused to take me into his confidence, but later he told me about his marriage, and the hole he was in. As soon as the murder was discovered, I realized that once the facts were known, suspicion could not fail to attach to Ralph—or, if not to him, to the girl he loved. That night I put the facts plainly before him. The thought of having possibly to give evidence which might incriminate his wife made him resolve at all costs to—to——"

I hesitated, and Ralph filled up the gap.

"To do a bunk," he said graphically. "You see, Ursula left me to go back to the house. I thought it possible that she might have attempted to have another interview with my stepfather. He had already been very rude to her that afternoon. It occurred to me that he might have so insulted her—in such an unforgivable manner—that without knowing what she was doing——"

He stopped. Ursula released her hand from his, and stepped back.

"You thought that, Ralph! You actually thought that I might have done it?"

"Let us get back to the culpable conduct of Dr. Sheppard," said Poirot dryly. "Dr. Sheppard consented to do what he could to help him. He was successful in hiding Captain Paton from the police."

"Where?" asked Raymond. "In his own house?"

"Ah, no, indeed," said Poirot. "You should ask yourself the question that I did. If the good doctor is concealing the young man, what place would he choose? It must necessarily be somewhere near at hand. I think of Cranchester. A hotel? No. Lodgings? Even more emphatically, no. Where, then? Ah! I have it. A nursing home. A home for the mentally unfit. I test my theory. I invent a nephew with mental trouble. I consult Mademoiselle Sheppard as to suitable homes. She gives me the names of two near Cranchester to which her brother has sent patients. I make inquiries. Yes, at one of them a patient was brought there by the doctor himself early on Saturday morning. That patient, though known by another name, I had no difficulty in identifying as Captain Paton. After certain necessary formalities, I was allowed to bring him away. He arrived at my house in the early hours of yesterday morning."

I looked at him ruefully.

"Caroline's Home Office expert," I murmured. "And to think I never guessed!"

"You see now why I drew attention to the reticence of your manuscript," murmured Poirot. "It was strictly truthful as far as it went—but it did not go very far, eh, my friend?"

I was too abashed to argue.

"Dr. Sheppard has been very loyal," said Ralph. "He has stood by me through thick and thin. He did what he thought was the best. I see now, from what M. Poirot has told me, that it was not really the best. I should have come forward and faced the music. You see, in the home, we never saw a newspaper. I knew nothing of what was going on."

"Dr. Sheppard has been a model of discretion," said Poirot dryly. "But me, I discover all the little secrets. It is my business."

"Now we can have your story of what happened that night," said Raymond impatiently.

"You know it already," said Ralph. "There's very little for me to add. I left the summer-house about nine-forty-five, and tramped about the lanes, trying to make up my mind as to what to do next—what line to take. I'm bound to admit that I've not the shadow of an alibi, but I give you my solemn word that I never went to the study, that I never saw my stepfather alive—or dead. Whatever the world thinks, I'd like all of you to believe me."

"No alibi," murmured Raymond. "That's bad. I believe you, of course, but—it's a bad business."

"It makes things very simple, though," said Poirot, in a cheerful voice. "Very simple indeed."

We all stared at him.

"You see what I mean? No? Just this—to save Captain Paton the real criminal must confess."

He beamed round at us all.

"But yes—I mean what I say. See now, I did not invite Inspector Raglan to be present. That was for a reason. I did not want to tell him all that I knew—at least I did not want to tell him to-night."

He leaned forward, and suddenly his voice and his whole personality changed. He suddenly became dangerous.

"I who speak to you—I know the murderer of Mr. Ackroyd is in this room now. It is to the murderer I speak. *To-morrow the truth goes to Inspector Raglan.* You understand?"

There was a tense silence. Into the midst of it came the old Breton woman with a telegram on a salver. Poirot tore it open.

Blunt's voice rose abrupt and resonant.

"The murderer is amongst us, you say? You know—which?"

Poirot had read the message. He crumpled it up in his hand.

"I know—now."

He tapped the crumpled ball of paper.

"What is that?" said Raymond sharply.

"A wireless message—from a steamer now on her way to the United States."

There was a dead silence. Poirot rose to his feet bowing.

"Messieurs et Mesdames, this reunion of mine is at an end. Remember—*the truth goes to Inspector Raglan in the morning.*"

CHAPTER 25

THE WHOLE TRUTH

A SLIGHT gesture from Poirot enjoined me to stay behind the rest. I obeyed, going over to the fire and thoughtfully stirring the big logs on it with the toe of my boot.

I was puzzled. For the first time I was absolutely at sea as to Poirot's meaning. For a moment I was inclined to think that the scene I had just witnessed was a gigantic piece of bombast—that he had been what he called "playing the comedy" with a view to making himself interesting and important. But, in spite of myself, I was forced to believe in an underlying reality. There had been real menace in his words—a certain indisputable sincerity. But I still believed him to be on entirely the wrong tack.

When the door shut behind the last of the party he came over to the fire.

"Well, my friend," he said quietly, "and what do you think of it all?"

"I don't know what to think," I said frankly. "What was the point? Why not go straight to Inspector Raglan with the truth instead of giving the guilty person this elaborate warning?"

Poirot sat down and drew out his case of tiny Russian cigarettes. He smoked for a minute or two in silence. Then:—

"Use your little gray cells," he said. "There is always a reason behind my actions."

I hesitated for a moment, and then I said slowly:

"The first one that occurs to me is that you yourself do not know who the guilty person is, but that you are sure that he is to be found amongst the people here to-night. Therefore your words were intended to force a confession from the unknown murderer?"

Poirot nodded approvingly.

"A clever idea, but not the truth."

"I thought, perhaps, that by making him believe you knew, you might force him out into the open—not necessarily by confession. He might try to silence you as he formerly silenced Mr. Ackroyd—before you could act to-morrow morning."

"A trap with myself as the bait! *Merci, mon ami,* but I am not sufficiently heroic for that."

"Then I fail to understand you. Surely you are running the risk of letting the murderer escape by thus putting him on his guard?"

Poirot shook his head.

"He cannot escape," he said gravely. "There is only one way out—and that way does not lead to freedom."

"You really believe that one of those people here to-night committed the murder?" I asked incredulously.

"Yes, my friend."

"Which one?"

There was a silence for some minutes. Then Poirot tossed the stump of his cigarette into the grate and began to speak in a quiet, reflective tone.

"I will take you the way that I have traveled myself. Step by step you shall accompany me, and see for yourself that all the facts point indisputably to one person. Now, to begin with, there were two facts and one little discrepancy in time which especially attracted my attention. The first fact was the telephone call. If Ralph Paton were indeed the murderer, the telephone call became meaningless and absurd. Therefore, I said to myself, Ralph Paton is not the murderer.

"I satisfied myself that the call could not have been sent by any one in the house, yet I was convinced that it was amongst those present on the fatal evening that I had to look for my criminal. Therefore I concluded that the telephone call must have been sent by an accomplice. I was not quite pleased with that deduction, but I let it stand for the minute.

"I next examined the *motive* for the call. That was difficult. I could only get at it by judging its *result*. Which was—that the murder was discovered that night instead of—in all probability—the following morning. You agree with that?"

"Ye-es," I admitted. "Yes. As you say, Mr. Ackroyd, having given orders that he was not to be disturbed, nobody would have been likely to go to the study that night."

"*Tres bien*. The affair marches, does it not? But matters were still obscure. What was the advantage of having the crime discovered that night in preference to the following morning? The only idea I could get hold of was that the murderer, knowing the crime was to be discovered at a certain time, could make sure of being present when the door was broken in—or at any rate immediately afterwards. And now we come to the second fact—the chair pulled out from the wall. Inspector Raglan dismissed that as of no importance. I, on the contrary, have always regarded it as of supreme importance.

"In your manuscript you have drawn a neat little plan of the study. If you had it with you this minute you would see that—the chair being drawn out in the position indicated by Parker—it would stand in a direct line between the door and the window."

"The window!" I said quickly.

"You, too, have my first idea. I imagined that the chair was drawn out so that something connected with the window should not be seen by any one entering through the door. But I soon abandoned that supposition, for though the chair was a grandfather with a high back, it obscured very little of the window—only the part between the sash and the ground. No, *mon ami*—but remember that just in front of the window there stood a table with books and magazines upon it. Now that table *was* completely hidden by the drawn-out chair—and immediately I had my first shadowy suspicion of the truth.

"Supposing that there had been something on that table not intended to be seen? Something placed there by the murderer? As yet I had no inkling of what that something might be. But I knew certain very interesting facts about it. For instance, it was something that the murderer had not been able to take away with him at the time that he committed the crime. At the same time it was vital that it should be removed as soon as possible after the crime had been discovered. And so—the telephone message, and the opportunity for the murderer to be on the spot when the body was discovered.

"Now four people were on the scene before the police arrived. Yourself, Parker, Major Blunt, and Mr. Raymond. Parker I eliminated at once, since at whatever time the crime was discovered, he was the one person certain to be on the spot. Also it was he who told me of the pulled-out chair. Parker, then, was cleared (of the murder, that is. I still thought it possible that he had been blackmailing Mrs. Ferrars). Raymond and Blunt, however, remained under suspicion since, if the crime had been discovered in the early hours of the morning, it was quite possible that they might have arrived on the scene too late to prevent the object on the round table being discovered.

"Now what was that object? You heard my arguments to-night in reference to the scrap of conversation overheard? As soon as I learned that a representative of a dictaphone company had called, the idea of a dictaphone took root in my mind. You heard what I said in this room not half an hour ago? They all agreed with my theory—but one vital fact seems to have escaped them. Granted that a dictaphone was being used by Mr. Ackroyd that night—why was no dictaphone found?"

"I never thought of that," I said.

"We know that a dictaphone was supplied to Mr. Ackroyd. But no dictaphone has been found amongst his effects. So, if something was taken from that table—why should not that something be the dictaphone? But there were certain difficulties in the way. The attention of every one was, of course, focused on the murdered man. I think any one could have gone to the table unnoticed by the other people in the room. But a dictaphone has a certain bulk—it cannot be slipped casually into a pocket. There must have been a receptacle of some kind capable of holding it.

"You see where I am arriving? The figure of the murderer is taking shape. A person who was on the scene straightway, but who might not have been if the crime had been discovered the following morning. A person carrying a receptacle into which the dictaphone might be fitted——"

I interrupted.

"But why remove the dictaphone? What was the point?"

"You are like Mr. Raymond. You take it for granted that what was heard at nine-thirty was Mr. Ackroyd's voice speaking into a dictaphone. But consider this useful invention for a little minute. You dictate into it, do you not? And at some later time a secretary or a typist turns it on, and the voice speaks again."

"You mean——" I gasped.

Poirot nodded.

"Yes, I mean that. *At nine-thirty Mr. Ackroyd was already dead.* It was the dictaphone speaking—not the man."

"And the murderer switched it on. Then he must have been in the room at that minute?"

"Possibly. But we must not exclude the likelihood of some mechanical device having been applied—something after the nature of a time lock, or even of a simple alarm clock. But in that case we must add two qualifications to our imaginary portrait of the murderer. It must be some one who knew of Mr. Ackroyd's purchase of the dictaphone and also some one with the necessary mechanical knowledge.

"I had got thus far in my own mind when we came to the footprints on the window ledge. Here there were three conclusions open to me. (1) They might really have been made by Ralph Paton. He had been at Fernly that night, and might have climbed into the study and found his uncle dead there. That was one hypothesis. (2) There was the possibility that the footmarks might have been made by somebody else who happened to have the same kind of studs in his shoes. But the inmates of the house had shoes soled with crepe rubber, and I declined to believe in the coincidence of some one from outside having the same kind of shoes as Ralph Paton wore. Charles Kent, as we know from the barmaid of the Dog and Whistle, had on a pair of boots 'clean dropping off him.' (3) Those prints were made by some one deliberately trying to throw suspicion on Ralph Paton. To test this last conclusion, it was necessary to ascertain certain facts. One pair of Ralph's shoes had been obtained from the Three Boars by the police. Neither Ralph nor any one else could have worn them that evening, since they were downstairs being cleaned. According to the police theory, Ralph was wearing another pair of the same kind, and I found out that it was true that he had two pairs. Now for my theory to be proved correct it was necessary for the murderer to have worn Ralph's shoes that evening—in which case Ralph must have been wearing yet a *third* pair of footwear of some kind. I could hardly suppose that he would bring three pairs of shoes all alike—the third pair of footwear were more likely to be boots. I got your sister to make inquiries on this point—laying some stress on the color, in order —I admit it frankly—to obscure the real reason for my asking.

"You know the result of her investigations. Ralph Paton *had* had a pair of boots with him. The first question I asked him when he came

THE MURDER OF ROGER ACKROYD

to my house yesterday morning was what he was wearing on his feet on the fatal night. He replied at once that he had worn *boots*—he was still wearing them, in fact—having nothing else to put on.

"So we get a step further in our description of the murderer—a person who had the opportunity to take these shoes of Ralph Paton's from the Three Boars that day."

He paused, and then said, with a slightly raised voice:—

"There is one further point. The murderer must have been a person who had the opportunity to purloin that dagger from the silver table. You might argue that any one in the house might have done so, but I will recall to you that Miss Ackroyd was very positive that the dagger was not there when she examined the silver table."

He paused again.

"Let us recapitulate—now that all is clear. A person who was at the Three Boars earlier that day, a person who knew Ackroyd well enough to know that he had purchased a dictaphone, a person who was of a mechanical turn of mind, who had the opportunity to take the dagger from the silver table before Miss Flora arrived, who had with him a receptacle suitable for hiding the dictaphone—such as a black bag, and who had the study to himself for a few minutes after the crime was discovered while Parker was telephoning for the police. In fact—*Dr. Sheppard!*"

CHAPTER 26

AND NOTHING BUT THE TRUTH

THERE WAS a dead silence for a minute and a half.

Then I laughed.

"You're mad," I said.

"No," said Poirot placidly. "I am not mad. It was the little discrepancy in time that first drew my attention to you—right at the beginning."

"Discrepancy in time?" I queried, puzzled.

"But yes. You will remember that every one agreed—you yourself included—that it took five minutes to walk from the lodge to the house—less if you took the short cut to the terrace. But you left the house at ten minutes to nine—both by your own statement and that of

Parker, and yet it was nine o'clock as you passed through the lodge gates. It was a chilly night—not an evening a man would be inclined to dawdle; why had you taken ten minutes to do a five-minutes' walk? All along I realized that we had only your statement for it that the study window was ever fastened. Ackroyd asked you if you had done so—he never looked to see. Supposing, then, that the study window was unfastened? Would there be time in that ten minutes for you to run round the outside of the house, change your shoes, climb in through the window, kill Ackroyd, and get to the gate by nine o'clock? I decided against that theory since in all probability a man as nervous as Ackroyd was that night would hear you climbing in, and then there would have been a struggle. But supposing that you killed Ackroyd *before* you left—as you were standing beside his chair? Then you go out of the front door, run round to the summer-house, take Ralph Paton's shoes out of the bag you brought up with you that night, slip them on, walk through the mud in them, and leave prints on the window ledge, you climb in, lock the study door on the inside, run back to the summer-house, change back into your own shoes, and race down to the gate. (I went through similar actions the other day, when you were with Mrs. Ackroyd—it took ten minutes exactly.) Then home—and an alibi—since you had timed the dictaphone for half-past nine."

"My dear Poirot," I said in a voice that sounded strange and forced to my own ears, "you've been brooding over this case too long. What on earth had I to gain by murdering Ackroyd?"

"Safety. It was you who blackmailed Mrs. Ferrars. Who could have had a better knowledge of what killed Mr. Ferrars than the doctor who was attending him? When you spoke to me that first day in the garden, you mentioned a legacy received about a year ago. I have been unable to discover any trace of a legacy. You had to invent some way of accounting for Mrs. Ferrars's twenty thousand pounds. It has not done you much good. You lost most of it in speculation—then you put the screw on too hard, and Mrs. Ferrars took a way out that you had not expected. If Ackroyd had learnt the truth he would have had no mercy on you—you were ruined for ever."

"And the telephone call?" I asked, trying to rally. "You have a plausible explanation of that also, I suppose?"

"I will confess to you that it was my greatest stumbling block when I found that a call had actually been put through to you from King's Abbot station. I at first believed that you had simply invented the story. It was a very clever touch, that. You must have some excuse for arriving at Fernly, finding the body, and so getting the chance to remove the dictaphone on which your alibi depended. I had a very vague notion of how it was worked when I came to see your sister that first day and inquired as to what patients you had seen on Friday morning. I had no thought of Miss Russell in my mind at that time. Her visit was a lucky coincidence, since it distracted your mind from the real object of my questions. I found what I was looking for. Among your patients that morning was the steward of an American liner. Who more suitable than he to be leaving for Liverpool by the train that evening? And afterwards he would be on the high seas, well out of the way. I noted that the *Orion* sailed on Saturday, and having obtained the name of the steward I sent him a wireless message asking a certain question. This is his reply you saw me receive just now."

He held out the message to me. It ran as follows:—

"Quite correct. Dr. Sheppard asked me to leave a note at a patient's house. I was to ring him up from the station with the reply. Reply was 'No answer.'"

"It was a clever idea," said Poirot. "The call was genuine. Your sister saw you take it. But there was only one man's word as to what was actually said—your own!"

I yawned.

"All this," I said, "is very interesting—but hardly in the sphere of practical politics."

"You think not? Remember what I said—the truth goes to Inspector Raglan in the morning. But, for the sake of your good sister, I am willing to give you the chance of another way out. There might be, for instance, an overdose of a sleeping draught. You comprehend me? But Captain Ralph Paton must be cleared—*ça va sans dire*. I should suggest that you finish that very interesting manuscript of yours—but abandoning your former reticence."

"You seem to be very prolific of suggestions," I remarked. "Are you sure you've quite finished."

"Now that you remind me of the fact, it is true that there is one thing more. It would be most unwise on your part to attempt to silence me as you silenced M. Ackroyd. That kind of business does not succeed against Hercule Poirot, you understand."

"My dear Poirot," I said, smiling a little, "whatever else I may be, I am not a fool."

I rose to my feet.

"Well, well," I said, with a slight yawn, "I must be off home. Thank you for a most interesting and instructive evening."

Poirot also rose and bowed with his accustomed politeness as I passed out of the room.

CHAPTER 27

APOLOGIA

FIVE A.M. I am very tired—but I have finished my task. My arm aches from writing.

A strange end to my manuscript. I meant it to be published some day as the history of one of Poirot's failures! Odd, how things pan out.

All along I've had a premonition of disaster, from the moment I saw Ralph Paton and Mrs. Ferrars with their heads together. I thought then that she was confiding in him; as it happened I was quite wrong there, but the idea persisted even after I went into the study with Ackroyd that night, until he told me the truth.

Poor old Ackroyd. I'm always glad that I gave him a chance. I urged him to read that letter before it was too late. Or let me be honest—didn't I subconsciously realize that with a pig-headed chap like him, it was my best chance of getting him *not* to read it? His nervousness that night was interesting psychologically. He knew danger was close at hand. And yet he never suspected *me*.

The dagger was an afterthought. I'd brought up a very handy little weapon of my own, but when I saw the dagger lying in the silver table, it occurred to me at once how much better it would be to use a weapon that couldn't be traced to me.

I suppose I must have meant to murder him all along. As soon as I heard of Mrs. Ferrars's death, I felt convinced that she would have told him everything before she died. When I met him and he seemed so agitated, I thought that perhaps he knew the truth, but that he couldn't bring himself to believe it, and was going to give me the chance of refuting it.

So I went home and took my precautions. If the trouble were after all only something to do with Ralph—well, no harm would have been done. The dictaphone he had given me two days before to adjust. Something had gone a little wrong with it, and I persuaded him to let me have a go at it, instead of sending it back. I did what I wanted to it, and took it up with me in my bag that evening.

I am rather pleased with myself as a writer. What could be neater, for instance, than the following:—

"The letters were brought in at twenty minutes to nine. It was just on ten minutes to nine when I left him, the letter still unread. I hesitated with my hand on the door handle, looking back and wondering if there was anything I had left undone."

All true, you see. But suppose I had put a row of stars after the first sentence! Would somebody then have wondered what exactly happened in that blank ten minutes?

When I looked round the room from the door, I was quite satisfied. Nothing had been left undone. The dictaphone was on the table by the window, timed to go off at nine-thirty (the mechanism of that little device was rather clever—based on the principle of an alarm clock), and the arm-chair was pulled out so as to hide it from the door.

I must admit that it gave me rather a shock to run into Parker just outside the door. I have faithfully recorded that fact.

Then later, when the body was discovered, and I had sent Parker to telephone for the police, what a judicious use of words: *"I did what little had to be done!"* It was quite little—just to shove the dictaphone into my bag and push back the chair against the wall in its proper place. I never dreamed that Parker would have noticed that chair. Logically, he ought to have been so agog over the body as to be blind to everything else. But I hadn't reckoned with the trained-servant complex.

I wish I could have known beforehand that Flora was going to say she'd seen her uncle alive at a quarter to ten. That puzzled me more than I can say. In fact, all through the case there have been things that puzzled me hopelessly. Every one seems to have taken a hand.

My greatest fear all through has been Caroline. I have fancied she might guess. Curious the way she spoke that day of my "strain of weakness."

Well, she will never know the truth. There is, as Poirot said, one way out. . . .

I can trust him. He and Inspector Raglan will manage it between them. I should not like Caroline to know. She is fond of me, and then, too, she is proud. . . . My death will be a grief to her, but grief passes. . . .

When I have finished writing, I shall enclose this whole manuscript in an envelope and address it to Poirot.

And then—what shall it be? Veronal? There would be a kind of poetic justice. Not that I take any responsibility for Mrs. Ferrars's death. It was the direct consequence of her own actions. I feel no pity for her.

I have no pity for myself either.

So let it be veronal.

But I wish Hercule Poirot had never retired from work and come here to grow vegetable marrows.

And Then There Were None

CHAPTER 1

IN THE CORNER of a first-class smoking carriage, Mr. Justice Wargrave, lately retired from the bench, puffed at a cigar and ran an interested eye through the political news in the *Times*.

He laid the paper down and glanced out of the window. They were running now through Somerset. He glanced at his watch—another two hours to go.

He went over in his mind all that had appeared in the papers about Indian Island. There had been its original purchase by an American millionaire who was crazy about yachting—and an account of the luxurious modern house he had built on this little island off the Devon coast. The unfortunate fact that the new third wife of the American millionaire was a bad sailor had led to the subsequent putting up of the house and island for sale. Various glowing advertisements of it had appeared in the papers. Then came the first bald statement that it had been bought—by a Mr. Owen. After that the rumours of the gossip writers had started. Indian Island had really been bought by Miss Gabrielle Turl, the Hollywood film star! She wanted to spend some months there free from all publicity! *Busy Bee* had hinted delicately that it was to be an abode for Royalty??! *Mr. Merryweather* had had it whispered to him that it had been bought for a honeymoon—Young Lord L—— had surrendered to Cupid at last! *Jonas* knew for a *fact* that it had been purchased by the Admiralty with a view to carrying out some very hush hush experiments!

Definitely, Indian Island was news!

From his pocket Mr. Justice Wargrave drew out a letter. The handwriting was practically illegible but words here and there stood out with unexpected clarity. *Dearest Lawrence . . . such years since I heard anything of you . . . must come to Indian Island . . . the most enchanting place . . . so much to talk over . . . old days . . .*

communion with Nature . . . bask in sunshine . . . 12.40 from Pad-dington . . . meet you at Oakbridge . . . and his correspondent signed herself with a flourish his *ever Constance Culmington.*

Mr. Justice Wargrave cast back in his mind to remember when ex-actly he had last seen Lady Constance Culmington. It must be seven —no, eight years ago. She had then been going to Italy to bask in the sun and be at one with Nature and the *contadini.* Later, he had heard, she had proceeded to Syria where she proposed to bask in yet stronger sun and live at one with Nature and the *bedouin.*

Constance Culmington, he reflected to himself, was exactly the sort of woman who *would* buy an island and surround herself with mys-tery! Nodding his head in gentle approval of his logic, Mr. Justice Wargrave allowed his head to nod. . . .

He slept. . . .

2

Vera Claythorne, in a third-class carriage with five other travellers in it, leaned her head back and shut her eyes. How hot it was travel-ling by train to-day! It would be nice to get to the sea! Really a great piece of luck getting this job. When you wanted a holiday post it nearly always meant looking after a swarm of children—secretarial holiday posts were much more difficult to get. Even the agency hadn't held out much hope.

And then the letter had come.

"I have received your name from the Skilled Women's Agency to-gether with their recommendation. I understand they know you per-sonally. I shall be glad to pay you the salary you ask and shall expect you to take up your duties on August 8th. The train is the 12.40 from Paddington and you will be met at Oakbridge station. I enclose five pound notes for expenses.

Yours truly,
Una Nancy Owen."

And at the top was the stamped address *Indian Island, Sticklehaven, Devon.* . . .

Indian Island! Why, there had been nothing else in the papers lately! All sorts of hints and interesting rumours. Though probably that was mostly untrue. But the house had certainly been built by a millionaire and was said to be absolutely the last word in luxury.

Vera Claythorne, tired by a recent strenuous term at school, thought to herself—"Being a games mistress in a third-class school isn't much of a catch. . . . If only I could get a job at some *decent* school."

And then, with a cold feeling round her heart, she thought: "But I'm lucky to have even this. After all, people don't like a Coroner's Inquest, even if the Coroner *did* acquit me of all blame!"

He had even complimented her on her presence of mind and courage, she remembered. For an inquest it couldn't have gone better. And Mrs. Hamilton had been kindness itself to her— Only Hugo— (*but she wouldn't think of Hugo!*)

Suddenly, in spite of the heat in the carriage she shivered and wished she wasn't going to the sea. A picture rose clearly before her mind. *Cyril's head, bobbing up and down, swimming to the rock.* . . . Up and down—up and down. . . . And herself, swimming in easy practised strokes after him—cleaving her way through the water but knowing, only too surely, that she wouldn't be in time. . . .

The sea—its deep warm blue—mornings spent lying out on the sands—Hugo—Hugo who had said he loved her. . . .

She must *not* think of Hugo. . . .

She opened her eyes and frowned across at the man opposite her. A tall man with a brown face, light eyes set rather close together and an arrogant almost cruel mouth.

She thought to herself:

"I bet he's been to some interesting parts of the world and seen some interesting things. . . ."

3

Philip Lombard, summing up the girl opposite in a mere flash of his quick moving eyes thought to himself:

"Quite attractive—a bit schoolmistressy perhaps. . . ."

A cool customer, he should imagine—and one who could hold her own—in love or war. He'd rather like to take her on. . . .

He frowned. No, cut out all that kind of stuff. This was business. He'd got to keep his mind on the job.

What exactly was up, he wondered? That little Jew had been damned mysterious.

"Take it or leave it, Captain Lombard."

He had said thoughtfully:

"A hundred guineas, eh?"

He had said it in a casual way as though a hundred guineas was nothing to him. *A hundred guineas* when he was literally down to his last square meal! He had fancied, though, that the little Jew had not been deceived—that was the damnable part about Jews, you couldn't deceive them about money—they *knew!*

He had said in the same casual tone:

"And you can't give me any further information?"

Mr. Isaac Morris had shaken his little bald head very positively.

"No, Captain Lombard, the matter rests there. It is understood by my client that your reputation is that of a good man in a tight place. I am empowered to hand you one hundred guineas in return for which you will travel to Sticklehaven, Devon. The nearest station is Oakbridge, you will be met there and motored to Sticklehaven where a motor launch will convey you to Indian Island. There you will hold yourself at the disposal of my client."

Lombard had said abruptly:

"For how long?"

"Not longer than a week at most."

Fingering his small moustache, Captain Lombard said:

"You understand I can't undertake anything—illegal?"

He had darted a very sharp glance at the other as he had spoken. There had been a very faint smile on the thick Semitic lips of Mr. Morris as he answered gravely:

"If anything illegal is proposed, you will, of course, be at perfect liberty to withdraw."

Damn the smooth little brute, he had smiled! It was as though he knew very well that in Lombard's past actions legality had not always been a *sine qua non*. . . .

Lombard's own lips parted in a grin.

By Jove, he'd sailed pretty near the wind once or twice! But he'd always got away with it! There wasn't much he drew the line at really. . . .

No, there wasn't much he'd draw the line at. He fancied that he was going to enjoy himself at Indian Island. . . .

4

In a non-smoking carriage Miss Emily Brent sat very upright as was her custom. She was sixty-five and she did not approve of lounging. Her father, a Colonel of the old school, had been particular about deportment.

The present generation was shamelessly lax—in their carriage, *and in every other way.* . . .

Enveloped in an aura of righteousness and unyielding principles, Miss Brent sat in her crowded third-class carriage and triumphed over its discomfort and its heat. Every one made such a fuss over things nowadays! They wanted injections before they had teeth pulled —they took drugs if they couldn't sleep—they wanted easy chairs and cushions and the girls allowed their figures to slop about anyhow and lay about half naked on the beaches in summer.

Miss Brent's lips set closely. She would like to make an example of certain people.

She remembered last year's summer holiday. This year, however, it would be quite different. Indian Island. . . .

Mentally she reread the letter which she had already read so many times.

Dear Miss Brent,

I do hope you remember me? We were together at Bellhaven Guest House in August some years ago, and we seemed to have so much in common.

I am starting a guest house of my own on an island off the coast of Devon. I think there is really an opening for a place where there is good plain cooking and a nice old-fashioned type of person. None of this nudity and gramophones half the night. I shall be very glad if you could see your way to spending your summer holiday on Indian Island—quite free—as my guest. Would early in August suit you? Perhaps the 8th.

Yours sincerely,

U. N. ——

What was the name? The signature was rather difficult to read. Emily Brent thought impatiently: "So many people write their signatures quite illegibly."

She let her mind run back over the people at Bellhaven. She had been there two summers running. There had been that nice middle-aged woman—Mrs.—Mrs.—now what *was* her name?—her father had been a Canon. And there had been a Miss Olton—Ormen— No, surely it was *Oliver!* Yes—Oliver.

Indian Island! There had been things in the paper about Indian Island—something about a film star—or was it an American million-aire?

Of course often those places went very cheap—islands didn't suit everybody. They thought the idea was romantic but when they came to live there they realized the disadvantages and were only too glad to sell.

Emily Brent thought to herself: *"I shall be getting a free holiday at any rate."*

With her income so much reduced and so many dividends not being paid, that was indeed something to take into consideration. If only she could remember a little more about Mrs.—or was it Miss—Oliver?

5

General Macarthur looked out of the carriage window. The train was just coming into Exeter where he had to change. Damnable, these slow branch line trains! This place, Indian Island, was really no distance at all as the crow flies.

He hadn't got it clear who this fellow Owen was. A friend of Spoof Leggard's, apparently—and of Johnny Dyer's.

—One or two of your old cronies are coming—would like to have a talk over old times.

Well, he'd enjoy a chat about old times. He'd had a fancy lately that fellows were rather fighting shy of him. All owing to that damned rumour! By God, it was pretty hard—nearly thirty years ago now! Armitage had talked, he supposed. Damned young pup! What did *he* know about it? Oh, well, no good brooding about these things! One fancied things sometimes—fancied a fellow was looking at you queerly.

This Indian Island now, he'd be interested to see it. A lot of gossip flying about. Looked as though there might be something in the rumour that the Admiralty or the War Office or the Air Force had got hold of it. . . .

Young Elmer Robson, the American millionaire, had actually built the place. Spent thousands on it, so it was said. Every mortal luxury. . . .

Exeter! And an hour to wait! And he didn't want to wait. He wanted to get on. . . .

6

Dr. Armstrong was driving his Morris across Salisbury Plain. He was very tired. . . . Success had its penalties. There had been a time when he had sat in his consulting room in Harley Street, correctly apparelled, surrounded with the most up-to-date appliances and the most luxurious furnishings and waited—waited through the empty days for his venture to succeed or fail. . . .

Well, it had succeeded! He'd been lucky! Lucky *and* skilful of course. He was a good man at his job—but that wasn't enough for success. You had to have luck as well. And he'd had it! An accurate diagnosis, a couple of grateful women patients—women with money and position—and word had got about. "You ought to try Armstrong —*quite* a young man—but *so* clever— Pam had been to all sorts of people for *years* and he put his finger on the trouble at once!" The ball had started rolling.

And now Dr. Armstrong had definitely arrived. His days were full. He had little leisure. And so, on this August morning, he was glad that he was leaving London and going to be for some days on an island off the Devon coast. Not that it was exactly a holiday. The letter he had received had been rather vague in its terms, but there was nothing vague about the accompanying cheque. A whacking fee. These Owens must be rolling in money. Some little difficulty, it seemed, a husband who was worried about his wife's health and wanted a report on it without her being alarmed. She wouldn't hear of seeing a doctor. Her nerves—

Nerves! The doctor's eyebrows went up. These women and their nerves! Well, it was good for business, after all. Half the women who consulted him had nothing the matter with them but boredom, but they wouldn't thank you for telling them so! And one could usually find something.

"A slightly uncommon condition of the—some long word—nothing at all serious—but it just needs putting right. A simple treatment."

Well, medicine was mostly faith-healing when it came to it. And he had a good manner—he could inspire hope and belief.

Lucky that he'd managed to pull himself together in time after that business ten—no, fifteen years ago. It had been a near thing, that! He'd been going to pieces. The shock had pulled him together. He'd cut out drink altogether. By Jove, it had been a near thing though. . . .

With a devastating ear-splitting blast on the horn an enormous Super Sports Dalmain car rushed past him at eighty miles an hour. Dr. Armstrong nearly went into the hedge. One of these young fools who tore round the country. He hated them. That had been a near shave, too. Damned young fool!

7

Tony Marston, roaring down into Mere, thought to himself:

"The amount of cars crawling about the roads is frightful. Always something blocking your way. *And* they will drive in the middle of the road! Pretty hopeless driving in England, anyway. . . . Not like France where you really *could* let out. . . ."

Should he stop here for a drink, or push on? Heaps of time! Only another hundred miles and a bit to go. He'd have a gin and ginger-beer. Fizzing hot day!

This island place ought to be rather good fun—if the weather lasted. Who *were* these Owens, he wondered? Rich and stinking, probably. Badger was rather good at nosing people like that out. Of course, he *had* to, poor old chap, with no money of his own. . . .

Hope they'd do one well in drinks. Never knew with these fellows who'd made their money and weren't born to it. Pity that story about Gabrielle Turl having bought Indian Island wasn't true. He'd like to have been in with that film star crowd.

Oh, well, he supposed there'd be a few girls there. . . .

Coming out of the Hotel, he stretched himself, yawned, looked up at the blue sky and climbed into the Dalmain.

Several young women looked at him admiringly—his six feet of well-proportioned body, his crisp hair, tanned face, and intensely blue eyes.

He let in the clutch with a roar and leapt up the narrow street. Old men and errand boys jumped for safety. The latter looked after the car admiringly.

Anthony Marston proceeded on his triumphal progress.

8

Mr. Blore was in the slow train from Plymouth. There was only one other person in his carriage, an elderly seafaring gentleman with a bleary eye. At the present moment he had dropped off to sleep.

Mr. Blore was writing carefully in a little notebook.

"That's the lot," he muttered to himself. "Emily Brent, Vera Claythorne, Dr. Armstrong, Anthony Marston, old Justice Wargrave, Philip Lombard, General Macarthur, C.M.G., D.S.O. Manservant and wife: Mr. and Mrs. Rogers."

He closed the notebook and put it back in his pocket. He glanced over at the corner and the slumbering man.

"Had one over the eight," diagnosed Mr. Blore accurately.

He went over things carefully and conscientiously in his mind.

"Job ought to be easy enough," he ruminated. "Don't see how I can slip up on it. Hope I look all right."

He stood up and scrutinized himself anxiously in the glass. The face reflected there was of a slightly military cast with a moustache. There was very little expression in it. The eyes were grey and set rather close together.

"Might be a Major," said Mr. Blore. "No, I forgot. There's that old military gent. He'd spot me at once.

"South Africa," said Mr. Blore, "that's my line! None of these people have anything to do with South Africa, and I've just been reading that travel folder so I can talk about it all right."

Fortunately there were all sorts and types of colonials. As a man of means from South Africa, Mr. Blore felt that he could enter into any society unchallenged.

Indian Island. He remembered Indian Island as a boy. . . . Smelly sort of rock covered with gulls—stood about a mile from the coast. It had got its name from its resemblance to a man's head—an American Indian profile.

Funny idea to go and build a house on it! Awful in bad weather! But millionaires were full of whims!

The old man in the corner woke up and said:

"You can't never tell at sea—never!"

Mr. Blore said soothingly, "That's right. You can't."

The old man hiccuped twice and said plaintively:

"There's a squall coming."

Mr. Blore said:

"No, no, mate, it's a lovely day."

The old man said angrily:

"There's a squall ahead. I can *smell* it."

"Maybe you're right," said Mr. Blore pacifically.

The train stopped at a station and the old fellow rose unsteadily.

"Thish where I get out." He fumbled with the window. Mr. Blore helped him.

The old man stood in the doorway. He raised a solemn hand and blinked his bleary eyes.

"Watch and pray," he said. "Watch and pray. The day of judgment is at hand."

He collapsed through the doorway onto the platform. From a recumbent position he looked up at Mr. Blore and said with immense dignity:

"I'm talking to *you*, young man. The day of judgment is very close at hand."

Subsiding onto his seat Mr. Blore thought to himself:

"He's nearer the day of judgment than I am!"

But there, as it happens, he was wrong. . . .

CHAPTER 2

OUTSIDE OAKBRIDGE STATION a little group of people stood in momentary uncertainty. Behind them stood porters with suitcases. One of these called "Jim!"

The driver of one of the taxis stepped forward.

"You'm for Indian Island, maybe?" he asked in a soft Devon voice. Four voices gave assent—and then immediately afterwards gave quick surreptitious glances at each other.

The driver said, addressing his remarks to Mr. Justice Wargrave as the senior member of the party:

"There are two taxis here, sir. One of them must wait till the slow train from Exeter gets in—a matter of five minutes—there's one gentleman coming by that. Perhaps one of you wouldn't mind waiting? You'd be more comfortable that way."

Vera Claythorne, her own secretarial position clear in her mind, spoke at once.

"I'll wait," she said, "if you will go on?" She looked at the other three, her glance and voice had that slight suggestion of command in it that comes from having occupied a position of authority. She might have been directing which tennis sets the girls were to play in.

Miss Brent said stiffly, "Thank you," bent her head and entered one of the taxis, the door of which the driver was holding open.

Mr. Justice Wargrave followed her.

Captain Lombard said:

"I'll wait with Miss—"

"Claythorne," said Vera.

"My name is Lombard, Philip Lombard."

The porters were piling luggage on the taxi. Inside, Mr. Justice Wargrave said with due legal caution:

"Beautiful weather we are having."

Miss Brent said:

"Yes, indeed."

A very distinguished old gentleman, she thought to herself. Quite unlike the usual type of man in seaside guest houses. Evidently Mrs. or Miss Oliver had good connections. . . .

Mr. Justice Wargrave inquired:

"Do you know this part of the world well?"

"I have been to Cornwall and to Torquay, but this is my first visit to this part of Devon."

The judge said:

"I also am unacquainted with this part of the world."

The taxi drove off.

The driver of the second taxi said:

"Like to sit inside while you're waiting?"

Vera said decisively:

"Not at all."

Captain Lombard smiled.

He said:

"That sunny wall looks more attractive. Unless you'd rather go inside the station?"

"No, indeed. It's so delightful to get out of that stuffy train."

He answered:

"Yes, travelling by train *is* rather trying in this weather."

Vera said conventionally:

"I do hope it lasts—the weather, I mean. Our English summers are so treacherous."

With a slight lack of originality Lombard asked:

"Do you know this part of the world well?"

"No, I've never been here before." She added quickly, conscientiously determined to make her position clear at once, "I haven't even seen my employer yet."

"Your employer?"

"Yes, I'm Mrs. Owen's secretary."

"Oh, I see." Just imperceptibly his manner changed. It was slightly more assured—easier in tone. He said: "Isn't that rather unusual?"

Vera laughed.

"Oh, no, I don't think so. Her own secretary was suddenly taken ill and she wired to an agency for a substitute and they sent me."

"So that was it. And suppose you don't like the post when you've got there?"

Vera laughed again.

"Oh, it's only temporary—a holiday post. I've got a permanent job at a girls' school. As a matter of fact I'm frightfully thrilled at the prospect of seeing Indian Island. There's been such a lot about it in the papers. Is it really very fascinating?"

Lombard said:

"I don't know. I haven't seen it."

"Oh, really? The Owens are frightfully keen on it, I suppose. What are they like? Do tell me."

Lombard thought: Awkward, this—am I supposed to have met them or not? He said quickly:

"There's a wasp crawling up your arm. No—keep quite still." He made a convincing pounce. "There. It's gone!"

"Oh, thank you. There are a lot of wasps about this summer."

"Yes, I suppose it's the heat. Who are we waiting for, do you know?"

"I haven't the least idea."

The loud drawn out scream of an approaching train was heard. Lombard said:

"That will be the train now."

2

It was a tall soldierly old man who appeared at the exit from the platform. His grey hair was clipped close and he had a neatly trimmed white moustache.

His porter, staggering slightly under the weight of the solid leather suitcase, indicated Vera and Lombard.

Vera came forward in a competent manner. She said:

"I am Mrs. Owen's secretary. There is a car here waiting." She added: "This is Mr. Lombard."

The faded blue eyes, shrewd in spite of their age, sized up Lombard. For a moment a judgment showed in them—had there been any one to read it.

"Good-looking fellow. Something just a little wrong about him. . . ."

The three of them got into the waiting taxi. They drove through the sleepy streets of little Oakbridge and continued about a mile on the main Plymouth road. Then they plunged into a maze of cross country lanes, steep, green and narrow.

General Macarthur said:

"Don't know this part of Devon at all. My little place is in East Devon—just on the border-line of Dorset."

Vera said:

"It really is lovely here. The hills and the red earth and everything so green and luscious looking."

Philip Lombard said critically:

"It's a bit shut in. . . . I like open country myself. Where you can see what's coming. . . ."

General Macarthur said to him:

"You've seen a bit of the world, I fancy?"

Lombard shrugged his shoulders disparagingly.

"I've knocked about here and there, sir."

He thought to himself: "He'll ask me now if I was old enough to be in the War. These old boys always do."

But General Macarthur did not mention the War.

3

They came up over a steep hill and down a zig-zag track to Sticklehaven—a mere cluster of cottages with a fishing boat or two drawn up on the beach.

Illuminated by the setting sun, they had their first glimpse of Indian Island jutting up out of the sea to the south.

Vera said, surprised:

"It's a long way out."

She had pictured it differently, close to shore, crowned with a beautiful white house. But there was no house visible, only the boldly silhouetted rock with its faint resemblance to a giant Indian's head. There was something sinister about it. She shivered faintly.

Outside a little inn, the Seven Stars, three people were sitting. There was the hunched elderly figure of the judge, the upright form of Miss Brent, and a third man—a big bluff man who came forward and introduced himself.

"Thought we might as well wait for you," he said. "Make one trip of it. Allow me to introduce myself. Name's Davis. Natal, South Africa's, my natal spot, ha, ha!"

He laughed breezily.

Mr. Justice Wargrave looked at him with active malevolence. He seemed to be wishing that he could order the court to be cleared. Miss Emily Brent was clearly not sure if she liked Colonials.

"Any one care for a little nip before we embark?" asked Mr. Davis hospitably.

Nobody assenting to this proposition, Mr. Davis turned and held up a finger.

"Mustn't delay, then. Our good host and hostess will be expecting us," he said.

He might have noticed that a curious constraint came over the other members of the party. It was as though the mention of their host and hostess had a curiously paralyzing effect upon the guests.

In response to Davis' beckoning finger, a man detached himself from a nearby wall against which he was leaning and came up to them. His rolling gait proclaimed him a man of the sea. He had a weather-beaten face and dark eyes with a slightly evasive expression. He spoke in his soft Devon voice.

"Will you be ready to be starting for the island, ladies and gentlemen? The boat's waiting. There's two gentlemen coming by car, but Mr. Owen's orders was not to wait for them as they might arrive at any time."

The party got up. Their guide led them along a small stone jetty. Alongside it a motor boat was lying.

Emily Brent said:

"That's a very small boat."

The boat's owner said persuasively:

"She's a fine boat, that, Ma'am. You could go to Plymouth in her as easy as winking."

Mr. Justice Wargrave said sharply:

"There are a good many of us."

"She'd take double the number, sir."

Philip Lombard said in his pleasant easy voice:

"It's quite all right. Glorious weather—no swell."

Rather doubtfully, Miss Brent permitted herself to be helped into the boat. The others followed suit. There was as yet no fraternizing among the party. It was as though each member of it was puzzled by the other members.

They were just about to cast loose when their guide paused, boathook in hand.

Down the steep track into the village a car was coming. A car so fantastically powerful, so superlatively beautiful that it had all the nature of an apparition. At the wheel sat a young man, his hair blown back by the wind. In the blaze of the evening light he looked, not a man, but a young God, a Hero God out of some Northern Saga.

He touched the horn and a great roar of sound echoed from the rocks of the bay.

It was a fantastic moment. In it, Anthony Marston seemed to be something more than mortal. Afterwards, more than one of those present remembered that moment.

4

Fred Narracott sat by the engine thinking to himself that this was a queer lot. Not at all his idea of what Mr. Owen's guests were likely to be. He'd expected something altogether more classy. Togged up women and gentlemen in yachting costume and all very rich and important looking.

Not at all like Mr. Elmer Robson's parties. A faint grin came to Fred Narracott's lips as he remembered the millionaire's guests. That had been a party if you like—and the drink they'd got through!

This Mr. Owen must be a very different sort of gentleman. Funny it was, thought Fred, that he'd never yet set eyes on Owen—or his Missus either. Never been down here yet, he hadn't. Everything ordered and paid for by that Mr. Morris. Instructions always very clear and payment prompt, but it was odd, all the same. The papers said there was some mystery about Owen. Mr. Narracott agreed with them.

Perhaps, after all, it *was* Miss Gabrielle Turl who had bought the island. But that theory departed from him as he surveyed his passengers. Not this lot—none of them looked likely to have anything to do with a film star.

He summed them up dispassionately.

One old maid—the sour kind—he knew them well enough. She was a Tartar, he could bet. Old military gentleman—real Army by the look of him. Nice looking young lady—but the ordinary kind, not glamourous—no Hollywood touch about her. That bluff cheery gent— *he* wasn't a real gentleman. Retired tradesman, that's what he is, thought Fred Narracott. The other gentleman, the lean hungry looking gentleman with the quick eyes, he was a queer one, he was. Just possible he *might* have something to do with the pictures.

No, there was only one satisfactory passenger in the boat. The last gentleman, the one who had arrived in the car (and what a car! A car such as had never been seen in Sticklehaven before. Must have cost hundreds and hundreds, a car like that.). He was the right kind. Born to money, he was. If the party had been all like him . . . he'd understand it. . . .

Queer business when you came to think of it—the whole thing was queer—very queer. . . .

5

The boat churned its way round the rock. Now at last the house came into view. The south side of the island was quite different. It shelved gently down to the sea. The house was there facing south—

low and square and modern-looking with rounded windows letting in all the light.

An exciting house—a house that lived up to expectation!

Fred Narracott shut off the engine, they nosed their way gently into a little natural inlet between rocks.

Philip Lombard said sharply:

"Must be difficult to land here in dirty weather."

Fred Narracott said cheerfully:

"Can't land on Indian Island when there's a southeasterly. Sometimes 'tis cut off for a week or more."

Vera Claythorne thought:

"The catering must be very difficult. That's the worst of an island. All the domestic problems are so worrying."

The boat grated against the rocks. Fred Narracott jumped out and he and Lombard helped the others to alight. Narracott made the boat fast to a ring in the rock. Then he led the way up steps cut in the rock.

General Macarthur said:

"Ha, delightful spot!"

But he felt uneasy. Damned odd sort of place.

As the party ascended the steps, and came out on a terrace above, their spirits revived. In the open doorway of the house a correct butler was awaiting them, and something about his gravity reassured them. And then the house itself was really most attractive, the view from the terrace magnificent. . . .

The butler came forward bowing slightly. He was a tall lank man, grey-haired and very respectable. He said:

"Will you come this way, please?"

In the wide hall drinks stood ready. Rows of bottles. Anthony Marston's spirits cheered up a little. He'd just been thinking this was a rum kind of show. None of *his* lot! What could old Badger have been thinking about to let him in for this? However the drinks were all right. Plenty of ice, too.

What was it the butler chap was saying?

Mr. Owen—unfortunately delayed—unable to get here till to-morrow. Instructions—everything they wanted—if they would like to go to their rooms? . . . Dinner would be at 8 o'clock. . . .

6

Vera had followed Mrs. Rogers upstairs. The woman had thrown open a door at the end of a passage and Vera had walked into a delightful bedroom with a big window that opened wide upon the sea and another looking east. She uttered a quick exclamation of pleasure.

Mrs. Rogers was saying:

"I hope you've got everything you want, Miss?"

Vera looked round. Her luggage had been brought up and had been unpacked. At one side of the room a door stood open into a pale blue tiled bathroom.

She said quickly:

"Yes, everything, I think."

"You'll ring the bell if you want anything, Miss?"

Mrs. Rogers had a flat monotonous voice. Vera looked at her curiously. What a white bloodless ghost of a woman! Very respectable looking, with her hair dragged back from her face and her black dress. Queer light eyes that shifted the whole time from place to place.

Vera thought:

"She looks frightened of her own shadow."

Yes, that was it—frightened!

She looked like a woman who walked in mortal fear. . . .

A little shiver passed down Vera's back. What on earth was the woman afraid of?

She said pleasantly:

"I'm Mrs. Owen's new secretary. I expect you know that."

Mrs. Rogers said:

"No, Miss, I don't know anything. Just a list of the ladies and gentlemen and what rooms they were to have."

Vera said:

"Mrs. Owen didn't mention me?"

Mrs. Rogers' eyelashes flickered.

"I haven't seen Mrs. Owen—not yet. We only came here two days ago."

Extraordinary people, these Owens, thought Vera. Aloud she said:

"What staff is there here?"

"Just me and Rogers, Miss."

Vera frowned. Eight people in the house—ten with the host and hostess—and only one married couple to do for them.

Mrs. Rogers said:

"I'm a good cook and Rogers is handy about the house. I didn't know, of course, that there was to be such a large party."

Vera said:

"But you can manage?"

"Oh, yes, Miss, I can manage. If there's to be large parties often, perhaps Mrs. Owen could get extra help in."

Vera said, "I expect so."

Mrs. Rogers turned to go. Her feet moved noiselessly over the floor. She drifted from the room like a shadow.

Vera went over to the window and sat down on the window seat. She was faintly disturbed. Everything—somehow—was a little queer. The absence of the Owens, the pale ghostlike Mrs. Rogers. And the guests! Yes, the guests were queer too. An oddly assorted party.

Vera thought:

"I wish I'd seen the Owens. . . . I wish I knew what they were like."

She got up and walked restlessly about the room.

A perfect bedroom decorated throughout in the modern style. Off white rugs on the gleaming parquet floor—faintly tinted walls—a long mirror surrounded by lights. A mantelpiece bare of ornaments save for an enormous block of white marble shaped like a bear, a piece of modern sculpture in which was inset a clock. Over it, in a gleaming chromium frame, was a big square of parchment—a poem.

She stood in front of the fireplace and read it. It was the old nursery rhyme that she remembered from her childhood days.

Ten little Indian boys went out to dine;
One choked his little self and then there were nine.

Nine little Indian boys sat up very late;
One overslept himself and then there were eight.

Eight little Indian boys travelling in Devon;
One said he'd stay there and then there were seven.

Seven little Indian boys chopping up sticks;
One chopped himself in halves and then there were six.

Six little Indian boys playing with a hive;
A bumblebee stung one and then there were five.

Five little Indian boys going in for law;
One got in Chancery and then there were four.

Four little Indian boys going out to sea;
A red herring swallowed one and then there were three.

Three little Indian boys walking in the Zoo;
A big bear hugged one and then there were two.

Two little Indian boys sitting in the sun;
One got frizzled up and then there was one.

One little Indian boy left all alone;
He went and hanged himself and then there were none.

Vera smiled. Of course! This was Indian Island!

She went and sat again by the window looking out to sea.

How big the sea was! From here there was no land to be seen any-where—just a vast expanse of blue water rippling in the evening sun.

The sea. . . . So peaceful to-day—sometimes so cruel. . . . The sea that dragged you down to its depths. Drowned. . . . Found drowned. . . . Drowned at sea. . . . Drowned—drowned—drowned. . . .

No, she wouldn't remember. . . . She would *not* think of it! All that was over. . . .

7

Dr. Armstrong came to Indian Island just as the sun was sinking into the sea. On the way across he had chatted to the boatman—a local man. He was anxious to find out a little about these people who owned Indian Island, but the man Narracott seemed curiously ill in-formed, or perhaps unwilling to talk.

So Dr. Armstrong chatted instead of the weather and of fishing.

He was tired after his long motor drive. His eyeballs ached. Driv-ing west you were driving against the sun.

Yes, he was very tired. The sea and perfect peace—that was what he needed. He would like, really, to take a long holiday. But he couldn't afford to do that. He could afford it financially, of course, but he couldn't afford to drop out. You were soon forgotten nowa-days. No, now that he had arrived, he must keep his nose to the grindstone.

He thought:

"All the same, this evening, I'll imagine to myself that I'm not going back—that I've done with London and Harley Street and all the rest of it."

There was something magical about an island—the mere word suggested fantasy. You lost touch with the world—an island was a world of its own. A world, perhaps, from which you might never return.

He thought:

"I'm leaving my ordinary life behind me."

And, smiling to himself, he began to make plans, fantastic plans for the future.

He was still smiling when he walked up the rock cut steps.

In a chair on the terrace an old gentleman was sitting and the sight of him was vaguely familiar to Dr. Armstrong. Where had he seen that frog-like face, that tortoise-like neck, that hunched up attitude—yes, and those pale shrewd little eyes? Of course—old Wargrave. He'd given evidence once before him. Always looked half asleep, but was shrewd as could be when it came to a point of law. Had great power with a jury—it was said he could make their minds up for them any day of the week. He'd got one or two unlikely convictions out of them. A hanging judge, some people said.

Funny place to meet him . . . here—out of the world.

8

Mr. Justice Wargrave thought to himself:

"Armstrong? Remember him in the witness box. Very correct and cautious. All doctors are damned fools. Harley Street ones are the worst of the lot." And his mind dwelt malevolently on a recent interview he had had with a suave personage in that very street.

Aloud he grunted:

"Drinks are in the hall."

Dr. Armstrong said:

"I must go and pay my respects to my host and hostess."

Mr. Justice Wargrave closed his eyes again, looking decidedly reptilian, and said:

"You can't do that."

Dr. Armstrong was startled.

"Why not?"

The judge said:

"No host and hostess. Very curious state of affairs. Don't understand this place."

Dr. Armstrong stared at him for a minute. When he thought the old gentleman had actually gone to sleep, Wargrave said suddenly:

"D'you know Constance Culmington?"

"Er—no, I'm afraid I don't."

"It's of no consequence," said the judge. "Very vague woman—and practically unreadable handwriting. I was just wondering if I'd come to the wrong house."

Dr. Armstrong shook his head and went on up to the house.

Mr. Justice Wargrave reflected on the subject of Constance Culmington. Undependable like all women.

His mind went on to the two women in the house, the tight-lipped old maid and the girl. He didn't care for the girl, cold-blooded young hussy. No, three women, if you counted the Rogers woman. Odd creature, she looked scared to death. Respectable pair and knew their job.

Rogers coming out on the terrace that minute, the judge asked him:

"Is Lady Constance Culmington expected, do you know?"

Rogers stared at him.

"No, sir, not to my knowledge."

The judge's eyebrows rose. But he only grunted.

He thought:

"Indian Island, eh? There's a nigger in the woodpile."

9

Anthony Marston was in his bath. He luxuriated in the steaming water. His limbs had felt cramped after his long drive. Very few thoughts passed through his head. Anthony was a creature of sensation—and of action.

He thought to himself:

"Must go through with it, I suppose," and thereafter dismissed everything from his mind.

Warm steaming water—tired limbs—presently a shave—a cocktail—dinner.

And after—?

10

Mr. Blore was tying his tie. He wasn't very good at this sort of thing.

Did he look all right? He supposed so.

Nobody had been exactly cordial to him. . . . Funny the way they all eyed each other—as though they *knew*. . . .

Well, it was up to him.

He didn't mean to bungle his job.

He glanced up at the framed nursery rhyme over the mantelpiece. Neat touch, having that there!

He thought:

Remember this island when I was a kid. Never thought I'd be doing this sort of a job in a house here. Good thing, perhaps, that one can't foresee the future. . . .

11

General Macarthur was frowning to himself.

Damn it all, the whole thing was deuced odd! Not at all what he'd been led to expect. . . .

For two pins he'd make an excuse and get away. . . . Throw up the whole business. . . .

But the motor boat had gone back to the mainland.

He'd have to stay.

That fellow Lombard now, he was a queer chap.

Not straight. He'd swear the man wasn't straight.

12

As the gong sounded, Philip Lombard came out of his room and walked to the head of the stairs. He moved like a panther, smoothly

and noiselessly. There was something of the panther about him altogether. A beast of prey—pleasant to the eye.

He was smiling to himself.

A week—eh?

He was going to enjoy that week.

13

In her bedroom, Emily Brent, dressed in black silk ready for dinner, was reading her Bible.

Her lips moved as she followed the words:

*"The heathen are sunk down in the pit that they made: in the net
which they hid is their own foot taken. The Lord is known by the
judgment which he executeth: the wicked is snared in the work of his
own hands. The wicked shall be turned into hell."*

Her tight lips closed. She shut the Bible.

Rising, she pinned a cairngorm brooch at her neck, and went down
to dinner.

CHAPTER 3

DINNER WAS drawing to a close.

The food had been good, the wine perfect. Rogers waited well.

Every one was in better spirits. They had begun to talk to each
other with more freedom and intimacy.

Mr. Justice Wargrave, mellowed by the excellent port, was being
amusing in a caustic fashion, Dr. Armstrong and Tony Marston were
listening to him. Miss Brent chatted to General Macarthur, they had
discovered some mutual friends. Vera Claythorne was asking Mr.
Davis intelligent questions about South Africa. Mr. Davis was quite
fluent on the subject. Lombard listened to the conversation. Once or
twice he looked up quickly, and his eyes narrowed. Now and then his
eyes played round the table, studying the others.

Anthony Marston said suddenly:

"Quaint, these things, aren't they?"

In the centre of the round table, on a circular glass stand, were some little china figures.

"Indians," said Tony. "Indian Island. I suppose that's the idea."

Vera leaned forward.

"I wonder. How many are there? Ten?"

"Yes—ten there are."

Vera cried:

"What fun! They're the ten little Indian boys of the nursery rhyme, I suppose. In my bedroom the rhyme is framed and hung up over the mantelpiece."

Lombard said:

"In my room, too."

"And mine."

"And mine."

Everybody joined the chorus. Vera said:

"It's an amusing idea, isn't it?"

Mr. Justice Wargrave grunted:

"Remarkably childish," and helped himself to port.

Emily Brent looked at Vera Claythorne. Vera Claythorne looked at Miss Brent. The two women rose.

In the drawing-room, the French windows were open onto the terrace and the sound of the sea murmuring against the rocks came up to them.

Emily Brent said: "Pleasant sound."

Vera said sharply: "I hate it."

Miss Brent's eyes looked at her in surprise. Vera flushed. She said, more composedly:

"I don't think this place would be very agreeable in a storm."

Emily Brent agreed.

"I've no doubt the house is shut up in winter," she said. "You'd never get servants to stay here for one thing."

Vera murmured:

"It must be difficult to get servants anyway."

Emily Brent said:

"Mrs. Oliver has been lucky to get these two. The woman's a good cook."

Vera thought:

"Funny how elderly people always get names wrong."

She said:

"Yes, I think Mrs. Owen has been very lucky indeed."

Emily Brent had brought a small piece of embroidery out of her bag. Now, as she was about to thread her needle, she paused. She said sharply:

"Owen? Did you say Owen?"

"Yes."

Emily Brent said sharply:

"I've never met any one called Owen in my life."

Vera stared.

"But surely—"

She did not finish her sentence. The door opened and the men joined them. Rogers followed them into the room with the coffee tray.

The judge came and sat down by Emily Brent. Armstrong came up to Vera. Tony Marston strolled to the open window. Blore studied with naïve surprise a statuette in brass—wondering perhaps if its bizarre angularities were really supposed to be the female figure. General Macarthur stood with his back to the mantelpiece. He pulled at his little white moustache. That had been a damned good dinner! His spirits were rising. Lombard turned over the pages of *Punch* that lay with other papers on a table by the wall.

Rogers went round with the coffee tray. The coffee was good—really black and very hot.

The whole party had dined well. They were satisfied with themselves and with life. The hands of the clock pointed to twenty minutes past nine. There was a silence—a comfortable replete silence.

Into that silence came The Voice. Without warning, inhuman, penetrating . . .

"Ladies and gentlemen! Silence, please!"

Every one was startled. They looked round—at each other, at the walls. Who was speaking?

The Voice went on—a high clear voice.

You are charged with the following indictments:

Edward George Armstrong, that you did upon the 14th day of March, 1925, cause the death of Louisa Mary Clees.

Emily Caroline Brent, that upon the 5th November, 1931, you were responsible for the death of Beatrice Taylor.

William Henry Blore, that you brought about the death of James Stephen Landor on October 10th, 1928.

Vera Elizabeth Claythorne, that on the 11th day of August, 1935, you killed Cyril Ogilvie Hamilton.

Philip Lombard, that upon a date in February, 1932, you were

*guilty of the death of twenty-one men, members of an East African
tribe.*

*John Gordon Macarthur, that on the 4th of January, 1917, you
deliberately sent your wife's lover, Arthur Richmond, to his death.*

*Anthony James Marston, that upon the 14th day of November
last, you were guilty of the murder of John and Lucy Combes.*

*Thomas Rogers and Ethel Rogers, that on the 6th of May, 1929,
you brought about the death of Jennifer Brady.*

*Lawrence John Wargrave, that upon the 10th day of June, 1930,
you were guilty of the murder of Edward Seton.*

Prisoners at the bar, have you anything to say in your defence?

2

The Voice had stopped.

There was a moment's petrified silence and then a resounding
crash! Rogers had dropped the coffee tray!

At the same moment, from somewhere outside the room there
came a scream and the sound of a thud.

Lombard was the first to move. He leapt to the door and flung it
open. Outside, lying in a huddled mass, was Mrs. Rogers.

Lombard called:

"Marston."

Anthony sprang to help him. Between them, they lifted up the
woman and carried her into the drawing-room.

Dr. Armstrong came across quickly. He helped them to lift her
onto the sofa and bent over her. He said quickly:

"It's nothing. She's fainted, that's all. She'll be round in a minute."

Lombard said to Rogers:

"Get some brandy."

Rogers, his face white, his hands shaking, murmured:

"Yes, sir," and slipped quickly out of the room.

Vera cried out:

"Who was that speaking? Where was he? It sounded—it sounded—"

General Macarthur spluttered out:

"What's going on here? What kind of a practical joke was that?"

His hand was shaking. His shoulders sagged. He looked suddenly
ten years older.

Blore was mopping his face with a handkerchief.

Only Mr. Justice Wargrave and Miss Brent seemed comparatively unmoved. Emily Brent sat upright, her head held high. In both cheeks was a spot of hard colour. The judge sat in his habitual pose, his head sunk down into his neck. With one hand he gently scratched his ear. Only his eyes were active, darting round and round the room, puzzled, alert with intelligence.

Again it was Lombard who acted. Armstrong being busy with the collapsed woman, Lombard was free once more to take the initiative.

He said:

"That voice? It sounded as though it were in the room."

Vera cried:

"Who was it? Who was it? It wasn't one of us."

Like the judge, Lombard's eyes wandered slowly round the room. They rested a minute on the open window, then he shook his head decisively. Suddenly his eyes lighted up. He moved forward swiftly to where a door near the fireplace led into an adjoining room.

With a swift gesture, he caught the handle and flung the door open. He passed through and immediately uttered an exclamation of satisfaction.

He said:

"Ah, here we are."

The others crowded after him. Only Miss Brent remained alone sitting erect in her chair.

Inside the second room a table had been brought up close to the wall which adjoined the drawing-room. On the table was a gramophone—an old-fashioned type with a large trumpet attached. The mouth of the trumpet was against the wall, and Lombard, pushing it aside, indicated where two or three small holes had been unobtrusively bored through the wall.

Adjusting the gramophone he replaced the needle on the record and immediately they heard again: *"You are charged with the following indictments—"*

Vera cried:

"Turn it off! Turn it off! It's horrible!"

Lombard obeyed.

Dr. Armstrong said, with a sigh of relief:

"A disgraceful and heartless practical joke, I suppose."

The small clear voice of Mr. Justice Wargrave murmured:

"So you think it's a joke, do you?"

The doctor stared at him.

"What else could it be?"

The hand of the judge gently stroked his upper lip.

He said:

"At the moment I'm not prepared to give an opinion."

Anthony Marston broke in. He said:

"Look here, there's one thing you've forgotten. Who the devil turned the thing on and set it going?"

Wargrave murmured:

"Yes, I think we must inquire into that."

He led the way back into the drawing-room. The others followed.

Rogers had just come in with a glass of brandy. Miss Brent was bending over the moaning form of Mrs. Rogers.

Adroitly Rogers slipped between the two women.

"Allow me, Madam, I'll speak to her. Ethel—Ethel—it's all right. All right, do you hear? Pull yourself together."

Mrs. Rogers' breath came in quick gasps. Her eyes, staring frightened eyes, went round and round the ring of faces. There was urgency in Rogers' tone.

"Pull yourself together, Ethel."

Dr. Armstrong spoke to her soothingly.

"You'll be all right now, Mrs. Rogers. Just a nasty turn."

She said:

"Did I faint, sir?"

"Yes."

"It was The Voice—that awful voice—*like a judgment*—"

Her face turned green again, her eyelids fluttered.

Dr. Armstrong said sharply:

"Where's that brandy?"

Rogers had put it down on a little table. Some one handed it to the doctor and he bent over the gasping woman with it.

"Drink this, Mrs. Rogers."

She drank, choking a little and gasping. The spirit did her good. The colour returned to her face. She said:

"I'm all right now. It just—gave me a turn."

Rogers said quickly:

"Of course it did. It gave me a turn too. Fair made me drop that tray. Wicked lies, it was! I'd like to know—"

He was interrupted. It was only a cough—a dry little cough but it had the effect of stopping him in full cry. He stared at Mr. Justice Wargrave and the latter coughed again. Then he said:

"Who put that record on the gramophone? Was it you, Rogers?"

Rogers cried:

"I didn't know what it was. Before God, I didn't know what it was, sir. If I had I'd never have done it."

The judge said drily:

"That is probably true. But I think you'd better explain, Rogers."

The butler wiped his face with a handkerchief. He said earnestly:

"I was just obeying orders, sir, that's all."

"Whose orders?"

"Mr. Owen's."

Mr. Justice Wargrave said:

"Let me get this quite clear. Mr. Owen's orders were—what exactly?"

Rogers said:

"I was to put a record on the gramophone. I'd find the record in the drawer and my wife was to start the gramophone when I'd gone into the drawing-room with the coffee tray."

The judge murmured:

"A very remarkable story."

Rogers cried:

"It's the truth, sir. I swear to God it's the truth. I didn't know what it was—not for a moment. It had a name on it—I thought it was just a piece of music."

Wargrave looked at Lombard.

"Was there a title on it?"

Lombard nodded. He grinned suddenly, showing his white pointed teeth.

He said:

"Quite right, sir. It was entitled *Swan Song*. . . ."

3

General Macarthur broke out suddenly. He exclaimed:

"The whole thing is preposterous—preposterous! Slinging accusations about like this! Something must be done about it. This fellow Owen whoever he is—"

Emily Brent interrupted. She said sharply:

"That's just it, who is he?"

The judge interposed. He spoke with the authority that a lifetime in the courts had given him. He said:

"That is exactly what we must go into very carefully. I should suggest that you get your wife to bed first of all, Rogers. Then come back here."

"Yes, sir."

Dr. Armstrong said:

"I'll give you a hand, Rogers."

Leaning on the two men, Mrs. Rogers tottered out of the room. When they had gone Tony Marston said:

"Don't know about you, sir, but I could do with a drink."

Lombard said:

"I agree."

Tony said:

"I'll go and forage."

He went out of the room.

He returned a second or two later.

"Found them all waiting on a tray outside ready to be brought in."

He set down his burden carefully. The next minute or two was spent in dispensing drinks. General Macarthur had a stiff whiskey and so did the judge. Every one felt the need of a stimulant. Only Emily Brent demanded and obtained a glass of water.

Dr. Armstrong re-entered the room.

"She's all right," he said. "I've given her a sedative to take. What's that, a drink? I could do with one."

Several of the men refilled their glasses. A moment or two later Rogers re-entered the room.

Mr. Justice Wargrave took charge of the proceedings. The room became an impromptu court of law.

The judge said:

"Now then, Rogers, we must get to the bottom of this. Who is this Mr. Owen?"

Rogers stared.

"He owns this place, sir."

"I am aware of the fact. What I want you to tell me is what you yourself know about the man."

Rogers shook his head.

"I can't say, sir. You see, I've never seen him."

There was a faint stir in the room.

General Macarthur said:

"You've never seen him? What d'yer mean?"

"We've only been here just under a week, sir, my wife and I. We were engaged by letter, through an agency. The Regina Agency in Plymouth."

Blore nodded.

"Old established firm," he volunteered.

Wargrave said:

"Have you got that letter?"

"The letter engaging us? No, sir. I didn't keep it."

"Go on with your story. You were engaged, as you say, by letter."

"Yes, sir. We were to arrive on a certain day. We did. Everything was in order here. Plenty of food in stock and everything very nice. Just needed dusting and that."

"What next?"

"Nothing, sir. We got orders—by letter again—to prepare the rooms for a houseparty and then yesterday by the afternoon post I got another letter from Mr. Owen. It said he and Mrs. Owen were detained and to do the best we could and it gave the instructions about dinner and coffee and putting on the gramophone record."

The judge said sharply:

"Surely you've got *that* letter?"

"Yes, sir, I've got it here."

He produced it from a pocket. The judge took it.

"H'm," he said. "Headed Ritz Hotel and typewritten."

With a quick movement Blore was beside him.

He said:

"If you'll just let me have a look."

He twitched it out of the other's hand, and ran his eye over it. He murmured:

"Coronation machine. Quite new—no defects. Ensign paper—the most widely used make. You won't get anything out of that. Might be fingerprints, but I doubt it."

Wargrave stared at him with sudden attention.

Anthony Marston was standing beside Blore looking over his shoulder. He said:

"Got some fancy Christian names, hasn't he? Ulick Norman Owen. Quite a mouthful."

The old judge said with a slight start:

"I am obliged to you, Mr. Marston. You have drawn my attention to a curious and suggestive point."

He looked round at the others and thrusting his neck forward like an angry tortoise, he said:

"I think the time has come for us all to pool our information. It would be well, I think, for everybody to come forward with all the information they have regarding the owner of this house." He paused and then went on. "We are all his guests. I think it would be profitable if each one of us were to explain exactly how that came about."

There was a moment's pause and then Emily Brent spoke with decision.

"There's something very peculiar about all this," she said. "I received a letter with a signature that was not very easy to read. It purported to be from a woman I had met at a certain summer resort two or three years ago. I took the name to be either Ogden or Oliver. I am acquainted with a Mrs. Oliver and also with a Miss Ogden. I am quite certain that I have never met, or become friendly with, anyone of the name of Owen."

Mr. Justice Wargrave said:

"You have that letter, Miss Brent?"

"Yes, I will fetch it for you."

She went away and returned a minute later with the letter.

The judge read it. He said:

"I begin to understand. . . . Miss Claythorne?"

Vera explained the circumstances of her secretarial engagement.

The judge said:

"Marston?"

Anthony said:

"Got a wire. From a pal of mine. Badger Berkeley. Surprised me at the time because I had an idea the old horse had gone to Norway. Told me to roll up here."

Again Wargrave nodded. He said:

"Dr. Armstrong?"

"I was called in professionally."

"I see. You had no previous acquaintanceship with the family?"

"No. A colleague of mine was mentioned in the letter."

The judge said:

"To give verisimilitude. . . . Yes, and that colleague, I presume, was momentarily out of touch with you?"

"Well—er—yes."

Lombard, who had been staring at Blore, said suddenly:

"Look here, I've just thought of something—"

The judge lifted a hand.

"In a minute—"

"But I—"

"We will take one thing at a time, Mr. Lombard. We are at present inquiring into the causes which have resulted in our being assembled here to-night. General Macarthur?"

Pulling at his moustache, the General muttered:

"Got a letter—from this fellow Owen—mentioned some old pals of mine who were to be here—hoped I'd excuse informal invitation. Haven't kept the letter, I'm afraid."

Wargrave said:

"Mr. Lombard?"

Lombard's brain had been active. Was he to come out in the open, or not? He made up his mind.

"Same sort of thing," he said. "Invitation, mentioned of mutual friends—I fell for it all right. I've torn up the letter."

Mr. Justice Wargrave turned his attention to Mr. Blore. His forefinger stroked his upper lip and his voice was dangerously polite.

He said: "Just now we had a somewhat disturbing experience. An apparently disembodied voice spoke to us all by name, uttering certain precise accusations against us. We will deal with those accusations presently. At the moment I am interested in a minor point. Amongst the names recited was that of William Henry Blore. But as far as we know there is no one named Blore amongst us. The name of Davis was *not* mentioned. What have you to say about that, Mr. Davis?"

Blore said sulkily:

"Cat's out of the bag, it seems. I suppose I'd better admit that my name isn't Davis."

"You are William Henry Blore?"

"That's right."

"I will add something," said Lombard. "Not only are you here under a false name, Mr. Blore, but in addition I've noticed this evening that you're a first-class liar. You claim to have come from Natal, South Africa. I know South Africa and Natal and I'm prepared to swear that you've never set foot in South Africa in your life."

All eyes were turned on Blore. Angry suspicious eyes. Anthony Marston moved a step nearer to him. His fists clenched themselves.

"Now then, you swine," he said. "Any explanation?"

Blore flung back his head and set his square jaw.

"You gentlemen have got me wrong," he said. "I've got my credentials and you can see them. I'm an ex-C.I.D. man. I run a detective agency in Plymouth. I was put on this job."

Mr. Justice Wargrave asked: "By whom?"

"This man Owen. Enclosed a handsome money order for expenses and instructed me as to what he wanted done. I was to join the houseparty, posing as a guest. I was given all your names. I was to watch you all."

"Any reason given?"

Blore said bitterly:

"Mrs. Owen's jewels. Mrs. Owen my foot! I don't believe there's any such person."

Again the forefinger of the judge stroked his lip, this time appreciatively.

"Your conclusions are, I think, justified," he said. "Ulick Norman Owen! In Miss Brent's letter, though the signature of the surname is a mere scrawl the Christian names are reasonably clear—Una Nancy —in either case, you notice, the same initials. Ulick Norman Owen— Una Nancy Owen—each time, that is to say, U. N. Owen. Or by a slight stretch of fancy, UNKNOWN!"

Vera cried:

"But this is fantastic—mad!"

The judge nodded gently.

He said:

"Oh, yes. I've no doubt in my own mind that we have been invited here by a madman—probably a dangerous homicidal lunatic."

CHAPTER 4

THERE WAS a moment's silence—a silence of dismay and bewilderment. Then the judge's small clear voice took up the thread once more.

"We will now proceed to the next stage of our inquiry. First, however, I will just add my own credentials to the list."

He took a letter from his pocket and tossed it onto the table.

"This purports to be from an old friend of mine, Lady Constance Culmington. I have not seen her for some years. She went to the East. It is exactly the kind of vague incoherent letter she would write, urging me to join her here and referring to her host and hostess in the vaguest of terms. The same technique, you will observe. I only mention it because it agrees with the other evidence—from all of which emerges one interesting point. *Whoever it was who enticed us here, that person knows or has taken the trouble to find out a good deal about us all.* He, whoever he may be, is aware of my friendship for

Lady Constance—and is familiar with her epistolary style. He knows something about Dr. Armstrong's colleagues and their present whereabouts. He knows the nickname of Mr. Marston's friend and the kind of telegrams he sends. He knows exactly where Miss Brent was two years ago for her holiday and the kind of people she met there. He knows all about General Macarthur's old cronies."

He paused. Then he said:

"*He knows, you see, a good deal.* And out of his knowledge concerning us, he has made certain definite accusations."

Immediately a babel broke out.

General Macarthur shouted:

"A pack of damn lies! Slander!"

Vera cried out:

"It's iniquitous!" Her breath came fast. "Wicked!"

Rogers said hoarsely:

"A lie—a wicked lie . . . we never did—neither of us. . . ."

Anthony Marston growled:

"Don't know what the damned fool was getting at!"

The upraised hand of Mr. Justice Wargrave calmed the tumult.

He said, picking his words with care:

"I wish to say this. Our unknown friend accuses me of the murder of one Edward Seton. I remember Seton perfectly well. He came up before me for trial in June of the year 1930. He was charged with the murder of an elderly woman. He was very ably defended and made a good impression on the jury in the witness box. Nevertheless, on the evidence, he was certainly guilty. I summed up accordingly, and the jury brought in a verdict of Guilty. In passing sentence of death I concurred with the verdict. An appeal was lodged on the grounds of misdirection. The appeal was rejected and the man was duly executed. I wish to say before you all that my conscience is perfectly clear on the matter. I did my duty and nothing more. I passed sentence on a rightly convicted murderer."

Armstrong was remembering now. The Seton case! The verdict had come as a great surprise. He had met Matthews, K.C., on one of the days of the trial dining at a restaurant. Matthews had been confident. "Not a doubt of the verdict. Acquittal practically certain." And then afterwards he had heard comments: "Judge was dead against him. Turned the jury right round and they brought him in guilty. Quite legal, though. Old Wargrave knows his law." "It was almost as though he had a private down on the fellow."

All these memories rushed through the doctor's mind. Before he could consider the wisdom of the question he had asked impulsively:

"Did you know Seton at all? I mean previous to the case."

The hooded reptilian eyes met his. In a clear cold voice the judge said:

"I knew nothing of Seton previous to the case."

Armstrong said to himself:

"The fellow's lying—I know he's lying."

2

Vera Claythorne spoke in a trembling voice.

She said:

"I'd like to tell you. About that child—Cyril Hamilton. I was nursery governess to him. He was forbidden to swim out far. One day, when my attention was distracted, he started off. I swam after him . . . I couldn't get there in time. . . . It was awful. . . . But it wasn't my fault. At the inquest the Coroner exonerated me. And his mother—she was so kind. If even she didn't blame me, why should—why should this awful thing be said? It's not fair—not fair . . ."

She broke down, weeping bitterly.

General Macarthur patted her shoulder.

He said:

"There, there, my dear. Of course it's not true. Fellow's a madman. A madman! Got a bee in his bonnet! Got hold of the wrong end of the stick all round."

He stood erect, squaring his shoulders. He barked out:

"Best really to leave this sort of thing unanswered. However, feel I ought to say—no truth—no truth whatever in what he said about—er—young Arthur Richmond. Richmond was one of my officers. I sent him on a reconnaissance. He was killed. Natural course of events in war time. Wish to say resent very much—slur on my wife. Best woman in the world. Absolutely—Caesar's wife!"

General Macarthur sat down. His shaking hand pulled at his moustache. The effort to speak had cost him a good deal.

Lombard spoke. His eyes were amused. He said:

"About those natives—"

Marston said:

"What about them?"

Philip Lombard grinned.

"Story's quite true! I left 'em! Matter of self-preservation. We were lost in the bush. I and a couple of other fellows took what food there was and cleared out."

General Macarthur said sternly:

"You abandoned your men—left them to starve?"

Lombard said:

"Not quite the act of a *pukka sahib,* I'm afraid. But self-preservation's a man's first duty. And natives don't mind dying, you know. They don't feel about it as Europeans do."

Vera lifted her face from her hands. She said, staring at him:

"You left them—to *die?*"

Lombard answered:

"I left them to die."

His amused eyes looked into her horrified ones.

Anthony Marston said in a slow puzzled voice:

"I've just been thinking—John and Lucy Combes. Must have been a couple of kids I ran over near Cambridge. Beastly bad luck."

Mr. Justice Wargrave said acidly:

"For them, or for you?"

Anthony said:

"Well, I was thinking—for me—but of course, you're right, sir, it was damned bad luck on them. Of course it was a pure accident. They rushed out of some cottage or other. I had my licence endorsed for a year. Beastly nuisance."

Dr. Armstrong said warmly:

"This speeding's all wrong—all wrong! Young men like you are a danger to the community."

Anthony shrugged his shoulders.

He said:

"Speed's come to stay. English roads are hopeless, of course. Can't get up a decent pace on them."

He looked round vaguely for his glass, picked it up off a table and went over to the side table and helped himself to another whiskey and soda. He said over his shoulder:

"Well, anyway, it wasn't my fault. Just an accident!"

3

The manservant, Rogers, had been moistening his lips and twisting his hands. He said now in a low deferential voice:

"If I might just say a word, sir."

Lombard said:

"Go ahead, Rogers."

Rogers cleared his throat and passed his tongue once more over his dry lips.

"There was a mention, sir, of me and Mrs. Rogers. And of Miss Brady. There isn't a word of truth in it, sir. My wife and I were with Miss Brady till she died. She was always in poor health, sir, always from the time we came to her. There was a storm, sir, that night—the night she was taken bad. The telephone was out of order. We couldn't get the doctor to her. I went for him, sir, on foot. But he got there too late. We'd done everything possible for her, sir. Devoted to her, we were. Any one will tell you the same. There was never a word said against us. Not a word."

Lombard looked thoughtfully at the man's twitching face, his dry lips, the fright in his eyes. He remembered the crash of the falling coffee tray. He thought, but did not say, "Oh, yeah?"

Blore spoke—spoke in his hearty bullying official manner. He said:

"Came into a little something at her death, though? Eh?"

Rogers drew himself up. He said stiffly:

"Miss Brady left us a legacy in recognition of our faithful services. And why not, I'd like to know?"

Lombard said:

"What about yourself, Mr. Blore?"

"What about me?"

"Your name was included in the list."

Blore went purple.

"Landor, you mean? That was the bank robbery—London and Commercial."

Mr. Justice Wargrave stirred. He said:

"I remember. It didn't come before me, but I remember the case. Landor was convicted on your evidence. You were the police officer in charge of the case?"

Blore said:

"I was."

"Landor got penal servitude for life and died in Dartmoor a year later. He was a delicate man."

Blore said:

"He was a crook. It was he who knocked out the night watchman. The case was quite clear against him."

Wargrave said slowly:

"You were complimented, I think, on your able handling of the case."

Blore said sulkily:

"I got my promotion."

He added in a thick voice:

"I was only doing my duty."

Lombard laughed—a sudden ringing laugh. He said:

"What a duty-loving, law-abiding lot we all seem to be! Myself excepted. What about you, doctor—and your little professional mistake? Illegal operation, was it?"

Emily Brent glanced at him in sharp distaste and drew herself away a little.

Dr. Armstrong, very much master of himself, shook his head good-humouredly.

"I'm at a loss to understand the matter," he said. "The name meant nothing to me when it was spoken. What was it—Clees? Close? I really can't remember having a patient of that name, or being connected with a death in any way. The thing's a complete mystery to me. Of course, it's a long time ago. It might possibly be one of my operation cases in hospital. They come too late, so many of these people. Then, when the patient dies, they always consider it's the surgeon's fault."

He sighed, shaking his head.

He thought:

Drunk—that's what it was—drunk. . . . And I operated! Nerves all to pieces—hands shaking. I killed her, all right. Poor devil—elderly woman—simple job if I'd been sober. Lucky for me there's loyalty in our profession. The Sister knew, of course—but she held her tongue. God, it gave me a shock! Pulled me up. But who could have known about it—after all these years?

4

There was a silence in the room. Everybody was looking, covertly or openly, at Emily Brent. It was a minute or two before she became aware of the expectation. Her eyebrows rose on her narrow forehead. She said:

"Are you waiting for me to say something? I have nothing to say."

The judge said:

"Nothing, Miss Brent?"

"Nothing."

Her lips closed tightly.

The judge stroked his face. He said mildly:

"You reserve your defence?"

Miss Brent said coldly:

"There is no question of defence. I have always acted in accordance with the dictates of my conscience. I have nothing with which to reproach myself."

There was an unsatisfied feeling in the air. But Emily Brent was not one to be swayed by public opinion. She sat unyielding.

The judge cleared his throat once or twice. Then he said:

"Our inquiry rests there. Now, Rogers, who else is there on this island besides ourselves and you and your wife?"

"Nobody, sir. Nobody at all."

"You're sure of that?"

"Quite sure, sir."

Wargrave said:

"I am not yet clear as to the purpose of our Unknown host in getting us to assemble here. But in my opinion this person, whoever he may be, is not sane in the accepted sense of the word.

"He may be dangerous. In my opinion it would be well for us to leave this place as soon as possible. I suggest that we leave to-night."

Rogers said:

"I beg your pardon, sir, but there's no boat on the island."

"No boat at all?"

"No, sir."

"How do you communicate with the mainland?"

"Fred Narracott, he comes over every morning, sir. He brings the bread and the milk and the post, and takes the orders."

Mr. Justice Wargrave said:

"Then in my opinion it would be well if we all left to-morrow morning as soon as Narracott's boat arrives."

There was a chorus of agreement with only one dissentient voice. It was Anthony Marston who disagreed with the majority.

"A bit unsporting, what?" he said. "Ought to ferret out the mystery before we go. Whole thing's like a detective story. Positively thrilling."

The judge said acidly:

"At my time of life, I have no desire for 'thrills,' as you call them."

Anthony said with a grin:

"The legal life's narrowing! I'm all for crime! Here's to it."

He picked up his drink and drank it off at a gulp.

Too quickly, perhaps. He choked—choked badly. His face contorted, turned purple. He gasped for breath—then slid down off his chair, the glass falling from his hand.

CHAPTER 5

IT WAS so sudden and so unexpected that it took every one's breath away. They remained stupidly staring at the crumpled figure on the floor.

Then Dr. Armstrong jumped up and went over to him, kneeling beside him. When he raised his head his eyes were bewildered.

He said in a low awe-struck whisper:

"My God! he's dead."

They didn't take it in. Not at once.

Dead? *Dead?* That young Norse God in the prime of his health and strength. Struck down all in a moment. Healthy young men didn't die like that, choking over a whiskey and soda. . . .

No, they couldn't take it in.

Dr. Armstrong was peering into the dead man's face. He sniffed at the blue twisted lips. Then he picked up the glass from which Anthony Marston had been drinking.

General Macarthur said:

"Dead? D'you mean the fellow just choked and—and died?"

The physician said:

"You can call it choking if you like. He died of asphyxiation right enough."

He was sniffing now at the glass. He dipped a finger into the dregs and very cautiously just touched the finger with the tip of his tongue.

His expression altered.

General Macarthur said:

"Never knew a man could die like that—just of a choking fit!"

Emily Brent said in a clear voice:

"In the midst of life we are in death."

Dr. Armstrong stood up. He said brusquely:

"No, a man doesn't die of a mere choking fit. Marston's death wasn't what we call a natural death."

Vera said almost in a whisper:

"Was there—something—in the whiskey?"

Armstrong nodded.

"Yes. Can't say exactly. Everything points to one of the Cyanides. No distinctive smell of Prussic Acid, probably Potassium Cyanide. It acts pretty well instantaneously."

The judge said sharply:

"It was in his glass?"

"Yes."

The doctor strode to the table where the drinks were. He removed the stopper from the whiskey and smelt and tasted it. Then he tasted the soda water. He shook his head.

"They're both all right."

Lombard said:

"You mean—he must have put the stuff in his glass *himself?*"

Armstrong nodded with a curiously dissatisfied expression. He said:

"Seems like it."

Blore said:

"Suicide, eh? That's a queer go."

Vera said slowly:

"You'd never think that *he* would kill himself. He was so alive. He was—oh—enjoying himself! When he came down the hill in his car this evening he looked—he looked—oh, I can't *explain!*"

But they knew what she meant. Anthony Marston, in the height of his youth and manhood, had seemed like a being who was immortal. And now, crumpled and broken, he lay on the floor.

Dr. Armstrong said:

"Is there any possibility other than suicide?"

Slowly every one shook his head. There could be no other explanation. The drinks themselves were untampered with. They had all seen Anthony Marston go across and help himself. It followed therefore that any Cyanide in the drink must have been put there by Anthony Marston himself.

And yet—why should Anthony Marston commit suicide?

Blore said thoughtfully:

"You know, doctor, it doesn't seem right to me. I shouldn't have said Mr. Marston was a suicidal type of gentleman."

Armstrong answered:

"I agree."

2

They had left it like that. What else was there to say?

Together Armstrong and Lombard had carried the inert body of Anthony Marston to his bedroom and had laid him there covered over with a sheet.

When they came downstairs again, the others were standing in a group, shivering a little, though the night was not cold.

Emily Brent said:

"We'd better go to bed. It's late."

It was past twelve o'clock. The suggestion was a wise one—yet every one hesitated. It was as though they clung to each other's company for reassurance.

The judge said:

"Yes, we must get some sleep."

Rogers said:

"I haven't cleared yet—in the dining-room."

Lombard said curtly:

"Do it in the morning."

Armstrong said to him:

"Is your wife all right?"

"I'll go and see, sir."

He returned a minute or two later.

"Sleeping beautiful, she is."

"Good," said the doctor. "Don't disturb her."

"No, sir. I'll just put things straight in the dining-room and make sure everything's locked up right, and then I'll turn in."

He went across the hall into the dining-room.

The others went upstairs, a slow unwilling procession.

If this had been an old house, with creaking wood, and dark shadows, and heavily panelled walls, there might have been an eerie feeling. But this house was the essence of modernity. There were no dark corners—no possible sliding panels—it was flooded with electric light—everything was new and bright and shining. There was nothing hidden in this house, nothing concealed. It had no atmosphere about it.

Somehow, that was the most frightening thing of all. . . .

They exchanged good-nights on the upper landing. Each of them went into his or her own room, and each of them automatically, almost without conscious thought, locked the door. . . .

3

In his pleasant softly tinted room, Mr. Justice Wargrave removed his garments and prepared himself for bed.

He was thinking about Edward Seton.

He remembered Seton very well. His fair hair, his blue eyes, his habit of looking you straight in the face with a pleasant air of straightforwardness. That was what had made so good an impression on the jury.

Llewellyn, for the Crown, had bungled it a bit. He had been over-vehement, had tried to prove too much.

Matthews, on the other hand, for the Defence, had been good. His points had told. His cross-examinations had been deadly. His handling of his client in the witness box had been masterly.

And Seton had come through the ordeal of cross-examination well. He had not got excited or over-vehement. The jury had been impressed. It had seemed to Matthews, perhaps, as though everything had been over bar the shouting.

The judge wound up his watch carefully and placed it by the bed.

He remembered exactly how he had felt sitting there—listening, making notes, appreciating everything, tabulating every scrap of evidence that told against the prisoner.

He'd enjoyed that case! Matthews' final speech had been first-class. Llewellyn, coming after it, had failed to remove the good impression that the defending counsel had made.

And then had come his own summing up. . . .

Carefully, Mr. Justice Wargrave removed his false teeth and

dropped them into a glass of water. The shrunken lips fell in. It was a cruel mouth now, cruel and predatory.

Hooding his eyes, the judge smiled to himself.

He'd cooked Seton's goose all right!

With a slightly rheumatic grunt, he climbed into bed and turned out the electric light.

4

Downstairs in the dining-room, Rogers stood puzzled.

He was staring at the china figures in the centre of the table.

He muttered to himself:

"That's a rum go! I could have sworn there were ten of them."

5

General Macarthur tossed from side to side.

Sleep would not come to him.

In the darkness he kept seeing Arthur Richmond's face.

He'd liked Arthur—he'd been damned fond of Arthur. He'd been pleased that Leslie liked him too.

Leslie was so capricious. Lots of good fellows that Leslie would turn up her nose at and pronounce dull. "Dull!" Just like that.

But she hadn't found Arthur Richmond dull. They'd got on well together from the beginning. They'd talked of plays and music and pictures together. She'd teased him, made fun of him, ragged him. And he, Macarthur, had been delighted at the thought that Leslie took quite a motherly interest in the boy.

Motherly indeed! Damn fool not to remember that Richmond was twenty-eight to Leslie's twenty-nine.

He'd loved Leslie. He could see her now. Her heart-shaped face, and her dancing deep grey eyes, and the brown curling mass of her hair. He'd loved Leslie and he'd believed in her absolutely.

Out there in France, in the middle of all the hell of it, he'd sat thinking of her, taken her picture out of the breast pocket of his tunic.

And then—he'd found out!

It had come about exactly in the way things happened in books. The letter in the wrong envelope. She'd been writing to them both and she'd put her letter to Richmond in the envelope addressed to her husband. Even now, all these years after, he could feel the shock of it—the pain. . . .

God, it had hurt!

And the business had been going on some time. The letter made that clear. Week-ends! Richmond's last leave. . . .

Leslie—Leslie and Arthur!

God damn the fellow! Damn his smiling face, his brisk "Yes, sir." Liar and hypocrite! Stealer of another man's wife!

It had gathered slowly—that cold murderous rage.

He'd managed to carry on as usual—to show nothing. He'd tried to make his manner to Richmond just the same.

Had he succeeded? He thought so. Richmond hadn't suspected. Inequalities of temper were easily accounted for out there, where men's nerves were continually snapping under the strain.

Only young Armitage had looked at him curiously once or twice. Quite a young chap, but he'd had perceptions, that boy.

Armitage, perhaps, had guessed—when the time came.

He'd sent Richmond deliberately to death. Only a miracle could have brought him through unhurt. That miracle didn't happen. Yes, he'd sent Richmond to his death and he wasn't sorry. It had been easy enough. Mistakes were being made all the time, officers being sent to death needlessly. All was confusion, panic. People might say afterwards, "Old Macarthur lost his nerve a bit, made some colossal blunders, sacrificed some of his best men." They couldn't say more.

But young Armitage was different. He'd looked at his commanding officer very oddly. He'd known, perhaps, that Richmond was being deliberately sent to death.

(And after the War was over—had Armitage talked?)

Leslie hadn't known. Leslie had wept for her lover (he supposed) but her weeping was over by the time he'd come back to England. He'd never told her that he'd found her out. They'd gone on together —only, somehow, she hadn't seemed very real any more. And then, three or four years later, she'd got double pneumonia and died.

That had been a long time ago. Fifteen years—sixteen years?

And he'd left the Army and come to live in Devon—bought the sort of little place he'd always meant to have. Nice neighbours— pleasant part of the world. There was a bit of shooting and fishing. He'd gone to church on Sundays. (But not the day that the lesson was read about David putting Uriah in the forefront of the battle. Somehow he couldn't face that. Gave him an uncomfortable feeling.)

Everybody had been very friendly. At first, that is. Later, he'd had an uneasy feeling that people were talking about him behind his back. They eyed him differently, somehow. As though they'd heard something—some lying rumour. . . .

(Armitage? Supposing Armitage had talked?)

He'd avoided people after that—withdrawn into himself. Unpleasant to feel that people were discussing you.

And all so long ago. So—so purposeless now. Leslie had faded into the distance and Arthur Richmond, too. Nothing of what had happened seemed to matter any more.

It made life lonely, though. He'd taken to shunning his old Army friends.

(If Armitage had talked, they'd know about it.)

And now—this evening—a hidden voice had blared out that old hidden story.

Had he dealt with it all right? Kept a stiff upper lip? Betrayed the right amount of feeling—indignation, disgust—but no guilt, no discomfiture? Difficult to tell.

Surely nobody could have taken the accusation seriously. There had been a pack of other nonsense, just as far-fetched. That charming girl—the voice had accused her of drowning a child! Idiotic! Some madman throwing crazy accusations about!

Emily Brent, too—actually a niece of old Tom Brent of the Regiment. It had accused *her* of murder! Any one could see with half an eye that the woman was as pious as could be—the kind that was hand and glove with parsons.

Damned curious business the whole thing! Crazy, nothing less.

Ever since they had got here—when was that? Why, damn it, it was only this afternoon! Seemed a good bit longer than that.

He thought: "I wonder when we shall get away again."

To-morrow, of course, when the motor boat came from the mainland.

Funny, just this minute he didn't want much to get away from the island. . . . To go back to the mainland, back to his little house, back to all the troubles and worries. Through the open window he could hear the waves breaking on the rocks—a little louder now than earlier in the evening. Wind was getting up, too.

He thought: Peaceful sound. Peaceful place. . . .

He thought: Best of an island is once you get there—you can't go any further . . . you've come to the end of things. . . .

He knew, suddenly, that he didn't want to leave the island.

6

Vera Claythorne lay in bed, wide awake, staring up at the ceiling. The light beside her was on. She was frightened of the dark.

She was thinking:

"Hugo . . . Hugo . . . Why do I feel you're so near to me to-night? . . . Somewhere quite close. . . .

"Where is he really? I don't know. I never shall know. He just went away—right away—out of my life."

It was no good trying not to think of Hugo. He was close to her. She *had* to think of him—to remember . . .

Cornwall . . .

The black rocks, the smooth yellow sand. Mrs. Hamilton, stout, good-humoured. Cyril, whining a little always, pulling at her hand.

"I want to swim out to the rock, Miss Claythorne. Why can't I swim out to the rock?"

Looking up—meeting Hugo's eyes watching her.

The evenings after Cyril was in bed . . .

"Come out for a stroll, Miss Claythorne."

"I think perhaps I will."

The decorous stroll down to the beach. The moonlight—the soft Atlantic air.

And then, Hugo's arms round her.

"I love you. I love you. You know I love you, Vera?"

Yes, she knew.

(Or thought she knew.)

"I can't ask you to marry me. I've not got a penny. It's all I can do to keep myself. Queer, you know, once, for three months I had the chance of being a rich man to look forward to. Cyril wasn't born until three months after Maurice died. If he'd been a girl . . ."

If the child had been a girl, Hugo would have come into everything. He'd been disappointed, he admitted.

"I hadn't built on it, of course. But it was a bit of a knock. Oh, well, luck's luck! Cyril's a nice kid. I'm awfully fond of him." And he

was fond of him, too. Always ready to play games or amuse his small nephew. No rancour in Hugo's nature.

Cyril wasn't really strong. A puny child—no stamina. The kind of child, perhaps, who wouldn't live to grow up. . . .

And then—?

"Miss Claythorne, why can't I swim to the rock?"

Irritating whiney repetition.

"It's too far, Cyril."

"But, Miss Claythorne . . ."

Vera got up. She went to the dressing-table and swallowed three aspirins.

She thought:

"I wish I had some proper sleeping stuff."

She thought:

"If *I* were doing away with myself I'd take an overdose of Veronal —something like that—not Cyanide!"

She shuddered as she remembered Anthony Marston's convulsed purple face.

As she passed the mantelpiece, she looked up at the framed doggerel.

Ten little Indian boys went out to dine;
One choked his little self and then there were nine.

She thought to herself:

"It's horrible—*just like us this evening.* . . ."

Why had Anthony Marston wanted to die?

She didn't want to die.

She couldn't imagine wanting to die. . . .

Death was for—the other people. . . .

CHAPTER 6

Dr. Armstrong was dreaming. . . .

It was very hot in the operating room. . . .

Surely they'd got the temperature too high? The sweat was rolling down his face. His hands were clammy. Difficult to hold the scalpel firmly. . . .

How beautifully sharp it was. . . .

Easy to do a murder with a knife like that. And of course he *was* doing a murder. . . .

The woman's body looked different. It had been a large unwieldy body. This was a spare meagre body. And the face was hidden.

Who was it that he had to kill?

He couldn't remember. But he *must* know! Should he ask Sister?

Sister was watching him. No, he couldn't ask her. She was suspicious, he could see that.

But who was it on the operating table?

They shouldn't have covered up the face like that. . . .

If he could only see the face. . . .

Ah! that was better. A young probationer was pulling off the handkerchief.

Emily Brent, of course. It was Emily Brent that he had to kill. How malicious her eyes were! Her lips were moving. What was she saying?

"In the midst of life we are in death. . . ."

She was laughing now. No, nurse, don't put the handkerchief back. I've got to see. I've got to give the anaesthetic. Where's the ether? I must have brought the ether with me. What have you done with the ether, Sister? Château Neuf du Pape? Yes, that will do quite as well.

Take the handkerchief away, nurse.

Of course! I knew it all the time! *It's Anthony Marston!* His face is purple and convulsed. But he's not dead—he's laughing. I tell you he's laughing! He's shaking the operating table.

Look out, man, look out. Nurse, steady it—steady—it—

With a start Dr. Armstrong woke up. It was morning. Sunlight was pouring into the room.

And some one was leaning over him—shaking him. It was Rogers. Rogers, with a white face, saying: "Doctor—doctor!"

Dr. Armstrong woke up completely.

He sat up in bed. He said sharply:

"What is it?"

"It's the wife, doctor. *I can't get her to wake.* My God! I can't get her to wake. And—and she don't look right to me."

Dr. Armstrong was quick and efficient. He wrapped himself in his dressing-gown and followed Rogers.

He bent over the bed where the woman was lying peacefully on her side. He lifted the cold hand, raised the eyelid. It was some few minutes before he straightened himself and turned from the bed.

Rogers whispered:

"Is—she—is she—?"

He passed a tongue over dry lips.

Armstrong nodded.

"Yes, she's gone."

His eyes rested thoughtfully on the man before him. Then they went to the table by the bed, to the washstand, then back to the sleeping woman.

Rogers said:

"Was it—was it—'er 'eart, doctor?"

Dr. Armstrong was a minute or two before replying. Then he said:

"What was her health like normally?"

Rogers said:

"She was a bit rheumaticky."

"Any doctor been attending her recently?"

"Doctor?" Rogers stared. "Not been to a doctor for years—neither of us."

"You'd no reason to believe she suffered from heart trouble?"

"No, doctor. I never knew of anything."

Armstrong said:

"Did she sleep well?"

Now Rogers' eyes evaded his. The man's hands came together and turned and twisted uneasily. He muttered.

"She didn't sleep extra well—no."

The doctor said sharply:

"Did she take things to make her sleep?"

Rogers stared at him, surprised.

"Take things? To make her sleep? Not that I knew of. I'm sure she didn't."

Armstrong went over to the washstand.

There were a certain number of bottles on it. Hair lotion, lavender water, cascara, glycerine of cucumber for the hands, a mouth wash, tooth paste and some Elliman's.

Rogers helped by pulling out the drawers of the dressing-table. From there they moved on to the chest of drawers. But there was no sign of sleeping draughts or tablets.

Rogers said:

"She didn't have nothing last night, sir, except what you gave her. . . ."

2

When the gong sounded for breakfast at nine o'clock it found every one up and awaiting the summons.

General Macarthur and the judge had been pacing the terrace outside, exchanging desultory comments on the political situation.

Vera Claythorne and Philip Lombard had been up to the summit of the island behind the house. There they had discovered William Henry Blore, standing staring at the mainland.

He said:

"No sign of that motor boat yet. I've been watching for it."

Vera said, smiling:

"Devon's a sleepy county. Things are usually late."

Philip Lombard was looking the other way, out to sea.

He said abruptly:

"What d'you think of the weather?"

Glancing up at the sky, Blore remarked:

"Looks all right to me."

Lombard pursed up his mouth into a whistle.

He said:

"It will come on to blow before the day's out."

Blore said:

"Squally—eh?"

From below them came the boom of a gong.

Philip Lombard said:

"Breakfast? Well, I could do with some."

As they went down the steep slope Blore said to Lombard in a ruminating voice:

"You know, it beats me—why that young fellow wanted to do himself in! I've been worrying about it all night."

Vera was a little ahead. Lombard hung back slightly. He said:

"Got any alternative theory?"

"I'd want some proof. Motive, to begin with. Well off I should say he was."

Emily Brent came out of the drawing-room door to meet them.

She said sharply:

"Is the boat coming?"

"Not yet," said Vera.

They went in to breakfast. There was a vast dish of eggs and bacon on the sideboard and tea and coffee.

Rogers held the door open for them to pass in, then shut it from the outside.

Emily Brent said:

"That man looks ill this morning."

Dr. Armstrong, who was standing by the window, cleared his throat. He said:

"You must excuse any—er—shortcomings this morning. Rogers has had to do the best he can for breakfast single-handed. Mrs. Rogers has—er—not been able to carry on this morning."

Emily Brent said sharply:

"What's the matter with the woman?"

Dr. Armstrong said easily:

"Let us start our breakfast. The eggs will be cold. Afterwards, there are several matters I want to discuss with you all."

They took the hint. Plates were filled, coffee and tea was poured. The meal began.

Discussion of the island was, by mutual consent, tabooed. They spoke instead in a desultory fashion of current events. The news from abroad, events in the world of sport, the latest reappearance of the Loch Ness monster.

Then, when plates were cleared, Dr. Armstrong moved back his chair a little, cleared his throat importantly and spoke.

He said:

"I thought it better to wait until you had had your breakfast before telling you of a sad piece of news. Mrs. Rogers died in her sleep."

There were startled and shocked ejaculations.

Vera exclaimed:

"How awful! Two deaths on this island since we arrived!"

Mr. Justice Wargrave, his eyes narrowed, said in his small precise clear voice:

"H'm—very remarkable—what was the cause of death?"

Armstrong shrugged his shoulders.

"Impossible to say offhand."

"There must be an autopsy?"

"I certainly couldn't give a certificate. I have no knowledge whatsoever of the woman's state of health."

Vera said:

"She was a very nervous-looking creature. And she had a shock last night. It might have been heart failure, I suppose?"

Dr. Armstrong said drily:

"Her heart certainly failed to beat—but what caused it to fail is the question."

One word fell from Emily Brent. It fell hard and clear into the listening group.

"Conscience!" she said.

Armstrong turned to her.

"What exactly do you mean by that, Miss Brent?"

Emily Brent, her lips tight and hard, said:

"You all heard. She was accused, together with her husband, of having deliberately murdered her former employer—an old lady."

"And you think?"

Emily Brent said:

"I think that that accusation was true. You all saw her last night. She broke down completely and fainted. The shock of having her wickedness brought home to her was too much for her. She literally died of fear."

Dr. Armstrong shook his head doubtfully.

"It is a possible theory," he said. "One cannot adopt it without more exact knowledge of her state of health. If there was cardiac weakness—"

Emily Brent said quietly:

"Call it, if you prefer, an Act of God."

Every one looked shocked. Mr. Blore said uneasily:

"That's carrying things a bit far, Miss Brent."

She looked at them with shining eyes. Her chin went up. She said:

"You regard it as impossible that a sinner should be struck down by the wrath of God! I do not!"

The judge stroked his chin. He murmured in a slightly ironic voice:

"My dear lady, in my experience of ill-doing, Providence leaves the work of conviction and chastisement to us mortals—and the process is often fraught with difficulties. There are no short cuts."

Emily Brent shrugged her shoulders.

Blore said sharply:

"What did she have to eat and drink last night after she went up to bed?"

Armstrong said:

"Nothing."

"She didn't take anything? A cup of tea? A drink of water? I'll bet you she had a cup of tea. That sort always does."

"Rogers assures me she had nothing whatsoever."

"Ah," said Blore. "But he *might* say so!"

His tone was so significant that the doctor looked at him sharply. Philip Lombard said:

"So that's your idea?"

Blore said aggressively:

"Well, why not? We all heard that accusation last night. May be sheer moonshine—just plain lunacy! On the other hand, it may not. Allow for the moment that it's true. Rogers and his missus polished off that old lady. Well, where does that get you? They've been feeling quite safe and happy about it—"

Vera interrupted. In a low voice she said:

"No, I don't think Mrs. Rogers ever felt safe."

Blore looked slightly annoyed at the interruption. "Just like a woman," his glance said.

He resumed:

"That's as may be. Anyway there's no active danger to them as far as they know. Then, last night, some unknown lunatic spills the beans. What happens? The woman cracks—she goes to pieces. Notice how her husband hung over her as she was coming round. Not all husbandly solicitude! Not on your life! He was like a cat on hot bricks. Scared out of his life as to what she might say.

"And there's the position for you! They've done a murder and got away with it. But if the whole thing's going to be raked up, what's going to happen? Ten to one, the woman will give the show away. She hasn't got the nerve to stand up and brazen it out. She's a living danger to her husband, that's what she is. He's all right. *He*'ll lie with a straight face till kingdom comes—but he can't be sure of *her!* And if *she* goes to pieces, his neck's in danger! So he slips something into a cup of tea and makes sure that her mouth is shut permanently."

Armstrong said slowly:

"There was no empty cup by her bedside—there was nothing there at all. I looked."

Blore snorted.

"Of course there wouldn't be! First thing he'd do when she'd drunk it would be to take that cup and saucer away and wash it up carefully."

There was a pause. Then General Macarthur said doubtfully:

"It may be so. But I should hardly think it possible that a man would do that—to his wife."

Blore gave a short laugh.

He said:

"When a man's neck's in danger, he doesn't stop to think too much about sentiment."

There was a pause. Before any one could speak, the door opened and Rogers came in.

He said, looking from one to the other:

"Is there anything more I can get you? I'm sorry there was so little toast, but we've run right out of bread. The new bread hasn't come over from the mainland yet."

Mr. Justice Wargrave stirred a little in his chair. He asked:

"What time does the motor boat usually come over?"

"Between seven and eight, sir. Sometimes it's a bit after eight. Don't know what Fred Narracott can be doing this morning. If he's ill he'd send his brother."

Philip Lombard said:

"What's the time now?"

"Ten minutes to ten, sir."

Lombard's eyebrows rose. He nodded slowly to himself.

Rogers waited a minute or two.

General Macarthur spoke suddenly and explosively.

"Sorry to hear about your wife, Rogers. Doctor's just been telling us."

Rogers inclined his head.

"Yes, sir. Thank you, sir."

He took up the empty bacon dish and went out.

Again there was a silence.

3

On the terrace outside Philip Lombard said:

"About this motor boat—"

Blore looked at him.

Blore nodded his head.

He said:

"I know what you're thinking, Mr. Lombard. I've asked myself the same question. Motor boat ought to have been here nigh on two hours ago. It hasn't come? Why?"

"Found the answer?" asked Lombard.

"It's not an accident—that's what I say. It's part and parcel of the whole business. It's all bound up together."

Philip Lombard said:

"It won't come, you think?"

A voice spoke behind him—a testy impatient voice.

"The motor boat's not coming," he said.

Blore turned his square shoulder slightly and viewed the last speaker thoughtfully.

"You think not too, General?"

General Macarthur said sharply:

"Of course it won't come. We're counting on the motor boat to take us off the island. That's the meaning of the whole business. *We're not going to leave the island.* . . . None of us will ever leave. . . . It's the end, you see—the end of everything. . . ."

He hesitated, then he said in a low strange voice:

"That's peace—real peace. To come to the end—not to have to go on. . . . Yes, peace. . . ."

He turned abruptly and walked away. Along the terrace, then down the slope towards the sea—obliquely—to the end of the island where loose rocks went out into the water.

He walked a little unsteadily, like a man who was only half awake.

Blore said:

"There goes another one who's balmy! Looks as though it'll end with the whole lot going that way."

Philip Lombard said:

"I don't fancy *you* will, Blore."

The ex-Inspector laughed.

"It would take a lot to send me off my head." He added drily: "And I don't think you'll be going that way either, Mr. Lombard."

Philip Lombard said:

"I feel quite sane at the minute, thank you."

4

Dr. Armstrong came out onto the terrace. He stood there hesitating. To his left were Blore and Lombard. To his right was Wargrave, slowly pacing up and down, his head bent down.

Armstrong, after a moment of indecision, turned towards the latter.

But at that moment Rogers came quickly out of the house.

"Could I have a word with you, sir, please?"

Armstrong turned.

He was startled at what he saw.

Rogers' face was working. Its colour was greyish green. His hands shook.

It was such a contrast to his restraint of a few minutes ago that Armstrong was quite taken aback.

"Please, sir, if I could have a word with you. Inside, sir."

The doctor turned back and re-entered the house with the frenzied butler. He said:

"What's the matter, man? Pull yourself together."

"In here, sir, come in here."

He opened the dining-room door. The doctor passed in. Rogers followed him and shut the door behind him.

"Well," said Armstrong, "what is it?"

The muscles of Rogers' throat were working. He was swallowing. He jerked out:

"There's things going on, sir, that I don't understand."

Armstrong said sharply: "Things? What things?"

"You'll think I'm crazy, sir. You'll say it isn't anything. But it's got to be explained, sir. It's got to be explained. Because it doesn't make any sense."

"Well, man, tell me what it is? Don't go on talking in riddles."

Rogers swallowed again.

He said:

"It's those little figures, sir. In the middle of the table. The little china figures. Ten of them, there were. I'll swear to that, ten of them."

Armstrong said:

"Yes, ten. We counted them last night at dinner."

Rogers came nearer.

"That's just it, sir. Last night, when I was clearing up, there wasn't but nine, sir. I noticed it and thought it queer. But that's all I thought. And now, sir, this morning. I didn't notice when I laid the breakfast. I was upset and all that.

"But now, sir, when I came to clear away. See for yourself if you don't believe me.

"There's only eight, sir! Only eight! It doesn't make sense, does it? *Only eight. . . ."*

CHAPTER 7

AFTER BREAKFAST, Emily Brent had suggested to Vera Claythorne that they should walk up to the summit again and watch for the boat. Vera had acquiesced.

The wind had freshened. Small white crests were appearing on the sea. There were no fishing boats out—and no sign of the motor boat.

The actual village of Sticklehaven could not be seen, only the hill above it, a jutting out cliff of red rock concealed the actual little bay.

Emily Brent said:

"The man who brought us out yesterday seemed a dependable sort of person. It is really very odd that he should be so late this morning."

Vera did not answer. She was fighting down a rising feeling of panic.

She said to herself angrily:

"You must keep cool. This isn't like you. You've always had excellent nerves."

Aloud she said after a minute or two:

"I wish he would come. I—I want to get away."

Emily Brent said drily:

"I've no doubt we all do."

Vera said:

"It's all so extraordinary. . . . There seems no—no meaning in it all."

The elderly woman beside her said briskly:

"I'm very annoyed with myself for being so easily taken in. Really that letter is absurd when one comes to examine it. But I had no doubts at the time—none at all."

Vera murmured mechanically:

"I suppose not."

"One takes things for granted too much," said Emily Brent.

Vera drew a deep shuddering breath.

She said:

"Do you really think—what you said at breakfast?"

"Be a little more precise, my dear. To what in particular are you referring?"

Vera said in a low voice:

"Do you really think that Rogers and his wife did away with that old lady?"

Emily Brent gazed thoughtfully out to sea. Then she said:

"Personally, I am quite sure of it. What do you think?"

"I don't know what to think."

Emily Brent said:

"Everything goes to support the idea. The way the woman fainted. And the man dropped the coffee tray, remember. Then the way he spoke about it—it didn't ring true. Oh, yes, I'm afraid they did it."

Vera said:

"The way she looked—scared of her own shadow! I've never seen a woman look so frightened. . . . She must have been always haunted by it. . . ."

Miss Brent murmured:

"I remember a text that hung in my nursery as a child. *'Be sure thy sin will find thee out.'* It's very true, that. *'Be sure thy sin will find thee out.'*"

Vera scrambled to her feet. She said:

"But, Miss Brent—Miss Brent—in that case—"

"Yes, my dear?"

"The others? What about the others?"

"I don't quite understand you."

"All the other accusations—they—*they* weren't true? But if it's true about the Rogerses—" She stopped, unable to make her chaotic thought clear.

Emily Brent's brow, which had been frowning perplexedly, cleared.

She said:

"Ah, I understand you now. Well, there is that Mr. Lombard. He admits to having abandoned twenty men to their deaths."

Vera said:

"They were only natives. . . ."

Emily Brent said sharply:

"Black or white, they are our brothers."

Vera thought:

"Our black brothers—our black brothers. Oh, I'm going to laugh. I'm hysterical. I'm not myself. . . ."

Emily Brent continued thoughtfully:

"Of course, some of the other accusations were very far-fetched and ridiculous. Against the judge, for instance, who was only doing his duty in his public capacity. And the ex-Scotland Yard man. My own case, too."

She paused and then went on:

"Naturally, considering the circumstances, I was not going to say anything last night. It was not a fit subject to discuss before gentlemen."

"No?"

Vera listened with interest. Miss Brent continued serenely:

"Beatrice Taylor was in service with me. *Not a nice girl*—as I found out too late. I was very much deceived in her. She had nice manners and was very clean and willing. I was very pleased with her. Of course all that was the sheerest hypocrisy! She was a loose girl with no morals. Disgusting! It was some time before I found out that she was what they call 'in trouble.'" She paused, her delicate nose wrinkling itself in distaste. "It was a great shock to me. Her parents were decent folk, too, who had brought her up very strictly. I'm glad to say they did not condone her behaviour."

Vera said, staring at Miss Brent:

"What happened?"

"Naturally I did not keep her an hour under my roof. No one shall ever say that I condoned immorality."

Vera said in a lower voice:

"What happened—to her?"

Miss Brent said:

"The abandoned creature, not content with having one sin on her conscience, committed a still graver sin. She took her own life."

Vera whispered, horror-struck:

"She killed herself?"

"Yes, she threw herself into the river."

Vera shivered.

She stared at the calm delicate profile of Miss Brent. She said:

"What did you feel like when you knew she'd done that? Weren't you sorry? Didn't you blame yourself?"

Emily Brent drew herself up.

"I? I had nothing with which to reproach myself."

Vera said:

"But if your—hardness—drove her to it."

Emily Brent said sharply:

"Her own action—her own sin—that was what drove her to it. If she had behaved like a decent modest young woman none of this would have happened."

She turned her face to Vera. There was no self-reproach, no uneasiness in those eyes. They were hard and self-righteous. Emily Brent sat on the summit of Indian Island, encased in her own armour of virtue.

The little elderly spinster was no longer slightly ridiculous to Vera. Suddenly—she was terrible.

2

Dr. Armstrong came out of the dining-room and once more came out on the terrace.

The judge was sitting in a chair now, gazing placidly out to sea.

Lombard and Blore were over to the left, smoking but not talking.

As before, the doctor hesitated for a moment. His eye rested speculatively on Mr. Justice Wargrave. He wanted to consult with some one. He was conscious of the judge's acute logical brain. But nevertheless he wavered. Mr. Justice Wargrave might have a good brain but he was an elderly man. At this juncture, Armstrong felt what was needed was a man of action.

He made up his mind.

"Lombard, can I speak to you for a minute?"

Philip started.

"Of course."

The two men left the terrace. They strolled down the slope towards the water. When they were out of earshot, Armstrong said:

"I want a consultation."

Lombard's eyebrows went up. He said:

"My dear fellow, I've no medical knowledge."

"No, no, I mean as to the general situation."

"Oh, that's different."

Armstrong said:

"Frankly, what do you think of the position?"

Lombard reflected a minute. Then he said:

"It's rather suggestive, isn't it?"

"What are your ideas on the subject of that woman? Do you accept Blore's theory?"

Philip puffed smoke into the air. He said:

"It's perfectly feasible—taken alone."

"Exactly."

Armstrong's tone sounded relieved. Philip Lombard was no fool. The latter went on:

"That is, accepting the premise that Mr. and Mrs. Rogers have successfully got away with murder in their time. And I don't see why they shouldn't. What do you think they did exactly? Poisoned the old lady?"

Armstrong said slowly:

"It might be simpler than that. I asked Rogers this morning what this Miss Brady had suffered from. His answer was enlightening. I don't need to go into medical details, but in a certain form of cardiac trouble, amyl nitrite is used. When an attack comes on an ampoule of amyl nitrite is broken and it is inhaled. If amyl nitrite were withheld—well, the consequences might easily be fatal."

Philip Lombard said thoughtfully:

"As simple as that. It must have been—rather tempting."

The doctor nodded.

"Yes, no positive action. No arsenic to obtain and administer—nothing definite—just—negation! And Rogers hurried through the night to fetch a doctor and they both felt confident that no one could ever know."

"And, even if any one knew, nothing could ever be proved against them," added Philip Lombard.

He frowned suddenly.

"Of course—that explains a good deal."

Armstrong said, puzzled:

"I beg your pardon."

Lombard said:

"I mean—it explains Indian Island. There are crimes that cannot be brought home to their perpetrators. Instance, the Rogerses'. Another instance, old Wargrave, who committed his murder strictly within the law."

Armstrong said sharply:

"You believe that story?"

Philip Lombard smiled.

"Oh, yes, I believe it. Wargrave murdered Edward Seton all right, murdered him as surely as if he'd stuck a stiletto through him! But he was clever enough to do it from the judge's seat in wig and gown. So in the ordinary way you can't bring his little crime home to him."

A sudden flash passed like lightning through Armstrong's mind.

"Murder in Hospital. Murder on the Operating Table. Safe—yes, safe as houses!"

Philip Lombard was saying:

"Hence—Mr. Owen—hence—Indian Island!"

Armstrong drew a deep breath.

"Now we're getting down to it. What's the real purpose of getting us all here?"

Philip Lombard said:

"What do *you* think?"

Armstrong said abruptly:

"Let's go back a minute to this woman's death. What are the possible theories? Rogers killed her because he was afraid she would give the show away. Second possibility: She lost her nerve and took an easy way out herself."

Philip Lombard said:

"Suicide, eh?"

"What do you say to that?"

Lombard said:

"It could have been—yes—*if it hadn't been for Marston's death.* Two suicides within twelve hours is a little *too* much to swallow! And if you tell me that Anthony Marston, a young bull with no nerves and precious little brains, got the wind up over having mowed down a couple of kids and deliberately put himself out of the way—well, the idea's laughable! And anyway, how did he get hold of the stuff? From all I've ever heard, Potassium Cyanide isn't the kind of stuff you take about with you in your waistcoat pocket. But that's your line of country."

Armstrong said:

"Nobody in their senses carries Potassium Cyanide. It might be done by some one who was going to take a wasps' nest."

"The ardent gardener or landowner, in fact? Again, not Anthony Marston. It strikes me that Cyanide is going to need a bit of explaining. Either Anthony Marston meant to do away with himself before he came here, and therefore came prepared—or else—"

Armstrong prompted him.

"Or else?"

Philip Lombard grinned.

"Why make me say it? When it's on the tip of your own tongue. *Anthony Marston was murdered, of course.*"

3

Dr. Armstrong drew a deep breath.

"And Mrs. Rogers?"

Lombard said slowly:

"I could believe in Anthony's suicide (with difficulty) if it weren't for Mrs. Rogers. I could believe in Mrs. Rogers' suicide (easily) if it weren't for Anthony Marston. I can believe that Rogers put his wife out of the way—if it were not for the unexplained death of Anthony Marston. But what we need is a theory to explain two deaths following rapidly on each other."

Armstrong said:

"I can perhaps give you some help towards that theory."

And he repeated the facts that Rogers had given him about the disappearance of the two little china figures.

Lombard said:

"Yes, little china Indian figures. . . . There were certainly ten last night at dinner. And now there are eight, you say?"

Dr. Armstrong recited:

"Ten little Indian boys going out to dine;
 One went and choked himself and then there were nine.

"Nine little Indian boys sat up very late;
 One overslept himself and then there were eight."

The two men looked at each other. Philip Lombard grinned and flung away his cigarette.

"Fits too damned well to be a coincidence! Anthony Marston dies of asphyxiation or choking last night after dinner, and Mother Rogers oversleeps herself with a vengeance."

"And therefore?" said Armstrong.

Lombard took him up.

"And therefore another kind of puzzle. The Nigger in the Wood-pile! X! Mr. Owen! U. N. Owen. One Unknown Lunatic at Large!"

"Ah!" Armstrong breathed a sigh of relief. "You agree. But you see what it involves? Rogers swore that there was no one but ourselves and he and his wife on the island."

"Rogers is wrong! Or possibly Rogers is lying!"

Armstrong shook his head.

"I don't think he's lying. The man's scared. He's scared nearly out of his senses."

Philip Lombard nodded.

He said:

"No motor boat this morning. That fits in. Mr. Owen's little arrangements again to the fore. Indian Island is to be isolated until Mr. Owen has finished his job."

Armstrong had gone pale. He said:

"You realize—the man must be a raving maniac!"

Philip Lombard said, and there was a new ring in his voice:

"There's one thing Mr. Owen didn't realize."

"What's that?"

"This island's more or less a bare rock. We shall make short work of searching it. We'll soon ferret out U. N. Owen, Esq."

Dr. Armstrong said warningly:

"He'll be dangerous."

Philip Lombard laughed.

"Dangerous? Who's afraid of the big bad wolf? *I'*ll be dangerous when I get hold of him!"

He paused and said:

"We'd better rope in Blore to help us. He'll be a good man in a pinch. Better not tell the women. As for the others, the General's ga ga, I think, and old Wargrave's forte is masterly inactivity. The three of us can attend to this job."

CHAPTER 8

BLORE WAS easily roped in. He expressed immediate agreement with their arguments.

"What you've said about those china figures, sir, makes all the difference. That's crazy, that is! There's only one thing. You don't think this Owen's idea might be to do the job by proxy, as it were?"

"Explain yourself, man."

"Well, I mean like this. After the racket last night this young Mr. Marston gets the wind up and poisons himself. And Rogers, *he* gets the wind up too and bumps off his wife! All according to U. N. O.'s plan."

Armstrong shook his head. He stressed the point about the Cyanide. Blore agreed.

"Yes, I'd forgotten that. Not a natural thing to be carrying about with you. But how did it get into his drink, sir?"

Lombard said:

"I've been thinking about that. Marston had several drinks that night. Between the time he had his last one and the time he finished the one before it, there was quite a gap. During that time his glass was lying about on some table or other. I think—though I can't be sure, it was on the little table near the window. The window was open. Somebody could have slipped a dose of the Cyanide into the glass."

Blore said unbelievingly:

"Without our all seeing him, sir?"

Lombard said drily:

"We were all—rather concerned elsewhere."

Armstrong said slowly:

"That's true. We'd all been attacked. We were walking about, moving about the room. Arguing, indignant, intent on our own business. I think it *could* have been done. . . ."

Blore shrugged his shoulders.

"Fact is, it must have been done! Now then, gentlemen, let's make a start. Nobody's got a revolver, by any chance? I suppose that's too much to hope for."

Lombard said:

"I've got one." He patted his pocket.

Blore's eyes opened very wide. He said in an over-casual tone:

"Always carry that about with you, sir?"

Lombard said:

"Usually. I've been in some tight places, you know."

"Oh," said Blore and added: "Well, you've probably never been in a tighter place than you are to-day! If there's a lunatic hiding on this island, he's probably got a young arsenal on him—to say nothing of a knife or dagger or two."

Armstrong coughed.

"You may be wrong there, Blore. Many homicidal lunatics are very quiet, unassuming people. Delightful fellows."

Blore said:

"I don't feel this one is going to be of that kind, Dr. Armstrong."

2

The three men started on their tour of the island.

It proved unexpectedly simple. On the northwest side, towards the coast, the cliffs fell sheer to the sea below, their surface unbroken.

On the rest of the island there were no trees and very little cover. The three men worked carefully and methodically, beating up and down from the highest point to the water's edge, narrowly scanning the least irregularity in the rock which might point to the entrance to a cave. But there were no caves.

They came at last, skirting the water's edge, to where General Macarthur sat looking out to sea. It was very peaceful here with the lap of the waves breaking over the rocks. The old man sat very upright, his eyes fixed on the horizon.

He paid no attention to the approach of the searchers. His oblivion of them made one at least faintly uncomfortable.

Blore thought to himself:

" 'Tisn't natural—looks as though he'd gone into a trance or something."

He cleared his throat and said in a would-be conversational tone:

"Nice peaceful spot you've found for yourself, sir."

The General frowned. He cast a quick look over his shoulder. He said:

"There is so little time—so little time. I really must insist that no one disturbs me."

Blore said genially:

"We won't disturb you. We're just making a tour of the island, so to speak. Just wondered, you know, if some one might be hiding on it."

The General frowned and said:

"You don't understand—you don't understand at all. Please go away."

Blore retreated. He said, as he joined the other two:

"He's crazy. . . . It's no good talking to him."

Lombard asked with some curiosity:

"What did he say?"

Blore shrugged his shoulders.

"Something about there being no time and that he didn't want to be disturbed."

Dr. Armstrong frowned.

He murmured:

"I wonder now. . . ."

3

The search of the island was practically completed. The three men stood on the highest point looking over towards the mainland. There were no boats out. The wind was freshening.

Lombard said:

"No fishing boats out. There's a storm coming. Damned nuisance you can't see the village from here. We could signal or do something."

Blore said:

"We might light a bonfire to-night."

Lombard said, frowning:

"The devil of it is that that's all probably been provided for."

"In what way, sir?"

"How do I know? Practical joke, perhaps. We're to be marooned here, no attention is to be paid to signals, etc. Possibly the village has been told there's a wager on. Some damn fool story anyway."

Blore said dubiously:

"Think they'd swallow that?"

Lombard said drily:

"It's easier of belief than the truth! If the village were told that the island was to be isolated until Mr. Unknown Owen had quietly murdered all his guests—do you think they'd believe that?"

Dr. Armstrong said:

"There are moments when I can't believe it myself. And yet—"

Philip Lombard, his lips curling back from his teeth, said:

"*And yet*—that's just it! You've said it, doctor!"

Blore was gazing down into the water.

He said:

"Nobody could have clambered down here, I suppose?"

Armstrong shook his head.

"I doubt it. It's pretty sheer. And where could he hide?"

Blore said:

"There might be a hole in the cliff. If we had a boat now, we could row round the island."

Lombard said:

"If we had a boat, we'd all be halfway to the mainland by now!"

"True enough, sir."

Lombard said suddenly:

"We can make sure of this cliff. There's only one place where there *could* be a recess—just a little to the right below here. If you fellows can get hold of a rope, you can let me down to make sure."

Blore said:

"Might as well *be* sure. Though it seems absurd—on the face of it! I'll see if I can get hold of something."

He started off briskly down to the house.

Lombard stared up at the sky. The clouds were beginning to mass themselves together. The wind was increasing.

He shot a sideways look at Armstrong. He said:

"You're very silent, doctor. What are you thinking?"

Armstrong said slowly:

"I was wondering exactly how mad old Macarthur was. . . ."

4

Vera had been restless all the morning. She had avoided Emily Brent with a kind of shuddering aversion.

Miss Brent herself had taken a chair just round the corner of the house so as to be out of the wind. She sat there knitting.

Every time Vera thought of her she seemed to see a pale drowned face with seaweed entangled in the hair. . . . A face that had once been pretty—impudently pretty perhaps—and which was now beyond the reach of pity or terror.

And Emily Brent, placid and righteous, sat knitting.

On the main terrace, Mr. Justice Wargrave sat huddled in a porter's chair. His head was poked down well into his neck.

When Vera looked at him, she saw a man standing in the dock—a young man with fair hair and blue eyes and a bewildered, frightened face. Edward Seton. And in imagination she saw the judge's old hands put the black cap on his head and begin to pronounce sentence. . . .

After a while Vera strolled slowly down to the sea. She walked along towards the extreme end of the island where an old man sat staring out to the horizon.

General Macarthur stirred at her approach. His head turned—there was a queer mixture of questioning and apprehension in his look. It startled her. He stared intently at her for a minute or two.

She thought to herself:

"How queer. It's almost as though he *knew*. . . ."

He said:

"Ah! it's you! You've come. . . ."

Vera sat down beside him. She said:

"Do you like sitting here looking out to sea?"

He nodded his head gently.

"Yes," he said. "It's pleasant. It's a good place, I think, to wait."

"To wait?" said Vera sharply. "What are you waiting for?"

He said gently:

"The end. But I think you know that, don't you? It's true, isn't it? We're all waiting for the end."

She said unsteadily:

"What do you mean?"

General Macarthur said gravely:

"*None of us are going to leave the island*. That's the plan. You know it, of course, perfectly. What, perhaps, you can't understand is the relief!"

Vera said wonderingly:

"The relief?"

He said:

"Yes. Of course, you're very young . . . you haven't got to that yet. But it does come! The blessed relief when you know that you've done with it all—that you haven't got to carry the burden any longer. You'll feel that too some day. . . ."

Vera said hoarsely:

"I don't understand you."

Her fingers worked spasmodically. She felt suddenly afraid of this quiet old soldier.

He said musingly:

"You see, I loved Leslie. I loved her very much. . . ."

Vera said questioningly:

"Was Leslie your wife?"

"Yes, my wife. . . . I loved her—and I was very proud of her. She was so pretty—and so gay."

He was silent for a minute or two, then he said:

"Yes, I loved Leslie. That's why I did it."

Vera said:

"You mean—" and paused.

General Macarthur nodded his head gently.

"It's not much good denying it now—not when we're all going to die. *I sent Richmond to his death.* I suppose, in a way, it was murder. Curious. *Murder*—and I've always been such a law-abiding man! But it didn't seem like that at the time. I had no regrets. 'Serves him damned well right!'—that's what I thought. But afterwards—"

In a hard voice, Vera said:

"Well, afterwards?"

He shook his head vaguely. He looked puzzled and a little distressed.

"I don't know. I—don't know. It was all different, you see. I don't know if Leslie ever guessed . . . I don't think so. But you see, I didn't know about her any more. She'd gone far away where I couldn't reach her. And then she died—and I was alone. . . ."

Vera said:

"Alone—alone—" and the echo of her voice came back to her from the rocks.

General Macarthur said:

"You'll be glad, too, when the end comes."

Vera got up. She said sharply:

"I don't know what you mean!"

He said:

"I *know*, my child, I *know*. . . ."

"You don't. You don't understand at all. . . ."

General Macarthur looked out to sea again. He seemed unconscious of her presence behind him.

He said very gently and softly:

"Leslie . . . ?"

5

When Blore returned from the house with a rope coiled over his arm, he found Armstrong where he had left him staring down into the depths.

Blore said breathlessly:

"Where's Mr. Lombard?"

Armstrong said carelessly:

"Gone to test some theory or other. He'll be back in a minute. Look here, Blore, I'm worried."

"I should say we were all worried."

The doctor waved an impatient hand.

"Of course—of course. I don't mean it that way. I'm thinking of old Macarthur."

"What about him, sir?"

Dr. Armstrong said grimly:

"What we're looking for is a madman. *What price Macarthur?*"

Blore said incredulously:

"You mean he's homicidal?"

Armstrong said doubtfully:

"I shouldn't have said so. Not for a minute. But of course I'm not a specialist in mental diseases. I haven't really had any conversation with him—I haven't studied him from that point of view."

Blore said doubtfully:

"Ga ga, yes! But I wouldn't have said—"

Armstrong cut in with a slight effort as of a man who pulls himself together.

"You're probably right! Damn it all, there *must* be some one hiding on the island. Ah! here comes Lombard."

They fastened the rope carefully.

Lombard said:

"I'll help myself all I can. Keep a lookout for a sudden strain on the rope."

After a minute or two, while they stood together watching Lombard's progress, Blore said:

"Climbs like a cat, doesn't he?"

There was something odd in his voice.

Dr. Armstrong said:

"I should think he must have done some mountaineering in his time."

"Maybe."

There was a silence and the ex-Inspector said:

"Funny sort of cove altogether. D'you know what I think?"

"What?"

"He's a wrong 'un!"

Armstrong said doubtfully:

"In what way?"

Blore grunted. Then he said:

"I don't know—exactly. But I wouldn't trust him a yard."

Dr. Armstrong said:

"I suppose he's led an adventurous life."

Blore said:

"I bet some of his adventures have had to be kept pretty dark." He paused and then went on: "Did you happen to bring a revolver along with you, doctor?"

Armstrong stared.

"Me? Good Lord, no. Why should I?"

Blore said:

"Why did Mr. Lombard?"

Armstrong said doubtfully:

"I suppose—habit."

Blore snorted.

A sudden pull came on the rope. For some moments they had their hands full. Presently, when the strain relaxed, Blore said:

"There are habits *and* habits! Mr. Lombard takes a revolver to out-of-the-way places, right enough, *and* a primus and a sleeping-bag and a supply of bug powder, no doubt! But habit wouldn't make him bring the whole outfit down here? It's only in books people carry revolvers around as a matter of course."

Dr. Armstrong shook his head perplexedly.

They leaned over and watched Lombard's progress. His search was thorough and they could see at once that it was futile. Presently he came up over the edge of the cliff. He wiped the perspiration from his forehead.

"Well," he said. "We're up against it. It's the house or nowhere."

6

The house was easily searched. They went through the few out-buildings first and then turned their attention to the building itself. Mrs. Rogers' yard measure discovered in the kitchen dresser assisted them. But there were no hidden spaces left unaccounted for. Everything was plain and straightforward, a modern structure devoid of concealments. They went through the ground floor first. As they mounted to the bedroom floor, they saw through the landing window Rogers carrying out a tray of cocktails to the terrace.

Philip Lombard said lightly:

"Wonderful animal, the good servant. Carries on with an impassive countenance."

Armstrong said appreciatively:

"Rogers is a first-class butler, I'll say that for him!"

Blore said:

"His wife was a pretty good cook, too. That dinner—last night—"

They turned in to the first bedroom.

Five minutes later they faced each other on the landing. No one hiding—no possible hiding-place.

Blore said:

"There's a little stair here."

Dr. Armstrong said:

"It leads up to the servants' room."

Blore said:

"There must be a place under the roof—for cisterns, water tank, etc. It's the best chance—and the only one!"

And it was then, as they stood there, that they heard the sound from above. A soft furtive footfall overhead.

They all heard it. Armstrong grasped Blore's arm. Lombard held up an admonitory finger.

"Quiet—listen."

It came again—some one moving softly, furtively, overhead.

Armstrong whispered:

"He's actually in the bedroom itself. The room where Mrs. Rogers' body is."

Blore whispered back:

"Of course! Best hiding-place he could have chosen! Nobody likely to go there. Now then—quiet as you can."

They crept stealthily upstairs.

On the little landing outside the door of the bedroom they paused again. Yes, some one was in the room. There was a faint creak from within.

Blore whispered:

"Now."

He flung open the door and rushed in, the other two close behind him.

Then all three stopped dead.

Rogers was in the room, his hands full of garments.

7

Blore recovered himself first. He said:

"Sorry—er—Rogers. Heard some one moving about in here, and thought—well—"

He stopped.

Rogers said:

"I'm sorry, gentlemen. I was just moving my things. I take it there will be no objection if I take one of the vacant guest chambers on the floor below? The smallest room."

It was to Armstrong that he spoke, and Armstrong replied:

"Of course. Of course. Get on with it."

He avoided looking at the sheeted figure lying on the bed.

Rogers said:

"Thank you, sir."

He went out of the room with his arm full of belongings and went down the stairs to the floor below.

Armstrong moved over to the bed and, lifting the sheet, looked down on the peaceful face of the dead woman. There was no fear there now. Just emptiness.

Armstrong said:

"Wish I'd got my stuff here. I'd like to know what drug it was."

Then he turned to the other two.

"Let's get finished. I feel it in my bones we're not going to find anything."

Blore was wrestling with the bolts of a low manhole.

He said:

"That chap moves damned quietly. A minute or two ago we saw him in the garden. None of us heard him come upstairs."

Lombard said:

"I suppose that's why we assumed it must be a stranger moving about up here."

Blore disappeared into a cavernous darkness. Lombard pulled a torch from his pocket and followed.

Five minutes later three men stood on an upper landing and looked at each other. They were dirty and festooned with cobwebs and their faces were grim.

There was no one on the island but their eight selves.

CHAPTER 9

LOMBARD SAID slowly:

"So we've been wrong—wrong all along! Built up a nightmare of superstition and fantasy all because of the coincidence of two deaths!"

Armstrong said gravely:

"And yet, you know, the argument holds. Hang it all, I'm a doctor, I know something about suicides. Anthony Marston wasn't a suicidal type."

Lombard said doubtfully:

"It couldn't, I suppose, have been an accident?"

Blore snorted, unconvinced.

"Damned queer sort of accident," he grunted.

There was a pause, then Blore said:

"About the woman—" and stopped.

"Mrs. Rogers?"

"Yes. It's possible, isn't it, that that might have been an accident?"

Philip Lombard said:

"An accident? In what way?"

Blore looked slightly embarrassed. His red-brick face grew a little deeper in hue. He said, almost blurting out the words:

"Look here, doctor, you did give her some dope, you know."

Armstrong stared at him.

"Dope? What do you mean?"

"Last night. You said yourself you'd give her something to make her sleep."

"Oh, that, yes. A harmless sedative."

"What was it exactly?"

"I gave her a mild dose of trional. A perfectly harmless preparation."

Blore grew redder still. He said:

"Look here—not to mince matters—you didn't give her an overdose, did you?"

Dr. Armstrong said angrily:

"I don't know what you mean."

Blore said:

"It's possible, isn't it, that you may have made a mistake? These things do happen once in a while."

Armstrong said sharply:

"I did nothing of the sort. The suggestion is ridiculous." He stopped and added in a cold biting tone: "Or do you suggest that I gave her an overdose on purpose?"

Philip Lombard said quickly:

"Look here, you two, got to keep our heads. Don't let's start slinging accusations about."

Blore said sullenly:

"I only suggested the doctor had made a mistake."

Dr. Armstrong smiled with an effort. He said, showing his teeth in a somewhat mirthless smile:

"Doctors can't afford to make mistakes of that kind, my friend."

Blore said deliberately:

"It wouldn't be the first you've made—if that gramophone record is to be believed!"

Armstrong went white. Philip Lombard said quickly and angrily to Blore:

"What's the sense of making yourself offensive? We're all in the same boat. We've got to pull together. What about your own pretty little spot of perjury?"

Blore took a step forward, his hands clenched. He said in a thick voice:

"Perjury be damned! That's a foul lie! You may try and shut me up, Mr. Lombard, but there's things I want to know—and one of them is about *you!*"

Lombard's eyebrows rose.

"About me?"

"Yes. I want to know why you brought a revolver down here on a pleasant social visit?"

Lombard said:

"You do, do you?"

"Yes, I do, Mr. Lombard."

Lombard said unexpectedly:

"You know, Blore, you're not nearly such a fool as you look."

"That's as may be. What about that revolver?"

Lombard smiled.

"I brought it because I expected to run into a spot of trouble."

Blore said suspiciously:

"You didn't tell us that last night."

Lombard shook his head.

"You were holding out on us?" Blore persisted.

"In a way, yes," said Lombard.

"Well, come on, out with it."

Lombard said slowly:

"I allowed you all to think that I was asked here in the same way as most of the others. That's not quite true. As a matter of fact I was approached by a little Jewboy—Morris his name was. He offered me a hundred guineas to come down here and keep my eyes open—said I'd got a reputation for being a good man in a tight place."

"Well?" Blore prompted impatiently.

Lombard said with a grin:

"That's all."

Dr. Armstrong said:

"But surely he told you more than that?"

"Oh, no, he didn't. Just shut up like a clam. I could take it or leave it—those were his words. I was hard up. I took it."

Blore looked unconvinced. He said:

"Why didn't you tell us all this last night?"

"My dear man—" Lombard shrugged eloquent shoulders. "How was I to know that last night wasn't exactly the eventuality I was here to cope with? I lay low and told a noncommittal story."

Dr. Armstrong said shrewdly:

"But now—you think differently?"

Lombard's face changed. It darkened and hardened. He said:

"Yes. I believe now that I'm in the same boat as the rest of you. That hundred guineas was just Mr. Owen's little bit of cheese to get me into the trap along with the rest of you."

He said slowly:

"*For we are in a trap*—I'll take my oath on that! Mrs. Rogers' death! Tony Marston's! The disappearing Indian boys on the dinner-table! Oh, yes, Mr. Owen's hand is plainly to be seen—*but where the devil is Mr. Owen himself?*"

Downstairs the gong pealed a solemn call to lunch.

2

Rogers was standing by the dining-room door. As the three men descended the stairs he moved a step or two forward. He said in a low anxious voice:

"I hope lunch will be satisfactory. There is cold ham and cold tongue, and I've boiled some potatoes. And there's cheese and biscuits and some tinned fruits."

Lombard said:

"Sounds all right. Stores are holding out, then?"

"There is plenty of food, sir—of a tinned variety. The larder is very well stocked. A necessity, that, I should say, sir, on an island where one may be cut off from the mainland for a considerable period."

Lombard nodded.

Rogers murmured as he followed the three men into the dining-room:

"It worries me that Fred Narracott hasn't been over to-day. It's peculiarly unfortunate, as you might say."

"Yes," said Lombard, "peculiarly unfortunate describes it very well."

Miss Brent came into the room. She had just dropped a ball of wool and was carefully rewinding the end of it.

As she took her seat at table she remarked:

"The weather is changing. The wind is quite strong and there are white horses on the sea."

Mr. Justice Wargrave came in. He walked with a slow measured tread. He darted quick looks from under his bushy eyebrows at the other occupants of the dining-room. He said:

"You have had an active morning."

There was a faint malicious pleasure in his voice.

Vera Claythorne hurried in. She was a little out of breath.

She said quickly:

"I hope you didn't wait for me. Am I late?"

Emily Brent said:

"You're not the last. The General isn't here yet."

They sat round the table.

Rogers addressed Miss Brent:

"Will you begin, Madam, or will you wait?"

Vera said:

"General Macarthur is sitting right down by the sea. I don't expect he would hear the gong there and anyway"—she hesitated—"he's a little vague to-day, I think."

Rogers said quickly:

"I will go down and inform him luncheon is ready."

Dr. Armstrong jumped up.

"I'll go," he said. "You others start lunch."

He left the room. Behind him he heard Rogers' voice.

"Will you take cold tongue or cold ham, Madam?"

3

The five people sitting round the table seemed to find conversation difficult. Outside sudden gusts of wind came up and died away.

Vera shivered a little and said:

"There is a storm coming."

Blore made a contribution to the discourse. He said conversationally:

"There was an old fellow in the train from Plymouth yesterday. *He* kept saying a storm was coming. Wonderful how they know weather, these old salts."

Rogers went round the table collecting the meat plates.

Suddenly, with the plates held in his hands, he stopped.

He said in an odd scared voice:

"There's somebody running. . . ."

They could all hear it—running feet along the terrace.

In that minute, they knew—knew without being told. . . .

As by common accord, they all rose to their feet. They stood looking towards the door.

Dr. Armstrong appeared, his breath coming fast.

He said:

"General Macarthur—"

"Dead!" The word burst from Vera explosively.

Armstrong said:

"Yes, he's dead. . . ."

There was a pause—a long pause.

Seven people looked at each other and could find no words to say.

4

The storm broke just as the old man's body was borne in through the door.

The others were standing in the hall.

There was a sudden hiss and roar as the rain came down.

As Blore and Armstrong passed up the stairs with their burden,

Vera Claythorne turned suddenly and went into the deserted dining-room.

It was as they had left it. The sweet course stood ready on the sideboard untasted.

Vera went up to the table. She was there a minute or two later when Rogers came softly into the room.

He started when he saw her. Then his eyes asked a question.

He said:

"Oh, Miss, I—I just came to see . . ."

In a loud harsh voice that surprised herself Vera said:

"You're quite right, Rogers. Look for yourself. *There are only seven*. . . ."

5

General Macarthur had been laid on his bed.

After making a last examination Armstrong left the room and came downstairs. He found the others assembled in the drawing-room.

Miss Brent was knitting. Vera Claythorne was standing by the window looking out at the hissing rain. Blore was sitting squarely in a chair, his hands on his knees. Lombard was walking restlessly up and down. At the far end of the room Mr. Justice Wargrave was sitting in a grandfather chair. His eyes were half closed.

They opened as the doctor came into the room. He said in a clear penetrating voice:

"Well, doctor?"

Armstrong was very pale. He said:

"No question of heart failure or anything like that. Macarthur was hit with a life preserver or some such thing on the back of the head."

A little murmur went round, but the clear voice of the judge was raised once more.

"Did you find the actual weapon used?"

"No."

"Nevertheless you are sure of your facts?"

"I am quite sure."

Mr. Justice Wargrave said quietly:

"We know now exactly where we are."

There was no doubt now who was in charge of the situation. This morning Wargrave had sat huddled in his chair on the terrace refraining from any overt activity. Now he assumed command with the ease born of a long habit of authority. He definitely presided over the court.

Clearing his throat, he once more spoke.

"This morning, gentlemen, whilst I was sitting on the terrace, I was an observer of your activities. There could be little doubt of your purpose. You were searching the island for an unknown murderer?"

"Quite right, sir," said Philip Lombard.

The judge went on.

"You had come, doubtless, to the same conclusion that I had— namely that the deaths of Anthony Marston and Mrs. Rogers were neither accidental nor were they suicides. No doubt you also reached a certain conclusion as to the purpose of Mr. Owen in enticing us to this island?"

Blore said hoarsely:

"He's a madman! A loony."

The judge coughed.

"That almost certainly. But it hardly affects the issue. Our main preoccupation is this—to save our lives."

Armstrong said in a trembling voice:

"There's no one on the island, I tell you. *No one!*"

The judge stroked his jaw.

He said gently:

"In the sense you mean, no. I came to that conclusion early this morning. I could have told you that your search would be fruitless. Nevertheless I am strongly of the opinion that 'Mr. Owen' (to give him the name he himself has adopted) *is* on the island. Very much so. Given the scheme in question which is neither more nor less than the execution of justice upon certain individuals for offences which the law cannot touch, *there is only one way in which that scheme could be accomplished.* Mr. Owen could only come to the island in one way.

"It is perfectly clear. *Mr. Owen is one of us. . . .*"

6

"Oh, no, no, no. . . ."

It was Vera who burst out—almost in a moan. The judge turned a keen eye on her.

He said:

"My dear young lady, this is no time for refusing to look facts in the face. We are all in grave danger. One of us is U. N. Owen. And we do not know which of us. Of the ten people who came to this island three are definitely cleared. Anthony Marston, Mrs. Rogers, and General Macarthur have gone beyond suspicion. There are seven of us left. Of those seven, one is, if I may so express myself, a bogus little Indian boy."

He paused and looked round.

"Do I take it that you all agree?"

Armstrong said:

"It's fantastic—but I suppose you're right."

Blore said:

"Not a doubt of it. And if you ask me, I've a very good idea—"

A quick gesture of Mr. Justice Wargrave's hand stopped him. The judge said quietly:

"We will come to that presently. At the moment all I wish to establish is that we are in agreement on the facts."

Emily Brent, still knitting, said:

"Your argument seems logical. I agree that one of us is possessed by a devil."

Vera murmured:

"I can't believe it. . . . I can't. . . ."

Wargrave said:

"Lombard?"

"I agree, sir, absolutely."

The judge nodded his head in a satisfied manner. He said:

"Now let us examine the evidence. To begin with, is there any reason for suspecting one particular person? Mr. Blore, you have, I think, something to say."

Blore was breathing hard. He said:

"Lombard's got a revolver. He didn't tell the truth—last night. He admits it."

Philip Lombard smiled scornfully.

He said:

"I suppose I'd better explain again."

He did so, telling the story briefly and succinctly.

Blore said sharply:

"What's to prove it? There's nothing to corroborate your story."

The judge coughed.

"Unfortunately," he said, "we are all in that position. There is only our own word to go upon."

He leant forward.

"You have none of you yet grasped what a very peculiar situation this is. To my mind there is only one course of procedure to adopt. Is there any one whom we can definitely eliminate from suspicion on the evidence which is in our possession?"

Dr. Armstrong said quickly:

"I am a well-known professional man. The mere idea that I can be suspected of—"

Again a gesture of the judge's hand arrested a speaker before he finished his speech. Mr. Justice Wargrave said in his small clear voice:

"I, too, am a well-known person! But, my dear sir, that proves less than nothing! Doctors have gone mad before now. Judges have gone mad. So," he added, looking at Blore, "have policemen!"

Lombard said:

"At any rate, I suppose you'll leave the women out of it."

The judge's eyebrows rose. He said in the famous "acid" tone that Counsel knew so well:

"Do I understand you to assert that women are not subject to homicidal mania?"

Lombard said irritably:

"Of course not. But all the same, it hardly seems possible—"

He stopped. Mr. Justice Wargrave still in the same thin sour voice addressed Armstrong.

"I take it, Dr. Armstrong, that a woman would have been physically capable of striking the blow that killed poor Macarthur?"

The doctor said calmly:

"Perfectly capable—given a suitable instrument, such as a rubber truncheon or cosh."

"It would require no undue exertion of force?"

"Not at all."

Mr. Justice Wargrave wriggled his tortoise-like neck. He said:

"The other two deaths have resulted from the administration of drugs. That, no one will dispute, is easily compassed by a person of the smallest physical strength."

Vera cried angrily:

"I think you're mad!"

His eyes turned slowly till they rested on her. It was the dispassionate stare of a man well used to weighing humanity in the balance. She thought:

"He's just seeing me as a—as a specimen. And"—the thought came to her with real surprise—"he doesn't like me much!"

In measured tones the judge was saying:

"My dear young lady, do try and restrain your feelings. I am not accusing you." He bowed to Miss Brent. "I hope, Miss Brent, that you are not offended by my insistence that *all* of us are equally under suspicion?"

Emily Brent was knitting. She did not look up. In a cold voice she said:

"The idea that I should be accused of taking a fellow creature's life—not to speak of the lives of *three* fellow creatures—is, of course, quite absurd to any one who knows anything of my character. But I quite appreciate the fact that we are all strangers to one another and that in those circumstances, nobody can be exonerated without the fullest proof. There is, as I have said, a devil amongst us."

The judge said:

"Then we are agreed. There can be no elimination on the ground of character or position alone."

Lombard said:

"What about Rogers?"

The judge looked at him unblinkingly.

"What about him?"

Lombard said:

"Well, to my mind, Rogers seems pretty well ruled out."

Mr. Justice Wargrave said:

"Indeed, and on what grounds?"

Lombard said:

"He hasn't got the brains for one thing. And for another his wife was one of the victims."

The judge's heavy eyebrows rose once more. He said:

"In my time, young man, several people have come before me accused of the murders of their wives—*and* have been found guilty."

"Oh! I agree. Wife murder is perfectly possible—almost natural, let's say! But not this particular kind! I can believe in Rogers killing his wife because he was scared of her breaking down and giving him away, or because he'd taken a dislike to her, or because he wanted to link up with some nice little bit rather less long in the tooth. But I can't see him as the lunatic Mr. Owen dealing out crazy justice and starting on his own wife for a crime they both committed."

Mr. Justice Wargrave said:

"You are assuming heresay to be evidence. We do not know that Rogers and his wife conspired to murder their employer. That may have been a false statement, made so that Rogers should appear to be in the same position as ourselves. Mrs. Rogers' terror last night may have been due to the fact that she realized her husband was mentally unhinged."

Lombard said:

"Well, have it your own way. U. N. Owen is one of us. No exceptions allowed. We all qualify."

Mr. Justice Wargrave said:

"My point is that there can be no exceptions allowed on the score of *character, position,* or *probability.* What we must now examine is the possibility of eliminating one or more persons on the *facts.* To put it simply, is there among us one or more persons who could not possibly have administered either Cyanide to Anthony Marston, or an overdose of sleeping draught to Mrs. Rogers, and who had no opportunity of striking the blow that killed General Macarthur?"

Blore's rather heavy face lit up. He leant forward.

"Now you're talking, sir!" he said. "That's the stuff! Let's go into it. As regards young Marston I don't think there's anything to be done. It's already been suggested that some one from outside slipped something into the dregs of his glass before he refilled it for the last time. A person actually in the room could have done that even more easily. I can't remember if Rogers was in the room, but any of the rest of us could certainly have done it."

He paused, then went on.

"Now take the woman Rogers. The people who stand out there are her husband and the doctor. Either of them could have done it as easy as winking—"

Armstrong sprang to his feet. He was trembling.

"I protest— This is absolutely uncalled for! I swear that the dose I gave the woman was perfectly—"

"Dr. Armstrong."

The small sour voice was compelling. The doctor stopped with a jerk in the middle of his sentence. The small cold voice went on.

"Your indignation is very natural. Nevertheless you must admit that the facts have got to be faced. Either you or Rogers *could* have administered a fatal dose with the greatest ease. Let us now consider the position of the other people present. What chance had I, had Inspector Blore, had Miss Brent, had Miss Claythorne, had Mr. Lombard of administering poison? Can any one of us be completely and entirely eliminated?" He paused. "I think not."

Vera said angrily:

"I was nowhere near the woman! All of you can swear to that."

Mr. Justice Wargrave waited a minute, then he said:

"As far as my memory serves me the facts were these—will any one please correct me if I make a misstatement? Mrs. Rogers was lifted onto the sofa by Anthony Marston and Mr. Lombard and Dr. Armstrong went to her. He sent Rogers for brandy. There was then a question raised as to where the voice we had just heard had come from. We all went into the next room with the exception of Miss Brent who remained in this room—alone with the unconscious woman."

A spot of colour came into Emily Brent's cheeks. She stopped knitting. She said:

"This is outrageous!"

The remorseless small voice went on.

"When we returned to this room, you, Miss Brent, were bending over the woman on the sofa."

Emily Brent said:

"Is common humanity a criminal offence?"

Mr. Justice Wargrave said:

"I am only establishing facts. Rogers then entered the room with the brandy which, of course, he could quite well have doctored before entering the room. The brandy was administered to the woman and shortly afterwards her husband and Dr. Armstrong assisted her up to bed where Dr. Armstrong gave her a sedative."

Blore said:

"That's what happened. Absolutely. And that lets out the judge, Mr. Lombard, myself and Miss Claythorne."

His voice was loud and jubilant. Mr. Justice Wargrave, bringing a cold eye to bear upon him, murmured:

"Ah, but does it? We must take into account *every possible eventuality*."

Blore stared. He said:

"I don't get you."

Mr. Justice Wargrave said:

"Upstairs in her room, Mrs. Rogers is lying in bed. The sedative that the doctor has given her begins to take effect. She is vaguely sleepy and acquiescent. Supposing that at that moment there is a tap on the door and some one enters bringing her, shall we say, a tablet, or a draught, with the message that 'the doctor says you're to take this.' Do you imagine for one minute that she would not have swallowed it obediently without thinking twice about it?"

There was a silence. Blore shifted his feet and frowned. Philip Lombard said:

"I don't believe in that story for a minute. Besides none of us left this room for hours afterwards. There was Marston's death and all the rest of it."

The judge said:

"Some one could have left his or her bedroom—later."

Lombard objected:

"But then Rogers would have been up there."

Dr. Armstrong stirred.

"No," he said. "Rogers went downstairs to clear up in the dining-room and pantry. Any one could have gone up to the woman's bedroom then without being seen."

Emily Brent said:

"Surely, doctor, the woman would have been fast asleep by then under the influence of the drug you had administered?"

"In all likelihood, yes. But it is not a certainty. Until you have prescribed for a patient more than once you cannot tell their reaction to different drugs. There is, sometimes, a considerable period before a sedative takes effect. It depends on the personal idiosyncrasy of the patient towards that particular drug."

Lombard said:

"Of course you *would* say that, doctor. Suits your book—eh?"

Again Armstrong's face darkened with anger.

But again that passionless cold little voice stopped the words on his lips.

"No good result can come from recrimination. Facts are what we have to deal with. It is established, I think, that there is a possibility of such a thing as I have outlined occurring. I agree that its probability value is not high; though there again, it depends on who that person might have been. The appearance of Miss Brent or of Miss Claythorne on such an errand would have occasioned no surprise in the patient's mind. I agree that the appearance of myself, or of Mr. Blore, or of Mr. Lombard could have been, to say the least of it, unusual, but I still think the visit would have been received without the awakening of any real suspicion."

Blore said:

"And that gets us—*where?*"

7

Mr. Justice Wargrave, stroking his lip and looking quite passionless and inhuman, said:

"We have now dealt with the second killing, and have established the fact that no one of us can be completely exonerated from suspicion."

He paused and went on.

"We come now to the death of General Macarthur. That took place this morning. I will ask any one who considers that he or she has an alibi to state it in so many words. I myself will state at once that I have no valid alibi. I spent the morning sitting on the terrace and meditating on the singular position in which we all find ourselves.

"I sat on that chair on the terrace for the whole morning until the gong went, but there were, I should imagine, several periods during the morning when I was quite unobserved and during which it would have been possible for me to walk down to the sea, kill the General, and return to my chair. There is only my word for the fact that I never left the terrace. In the circumstances that is not enough. There must be *proof*."

Blore said:

"I was with Mr. Lombard and Dr. Armstrong all the morning. They'll bear me out."

Dr. Armstrong said:

"You went to the house for a rope."

Blore said:

"Of course, I did. Went straight there and straight back. You know I did."

Armstrong said:

"You were a long time. . . ."

Blore turned crimson.

He said:

"What the hell do you mean by that, Dr. Armstrong?"

Armstrong repeated:

"I only said you were a long time."

"Had to find it, didn't I? Can't lay your hands on a coil of rope all in a minute."

Mr. Justice Wargrave said:

"During Inspector Blore's absence, were you two gentlemen together?"

Armstrong said hotly:

"Certainly. That is, Lombard went off for a few minutes. I remained where I was."

Lombard said with a smile:

"I wanted to test the possibilities of heliographing to the mainland. Wanted to find the best spot. I was only absent a minute or two."

Armstrong nodded. He said:

"That's right. Not long enough to do a murder, I assure you."

The judge said:

"Did either of you two glance at your watches?"

"Well, no."

Philip Lombard said:

"I wasn't wearing one."

The judge said evenly:

"A minute or two is a vague expression."

He turned his head to the upright figure with the knitting lying on her lap.

"Miss Brent?"

Emily Brent said:

"I took a walk with Miss Claythorne up to the top of the island. Afterwards I sat on the terrace in the sun."

The judge said:

"I don't think I noticed you there."

"No, I was round the corner of the house to the east. It was out of the wind there."

"And you sat there till lunch time?"

"Yes."

"Miss Claythorne?"

Vera answered readily and clearly.

"I was with Miss Brent early this morning. After that I wandered about a bit. Then I went down and talked to General Macarthur."

Mr. Justice Wargrave interrupted. He said:

"What time was that?"

Vera for the first time was vague. She said:

"I don't know. About an hour before lunch, I think—or it might have been less."

Blore asked:

"Was it after we'd spoken to him or before?"

Vera said:

"I don't know. He—he was very queer."

She shivered.

"In what way was he queer?" the judge wanted to know.

Vera said in a low voice:

"He said we were all going to die—he said he was waiting for the end. He—he frightened me. . . ."

The judge nodded. He said:

"What did you do next?"

"I went back to the house. Then, just before lunch, I went out again and up behind the house. I've been terribly restless all day."

Mr. Justice Wargrave stroked his chin. He said:

"There remains Rogers. Though I doubt if his evidence will add anything to our sum of knowledge."

Rogers, summoned before the court, had very little to tell. He had been busy all the morning about household duties and with the preparation of lunch. He had taken cocktails onto the terrace before lunch and had then gone up to remove his things from the attic to another room. He had not looked out of the window during the morning and had seen nothing that could have any bearing upon the death of General Macarthur. He would swear definitely that there had been eight china figures upon the dining-table when he laid the table for lunch.

At the conclusion of Rogers' evidence there was a pause.

Mr. Justice Wargrave cleared his throat.

Lombard murmured to Vera Claythorne:

"The summing up will now take place!"

The judge said:

"We have inquired into the circumstances of these three deaths to the best of our ability. Whilst probability in some cases is against certain people being implicated, yet we cannot say definitely that any one person can be considered as cleared of all complicity. I reiterate my positive belief that of the seven persons assembled in this room one is a dangerous and probably insane criminal. There is no evidence before us as to who that person is. All we can do at the present juncture is to consider what measures we can take for communicating with the mainland for help, and in the event of help being delayed (as is only too possible given the state of the weather) what measures we must adopt to ensure our safety.

"I would ask you all to consider this carefully and to give me any suggestions that may occur to you. In the meantime I warn everybody to be upon his or her guard. So far the murderer has had an easy task, since his victims have been unsuspicious. From now on, it is our task to suspect each and every one amongst us. Forewarned is forearmed. Take no risks and be alert to danger. That is all."

Philip Lombard murmured beneath his breath:

"The court will now adjourn. . . ."

CHAPTER 10

"Do you believe it?" Vera asked.

She and Philip Lombard sat on the window-sill of the living-room. Outside the rain poured down and the wind howled in great shuddering gusts against the window-panes.

Philip Lombard cocked his head slightly on one side before answering. Then he said:

"You mean, do I believe that old Wargrave is right when he says it's one of us?"

"Yes."

Philip Lombard said slowly:

"It's difficult to say. Logically, you know, he's right, and yet—"

Vera took the words out of his mouth.

"And yet it seems so incredible!"

Philip Lombard made a grimace.

"The whole thing's incredible! But after Macarthur's death there's no more doubt as to one thing. There's no question now of accidents or suicides. It's definitely murder. Three murders up to date."

Vera shivered. She said:

"It's like some awful dream. I keep feeling that things like this *can't* happen!"

He said with understanding:

"I know. Presently a tap will come on the door, and early morning tea will be brought in."

Vera said:

"Oh, how I wish that could happen!"

Philip Lombard said gravely:

"Yes, but it won't! We're all in the dream! And we've got to be pretty much upon our guard from now on."

Vera said, lowering her voice:

"If—if it *is* one of them—which do you think it is?"

Philip Lombard grinned suddenly. He said:

"I take it you are excepting our two selves? Well, that's all right. I know very well that I'm not the murderer, and I don't fancy that there's anything insane about you, Vera. You strike me as being one of the sanest and most level-headed girls I've come across. I'd stake my reputation on your sanity."

With a slightly wry smile, Vera said:

"Thank you."

He said:

"Come now, Miss Vera Claythorne, aren't you going to return the compliment?"

Vera hesitated a minute, then she said:

"You've admitted, you know, that you don't hold human life particularly sacred, but all the same I can't see you as—as the man who dictated that gramophone record."

Lombard said:

"Quite right. If I were to commit one or more murders it would be solely for what I could get out of them. This mass clearance isn't my line of country. Good, then we'll eliminate ourselves and concentrate on our five fellow prisoners. Which of them is U. N. Owen? Well, at a guess, and with absolutely nothing to go upon, I'd plump for Wargrave!"

"Oh!" Vera sounded surprised. She thought a minute or two and then said, "Why?"

"Hard to say exactly. But to begin with, he's an old man and he's been presiding over courts of law for years. That is to say, he's played God Almighty for a good many months every year. That must go to a man's head eventually. He gets to see himself as all powerful, as holding the power of life and death—and it's possible that his brain might snap and he might want to go one step farther and be Executioner and Judge Extraordinary."

Vera said slowly:

"Yes, I suppose that's *possible*. . . ."

Lombard said:

"Who do you plump for?"

Without any hesitation Vera answered:

"Dr. Armstrong."

Lombard gave a low whistle.

"The doctor, eh? You know, I should have put him last of all."

Vera shook her head.

"Oh, no! Two of the deaths have been poison. That rather points to a doctor. And then you can't get over the fact that the only thing we are absolutely certain Mrs. Rogers had was the sleeping draught that *he* gave her."

Lombard admitted:

"Yes, that's true."

Vera persisted:

"If a doctor went mad, it would be a long time before any one suspected. And doctors overwork and have a lot of strain."

Philip Lombard said:

"Yes, but I doubt if he could have killed Macarthur. He wouldn't have had time during that brief interval when I left him—not, that is, unless he fairly hared down there and back again, and I doubt if he's in good enough training to do that and show no signs of it."

Vera said:

"He didn't do it then. He had an opportunity later."

"When?"

"When he went down to call the General to lunch."

Philip whistled again very softly. He said:

"So you think he did it then? Pretty cool thing to do."

Vera said impatiently:

"What risk was there? He's the only person here with medical knowledge. He can swear the body's been dead at least an hour and who's to contradict him?"

Philip looked at her thoughtfully.

"You know," he said, "that's a clever idea of yours. I wonder—"

2

"Who is it, Mr. Blore? That's what I want to know. Who is it?"

Rogers' face was working. His hands were clenched round the polishing leather that he held in his hand.

Ex-Inspector Blore said:

"Eh, my lad, that's the question!"

"One of us, 'is lordship said. Which one? That's what I want to know. Who's the fiend in 'uman form?"

"That," said Blore, "is what we all would like to know."

Rogers said shrewdly:

"But you've got an idea, Mr. Blore. You've got an idea, 'aven't you?"

"I may have an idea," said Blore slowly. "But that's a long way from being sure. I may be wrong. All I can say is that if I'm right the person in question is a very cool customer—a very cool customer indeed."

Rogers wiped the perspiration from his forehead. He said hoarsely:

"It's like a bad dream, that's what it is."

Blore said, looking at him curiously:

"Got any ideas yourself, Rogers?"

The butler shook his head. He said hoarsely:

"I don't know. I don't know at all. And that's what's frightening the life out of me. To have no idea . . ."

3

Dr. Armstrong said violently:

"We must get out of here—we must—we must! At all costs!"

Mr. Justice Wargrave looked thoughtfully out of the smoking-room window. He played with the cord of his eyeglasses. He said:

"I do not, of course, profess to be a weather prophet. But I should say that it is very unlikely that a boat could reach us—even if they knew of our plight—under twenty-four hours—and even then only if the wind drops."

Dr. Armstrong dropped his head in his hands and groaned.

He said:

"And in the meantime we may all be murdered in our beds?"

"I hope not," said Mr. Justice Wargrave. "I intend to take every possible precaution against such a thing happening."

It flashed across Dr. Armstrong's mind that an old man like the judge, was far more tenacious of life than a younger man would be. He had often marvelled at that fact in his professional career. Here was he, junior to the judge by perhaps twenty years, and yet with a vastly inferior sense of self-preservation.

Mr. Justice Wargrave was thinking:

"Murdered in our beds! These doctors are all the same—they think in *clichés*. A thoroughly commonplace mind."

The doctor said:

"There have been three victims already, remember."

"Certainly. But you must remember that they were unprepared for the attack. We are forewarned."

Dr. Armstrong said bitterly:

"What can we do? Sooner or later—"

"I think," said Mr. Justice Wargrave, "that there are several things we can do."

Armstrong said:

"We've no idea, even, who it can be—"

The judge stroked his chin and murmured:

"Oh, you know, I wouldn't quite say that."

Armstrong stared at him.

"Do you mean you *know?*"

Mr. Justice Wargrave said cautiously:

"As regards actual evidence, such as is necessary in court, I admit that I have none. But it appears to me, reviewing the whole business, that one particular person is sufficiently clearly indicated. Yes, I think so."

Armstrong stared at him.

He said:

"I don't understand."

4

Miss Brent was upstairs in her bedroom.

She took up her Bible and went to sit by the window.

She opened it. Then, after a minute's hesitation, she set it aside and went over to the dressing-table. From a drawer in it she took out a small black-covered notebook.

She opened it and began writing.

"A terrible thing has happened. General Macarthur is dead. (His cousin married Elsie MacPherson.) There is no doubt but that he was murdered. After luncheon the judge made us a most interesting speech. He is convinced that the murderer is one of us. That means that one of us is possessed by a devil. I had already suspected that. Which of us is it? They are all asking themselves that. I alone know. . . ."

She sat for some time without moving. Her eyes grew vague and filmy. The pencil straggled drunkenly in her fingers. In shaking loose capitals she wrote:

THE MURDERER'S NAME IS BEATRICE TAYLOR. . . .

Her eyes closed.

Suddenly, with a start, she awoke. She looked down at the note-

book. With an angry exclamation she scored through the vague unevenly scrawled characters of the last sentence.

She said in a low voice:

"Did *I* write that? Did I? *I must be going mad. . . .*"

5

The storm increased. The wind howled against the side of the
house.

Every one was in the living-room. They sat listlessly huddled together. And, surreptitiously, they watched each other.

When Rogers brought in the tea-tray, they all jumped.

He said:

"Shall I draw the curtains? It would make it more cheerful like."

Receiving an assent to this, the curtains were drawn and the lamps
turned on. The room grew more cheerful. A little of the shadow
lifted. Surely, by to-morrow, the storm would be over and some one
would come—a boat would arrive. . . .

Vera Claythorne said:

"Will you pour out tea, Miss Brent?"

The elder woman replied:

"No, you do it, dear. That tea-pot is so heavy. And I have lost two
skeins of my grey knitting-wool. So annoying."

Vera moved to the tea-table. There was a cheerful rattle and clink
of china. Normality returned.

Tea! Blessed ordinary everyday afternoon tea! Philip Lombard
made a cheery remark. Blore responded. Dr. Armstrong told a hu-
morous story. Mr. Justice Wargrave, who ordinarily hated tea, sipped
approvingly.

Into this relaxed atmosphere came Rogers.

And Rogers was upset. He said nervously and at random:

"Excuse me, sir, but does any one know what's become of the
bathroom curtain?"

Lombard's head went up with a jerk.

"The bathroom curtain? What the devil do you mean, Rogers?"

"It's gone, sir, clean vanished. I was going round drawing all the
curtains and the one in the lav—bathroom wasn't there any longer."

Mr. Justice Wargrave asked:

"Was it there this morning?"

"Oh, yes, sir."

Blore said:

"What kind of a curtain was it?"

"Scarlet oilsilk, sir. It went with the scarlet tiles."

Lombard said:

"And it's gone?"

"Gone, sir."

They stared at each other.

Blore said heavily:

"Well—after all—what of it? It's mad—but so's everything else. Anyway, it doesn't matter. You can't kill anybody with an oilsilk curtain. Forget about it."

Rogers said:

"Yes, sir, thank you, sir."

He went out, shutting the door behind him.

Inside the room, the pall of fear had fallen anew.

Again, surreptitiously, they watched each other.

6

Dinner came, was eaten, and cleared away. A simple meal, mostly out of tins.

Afterwards, in the living-room, the strain was almost too great to be borne.

At nine o'clock, Emily Brent rose to her feet.

She said:

"I'm going to bed."

Vera said:

"I'll go to bed too."

The two women went up the stairs and Lombard and Blore came with them. Standing at the top of the stairs, the two men watched the women go into their respective rooms and shut the doors. They heard the sound of two bolts being shot and the turning of two keys.

Blore said with a grin:

"No need to tell 'em to lock their doors!"

Lombard said:

"Well, *they*'re all right for the night, at any rate!"

He went down again and the other followed him.

7

The four men went to bed an hour later. They went up together. Rogers, from the dining-room where he was setting the table for breakfast, saw them go up. He heard them pause on the landing above.

Then the judge's voice spoke.

"I need hardly advise you, gentlemen, to lock your doors."

Blore said:

"And, what's more, put a chair under the handle. There are ways of turning locks from the outside."

Lombard murmured:

"My dear Blore, the trouble with you is you know too much!"

The judge said gravely:

"Good-night, gentlemen. May we all meet safely in the morning!"

Rogers came out of the dining-room and slipped halfway up the stairs. He saw four figures pass through four doors and heard the turning of four locks and the shooting of four bolts.

He nodded his head.

"That's all right," he muttered.

He went back into the dining-room. Yes, everything was ready for the morning. His eye lingered on the centre plaque of looking-glass and the seven little china figures.

A sudden grin transformed his face.

He murmured:

"I'll see no one plays tricks to-night, at any rate."

Crossing the room he locked the door to the pantry. Then going through the other door to the hall he pulled the door to, locked it and slipped the key into his pocket.

Then, extinguishing the lights, he hurried up the stairs and into his new bedroom.

There was only one possible hiding-place in it, the tall wardrobe, and he looked into that immediately. Then, locking and bolting the door, he prepared for bed.

He said to himself:

"No more Indian tricks to-night. I've seen to that. . . ."

PHILIP LOMBARD had the habit of waking at daybreak. He did so on this particular morning. He raised himself on an elbow and listened. The wind had somewhat abated but was still blowing. He could hear no sound of rain. . . .

At eight o'clock the wind was blowing more strongly, but Lombard did not hear it. He was asleep again.

At nine-thirty he was sitting on the edge of his bed looking at his watch. He put it to his ear. Then his lips drew back from his teeth in that curious wolf-like smile characteristic of the man.

He said very softly:

"I think the time has come to do something about this."

At twenty-five minutes to ten he was tapping on the closed door of Blore's room.

The latter opened it cautiously. His hair was tousled and his eyes were still dim with sleep.

Philip Lombard said affably:

"Sleeping the clock round? Well, shows you've got an easy conscience."

Blore said shortly:

"What's the matter?"

Lombard answered:

"Anybody called you—or brought you any tea? Do you know what time it is?"

Blore looked over his shoulder at a small travelling clock by his bedside.

He said:

"Twenty-five to ten. Wouldn't have believed I could have slept like that. Where's Rogers?"

Philip Lombard said:

"It's a case of echo answers where?"

"What d'you mean?" asked the other sharply.

Lombard said:

"I mean that Rogers is missing. He isn't in his room or anywhere else. And there's no kettle on and the kitchen fire isn't even lit."

Blore swore under his breath. He said:

"Where the devil can he be? Out on the island somewhere? Wait till I get some clothes on. See if the others know anything."

Philip Lombard nodded. He moved along the line of closed doors.

He found Armstrong up and nearly dressed. Mr. Justice Wargrave, like Blore, had to be roused from sleep. Vera Claythorne was dressed. Emily Brent's room was empty.

The little party moved through the house. Rogers' room, as Philip Lombard had already ascertained, was untenanted. The bed had been slept in, and his razor and sponge and soap were wet.

Lombard said:

"He got up all right."

Vera said in a low voice which she tried to make firm and assured:

"You don't think he's—hiding somewhere—waiting for us?"

Lombard said:

"My dear girl, I'm prepared to think anything of any one! My advice is that we keep together until we find him."

Armstrong said:

"He must be out on the island somewhere."

Blore who had joined them, dressed, but still unshaved, said:

"Where's Miss Brent got to—that's another mystery?"

But as they arrived in the hall, Emily Brent came in through the front door. She had on a mackintosh. She said:

"The sea is as high as ever. I shouldn't think any boat could put out to-day."

Blore said:

"Have you been wandering about the island alone, Miss Brent? Don't you realize that that's an exceedingly foolish thing to do?"

Emily Brent said:

"I assure you, Mr. Blore, that I kept an extremely sharp lookout."

Blore grunted. He said:

"Seen anything of Rogers?"

Miss Brent's eyebrows rose.

"Rogers? No, I haven't seen him this morning. Why?"

Mr. Justice Wargrave, shaved, dressed and with his false teeth in position, came down the stairs. He moved to the open dining-room door. He said:

"Ha, laid the table for breakfast, I see."

Lombard said:

"He might have done that last night."

They all moved inside the room, looking at the neatly set plates and cutlery. At the row of cups on the sideboard. At the felt mats placed ready for the coffee urn.

It was Vera who saw it first. She caught the judge's arm and the grip of her athletic fingers made the old gentleman wince.

She cried out:

"The Indians! Look!"

There were only six china figures in the middle of the table.

2

They found him shortly afterwards.

He was in the little wash-house across the yard. He had been chopping sticks in preparation for lighting the kitchen fire. The small chopper was still in his hand. A bigger chopper, a heavy affair, was leaning against the door—the metal of it stained a dull brown. It corresponded only too well with the deep wound in the back of Rogers' head. . . .

3

"Perfectly clear," said Armstrong. "The murderer must have crept up behind him, swung the chopper once and brought it down on his head as he was bending over."

Blore was busy on the handle of the chopper and the flour sifter from the kitchen.

Mr. Justice Wargrave asked:

"Would it have needed great force, doctor?"

Armstrong said gravely:

"A woman could have done it if that's what you mean." He gave a quick glance round. Vera Claythorne and Emily Brent had retired to the kitchen. "The girl could have done it easily—she's an athletic type. In appearance Miss Brent is fragile looking, but that type of woman has often a lot of wiry strength. And you must remember that any one who's mentally unhinged has a good deal of unsuspected strength."

The judge nodded thoughtfully.

Blore rose from his knees with a sigh. He said:

"No fingerprints. Handle was wiped afterwards."

A sound of laughter was heard—they turned sharply. Vera Claythorne was standing in the yard. She cried out in a high shrill voice, shaken with wild bursts of laughter:

"Do they keep bees on this island? Tell me that. Where do we go for honey? Ha! ha!"

They stared at her uncomprehendingly. It was as though the sane well-balanced girl had gone mad before their eyes. She went on in that high unnatural voice.

"Don't stare like that! As though you thought I was mad. It's sane enough what I'm asking. Bees, hives, bees! Oh, don't you understand? Haven't you read that idiotic rhyme? It's up in all your bedrooms—put there for you to study! We might have come here straightaway if we'd had sense. *Seven little Indian boys chopping up sticks.* And the next verse. I know the whole thing by heart, I tell you! *Six little Indian boys playing with a hive.* And that's why I'm asking—do they keep bees on this island?—isn't it funny?—isn't it damned funny . . . ?"

She began laughing wildly again. Dr. Armstrong strode forward. He raised his hand and struck her a flat blow on the cheek.

She gasped, hiccuped—and swallowed. She stood motionless a minute, then she said:

"Thank you . . . I'm all right now."

Her voice was once more calm and controlled—the voice of the efficient games mistress.

She turned and went across the yard into the kitchen saying: "Miss Brent and I are getting you breakfast. Can you—bring some sticks to light the fire?"

The marks of the doctor's hand stood out red on her cheek.

As she went into the kitchen Blore said:

"Well, you dealt with that all right, doctor."

Armstrong said apologetically:

"Had to! We can't cope with hysteria on the top of everything else."

Philip Lombard said:

"She's not a hysterical type."

Armstrong agreed.

"Oh, no. Good healthy sensible girl. Just the sudden shock. It might happen to anybody."

Rogers had chopped a certain amount of firewood before he had been killed. They gathered it up and took it into the kitchen. Vera and Emily Brent were busy. Miss Brent was raking out the stove. Vera was cutting the rind off the bacon.

Emily Brent said:

"Thank you. We'll be as quick as we can—say half an hour to three quarters. The kettle's got to boil."

4

Ex-Inspector Blore said in a low hoarse voice to Philip Lombard:
"Know what I'm thinking?"

Philip Lombard said:

"As you're just about to tell me, it's not worth the trouble of guessing."

Ex-Inspector Blore was an earnest man. A light touch was incomprehensible to him. He went on heavily:

"There was a case in America. Old gentleman and his wife—both killed with an axe. Middle of the morning. Nobody in the house but the daughter and the maid. Maid, it was proved, couldn't have done it. Daughter was a respectable middle-aged spinster. Seemed incredible. So incredible that they acquitted her. But they never found any other explanation." He paused. "I thought of that when I saw the axe —and then when I went into the kitchen and saw her there so neat and calm. Hadn't turned a hair! That girl, coming all over hysterical —well, that's natural—the sort of thing you'd expect—don't you think so?"

Philip Lombard said laconically:

"It might be."

Blore went on.

"But the other! So neat and prim—wrapped up in that apron—Mrs. Rogers' apron, I suppose—saying: 'Breakfast will be ready in half an hour or so.' If you ask me that woman's as mad as a hatter! Lots of elderly spinsters go that way—I don't mean go in for homicide on the grand scale, but go queer in their heads. Unfortunately it's taken her this way. Religious mania—thinks she's God's instrument, something of that kind! She sits in her room, you know, reading her Bible."

Philip Lombard sighed and said:

"That's hardly proof positive of an unbalanced mentality, Blore."

But Blore went on, ploddingly, perseveringly:

"And then she was out—in her mackintosh, said she'd been down to look at the sea."

The other shook his head.

He said:

"Rogers was killed as he was chopping firewood—that is to say first thing when he got up. Miss Brent wouldn't have needed to wander about outside for hours afterwards. If you ask me, the murderer of Rogers would take jolly good care to be rolled up in bed snoring."

Blore said:

"You're missing the point, Mr. Lombard. If the woman was innocent she'd be too dead scared to go wandering about by herself. She'd only do that *if she knew that she had nothing to fear*. That's to say *if she herself is the criminal*."

Philip Lombard said:

"That's a good point. . . . Yes, I hadn't thought of that."

He added with a faint grin:

"Glad you don't still suspect me."

Blore said rather shamefacedly:

"I did start by thinking of you—that revolver—and the queer story you told—or didn't tell. But I've realized now that that was really a bit too obvious." He paused and said: "Hope you feel the same about me."

Philip said thoughtfully:

"I may be wrong, of course, but I can't feel that you've got enough imagination for this job. All I can say is, if you're the criminal, you're a damned fine actor and I take my hat off to you." He lowered his voice. "Just between ourselves, Blore, and taking into account that we'll probably both be a couple of stiffs before another day is out, you did indulge in that spot of perjury, I suppose?"

Blore shifted uneasily from one foot to the other. He said at last:

"Doesn't seem to make much odds now. Oh, well, here goes. Landor was innocent right enough. The gang had got me squared and between us we got him put away for a stretch. Mind you, I wouldn't admit this—"

"If there were any witnesses," finished Lombard with a grin. "It's just between you and me. Well, I hope you made a tidy bit out of it."

"Didn't make what I should have done. Mean crowd, the Purcell gang. I got my promotion, though."

"And Landor got penal servitude and died in prison."

"I couldn't know he was going to die, could I?" demanded Blore.

"No, that was your bad luck."

"Mine? His, you mean."

"Yours, too. Because, as a result of it, it looks as though your own life is going to be cut unpleasantly short."

"Me?" Blore stared at him. "Do you think I'm going to go the way of Rogers and the rest of them? Not me! I'm watching out for myself pretty carefully, I can tell you."

Lombard said:

"Oh, well—I'm not a betting man. And anyway if you were dead I wouldn't get paid."

"Look here, Mr. Lombard, what do you mean?"

Philip Lombard showed his teeth. He said:

"I mean, my dear Blore, that in my opinion you haven't got a chance!"

"What?"

"Your lack of imagination is going to make you absolutely a sitting target. A criminal of the imagination of U. N. Owen can make rings round you any time he—or she—wants to."

Blore's face went crimson. He demanded angrily:

"And what about you?"

Philip Lombard's face went hard and dangerous.

He said:

"I've a pretty good imagination of my own. I've been in tight places before now and got out of them! I think—I won't say more than that but I *think* I'll get out of this one."

5

The eggs were in the frying-pan. Vera, at the stove, thought to herself:

"Why did I make a hysterical fool of myself? That was a mistake. Keep calm, my girl, keep calm."

After all, she'd always prided herself on her levelheadedness!

"Miss Claythorne was wonderful—kept her head—started off swimming after Cyril at once."

Why think of that now? All that was over—over. . . . Cyril had disappeared long before she got near the rock. She had felt the current take her, sweeping her out to sea. She had let herself go with it—swimming quietly, floating—till the boat arrived at last. . . .

They had praised her courage and her *sang-froid*. . . .

But not Hugo. Hugo had just—looked at her. . . .

God, how it hurt, even now, to think of Hugo. . . .

Where was he? What was he doing? Was he engaged—married?

Emily Brent said sharply:

"Vera, that bacon is burning."

"Oh, sorry, Miss Brent, so it is. How stupid of me."

Emily Brent lifted out the last egg from the sizzling fat.

Vera, putting fresh pieces of bacon in the frying-pan, said curiously:

"You're wonderfully calm, Miss Brent."

Emily Brent said, pressing her lips together:

"I was brought up to keep my head and never to make a fuss."

Vera thought mechanically:

"Repressed as a child. . . . That accounts for a lot. . . ."

She said:

"Aren't you afraid?"

She paused and then added:

"Or don't you mind dying?"

Dying! It was as though a sharp little gimlet had run into the solid congealed mass of Emily Brent's brain. Dying? But *she* wasn't going to die! The others would die—yes—but not she, Emily Brent. This girl didn't understand! Emily wasn't afraid, naturally—none of the Brents were afraid. All her people were Service people. They faced death unflinchingly. They led upright lives just as she, Emily Brent, had led an upright life. . . . She had never done anything to be ashamed of. . . . And so, naturally, *she* wasn't going to die. . . .

"The Lord is mindful of his own." "Thou shalt not be afraid for the terror by night; nor for the arrow that flieth by day. . . ." It was daylight now—there was no terror. *"We shall none of us leave this island."* Who had said that? General Macarthur, of course, whose cousin had married Elsie MacPherson. He hadn't seemed to *care*. He had seemed—actually—to *welcome* the idea! Wicked! Almost impious to feel that way. Some people thought so little of death that they actually took their own lives. *Beatrice Taylor*. . . . Last night she had dreamed of Beatrice—dreamt that she was outside pressing her face against the window and moaning, asking to be let in. But Emily Brent hadn't wanted to let her in. Because, if she did, something terrible would happen. . . .

Emily came to herself with a start. That girl was looking at her very strangely. She said in a brisk voice:

"Everything's ready, isn't it? We'll take the breakfast in."

6

Breakfast was a curious meal. Every one was very polite.

"May I get you some more coffee, Miss Brent?"

"Miss Claythorne, a slice of ham?"

"Another piece of bacon?"

Six people, all outwardly self-possessed and normal.

And within? Thoughts that ran round in a circle like squirrels in a cage. . . .

"What next? What next? Who? Which?"

"Would it work? I wonder. It's worth trying. If there's time. My God, if there's time. . . ."

"Religious mania, that's the ticket. . . . Looking at her, though, you can hardly believe it. . . . Suppose I'm wrong. . . ."

"It's crazy—everything's crazy. I'm going crazy. Wool disappearing —red silk curtains—it doesn't make sense. I can't get the hang of it. . . ."

"The damned fool, he believed every word I said to him. It was easy. . . . I must be careful, though, very careful."

"Six of those little china figures . . . only six—how many will there be by to-night? . . ."

"Who'll have the last egg?"

"Marmalade?"

"Thanks, can I give you some ham?"

Six people, behaving normally at breakfast. . . .

CHAPTER 12

THE MEAL was over.

Mr. Justice Wargrave cleared his throat. He said in a small authoritative voice:

"It would be advisable, I think, if we met to discuss the situation. Shall we say in half an hour's time in the drawing-room?"

Every one made a sound suggestive of agreement.

Vera began to pile plates together.

She said:

"I'll clear away and wash up."

Philip Lombard said:

"We'll bring the stuff out to the pantry for you."

"Thanks."

Emily Brent, rising to her feet, sat down again. She said:

"Oh, dear."

The judge said:

"Anything the matter, Miss Brent?"

Emily said apologetically:

"I'm sorry. I'd like to help Miss Claythorne, but I don't know how it is. I feel just a little giddy."

"Giddy, eh?" Dr. Armstrong came towards her. "Quite natural. Delayed shock. I can give you something to—"

"No!"

The word burst from her lips like an exploding shell.

It took every one aback. Dr. Armstrong flushed a deep red.

There was no mistaking the fear and suspicion in her face. He said stiffly:

"Just as you please, Miss Brent."

She said:

"I don't wish to take anything—anything at all. I will just sit here quietly till the giddiness passes off."

They finished clearing away the breakfast things.

Blore said:

"I'm a domestic sort of man. I'll give you a hand, Miss Claythorne."

Vera said: "Thank you."

Emily Brent was left alone sitting in the dining-room.

For a while she heard a faint murmur of voices from the pantry.

The giddiness was passing. She felt drowsy now, as though she could easily go to sleep.

There was a buzzing in her ears—or was it a real buzzing in the room?

She thought:

"It's like a bee—a bumblebee."

Presently she saw the bee. It was crawling up the window-pane.

Vera Claythorne had talked about bees this morning.

Bees and honey. . . .

She liked honey. Honey in the comb, and strain it yourself through a muslin bag. Drip, drip, drip. . . .

There was somebody in the room . . . somebody all wet and dripping. . . . *Beatrice Taylor came from the river*. . . .

She had only to turn her head and she would see her.

But she couldn't turn her head. . . .

If she were to call out . . .

But she couldn't call out. . . .

There was no one else in the house. She was all alone. . . .

She heard footsteps—soft dragging footsteps coming up behind her. The stumbling footsteps of the drowned girl. . . .

There was a wet dank smell in her nostrils. . . .

On the window-pane the bee was buzzing—buzzing. . . .
And then she felt the prick.
The bee sting on the side of her neck. . . .

2

In the drawing-room they were waiting for Emily Brent.
Vera Claythorne said:
"Shall I go and fetch her?"
Blore said quickly:
"Just a minute."
Vera sat down again. Every one looked inquiringly at Blore.
He said:
"Look here, everybody, my opinion's this: we needn't look farther for the author of these deaths than the dining-room at this minute. I'd take my oath that woman's the one we're after!"
Armstrong said:
"And the motive?"
"Religious mania. What do you say, doctor?"
Armstrong said:
"It's perfectly possible. I've nothing to say against it. But of course we've no proof."
Vera said:
"She was very odd in the kitchen when we were getting breakfast. Her eyes—" She shivered.
Lombard said:
"You can't judge her by that. We're all a bit off our heads by now!"
Blore said:
"There's another thing. She's the only one who wouldn't give an explanation after that gramophone record. Why? Because she hadn't any to give."
Vera stirred in her chair. She said:
"That's not quite true. She told me—afterwards."
Wargrave said:
"What did she tell you, Miss Claythorne?"
Vera repeated the story of Beatrice Taylor.
Mr. Justice Wargrave observed:
"A perfectly straightforward story. I personally should have no difficulty in accepting it. Tell me, Miss Claythorne, did she appear to

be troubled by a sense of guilt or a feeling of remorse for her attitude in the matter?"

"None whatever," said Vera. "She was completely unmoved."

Blore said:

"Hearts as hard as flints, these righteous spinsters! Envy, mostly!"

Mr. Justice Wargrave said:

"It is now five minutes to eleven. I think we should summon Miss Brent to join our conclave."

Blore said:

"Aren't you going to take any action?"

The judge said:

"I fail to see what action we can take. Our suspicions are, at the moment, only suspicions. I will, however, ask Dr. Armstrong to observe Miss Brent's demeanour very carefully. Let us now go into the dining-room."

They found Emily Brent sitting in the chair in which they had left her. From behind they saw nothing amiss, except that she did not seem to hear their entrance into the room.

And then they saw her face—suffused with blood, with blue lips and staring eyes.

Blore said:

"My God, she's dead!"

3

The small quiet voice of Mr. Justice Wargrave said:

"One more of us acquitted—too late!"

Armstrong was bent over the dead woman. He sniffed the lips, shook his head, peered into the eyelids.

Lombard said impatiently:

"How did she die, doctor? She was all right when we left her here!"

Armstrong's attention was riveted on a mark on the right side of the neck.

He said:

"That's the mark of a hypodermic syringe."

There was a buzzing sound from the window. Vera cried:

"Look—a bee—*a bumblebee*. Remember what I said this morning!"

Armstrong said grimly:

"It wasn't that bee that stung her! A human hand held the syringe."

The judge asked:

"What poison was injected?"

Armstrong answered:

"At a guess, one of the Cyanides. Probably Potassium Cyanide, same as Anthony Marston. She must have died almost immediately by asphyxiation."

Vera cried:

"But that *bee?* It can't be *coincidence?*"

Lombard said grimly:

"Oh, no, it isn't coincidence! It's our murderer's touch of local colour! He's a playful beast. Likes to stick to his damnable nursery jingle as closely as possible!"

For the first time his voice was uneven, almost shrill. It was as though even his nerves, seasoned by a long career of hazards and dangerous undertakings, had given out at last.

He said violently:

"It's mad!—absolutely mad—we're all mad!"

The judge said calmly:

"We have still, I hope, our reasoning powers. *Did any one bring a hypodermic syringe to this house?*"

Dr. Armstrong, straightening himself, said in a voice that was not too well assured:

"Yes, I did."

Four pairs of eyes fastened on him. He braced himself against the deep hostile suspicion of those eyes. He said:

"Always travel with one. Most doctors do."

Mr. Justice Wargrave said calmly:

"Quite so. Will you tell us, doctor, where that syringe is now?"

"In the suitcase in my room."

Wargrave said:

"We might, perhaps, verify that fact."

The five of them went upstairs, a silent procession.

The contents of the suitcase were turned out on the floor.

The hypodermic syringe was not there.

4

Armstrong said violently:

"Somebody must have taken it!"

There was silence in the room.

Armstrong stood with his back to the window. Four pairs of eyes were on him, black with suspicion and accusation. He looked from Wargrave to Vera and repeated helplessly—weakly:

"I tell you some one must have taken it."

Blore was looking at Lombard who returned his gaze.

The judge said:

"There are five of us here in this room. *One of us is a murderer.* The position is fraught with grave danger. Everything must be done in order to safeguard the four of us who are innocent. I will now ask you, Dr. Armstrong, what drugs you have in your possession?"

Armstrong replied:

"I have a small medicine case here. You can examine it. You will find some sleeping stuff—trional and sulphonal tablets—a packet of bromide, bicarbonate of soda, aspirin. Nothing else. I have no Cyanide in my possession."

The judge said:

"I have, myself, some sleeping tablets—sulphonal, I think they are. I presume they would be lethal if a sufficiently large dose were given. You, Mr. Lombard, have in your possession a revolver."

Philip Lombard said sharply:

"What if I have?"

"Only this. I propose that the doctor's supply of drugs, my own sulphonal tablets, your revolver and anything else of the nature of drugs or firearms should be collected together and placed in a safe place. That after this is done, we should each of us submit to a search —both of our persons and of our effects."

Lombard said:

"I'm damned if I'll give up my revolver!"

Wargrave said sharply:

"Mr. Lombard, you are a very strongly built and powerful young man, but ex-Inspector Blore is also a man of powerful physique. I do not know what the outcome of a struggle between you would be but I can tell you this. On Blore's side, assisting him to the best of our ability will be myself, Dr. Armstrong and Miss Claythorne. You will ap-

preciate, therefore, that the odds against you if you choose to resist
will be somewhat heavy."

Lombard threw his head back. His teeth showed in what was almost a snarl.

"Oh, very well then. Since you've got it all taped out."

Mr. Justice Wargrave nodded his head.

"You are a sensible young man. Where is this revolver of yours?"

"In the drawer of the table by my bed."

"Good."

"I'll fetch it."

"I think it would be desirable if we went with you."

Philip said with a smile that was still nearer a snarl:

"Suspicious devil, aren't you?"

They went along the corridor to Lombard's room.

Philip strode across to the bed-table and jerked open the drawer.
Then he recoiled with an oath.

The drawer of the bed-table was empty.

5

"Satisfied?" asked Lombard.

He had stripped to the skin and he and his room had been meticulously searched by the other three men. Vera Claythorne was outside
in the corridor.

The search proceeded methodically. In turn, Armstrong, the judge
and Blore submitted to the same test.

The four men emerged from Blore's room and approached Vera. It
was the judge who spoke.

"I hope you will understand, Miss Claythorne, that we can make
no exceptions. That revolver must be found. You have, I presume, a
bathing dress with you?"

Vera nodded.

"Then I will ask you to go into your room and put it on and then
come out to us here."

Vera went into her room and shut the door. She reappeared in
under a minute dressed in a tight-fitting silk rucked bathing dress.

Wargrave nodded approval.

"Thank you, Miss Claythorne. Now if you will remain here, we
will search your room."

Vera waited patiently in the corridor until they emerged. Then she went in, dressed, and came out to where they were waiting.

The judge said:

"We are now assured of one thing. There are no lethal weapons or drugs in the possession of any of us five. That is one point to the good. We will now place the drugs in a safe place. There is, I think, a silver chest, is there not, in the pantry?"

Blore said:

"That's all very well, but who's to have the key? You, I suppose."

Mr. Justice Wargrave made no reply.

He went down to the pantry and the others followed him. There was a small case there designed for the purpose of holding silver and plate. By the judge's directions, the various drugs were placed in this and it was locked. Then, still on Wargrave's instructions, the chest was lifted into the plate cupboard and this in turn was locked. The judge then gave the key of the chest to Philip Lombard and the key of the cupboard to Blore.

He said:

"You two are the strongest physically. It would be difficult for either of you to get the key from the other. It would be impossible for any of us three to do so. To break open the cupboard—or the plate chest—would be a noisy and cumbrous proceeding and one which could hardly be carried out without attention being attracted to what was going on."

He paused, then went on:

"We are still faced by one very grave problem. *What has become of Mr. Lombard's revolver?*"

Blore said:

"Seems to me its owner is the most likely person to know that."

A white dint showed in Philip Lombard's nostrils. He said:

"You damned pig-headed fool! I tell you it's been stolen from me!"

Wargrave asked:

"When did you see it last?"

"Last night. It was in the drawer when I went to bed—ready in case anything happened."

The judge nodded.

He said:

"It must have been taken this morning during the confusion of searching for Rogers or after his dead body was discovered."

Vera said:

"It must be hidden somewhere about the house. We must look for
it."

Mr. Justice Wargrave's finger was stroking his chin. He said:

"I doubt if our search will result in anything. Our murderer has
had plenty of time to devise a hiding-place. I do not fancy we shall
find that revolver easily."

Blore said forcefully:

"I don't know where the revolver is, but I'll bet I know where
something else is—that hypodermic syringe. Follow me."

He opened the front door and led the way round the house.

A little distance away from the dining-room window he found the
syringe. Beside it was a smashed china figure—a fifth broken Indian
boy.

Blore said in a satisfied voice:

"Only place it could be. After he'd killed her, he opened the window and threw out the syringe and picked up the china figure from
the table and followed on with that."

There were no prints on the syringe. It had been carefully wiped.

Vera said in a determined voice:

"Now let us look for the revolver."

Mr. Justice Wargrave said:

"By all means. But in doing so let us be careful to keep together.
Remember, if we separate, the murderer gets his chance."

They searched the house carefully from attic to cellars, but without
result. The revolver was still missing.

CHAPTER 13

"One of us . . . One of us . . . One of us . . ."

Three words, endlessly repeated, dinning themselves hour after
hour into receptive brains.

Five people—five frightened people. Five people who watched each
other, who now hardly troubled to hide their state of nervous tension.

There was little pretence now—no formal veneer of conversation.
They were five enemies linked together by a mutual instinct of self-
preservation.

And all of them, suddenly, looked less like human beings. They
were reverting to more bestial types. Like a wary old tortoise, Mr.
Justice Wargrave sat hunched up, his body motionless, his eyes keen

and alert. Ex-Inspector Blore looked coarser and clumsier in build. His walk was that of a slow padding animal. His eyes were bloodshot. There was a look of mingled ferocity and stupidity about him. He was like a beast at bay ready to charge its pursuers. Philip Lombard's senses seemed heightened, rather than diminished. His ears reacted to the slightest sound. His step was lighter and quicker, his body was lithe and graceful. And he smiled often, his lips curling back from his long white teeth.

Vera Claythorne was very quiet. She sat most of the time huddled in a chair. Her eyes stared ahead of her into space. She looked dazed. She was like a bird that has dashed its head against glass and that has been picked up by a human hand. It crouches there, terrified, unable to move, hoping to save itself by its immobility.

Armstrong was in a pitiable condition of nerves. He twitched and his hands shook. He lighted cigarette after cigarette and stubbed them out almost immediately. The forced inaction of their position seemed to gall him more than the others. Every now and then he broke out into a torrent of nervous speech.

"We—we shouldn't just sit here doing nothing! There must be *something*—surely, surely, there is *something* that we can do? If we lit a bonfire—"

Blore said heavily:

"In this weather?"

The rain was pouring down again. The wind came in fitful gusts. The depressing sound of the pattering rain nearly drove them mad.

By tacit consent, they had adopted a plan of campaign. They all sat in the big drawing-room. Only one person left the room at a time. The other four waited till the fifth returned.

Lombard said:

"It's only a question of time. The weather will clear. Then we can do something—signal—light fires—make a raft—something!"

Armstrong said with a sudden cackle of laughter:

"A question of time—*time?* We can't afford time! We shall all be dead. . . ."

Mr. Justice Wargrave said, and his small clear voice was heavy with passionate determination:

"Not if we are careful. *We must be very careful.* . . ."

The mid-day meal had been duly eaten—but there had been no conventional formality about it. All five of them had gone to the kitchen. In the larder they had found a great store of tinned foods. They had opened a tin of tongue and two tins of fruit. They had eaten standing round the kitchen table. Then, herding close together, they had returned to the drawing-room—to sit there—sit—watching each other. . . .

And by now the thoughts that ran through their brains were abnormal, feverish, diseased. . . .

"It's Armstrong . . . I saw him looking at me sideways just then . . . his eyes are mad . . . quite mad. . . . Perhaps he isn't a doctor at all. . . . That's it, of course! . . . He's a lunatic, escaped from some doctor's house—pretending to be a doctor. . . . It's true . . . shall I tell them? . . . Shall I scream out? . . . No, it won't do to put him on his guard. . . . Besides he can seem so sane. . . . What time is it? . . . Only a quarter past three! . . . Oh, God, I shall go mad myself. . . . *Yes, it's Armstrong*. . . . He's watching me now. . . ."

"They won't get *me! I* can take care of myself. . . . I've been in tight places before. . . . Where the hell is that revolver? . . . Who took it? . . . Who's got it? . . . Nobody's got it—we know that. We were all searched. . . . Nobody *can* have it. . . . *But some one knows where it is.* . . ."

"They're going mad . . . they'll all go mad. . . . Afraid of death . . . we're all afraid of death . . . *I'm* afraid of death. . . . Yes, but that doesn't stop death coming. . . . *'The hearse is at the door, sir.'* Where did I read that? The girl . . . I'll watch the girl. Yes, I'll watch the girl. . . ."

"Twenty to four . . . only twenty to four . . . perhaps the clock has stopped. . . . I don't understand—no, I don't understand. . . . This sort of thing can't happen . . . *it is happening.* . . . Why don't we wake up? Wake up—Judgment Day—no, not that! If I could only think. . . . My head—something's happening in my head—it's going to burst—it's going to split. . . . This sort of thing can't happen. . . . What's the time? Oh, God! it's only a quarter to four."

"I must keep my head . . . I must keep my head. . . . If only I keep my head . . . It's all perfectly clear—all worked out. But nobody must suspect. It may do the trick. It must! Which one? That's the question—which one? I think—yes, I rather think—yes—*him.*"

When the clock struck five they all jumped.

Vera said:

"Does any one—want tea?"

There was a moment's silence. Blore said:

"I'd like a cup."

Vera rose. She said:

"I'll go and make it. You can all stay here."

Mr. Justice Wargrave said gently:

"I think, my dear young lady, we would all prefer to come and watch you make it."

Vera stared, then gave a short rather hysterical laugh.

She said:

"Of course! You would!"

Five people went into the kitchen. Tea was made and drunk by Vera and Blore. The other three had whiskey—opening a fresh bottle and using a siphon from a nailed up case.

The judge murmured with a reptilian smile:

"We must be very careful. . . ."

They went back again to the drawing-room. Although it was summer the room was dark. Lombard switched on the lights but they did not come on. He said:

"Of course! The engine's not been run to-day since Rogers hasn't been there to see to it."

He hesitated and said:

"We could go out and get it going, I suppose."

Mr. Justice Wargrave said:

"There are packets of candles in the larder, I saw them, better use those."

Lombard went out. The other four sat watching each other.

He came back with a box of candles and a pile of saucers. Five candles were lit and placed about the room.

The time was a quarter to six.

2

At twenty past six, Vera felt that to sit there longer was unbearable. She would go to her room and bathe her aching head and temples in cold water.

She got up and went towards the door. Then she remembered and came back and got a candle out of the box. She lighted it, let a little wax pour into a saucer and stuck the candle firmly to it. Then she went out of the room, shutting the door behind her and leaving the four men inside.

She went up the stairs and along the passage to her room.

As she opened her door, she suddenly halted and stood stock still. Her nostrils quivered.

The sea . . . The smell of the sea at St. Tredennick . . .

That was it. She could not be mistaken. Of course one smelt the

sea on an island anyway, but this was different. It was the smell there
had been on the beach that day—with the tide out and the rocks
covered with seaweed drying in the sun.

"Can I swim out to the island, Miss Claythorne?"

"Why can't I swim out to the island? . . ."

Horrid whiny spoilt little brat! If it weren't for him, Hugo would be
rich . . . able to marry the girl he loved. . . .

Hugo . . .

*Surely—surely—Hugo was beside her? No, waiting for her in the
room. . . .*

She made a step forward. The draught from the window caught
the flame of the candle. It flickered and went out. . . .

In the dark she was suddenly afraid. . . .

"Don't be a fool," Vera Claythorne urged herself. "It's all right.
The others are downstairs. All four of them. There's no one in the
room. There can't be. You're imagining things, my girl."

But that smell—that smell of the beach at St. Tredennick . . . that
wasn't imagined. *It was true.* . . .

And there *was* some one in the room. . . . She had heard something—surely she had heard something. . . .

And then, as she stood there, listening—a cold, clammy hand
touched her throat—a wet hand, smelling of the sea. . . .

3

Vera screamed. She screamed and screamed—screams of the utmost terror—wild desperate cries for help.

She did not hear the sounds from below, of a chair being over-
turned, of a door opening, of men's feet running up the stairs. She
was conscious only of supreme terror.

Then, restoring her sanity, lights flickered in the doorway—candles
—men hurrying into the room.

"What the devil?" "What's happened?" "Good God, what is it?"

She shuddered, took a step forward, collapsed on the floor.

She was only half aware of some one bending over her, of some
one forcing her head down between her knees.

Then at a sudden exclamation, a quick "My God, look at that!"
her senses returned. She opened her eyes and raised her head. She
saw what it was the men with the candles were looking at.

A broad ribbon of wet seaweed was hanging down from the ceiling. It was that which in the darkness had swayed against her throat. It was that which she had taken for a clammy hand, a drowned hand come back from the dead to squeeze the life out of her! . . .

She began to laugh hysterically. She said:

"It was seaweed—only seaweed—and that's what the smell was. . . ."

And then the faintness came over her once more—waves upon waves of sickness. Again some one took her head and forced it between her knees.

Aeons of time seemed to pass. They were offering her something to drink—pressing the glass against her lips. She smelt brandy.

She was just about to gulp the spirit gratefully down when, suddenly, a warning note—like an alarm bell—sounded in her brain. She sat up, pushing the glass away.

She said sharply:

"Where did this come from?"

Blore's voice answered. He stared a minute before speaking. He said:

"I got it from downstairs."

Vera cried:

"I won't drink it. . . ."

There was a moment's silence, then Lombard laughed.

He said with appreciation:

"Good for you, Vera! You've got your wits about you—even if you have been scared half out of your life. I'll get a fresh bottle that hasn't been opened."

He went swiftly out.

Vera said uncertainly:

"I'm all right now. I'll have some water."

Armstrong supported her as she struggled to her feet. She went over to the basin, swaying and clutching at him for support. She let the cold tap run and then filled the glass.

Blore said resentfully:

"That brandy's all right."

Armstrong said:

"How do you know?"

Blore said angrily:

"I didn't put anything in it. That's what you're getting at, I suppose."

Armstrong said:

"I'm not saying you did. You might have done it, or some one might have tampered with the bottle for just this emergency."

Lombard came swiftly back into the room.

He had a new bottle of brandy in his hands and a corkscrew.

He thrust the sealed bottle under Vera's nose.

"There you are, my girl. Absolutely no deception." He peeled off the tin foil and drew the cork. "Lucky there's a good supply of spirits in the house. Thoughtful of U. N. Owen."

Vera shuddered violently.

Armstrong held the glass while Philip poured the brandy into it. He said:

"You'd better drink this, Miss Claythorne. You've had a nasty shock."

Vera drank a little of the spirit. The colour came back to her face.

Philip Lombard said with a laugh:

"Well, here's one murder that hasn't gone according to plan!"

Vera said almost in a whisper:

"You think—that was what was meant?"

Lombard nodded.

"Expected you to pass out through fright! Some people would have, wouldn't they, doctor?"

Armstrong did not commit himself. He said doubtfully:

"H'm, impossible to say. Young healthy subject—no cardiac weakness. Unlikely. On the other hand—"

He picked up the glass of brandy that Blore had brought. He dipped a finger in it, tasted it gingerly. His expression did not alter. He said dubiously: "H'm, tastes all right."

Blore stepped forward angrily. He said:

"If you're saying that I tampered with that, I'll knock your ruddy block off."

Vera, her wits revived by the brandy, made a diversion by saying:

"Where's the judge?"

The three men looked at each other.

"*That's odd*. . . . Thought he came up with us."

Blore said:

"*So did I*. . . . What about it, doctor? You came up the stairs behind me."

Armstrong said:

"I thought he was following me. . . . Of course, he'd be bound to go slower than we did. He's an old man."

They looked at each other again.

Lombard said:

"It's damned odd. . . ."

Blore cried:

"We must look for him."

He started for the door. The others followed him, Vera last.

As they went down the stairs Armstrong said over his shoulder:

"Of course he *may* have stayed in the living-room. . . ."

They crossed the hall. Armstrong called out loudly:

"Wargrave, Wargrave, where are you?"

There was no answer. A deadly silence filled the house apart from the gentle patter of the rain.

Then, in the entrance to the drawing-room door, Armstrong stopped dead. The others crowded up and looked over his shoulder.

Somebody cried out.

Mr. Justice Wargrave was sitting in his high-backed chair at the end of the room. Two candles burnt on either side of him. But what shocked and startled the onlookers was the fact that he sat there robed in scarlet with a judge's wig upon his head. . . .

Dr. Armstrong motioned to the others to keep back. He himself walked across to the silent staring figure, reeling a little as he walked like a drunken man.

He bent forward, peering into the still face. Then, with a swift movement, he raised the wig. It fell to the floor, revealing the high bald forehead with, in the very middle, a round stained mark from which something had trickled. . . .

Dr. Armstrong raised the limp hand and felt for the pulse. Then he turned to the others.

He said—and his voice was expressionless, dead, far away:

"*He's been shot.* . . ."

Blore said:

"God—*the revolver!*"

The doctor said, still in the same lifeless voice:

"Got him through the head. Instantaneous."

Vera stooped to the wig. She said, and her voice shook with horror:

"*Miss Brent's missing grey wool.* . . ."

Blore said:

"And the scarlet curtain that was missing from the bath-room. . . ."

Vera whispered:

"So this is what they wanted them for. . . ."

Suddenly Philip Lombard laughed—a high unnatural laugh.

" 'Five little Indian boys going in for law; one got in Chancery and then there were four.' That's the end of Mr. Bloody Justice War-grave. No more pronouncing sentence for him! No more putting on of the black cap! Here's the last time *he*'ll ever sit in court! No more summing up and sending innocent men to death. How Edward Seton would laugh if he were here! God, how he'd laugh!"

His outburst shocked and startled the others.

Vera cried:

"Only this morning you said *he* was the one!"

Philip Lombard's face changed—sobered.

He said in a low voice:

"I know I did. . . . Well, I was wrong. Here's one more of us who's been proved innocent—*too late!*"

CHAPTER 14

THEY HAD CARRIED Mr. Justice Wargrave up to his room and laid him on the bed.

Then they had come down again and had stood in the hall looking at each other.

Blore said heavily:

"What do we do now?"

Lombard said briskly:

"Have something to eat. We've got to eat, you know."

Once again they went into the kitchen. Again they opened a tin of tongue. They ate mechanically, almost without tasting.

Vera said:

"I shall never eat tongue again."

They finished the meal. They sat round the kitchen table staring at each other.

Blore said:

"Only four of us now. . . . *Who'll be the next?*"

Armstrong stared. He said, almost mechanically:

"We must be very careful—" and stopped.

Blore nodded.

"That's what *he* said. . . . And now he's dead!"

Armstrong said:

"How did it happen, I wonder?"

Lombard swore. He said:

"A damned clever double cross! That stuff was planted in Miss

Claythorne's room and it worked just as it was intended to. Every one dashes up there thinking *she's* being murdered. And so—in the confusion—some one—caught the old boy off his guard."

Blore said:

"Why didn't any one hear the shot?"

Lombard shook his head.

"Miss Claythorne was screaming, the wind was howling, we were running about and calling out. No, it wouldn't be heard." He paused. "But that trick's not going to work again. He'll have to try something else next time."

Blore said:

"He probably will."

There was an unpleasant tone in his voice. The two men eyed each other.

Armstrong said:

"Four of us, and we don't know which . . ."

Blore said:

"*I* know. . . ."

Vera said:

"I haven't the least doubt. . . ."

Armstrong said slowly:

"I suppose I do know really. . . ."

Philip Lombard said:

"I think I've got a pretty good idea now. . . ."

Again they all looked at each other. . . .

Vera staggered to her feet. She said:

"I feel awful. I must go to bed. . . . I'm dead beat."

Lombard said:

"Might as well. No good sitting watching each other."

Blore said:

"*I*'ve no objection. . . ."

The doctor murmured:

"The best thing to do—although I doubt if any of us will sleep."

They moved to the door. Blore said:

"*I wonder where that revolver is now? . . .*"

2

They went up the stairs.

The next move was a little like a scene in a farce.

Each one of the four stood with a hand on his or her bedroom door handle. Then, as though at a signal, each one stepped into the room and pulled the door shut. There were sounds of bolts and locks, of the moving of furniture.

Four frightened people were barricaded in until morning.

3

Philip Lombard drew a breath of relief as he turned from adjusting a chair under the door handle.

He strolled across to the dressing-table.

By the light of the flickering candle he studied his face curiously. He said softly to himself:

"Yes, this business has got you rattled all right."

His sudden wolf-like smile flashed out.

He undressed quickly.

He went over to the bed, placing his wrist-watch on the table by the bed.

Then he opened the drawer of the table.

He stood there, staring down at the revolver that was inside it. . . .

4

Vera Claythorne lay in bed.

The candle still burned beside her.

As yet she could not summon the courage to put it out.

She was afraid of the dark. . . .

She told herself again and again: *"You're all right until morning. Nothing happened last night. Nothing will happen to-night. Nothing can happen. You're locked and bolted in. No one can come near you. . . ."*

And she thought suddenly:

"Of course! I can stay here! Stay here locked in! Food doesn't really matter! I can stay here—safely—till help comes! Even if it's a day —or two days. . . ."

Stay here. Yes, but could she stay here? Hour after hour—with no one to speak to, with nothing to do but *think*. . . .

She'd begin to think of Cornwall—of Hugo—of—of what she'd said to Cyril.

Horrid whiny little boy, always pestering her. . . .

"Miss Claythorne, why can't I swim out to the rock? I can. I know I can."

Was it her voice that had answered?

"Of course you can, Cyril, really. I know that."

"Can I go then, Miss Claythorne?"

"Well, you see, Cyril, your mother gets so nervous about you. I'll tell you what. To-morrow you can swim out to the rock. I'll talk to your mother on the beach and distract her attention. And then, when she looks for you, there you'll be standing on the rock waving to her! It *will* be a surprise!"

"Oh, good egg, Miss Claythorne! That will be a lark!"

She'd said it now. To-morrow! Hugo was going to Newquay. When he came back—it would be all over. . . .

Yes, but supposing it wasn't? Supposing it went wrong? Cyril might be rescued in time. And then—then he'd say, *"Miss Claythorne said I could."* Well, what of it? One must take *some* risk! If the worst happened she'd brazen it out. *"How can you tell such a wicked lie, Cyril? Of course I never said any such thing!"* They'd believe her all right. Cyril often told stories. He was an untruthful child. Cyril would know, of course. But that didn't matter. . . . And anyway nothing *would* go wrong. She'd pretend to swim out after him. But she'd arrive too late. . . . Nobody would ever suspect. . . .

Had Hugo suspected? Was that why he had looked at her in that queer far-off way . . . ? Had Hugo known?

Was that why he had gone off after the inquest so hurriedly?

He hadn't answered the one letter she had written to him. . . .

Hugo . . .

Vera turned restlessly in bed. No, no, she mustn't think of Hugo. It hurt too much! That was all over, over and done with. . . . Hugo must be forgotten. . . .

Why, this evening, had she suddenly felt that Hugo was in the room with her?

She stared up at the ceiling, stared at the big black hook in the middle of the room.

She'd never noticed that hook before.

The seaweed had hung from that. . . .

She shivered as she remembered that cold clammy touch on her neck. . . .

She didn't like that hook on the ceiling. It drew your eyes, fascinated you . . . a big black hook. . . .

5

Ex-Inspector Blore sat on the side of his bed.

His small eyes, red-rimmed and bloodshot, were alert in the solid mass of his face. He was like a wild boar waiting to charge.

He felt no inclination to sleep.

The menace was coming very near now. . . . Six out of ten!

For all his sagacity, for all his caution and astuteness, the old judge had gone the way of the rest.

Blore snorted with a kind of savage satisfaction.

"What was it the old geezer had said?"

"We must be very careful. . . ."

Self-righteous smug old hypocrite. Sitting up in court feeling like God Almighty. He'd got his all right. . . . No more being careful for him.

And now there were four of them. The girl, Lombard, Armstrong and himself.

Very soon another of them would go. . . . But it wouldn't be William Henry Blore. He'd see to that all right.

(But the revolver. . . . What about the revolver? That was the disturbing factor—the revolver!)

Blore sat on his bed, his brow furrowed, his little eyes creased and puckered while he pondered the problem of the revolver. . . .

In the silence he could hear the clocks strike downstairs.

Midnight.

He relaxed a little now—even went so far as to lie down on his bed. But he did not undress.

He lay there, thinking. Going over the whole business from the beginning, methodically, painstakingly, as he had been wont to do in his police officer days. It was thoroughness that paid in the end.

The candle was burning down. Looking to see if the matches were within easy reach of his hand, he blew it out.

Strangely enough, he found the darkness disquieting. It was as though a thousand age-old fears awoke and struggled for supremacy in his brain. Faces floated in the air—the judge's face crowned with that mockery of grey wool—the cold dead face of Mrs. Rogers—the convulsed purple face of Anthony Marston. . . .

Another face—pale, spectacled, with a small straw-coloured moustache. . . .

A face he had seen sometime or other—but when? Not on the island. No, much longer ago than that.

Funny, that he couldn't put a name to it. . . . Silly sort of face really—fellow looked a bit of a mug.

Of course!

It came to him with a real shock.

Landor!

Odd to think he'd completely forgotten what Landor looked like. Only yesterday he'd been trying to recall the fellow's face, and hadn't been able to.

And now here it was, every feature clear and distinct, as though he had seen it only yesterday. . . .

Landor had had a wife—a thin slip of a woman with a worried face. There'd been a kid too, a girl about fourteen. For the first time, he wondered what had become of them. . . .

(The revolver. What had become of the revolver? That was much more important. . . .)

The more he thought about it the more puzzled he was. . . . He didn't understand this revolver business. . . .

Somebody in the house had got that revolver. . . .

Downstairs a clock struck one.

Blore's thoughts were cut short. He sat up on the bed, suddenly alert. For he had heard a sound—a very faint sound—somewhere outside his bedroom door.

There was some one moving about in the darkened house.

The perspiration broke out on his forehead. Who was it, moving secretly and silently along the corridors? Some one who was up to no good, he'd bet that!

Noiselessly, in spite of his heavy build, he dropped off the bed and with two strides was standing by the door listening.

But the sound did not come again. Nevertheless Blore was convinced that he was not mistaken. He had heard a footfall just outside his door. The hair rose slightly on his scalp. He knew fear again. . . .

Some one creeping about stealthily in the night. . . .

He listened—but the sound was not repeated.

And now a new temptation assailed him. He wanted, desperately, to go out and investigate. If he could only see who it was prowling about in the darkness.

But to open his door would be the action of a fool. Very likely that was exactly what the other was waiting for. He might even have meant Blore to hear what he had heard, counting on him coming out to investigate.

Blore stood rigid—listening. He could hear sounds everywhere now, cracks, rustles, mysterious whispers—but his dogged realistic brain knew them for what they were—the creations of his own heated imagination.

And then suddenly he heard something that was *not* imagination. Footsteps, very soft, very cautious, but plainly audible to a man listening with all his ears as Blore was listening.

They came softly along the corridor (both Lombard's and Armstrong's rooms were further from the stair-head than his). They passed his door without hesitating or faltering.

And as they did so, Blore made up his mind.

He meant to see who it was! The footsteps had definitely passed his door going to the stairs. Where was the man going?

When Blore acted, he acted quickly, surprisingly so for a man who looked so heavy and slow. He tiptoed back to the bed, slipped matches into his pocket, detached the plug of the electric lamp by his bed, and picked it up winding the flex round it. It was a chromium affair with a heavy ebonite base—a useful weapon.

He sprinted noiselessly across the room, removed the chair from under the door handle and with precaution unlocked and unbolted the door. He stepped out into the corridor. There was a faint sound in the hall below. Blore ran noiselessly in his stockinged feet to the head of the stairs.

At that moment he realized why it was he had heard all these sounds so clearly. The wind had died down completely and the sky must have cleared. There was faint moonlight coming in through the landing window and it illuminated the hall below.

Blore had an instantaneous glimpse of a figure just passing out through the front door.

In the act of running down the stairs in pursuit, he paused.

Once again, he had nearly made a fool of himself! This was a trap, perhaps, to lure him out of the house!

But what the other man didn't realize was that he had made a mistake, had delivered himself neatly into Blore's hands.

For, of the three tenanted rooms upstairs, *one must now be empty.* All that had to be done was to ascertain *which!*

Blore went swiftly back along the corridor.

He paused first at Dr. Armstrong's door and tapped. There was no answer.

He waited a minute, then went on to Philip Lombard's room.

Here the answer came at once.

"Who's there?"

"It's Blore. I don't think Armstrong is in his room. Wait a minute."

He went on to the door at the end of the corridor. Here he tapped again.

"Miss Claythorne. Miss Claythorne."

Vera's voice, startled, answered him.

"Who is it? What's the matter?"

"It's all right, Miss Claythorne. Wait a minute. I'll come back."

He raced back to Lombard's room. The door opened as he did so. Lombard stood there. He held a candle in his left hand. He had pulled on his trousers over his pyjamas. His right hand rested in the pocket of his pyjama jacket. He said sharply:

"What the hell's all this?"

Blore explained rapidly. Lombard's eyes lit up.

"*Armstrong—eh?* So *he's* our pigeon!" He moved along to Armstrong's door. "Sorry, Blore, but I don't take anything on trust."

He rapped sharply on the panel.

"Armstrong—Armstrong."

There was no answer.

Lombard dropped to his knees and peered through the keyhole. He inserted his little finger gingerly into the lock.

He said:

"Key's not in the door on the inside."

Blore said:

"That means he locked it on the outside and took it with him."

Philip nodded:

"Ordinary precaution to take. *We'll get him, Blore.* . . . This time, *we'll get him!* Half a second."

He raced along to Vera's room.

"Vera."

"Yes."

"We're hunting Armstrong. He's out of his room. Whatever you do, *don't open your door*. Understand?"

"Yes, I understand."

"If Armstrong comes along and says that I've been killed, or Blore's been killed, *pay no attention*. See? Only open your door if *both Blore and I* speak to you. Got that?"

Vera said:

"Yes. I'm not a complete fool."

Lombard said:

"Good."

He joined Blore. He said:

"And now—after him! The hunt's up!"

Blore said:

"We'd better be careful. He's got a revolver, remember."

Philip Lombard racing down the stairs chuckled.

He said:

"That's where you're wrong." He undid the front door, remarking:
"Latch pushed back—so that he could get in again easily."

He went on:

"I've got that revolver!" He took it half out of his pocket as he
spoke. "Found it put back in my drawer to-night."

Blore stopped dead on the doorstep. His face changed. Philip
Lombard saw it.

He said impatiently:

"Don't be a damned fool, Blore! I'm not going to shoot you! Go
back and barricade yourself in if you like! I'm off after Armstrong."

He started off into the moonlight. Blore, after a minute's hesitation, followed him.

He thought to himself:

"I suppose I'm asking for it. But after all—"

After all he had tackled criminals armed with revolvers before
now. Whatever else he lacked, Blore did not lack courage. Show him
the danger and he would tackle it pluckily. He was not afraid of danger in the open, only of danger undefined and tinged with the supernatural.

6

Vera, left to wait results, got up and dressed.

She glanced over once or twice at the door. It was a good solid
door. It was both bolted and locked and had an oak chair wedged
under the handle.

It could not be broken open by force. Certainly not by Dr.
Armstrong. He was not a physically powerful man.

If she were Armstrong intent on murder, it was cunning that she
would employ, not force.

She amused herself by reflecting on the means he might employ.

He might, as Philip had suggested, announce that one of the other two men was dead. Or he might possibly pretend to be mortally wounded himself, might drag himself groaning to her door.

There were other possibilities. He might inform her that the house was on fire. More, he might actually set the house on fire. . . . Yes, that would be a possibility. Lure the other two men out of the house, then, having previously laid a trail of petrol, he might set light to it. And she, like an idiot, would remain barricaded in her room until it was too late.

She crossed over to the window. Not too bad. At a pinch one could escape that way. It would mean a drop—but there was a handy flower-bed.

She sat down and picking up her diary began to write in it in a clear flowing hand.

One must pass the time.

Suddenly she stiffened to attention. She had heard a sound. It was, she thought, a sound like breaking glass. And it came from somewhere downstairs.

She listened hard, but the sound was not repeated.

She heard, or thought she heard, stealthy sounds of footsteps, the creak of stairs, the rustle of garments—but there was nothing definite, and she concluded, as Blore had done earlier, that such sounds had their origin in her own imagination.

But presently she heard sounds of a more concrete nature. People moving about downstairs—the murmur of voices. Then the very decided sound of some one mounting the stairs—doors opening and shutting—feet going up to the attic overhead. More noises from there.

Finally the steps came along the passage. Lombard's voice said:

"Vera? You all right?"

"Yes. What's happened?"

Blore's voice said:

"Will you let us in?"

Vera went to the door. She removed the chair, unlocked the door and slid back the bolt. She opened the door. The two men were breathing hard, their feet and the bottom of their trousers were soaking wet.

She said again:

"What's happened?"

Lombard said:

"*Armstrong's disappeared.* . . ."

7

Vera cried:

"What?"

Lombard said:

"Vanished clean off the island."

Blore concurred:

"Vanished—that's the word! Like some damned conjuring trick."

Vera said impatiently:

"Nonsense! He's hiding somewhere!"

Blore said:

"No, he isn't! I tell you, there's nowhere to hide on this island. It's as bare as your hand! There's moonlight outside. As clear as day it is. *And he's not to be found.*"

Vera said:

"He doubled back into the house."

Blore said:

"We thought of that. We've searched the house too. You must have heard us. *He's not here,* I tell you. He's gone—clean vanished, vamoosed. . . ."

Vera said incredulously:

"I don't believe it."

Lombard said:

"It's true, my dear."

He paused and then said:

"There's one other little fact. A pane in the dining-room window has been smashed—*and there are only three little Indian boys on the table.*"

CHAPTER 15

THREE PEOPLE sat eating breakfast in the kitchen.

Outside, the sun shone. It was a lovely day. The storm was a thing of the past.

And with the change in the weather, a change had come in the mood of the prisoners on the island.

They felt now like people just awakening from a nightmare. There was danger, yes, but it was danger in daylight. That paralyzing atmosphere of fear that had wrapped them round like a blanket yesterday while the wind howled outside was gone.

Lombard said:

"We'll try heliographing to-day with a mirror from the highest point of the island. Some bright lad wandering on the cliff will recognize S O S when he sees it, I hope. In the evening we could try a bonfire—only there isn't much wood—and anyway they might just think it was song and dance and merriment."

Vera said:

"Surely some one can read Morse. And then they'll come to take us off. Long before this evening."

Lombard said:

"The weather's cleared all right, but the sea hasn't gone down yet. Terrific swell on! They won't be able to get a boat near the island before to-morrow."

Vera cried:

"Another night in this place!"

Lombard shrugged his shoulders.

"May as well face it! Twenty-four hours will do it, I think. If we can last out that, we'll be all right."

Blore cleared his throat. He said:

"We'd better come to a clear understanding. *What's happened to Armstrong?*"

Lombard said:

"Well, we've got one piece of evidence. Only three little Indian boys left on the dinner-table. It looks as though Armstrong had got his quietus."

Vera said:

"Then why haven't you found his dead body?"

Blore said:

"Exactly."

Lombard shook his head. He said:

"It's damned odd—no getting over it."

Blore said doubtfully:

"It might have been thrown into the sea."

Lombard said sharply:

"By whom? You? Me? You saw him go out of the front door. You come along and find me in my room. We go out and search together. When the devil had I time to kill him and carry his body round the island?"

Blore said:

"I don't know. But I do know one thing."

Lombard said:

"What's that?"

Blore said:

"The revolver. It was your revolver. It's in your possession now. There's nothing to show that it hasn't been in your possession all along."

"Come now, Blore, we were all searched."

"Yes, you'd hidden it away before that happened. Afterwards you just took it back again."

"My good blockhead, I swear to you that it was put back in my drawer. Greatest surprise I ever had in my life when I found it there."

Blore said:

"You ask us to believe a thing like that! Why the devil should Armstrong, or any one else for that matter, put it back?"

Lombard raised his shoulders hopelessly.

"I haven't the least idea. It's just crazy. The last thing one would expect. There seems no point in it."

Blore agreed.

"No, there isn't. You might have thought of a better story."

"Rather proof that I'm telling the truth, isn't it?"

"I don't look at it that way."

Philip said:

"You wouldn't."

Blore said:

"Look here, Mr. Lombard, if you're an honest man, as you pretend—"

Philip murmured:

"When did I lay claims to being an honest man? No, indeed, I never said that."

Blore went on stolidly:

"If you're speaking the truth—there's only one thing to be done. As long as you have that revolver, Miss Claythorne and I are at your mercy. The only fair thing is to put that revolver with the other things that are locked up—and you and I will hold the two keys still."

Philip Lombard lit a cigarette.

As he puffed smoke, he said:

"Don't be an ass."

"You won't agree to that?"

"No, I won't. That revolver's mine. I need it to defend myself—and I'm going to keep it."

Blore said:

"In that case we're bound to come to one conclusion."

"That I'm U. N. Owen? Think what you damned well please. But I'll ask you, if that's so, why I didn't pot you with the revolver last night? I could have, about twenty times over."

Blore shook his head.

He said:

"I don't know—and that's a fact. You must have had some reason."

Vera had taken no part in the discussion. She stirred now and said:

"I think you're both behaving like a pair of idiots."

Lombard looked at her.

"What's this?"

Vera said:

"You've forgotten the nursery rhyme. Don't you see there's a clue there?"

She recited in a meaning voice:

"Four little Indian boys going out to sea;
A red herring swallowed one and then there were three."

She went on:

"*A red herring*—that's the vital clue. *Armstrong's not dead.* . . . He took away the china Indian to make you think he was. You may say what you like—Armstrong's on the island still. His disappearance is just a red herring across the track. . . ."

Lombard sat down again.

He said:

"You know, you may be right."

Blore said:

"Yes, but if so, where is he? We've searched the place. Outside and inside."

Vera said scornfully:

"We all searched for the revolver, didn't we, and couldn't find it? But it was somewhere all the time!"

Lombard murmured:

"There's a slight difference in size, my dear, between a man and a revolver."

Vera said:

"I don't care—I'm sure I'm right."

Blore murmured:

330

"Rather giving himself away, wasn't it? Actually mentioning a red herring in the verse. He could have written it up a bit different."

Vera cried:

"But don't you *see,* he's *mad?* It's all mad! The whole thing of going by the rhyme is mad! Dressing up the judge, killing Rogers when he was chopping sticks—drugging Mrs. Rogers so that she overslept herself—arranging for a bumblebee when Miss Brent died! It's like some horrible child playing a game. It's all got to fit in."

Blore said:

"Yes, you're right." He thought a minute. "At any rate there's no Zoo on the island. He'll have a bit of trouble getting over that."

Vera cried:

"Don't you see? *We're the Zoo.* . . . Last night, we were hardly human any more. *We're the Zoo.* . . ."

2

They spent the morning on the cliffs, taking it in turns to flash a mirror at the mainland.

There were no signs that any one saw them. No answering signals. The day was fine, with a slight haze. Below the sea heaved in a gigantic swell. There were no boats out.

They had made another abortive search of the island. There was no trace of the missing physician.

Vera looked up at the house from where they were standing.

She said, her breath coming with a slight catch in it:

"One feels safer here, out in the open. . . . Don't let's go back into the house again."

Lombard said:

"Not a bad idea. We're pretty safe here, no one can get at us without our seeing him a long time beforehand."

Vera said:

"We'll stay here."

Blore said:

"Have to pass the night somewhere. We'll have to go back to the house then."

Vera shuddered.

"I can't bear it. I *can't* go through another night!"

Philip said:

"You'll be safe enough—locked in your room."

Vera murmured: "I suppose so."

She stretched out her hands, murmuring:

"It's lovely—to feel the sun again. . . ."

She thought:

"How odd. . . . I'm almost happy. And yet I suppose I'm actually in danger. . . . Somehow—now—nothing seems to matter . . . not in daylight. . . . I feel full of power—I feel that I can't die. . . ."

Blore was looking at his wrist-watch. He said:

"It's two o'clock. What about lunch?"

Vera said obstinately:

"I'm not going back to the house. I'm going to stay here—in the open."

"Oh, come now, Miss Claythorne. Got to keep your strength up, you know."

Vera said:

"If I even see a tinned tongue, I shall be sick! I don't want any food. People go days on end with nothing sometimes when they're on a diet."

Blore said:

"Well, I need my meals regular. What about you, Mr. Lombard?"

Philip said:

"You know, I don't relish the idea of tinned tongue particularly. I'll stay here with Miss Claythorne."

Blore hesitated. Vera said:

"I shall be quite all right. I don't think he'll shoot me as soon as your back is turned if that's what you're afraid of."

Blore said:

"It's all right if you say so. But we agreed we ought not to separate."

Philip said:

"You're the one who wants to go into the lion's den. I'll come with you if you like?"

"No, you won't," said Blore. "You'll stay here."

Philip laughed.

"So you're still afraid of me? Why, I could shoot you both this very minute if I liked."

Blore said:

"Yes, but that wouldn't be according to plan. It's one at a time, and it's got to be done in a certain way."

"Well," said Philip, "you seem to know all about it."

"Of course," said Blore, "it's a bit jumpy going up to the house alone—"

Philip said softly:

"And therefore, *will I lend you my revolver?* Answer, no, I will *not!* Not quite so simple as that, thank you."

Blore shrugged his shoulders and began to make his way up the steep slope to the house.

Lombard said softly:

"Feeding time at the Zoo! The animals are very regular in their habits!"

Vera said anxiously:

"Isn't it very risky, what he's doing?"

"In the sense you mean—no, I don't think it is! Armstrong's not armed, you know, and anyway Blore is twice a match for him in physique and he's very much on his guard. And anyway it's a sheer impossibility that Armstrong can be in the house. I *know* he's not there."

"But—what other solution is there?"

Philip said softly:

"There's Blore."

"Oh—do you really think—?"

"Listen, my girl. You heard Blore's story. You've got to admit that if it's true, *I can't possibly have had anything to do with Armstrong's disappearance.* His story clears me. *But it doesn't clear him.* We've only *his* word for it that he heard footsteps and saw a man going downstairs and out at the front door. The whole thing may be a lie. He may have got rid of Armstrong a couple of hours before that."

"How?"

Lombard shrugged his shoulders.

"That we don't know. But if you ask me, we've only one danger to fear—and that danger is Blore! What do we know about the man? Less than nothing! All this ex-policeman story may be bunkum! He may be anybody—a mad millionaire—a crazy business man—an escaped inmate of Broadmoor. One thing's certain. He *could* have done every one of these crimes."

Vera had gone rather white. She said in a slightly breathless voice:

"And supposing he gets—us?"

Lombard said softly, patting the revolver in his pocket:

"I'm going to take very good care he doesn't."

Then he looked at her curiously.

"Touching faith in me, haven't you, Vera? Quite sure I wouldn't shoot you?"

Vera said:

"One has got to trust some one. . . . As a matter of fact I think you're wrong about Blore. I still think it's Armstrong."

She turned to him suddenly.

"Don't you feel—all the time—that there's *some one*. Some one watching and waiting?"

Lombard said slowly:

"That's just nerves."

Vera said eagerly:

"Then you *have* felt it?"

She shivered. She bent a little closer.

"Tell me—you don't think—" She broke off, went on: "I read a story once—about two judges that came to a small American town—from the Supreme Court. They administered justice—Absolute Justice. *Because—they didn't come from this world at all. . . .*"

Lombard raised his eyebrows.

He said:

"Heavenly visitants, eh? No, I don't believe in the supernatural. This business is human enough."

Vera said in a low voice:

"Sometimes—I'm not sure. . . ."

Lombard looked at her. He said:

"That's conscience. . . ." After a moment's silence he said very quietly: "So you *did* drown that kid after all?"

Vera said vehemently:

"I didn't! I didn't! You've no right to say that!"

He laughed easily.

"Oh, yes, you did, my good girl! I don't know why. Can't imagine. There was a man in it probably. Was that it?"

A sudden feeling of lassitude, of intense weariness, spread over Vera's limbs. She said in a dull voice:

"Yes—there was a man in it. . . ."

Lombard said softly:

"Thanks. That's what I wanted to know. . . ."

Vera sat up suddenly. She exclaimed:

"What was that? It wasn't an earthquake?"

Lombard said:

"No, no. Queer, though—a thud shook the ground. And I thought —did you hear a sort of cry? I did."

They stared up at the house.

Lombard said:

"It came from there. We'd better go up and see."

"No, no, I'm not going."

"Please yourself. I am."

Vera said desperately:

"All right. I'll come with you."

They walked up the slope to the house. The terrace was peaceful and innocuous-looking in the sunshine. They hesitated there a minute, then instead of entering by the front door, they made a cautious circuit of the house.

They found Blore. He was spread-eagled on the stone terrace on the east side, his head crushed and mangled by a great block of white marble.

Philip looked up. He said:

"Whose is that window just above?"

Vera said in a low shuddering voice:

"It's mine—and *that's the clock from my mantelpiece*. . . . I remember now. It was—shaped like a bear."

She repeated and her voice shook and quavered:

"It was shaped like a bear. . . ."

3

Philip grasped her shoulder.

He said, and his voice was urgent and grim:

"This settles it. Armstrong is in hiding somewhere in that house. I'm going to get him."

But Vera clung to him. She cried:

"Don't be a fool. It's *us* now! We're next! He *wants* us to look for him! He's *counting* on it!"

Philip stopped. He said thoughtfully:

"There's something in that."

Vera cried:

"At any rate, you do admit now I was right."

He nodded.

"Yes—you win! It's Armstrong all right. But where the devil did he hide himself? We went over the place with a fine-tooth comb."

Vera said urgently:

"If you didn't find him last night, you *won't find him now*. . . . That's common-sense."

Lombard said reluctantly:

"Yes, but—"

"He must have prepared a secret place beforehand—naturally—of course it's just what he would do. You know, like a Priest's Hole in old manor houses."

"This isn't an old house of that kind."

"He could have had one made."

Philip Lombard shook his head.

He said:

"We measured the place—that first morning. I'll swear there's no space unaccounted for."

Vera said:

"There must be. . . ."

Lombard said:

"I'd like to see—"

Vera cried:

"Yes, you'd like to see! And he knows that! He's in there—waiting for you."

Lombard said, half bringing out the revolver from his pocket:

"I've got this, you know."

"You said Blore was all right—that he was more than a match for Armstrong. So he was physically, and he was on the lookout too. But what you don't seem to realize is that Armstrong is *mad!* And a madman has all the advantages on his side. He's twice as cunning as any one sane can be."

Lombard put back the revolver in his pocket. He said:

"Come on, then."

4

Lombard said at last:

"What are we going to do when night comes?"

Vera didn't answer. He went on accusingly:

"You haven't thought of that?"

She said helplessly:

"What *can* we do? Oh, my God, I'm *frightened*. . . ."

Philip Lombard said thoughtfully:

"It's fine weather. There will be a moon. We must find a place—up by the top cliffs perhaps. We can sit there and wait for morning. *We mustn't go to sleep*. . . . We must watch the whole time. And if any one comes up towards us, I shall shoot!"

He paused:

"You'll be cold, perhaps, in that thin dress?"

Vera said with a raucous laugh:

"Cold? I should be colder if I were dead!"

Philip Lombard said quietly:

"Yes, that's true. . . ."

Vera moved restlessly.

She said:

"I shall go mad if I sit here any longer. Let's move about."

"All right."

They paced slowly up and down, along the line of the rocks overlooking the sea. The sun was dropping towards the west. The light was golden and mellow. It enveloped them in a golden glow.

Vera said, with a sudden nervous little giggle:

"Pity we can't have a bathe. . . ."

Philip was looking down towards the sea. He said abruptly:

"What's that, there? You see—by that big rock? No—a little further to the right."

Vera stared. She said:

"It looks like somebody's clothes!"

"A bather, eh?" Lombard laughed. "Queer. I suppose it's only seaweed."

Vera said:

"Let's go and look."

"It is clothes," said Lombard as they drew nearer. "A bundle of them. That's a boot. Come on, let's scramble along here."

They scrambled over the rocks.

Vera stopped suddenly. She said:

"It's not clothes—it's a man. . . ."

The man was wedged between two rocks, flung there by the tide earlier in the day.

Lombard and Vera reached it in a last scramble. They bent down.

A purple discoloured face—a hideous drowned face. . . .

Lombard said:

"My God! it's *Armstrong.* . . ."

CHAPTER 16

AEONS PASSED . . . worlds spun and whirled. . . . Time was motionless. . . . It stood still—it passed through a thousand ages. . . .

No, it was only a minute or so. . . .

Two people were standing looking down on a dead man. . . .

Slowly, very slowly, Vera Claythorne and Philip Lombard lifted their heads and looked into each other's eyes. . . .

2

Lombard laughed.

He said:

"So that's it, is it, Vera?"

Vera said:

"There's no one on the island—no one at all—*except us two*. . . ."

Her voice was a whisper—nothing more.

Lombard said:

"Precisely. So we know where we are, don't we?"

Vera said:

"How was it worked—that trick with the marble bear?"

He shrugged his shoulders.

"A conjuring trick, my dear—a very good one. . . ."

Their eyes met again.

Vera thought:

"*Why did I never see his face properly before. A wolf—that's what it is—a wolf's face. . . . Those horrible teeth. . . .*"

Lombard said, and his voice was a snarl—dangerous—menacing:

"This is the end, you understand. We've come to the truth now. *And it's the end. . . .*"

Vera said quietly:

"I understand. . . ."

She stared out to sea. General Macarthur had stared out to sea—when—only yesterday? Or was it the day before? He too had said, "*This is the end. . . .*"

He had said it with acceptance—almost with welcome.

But to Vera the words—the thought—brought rebellion.

No, it should not be the end.

She looked down at the dead man. She said:

"Poor Dr. Armstrong. . . ."

Lombard sneered.

He said:

"What's this? Womanly pity?"

Vera said:

"Why not? Haven't *you* any pity?"

He said:

"I've no pity for you. Don't expect it!"

Vera looked down again at the body. She said:

"We must move him. Carry him up to the house."

"To join the other victims, I suppose? All neat and tidy. As far as I'm concerned he can stay where he is."

Vera said:

"At any rate, let's get him out of reach of the sea."

Lombard laughed. He said:

"If you like."

He bent—tugging at the body. Vera leaned against him, helping him. She pulled and tugged with all her might.

Lombard panted:

"Not such an easy job."

They managed it, however, drawing the body clear of high water mark.

Lombard said as he straightened up:

"Satisfied?"

Vera said:

"Quite."

Her tone warned him. He spun round. Even as he clapped his hand to his pocket he knew that he would find it empty.

She had moved a yard or two away and was facing him, revolver in hand.

Lombard said:

"So that's the reason for your womanly solicitude! You wanted to pick my pocket."

She nodded.

She held it steadily and unwaveringly.

Death was very near to Philip Lombard now. It had never, he knew, been nearer.

Nevertheless he was not beaten yet.

He said authoritatively:

"Give that revolver to me."

Vera laughed.

Lombard said:

"Come on, hand it over."

His quick brain was working. Which way—which method—talk her over—lull her into security—or a swift dash—

All his life Lombard had taken the risky way. He took it now.

He spoke slowly, argumentatively.

"Now look here, my dear girl, you just listen—"

And then he sprang. Quick as a panther—as any other feline creature. . . .

Automatically Vera pressed the trigger. . . .

Lombard's leaping body stayed poised in mid-spring, then crashed heavily to the ground.

Vera came warily forward, the revolver ready in her hand.

But there was no need of caution.

Philip Lombard was dead—shot through the heart. . . .

3

Relief possessed Vera—enormous exquisite relief.

At last it was over.

There was no more fear—no more steeling of her nerves. . . .

She was alone on the island. . . .

Alone with nine dead bodies. . . .

But what did that matter? *She* was alive. . . .

She sat there—exquisitely happy—exquisitely at peace. . . .

No more fear. . . .

4

The sun was setting when Vera moved at last. Sheer reaction had kept her immobile. There had been no room in her for anything but the glorious sense of safety.

She realized now that she was hungry and sleepy. Principally sleepy. She wanted to throw herself on her bed and sleep and sleep and sleep. . . .

To-morrow, perhaps, they would come and rescue her—but she

didn't really mind. She didn't mind staying here. Not now that she was alone. . . .

Oh! blessed, blessed peace. . . .

She got to her feet and glanced up at the house.

Nothing to be afraid of any longer! No terrors waiting for her! Just an ordinary well-built modern house. And yet, a little earlier in the day, she had not been able to look at it without shivering. . . .

Fear—what a strange thing fear was. . . .

Well, it was over now. She had conquered—had triumphed over the most deadly peril. By her own quick-wittedness and adroitness she had turned the tables on her would-be destroyer.

She began to walk up towards the house.

The sun was setting, the sky to the west was streaked with red and orange. It was beautiful and peaceful. . . .

Vera thought:

"The whole thing might be a dream. . . ."

How tired she was—terribly tired. Her limbs ached, her eyelids were drooping. Not to be afraid any more. . . . To sleep. Sleep . . . sleep . . . sleep. . . .

To sleep safely since she was alone on the island. One little Indian boy left all alone.

She smiled to herself.

She went in at the front door. The house, too, felt strangely peaceful.

Vera thought:

"Ordinarily one wouldn't care to sleep where there's a dead body in practically every bedroom!"

Should she go to the kitchen and get herself something to eat?

She hesitated a moment, then decided against it. She was really too tired. . . .

She paused by the dining-room door. There were still three little china figures in the middle of the table.

Vera laughed.

She said:

"You're behind the times, my dears."

She picked up two of them and tossed them out through the window. She heard them crash on the stone of the terrace.

The third little figure she picked up and held in her hand.

She said:

"You can come with me. We've won, my dear! We've won!"

The hall was dim in the dying light.

Vera, the little Indian clasped in her hand, began to mount the stairs. Slowly, because her legs were suddenly very tired.

"One little Indian boy left all alone." How did it end? Oh, yes! *"He got married and then there were none."*

Married. . . . Funny, how she suddenly got the feeling again that Hugo was in the house. . . .

Very strong. Yes, Hugo was upstairs waiting for her.

Vera said to herself:

"Don't be a fool. You're so tired that you're imagining the most fantastic things. . . ."

Slowly up the stairs. . . .

At the top of them something fell from her hand, making hardly any noise on the soft pile carpet. She did not notice that she had dropped the revolver. She was only conscious of clasping a little china figure.

How very quiet the house was. And yet—it didn't seem like an empty house. . . .

Hugo, upstairs, waiting for her. . . .

"One little Indian boy left all alone." What was the last line again? Something about being married—or was it something else?

She had come now to the door of her room. Hugo was waiting for her inside—she was quite sure of it.

She opened the door. . . .

She gave a gasp. . . .

What was that—hanging from the hook in the ceiling? *A rope with a noose all ready? And a chair to stand upon—a chair that could be kicked away. . . .*

That was what Hugo wanted. . . .

And of course that was the last line of the rhyme.

"He went and hanged himself and then there were none. . . ."

The little china figure fell from her hand. It rolled unheeded and broke against the fender.

Like an automaton Vera moved forward. This was the end—here where the cold wet hand (Cyril's hand, of course) had touched her throat. . . .

"You can go to the rock, Cyril. . . ."

That was what murder was—as easy as that!

But afterwards you went on remembering. . . .

She climbed up on the chair, her eyes staring in front of her like a sleepwalker's. . . . She adjusted the noose round her neck.

Hugo was there to see she did what she had to do.

She kicked away the chair. . . .

EPILOGUE

Sir Thomas Legge, Assistant Commissioner at Scotland Yard, said irritably:

"But the whole thing's incredible!"

Inspector Maine said respectfully:

"I know, sir."

The A.C. went on:

"Ten people dead on an island and not a living soul on it. It doesn't make sense!"

Inspector Maine said stolidly:

"Nevertheless, it *happened,* sir."

Sir Thomas Legge said:

"Damn it all, Maine, somebody must have killed 'em."

"That's just our problem, sir."

"Nothing helpful in the doctor's report?"

"No, sir. Wargrave and Lombard were shot, the first through the head, the second through the heart. Miss Brent and Marston died of Cyanide poisoning. Mrs. Rogers died of an overdose of Chloral. Rogers' head was split open. Blore's head was crushed in. Armstrong died of drowning. Macarthur's skull was fractured by a blow on the back of the head and Vera Claythorne was hanged."

The A.C. winced. He said:

"Nasty business—all of it."

He considered for a minute or two. He said irritably:

"Do you mean to say that you haven't been able to get anything helpful out of the Sticklehaven people. Dash it, they must know something."

Inspector Maine shrugged his shoulders.

"They're ordinary decent seafaring folk. They know that the island was bought by a man called Owen—and that's about all they do know."

"Who provisioned the island and made all the necessary arrangements?"

"Man called Morris. Isaac Morris."

"And what does he say about it all?"

"He can't say anything, sir, he's dead."

The A.C. frowned.

"Do we know anything about this Morris?"

"Oh, yes, sir, we know about him. He wasn't a very savoury gentleman, Mr. Morris. He was implicated in that share-pushing fraud of Bennito's three years ago—we're sure of that though we can't prove it. And he was mixed up in the dope business. And again we can't prove it. He was a very careful man, Morris."

"And he was behind this island business?"

"Yes, sir, he put through the sale—though he made it clear that he was buying Indian Island for a third party, unnamed."

"Surely there's something to be found out on the financial angle, there?"

Inspector Maine smiled.

"Not if you knew Morris! He can wangle figures until the best chartered accountant in the country wouldn't know if he was on his head or his heels! We've had a taste of that in the Bennito business. No, he covered his employer's tracks all right."

The other man sighed. Inspector Maine went on:

"It was Morris who made all the arrangements down at Sticklehaven. Represented himself as acting for 'Mr. Owen.' And it was he who explained to the people down there that there was some experiment on—some bet about living on a 'desert island' for a week—and that no notice was to be taken of any appeal for help from out there."

Sir Thomas Legge stirred uneasily. He said:

"And you're telling me that those people didn't smell a rat? Not even then?"

Maine shrugged his shoulders. He said:

"You're forgetting, sir, that Indian Island previously belonged to young Elmer Robson, the American. He had the most extraordinary parties down there. I've no doubt the local people's eyes fairly popped out over them. But they got used to it and they'd begun to feel that anything to do with Indian Island would necessarily be incredible. It's natural, that, sir, when you come to think of it."

The Assistant Commissioner admitted gloomily that he supposed it was.

Maine said:

"Fred Narracott—that's the man who took the party out there—did say one thing that was illuminating. He said he was surprised to see what sort of people these were. 'Not at all like Mr. Robson's parties.' I think it was the fact that they were all so normal and so quiet that made him override Morris' orders and take out a boat to the island after he'd heard about the S O S signals."

"When did he and the other men go?"

"The signals were seen by a party of boy scouts on the morning of the 11th. There was no possibility of getting out there that day. The men got there on the afternoon of the 12th at the first moment possible to run a boat ashore there. They're all quite positive that nobody could have left the island before they got there. There was a big sea on after the storm."

"Couldn't some one have swum ashore?"

"It's over a mile to the coast and there were heavy seas and big breakers inshore. And there were a lot of people, boy scouts and others on the cliffs looking out towards the island and watching."

The A.C. sighed. He said:

"What about that gramophone record you found in the house? Couldn't you get hold of anything there that might help?"

Inspector Maine said:

"I've been into that. It was supplied by a firm that do a lot of theatrical stuff and film effects. It was sent to U. N. Owen, Esq., c/o Isaac Morris, and was understood to be required for the amateur performance of a hitherto unacted play. The typescript of it was returned with the record."

Legge said:

"And what about the subject matter, eh?"

Inspector Maine said gravely:

"I'm coming to that, sir."

He cleared his throat.

"I've investigated those accusations as thoroughly as I can.

"Starting with the Rogerses who were the first to arrive on the island. They were in service with a Miss Brady who died suddenly. Can't get anything definite out of the doctor who attended her. He says they certainly didn't poison her, or anything like that, but his personal belief is that there *was* some funny business—that she died as the result of neglect on their part. Says it's the sort of thing that's quite impossible to prove.

"Then there is Mr. Justice Wargrave. That's O.K. He was the judge who sentenced Seton.

"By the way, Seton was guilty—unmistakably guilty. Evidence turned up later after he was hanged which proved that beyond any shadow of doubt. But there was a good deal of comment at the time—nine people out of ten thought Seton was innocent and that the judge's summing up had been vindictive.

"The Claythorne girl, I find, was governess in a family where a death occurred by drowning. However, she doesn't seem to have had anything to do with it, and as a matter of fact she behaved very well, swam out to the rescue and was actually carried out to sea and only just rescued in time."

"Go on," said the A.C. with a sigh.

Maine took a deep breath.

"Dr. Armstrong now. Well-known man. Had a consulting room in Harley Street. Absolutely straight and aboveboard in his profession. Haven't been able to trace any record of an illegal operation or anything of that kind. It's true that there *was* a woman called Clees who was operated on by him way back in 1925 at Leithmore, when he was attached to the hospital there. Peritonitis and she died on the operating table. Maybe he wasn't very skilful over the op.—after all he hadn't much experience—but after all clumsiness isn't a criminal offence. There was certainly no motive.

"Then there's Miss Emily Brent. Girl, Beatrice Taylor, was in service with her. Got pregnant, was turned out by her mistress and went and drowned herself. Not a nice business—but again not criminal."

"That," said the A.C., "seems to be the point. U. N. Owen dealt with cases that the law couldn't touch."

Maine went stolidly on with his list.

"Young Marston was a fairly reckless car driver—had his licence endorsed twice and he ought to have been prohibited from driving, in my opinion. That's all there is to him. The two names John and Lucy Combes were those of two kids he knocked down and killed near Cambridge. Some friends of his gave evidence for him and he was let off with a fine.

"Can't find anything definite about General Macarthur. Fine record—war service—all the rest of it. Arthur Richmond was serving under him in France and was killed in action. No friction of any kind between him and the General. They were close friends as a matter of fact. There were some blunders made about that time—commanding officers sacrificed men unnecessarily—possibly this was a blunder of that kind."

"Possibly," said the A.C.

"Now, Philip Lombard. Lombard has been mixed up in some very curious shows abroad. He's sailed very near the law once or twice.

Got a reputation for daring and for not being over-scrupulous. Sort of fellow who might do several murders in some quiet out-of-the-way spot.

"Then we come to Blore." Maine hesitated. "He of course was one of our lot."

The other man stirred.

"Blore," said the Assistant Commissioner forcibly, "was a bad hat!"

"You think so, sir?"

The A.C. said:

"I always thought so. But he was clever enough to get away with it. It's my opinion that he committed black perjury in the Landor case. I wasn't happy about it at the time. But I couldn't find anything. I put Harris onto it and *he* couldn't find anything but I'm still of the opinion that there was something to find if we'd known how to set about it. The man wasn't straight."

There was a pause, then Sir Thomas Legge said:

"And Isaac Morris is dead, you say? When did he die?"

"I thought you'd soon come to that, sir. Isaac Morris died on the night of August 8th. Took an overdose of sleeping stuff—one of the barbiturates, I understand. There wasn't anything to show whether it was accident or suicide."

Legge said slowly:

"Care to know what I think, Maine?"

"Perhaps I can guess, sir."

Legge said heavily:

"That death of Morris' is a damned sight too opportune!"

Inspector Maine nodded. He said:

"I thought you'd say that, sir."

The Assistant Commissioner brought down his fist with a bang on the table. He cried out:

"The whole thing's fantastic—impossible. Ten people killed on a bare rock of an island—and we don't know who did it, or why, or how."

Maine coughed. He said:

"Well, it's not quite like that, sir. We do know *why,* more or less. Some fanatic with a bee in his bonnet about justice. He was out to get people who were beyond the reach of the law. He picked ten people—whether they were really guilty or not doesn't matter—"

The Commissioner stirred. He said sharply:

"Doesn't it? It seems to me—"

He stopped. Inspector Maine waited respectfully. With a sigh Legge shook his head.

"Carry on," he said. "Just for a minute I felt I'd got somewhere. Got, as it were, the clue to the thing. It's gone now. Go ahead with what you were saying."

Maine went on:

"There were ten people to be—executed, let's say. They *were* executed. U. N. Owen accomplished his task. And somehow or other he spirited himself off that island into thin air."

The A.C. said:

"First-class vanishing trick. But you know, Maine, there must be an explanation."

Maine said:

"You're thinking, sir, that if the man wasn't on the island, he couldn't have left the island, and according to the account of the interested parties he never was on the island. Well, then the only explanation possible is that he was actually one of the ten."

The A.C. nodded.

Maine said earnestly:

"We thought of that, sir. We went into it. Now, to begin with, we're not quite in the dark as to what happened on Indian Island. Vera Claythorne kept a diary, so did Emily Brent. Old Wargrave made some notes—dry legal cryptic stuff, but quite clear. And Blore made notes too. All those accounts tally. The deaths occurred in this order: Marston, Mrs. Rogers, Macarthur, Rogers, Miss Brent, Wargrave. After his death Vera Claythorne's diary states that Armstrong left the house in the night and that Blore and Lombard had gone after him. Blore has one more entry in his notebook. Just two words: 'Armstrong disappeared.'

"Now, sir, it seemed to me, taking everything into account, that we might find here a perfectly good solution. Armstrong was drowned, you remember. Granting that Armstrong was mad, what was to prevent him having killed off all the others and then committed suicide by throwing himself over the cliff, or perhaps while trying to swim to the mainland?

"That was a good solution—but it won't do. No, sir, it won't do. First of all there's the police surgeon's evidence. He got to the island early on the morning of August 13th. He couldn't say much to help us. All he could say was that all the people had been dead at least thirty-six hours and probably a good deal longer. But he was fairly definite about Armstrong. Said he must have been from eight to ten hours in the water before his body was washed up. That works out at this, that Armstrong must have gone into the sea sometime during the night of the 10th-11th—and I'll explain why. We found the point where the body was washed up—it had been wedged between two rocks and there were bits of cloth, hair, etc., on them. It must have been deposited there at high water on the 11th—that's to say round about 11 o'clock A.M. After that, the storm subsided, and succeeding high water marks are considerably lower.

"You might say, I suppose, that Armstrong managed to polish off the other three *before* he went into the sea that night. But there's another point and one you can't get over. *Armstrong's body had been dragged above high water mark.* We found it well above the reach of any tide. And it was laid out straight on the ground—all neat and tidy.

"So that settles one point definitely. *Some one* was alive on the island *after Armstrong was dead.*"

He paused and then went on.

"And that leaves—just what exactly? Here's the position early on the morning of the 11th. Armstrong has 'disappeared' (*drowned*). That leaves us three people. Lombard, Blore and Vera Claythorne. Lombard was shot. His body was down by the sea—near Armstrong's. Vera Claythorne was found hanged in her own bedroom. Blore's body was on the terrace. His head was crushed in by a heavy marble clock that it seems reasonable to suppose fell on him from the window above."

The A.C. said sharply:

"Whose window?"

"Vera Claythorne's. Now, sir, let's take each of these cases separately. First Philip Lombard. Let's say *he* pushed over that lump of marble onto Blore—then he doped Vera Claythorne and strung her up. Lastly, he went down to the seashore and shot himself.

"But if so, *who took away the revolver from him?* For that revolver was found up in the house just inside the door at the top of the stairs—Wargrave's room."

The A.C. said:

"Any fingerprints on it?"

"Yes, sir, Vera Claythorne's."

"But, man alive, then—"

"I know what you're going to say, sir. That it was Vera Claythorne. That she shot Lombard, took the revolver back to the house, toppled the marble block onto Blore and then—hanged herself.

"And that's quite all right—up to a point. There's a chair in her bedroom and on the seat of it there are marks of seaweed same as on her shoes. Looks as though she stood on the chair, adjusted the rope round her neck and kicked away the chair.

"*But that chair wasn't found kicked over*. It was, like all the other chairs, neatly put back against the wall. That was done *after Vera Claythorne's death*—by *some one else*.

"That leaves us with Blore and if you tell me that after shooting Lombard and inducing Vera Claythorne to hang herself he then went out and pulled down a whacking great block of marble on himself by tying a string to it or something like that—well, I simply don't believe you. Men don't commit suicide that way—and what's more Blore wasn't that kind of man. *We* knew Blore—and he was not the man that you'd ever accuse of a desire for abstract justice."

The Assistant Commissioner said:

"I agree."

Inspector Maine said:

"And therefore, sir, there must have been *some one else* on the island. Some one who tidied up when the whole business was over. But where was he all the time—and where did he go to? The Sticklehaven people are absolutely certain that no one could have left the island before the rescue boat got there. But in that case—"

He stopped.

The Assistant Commissioner said:

"In that case—"

He sighed. He shook his head. He leant forward.

"But in that case," he said, "*who killed them?*"

A MANUSCRIPT DOCUMENT SENT
TO SCOTLAND YARD BY THE MASTER OF
THE *EMMA JANE,* FISHING TRAWLER

FROM MY earliest youth I realized that my nature was a mass of contradictions. I have, to begin with, an incurably romantic imagination. The practice of throwing a bottle into the sea with an important document inside was one that never failed to thrill me when reading adventure stories as a child. It thrills me still—and for that reason I have adopted this course—writing my confession, enclosing it in a bottle, sealing the latter, and casting it into the waves. There is, I suppose, a hundred to one chance that my confession may be found—and then (or do I flatter myself?) a hitherto unsolved murder mystery will be explained.

I was born with other traits besides my romantic fancy. I have a definite sadistic delight in seeing or causing death. I remember experiments with wasps—with various garden pests. . . . From an early age I knew very strongly the lust to kill.

But side by side with this went a contradictory trait—a strong sense of justice. It is abhorrent to me that an innocent person or creature should suffer or die by any act of mine. I have always felt strongly that right should prevail.

It may be understood—I think a psychologist would understand—that with my mental makeup being what it was, I adopted the law as a profession. The legal profession satisfied nearly all my instincts.

Crime and its punishment has always fascinated me. I enjoy reading every kind of detective story and thriller. I have devised for my own private amusement the most ingenious ways of carrying out a murder.

When in due course I came to preside over a court of law, that other secret instinct of mine was encouraged to develop. To see a wretched criminal squirming in the dock, suffering the tortures of the damned, as his doom came slowly and slowly nearer, was to me an exquisite pleasure. Mind you, I took no pleasure in seeing an *inno-cent* man there. On at least two occasions I stopped cases where to my mind the accused was palpably innocent, directing the jury that there was no case. Thanks, however, to the fairness and efficiency of our police force, the majority of the accused persons who have come before me to be tried for murder, have been guilty.

I will say here that such was the case with the man Edward Seton. His appearance and manner were misleading and he created a good impression on the jury. But not only the evidence, which was clear, though unspectacular, but my own knowledge of criminals told me without any doubt that the man had actually committed the crime with which he was charged, the brutal murder of an elderly woman who trusted him.

I have a reputation as a hanging judge, but that is unfair. I have always been strictly just and scrupulous in my summing up of a case.

All I have done is to protect the jury against the emotional effect of emotional appeals by some of our more emotional counsel. I have drawn their attention to the actual evidence.

For some years past I have been aware of a change within myself, a lessening of control—a desire to act instead of to judge.

I have wanted—let me admit it frankly—*to commit a murder my-self*. I recognized this as the desire of the artist to express himself! I was, or could be, an artist in crime! My imagination, sternly checked by the exigencies of my profession, waxed secretly to colossal force.

I must—I must—I *must*—commit a murder! And what is more, it must be no ordinary murder! It must be a fantastical crime—something stupendous—out of the common! In that one respect, I have still, I think, an adolescent's imagination.

I wanted something theatrical, impossible!

I wanted to kill. . . . Yes, I wanted to kill. . . .

But—incongruous as it may seem to some—I was restrained and hampered by my innate sense of justice. The innocent must not suffer.

And then, quite suddenly, the idea came to me—started by a chance remark uttered during casual conversation. It was a doctor to whom I was talking—some ordinary undistinguished G.P. He mentioned casually how often murder must be committed which the law was unable to touch.

And he instanced a particular case—that of an old lady, a patient of his who had recently died. He was, he said, himself convinced that her death was due to the withholding of a restorative drug by a married couple who attended on her and who stood to benefit very substantially by her death. That sort of thing, he explained, was quite impossible to prove, but he was nevertheless quite sure of it in his own mind. He added that there were many cases of a similar nature going on all the time—cases of deliberate murder—and all quite untouchable by the law.

That was the beginning of the whole thing. I suddenly saw my way clear. And I determined to commit not one murder, but murder on a grand scale.

A childish rhyme of my infancy came back into my mind—the rhyme of the ten little Indian boys. It had fascinated me as a child of two—the inexorable diminishment—the sense of inevitability.

I began, secretly, to collect victims. . . .

I will not take up space here by going into details of how this was accomplished. I had a certain routine line of conversation which I employed with nearly every one I met—and the results I got were really surprising. During the time I was in a nursing home I collected the case of Dr. Armstrong—a violently teetotal sister who attended on me being anxious to prove to me the evils of drink by recounting to me a case many years ago in hospital when a doctor under the influence of alcohol had killed a patient on whom he was operating. A careless question as to where the sister in question had trained, etc., soon gave me the necessary data. I tracked down the doctor and the patient mentioned without difficulty.

A conversation between two old military gossips in my Club put me on the track of General Macarthur. A man who had recently returned from the Amazon gave me a devastating résumé of the activities of one Philip Lombard. An indignant *mem sahib* in Majorca recounted the tale of the Puritan Emily Brent and her wretched servant girl. Anthony Marston I selected from a large group of people who had committed similar offences. His complete callousness and his inability to feel any responsibility for the lives he had taken made him, I considered, a type dangerous to the community and unfit to live. Ex-Inspector Blore came my way quite naturally, some of my professional brethren discussing the Landor case with freedom and vigour. I took a serious view of his offence. The police, as servants of the law, must be of a high order of integrity. For their word is perforce believed by virtue of their profession.

Finally there was the case of Vera Claythorne. It was when I was crossing the Atlantic. At a late hour one night the sole occupants of the smoking-room were myself and a good-looking young man called Hugo Hamilton.

Hugo Hamilton was unhappy. To assuage that unhappiness he had taken a considerable quantity of drink. He was in the maudlin confidential stage. Without much hope of any result I automatically started my routine conversational gambit. The response was startling. I can remember his words now. He said:

"You're right. Murder isn't what most people think—giving some one a dollop of arsenic—pushing them over a cliff—that sort of stuff." He leaned forward, thrusting his face into mine. He said: "I've known a murderess—known her, I tell you. And what's more I was crazy about her. . . . God help me, sometimes I think I still am. . . . It's Hell, I tell you—Hell— You see, she did it more or less for me. . . . Not that I ever dreamed. Women are fiends—absolute fiends—you wouldn't think a girl like that—a nice straight jolly girl— you wouldn't think she'd do that, would you? That she'd take a kid out to sea and let it drown—you wouldn't think a *woman* could do a thing like that?"

I said to him:

"Are you sure she did do it?"

He said and in saying it he seemed suddenly to sober up:

"I'm quite sure. Nobody else ever thought of it. But I knew the moment I looked at her—when I got back—after . . . And she knew I knew. . . . What she didn't realize was that I loved that kid. . . ."

He didn't say any more, but it was easy enough for me to trace back the story and reconstruct it.

I needed a tenth victim. I found him in a man named Morris. He was a shady little creature. Amongst other things he was a dope pedlar and he was responsible for inducing the daughter of friends of mine to take to drugs. She committed suicide at the age of twenty-one.

During all this time of search my plan had been gradually maturing in my mind. It was now complete and the coping stone to it was an interview I had with a doctor in Harley Street. I have mentioned that I underwent an operation. My interview in Harley Street told me that another operation would be useless. My medical adviser wrapped up the information very prettily, but I am accustomed to getting at the truth of a statement.

I did not tell the doctor of my decision—that my death should not be a slow and protracted one as it would be in the course of nature. No, my death should take place in a blaze of excitement. I would *live* before I died.

And now to the actual mechanics of the crime of Indian Island. To acquire the island, using the man Morris to cover my tracks, was easy enough. He was an expert in that sort of thing. Tabulating the information I had collected about my prospective victims, I was able to concoct a suitable bait for each. None of my plans miscarried. All my guests arrived at Indian Island on the 8th of August. The party included myself.

Morris was already accounted for. He suffered from indigestion. Before leaving London I gave him a capsule to take last thing at night which had, I said, done wonders for my own gastric juices. He accepted it unhesitatingly—the man was a slight hypochondriac. I had no fear that he would leave any compromising documents or memoranda behind. He was not that sort of man.

The order of death upon the island had been subjected by me to special thought and care. There were, I considered, amongst my guests, varying degrees of guilt. Those whose guilt was the lightest should, I decided, pass out first, and not suffer the prolonged mental strain and fear that the more cold-blooded offenders were to suffer.

Anthony Marston and Mrs. Rogers died first, the one instantaneously, the other in a peaceful sleep. Marston, I recognized, was a type born without that feeling of moral responsibility which most of us have. He was amoral—pagan. Mrs. Rogers, I had no doubt, had acted very largely under the influence of her husband.

I need not describe closely how those two met their deaths. The police will have been able to work that out quite easily. Potassium Cyanide is easily obtained by householders for putting down wasps. I had some in my possession and it was easy to slip it into Marston's almost empty glass during the tense period after the gramophone recital.

I may say that I watched the faces of my guests closely during that indictment and I had no doubt whatever, after my long court experience, that one and all were guilty.

During recent bouts of pain, I had been ordered a sleeping draught —Chloral Hydrate. It had been easy for me to suppress this until I had a lethal amount in my possession. When Rogers brought up some brandy for his wife, he set it down on a table and in passing that table I put the stuff into the brandy. It was easy, for at that time suspicion had not begun to set in.

General Macarthur met his death quite painlessly. He did not hear me come up behind him. I had, of course, to choose my time for leaving the terrace very carefully, but everything was successful.

As I had anticipated, a search was made of the island and it was discovered that there was no one on it but our seven selves. That at once created an atmosphere of suspicion. According to my plan I should shortly need an ally. I selected Dr. Armstrong for that part. He was a gullible sort of man, he knew me by sight and reputation and it was inconceivable to him that a man of my standing should actually be a murderer! All his suspicions were directed against Lombard and I pretended to concur in these. I hinted to him that I had a scheme by which it might be possible to trap the murderer into incriminating himself.

Though a search had been made of every one's room, no search had as yet been made of the persons themselves. But that was bound to come soon.

I killed Rogers on the morning of August 10th. He was chopping sticks for lighting the fire and did not hear me approach. I found the key to the dining-room door in his pocket. He had locked it the night before.

In the confusion attending the finding of Rogers' body I slipped into Lombard's room and abstracted his revolver. I knew that he would have one with him—in fact, I had instructed Morris to suggest as much when he interviewed him.

At breakfast I slipped my last dose of Chloral into Miss Brent's coffee when I was refilling her cup. We left her in the dining-room. I slipped in there a little while later—she was nearly unconscious and it was easy to inject a strong solution of Cyanide into her. The bumble-bee business was really rather childish—but somehow, you know, it pleased me. I liked adhering as closely as possible to my nursery rhyme.

Immediately after this what I had already foreseen happened—indeed I believe I suggested it myself. We all submitted to a rigorous search. I had safely hidden away the revolver, and had no more Cyanide or Chloral in my possession.

It was then that I intimated to Armstrong that we must carry our plan into effect. It was simply this—*I must appear to be the next victim.* That would perhaps rattle the murderer—at any rate once I was supposed to be dead I could move about the house and spy upon the unknown murderer.

Armstrong was keen on the idea. We carried it out that evening. A little plaster of red mud on the forehead—the red curtain and the wool and the stage was set. The lights of the candles were very flickering and uncertain and the only person who would examine me closely was Armstrong.

It worked perfectly. Miss Claythorne screamed the house down when she found the seaweed which I had thoughtfully arranged in her room. They all rushed up, and I took up my pose of a murdered man.

The effect on them when they found me was all that could be desired. Armstrong acted his part in the most professional manner. They carried me upstairs and laid me on my bed. Nobody worried about me, they were all too deadly scared and terrified of each other.

I had a rendezvous with Armstrong outside the house at a quarter to two. I took him up a little way behind the house on the edge of the cliff. I said that here we could see if any one else approached us, and we should not be seen from the house as the bedrooms faced the other way. He was still quite unsuspicious—and yet he ought to have been warned— If he had only remembered the words of the nursery rhyme, "A red herring swallowed one . . ." He took the red herring all right.

It was quite easy. I uttered an exclamation, leant over the cliff, told him to look, wasn't that the mouth of a cave? He leant right over. A quick vigorous push sent him off his balance and splash into the heaving sea below. I returned to the house. It must have been my footfall that Blore heard. A few minutes after I had returned to Armstrong's room I left it, this time making a certain amount of noise so that some one *should* hear me. I heard a door open as I got to the bottom of the stairs. They must have just glimpsed my figure as I went out of the front door.

It was a minute or two before they followed me. I had gone straight round the house and in at the dining-room window which I had left open. I shut the window and later I broke the glass. Then I went upstairs and laid myself out again on my bed.

I calculated that they would search the house again, but I did not think they would look closely at any of the corpses, a mere twitch aside of the sheet to satisfy themselves that it was not Armstrong masquerading as a body. This is exactly what occurred.

I forgot to say that I returned the revolver to Lombard's room. It may be of interest to some one to know where it was hidden during the search. There was a big pile of tinned food in the larder. I opened the bottommost of the tins—biscuits I think it contained, bedded in the revolver and replaced the strip of adhesive tape.

I calculated, and rightly, that no one would think of working their way through a pile of apparently untouched foodstuffs, especially as all the top tins were soldered.

The red curtain I had concealed by laying it flat on the seat of one of the drawing-room chairs under the chintz cover and the wool in the seat cushion, cutting a small hole.

And now came the moment that I had anticipated—three people who were so frightened of each other that anything might happen—

and one of them had a revolver. I watched them from the windows of the house. When Blore came up alone I had the big marble clock poised ready. *Exit Blore.* . . .

From my window I saw Vera Claythorne shoot Lombard. A daring and resourceful young woman. I always thought she was a match for him and more. As soon as that had happened I set the stage in her bedroom.

It was an interesting psychological experiment. Would the consciousness of her own guilt, the state of nervous tension consequent on having just shot a man, be sufficient, together with the hypnotic suggestion of the surroundings, to cause her to take her own life? I thought it would. I was right. Vera Claythorne hanged herself before my eyes where I stood in the shadow of the wardrobe.

And now for the last stage. I came forward, picked up the chair and set it against the wall. I looked for the revolver and found it at the top of the stairs where the girl had dropped it. I was careful to preserve her fingerprints on it.

And now?

I shall finish writing this. I shall enclose it and seal it in a bottle and I shall throw the bottle into the sea.

Why?

Yes, why? . . .

It was my ambition to *invent* a murder mystery that no one could solve.

But no artist, I now realize, can be satisfied with art alone. There is a natural craving for recognition which cannot be gainsaid.

I have, let me confess it in all humility, a pitiful human wish that some one should know just how clever I have been. . . .

In all this, I have assumed that the mystery of Indian Island will remain unsolved. It may be, of course, that the police will be cleverer than I think. There are, after all, three clues. One: the police are perfectly aware that Edward Seton was guilty. They know, therefore, that one of the ten people on the island was not a murderer in any sense of the word, and it follows, paradoxically, that that person must logically be *the* murderer. The second clue lies in the seventh verse of the nursery rhyme. Armstrong's death is associated with a "red herring" which he swallowed—or rather which resulted in swallowing him! That is to say that at that stage of the affair some hocus-pocus is clearly indicated—and that Armstrong was deceived by it and sent to his death. That might start a promising line of inquiry. For at that period there are only four persons and of those four I am clearly the only one likely to inspire him with confidence.

The third is symbolical. The manner of my death marking me on the forehead. The brand of Cain.

There is, I think, little more to say.

After entrusting my bottle and its message to the sea I shall go to my room and lay myself down on the bed. To my eyeglasses is attached what seems a length of fine black cord—but it is elastic cord. I shall lay the weight of the body on the glasses. The cord I shall loop round the door-handle and attach it, not too solidly, to the revolver. What I think will happen is this.

My hand, protected with a handkerchief, will press the trigger. My hand will fall to my side, the revolver, pulled by the elastic will recoil to the door, jarred by the door-handle it will detach itself from the elastic and fall. The elastic, released, will hang down innocently from the eyeglasses on which my body is lying. A handkerchief lying on the floor will cause no comment whatever.

I shall be found, laid neatly on my bed, shot through the forehead in accordance with the record kept by my fellow victims. Times of death cannot be stated with any accuracy by the time our bodies are examined.

When the sea goes down, there will come from the mainland boats and men.

And they will find ten dead bodies and an unsolved problem on Indian Island.

Signed

LAWRENCE WARGRAVE.

The Witness
for the Prosecution

MR. MAYHERNE ADJUSTED his pince-nez and cleared his throat with a little dry-as-dust cough that was wholly typical of him. Then he looked again at the man opposite him, the man charged with willful murder.

Mr. Mayherne was a small man, precise in manner, neatly, not to say foppishly dressed, with a pair of very shrewd and piercing gray eyes. By no means a fool. Indeed, as a solicitor, Mr. Mayherne's reputation stood very high. His voice, when he spoke to his client, was dry but not unsympathetic.

"I must impress upon you again that you are in very grave danger, and that the utmost frankness is necessary."

Leonard Vole, who had been staring in a dazed fashion at the blank wall in front of him, transferred his glance to the solicitor.

"I know," he said hopelessly. "You keep telling me so. But I can't seem to realize yet that I'm charged with murder—*murder*. And such a dastardly crime, too."

Mr. Mayherne was practical, not emotional. He coughed again, took off his pince-nez, polished them carefully, and replaced them on his nose. Then he said, "Yes, yes, yes. Now, my dear Mr. Vole, we're going to make a determined effort to get you off—and we shall succeed—we shall succeed. But I must have all the facts. I must know just how damaging the case against you is likely to be. Then we can fix upon the best line of defense."

Still the young man looked at him in the same dazed, hopeless fashion. To Mr. Mayherne the case had seemed black enough, and the guilt of the prisoner assured. Now, for the first time, he felt a doubt.

"You think I'm guilty," said Leonard Vole, in a low voice. "But, by God, I swear I'm not! It looks pretty black against me, I know that. I'm like a man caught in a net—the meshes of it all round me, entangling me whichever way I turn. But I didn't do it, Mr. Mayherne, I didn't do it!"

In such a position a man was bound to protest his innocence. Mr. Mayherne knew that. Yet, in spite of himself, he was impressed. It might be, after all, that Leonard Vole was innocent.

"You are right, Mr. Vole," he said gravely. "The case does look very black against you. Nevertheless, I accept your assurance. Now, let us get to facts. I want you to tell me in your own words exactly how you came to make the acquaintance of Miss Emily French."

"It was one day in Oxford Street. I saw an elderly lady crossing the road. She was carrying a lot of parcels. In the middle of the street she dropped them, tried to recover them, found a bus was almost on top of her, and just managed to reach the curb safely, dazed and bewildered by people having shouted at her. I recovered her parcels, wiped the mud off them as best I could, retied the string of one, and returned them to her."

"There was no question of your having saved her life?"

"Oh, dear me, no! All I did was to perform a common act of courtesy. She was extremely grateful, thanked me warmly, and said something about my manners not being those of most of the younger generation—I can't remember the exact words. Then I lifted my hat and went on. I never expected to see her again. But life is full of coincidences. That very evening I came across her at a party at a friend's house. She recognized me at once and asked that I should be introduced to her. I then found out that she was a Miss Emily French and that she lived at Cricklewood. I talked to her for some time. She was, I imagine, an old lady who took sudden and violent fancies to people. She took one to me on the strength of a perfectly simple action which anyone might have performed. On leaving, she shook me warmly by the hand and asked me to come and see her. I replied, of course, that I should be very pleased to do so, and she then urged me to name a day. I did not want particularly to go, but it would have seemed churlish to refuse, so I fixed on the following Saturday. After she had gone, I learned something about her from my friends. That she was rich, eccentric, lived alone with one maid, and owned no less than eight cats."

"I see," said Mr. Mayherne. "The question of her being well off came up as early as that?"

"If you mean that I inquired—" began Leonard Vole hotly, but Mr. Mayherne stilled him with a gesture.

"I have to look at the case as it will be presented by the other side. An ordinary observer would not have supposed Miss French to be a lady of means. She lived poorly, almost humbly. Unless you had been told the contrary, you would in all probability have considered her to be in poor circumstances—at any rate to begin with. Who was it exactly who told you that she was well off?"

"My friend, George Harvey, at whose house the party took place."

"Is he likely to remember having done so?"

"I really don't know. Of course it is some time ago now."

"Quite so, Mr. Vole. You see, the first aim of the prosecution will be to establish that you were in low water financially—that is true, is it not?"

Leonard Vole flushed.

"Yes," he said, in a low voice. "I'd been having a run of infernal bad luck just then."

"Quite so," said Mr. Mayherne again. "That being, as I say, in low water financially, you met this rich old lady and cultivated her acquaintance assiduously. Now if we are in a position to say that you had no idea she was well off, and that you visited her out of pure kindness of heart—"

"Which is the case."

"I dare say. I am not disputing the point. I am looking at it from the outside point of view. A great deal depends on the memory of Mr. Harvey. Is he likely to remember that conversation or is he not? Could he be confused by counsel into believing that it took place later?"

Leonard Vole reflected for some minutes. Then he said steadily enough, but with a rather pale face, "I do not think that that line would be successful, Mr. Mayherne. Several of those present heard his remark, and one or two of them chaffed me about my conquest of a rich old lady."

The solicitor endeavored to hide his disappointment with a wave of the hand.

"Unfortunate," he said. "But I congratulate you upon your plain speaking, Mr. Vole. It is to you I look to guide me. Your judgment is quite right. To persist in the line I spoke of would have been disastrous. We must leave that point. You made the acquaintance of Miss French, you called upon her, the acquaintanceship progressed. We want a clear reason for all this. Why did you, a young man of thirty-three, good-looking, fond of sport, popular with your friends, devote so much of your time to an elderly woman with whom you could hardly have anything in common?"

Leonard Vole flung out his hands in a nervous gesture.

"I can't tell you—I really can't tell you. After the first visit, she pressed me to come again, spoke of being lonely and unhappy. She made it difficult for me to refuse. She showed so plainly her fondness and affection for me that I was placed in an awkward position. You see, Mr. Mayherne, I've got a weak nature—I drift—I'm one of those people who can't say no. And believe me or not, as you like, after the third or fourth visit I paid her I found myself getting genuinely fond of the old thing. My mother died when I was young, an aunt brought me up, and she, too, died before I was fifteen. If I told you that I genuinely enjoyed being mothered and pampered, I dare say you'd only laugh."

Mr. Mayherne did not laugh. Instead he took off his pince-nez again and polished them, a sign with him that he was thinking deeply.

"I accept your explanation, Mr. Vole," he said at last. "I believe it to be psychologically probable. Whether a jury would take that view of it is another matter. Please continue your narrative. When was it that Miss French first asked you to look into her business affairs?"

"After my third or fourth visit to her. She understood very little of money matters, and was worried about some investments."

Mr. Mayherne looked up sharply.

"Be careful, Mr. Vole. The maid, Janet Mackenzie, declares that her mistress was a good woman of business and transacted all her own affairs, and this is borne out by the testimony of her bankers."

"I can't help that," said Vole earnestly. "That's what she said to me."

Mr. Mayherne looked at him for a moment or two in silence. Though he had no intention of saying so, his belief in Leonard Vole's innocence was at that moment strengthened. He knew something of the mentality of elderly ladies. He saw Miss French, infatuated with the good-looking young man, hunting about for pretexts that would bring him to the house. What more likely than that she should plead ignorance of business, and beg him to help her with her money affairs? She was enough of a woman of the world to realize that any man is slightly flattered by such an admission of his superiority. Leonard Vole had been flattered. Perhaps, too, she had not been averse to letting this young man know that she was wealthy. Emily French had been a strong-willed old woman, willing to pay her price for what she wanted. All this passed rapidly through Mr. Mayherne's mind, but he gave no indication of it, and asked instead a further question.

"And did you handle her affairs for her at her request?"

"I did."

"Mr. Vole," said the solicitor, "I am going to ask you a very seri-

ous question, and one to which it is vital I should have a truthful answer. You were in low water financially. You had the handling of an
old lady's affairs—an old lady who, according to her own statement,
knew little or nothing of business. Did you at any time, or in any
manner, convert to your own use the securities which you handled?
Did you engage in any transaction for your own pecuniary advantage
which will not bear the light of day?" He quelled the other's response. "Wait a minute before you answer. There are two courses
open to us. Either we can make a feature of your probity and honesty
in conducting her affairs while pointing out how unlikely it is that you
would commit murder to obtain money which you might have obtained by such infinitely easier means. If, on the other hand, there is
anything in your dealings which the prosecution will get hold of—if,
to put it baldly, it can be proved that you swindled the old lady in any
way, we must take the line that you had no motive for the murder,
since she was already a profitable source of income to you. You perceive the distinction. Now, I beg of you, take your time before you
reply."

But Leonard Vole took no time at all.

"My dealings with Miss French's affairs were all perfectly fair and
above board. I acted for her interests to the very best of my ability,
as anyone will find who looks into the matter."

"Thank you," said Mr. Mayherne. "You relieve my mind very
much. I pay you the compliment of believing that you are far too
clever to lie to me over such an important matter."

"Surely," said Vole eagerly, "the strongest point in my favor is the
lack of motive. Granted that I cultivated the acquaintanceship of a
rich old lady in the hopes of getting money out of her—that, I gather,
is the substance of what you have been saying—surely her death frus-
trates all my hopes?"

The solicitor looked at him steadily. Then, very deliberately, he
repeated his unconscious trick with his pince-nez. It was not until
they were firmly replaced on his nose that he spoke.

"Are you not aware, Mr. Vole, that Miss French left a will under
which you are the principal beneficiary?"

"What?" The prisoner sprang to his feet. His dismay was obvious
and unforced. "My God! What are you saying? She left her money
to me?"

Mr. Mayherne nodded slowly. Vole sank down again, his head in
his hands.

"You pretend you know nothing of this will?"

"Pretend? There's no pretense about it. I knew nothing about it."

"What would you say if I told you that the maid, Janet Mackenzie, swears that you *did* know? That her mistress told her distinctly that she had consulted you in the matter, and told you of her intentions?"

"Say? That she's lying! No, I go too fast. Janet is an elderly woman. She was a faithful watchdog to her mistress, and she didn't like me. She was jealous and suspicious. I should say that Miss French confided her intentions to Janet, and that Janet either mistook something she said, or else was convinced in her own mind that I had persuaded the old lady into doing it. I dare say that she herself believes now that Miss French actually told her so."

"You don't think she dislikes you enough to lie deliberately about the matter?"

Leonard Vole looked shocked and startled.

"No, indeed! Why should she?"

"I don't know," said Mr. Mayherne thoughtfully. "But she's very bitter against you."

The wretched young man groaned again.

"I'm beginning to see," he muttered. "It's frightful. I made up to her, that's what they'll say, I got her to make a will leaving her money to me, and then I go there that night, and there's nobody in the house—they find her the next day—oh, my God, it's awful!"

"You are wrong about there being nobody in the house," said Mr. Mayherne. "Janet, as you remember, was to go out for the evening. She went, but about half past nine she returned to fetch the pattern of a blouse sleeve which she had promised to a friend. She let herself in by the back door, went upstairs and fetched it, and went out again. She heard voices in the sitting-room, though she could not distinguish what they said, but she will swear that one of them was Miss French's and one was a man's."

"At half past nine," said Leonard Vole. "At half past nine—" He sprang to his feet. "But then I'm saved—saved—"

"What do you mean, saved?" cried Mr. Mayherne, astonished.

"By half past nine I was at home again! My wife can prove that. I left Miss French about five minutes to nine. I arrived home about twenty past nine. My wife was there waiting for me. Oh, thank God—thank God! And bless Janet Mackenzie's sleeve pattern."

In his exuberance, he hardly noticed that the grave expression on the solicitor's face had not altered. But the latter's words brought him down to earth with a bump.

"Who, then, in your opinion, murdered Miss French?"

"Why, a burglar, of course, as was thought at first. The window was forced, you remember. She was killed with a heavy blow from a crowbar, and the crowbar was found lying on the floor beside the body. And several articles were missing. But for Janet's absurd suspicions and dislike of me, the police would never have swerved from the right track."

"That will hardly do, Mr. Vole," said the solicitor. "The things that were missing were mere trifles of no value, taken as a blind. And the marks on the window were not at all conclusive. Besides, think for yourself. You say you were no longer in the house by half past nine. Who, then, was the man Janet heard talking to Miss French in the sitting-room? She would hardly be having an amicable conversation with a burglar."

"No," said Vole. "No—" He looked puzzled and discouraged. "But, anyway," he added with reviving spirit, "it lets me out. I've got an alibi. You must see Romaine—my wife—at once."

"Certainly," acquiesced the lawyer. "I should already have seen Mrs. Vole but for her being absent when you were arrested. I wired to Scotland at once, and I understand that she arrives back tonight. I am going to call upon her immediately I leave here."

Vole nodded, a great expression of satisfaction settling down over his face.

"Yes, Romaine will tell you. My God! it's a lucky chance that."

"Excuse me, Mr. Vole, but you are very fond of your wife?"

"Of course."

"And she of you?"

"Romaine is devoted to me. She'd do anything in the world for me."

He spoke enthusiastically, but the solicitor's heart sank a little lower. The testimony of a devoted wife—would it gain credence?

"Was there anyone else who saw you return at nine-twenty? A maid, for instance?"

"We have no maid."

"Did you meet anyone in the street on the way back?"

"Nobody I knew. I rode part of the way in a bus. The conductor might remember."

Mr. Mayherne shook his head doubtfully.

"There is no one, then, who can confirm your wife's testimony?"

"No. But it isn't necessary, surely?"

"I dare say not. I dare say not," said Mr. Mayherne hastily. "Now there's just one thing more. Did Miss French know that you were a married man?"

"Oh, yes."

"Yet you never took your wife to see her. Why was that?"

For the first time, Leonard Vole's answer came halting and uncertain.

"Well—I don't know."

"Are you aware that Janet Mackenzie says her mistress believed you to be single, and contemplated marrying you in the future?"

Vole laughed. "Absurd! There was forty years' difference in age between us."

"It has been done," said the solicitor dryly. "The fact remains. Your wife never met Miss French?"

"No—" Again the constraint.

"You will permit me to say," said the lawyer, "that I hardly understand your attitude in the matter."

Vole flushed, hesitated, and then spoke.

"I'll make a clean breast of it. I was hard up, as you know. I hoped that Miss French might lend me some money. She was fond of me, but she wasn't at all interested in the struggles of a young couple. Early on, I found that she had taken it for granted that my wife and I didn't get on—were living apart. Mr. Mayherne—I wanted the money —for Romaine's sake. I said nothing, and allowed the old lady to think what she chose. She spoke of my being an adopted son to her. There was never any question of marriage—that must be just Janet's imagination."

"And that is all?"

"Yes—that is all."

Was there just a shade of hesitation in the words? The lawyer fancied so. He rose and held out his hand.

"Good-by, Mr. Vole." He looked into the haggard young face and spoke with an unusual impulse. "I believe in your innocence in spite of the multitude of facts arrayed against you. I hope to prove it and vindicate you completely."

Vole smiled back at him.

"You'll find the alibi is all right," he said cheerfully.

Again he hardly noticed that the other did not respond.

"The whole thing hinges a good deal on the testimony of Janet Mackenzie," said Mr. Mayherne. "She hates you. That much is clear."

"She can hardly hate me," protested the young man.

The solicitor shook his head as he went out. *Now for Mrs. Vole,* he said to himself. He was seriously disturbed by the way the thing was shaping.

The Voles lived in a small shabby house near Paddington Green. It was to this house that Mr. Mayherne went.

In answer to his ring, a big slatternly woman, obviously a char-woman, answered the door.

"Mrs. Vole? Has she returned yet?"

"Got back an hour ago. But I dunno if you can see her."

"If you will take my card to her," said Mr. Mayherne quietly, "I am quite sure that she will do so."

The woman looked at him doubtfully, wiped her hand on her apron, and took the card. Then she closed the door in his face and left him on the step outside.

In a few minutes, however, she returned with a slightly altered manner.

"Come inside, please."

She ushered him into a tiny drawing-room. Mr. Mayherne, ex-amining a drawing on the wall, started up suddenly to face a tall, pale woman who had entered so quietly that he had not heard her.

"Mr. Mayherne? You are my husband's solicitor, are you not? You have come from him? Will you please sit down?"

Until she spoke he had not realized that she was not English. Now, observing her more closely, he noticed the high cheekbones, the dense blue-black of the hair, and an occasional very slight movement of the hands that was distinctly foreign. A strange woman, very quiet. So quiet as to make one uneasy. From the very first Mr. Mayherne was conscious that he was up against something that he did not un-derstand.

"Now, my dear Mrs. Vole," he began, "you must not give way—"

He stopped. It was so very obvious that Romaine Vole had not the slightest intention of giving way. She was perfectly calm and com-posed.

"Will you please tell me about it?" she said. "I must know every-thing. Do not think to spare me. I want to know the worst." She hesi-tated, then repeated in a lower tone, with a curious emphasis which the lawyer did not understand, "I want to know the worst."

Mr. Mayherne went over his interview with Leonard Vole. She listened attentively, nodding her head now and then.

"I see," she said, when he had finished. "He wants me to say that he came in at twenty minutes past nine that night?"

"He did come in at that time?" said Mr. Mayherne sharply.

"That is not the point," she said coldly. "Will my saying so acquit him? Will they believe me?"

Mr. Mayherne was taken aback. She had gone so quickly to the core of the matter.

"That is what I want to know," she said. "Will it be enough? Is there anyone else who can support my evidence?"

There was a suppressed eagerness in her manner that made him vaguely uneasy.

"So far there is no one else," he said reluctantly.

"I see," said Romaine Vole.

She sat for a minute or two perfectly still. A little smile played over her lips.

The lawyer's feeling of alarm grew stronger and stronger.

"Mrs. Vole—" he began. "I know what you must feel—"

"Do you?" she asked. "I wonder."

"In the circumstances—"

"In the circumstances—I intend to play a lone hand."

He looked at her in dismay.

"But, my dear Mrs. Vole—you are overwrought. Being so devoted to your husband—"

"I beg your pardon?"

The sharpness of her voice made him start. He repeated in a hesitating manner, "Being so devoted to your husband—"

Romaine Vole nodded slowly, the same strange smile on her lips.

"Did he tell you that I was devoted to him?" she asked softly. "Ah! yes, I can see he did. How stupid men are! Stupid—stupid—stupid—"

She rose suddenly to her feet. All the intense emotion that the lawyer had been conscious of in the atmosphere was now concentrated in her tone.

"I hate him, I tell you! I hate him. I hate him. I hate him! I would like to see him hanged by the neck till he is dead."

The lawyer recoiled before her and the smoldering passion in her eyes.

She advanced a step nearer and continued vehemently.

"Perhaps I shall see it. Supposing I tell you that he did not come in that night at twenty past nine, but at twenty past ten? You say that he tells you he knew nothing about the money coming to him. Supposing I tell you he knew all about it, and counted on it, and committed murder to get it? Supposing I tell you that he admitted to me that night when he came in what he had done? That there was blood on his coat? What then? Supposing that I stand up in court and say all these things?"

Her eyes seemed to challenge him. With an effort he concealed his growing dismay, and endeavored to speak in a rational tone.

"You cannot be asked to give evidence against your husband—"

"He is not my husband!"

The words came out so quickly that he fancied he had misunderstood her.

"I beg your pardon? I—"

"He is not my husband."

The silence was so intense that you could have heard a pin drop.

"I was an actress in Vienna. My husband is alive but in a madhouse. So we could not marry. I am glad now." She nodded defiantly.

"I should like you to tell me one thing," said Mr. Mayherne. He contrived to appear as cool and unemotional as ever. "Why are you so bitter against Leonard Vole?"

She shook her head, smiling a little.

"Yes, you would like to know. But I shall not tell you. I will keep my secret."

Mr. Mayherne gave his dry little cough and rose.

"There seems no point in prolonging this interview," he remarked. "You will hear from me again after I have communicated with my client."

She came closer to him, looking into his eyes with her own wonderful dark ones.

"Tell me," she said, "did you believe—honestly—that he was innocent when you came here today?"

"I did," said Mr. Mayherne.

"You poor little man." She laughed.

"And I believe so still," finished the lawyer. "Good evening, madam."

He went out of the room, taking with him the memory of her startled face. *This is going to be the devil of a business,* said Mr. Mayherne to himself as he strode along the street.

Extraordinary, the whole thing. An extraordinary woman. A very dangerous woman. Women were the devil when they got their knife into you.

What was to be done? That wretched young man hadn't a leg to stand upon. Of course, possibly he did commit the crime.

No, said Mr. Mayherne to himself. *No—there's almost too much evidence against him. I don't believe this woman. She was trumping up the whole story. But she'll never bring it into court.*

He wished he felt more conviction on the point.

The police court proceedings were brief and dramatic. The principal witnesses for the prosecution were Janet Mackenzie, maid to the dead woman, and Romaine Heilger, Austrian subject, the mistress of the prisoner.

Mr. Mayherne sat in court and listened to the damning story that the latter told. It was on the lines she had indicated to him in their interview.

The prisoner reserved his defense and was committed for trial.

Mr. Mayherne was at his wits' end. The case against Leonard Vole was black beyond words. Even the famous K.C. who was engaged for the defense held out little hope.

"If we can shake that Austrian woman's testimony, we might do something," he said dubiously. "But it's a bad business."

Mr. Mayherne had concentrated his energies on one single point. Assuming Leonard Vole to be speaking the truth, and to have left the murdered woman's house at nine o'clock, who was the man Janet heard talking to Miss French at half past nine?

The only ray of light was in the shape of a scapegrace nephew who had in bygone days cajoled and threatened his aunt out of various sums of money. Janet Mackenzie, the solicitor learned, had always been attached to this young man, and had never ceased urging his claims upon her mistress. It certainly seemed possible that it was this nephew who had been with Miss French after Leonard Vole left, especially as he was not to be found in any of his old haunts.

In all other directions, the lawyer's researches had been negative in their result. No one had seen Leonard Vole entering his own house, or leaving that of Miss French. No one had seen any other man enter or leave the house in Cricklewood. All inquiries drew blank.

It was the eve of the trial when Mr. Mayherne received the letter which was to lead his thoughts in an entirely new direction.

It came by the six-o'clock post. An illiterate scrawl, written on common paper and enclosed in a dirty envelope with the stamp stuck on crooked.

Mr. Mayherne read it through once or twice before he grasped its meaning.

Dear Mister:

Youre the lawyer chap wot acts for the young feller. If you want that painted foreign hussy showd up for wot she is an her pack of lies you come to 16 Shaw's Rents Stepney to-night It ull cawst you 2 hundred quid Arsk for Missis Mogson.

The solicitor read and reread this strange epistle. It might, of course, be a hoax, but when he thought it over, he became increasingly convinced that it was genuine, and also convinced that it was the one hope for the prisoner. The evidence of Romaine Heilger damned him completely, and the line the defense meant to pursue, the line that the evidence of a woman who had admittedly lived an immoral life was not to be trusted, was at best a weak one.

Mr. Mayherne's mind was made up. It was his duty to save his client at all costs. He must go to Shaw's Rents.

He had some difficulty in finding the place, a ramshackle building in an evil-smelling slum, but at last he did so, and on inquiry for Mrs. Mogson was sent up to a room on the third floor. On this door he knocked, and getting no answer, knocked again.

At this second knock, he heard a shuffling sound inside, and presently the door was opened cautiously half an inch and a bent figure peered out.

Suddenly the woman, for it was a woman, gave a chuckle and opened the door wider.

"So it's you, dearie," she said, in a wheezy voice. "Nobody with you, is there? No playing tricks? That's right. You can come in—you can come in."

With some reluctance the lawyer stepped across the threshold into the small, dirty room, with its flickering gas jet. There was an untidy unmade bed in a corner, a plain deal table, and two rickety chairs. For the first time Mr. Mayherne had a full view of the tenant of this unsavory apartment. She was a woman of middle age, bent in figure, with a mass of untidy gray hair and a scarf wound tightly round her face. She saw him looking at this and laughed again, the same curious, toneless chuckle.

"Wondering why I hide my beauty, dear? He, he, he. Afraid it may tempt you, eh? But you shall see—you shall see."

She drew aside the scarf, and the lawyer recoiled involuntarily before the almost formless blur of scarlet. She replaced the scarf again.

"So you're not wanting to kiss me, dearie? He, he, I don't wonder. And yet I was a pretty girl once—not so long ago as you'd think, either. Vitriol, dearie, vitriol—that's what did that. Ah! but I'll be even with 'em—"

She burst into a hideous torrent of profanity which Mr. Mayherne tried vainly to quell. She fell silent at last, her hands clenching and unclenching themselves nervously.

"Enough of that," said the lawyer sternly. "I've come here because I have reason to believe you can give me information which will clear my client, Leonard Vole. Is that the case?"

Her eyes leered at him cunningly.

"What about the money, dearie?" she wheezed. "Two hundred quid, you remember."

"It is your duty to give evidence, and you can be called upon to do so."

"That won't do, dearie. I'm an old woman, and I know nothing. But you give me two hundred quid, and perhaps I can give you a hint or two. See?"

"What kind of hint?"

"What should you say to a letter? A letter from *her*. Never mind how I got hold of it. That's my business. It'll do the trick. But I want my two hundred quid."

Mr. Mayherne looked at her coldly, and made up his mind.

"I'll give you ten pounds, nothing more. And only that if this letter is what you say it is."

"Ten pounds?" She screamed and raved at him.

"Twenty," said Mr. Mayherne, "and that's my last word."

He rose as if to go. Then, watching her closely, he drew out a pocketbook, and counted out twenty one-pound notes.

"You see," he said. "That is all I have with me. You can take it or leave it."

But already he knew that the sight of the money was too much for her. She cursed and raved impotently, but at last she gave in. Going over to the bed, she drew something out from beneath the tattered mattress.

"Here you are, damn you!" she snarled. "It's the top one you want."

It was a bundle of letters that she threw to him, and Mr. Mayherne untied them and scanned them in his usual cool, methodical manner. The woman, watching him eagerly, could gain no clue from his impassive face.

He read each letter through, then returned again to the top one and read it a second time. Then he tied the whole bundle up again carefully.

They were love letters, written by Romaine Heilger, and the man they were written to was not Leonard Vole. The top letter was dated the day of the latter's arrest.

"I spoke true, dearie, didn't I?" whined the woman. "It'll do for her, that letter?"

Mr. Mayherne put the letters in his pocket, then he asked a question.

"How did you get hold of this correspondence?"

"That's telling," she said with a leer. "But I know something more. I heard in court what that hussy said. Find out where she was at twenty past ten, the time she says she was at home. Ask at the Lion

Road Cinema. They'll remember—a fine upstanding girl like that—curse her!"

"Who is the man?" asked Mr. Mayherne. "There's only a Christian name here."

The other's voice grew thick and hoarse, her hands clenched and unclenched. Finally she lifted one to her face.

"He's the man that did this to me. Many years ago now. She took him away from me—a chit of a girl she was then. And when I went after him—and went for him, too—he threw the cursed stuff at me! And she laughed—damn her! I've had it in for her for years. Followed her, I have, spied upon her. And now I've got her! She'll suffer for this, won't she, Mr. Lawyer? She'll suffer?"

"She will probably be sentenced to a term of imprisonment for perjury," said Mr. Mayherne quietly.

"Shut away—that's what I want. You're going, are you? Where's my money? Where's that good money?"

Without a word, Mr. Mayherne put down the notes on the table. Then, drawing a deep breath, he turned and left the squalid room. Looking back, he saw the old woman crooning over the money.

He wasted no time. He found the cinema in Lion Road easily enough, and, shown a photograph of Romaine Heilger, the commissionaire recognized her at once. She had arrived at the cinema with a man some time after ten o'clock on the evening in question. He had not noticed her escort particularly, but he remembered the lady who had spoken to him about the picture that was showing. They stayed until the end, about an hour later.

Mr. Mayherne was satisfied. Romaine Heilger's evidence was a tissue of lies from beginning to end. She had evolved it out of her passionate hatred. The lawyer wondered whether he would ever know what lay behind that hatred. What had Leonard Vole done to her? He had seemed dumfounded when the solicitor had reported her attitude to him. He had declared earnestly that such a thing was incredible—yet it had seemed to Mr. Mayherne that after the first astonishment his protests had lacked sincerity.

He did know. Mr. Mayherne was convinced of it. He knew, but he had no intention of revealing the fact. The secret between those two remained a secret. Mr. Mayherne wondered if some day he should come to learn what it was.

The solicitor glanced at his watch. It was late, but time was everything. He hailed a taxi and gave an address.

"Sir Charles must know of this at once," he murmured to himself as he got in.

The trial of Leonard Vole for the murder of Emily French aroused widespread interest. In the first place the prisoner was young and good-looking, then he was accused of a particularly dastardly crime, and there was the further interest of Romaine Heilger, the principal witness for the prosecution. There had been pictures of her in many papers, and several fictitious stories as to her origin and history.

The proceedings opened quietly enough. Various technical evidence came first. Then Janet Mackenzie was called. She told substantially the same story as before. In cross-examination counsel for the defense succeeded in getting her to contradict herself once or twice over her account of Vole's association with Miss French; he emphasized the fact that though she had heard a man's voice in the sitting-room that night, there was nothing to show that it was Vole who was there, and he managed to drive home a feeling that jealousy and dislike of the prisoner were at the bottom of a good deal of her evidence.

Then the next witness was called.

"Your name is Romaine Heilger?"

"Yes."

"You are an Austrian subject?"

"Yes."

"For the last three years you have lived with the prisoner and passed yourself off as his wife?"

Just for a moment Romaine Heilger's eyes met those of the man in the dock. Her expression held something curious and unfathomable.

"Yes."

The questions went on. Word by word the damning facts came out. On the night in question the prisoner had taken out a crowbar with him. He had returned at twenty minutes past ten, and had confessed to having killed the old lady. His cuffs had been stained with blood, and he had burned them in the kitchen stove. He had terrorized her into silence by means of threats.

As the story proceeded, the feeling of the court which had, to begin with, been slightly favorable to the prisoner, now set dead against him. He himself sat with downcast head and moody air, as though he knew he were doomed.

Yet it might have been noted that her own counsel sought to restrain Romaine's animosity. He would have preferred her to be more unbiased.

Formidable and ponderous, counsel for the defense arose.

He put it to her that her story was a malicious fabrication from start to finish, that she had not even been in her own house at the time in question, that she was in love with another man and was deliberately seeking to send Vole to his death for a crime he did not commit.

Romaine denied these allegations with superb insolence.

Then came the surprising denouement, the production of the letter. It was read aloud in court in the midst of a breathless stillness.

"Max, beloved, the Fates have delivered him into our hands! He has been arrested for murder—but, yes, the murder of an old lady! Leonard, who would not hurt a fly! At last I shall have my revenge. The poor chicken! I shall say that he came in that night with blood upon him—that he confessed to me. I shall hang him, Max—and when he hangs he will know and realize that it was Romaine who sent him to his death. And then—happiness, Beloved! Happiness at last!"

There were experts present ready to swear that the handwriting was that of Romaine Heilger, but they were not needed. Confronted with the letter, Romaine broke down utterly and confessed everything. Leonard Vole had returned to the house at the time he said, twenty past nine. She had invented the whole story to ruin him.

With the collapse of Romaine Heilger, the case for the Crown collapsed also. Sir Charles called his few witnesses, the prisoner himself went into the box and told his story in a manly straightforward manner, unshaken by cross-examination.

The prosecution endeavored to rally, but without great success. The judge's summing up was not wholly favorable to the prisoner, but a reaction had set in and the jury needed little time to consider their verdict.

"We find the prisoner not guilty."

Leonard Vole was free!

Little Mr. Mayherne hurried from his seat. He must congratulate his client.

He found himself polishing his pince-nez vigorously, and checked himself. His wife had told him only the night before that he was getting a habit of it. Curious things, habits. People themselves never knew they had them.

An interesting case—a very interesting case. That woman, now, Romaine Heilger.

The case was dominated for him still by the exotic figure of Romaine Heilger. She had seemed a pale, quiet woman in the house at Paddington, but in court she had flamed out against the sober background, flaunting herself like a tropical flower.

If he closed his eyes he could see her now, tall and vehement, her exquisite body bent forward a little, her right hand clenching and unclenching itself unconsciously all the time.

Curious things, habits. That gesture of hers with the hand was her habit, he supposed. Yet he had seen someone else do it quite lately. Who was it now? Quite lately—

He drew in his breath with a gasp as it came back to him. The woman in Shaw's Rents—

He stood still, his head whirling. It was impossible—impossible— Yet, Romaine Heilger was an actress.

The K.C. came up behind him and clapped him on the shoulder. "Congratulated our man yet? He's had a narrow shave, you know. Come along and see him."

But the little lawyer shook off the other's hand.

He wanted one thing only—to see Romaine Heilger face to face.

He did not see her until some time later, and the place of their meeting is not relevant.

"So you guessed," she said, when he had told her all that was in his mind. "The face? Oh! that was easy enough, and the light of that gas jet was too bad for you to see the make-up."

"But why—why—"

"Why did I play a lone hand?" She smiled a little, remembering the last time she had used the words.

"Such an elaborate comedy!"

"My friend—I had to save him. The evidence of a woman devoted to him would not have been enough—you hinted as much yourself. But I know something of the psychology of crowds. Let my evidence be wrung from me, as an admission, damning me in the eyes of the law, and a reaction in favor of the prisoner would immediately set in."

"And the bundle of letters?"

"One alone, the vital one, might have seemed like a—what do you call it?—put-up job."

"Then the man called Max?"

"Never existed, my friend."

"I still think," said little Mr. Mayherne, in an aggrieved manner, "that we could have got him off by the—er—normal procedure."

"I dared not risk it. You see you thought he was innocent—"

"And you knew it? I see," said little Mr. Mayherne.

"My dear Mr. Mayherne," said Romaine, "you do not see at all. I knew—he was guilty!"

Death on the Nile

CHAPTER 1

"LINNET RIDGEWAY!"

"That's *her!*" said Mr. Burnaby, the landlord of the Three Crowns. He nudged his companion.

The two men stared with round bucolic eyes and slightly open mouths.

A big scarlet Rolls Royce had just stopped in front of the local post office.

A girl jumped out, a girl without a hat and wearing a frock that looked (but only *looked*) simple. A girl with golden hair and straight autocratic features—a girl with a lovely shape—a girl such as was seldom seen in Malton-under-Wode.

With a quick imperative step she passed into the post office.

"That's her!" said Mr. Burnaby again. And he went on in a low awed voice: "Millions she's got. . . . Going to spend thousands on the place. Swimming pools there's going to be, and Italian gardens and a ballroom and half of the house pulled down and rebuilt. . . ."

"She'll bring money into the town," said his friend. He was a lean seedy-looking man. His tone was envious and grudging.

Mr. Burnaby agreed.

"Yes, it's a great thing for Malton-under-Wode. A great thing it is."

Mr. Burnaby was complacent about it.

"Wake us all up proper," he added.

"Bit of a difference from Sir George," said the other.

"Ah, it was the 'orses did for him," said Mr. Burnaby indulgently. "Never 'ad no luck."

"What did he get for the place?"

"A cool sixty thousand, so I've heard."

The lean man whistled.

Mr. Burnaby went on triumphantly: "And they say she'll have spent another sixty thousand before she's finished!"

"Wicked!" said the lean man. "Where'd she *get* all that money from?"

"America, so I've heard. Her mother was the only daughter of one of those millionaire blokes. Quite like the Pictures, isn't it?"

The girl came out of the post office and climbed into the car.

As she drove off the lean man followed her with his eyes. He muttered:

"It seems all wrong to me—her looking like that. Money *and* looks —it's too much! If a girl's as rich as that she's no right to be a good-looker as well. And she *is* a good-looker. . . . Got everything, that girl has. Doesn't seem fair. . . ."

2

Extract from the Social column of the *Daily Blague.*

Among those supping at Chez Ma Tante I noticed beautiful Linnet Ridgeway. She was with the Hon. Joanna Southwood, Lord Windle-sham and Mr. Toby Bryce. Miss Ridgeway, as everyone knows, is the daughter of Melhuish Ridgeway who married Anna Hartz. She inherits from her grandfather, Leopold Hartz, an immense fortune. The lovely Linnet is the sensation of the moment and it is rumoured that an engagement may be announced shortly. Certainly Lord Windlesham seemed very épris!!

3

The Hon. Joanna Southwood said:

"Darling, I think it's going to be all perfectly *marvellous!*"

She was sitting in Linnet Ridgeway's bedroom at Wode Hall.

From the window the eye passed over the gardens to open country with blue shadows of woodlands.

"It's rather perfect, isn't it?" said Linnet.

She leaned her arms on the window sill. Her face was eager, alive, dynamic. Beside her, Joanna Southwood seemed, somehow, a little dim—a tall thin young woman of twenty-seven, with a long clever face and freakishly plucked eyebrows.

"And you've done so much in the time! Did you have lots of archi-tects and things?"

"Three."

"What are architects like? I don't think I've ever seen any."

"They were all right. I found them rather unpractical sometimes."

"Darling, you soon put *that* right! You are the *most* practical crea-ture!"

Joanna picked up a string of pearls from the dressing-table.

"I suppose these are real, aren't they, Linnet?"

"Of course."

"I know it's 'of course' to you, my sweet, but it wouldn't be to most people. Heavily cultured or even Woolworth! Darling, they re-ally are *incredible,* so exquisitely matched. They must be worth the *most* fabulous sums!"

"Rather vulgar, you think?"

"No, not at all—just pure beauty. What *are* they worth?"

"About fifty thousand."

"What a lovely lot of money! Aren't you afraid of having them stolen?"

"No, I always wear them—and anyway they're insured."

"Let me wear them till dinner time, will you, darling? It would give me such a thrill."

Linnet laughed.

"Of course if you like."

"You know, Linnet, I really do envy you. You've simply got *ev-erything*. Here you are at twenty, your own mistress, with any amount of money, looks, superb health. You've even got *brains!* When are you twenty-one?"

"Next June. I shall have a grand coming-of-age party in London."

"And then are you going to marry Charles Windlesham? All the dreadful little gossip writers are getting so excited about it. And he really is frightfully devoted."

Linnet shrugged her shoulders.

"I don't know. I don't really want to marry anyone yet."

"Darling, how right you are! It's never quite the same afterward, is it?"

The telephone shrilled and Linnet went to it.

"Yes? Yes?"

The butler's voice answered her.

"Miss de Bellefort is on the line. Shall I put her through?"

"Bellefort? Oh, of course, yes, put her through."

A click and a voice, an eager, soft, slightly breathless voice: "Hullo, is that Miss Ridgeway? *Linnet!*"

"*Jackie darling!* I haven't heard anything of you for ages and *ages!*"

"I know. It's awful. Linnet, I want to see you terribly."

"Darling, can't you come down here? My new toy. I'd love to show it to you."

"That's just what I want to do."

"Well, jump into a train or a car."

"Right, I will. A frightfully dilapidated two-seater. I bought it for fifteen pounds, and some days it goes beautifully. But it has moods. If I haven't arrived by tea time you'll know it's had a mood. So long, my sweet."

Linnet replaced the receiver. She crossed back to Joanna.

"That's my oldest friend, Jacqueline de Bellefort. We were together at a convent in Paris. She's had the most terribly bad luck. Her father was a French Count, her mother was American—a Southerner. The father went off with some woman, and her mother lost all her money in the Wall Street crash. Jackie was left absolutely broke. I don't know how she's managed to get along the last two years."

Joanna was polishing her deep-blood-coloured nails with her friend's nail pad. She leant back with her head on one side scrutinizing the effect.

"Darling," she drawled, "won't that be rather *tiresome?* If any misfortunes happen to my friends I always drop them *at once!* It sounds heartless, but it saves such a lot of trouble later! They always want to borrow money off you, or else they start a dressmaking business and you have to get the most terrible clothes from them. Or they paint lampshades, or do Batik scarves."

"So if I lost all my money, you'd drop me tomorrow?"

"Yes, darling, I would. You can't say I'm not honest about it! I only like successful people. And you'll find that's true of nearly everybody—only most people won't admit it. They just say that really they can't put up with Mary or Emily or Pamela any more! 'Her troubles have made her so *bitter* and peculiar, poor dear!'"

"How beastly you are, Joanna!"

"I'm only on the make, like everyone else."

"*I'm* not on the make!"

"For obvious reasons! You don't have to be sordid when good-looking, middle-aged American trustees pay you over a vast allowance every quarter."

"And you're wrong about Jacqueline," said Linnet. "She's not a sponge. I've wanted to help her, but she won't let me. She's as proud as the devil."

"What's she in such a hurry to see you for? I'll bet she wants something! You just wait and see."

"She sounded excited about something," admitted Linnet. "Jackie always did get frightfully worked up over things. She once stuck a penknife into someone!"

"Darling, how thrilling!"

"A boy who was teasing a dog. Jackie tried to get him to stop. He wouldn't. She pulled him and shook him but he was much stronger than she was, and at last she whipped out a penknife and plunged it right into him. There was the *most* awful row!"

"I should think so. It sounds most uncomfortable!"

Linnet's maid entered the room. With a murmured word of apology, she took down a dress from the wardrobe and went out of the room with it.

"What's the matter with Marie?" asked Joanna. "She's been crying."

"Poor thing. You know I told you she wanted to marry a man who has a job in Egypt. She didn't know much about him, so I thought I'd better make sure he was all right. It turned out that he had a wife already—and three children."

"What a lot of enemies you must make, Linnet."

"Enemies?" Linnet looked surprised.

Joanna nodded and helped herself to a cigarette.

"Enemies, my sweet. You're so devastatingly efficient. And you're so frightfully good at doing the right thing."

Linnet laughed.

"Why, I haven't got an enemy in the world!"

4

Lord Windlesham sat under the cedar tree. His eyes rested on the graceful proportions of Wode Hall. There was nothing to mar its old-world beauty; the new buildings and additions were out of sight round the corner. It was a fair and peaceful sight bathed in the Autumn sunshine. Nevertheless, as he gazed, it was no longer Wode Hall that Charles Windlesham saw. Instead, he seemed to see a more imposing Elizabethan mansion, a long sweep of park, a more bleak background. . . . It was his own family seat, Charltonbury, and in the foreground stood a figure—a girl's figure, with bright golden hair and an eager confident face . . . Linnet as mistress of Charltonbury!

He felt very hopeful. That refusal of hers had not been at all a definite refusal. It had been little more than a plea for time. Well, he could afford to wait a little. . . .

How amazingly suitable the whole thing was. It was certainly advisable that he should marry money, but not such a matter of necessity that he could regard himself as forced to put his own feelings on one side. And he loved Linnet. He would have wanted to marry her even if she had been practically penniless, instead of one of the richest girls in England. Only, fortunately, she *was* one of the richest girls in England. . . .

His mind played with attractive plans for the future. The Mastership of the Roxdale perhaps, the restoration of the west wing, no need to let the Scotch shooting. . . .

Charles Windlesham dreamed in the sun.

5

It was four o'clock when the dilapidated little two-seater stopped with a sound of crunching gravel. A girl got out of it—a small slender creature with a mop of dark hair. She ran up the steps and tugged at the bell.

A few minutes later she was being ushered into the long stately drawing-room, and an ecclesiastical butler was saying with the proper mournful intonation, "Miss de Bellefort."

"Linnet!"

"Jackie!"

Windlesham stood a little aside, watching sympathetically as this fiery little creature flung herself open-armed upon Linnet.

"Lord Windlesham—Miss de Bellefort—my best friend."

A pretty child, he thought—not really pretty but decidedly attractive, with her dark curly hair and her enormous eyes. He murmured a few tactful nothings and then managed unobtrusively to leave the two friends together.

Jacqueline pounced—in a fashion that Linnet remembered as being characteristic of her.

"Windlesham? Windlesham? *That's* the man the papers always say you're going to marry! Are you, Linnet? *Are* you?"

Linnet murmured, "Perhaps."

"Darling—I'm so glad! He looks nice."

"Oh, don't make up your mind about it—I haven't made up my own mind yet."

"Of course not! Queens always proceed with due deliberation to the choosing of a consort!"

"Don't be ridiculous, Jackie."

"But you *are* a queen, Linnet! You always were. *Sa Majesté, la reine Linette. Linette la blonde!* And I—*I*'m the Queen's confidante! The trusted Maid of Honour."

"What nonsense you talk, Jackie darling! Where have you been all this time? You just disappear. And you never write."

"I hate writing letters. Where have I been? Oh, about three parts submerged, darling. In JOBS, you know. Grim jobs with grim women!"

"Darling, I wish you'd—"

"Take the Queen's bounty? Well, frankly, darling, that's what I'm here for. No, not to borrow money. It's not got to that yet! But I've come to ask a great big important favour!"

"Go on."

"If you're going to marry the Windlesham man, you'll understand, perhaps."

Linnet looked puzzled for a minute; then her face cleared.

"Jackie, do you mean—"

"Yes, darling, *I'm engaged!*"

"So that's it! I thought you were looking particularly alive somehow. You always do, of course, but even more than usual."

"That's just what I feel like."

"Tell me all about him."

"His name's Simon Doyle. He's big and square and incredibly simple and boyish and utterly adorable! He's poor—got no money. He's what you call 'county' all right—but very impoverished county—a younger son and all that. His people come from Devonshire. He loves country and country things. And for the last five years he's been in the city in a stuffy office. And now they're cutting down and he's out of a job. Linnet, I shall *die* if I can't marry him! I shall die! I shall die! I shall *die*. . . ."

"Don't be ridiculous, Jackie."

"I shall die, I tell you! I'm crazy about him. He's crazy about me. We can't live without each other."

"Darling, you *have* got it badly!"

"I know. It's awful, isn't it? This love business gets hold of you and you can't do anything about it."

She paused for a minute. Her dark eyes dilated, looked suddenly tragic. She gave a little shiver.

"It's—even frightening sometimes! Simon and I were made for each other. I shall never care for anyone else. And *you*'ve got to help us, Linnet. I heard you'd bought this place and it put an idea into my head. Listen, you'll have to have a land agent—perhaps two. I want you to give the job to Simon."

"Oh!" Linnet was startled.

Jacqueline rushed on: "He's got all that sort of thing at his finger-tips. He knows all about estates—was brought up on one. And he's got his business training too. Oh, Linnet, you will give him a job, won't you, for love of me? If he doesn't make good, sack him. But he will. And we can live in a little house, and I shall see lots of you, and everything in the garden will be too, too divine."

She got up.

"Say you will, Linnet. Say you will. Beautiful Linnet! Tall golden Linnet! My own very special Linnet! Say you will!"

"Jackie—"

"You will?"

Linnet burst out laughing.

"Ridiculous Jackie! Bring along your young man and let me have a look at him and we'll talk it over."

Jackie darted at her, kissing her exuberantly:

"*Darling* Linnet—you're a real friend! I knew you were. You wouldn't let me down—ever. You're just the loveliest thing in the world. Good-bye."

"But, Jackie, you're *staying*."

"Me? No, I'm not. I'm going back to London, and tomorrow I'll come back and bring Simon and we'll settle it all up. You'll adore him. He really is a *pet*."

"But can't you wait and just have tea?"

"No, I can't wait, Linnet. I'm too excited. I must get back and tell Simon. I know I'm mad, darling, but I can't help it. Marriage will cure me, I expect. It always seems to have a very sobering effect on people."

She turned at the door, stood a moment, then rushed back for a last quick birdlike embrace.

"Dear Linnet—there's no one like you."

6

M. Gaston Blondin, the proprietor of that modish little restaurant Chez Ma Tante, was not a man who delighted to honour many of his *clientéle*. The rich, the beautiful, the notorious and the well-born might wait in vain to be signalled out and paid special attention. Only in the rarest cases did M. Blondin, with gracious condescension, greet a guest, accompany him to a privileged table, and exchange with him suitable and apposite remarks.

On this particular night, M. Blondin had exercised his royal prerogative three times—once for a Duchess, once for a famous racing peer, and once for a little man of comical appearance with immense black moustaches, who, a casual onlooker would have thought, could bestow no favour on Chez Ma Tante by his presence there.

M. Blondin, however, was positively fulsome in his attentions. Though clients had been told for the last half hour that a table was not to be had, one now mysteriously appeared, placed in a most favourable position. M. Blondin conducted the client to it with every appearance of *empressement*.

"But naturally, for *you* there is *always* a table, Monsieur Poirot! How I wish that you would honour us oftener."

Hercule Poirot smiled, remembering that past incident wherein a dead body, a waiter, M. Blondin, and a very lovely lady had played a part.

"You are too amiable, Monsieur Blondin," he said.

"And you are alone, Monsieur Poirot?"

"Yes, I am alone."

"Oh, well, Jules here will compose for you a little meal that will be a poem—positively a poem! Women, however charming, have this disadvantage: they distract the mind from food! You will enjoy your dinner, Monsieur Poirot; I promise you that. Now, as to wine—"

A technical conversation ensued. Jules, the *maître d'hôtel*, assisting.

Before departing, M. Blondin lingered a moment, lowering his voice confidentially.

"You have grave affairs on hand?"

Poirot shook his head.

"I am, alas, a man of leisure," he said sadly. "I have made the economies in my time and I have now the means to enjoy a life of idleness."

"I envy you."

"No, no, you would be unwise to do so. I can assure you, it is not so gay as it sounds." He sighed. "How true is the saying that man was forced to invent work in order to escape the strain of having to think."

M. Blondin threw up his hands.

"But there is so much! There is travel!"

"Yes, there is travel. Already I have done not so badly. This winter I shall visit Egypt, I think. The climate, they say, is superb! One will escape from the fogs, the greyness, the monotony of the constantly falling rain."

"Ah! Egypt," breathed M. Blondin.

"One can even voyage there now, I believe, by train, escaping all sea travel except the Channel."

"Ah, the sea, it does not agree with you?"

Hercule Poirot shook his head and shuddered slightly.

"I, too," said M. Blondin with sympathy. "Curious the effect it has upon the stomach."

"But only upon certain stomachs! There are people on whom the motion makes no impression whatever. They actually *enjoy* it!"

"An unfairness of the good God," said M. Blondin.

He shook his head sadly, and, brooding on the impious thought, withdrew.

Smooth-footed, deft-handed waiters ministered to the table. Toast Melba, butter, an ice pail, all the adjuncts to a meal of quality.

The Negro orchestra broke into an ecstasy of strange discordant noises. London danced.

Hercule Poirot looked on, registering impressions in his neat orderly mind.

How bored and weary most of the faces were! Some of those stout men, however, were enjoying themselves . . . whereas a patient endurance seemed to be the sentiment exhibited on their partners' faces. The fat woman in purple was looking radiant. . . . Undoubtedly the fat had certain compensations in life . . . a zest—a gusto—denied to those of more fashionable contours.

A good sprinkling of young people—some vacant looking—some bored—some definitely unhappy. How absurd to call youth the time of happiness—youth, the time of greatest vulnerability!

His glance softened as it rested on one particular couple. A well-matched pair—tall broad-shouldered man, slender delicate girl. Two bodies that moved in a perfect rhythm of happiness. Happiness in the place, the hour, and in each other.

The dance stopped abruptly. Hands clapped and it started again. After a second *encore* the couple returned to their table close by Poirot. The girl was flushed, laughing. As she sat, he could study her face, lifted laughing to her companion.

There was something else beside laughter in her eyes. Hercule Poirot shook his head doubtfully.

"She cares too much, that little one," he said to himself. "It is not safe. No, it is not safe."

And then a word caught his ear, "Egypt."

Their voices came to him clearly—the girl's young, fresh, arrogant, with just a trace of soft-sounding foreign R's, and the man's pleasant, low-toned, well-bred English.

"I'm *not* counting my chickens before they're hatched, Simon. I tell you Linnet won't let us down!"

"*I* might let *her* down."

"Nonsense—it's just the right job for you."

"As a matter of fact I think it is. . . . I haven't really any doubts as to my capability. And I mean to make good—for *your* sake!"

The girl laughed softly, a laugh of pure happiness.

"We'll wait three months—to make sure you don't get the sack—and then—"

"And then I'll endow thee with my worldly goods—that's the hang of it, isn't it?"

"And, as I say, we'll go to Egypt for our honeymoon. Damn the expense! I've always wanted to go to Egypt all my life. The Nile and the pyramids and the sand . . ."

He said, his voice slightly indistinct: "We'll see it together, Jackie . . . together. Won't it be marvellous?"

"I wonder. Will it be as marvellous to you as it is to me? Do you really care—as much as I do?"

Her voice was suddenly sharp—her eyes dilated—almost with fear. The man's answer came quickly crisp, "Don't be absurd, Jackie." But the girl repeated, "I wonder. . . ."

Then she shrugged her shoulders.

"Let's dance."

Hercule Poirot murmured to himself:

"*Un qui aime et un qui se laisse aimer*. Yes, I wonder too."

7

Joanna Southwood said, "And suppose he's a terrible tough?"

Linnet shook her head. "Oh, he won't be. I can trust Jacqueline's taste."

Joanna murmured, "Ah, but people don't run true to form in love affairs."

Linnet shook her head impatiently. Then she changed the subject. "I must go and see Mr. Pierce about those plans."

"Plans?"

"Yes, some dreadful insanitary old cottages. I'm having them pulled down and the people moved."

"How sanitary and public-spirited of you, darling!"

"They'd have had to go anyway. Those cottages would have overlooked my new swimming pool."

"Do the people who lived in them like going?"

"Most of them are delighted. One or two are being rather stupid about it—really tiresome in fact. They don't seem to realize how vastly improved their living conditions will be!"

"But you're being quite high-handed about it, I presume."

"My dear Joanna, it's to their advantage really."

"Yes, dear, I'm sure it is. Compulsory benefit."

Linnet frowned. Joanna laughed.

"Come now, you *are* a tyrant, admit it. A beneficent tyrant if you like!"

"I'm not the least bit a tyrant."

"But you like your own way!"

"Not especially."

"Linnet Ridgeway, can you look me in the face and tell me of *any one occasion* on which you've failed to do exactly as you wanted?"

"Heaps of times."

"Oh, yes, 'heaps of times'—just like that—but no concrete example. And you simply can't think up one, darling, however hard you try! The triumphal progress of Linnet Ridgeway in her golden car."

Linnet said sharply, "You think I'm selfish?"

"No—just irresistible. The combined effect of money and charm. Everything goes down before you. What you can't buy with cash you buy with a smile. Result: Linnet Ridgeway, the Girl Who Has Everything."

"Don't be ridiculous, Joanna!"

"Well, haven't you got everything?"

"I suppose I have. . . . It sounds rather disgusting, somehow!"

"Of course it's disgusting, darling! You'll probably get terribly bored and blasé by and by. In the meantime, enjoy the triumphal progress in the golden car. Only I wonder, I really do wonder, what will happen when you want to go down a street which has a board up saying 'No Thoroughfare.' "

"Don't be idiotic, Joanna." As Lord Windlesham joined them, Linnet said, turning to him, "Joanna is saying the nastiest things to me."

"All spite, darling, all spite," said Joanna vaguely as she got up from her seat.

She made no apology for leaving them. She had caught the glint in Windlesham's eye.

He was silent for a minute or two. Then he went straight to the point.

"Have you come to a decision, Linnet?"

Linnet said slowly: "Am I being a brute? I suppose, if I'm not sure, I ought to say 'No'—"

He interrupted her.

"Don't say it. You shall have time—as much time as you want. But I think, you know, we should be happy together."

"You see," Linnet's tone was apologetic, almost childish, "I'm enjoying myself so much—especially with all this." She waved a hand. "I wanted to make Wode Hall into my real ideal of a country house, and I do think I've got it nice, don't you?"

"It's beautiful. Beautifully planned. Everything perfect. You're very clever, Linnet."

He paused a minute and went on: "And you like Charltonbury, don't you? Of course it wants modernizing and all that—but you're so clever at that sort of thing. You'd enjoy it."

"Why, of course, Charltonbury's divine."

She spoke with ready enthusiasm, but inwardly she was conscious of a sudden chill. An alien note had sounded, disturbing her complete satisfaction with life. She did not analyse the feeling at the moment, but later, when Windlesham had gone into the house, she tried to probe into the recesses of her mind.

Charltonbury—yes, that was it—she had resented the mention of Charltonbury. But why? Charltonbury was modestly famous. Windlesham's ancestors had held it since the time of Elizabeth. To be mistress of Charltonbury was a position unsurpassed in society. Windlesham was one of the most desirable partis in England.

Naturally he couldn't take Wode seriously. . . . It was not in any way to be compared with Charltonbury.

Ah, but Wode was *hers!* She had seen it, acquired it, rebuilt and re-dressed it, lavished money on it. It was her own possession—her kingdom.

But in a sense it wouldn't count if she married Windlesham. What would they want with two country places? And of the two, naturally Wode Hall would be the one to be given up.

She, Linnet Ridgeway, wouldn't exist any longer. She would be Countess of Windlesham, bringing a fine dowry to Charltonbury and its master. She would be queen consort, not queen any longer.

"I'm being ridiculous," said Linnet to herself.

But it was curious how she did hate the idea of abandoning Wode. . . .

And wasn't there something else nagging at her?

Jackie's voice with that queer blurred note in it saying: "I shall *die* if I can't marry him! I shall die. I shall die . . ."

So positive, so earnest. Did she, Linnet, feel like that about Windlesham? Assuredly she didn't. Perhaps she could never feel like that about anyone. It must be—rather wonderful—to feel like that. . . .

The sound of a car came through the open window.

Linnet shook herself impatiently. That must be Jackie and her young man. She'd go out and meet them.

She was standing in the open doorway as Jacqueline and Simon Doyle got out of the car.

"Linnet!" Jackie ran to her. "This is Simon. Simon, here's Linnet. She's just the most wonderful person in the world."

Linnet saw a tall, broad-shouldered young man, with very dark blue eyes, crisply curling brown hair, a square chin and a boyish, appealingly simple smile. . . .

She stretched out a hand. The hand that clasped hers was firm and warm. . . . She liked the way he looked at her, the *naïve* genuine admiration. . . .

Jackie had told him she was wonderful, and he clearly thought that she was wonderful. . . .

A warm sweet feeling of intoxication ran through her veins.

"Isn't this all lovely?" she said. "Come in, Simon, and let me welcome my new land agent properly."

And as she turned to lead the way she thought: "I'm frightfully—

frightfully happy. I like Jackie's young man . . . I like him enormously. . . ."

And then with a sudden pang, "Lucky Jackie. . . ."

8

Tim Allerton leant back in his wicker chair and yawned as he
looked out over the sea. He shot a quick sidelong glance at his
mother.

Mrs. Allerton was a good-looking, white-haired woman of fifty. By
imparting an expression of pinched severity to her mouth every time
she looked at her son, she sought to disguise the fact of her intense
affection for him. Even total strangers were seldom deceived by this
device and Tim himself saw through it perfectly.

He said, "Do you really like Majorca, Mother?"

"Well," Mrs. Allerton considered, "it's cheap."

"And cold," said Tim with a slight shiver.

He was a tall, thin young man, with dark hair and a rather narrow
chest. His mouth had a very sweet expression; his eyes were sad and
his chin was indecisive. He had long delicate hands.

Threatened by consumption some years ago, he had never displayed a really robust physique. He was popularly supposed "to
write," but it was understood among his friends that inquiries as to
literary output were not encouraged.

"What are you thinking of, Tim?"

Mrs. Allerton was alert. Her bright, dark-brown eyes looked suspicious.

Tim Allerton grinned at her.

"I was thinking of Egypt."

"Egypt?"

Mrs. Allerton sounded doubtful.

"Real warmth, darling. Lazy golden sands. The Nile. I'd like to go
up the Nile, wouldn't you?"

"Oh, I'd *like* it." Her tone was dry. "But Egypt's expensive, my
dear. Not for those who have to count the pennies."

Tim laughed. He rose, stretched himself. Suddenly he looked alive
and eager. There was an excited note in his voice.

"The expense will be my affair. Yes, darling. A little flutter on the
Stock Exchange. With thoroughly satisfactory results. I heard this
morning."

"This morning?" said Mrs. Allerton sharply. "You only had one letter and that—"

She stopped and bit her lip.

Tim looked momentarily undecided whether to be amused or annoyed. Amusement gained the day.

"And that was from Joanna," he finished coolly. "Quite right, Mother. What a Queen of detectives you'd make! The famous Hercule Poirot would have to look to his laurels if you were about."

Mrs. Allerton looked rather cross.

"I just happened to see the handwriting—"

"And knew it wasn't that of a stockbroker? Quite right. As a matter of fact it was yesterday I heard from them. Poor Joanna's handwriting *is* rather noticeable—sprawls about all over the envelope like an inebriated spider."

"What does Joanna say? Any news?"

Mrs. Allerton strove to make her voice sound casual and ordinary. The friendship between her son and his second cousin, Joanna Southwood, always irritated her. Not, as she put it to herself, that there was "anything in it." She was quite sure there wasn't. Tim had never manifested a sentimental interest in Joanna, nor she in him. Their mutual attraction seemed to be founded on gossip and the possession of a large number of friends and acquaintances in common. They both liked people and discussing people. Joanna had an amusing if caustic tongue.

It was not because Mrs. Allerton feared that Tim might fall in love with Joanna that she found herself always becoming a little stiff in manner if Joanna were present or when letters from her arrived.

It was some other feeling hard to define—perhaps an unacknowledged jealousy in the unfeigned pleasure Tim always seemed to take in Joanna's society. He and his mother were such perfect companions that the sight of him absorbed and interested in another woman always startled Mrs. Allerton slightly. She fancied, too, that her own presence on these occasions set some barrier between the two members of the younger generation. Often she had come upon them eagerly absorbed in some conversation and, at sight of her, their talk had wavered, had seemed to include her rather too purposefully and as in duty bound. Quite definitely, Mrs. Allerton did not like Joanna Southwood. She thought her insincere, affected and essentially superficial. She found it very hard to prevent herself saying so in unmeasured tones.

In answer to her question, Tim pulled the letter out of his pocket and glanced through it. It was quite a long letter, his mother noted.

"Nothing much," he said. "The Devenishes are getting a divorce. Old Monty's been had up for being drunk in charge of a car. Windlesham's gone to Canada. Seems he was pretty badly hit when Linnet Ridgeway turned him down. She's definitely going to marry this land agent person."

"How extraordinary! Is he very dreadful?"

"No, no, not at all. He's one of the Devonshire Doyles. No money, of course—and he was actually engaged to one of Linnet's best friends. Pretty thick, that."

"I don't think it's at all nice," said Mrs. Allerton, flushing.

Tim flashed her a quick affectionate glance.

"I know, darling. You don't approve of snaffling other people's husbands and all that sort of thing."

"In my day we had our standards," said Mrs. Allerton. "And a very good thing too! Nowadays young people seem to think they can just go about doing anything they choose."

Tim smiled.

"They don't only think it. They do it. *Vide* Linnet Ridgeway!"

"Well, I think it's horrid!"

Tim twinkled at her.

"Cheer up, you old die-hard! Perhaps I agree with you. Anyway, *I* haven't helped myself to anyone's wife or fiancée yet."

"I'm sure you'd never do such a thing," said Mrs. Allerton. She added with spirit, "I've brought you up properly."

"So the credit is yours, not mine."

He smiled teasingly at her as he folded the letter and put it away again. Mrs. Allerton let the thought just flash across her mind: "Most letters he shows to me. He only reads me snippets from Joanna's."

But she put the unworthy thought away from her, and decided, as ever, to behave like a gentlewoman.

"Is Joanna enjoying life?" she asked.

"So so. Says she thinks of opening a delicatessen shop in Mayfair."

"She always talks about being hard up," said Mrs. Allerton with a tinge of spite, "but she goes about everywhere and her clothes must cost her a lot. She's always beautifully dressed."

"Ah, well," said Tim, "she probably doesn't pay for them. No, Mother, I don't mean what your Edwardian mind suggests to you. I just mean quite literally that she leaves her bills unpaid."

Mrs. Allerton sighed.

"I never know how people manage to do that."

"It's a kind of special gift," said Tim. "If only you have sufficiently extravagant tastes, and absolutely no sense of money values, people will give you any amount of credit."

"Yes, but you come to the Bankruptcy Court in the end like poor Sir George Wode."

"You have a soft spot for that old horse coper—probably because he called you a rosebud in eighteen seventy-nine at a dance."

"I wasn't born in eighteen seventy-nine," Mrs. Allerton retorted with spirit. "Sir George has charming manners, and I won't have you calling him a horse coper."

"I've heard funny stories about him from people that know."

"You and Joanna don't mind what you say about people; anything will do so long as it's sufficiently ill-natured."

Tim raised his eyebrows.

"My dear, you're quite heated. I didn't know old Wode was such a favourite of yours."

"You don't realize how hard it is for him, having to sell Wode Hall. He cared terribly about that place."

Tim suppressed the easy retort. After all, who was he to judge? Instead he said thoughtfully:

"You know, I think you're not far wrong there. Linnet asked him to come down and see what she'd done to the place, and he refused quite rudely."

"Of course. She ought to have known better than to ask him."

"And I believe he's quite venomous about her—mutters things under his breath whenever he sees her. Can't forgive her for having given him an absolutely top price for the worm-eaten family estate."

"And you can't understand that?" Mrs. Allerton spoke sharply.

"Frankly," said Tim calmly, "I can't. Why live in the past? Why cling on to things that have been?"

"What are you going to put in their place?"

He shrugged his shoulders. "Excitement, perhaps. Novelty. The joy of never knowing what may turn up from day to day. Instead of inheriting a useless tract of land, the pleasure of making money for yourself—by your own brains and skill."

"A successful deal on the Stock Exchange in fact!"

He laughed. "Why not?"

"And what about an equal *loss* on the Stock Exchange?"

"That, dear, is rather tactless. And quite inappropriate today. . . . What about this Egypt plan?"

"Well—"

He cut in, smiling at her: "That's settled. We've both always wanted to see Egypt."

"When do you suggest?"

"Oh, next month. January's about the best time there. We'll enjoy the delightful society in this hotel a few weeks longer."

"Tim," said Mrs. Allerton reproachfully. Then she added guiltily: "I'm afraid I promised Mrs. Leech that you'd go with her to the police station. She doesn't understand any Spanish."

Tim made a grimace.

"About her ring? The blood-red ruby of the horse leech's daughter? Does she still persist in thinking it's been stolen? I'll go if you like, but it's a waste of time. She'll only get some wretched chambermaid into trouble. I distinctly saw it on her finger when she went into the sea that day. It came off in the water and she never noticed."

"She says she is quite sure she took it off and left it on her dressing-table."

"Well, she didn't. I saw it with my own eyes. The woman's a fool. Any woman's a fool who goes prancing into the sea in December, pretending the water's quite warm just because the sun happens to be shining rather brightly at the moment. Stout women oughtn't to be allowed to bathe anyway; they look so revolting in bathing dresses."

Mrs. Allerton murmured, "I really feel I ought to give up bathing."

Tim gave a shout of laughter.

"You? You can give most of the young things points and to spare."

Mrs. Allerton sighed and said, "I wish there were a few more young people for you here."

Tim Allerton shook his head decidedly.

"I don't. You and I get along rather comfortably without outside distractions."

"You'd like it if Joanna were here."

"I wouldn't." His tone was unexpectedly resolute. "You're all wrong there. Joanna amuses me, but I don't really like her, and to have her around much gets on my nerves. I'm thankful she isn't here. I should be quite resigned if I were never to see Joanna again."

He added, almost below his breath, "There's only one woman in the world I've got a real respect and admiration for, and I think, Mrs. Allerton, you know very well who that woman is."

His mother blushed and looked quite confused.

Tim said gravely: "There aren't very many really nice women in the world. You happen to be one of them."

9

In an apartment overlooking Central Park in New York, Mrs. Robson exclaimed: "If that isn't just too lovely! You really are the luckiest girl, Cornelia."

Cornelia Robson flushed responsively. She was a big clumsy-looking girl with brown doglike eyes.

"Oh, it will be wonderful!" she gasped.

Old Miss Van Schuyler inclined her head in a satisfied fashion at this correct attitude on the part of poor relations.

"I've always dreamed of a trip to Europe," sighed Cornelia, "but I just didn't feel I'd ever get there."

"Miss Bowers will come with me as usual, of course," said Miss Van Schuyler, "but as a social companion I find her limited—very limited. There are many little things that Cornelia can do for me."

"I'd just love to, Cousin Marie," said Cornelia eagerly.

"Well, well, then that's settled," said Miss Van Schuyler. "Just run and find Miss Bowers, my dear. It's time for my eggnog."

Cornelia departed. Her mother said: "My dear Marie, I'm really *most* grateful to you! You know I think Cornelia suffers a lot from not being a social success. It makes her feel kind of mortified. If I could afford to take her to places—but you know how it's been since Ned died."

"I'm very glad to take her," said Miss Van Schuyler. "Cornelia has always been a nice handy girl, willing to run errands, and not so selfish as some of these young people nowadays."

Mrs. Robson rose and kissed her rich relative's wrinkled and slightly yellow face.

"I'm just ever so grateful," she declared.

On the stairs she met a tall capable looking woman who was carrying a glass containing a yellow foamy liquid.

"Well, Miss Bowers, so you're off to Europe?"

"Why, yes, Mrs. Robson."

"What a lovely trip!"

"Why, yes, I should think it would be very enjoyable."

"But you've been abroad before?"

"Oh, yes, Mrs. Robson. I went over to Paris with Miss Van Schuyler last Fall. But I've never been to Egypt before."

Mrs. Robson hesitated.

"I do hope—there won't be any—trouble."

She had lowered her voice. Miss Bowers, however, replied in her usual tone:

"Oh, *no,* Mrs. Robson; I shall take good care of *that.* I keep a very sharp look-out always."

But there was still a faint shadow on Mrs. Robson's face as she slowly continued down the stairs.

10

In his office down town Mr. Andrew Pennington was opening his personal mail. Suddenly his fist clenched itself and came down on his desk with a bang; his face crimsoned and two big veins stood out on his forehead. He pressed a buzzer on his desk and a smart looking stenographer appeared with commendable promptitude.

"Tell Mr. Rockford to step in here."

"Yes, Mr. Pennington."

A few minutes later, Sterndale Rockford, Pennington's partner, entered the office. The two men were not unlike—both tall, spare, with greying hair and clean-shaven, clever faces.

"What's up, Pennington?"

Pennington looked up from the letter he was re-reading. He said, "Linnet's married. . . ."

"*What?*"

"You heard what I said! Linnet Ridgeway's *married!*"

"How? When? Why didn't we hear about it?"

Pennington glanced at the calendar on his desk.

"She wasn't married when she wrote this letter, but she's married now. Morning of the fourth. That's today."

Rockford dropped into a chair.

"Whew! No warning? Nothing? Who's the man?"

Pennington referred again to the letter.

"Doyle. Simon Doyle."

"What sort of a fellow is he? Ever heard of him?"

"No. She doesn't say much. . . ." He scanned the lines of clear, upright handwriting. "Got an idea there's something hole-and-corner about the business. . . . That doesn't matter. The whole point is, she's married."

The eyes of the two men met. Rockford nodded.

"This needs a bit of thinking out," he said quietly.

"What are we going to do about it?"

"I'm asking you."

The two men sat silent. Then Rockford asked, "Got any plan?"

Pennington said slowly: "The *Normandie* sails today. One of us could just make it."

"You're crazy! What's the big idea?"

Pennington began, "Those British lawyers—" and stopped.

"What about 'em? Surely you're not going over to tackle 'em? You're mad!"

"I'm not suggesting that you—or I—should go to England."

"What's the big idea, then?"

Pennington smoothed out the letter on the table.

"Linnet's going to Egypt for her honeymoon. Expects to be there a month or more. . . ."

"Egypt—eh?"

Rockford considered. Then he looked up and met the other's glance.

"Egypt," he said; "*that's* your idea!"

"Yes—a chance meeting. Over on a trip. Linnet and her husband—honeymoon atmosphere. It might be done."

Rockford said doubtfully, "She's sharp, Linnet is . . . but—"

Pennington went on softly, "I think there might be ways of—managing it."

Again their eyes met. Rockford nodded.

"All right, big boy."

Pennington looked at the clock.

"We'll have to hustle—whichever of us is going."

"You go," said Rockford promptly. "You always made a hit with Linnet. 'Uncle Andrew.' That's the ticket!"

Pennington's face had hardened. He said, "I hope I can pull it off."

"You've got to pull it off," his partner said. "The situation's critical. . . ."

11

William Carmichael said to the thin, weedy youth who opened the door inquiringly, "Send Mr. Jim to me, please."

Jim Fanthorp entered the room and looked inquiringly at his uncle. The older man looked up with a nod and a grunt.

"Humph, there you are."

"You asked for me?"

"Just cast an eye over this."

The young man sat down and drew the sheaf of papers toward him. The elder man watched him.

"Well?"

The answer came promptly, "Looks fishy to me, sir."

Again the senior partner of Carmichael, Grant & Carmichael uttered his characteristic grunt.

Jim Fanthorp re-read the letter which had just arrived by air mail from Egypt:

. . . It seems wicked to be writing business letters on such a day. We have spent a week at Mena House and made an expedition to the Fayum. The day after tomorrow we are going up the Nile to Luxor and Assuan by steamer, and perhaps on to Khartûm. When we went into Cook's this morning to see about our tickets who do you think was the first person I saw?—my American trustee, Andrew Pennington. I think you met him two years ago when he was over. I had no idea he was in Egypt and he had no idea that I was! Nor that I was married! My letter, telling him of my marriage, must just have missed him. He is actually going up the Nile on the same trip that we are. Isn't it a coincidence? Thank you so much for all you have done in this busy time. I—

As the young man was about to turn the page, Mr. Carmichael took the letter from him.

"That's all," he said. "The rest doesn't matter. Well, what do you think?"

His nephew considered for a moment—then he said:

"Well—I think—not a coincidence. . . ."

The other nodded approval.

"Like a trip to Egypt?" he barked out.

"You think that's advisable?"

"I think there's no time to lose."

"But why me?"

"Use your brains, boy; use your brains. Linnet Ridgeway has never met you; no more has Pennington. If you go by air you may get there in time."

"I—I don't like it, sir. What am I to do?"

"Use your eyes. Use your ears. Use your brains—if you've got any. And, if necessary—act."

"I—I don't like it."

"Perhaps not—but you've got to do it."

"It's—necessary?"

"In my opinion," said Mr. Carmichael, "it's absolutely vital."

12

Mrs. Otterbourne, readjusting the turban of native material that she wore draped round her head, said fretfully:

"I really don't see why we shouldn't go on to Egypt. I'm sick and tired of Jerusalem."

As her daughter made no reply, she said, "You might at least answer when you're spoken to."

Rosalie Otterbourne was looking at a newspaper reproduction of a face. Below it was printed:

Mrs. Simon Doyle, who before her marriage was the well-known society beauty, Miss Linnet Ridgeway. Mr. and Mrs. Doyle are spending their holiday in Egypt.

Rosalie said, "You'd like to move on to Egypt, Mother?"

"Yes, I would," Mrs. Otterbourne snapped. "I consider they've treated us in a most cavalier fashion here. My being here is an advertisement—I ought to get a special reduction in terms. When I hinted as much, I consider they were most impertinent—*most* impertinent. I told them exactly what I thought of them."

The girl sighed. She said: "One place is very like another. I wish we could get right away."

"And this morning," went on Mrs. Otterbourne, "the manager actually had the impertinence to tell me that all the rooms had been booked in advance and that he would require ours in two days' time."

"So we've got to go somewhere."

"Not at all. I'm quite prepared to fight for my rights."

Rosalie murmured: "I suppose we might as well go on to Egypt. It doesn't make any difference."

"It's certainly not a matter of life or death," agreed Mrs. Otterbourne.

But there she was quite wrong—for a matter of life and death was exactly what it was.

Part Two — EGYPT

CHAPTER 1

"THAT'S Hercule Poirot, the detective," said Mrs. Allerton.

She and her son were sitting in brightly painted scarlet basket chairs outside the Cataract Hotel at Assuan. They were watching the retreating figures of two people—a short man dressed in a white silk suit and a tall slim girl.

Tim Allerton sat up in an unusually alert fashion.

"That funny little man?" he asked incredulously.

"That funny little man!"

"What on earth's he doing out here?" Tim asked.

His mother laughed. "Darling, you sound quite excited. Why do men enjoy crime so much? I hate detective stories and never read them. But I don't think Monsieur Poirot is here with any ulterior motive. He's made a good deal of money and he's seeing life, I fancy."

"Seems to have an eye for the best looking girl in the place."

Mrs. Allerton tilted her head a little on one side as she considered the retreating backs of M. Poirot and his companion.

The girl by his side overtopped him by some three inches. She walked well, neither stiffly nor slouchingly.

"I suppose she *is* quite good-looking," said Mrs. Allerton.

She shot a little glance sideways at Tim. Somewhat to her amusement the fish rose at once.

"She's more than quite. Pity she looks so bad-tempered and sulky."

"Perhaps that's just expression, dear."

"Unpleasant young devil, I think. But she's pretty enough."

The subject of these remarks was walking slowly by Poirot's side. Rosalie Otterbourne was twirling an unopened parasol, and her expression certainly bore out what Tim had just said. She looked both sulky and bad-tempered. Her eyebrows were drawn together in a frown, and the scarlet line of her mouth was drawn downward.

They turned to the left out of the hotel gate and entered the cool shade of the public gardens.

Hercule Poirot was prattling gently, his expression that of beatific good humour. He wore a white silk suit, carefully pressed, and a panama hat and carried a highly ornamental fly whisk with a sham amber handle.

"—it enchants me," he was saying. "The black rocks of Elephantine, and the sun, and the little boats on the river. Yes, it is good to be alive."

He paused and then added, "You do not find it so, Mademoiselle?"

Rosalie Otterbourne said shortly: "It's all right, I suppose. I think Assuan's a gloomy sort of place. The hotel's half empty, and everyone's about a hundred—"

She stopped—biting her lip.

Hercule Poirot's eyes twinkled.

"It is true, yes, I have one leg in the grave."

"I—I wasn't thinking of you," said the girl. "I'm sorry. That sounded rude."

"Not at all. It is natural you should wish for companions of your own age. Ah, well, there is *one* young man, at least."

"The one who sits with his mother all the time? I like *her*—but I think he looks dreadful—so conceited!"

Poirot smiled.

"And I—am I conceited?"

"Oh, I don't think so."

She was obviously uninterested—but the fact did not seem to annoy Poirot. He merely remarked with placid satisfaction, "My best friend says that I am very conceited."

"Oh, well," said Rosalie vaguely, "I suppose you have something to be conceited about. Unfortunately crime doesn't interest me in the least."

Poirot said solemnly, "I am delighted to learn that you have no guilty secret to hide."

Just for a moment the sulky mask of her face was transformed as she shot him a swift questioning glance. Poirot did not seem to notice it as he went on:

"Madame, your mother, was not at lunch today. She is not indisposed, I trust?"

"This place doesn't suit her," said Rosalie briefly. "I shall be glad when we leave."

"We are fellow passengers, are we not? We both make the excursion up to Wâdi Halfa and the Second Cataract?"

"Yes."

They came out from the shade of the gardens onto a dusty stretch of road bordered by the river. Five watchful bead sellers, two vendors of postcards, three sellers of plaster scarabs, a couple of donkey boys and some detached but hopeful infantile riff-raff closed in upon them.

"You want beads, sir? Very good, sir. Very cheap. . . ."

"Lady, you want scarab? Look—great queen—very lucky. . . ."

"You look, sir—real lapis. Very good, very cheap. . . ."

"You want ride donkey, sir? This very good donkey. This donkey Whisky and Soda, sir. . . ."

"You want to go granite quarries, sir? This very good donkey. Other donkey very bad, sir, that donkey fall down. . . ."

"You want postcard—very cheap—very nice. . . ."

"Look, lady. . . . Only ten piastres—very cheap—lapis—this ivory. . . ."

"This very good fly whisk—this all amber. . . ."

"You go out in boat, sir? I got very good boat, sir. . . ."

"You ride back to hotel, lady? This first class donkey. . . ."

Hercule Poirot made vague gestures to rid himself of this human cluster of flies. Rosalie stalked through them like a sleep walker.

"It's best to pretend to be deaf and blind," she remarked.

The infantile riff-raff ran alongside murmuring plaintively: "Bakshish? Bakshish? Hip hip hurrah—very good, very nice. . . ."

Their gaily coloured rags trailed picturesquely, and the flies lay in clusters on their eyelids. They were the most persistent. The others fell back and launched a fresh attack on the next comer.

Now Poirot and Rosalie only ran the gauntlet of the shops—suave, persuasive accents here. . . .

"You visit my shop today, sir?" "You want that ivory crocodile, sir?" "You not been in my shop yet, sir? I show you very beautiful things."

They turned into the fifth shop and Rosalie handed over several rolls of films—the object of the walk.

Then they came out again and walked toward the river's edge.

One of the Nile steamers was just mooring. Poirot and Rosalie looked interestedly at the passengers.

"Quite a lot, aren't there?" commented Rosalie.

She turned her head as Tim Allerton came up and joined them. He was a little out of breath as though he had been walking fast.

They stood there for a moment or two and then Tim spoke.

"An awful crowd as usual, I suppose," he remarked disparagingly, indicating the disembarking passengers.

"They're usually quite terrible," agreed Rosalie.

All three wore the air of superiority assumed by people who are already in a place when studying new arrivals.

"Hullo!" exclaimed Tim, his voice suddenly excited. "I'm damned if that isn't Linnet Ridgeway."

If the information left Poirot unmoved, it stirred Rosalie's interest. She leaned forward and her sulkiness quite dropped from her as she asked: "Where? That one in white?"

"Yes, there with the tall man. They're coming ashore now. He's the new husband, I suppose. Can't remember her name now."

"Doyle," said Rosalie. "Simon Doyle. It was in all the newspapers. She's simply rolling, isn't she?"

"Only about the richest girl in England," replied Tim cheerfully.

The three lookers-on were silent watching the passengers come ashore. Poirot gazed with interest at the subject of the remarks of his companions. He murmured, "She is beautiful."

"Some people have got everything," said Rosalie bitterly.

There was a queer grudging expression on her face as she watched the other girl come up the gangplank.

Linnet Doyle was looking as perfectly turned out as if she were stepping onto the centre of the stage of a Revue. She had something too of the assurance of a famous actress. She was used to being looked at, to being admired, to being the centre of the stage wherever she went.

She was aware of the keen glances bent upon her—and at the same time almost unaware of them; such tributes were part of her life.

She came ashore playing a rôle, even though she played it unconsciously. The rich beautiful society bride on her honeymoon. She turned, with a little smile and a light remark, to the tall man by her side. He answered, and the sound of his voice seemed to interest Hercule Poirot. His eyes lit up and he drew his brows together.

The couple passed close to him. He heard Simon Doyle say:

"We'll try and make time for it, darling. We can easily stay a week or two if you like it here."

His face was turned toward her, eager, adoring, a little humble.

Poirot's eyes ran over him thoughtfully—the square shoulders, the bronzed face, the dark blue eyes, the rather childlike simplicity of the smile.

"Lucky devil," said Tim after they had passed. "Fancy finding an heiress who hasn't got adenoids and flat feet!"

"They look frightfully happy," said Rosalie with a note of envy in her voice. She added suddenly, but so low that Tim did not catch the words, "It isn't fair."

Poirot heard, however. He had been frowning somewhat perplexedly but now he flashed a quick glance toward her.

Tim said, "I must collect some stuff for my mother now."

He raised his hat and moved off. Poirot and Rosalie retraced their steps slowly in the direction of the hotel, waving aside fresh proffers of donkeys.

"So it is not fair, Mademoiselle?" asked Poirot gently.

The girl flushed angrily.

"I don't know what you mean."

"I am repeating what you said just now under your breath. Oh, yes, you did."

Rosalie Otterbourne shrugged her shoulders.

"It really seems a little too much for one person. Money, good looks, marvellous figure and—"

She paused and Poirot said:

"And love? Eh? And love? But you do not know—she may have been married for her money!"

"Didn't you see the way he looked at her?"

"Oh, yes, Mademoiselle. I saw all there was to see—indeed I saw something that you did not."

"What was that?"

Poirot said slowly: "I saw, Mademoiselle, dark lines below a woman's eyes. I saw a hand that clutched a sunshade so tight that the knuckles were white. . . ."

Rosalie was staring at him.

"What do you mean?"

"I mean that all is not the gold that glitters. I mean that, though this lady is rich and beautiful and beloved, there is all the same *something* that is not right. And I know something else."

"Yes?"

"I know," said Poirot, frowning, "that somewhere, at some time, I have heard that voice before—the voice of Monsieur Doyle—and I wish I could remember where."

But Rosalie was not listening. She had stopped dead. With the point of her sunshade she was tracing patterns in the loose sand. Suddenly she broke out fiercely:

"I'm odious. I'm quite odious. I'm just a beast through and

through. I'd like to tear the clothes off her back and stamp on her lovely, arrogant, self-confident face. I'm just a jealous cat—but that's what I feel like. She's so horribly successful and poised and assured."

Hercule Poirot looked a little astonished by the outburst. He took her by the arm and gave her a friendly little shake.

"*Tenez*—you will feel better for having said that!"

"I just hate her! I've never hated anyone so much at first sight."

"Magnificent!"

Rosalie looked at him doubtfully. Then her mouth twitched and she laughed.

"*Bien*," said Poirot, and laughed too.

They proceeded amicably back to the hotel.

"I must find Mother," said Rosalie, as they came into the cool, dim hall.

Poirot passed out on the other side onto the terrace overlooking the Nile. Here were little tables set for tea, but it was early still. He stood for a few moments looking at the river, then strolled down through the gardens.

Some people were playing tennis in the hot sun. He paused to watch them for a while, then went on down the steep path. It was there, sitting on a bench overlooking the Nile, that he came upon the girl of Chez Ma Tante. He recognized her at once. Her face, as he had seen it that night, was securely etched upon his memory. The expression on it now was very different. She was paler, thinner, and there were lines that told of a great weariness and misery of spirit.

He drew back a little. She had not seen him, and he watched her for a while without her suspecting his presence. Her small foot tapped impatiently on the ground. Her eyes, dark with a kind of smouldering fire, had a queer kind of suffering dark triumph in them. She was looking out across the Nile where the white-sailed boats glided up and down the river.

A face—and a voice. He remembered them both. This girl's face and the voice he had heard just now, the voice of a newly made bridegroom. . . .

And even as he stood there considering the unconscious girl, the next scene in the drama was played.

Voices sounded above. The girl on the seat started to her feet. Linnet Doyle and her husband came down the path. Linnet's voice was happy and confident. The look of strain and tenseness of muscle had quite disappeared. Linnet was happy.

The girl who was standing there took a step or two forward. The other two stopped dead.

"Hullo, Linnet," said Jacqueline de Bellefort. "So here you are! We never seem to stop running into each other. Hullo, Simon, how are you?"

Linnet Doyle had shrunk back against the rock with a little cry. Simon Doyle's good-looking face was suddenly convulsed with rage. He moved forward as though he would have liked to strike the slim girlish figure.

With a quick birdlike turn of her head she signalled her realization of a stranger's presence. Simon turned his head and noticed Poirot. He said awkwardly, "Hullo, Jacqueline; we didn't expect to see you here."

The words were unconvincing in the extreme.

The girl flashed white teeth at them.

"Quite a surprise?" she asked. Then, with a little nod, she walked up the path.

Poirot moved delicately in the opposite direction. As he went he heard Linnet Doyle say:

"Simon—for God's sake! Simon—what can we do?"

CHAPTER 2

DINNER was over. The terrace outside the Cataract Hotel was softly lit. Most of the guests staying at the hotel were there sitting at little tables.

Simon and Linnet Doyle came out, a tall, distinguished looking grey-haired man, with a keen, clean-shaven American face, beside them.

As the little group hesitated for a moment in the doorway, Tim Allerton rose from his chair near by and came forward.

"You don't remember me, I'm sure," he said pleasantly to Linnet, "but I'm Joanna Southwood's cousin."

"Of course—how stupid of me! You're Tim Allerton. This is my husband"—a faint tremor in the voice, pride, shyness?—"and this is my American trustee, Mr. Pennington."

Tim said, "You must meet my mother."

A few minutes later they were sitting together in a party—Linnet in the corner, Tim and Pennington each side of her, both talking to her, vying for her attention. Mrs. Allerton talked to Simon Doyle.

The swing doors revolved. A sudden tension came into the beautiful upright figure sitting in the corner between the two men. Then it relaxed as a small man came out and walked across the terrace.

Mrs. Allerton said: "You're not the only celebrity here, my dear. That funny little man is Hercule Poirot."

She had spoken lightly, just out of instinctive social tact to bridge an awkward pause, but Linnet seemed struck by the information.

"Hercule Poirot? Of course—I've heard of him. . . ."

She seemed to sink into a fit of abstraction. The two men on either side of her were momentarily at a loss.

Poirot had strolled across to the edge of the terrace, but his attention was immediately solicited.

"Sit down, Monsieur Poirot. What a lovely night."

He obeyed.

"Mais oui, Madame, it is indeed beautiful."

He smiled politely at Mrs. Otterbourne. What draperies of black ninon and that ridiculous turban effect! Mrs. Otterbourne went on in her high complaining voice:

"Quite a lot of notabilities here now, aren't there? I expect we shall see a paragraph about it in the papers soon. Society beauties, famous novelists—"

She paused with a slight mock-modest laugh.

Poirot felt, rather than saw, the sulky frowning girl opposite him flinch and set her mouth in a sulkier line than before.

"You have a novel on the way at present, Madame?" he inquired.

Mrs. Otterbourne gave her little self-conscious laugh again.

"I'm being dreadfully lazy. I really must set to. My public is getting terribly impatient—and my publisher, poor man! Appeals by every post! Even cables!"

Again he felt the girl shift in the darkness.

"I don't mind telling you, Monsieur Poirot, I am partly here for local colour. *Snow on the Desert's Face*—that is the title of my new book. Powerful—suggestive. Snow—on the desert—melted in the first flaming breath of passion."

Rosalie got up, muttering something, and moved away down into the dark garden.

"One must be strong," went on Mrs. Otterbourne, wagging the turban emphatically. "Strong meat—that is what my books are—all important. Libraries banned—no matter! I speak the truth. Sex—ah! Monsieur Poirot—why is everyone so afraid of sex? The pivot of the universe! You have read my books?"

"Alas, Madame! You comprehend, I do not read many novels. My work—"

Mrs. Otterbourne said firmly: "I must give you a copy of *Under the Fig Tree*. I think you will find it significant. It is outspoken—but it is *real!*"

"That is most kind of you, Madame. I will read it with pleasure."

Mrs. Otterbourne was silent a minute or two. She fidgeted with a long chain of beads that was wound twice round her neck. She looked swiftly from side to side.

"Perhaps—I'll just slip up and get it for you now."

"Oh, Madame, pray do not trouble yourself. Later—"

"No, no. It's no trouble." She rose. "I'd like to show you—"

"What is it, Mother?"

Rosalie was suddenly at her side.

"Nothing, dear. I was just going up to get a book for Monsieur Poirot."

"The *Fig Tree*? I'll get it."

"You don't know where it is, dear. I'll go."

"Yes, I do."

The girl went swiftly across the terrace and into the hotel.

"Let me congratulate you, Madame, on a very lovely daughter," said Poirot, with a bow.

"Rosalie? Yes, yes—she is good-looking. But she's very *hard,* Monsieur Poirot. And no sympathy with illness. She always thinks she knows best. She imagines she knows more about my health than I do myself—"

Poirot signalled to a passing waiter.

"A liqueur, Madame? A chartreuse? A crème de menthe?"

Mrs. Otterbourne shook her head vigorously.

"No, no. I am practically a teetotaller. You may have noticed I never drink anything but water—or perhaps lemonade. I cannot bear the taste of spirits."

"Then may I order you a lemon squash, Madame?"

He gave the order—one lemon squash and one Benedictine.

The swing door revolved. Rosalie passed through and came toward them, a book in her hand.

"Here you are," she said. Her voice was quite expressionless—almost remarkably so.

"Monsieur Poirot has just ordered me a lemon squash," said her mother.

"And you, Mademoiselle, what will you take?"

"Nothing." She added, suddenly conscious of the curtness, "Nothing, thank you."

Poirot took the volume which Mrs. Otterbourne held out to him. It still bore its original jacket, a gaily coloured affair representing a lady, with smartly shingled hair and scarlet fingernails, sitting on a tiger skin, in the traditional costume of Eve. Above her was a tree with the leaves of an oak, bearing large and improbably coloured apples.

It was entitled *Under the Fig Tree,* by Salome Otterbourne. On the inside was a publisher's blurb. It spoke enthusiastically of the superb courage and realism of this study of a modern woman's love life. "Fearless, unconventional, realistic," were the adjectives used.

Poirot bowed and murmured, "I am honoured, Madame."

As he raised his head, his eyes met those of the authoress's daughter. Almost involuntarily he made a little movement. He was astonished and grieved at the eloquent pain they revealed.

It was at that moment that the drinks arrived and created a welcome diversion.

Poirot lifted his glass gallantly.

"*A votre santé, Madame—Mademoiselle.*"

Mrs. Otterbourne, sipping her lemonade, murmured, "So refreshing—delicious!"

Silence fell on the three of them. They looked down to the shining black rocks in the Nile. There was something fantastic about them in the moonlight. They were like vast prehistoric monsters lying half out of the water. A little breeze came up suddenly and as suddenly died away. There was a feeling in the air of hush—of expectancy.

Hercule Poirot brought his gaze back to the terrace and its occupants. Was he wrong, or was there the same hush of expectancy there? It was like a moment on the stage when one is waiting for the entrance of the leading lady.

And just at that moment the swing doors began to revolve once more. This time it seemed as though they did so with a special air of importance. Everyone had stopped talking and was looking toward them.

A dark slender girl in a wine coloured evening frock came through. She paused for a minute, then walked deliberately across the terrace and sat down at an empty table. There was nothing flaunting, nothing out of the way about her demeanour, and yet it had somehow the studied affect of a stage entrance.

"Well," said Mrs. Otterbourne. She tossed her turbaned head. "She seems to think she is somebody, that girl!"

Poirot did not answer. He was watching. The girl had sat down in a place where she could look deliberately across at Linnet Doyle. Presently, Poirot noticed, Linnet Doyle leant forward and said something and a moment later got up and changed her seat. She was now sitting facing in the opposite direction.

Poirot nodded thoughtfully to himself.

It was about five minutes later that the other girl changed her seat to the opposite side of the terrace. She sat smoking and smiling quietly, the picture of contented ease. But always, as though unconsciously, her meditative gaze was on Simon Doyle's wife.

After a quarter of an hour Linnet Doyle got up abruptly and went into the hotel. Her husband followed her almost immediately.

Jacqueline de Bellefort smiled and twisted her chair round. She lit a cigarette and stared out over the Nile. She went on smiling to herself.

CHAPTER 3

"MONSIEUR POIROT."

Poirot got hastily to his feet. He had remained sitting out on the terrace alone after everyone else had left. Lost in meditation he had been staring at the smooth shiny black rocks when the sound of his name recalled him to himself.

It was a well-bred, assured voice, a charming voice, although perhaps a trifle arrogant.

Hercule Poirot, rising quickly, looked into the commanding eyes of Linnet Doyle. She wore a wrap of rich purple velvet over her white satin gown and she looked more lovely and more regal than Poirot had imagined possible.

"You are Monsieur Hercule Poirot?" said Linnet.

It was hardly a question.

"At your service, Madame."

"You know who I am, perhaps?"

"Yes, Madame. I have heard your name. I know exactly who you are."

Linnet nodded. That was only what she had expected. She went on, in her charming autocratic manner: "Will you come with me into the card room, Monsieur Poirot? I am very anxious to speak to you."

"Certainly, Madame."

She led the way into the hotel. He followed. She led him into the deserted card room and motioned him to close the door. Then she sank down on a chair at one of the tables and he sat down opposite her.

She plunged straightaway into what she wanted to say. There were no hesitations. Her speech came flowingly.

"I have heard a great deal about you, Monsieur Poirot, and I know that you are a very clever man. It happens that I am urgently in need of someone to help me—and I think very possibly that you are the man who could do it."

Poirot inclined his head.

"You are very amiable, Madame, but you see, I am on holiday, and when I am on holiday I do not take cases."

"That could be arranged."

It was not offensively said—only with the quiet confidence of a young woman who had always been able to arrange matters to her satisfaction.

Linnet Doyle went on: "I am the subject, Monsieur Poirot, of an intolerable persecution. That persecution has got to stop! My own idea was to go to the police about it, but my—my husband seems to think that the police would be powerless to do anything."

"Perhaps—if you would explain a little further?" murmured Poirot politely.

"Oh, yes, I will do so. The matter is perfectly simple."

There was still no hesitation—no faltering. Linnet Doyle had a clear-cut businesslike mind. She only paused a minute so as to present the facts as concisely as possible.

"Before I met my husband, he was engaged to a Miss de Bellefort. She was also a friend of mine. My husband broke off his engagement to her—they were not suited in any way. She, I am sorry to say, took it rather hard. . . . I—am very sorry about that—but these things cannot be helped. She made certain—well, threats—to which I paid very little attention, and which, I may say, she has not attempted to carry out. But instead she has adopted the extraordinary course of—of following us about wherever we go."

Poirot raised his eyebrows.

"Ah—rather an unusual—er—revenge."

"Very unusual—and very ridiculous! But also—annoying."

She bit her lip.

Poirot nodded.

"Yes, I can imagine that. You are, I understand, on your honeymoon?"

"Yes. It happened—the first time—at Venice. She was there—at Danielli's. I thought it was just coincidence. Rather embarrassing, but that was all. Then we found her on board the boat at Brindisi. We—we understood that she was going on to Palestine. We left her, as we thought, on the boat. But—but when we got to Mena House she was there—waiting for us."

Poirot nodded.

"And now?"

"We came up the Nile by boat. I—I was half expecting to find her on board. When she wasn't there I thought she had stopped being so —so childish. But when we got here—she—she was here—waiting."

Poirot eyed her keenly for a moment. She was still perfectly composed, but the knuckles of the hand that was gripping the table were white with the force of her grip.

He said, "And you are afraid this state of things may continue?"

"Yes." She paused. "Of course the whole thing is idiotic! Jacqueline is making herself utterly ridiculous. I am surprised she hasn't got more pride—more dignity."

Poirot made a slight gesture.

"There are times, Madame, when pride and dignity—they go by the board! There are other—stronger emotions."

"Yes, possibly." Linnet spoke impatiently. "But what on earth can she hope to *gain* by all this?"

"It is not always a question of gain, Madame."

Something in his tone struck Linnet disagreeably. She flushed and said quickly: "You are right. A discussion of motives is beside the point. The crux of the matter is that this has got to be stopped."

"And how do you propose that that should be accomplished, Madame?" Poirot asked.

"Well—naturally—my husband and I cannot continue being subjected to this annoyance. There must be some kind of legal redress against such a thing."

She spoke impatiently. Poirot looked at her thoughtfully as he asked: "Has she threatened you in actual words in public? Used insulting language? Attempted any bodily harm?"

"No."

"Then, frankly, Madame, I do not see what you can do. If it is a young lady's pleasure to travel in certain places, and those places are the same where you and your husband find yourselves—*eh bien*—what of it? The air is free to all! There is no question of her forcing herself upon your privacy? It is always in public that these encounters take place?"

"You mean there is nothing that I can do about it?"

Linnet sounded incredulous.

Poirot said placidly: "Nothing at all as far as I can see. Mademoiselle de Bellefort is within her rights."

"But—but it is maddening! It is *intolerable* that I should have to put up with this!"

Poirot said drily, "I sympathize with you, Madame—especially as I imagine that you have not often had to put up with things."

Linnet was frowning.

"There *must* be some way of stopping it," she murmured.

Poirot shrugged his shoulders.

"You can always leave—move on somewhere else," he suggested.

"Then she will follow!"

"Very possibly—yes."

"It's absurd!"

"Precisely."

"Anyway, why should I—we—run away? As though—as though—" She stopped.

"Exactly, Madame. As though—! It is all there, is it not?"

Linnet lifted her head and stared at him.

"What do you mean?"

Poirot altered his tone. He leant forward; his voice was confidential, appealing. He said very gently, "Why do you mind so much, Madame?"

"Why? But it's maddening! Irritating to the last degree! I've told you why!"

Poirot shook his head.

"Not altogether."

"What do you mean?" Linnet asked again.

Poirot leant back, folded his arms and spoke in a detached impersonal manner.

"*Ecoutez,* Madame. I will recount to you a little history. It is that one day, a month or two ago, I am dining in a restaurant in London. At the table next to me are two people, a man and a girl. They are very happy, so it seems, very much in love. They talk with confidence of the future. It is not that I listen to what is not meant for me; they are quite oblivious of who hears them and who does not. The man's back is to me, but I can watch the girl's face. It is very intense. She is in love—heart, soul and body—and she is not of those who love lightly and often. With her it is clearly the life and the death. They are engaged to be married, these two; that is what I gather; and they talk of where they shall pass the days of their honeymoon. They plan to go to Egypt."

He paused. Linnet said sharply, "Well?"

Poirot went on: "That is a month or two ago, but the girl's face—I do not forget it. I know that I shall remember if I see it again. And I remember too the man's voice. And I think you can guess, Madame, when it is I see the one and hear the other again. It is here in Egypt. The man is on his honeymoon, yes—but he is on his honeymoon with another woman."

Linnet said sharply: "What of it? I had already mentioned the facts."

"The facts—yes."

"Well then?"

Poirot said slowly: "The girl in the restaurant mentioned a friend—a friend who, she was very positive, would not let her down. That friend, I think, was you, Madame."

Linnet flushed.

"Yes. I told you we had been friends."

"And she trusted you?"

"Yes."

She hesitated for a moment, biting her lip impatiently; then, as Poirot did not seem disposed to speak, she broke out:

"Of course the whole thing was very unfortunate. But these things happen, Monsieur Poirot."

"Ah! yes, they happen, Madame." He paused. "You are of the Church of England I presume?"

"Yes." Linnet looked slightly bewildered.

"Then you have heard portions of the Bible read aloud in church. You have heard of King David and of the rich man who had many flocks and herds and the poor man who had one ewe lamb—and of how the rich man took the poor man's one ewe lamb. That was something that happened, Madame."

Linnet sat up. Her eyes flashed angrily.

"I see perfectly what you are driving at, Monsieur Poirot! You think, to put it vulgarly, that I stole my friend's young man. Looking at the matter sentimentally—which is, I suppose, the way people of your generation cannot help looking at things—that is possibly true. But the real hard truth is different. I don't deny that Jackie was passionately in love with Simon, but I don't think you take into account that he may not have been equally devoted to her. He was very fond of her, but I think that even before he met me he was beginning to feel that he had made a mistake. Look at it clearly, Monsieur Poirot. Simon discovers that it is I he loves, not Jackie. What is he to do? Be heroically noble and marry a woman he does not care for—and thereby probably ruin three lives—for it is doubtful whether he could make Jackie happy under those circumstances? If he were actually married to her when he met me I agree that it *might* be his duty to stick to her—though I'm not really sure of that. If one person is unhappy the other suffers too. But an engagement is not really binding. If a mistake has been made, then surely it is better to face the fact before it is too late. I admit that it was very hard on Jackie, and I'm terribly sorry about it—but there it is. It was inevitable."

"I wonder."

She stared at him.

"What do you mean?"

"It is very sensible, very logical—all that you say! But it does not explain one thing."

"What is that?"

"Your own attitude, Madame. See you, this pursuit of you, you might take it in two ways. It might cause you annoyance—yes, or it might stir your pity—that your friend should have been so deeply hurt as to throw all regards for the conventions aside. But that is not the way you react. No, to you this persecution is *intolerable*—and why? It can be for one reason only—that you feel a sense of guilt."

Linnet sprang to her feet.

"How dare you? Really, Monsieur Poirot, this is going too far."

"But I do dare, Madame! I am going to speak to you quite frankly. I suggest to you that, although you may have endeavoured to gloss over the fact to yourself, you did deliberately set about taking your husband from your friend. I suggest that you felt strongly attracted to him at once. But I suggest that there was a moment when you hesitated, when you realized that there was a *choice*—that you could refrain or go on. I suggest that the initiative rested with *you*—not with Monsieur Doyle. You are beautiful, Madame; you are rich; you are clever, intelligent—and you have charm. You could have exercised that charm or you could have restrained it. You had everything, Madame, that life can offer. Your friend's life was bound up in one person. You knew that, but, though you hesitated, you did not hold your hand. You stretched it out and, like the rich man in the Bible, you took the poor man's one ewe lamb."

There was a silence. Linnet controlled herself with an effort and said in a cold voice, "All this is quite beside the point!"

"No, it is not beside the point. I am explaining to you just why the unexpected appearances of Mademoiselle de Bellefort have upset you so much. It is because, though she may be unwomanly and undignified in what she is doing, you have the inner conviction that she has right on her side."

"That's not true!"

Poirot shrugged his shoulders.

"You refuse to be honest with yourself."

"Not at all."

Poirot said gently, "I should say, Madame, that you have had a happy life, that you have been generous and kindly in your attitude toward others."

"I have tried to be," said Linnet. The impatient anger died out of her face. She spoke simply—almost forlornly.

"And that is why the feeling that you have deliberately caused injury to someone upsets you so much, and why you are so reluctant to admit the fact. Pardon me if I have been impertinent, but the psychology, it is the most important fact in a case."

Linnet said slowly: "Even supposing what you say were true—and I don't admit it, mind—what can be done about it now? One can't alter the past; one must deal with things as they are."

Poirot nodded.

"You have the clear brain. Yes, one cannot go back over the past. One must accept things as they are. And sometimes, Madame, that is all one can do—accept the consequences of one's past deeds."

"You mean," asked Linnet incredulously, "that I can do nothing—*nothing?*"

"You must have courage, Madame; that is what it seems like to me."

Linnet said slowly:

"Couldn't you—talk to Jackie—to Miss de Bellefort? Reason with her?"

"Yes, I could do that. I will do that if you would like me to do so. But do not expect much result. I fancy that Mademoiselle de Bellefort is so much in the grip of a fixed idea that nothing will turn her from it."

"But surely we can do *something* to extricate ourselves?"

"You could, of course, return to England and establish yourself in your own house."

"Even then, I suppose, Jacqueline is capable of planting herself in the village, so that I should see her every time I went out of the grounds."

"True."

"Besides," said Linnet slowly, "I don't think that Simon would agree to run away."

"What is his attitude in this?"

"He's furious—simply furious."

Poirot nodded thoughtfully.

Linnet said appealingly, "You will—talk to her?"

"Yes, I will do that. But it is my opinion that I shall not be able to accomplish anything."

Linnet said violently: "Jackie is extraordinary! One can't tell what she will do!"

"You spoke just now of certain threats she had made. Would you tell me what those threats were?"

Linnet shrugged her shoulders.

"She threatened to—well—kill us both. Jackie can be rather—Latin sometimes."

"I see." Poirot's tone was grave.

Linnet turned to him appealingly.

"You will act for me?"

"No, Madame." His tone was firm. "I will not accept a commission from you. I will do what I can in the interests of humanity. That, yes. There is here a situation that is full of difficulty and danger. I will do what I can to clear it up—but I am not very sanguine as to my chance of success."

Linnet Doyle said slowly, "But you will not act for *me?*"

"No, Madame," said Hercule Poirot.

CHAPTER 4

HERCULE POIROT found Jacqueline de Bellefort sitting on the rocks directly overlooking the Nile. He had felt fairly certain that she had not retired for the night and that he would find her somewhere about the grounds of the hotel.

She was sitting with her chin cupped in the palms of her hands, and she did not turn her head or look round at the sound of his approach.

"Mademoiselle de Bellefort?" asked Poirot. "You permit that I speak to you for a little moment?"

Jacqueline turned her head slightly. A faint smile played round her lips.

"Certainly," she said. "You are Monsieur Hercule Poirot, I think? Shall I make a guess? You are acting for Mrs. Doyle, who has promised you a large fee if you succeed in your mission."

Poirot sat down on the bench near her.

"Your assumption is partially correct," he said, smiling. "I have just come from Madame Doyle, but I am not accepting any fee from her and, strictly speaking, I am not acting for her."

"Oh!"

Jacqueline studied him attentively.

"Then why have you come?" she asked abruptly.

Hercule Poirot's reply was in the form of another question.

"Have you ever seen me before, Mademoiselle?"

She shook her head.

"No, I do not think so."

"Yet I have seen you. I sat next to you once at Chez Ma Tante. You were there with Monsieur Simon Doyle."

A strange masklike expression came over the girl's face. She said, "I remember that evening. . . ."

"Since then," said Poirot, "many things have occurred."

"As you say, many things have occurred."

Her voice was hard with an undertone of desperate bitterness.

"Mademoiselle, I speak as a friend. Bury your dead!"

She looked startled.

"What do you mean?"

"Give up the past! Turn to the future! What is done is done. Bitterness will not undo it."

"I'm sure that that would suit dear Linnet admirably."

Poirot made a gesture.

"I am not thinking of her at this moment! I am thinking of *you*. You have suffered—yes—but what you are doing now will only prolong that suffering."

She shook her head.

"You're wrong. There are times when I almost enjoy myself."

"And that, Mademoiselle, is the worst of all."

She looked up swiftly.

"You're not stupid," she said. She added slowly, "I believe you mean to be kind."

"Go home, Mademoiselle. You are young; you have brains; the world is before you."

Jacqueline shook her head slowly.

"You don't understand—or you won't. Simon is my world."

"Love is not everything, Mademoiselle," Poirot said gently. "It is only when we are young that we think it is."

But the girl still shook her head.

"You don't understand." She shot him a quick look. "You know all about it, of course? You've talked to Linnet? And you were in the restaurant that night. . . . Simon and I loved each other."

"I know that you loved him."

She was quick to perceive the inflection of his words. She repeated with emphasis:

"*We loved each other*. And I loved Linnet. . . . I trusted her. She was my best friend. All her life Linnet has been able to buy everything she wanted. She's never denied herself anything. When she saw Simon she wanted him—and she just took him."

"And he allowed himself to be—bought?"

Jacqueline shook her dark head slowly.

"No, it's not quite like that. If it were, I shouldn't be here now. . . . You're suggesting that Simon isn't worth caring for. . . . If he'd married Linnet for her money, that would be true. But he didn't marry her for her money. It's more complicated than that. There's such a thing as *glamour,* Monsieur Poirot. And money helps that. Linnet had an 'atmosphere,' you see. She was the queen of a kingdom—the young princess—luxurious to her fingertips. It was like a stage setting. She had the world at her feet, one of the richest and most sought after peers in England wanting to marry her. And she stoops instead to the obscure Simon Doyle. . . . Do you wonder it went to his head?" She made a sudden gesture. "Look at the moon up there. You see her very plainly, don't you? She's very real. But if the sun were to shine you wouldn't be able to see her at all. It was rather like that. I was the moon. . . . When the sun came out, Simon couldn't see me any more. . . . He was dazzled. He couldn't see anything but the sun—Linnet."

She paused and then went on: "So you see it was—glamour. She went to his head. And then there's her complete assurance—her habit of command. She's so sure of herself that she makes other people sure. Simon was weak, perhaps; but then he's a very simple person. He would have loved me and me only if Linnet hadn't come along and snatched him up in her golden chariot. And I know—I know perfectly—that he wouldn't ever have fallen in love with her if she hadn't made him."

"That is what you think—yes."

"I *know* it. He loved me—he will always love me."

Poirot said, "Even now?"

A quick answer seemed to rise to her lips, then be stifled. She looked at Poirot and a deep burning colour spread over her face. She looked away; her head dropped down. She said in a low stifled voice:

"Yes, I know. He hates me now. Yes, hates me. . . . He'd better be careful!"

With a quick gesture she fumbled in a little silk bag that lay on the seat. Then she held out her hand. On the palm of it was a small pearl-handled pistol—a dainty toy it looked.

"Nice little thing, isn't it?" she said. "Looks too foolish to be real, but it is real! One of those bullets would kill a man or a woman. And I'm a good shot." She smiled a faraway, reminiscent smile. "When I went home as a child with my mother, to South Carolina, my grandfather taught me to shoot. He was the old-fashioned kind that believes in shooting—especially where honour is concerned. My father, too, he fought several duels as a young man. He was a good swordsman. He killed a man once. That was over a woman. So you see, Monsieur Poirot"—she met his eyes squarely—"I've hot blood in me! I bought this when it first happened. I meant to kill one or other of them—the trouble was I couldn't decide which. Both of them would have been unsatisfactory. If I'd thought Linnet would have looked afraid—but she's got plenty of physical courage. She can stand up to physical action. And then I thought I'd—wait! That appealed to me more and more. After all, I could do it any time; it would be more fun to wait and—think about it! And then this idea came to my mind —to follow them! Whenever they arrived at some faraway spot and were together and happy, they should see *Me!* And it worked! It got Linnet badly—in a way nothing else could have done! It got right under her skin. . . . That was when I began to enjoy myself. . . . And there's nothing she can do about it! I'm always perfectly pleasant and polite! There's not a word they can take hold of! It's poisoning everything—everything—for them."

Her laugh rang out, clear and silvery.

Poirot grasped her arm.

"Be quiet. Quiet, I tell you."

Jacqueline looked at him.

"Well?" she asked. Her smile was definitely challenging.

"Mademoiselle, I beseech you, do not do what you are doing."

"Leave dear Linnet alone, you mean?"

"It is deeper than that. Do not open your heart to evil."

Her lips fell apart; a look of bewilderment came into her eyes.

Poirot went on gravely: "Because—if you do—evil will come. . . . Yes, very surely evil will come. . . . It will enter in and make its home within you, and after a little while it will no longer be possible to drive it out."

Jacqueline stared at him. Her glance seemed to waver, to flicker uncertainly.

She said, "I—don't know—" Then she cried out defiantly, "You can't stop me."

"No," said Hercule Poirot. "I cannot stop you." His voice was sad.

"Even if I were to—kill her, you couldn't stop me."

"No—not if you were willing to pay the price."

Jacqueline de Bellefort laughed.

"Oh, I'm not afraid of death! What have I got to live for, after all? I suppose you believe it's very wrong to kill a person who has injured you—even if they've taken away everything you had in the world?"

Poirot said steadily: "Yes, Mademoiselle. I believe it is the unforgivable offence—to kill."

Jacqueline laughed again.

"Then you ought to approve of my present scheme of revenge; because, you see, as long as it works, I shan't use that pistol. . . . But I'm afraid—yes, afraid sometimes—it all goes red—I want to hurt her—to stick a knife into her, to put my dear little pistol close against her head and then—just press with my finger—*Oh!*"

The exclamation startled him.

"What is it, Mademoiselle?"

She had turned her head and was staring into the shadows.

"Someone—standing over there. He's gone now."

Hercule Poirot looked round sharply.

The place seemed quite deserted.

"There seems no one here but ourselves, Mademoiselle." He got up. "In any case I have said all I came to say. I wish you goodnight."

Jacqueline got up too. She said almost pleadingly, "You do understand—that I can't do what you ask me to do?"

Poirot shook his head.

"No—for you could do it! There is always a moment! Your friend Linnet—there was a moment, too, in which she could have held her hand. . . . She let it pass by. And if one does that, then one is committed to the enterprise and there comes no second chance."

"No second chance. . . ." said Jacqueline de Bellefort.

She stood brooding for a moment; then she lifted her head defiantly.

"Good-night, Monsieur Poirot."

He shook his head sadly and followed her up the path to the hotel.

CHAPTER 5

ON THE FOLLOWING morning Simon Doyle joined Hercule Poirot as the latter was leaving the hotel to walk down to the town.

"Good-morning, Monsieur Poirot."

"Good-morning, Monsieur Doyle."

"You going to the town? Mind if I stroll along with you?"

"But certainly. I shall be delighted."

The two men walked side by side, passed out through the gateway and turned into the cool shade of the gardens. Then Simon removed his pipe from his mouth and said, "I understand, Monsieur Poirot, that my wife had a talk with you last night?"

"That is so."

Simon Doyle was frowning a little. He belonged to that type of men of action who find it difficult to put thoughts into words and who have trouble in expressing themselves clearly.

"I'm glad of one thing," he said. "You've made her realize that we're more or less powerless in the matter."

"There is clearly no legal redress," agreed Poirot.

"Exactly. Linnet didn't seem to understand that." He gave a faint smile. "Linnet's been brought up to believe that every annoyance can automatically be referred to the police."

"It would be pleasant if such were the case," said Poirot.

There was a pause. Then Simon said suddenly, his face going very red as he spoke:

"It's—it's infamous that she should be victimized like this! She's done nothing! If anyone likes to say I behaved like a cad, they're welcome to say so! I suppose I did. But I won't have the whole thing visited on Linnet. She had nothing whatever to do with it."

Poirot bowed his head gravely but said nothing.

"Did you—er—have you—talked to Jackie—Miss de Bellefort?"

"Yes, I have spoken with her."

"Did you get her to see sense?"

"I'm afraid not."

Simon broke out irritably: "Can't she see what an ass she's making of herself? Doesn't she realize that no decent woman would behave as she is doing? Hasn't she got any pride or self-respect?"

Poirot shrugged his shoulders.

"She has only a sense of—injury, shall we say?" he replied.

"Yes, but damn it all, man, decent girls don't behave like this! I admit I was entirely to blame. I treated her damned badly and all that. I should quite understand her being thoroughly fed up with me and never wishing to see me again. But this following me round—it's —it's *indecent!* Making a show of herself! What the devil does she hope to get out of it?"

"Perhaps—revenge!"

"Idiotic! I'd really understand better if she'd tried to do something melodramatic—like taking a pot shot at me."

"You think that would be more like her—yes?"

"Frankly I do. She's hot-blooded—and she's got an ungovernable temper. I shouldn't be surprised at her doing anything while she was in a white-hot rage. But this spying business—" He shook his head.

"It is more subtle—yes! It is intelligent!"

Doyle stared at him.

"You don't understand. It's playing hell with Linnet's nerves."

"And yours?"

Simon looked at him with momentary surprise.

"Me? I'd like to wring the little devil's neck."

"There is nothing, then, of the old feeling left?"

"My dear Monsieur Poirot—how can I put it? It's like the moon when the sun comes out. You don't know it's there any more. When once I'd met Linnet—Jackie didn't exist."

"*Tiens, c'est drôle ça!*" muttered Poirot.

"I beg your pardon."

"Your simile interested me, that is all."

Again flushing, Simon said: "I suppose Jackie told you that I'd only married Linnet for her money? Well, that's a damned lie! I wouldn't marry any woman for money! What Jackie doesn't understand is that it's difficult for a fellow when—when—a woman cares for him as she cared for me."

"Ah?"

Poirot looked up sharply.

Simon blundered on, "It—it—sounds a caddish thing to say, but Jackie was *too* fond of me!"

"*Un qui aime et un qui se laisse aimer,*" murmured Poirot.

"Eh? What's that you say? You see a man doesn't want to feel that a woman cares more for him than he does for her." His voice grew warm as he went on. "He doesn't want to feel *owned,* body and soul. It's that damned *possessive* attitude! This man is *mine*—he *belongs* to me! That's the sort of thing I can't stick—no man could stick! He wants to get away—to get free. He wants to own his woman; he doesn't want *her* to own *him*."

He broke off, and with fingers that trembled slightly he lit a cigarette.

Poirot said, "And it is like that that you felt with Mademoiselle Jacqueline?"

"Eh?" Simon stared and then admitted: "Er—yes—well, yes, as a matter of fact I did. She doesn't realize that, of course. And it's not the sort of thing I could ever tell her. But I *was* feeling restless—and then I met Linnet, and she just swept me off my feet! I'd never seen anything so lovely. It was all so amazing. Everyone kowtowing to her —and then her singling out a poor chump like me."

His tone held boyish awe and astonishment.

"I see," said Poirot. He nodded thoughtfully. "Yes—I see."

"Why can't Jackie take it like a man?" demanded Simon resentfully.

A very faint smile twitched Poirot's upper lip.

"Well, you see, Monsieur Doyle, to begin with she is *not* a man."

"No, no—but I meant take it like a good sport! After all, you've got to take your medicine when it comes to you. The fault's all mine, I admit. But there it is! If you no longer care for a girl, it's simply madness to marry her. And, now that I see what Jackie's really like and the lengths she is likely to go to, I feel I've had rather a lucky escape."

"The lengths she is likely to go to," Poirot repeated thoughtfully. "Have you an idea, Monsieur Doyle, what those lengths are?"

Simon frowned, then shook his head.

"No—at least, what do you mean?"

"You know she carries a pistol about with her."

Simon looked at him, rather startled.

"I don't believe she'll use that—now. She might have done so earlier. But I believe it's got past that. She's just spiteful now—trying to take it out of us both."

Poirot shrugged his shoulders.

"It may be so," he said doubtfully.

"It's Linnet I'm worrying about," declared Simon, somewhat unnecessarily.

"I quite realize that," said Poirot.

"I'm not really afraid of Jackie doing any melodramatic shooting stuff, but this spying and following business has absolutely got Linnet on the raw. I'll tell you the plan I've made, and perhaps you can suggest improvements on it. To begin with, I've announced fairly openly that we're going to stay here ten days. But tomorrow the steamer *Karnak* starts from Shellâl to Wâdi Halfa. I propose to book passages on that under an assumed name. Tomorrow we'll go on an excursion to Philae. Linnet's maid can take the luggage. We'll join the *Karnak* at Shellâl. When Jackie finds we don't come back, it will be too late— we shall be well on our way. She'll assume we have given her the slip and gone back to Cairo. In fact I might even bribe the porter to say so. Inquiry at the tourist offices won't help her, because our names won't appear. How does that strike you?"

"It is well imagined, yes. And suppose she waits here till you return?"

"We may not return. We could go on to Khartûm and then perhaps by air to Kenya. She can't follow us all over the globe."

"No; there must come a time when financial reasons forbid. She has very little money, I understand."

Simon looked at him with admiration.

"That's clever of you. Do you know, I hadn't thought of that. Jackie's as poor as they make them."

"And yet she has managed to follow you so far?"

Simon said doubtfully:

"She's got a small income, of course. Something under two hundred a year, I imagine. I suppose—yes, I suppose she must have sold out the capital to do what she's doing."

"So that the time will come when she has exhausted her resources and is quite penniless?"

"Yes. . . ."

Simon wriggled uneasily. The thought seemed to make him uncomfortable. Poirot watched him attentively.

"No," he remarked. "No, it is not a pretty thought. . . ."

Simon said rather angrily, "Well, *I* can't help it!" Then he added, "What do you think of my plan?"

"I think it may work, yes. But it is, of course, a *retreat*."

Simon flushed.

"You mean, we're running away? Yes, that's true. . . . But Linnet—"

Poirot watched him, then gave a short nod.

"As you say, it may be the best way. But remember, Mademoiselle de Bellefort has brains."

Simon said sombrely: "Someday, I feel, we've got to make a stand and fight it out. Her attitude isn't reasonable."

"Reasonable, *mon Dieu!*" cried Poirot.

"There's no reason why women shouldn't behave like rational beings," Simon asserted stolidly.

Poirot said drily: "Quite frequently they do. That is even more upsetting!" He added: "I, too, shall be on the *Karnak*. It is part of my itinerary."

"Oh!" Simon hesitated, then said, choosing his words with some embarrassment: "That isn't—isn't—er—on our account in any way? I mean I wouldn't like to think—"

Poirot disabused him quickly.

"Not at all. It was all arranged before I left London. I always make my plans well in advance."

"You don't just move on from place to place as the fancy takes you? Isn't the latter really pleasanter?"

"Perhaps. But to succeed in life every detail should be arranged well beforehand."

Simon laughed and said, "That is how the more skilful murderer behaves, I suppose."

"Yes—though I must admit that the most brilliant crime I remember and one of the most difficult to solve was committed on the spur of the moment."

Simon said boyishly, "You must tell us something about your cases on board the *Karnak*."

"No, no; that would be to talk—what do you call it—the shop."

"Yes, but your kind of shop is rather thrilling. Mrs. Allerton thinks so. She's longing to get a chance to cross-question you."

"Mrs. Allerton? That is the charming grey-haired woman who has such a devoted son?"

"Yes. She'll be on the *Karnak* too."

"Does she know that you—?"

"Certainly not," said Simon with emphasis. "Nobody knows. I've gone on the principle that it's better not to trust anybody."

"An admirable sentiment—and one which I always adopt. By the way, the third member of your party, the tall grey-haired man—"

"Pennington?"

"Yes. He is travelling with you?"

Simon said grimly: "Not very usual on a honeymoon, you were thinking? Pennington is Linnet's American trustee. We ran across him by chance in Cairo."

"*Ah vraiment!* You permit a question? She is of age, Madame your wife?"

Simon looked amused.

"She isn't actually twenty-one yet—but she hadn't got to ask anyone's consent before marrying me. It was the greatest surprise to Pennington. He left New York on the *Carmanic* two days before Linnet's letter got there telling him of our marriage, so he knew nothing about it."

"The *Carmanic*—" murmured Poirot.

"It was the greatest surprise to him when we ran into him at Shepheard's in Cairo."

"That was indeed the coincidence!"

"Yes, and we found that he was coming on this Nile trip—so naturally we foregathered; couldn't have done anything else decently. Besides that, it's been—well, a relief in some ways." He looked embarrassed again. "You see Linnet's been all strung up—expecting Jackie to turn up anywhere and everywhere. While we were alone together, the subject kept coming up. Andrew Pennington's a help that way; we have to talk of outside matters."

"Your wife has not confided in Mr. Pennington?"

"No." Simon's jaw looked aggressive. "It's nothing to do with anyone else. Besides, when we started on this Nile trip we thought we'd seen the end of the business."

Poirot shook his head.

"You have not seen the end of it yet. No—the end is not yet at hand. I am very sure of that."

"I say, Monsieur Poirot, you're not very encouraging."

Poirot looked at him with a slight feeling of irritation. He thought to himself: "The Anglo Saxon, he takes nothing seriously but playing games! He does not grow up."

Linnet Doyle—Jacqueline de Bellefort—both of them took the business seriously enough. But in Simon's attitude he could find nothing but male impatience and annoyance. He said: "You will permit me an impertinent question? Was it your idea to come to Egypt for your honeymoon?"

Simon flushed.

"No, of course not. As a matter of fact I'd rather have gone anywhere else, but Linnet was absolutely set upon it. And so—and so—"

He stopped rather lamely.

"Naturally," said Poirot gravely.

He appreciated the fact that, if Linnet Doyle was set upon anything, that thing had to happen.

He thought to himself: "I have now heard three separate accounts of the affair—Linnet Doyle's, Jacqueline de Bellefort's, Simon Doyle's. Which of them is nearest to the truth?"

CHAPTER 6

Simon and Linnet Doyle set off on their expedition to Philae about eleven o'clock the following morning. Jacqueline de Bellefort, sitting on the hotel balcony, watched them set off in the picturesque sailing boat. What she did not see was the departure of a car—laden with luggage, and in which sat a demure-looking maid—from the front door of the hotel. It turned to the right in the direction of Shellâl.

Hercule Poirot decided to pass the remaining two hours before lunch on the island of Elephantine, immediately opposite the hotel.

He went down to the landing stage. There were two men just stepping into one of the hotel boats, and Poirot joined them. The men were obviously strangers to each other. The younger of them had arrived by train the day before. He was a tall, dark-haired young man, with a thin face and a pugnacious chin. He was wearing an extremely dirty pair of grey flannel trousers and a high-necked polo jumper singularly unsuited to the climate. The other was a slightly podgy middle-aged man who lost no time in entering into conversation with Poirot in idiomatic but slightly broken English. Far from taking part in the conversation, the younger man merely scowled at them both and then deliberately turned his back on them and proceeded to admire the agility with which the Nubian boatman steered the boat with his toes as he manipulated the sail with his hands.

It was very peaceful on the water, the great smooth slippery black rocks gliding by and the soft breeze fanning their faces. Elephantine was reached very quickly and on going ashore Poirot and his loquacious acquaintance made straight for the Museum. By this time the latter had produced a card which he handed to Poirot with a little bow. It bore the inscription:

Signor Guido Richetti, Archeologo.

Not to be outdone, Poirot returned the bow and extracted his own card. These formalities completed, the two men stepped into the Museum together, the Italian pouring forth a stream of erudite information. They were by now conversing in French.

The young man in the flannel trousers strolled listlessly round the Museum, yawning from time to time, and then escaped to the outer air.

Poirot and Signor Richetti at last followed him. The Italian was energetic in examining the ruins, but presently Poirot, espying a green-lined sunshade which he recognized on the rocks down by the river, escaped in that direction.

Mrs. Allerton was sitting on a large rock, a sketch-book by her side and a book on her lap.

Poirot removed his hat politely and Mrs. Allerton at once entered into conversation.

"Good-morning," she said. "I suppose it would be quite impossible to get rid of some of these awful children."

A group of small black figures surrounded her, all grinning and posturing and holding out imploring hands as they lisped "Bakshish" at intervals, hopefully.

"I thought they'd get tired of me," said Mrs. Allerton sadly. "They've been watching me for over two hours now—and they close in on me little by little; and then I yell 'Imshi' and brandish my sunshade at them and they scatter for a minute or two. And then they come back and stare and stare, and their eyes are simply disgusting, and so are their noses, and I don't believe I really like children—not unless they're more or less washed and have the rudiments of manners."

She laughed ruefully.

Poirot gallantly attempted to disperse the mob for her, but without avail. They scattered and then reappeared, closing in once more.

"If there were only any peace in Egypt, I should like it better," said Mrs. Allerton. "But you can never be alone anywhere. Someone is always pestering you for money, or offering you donkeys, or beads, or expeditions to native villages, or duck shooting."

"It is the great disadvantage, that is true," agreed Poirot.

He spread his handkerchief cautiously on the rock and sat somewhat gingerly upon it.

"Your son is not with you this morning?" he went on.

"No, Tim had some letters to get off before we leave. We're doing the trip to the Second Cataract, you know."

"I, too."

"I'm so glad. I want to tell you that I'm quite thrilled to meet you. When we were in Majorca, there was a Mrs. Leech there, and she was telling us the most wonderful things about you. She'd lost a ruby ring bathing, and she was just lamenting that you weren't there to find it for her."

"Ah, *parbleu*, but I am not the diving seal!"

They both laughed.

Mrs. Allerton went on:

"I saw you from my window walking down the drive with Simon

Doyle this morning. Do tell me what you make of him? We're all so excited about him."

"Ah? Truly?"

"Yes. You know his marriage to Linnet Ridgeway was the greatest surprise. She was supposed to be going to marry Lord Windlesham and then suddenly she gets engaged to this man no one had ever heard of!"

"You know her well, Madame?"

"No, but a cousin of mine, Joanna Southwood, is one of her best friends."

"Ah, yes, I have read that name in the papers." He was silent a moment and then went on, "She is a young lady very much in the news, Mademoiselle Joanna Southwood."

"Oh, she knows how to advertise herself all right," snapped Mrs. Allerton.

"You do not like her, Madame?"

"That was a nasty remark of mine." Mrs. Allerton looked penitent. "You see I'm old-fashioned. I don't like her much. Tim and she are the greatest friends, though."

"I see," said Poirot.

His companion shot a quick look at him. She changed the subject.

"How very few young people there are out here! That pretty girl with the chestnut hair and the appalling mother in the turban is almost the only young creature in the place. You have talked to her a good deal, I notice. She interests me, that child."

"Why is that, Madame?"

"I feel sorry for her. You can suffer so much when you are young and sensitive. I think she is suffering."

"Yes, she is not happy, poor little one."

"Tim and I call her the 'sulky girl.' I've tried to talk to her once or twice, but she's snubbed me on each occasion. However I believe she's going on this Nile trip too, and I expect we'll have to be more or less all matey together, shan't we?"

"It is a possible contingency, Madame."

"I'm very matey really—people interest me enormously. All the different types." She paused, then said: "Tim tells me that that dark girl—her name is de Bellefort—is the girl who was engaged to Simon Doyle. It's rather awkward for them—meeting like this."

"It is awkward—yes," agreed Poirot.

Mrs. Allerton shot a quick glance at him.

"You know, it may sound foolish, but she almost frightened me. She looked so—intense."

Poirot nodded his head slowly.

"You were not far wrong, Madame. A great force of emotion is always frightening."

"Do people interest you too, Monsieur Poirot? Or do you reserve your interest for potential criminals?"

"Madame—that category would not leave many people outside it."

Mrs. Allerton looked a trifle startled.

"Do you really mean that?"

"Given the particular incentive, that is to say," Poirot added.

"Which would differ?"

"Naturally."

Mrs. Allerton hesitated—a little smile on her lips.

"Even I perhaps?"

"Mothers, Madame, are particularly ruthless when their children are in danger."

She said gravely, "I think that's true—yes, you're quite right."

She was silent a minute or two, then she said, smiling: "I'm trying to imagine motives for crime suitable for everyone in the hotel. It's quite entertaining. Simon Doyle for instance?"

Poirot said, smiling: "A very simple crime—a direct shortcut to his objective. No subtlety about it."

"And therefore very easily detected?"

"Yes; he would not be ingenious."

"And Linnet?"

"That would be like the Queen in your *Alice in Wonderland,* 'Off with her head.' "

"Of course. The divine right of monarchy! Just a little bit of the Naboth's vineyard touch. And the dangerous girl—Jacqueline de Bellefort—could *she* do a murder?"

Poirot hesitated for a minute or two, then he said doubtfully, "Yes, I think she could."

"But you're not sure?"

"No. She puzzles me, that little one."

"I don't think Mr. Pennington could do one, do you? He looks so desiccated and dyspeptic—with no red blood in him."

"But possibly a strong sense of self-preservation."

"Yes, I suppose so. And poor Mrs. Otterbourne in her turban?"

"There is always vanity."

"As a motive for murder?" Mrs. Allerton asked doubtfully.

"Motives for murder are sometimes very trivial, Madame."

"What are the most usual motives, Monsieur Poirot?"

"Most frequent—money. That is to say, gain in its various

ramifications. Then there is revenge—and love, and fear, and pure hate, and beneficence—"

"Monsieur Poirot!"

"Oh, yes, Madame. I have known of—shall we say A?—being removed by B solely in order to benefit C. Political murders often come under that heading. Someone is considered to be harmful to civilization and is removed on that account. Such people forget that life and death are the affair of the good God."

He spoke gravely.

Mrs. Allerton said quietly: "I am glad to hear you say that. All the same, God chooses his instruments."

"There is danger in thinking like that, Madame."

She adopted a lighter tone.

"After this conversation, Monsieur Poirot, I shall wonder that there is anyone left alive!"

She got up.

"We must be getting back. We have to start immediately after lunch."

When they reached the landing stage they found the young man in the polo jumper just taking his place in the boat. The Italian was already waiting. As the Nubian boatman cast the sail loose and they started, Poirot addressed a polite remark to the stranger.

"There are very wonderful things to be seen in Egypt, are there not?"

The young man was now smoking a somewhat noisome pipe. He removed it from his mouth and remarked briefly and very emphatically, in astonishingly well-bred accents, "They make me sick."

Mrs. Allerton put on her pince-nez and surveyed him with pleasurable interest.

"Indeed? And why is that?" Poirot asked.

"Take the Pyramids. Great blocks of useless masonry, put up to minister to the egoism of a despotic bloated king. Think of the sweated masses who toiled to build them and died doing it. It makes me sick to think of the suffering and torture they represent."

Mrs. Allerton said cheerfully, "You'd rather have no Pyramids, no Parthenon, no beautiful tombs or temples—just the solid satisfaction of knowing that people got three meals a day and died in their beds."

The young man directed his scowl in her direction.

"I think human beings matter more than stones."

"But they do not endure as well," remarked Hercule Poirot.

"I'd rather see a well fed worker than any so-called work of art. What matters is the future—not the past."

This was too much for Signor Richetti, who burst into a torrent of impassioned speech not too easy to follow.

The young man retorted by telling everybody exactly what he thought of the capitalist system. He spoke with the utmost venom.

When the tirade was over they had arrived at the hotel landing stage.

Mrs. Allerton murmured cheerfully, "Well, well," and stepped ashore. The young man directed a baleful glance after her.

In the hall of the hotel Poirot encountered Jacqueline de Bellefort. She was dressed in riding clothes. She gave him an ironical little bow.

"I'm going donkey riding. Do you recommend the native villages, Monsieur Poirot?"

"Is that your excursion today, Mademoiselle? *Eh bien,* they are picturesque—but do not spend large sums on native curios."

"Which are shipped here from Europe? No, I am not so easy to deceive as that."

With a little nod she passed out into the brilliant sunshine.

Poirot completed his packing—a very simple affair, since his possessions were always in the most meticulous order. Then he repaired to the dining-room and ate an early lunch.

After lunch the hotel bus took the passengers for the Second Cataract to the station where they were to catch the daily express from Cairo on to Shellâl—a ten-minute run.

The Allertons, Poirot, the young man in the dirty flannel trousers and the Italian were the passengers. Mrs. Otterbourne and her daughter had made the expedition to the Dam and to Philae and would join the steamer at Shellâl.

The train from Cairo and Luxor was about twenty minutes late. However, it arrived at last, and the usual scenes of wild activity occurred. Native porters taking suitcases out of the train collided with other porters putting them in.

Finally, somewhat breathless, Poirot found himself, with an assortment of his own, the Allertons' and some totally unknown luggage, in one compartment, while Tim and his mother were elsewhere with the remains of the assorted baggage.

The compartment in which Poirot found himself was occupied by an elderly lady with a very wrinkled face, a stiff white stock, a good many diamonds and an expression of reptilian contempt for the majority of mankind.

She treated Poirot to an aristocratic glare and retired behind the pages of an American magazine. A big rather clumsy young woman of under thirty was sitting opposite her. She had eager brown eyes, rather like a dog's, untidy hair, and a terrific air of willingness to please. At intervals the old lady looked over the top of her magazine and snapped an order at her.

"Cornelia, collect the rugs." "When we arrive look after my dressing-case. On no account let anyone else handle it." "Don't forget my paper-cutter."

The train run was brief. In ten minutes' time they came to rest on the jetty where the S. S. *Karnak* was awaiting them. The Otterbournes were already on board.

The *Karnak* was a smaller steamer than the *Papyrus* and the *Lotus,* the First Cataract steamers, which are too large to pass through the locks of the Assuan dam. The passengers went on board and were shown their accommodation. Since the boat was not full, most of the passengers had accommodation on the promenade deck. The entire forward part of this deck was occupied by an observation saloon, all glass-enclosed, where the passengers could sit and watch the river unfold before them. On the deck below were a smoking-room and a small drawing-room and on the deck below that, the dining-saloon.

Having seen his possessions disposed in his cabin, Poirot came out on the deck again to watch the process of departure. He joined Rosalie Otterbourne, who was leaning over the side.

"So now we journey into Nubia. You are pleased, Mademoiselle?"

The girl drew a deep breath.

"Yes. I feel that one's really getting away from things at last."

She made a gesture with her hand. There was a savage aspect about the sheet of water in front of them, the masses of rock without vegetation that came down to the water's edge—here and there a trace of houses abandoned and ruined as a result of the damming up of the waters. The whole scene had a melancholy, almost sinister charm.

"Away from *people,*" said Rosalie Otterbourne.

"Except those of our own number, Mademoiselle?"

She shrugged her shoulders. Then she said: "There's something about this country that makes me feel—wicked. It brings to the surface all the things that are boiling inside one. Everything's so unfair—so unjust."

"I wonder. You cannot judge by material evidence."

Rosalie muttered: "Look at—at some people's mothers—and look at mine. There is no God but Sex, and Salome Otterbourne is its Prophet." She stopped. "I shouldn't have said that, I suppose."

Poirot made a gesture with his hands.

"Why not say it—to me? I am one of those who hear many things. If, as you say, you boil inside—like the jam—*eh bien,* let the scum come to the surface, and then one can take it off with a spoon, so."

He made the gesture of dropping something into the Nile.

"There, it has gone."

"What an extraordinary man you are!" Rosalie said. Her sulky mouth twisted into a smile. Then she suddenly stiffened as she exclaimed: "Why, here are Mrs. Doyle and her husband! I'd no idea *they* were coming on this trip!"

Linnet had just emerged from a cabin half way down the deck. Simon was behind her. Poirot was almost startled by the look of her—so radiant, so assured. She looked positively arrogant with happiness. Simon Doyle, too, was a transformed being. He was grinning from ear to ear and looking like a happy schoolboy.

"This is grand," he said as he too leaned on the rail. "I'm really looking forward to this trip, aren't you, Linnet? It feels somehow, so much less touristy—as though we were really going into the heart of Egypt."

His wife responded quickly: "I know. It's so much—wilder, somehow."

Her hand slipped through his arm. He pressed it close to his side. "We're off, Lin," he murmured.

The steamer was drawing away from the jetty. They had started on their seven-day journey to the Second Cataract and back.

Behind them a light silvery laugh rang out. Linnet whipped round. Jacqueline de Bellefort was standing there. She seemed amused.

"Hullo, Linnet! I didn't expect to find *you* here. I thought you said you were staying at Assuan another ten days. This is a surprise!"

"You—you didn't—" Linnet's tongue stammered. She forced a ghastly conventional smile. "I—I didn't expect to see you either."

"No?"

Jacqueline moved away to the other side of the boat. Linnet's grasp on her husband's arm tightened.

"Simon—Simon—"

All Doyle's good-natured pleasure had gone. He looked furious. His hands clenched themselves in spite of his effort at self-control.

The two of them moved a little away. Without turning his head Poirot caught scraps of disjointed words:

". . . turn back . . . impossible . . . we could . . ." and then, slightly louder, Doyle's voice, despairing but grim: "We can't run away for ever, Lin. We've got to go through with it now. . . ."

It was some hours later. Daylight was just fading. Poirot stood in the glass-enclosed saloon looking straight ahead. The *Karnak* was going through a narrow gorge. The rocks came down with a kind of sheer ferocity to the river flowing deep and swift between them. They were in Nubia now.

He heard a movement and Linnet Doyle stood by his side. Her fingers twisted and untwisted themselves; she looked as he had never yet seen her look. There was about her the air of a bewildered child. She said:

"Monsieur Poirot, I'm afraid—I'm afraid of everything. I've never felt like this before. All these wild rocks and the awful grimness and starkness. Where are we going? What's going to happen? I'm afraid, I tell you. Everyone hates me. I've never felt like that before. I've always been nice to people—I've done things for them—and they hate me—lots of people hate me. Except for Simon, I'm surrounded by enemies. . . . It's terrible to feel—that there are people who hate you. . . ."

"But what is all this, Madame?"

She shook her head.

"I suppose—it's nerves. . . . I just feel that—everything's unsafe all round me."

She cast a quick nervous glance over her shoulder. Then she said abruptly: "How will all this end? We're caught here. Trapped! There's no way out. We've got to go on. I—I don't know where I am."

She slipped down onto a seat. Poirot looked down on her gravely; his glance was not untinged with compassion.

"How did she know we were coming on this boat?" she said. "How could she have known?"

Poirot shook his head as he answered, "She has brains, you know."

"I feel as though I shall never escape from her."

Poirot said: "There is one plan you might have adopted. In fact I am surprised that it did not occur to you. After all, with you, Madame, money is no object. Why did you not engage your own private dahabiyeh?"

Linnet shook her head rather helplessly.

"If we'd known about all this—but you see we didn't—then. And it was difficult. . . ." She flashed out with sudden impatience: "Oh! you don't understand half my difficulties. I've got to be careful with Simon. . . . He's—he's absurdly sensitive—about money. About my having so much! He wanted me to go to some little place in Spain with him—he—he wanted to pay all our honeymoon expenses himself. As if it *mattered!* Men are stupid! He's got to get used to—to—living comfortably. The mere idea of a dahabiyeh upset him—the—the needless expense. I've got to educate him—gradually."

She looked up, bit her lip vexedly, as though feeling that she had been led into discussing her difficulties rather too unguardedly.

She got up.

"I must change. I'm sorry, Monsieur Poirot. I'm afraid I've been talking a lot of foolish nonsense."

CHAPTER 7

MRS. ALLERTON, looking quiet and distinguished in her simple black lace evening gown, descended two decks to the dining-room. At the door of it her son caught her up.

"Sorry, darling. I thought I was going to be late."

"I wonder where we sit." The saloon was dotted with little tables. Mrs. Allerton paused till the steward, who was busy seating a party of people, could attend to them.

"By the way," she added, "I asked little Hercule Poirot to sit at our table."

"Mother, you didn't!" Tim sounded really taken aback and annoyed.

His mother stared at him in surprise. Tim was usually so easy-going.

"My dear, do you mind?"

"Yes, I do. He's an unmitigated little bounder!"

"Oh, no, Tim! I don't agree with you."

"Anyway, what do we want to get mixed up with an outsider for? Cooped up like this on a small boat, that sort of thing is always a bore. He'll be with us morning, noon and night."

"I'm sorry, dear." Mrs. Allerton looked distressed. "I thought really it would amuse you. After all, he must have had a varied experience. And you love detective stories."

Tim grunted.

"I wish you wouldn't have these bright ideas, Mother. We can't get out of it now, I suppose?"

"Really, Tim, I don't see how we can."

"Oh, well, we shall have to put up with it, I suppose."

The steward came to them at this minute and led them to a table. Mrs. Allerton's face wore rather a puzzled expression as she followed him. Tim was usually so easy-going and good-tempered. This outburst was quite unlike him. It wasn't as though he had the ordinary Britisher's dislike—and mistrust—of foreigners. Tim was very cosmopolitan. Oh, well—she sighed. Men were incomprehensible! Even one's nearest and dearest had unsuspected reactions and feelings.

As they took their places, Hercule Poirot came quickly and silently into the dining-saloon. He paused with his hand on the back of the third chair.

"You really permit, Madame, that I avail myself of your kind suggestion?"

"Of course. Sit down, Monsieur Poirot."

"You are most amiable."

She was uneasily conscious that, as he seated himself, he shot a swift glance at Tim, and that Tim had not quite succeeded in masking a somewhat sullen expression.

Mrs. Allerton set herself to produce a pleasant atmosphere. As they drank their soup, she picked up the passenger list which had been placed beside her plate.

"Let's try and identify everybody," she suggested cheerfully. "I always think that's rather fun."

She began reading: "Mrs. Allerton, Mr. T. Allerton. That's easy enough! Miss de Bellefort. They've put her at the same table as the Otterbournes, I see. I wonder what she and Rosalie will make of each other. Who comes next? Dr. Bessner. Dr. Bessner? Who can identify Dr. Bessner?"

She bent her glance on a table at which four men sat together.

"I think he must be the fat one with the closely shaved head and the moustache. A German, I should imagine. He seems to be enjoying his soup very much." Certain succulent noises floated across to them.

Mrs. Allerton continued: "Miss Bowers? Can we make a guess at Miss Bowers? There are three or four women— No, we'll leave her for the present. Mr. and Mrs. Doyle. Yes, indeed, the lions of this trip. She really is very beautiful, and what a perfectly lovely frock she is wearing."

Tim turned round in his chair. Linnet and her husband and Andrew Pennington had been given a table in the corner. Linnet was wearing a white dress and pearls.

"It looks frightfully simple to me," said Tim. "Just a length of stuff with a kind of cord round the middle."

"Yes, darling," said his mother. "A very nice manly description of an eighty-guinea model."

"I can't think why women pay so much for their clothes," Tim said. "It seems absurd to me."

Mrs. Allerton proceeded with her study of her fellow passengers.

"Mr. Fanthorp must be one of the four at that table. The intensely quiet young man who never speaks. Rather a nice face, cautious but intelligent."

Poirot agreed.

"He is intelligent—yes. He does not talk, but he listens very attentively, and he also watches. Yes, he makes good use of his eyes. Not quite the type you would expect to find travelling for pleasure in this part of the world. I wonder what he is doing here."

"Mr. Ferguson," read Mrs. Allerton. "I feel that Ferguson must be our anti-capitalist friend. Mrs. Otterbourne, Miss Otterbourne. We know all about them. Mr. Pennington? Alias Uncle Andrew. He's a good-looking man, I think—"

"Now, Mother," said Tim.

"I think he's very good-looking in a dry sort of way," said Mrs. Allerton. "Rather a ruthless jaw. Probably the kind of man one reads about in the paper, who operates on Wall Street—or is it *in* Wall Street? I'm sure he must be extremely rich. Next—Monsieur Hercule Poirot—whose talents are really being wasted. Can't you get up a crime for Monsieur Poirot, Tim?"

But her well-meant banter only seemed to annoy her son anew. He scowled and Mrs. Allerton hurried on: "Mr. Richetti. Our Italian archaeological friend. Then Miss Robson and last of all Miss Van Schuyler. The last's easy. The very ugly old American lady who obviously feels herself the queen of the boat and who is clearly going to be very exclusive and speak to nobody who doesn't come up to the most exacting standards! She's rather marvellous, isn't she, really? A kind of period piece. The two women with her must be Miss Bowers and Miss Robson—perhaps a secretary, the thin one with pince-nez, and a poor relation, the rather pathetic young woman who is obviously enjoying herself in spite of being treated like a black slave. I think Robson's the secretary woman and Bowers is the poor relation."

"Wrong, Mother," said Tim, grinning. He had suddenly recovered his good humour.

"How do you know?"

"Because I was in the lounge before dinner and the old bean said to the companion woman: 'Where's Miss Bowers? Fetch her at once, Cornelia.' And away trotted Cornelia like an obedient dog."

"I shall have to talk to Miss Van Schuyler," mused Mrs. Allerton.

Tim grinned again.

"She'll snub you, Mother."

"Not at all. I shall pave the way by sitting near her and conversing, in low (but penetrating), well-bred tones, about any titled relations and friends I can remember. I think a casual mention of your second cousin, once removed, the Duke of Glasgow, would probably do the trick."

"How unscrupulous you are, Mother!"

Events after dinner were not without their amusing side to a student of human nature.

The socialistic young man (who turned out to be Mr. Ferguson as deduced) retired to the smoking-room, scorning the assemblage of passengers in the observation saloon on the top deck.

Miss Van Schuyler duly secured the best and most undraughty position there by advancing firmly on a table at which Mrs. Otterbourne was sitting and saying, "You'll excuse me, I am sure, but I *think* my knitting was left here!"

Fixed by a hypnotic eye, the turban rose and gave ground. Miss Van Schuyler established herself and her suite. Mrs. Otterbourne sat down near by and hazarded various remarks, which were met with such chilling politeness that she soon gave up. Miss Van Schuyler then sat in glorious isolation. The Doyles sat with the Allertons. Dr. Bessner retained the quiet Mr. Fanthorp as a companion. Jacqueline de Bellefort sat by herself with a book. Rosalie Otterbourne was restless. Mrs. Allerton spoke to her once or twice and tried to draw her into their group, but the girl responded ungraciously.

M. Hercule Poirot spent his evening listening to an account of Mrs. Otterbourne's mission as a writer.

On his way to his cabin that night he encountered Jacqueline de Bellefort. She was leaning over the rail and, as she turned her head, he was struck by the look of acute misery on her face. There was now no insouciance, no malicious defiance, no dark flaming triumph.

"Good-night, Mademoiselle."

"Good-night, Monsieur Poirot." She hesitated, then said, "You were surprised to find me here?"

"I was not so much surprised as sorry—very sorry. . . ."

He spoke gravely.

"You mean sorry—for *me?*"

"That is what I meant. You have chosen, Mademoiselle, the dangerous course. . . . As we here in this boat have embarked on a journey, so you too have embarked on your own private journey—a journey on a swift-moving river, between dangerous rocks, and heading for who knows what currents of disaster. . . ."

"Why do you say all this?"

"Because it is true. . . . You have cut the bonds that moored you to safety. I doubt now if you could turn back if you would."

She said very slowly, "That is true. . . ."

Then she flung her head back.

"Ah, well—one must follow one's star, wherever it leads."

"Beware, Mademoiselle, that it is not a false star. . . ."

She laughed and mimicked the parrot cry of the donkey boys:

"That very bad star, sir! That star fall down. . . ."

He was just dropping off to sleep when the murmur of voices awoke him. It was Simon Doyle's voice he heard, repeating the same words he had used when the steamer left Shellâl.

"We've got to go through with it now. . . ."

"Yes," thought Hercule Poirot to himself, "we have got to go through with it now. . . ."

He was not happy.

CHAPTER 8

THE STEAMER arrived early next morning at Ez-Sebûa.

Cornelia Robson, her face beaming, a large flapping hat on her head, was one of the first to hurry on shore. Cornelia was not good at snubbing people. She was of an amiable disposition and disposed to like all her fellow creatures.

The sight of Hercule Poirot, in a white suit, pink shirt, large black bow tie and a white topee, did not make her wince as the aristocratic Miss Van Schuyler would assuredly have winced. As they walked together up an avenue of sphinxes, she responded readily to his conventional opening.

"Your companions are not coming ashore to view the temple?"

"Well, you see, Cousin Marie—that's Miss Van Schuyler—never gets up very early. She has to be very, very careful of her health. And of course she wanted Miss Bowers, that's her hospital nurse, to do things for her. And she said, too, that this isn't one of the best temples—but she was frightfully kind and said it would be quite all right for me to come."

"That was very gracious of her," said Poirot drily.

The ingenuous Cornelia agreed unsuspectingly.

"Oh, she's very kind. It's simply wonderful of her to bring me on this trip. I do feel I'm a lucky girl. I just could hardly believe it when she suggested to Mother that I should come too."

"And you have enjoyed it—yes?"

"Oh, it's been wonderful! I've seen Italy—Venice and Padua and Pisa—and then Cairo—only Cousin Marie wasn't very well in Cairo, so I couldn't get around much, and now this wonderful trip up to Wâdi Halfa and back."

Poirot said, smiling, "You have the happy nature, Mademoiselle."

He looked thoughtfully from her to the silent, frowning Rosalie, who was walking ahead by herself.

"She's very nice-looking, isn't she?" said Cornelia, following his glance. "Only kind of scornful looking. She's very English, of course. She's not as lovely as Mrs. Doyle. I think Mrs. Doyle's the loveliest, the most elegant woman I've ever seen! And her husband just worships the ground she walks on, doesn't he? I think that grey-haired lady is kind of distinguished looking, don't you? She's cousin to a Duke, I believe. She was talking about him right near us last night. But she isn't actually titled herself, is she?"

She prattled on until the dragoman in charge called a halt and began to intone: "This temple was dedicated to Egyptian God Amun and the Sun God Rē-Harakhte—whose symbol was hawk's head . . ."

It droned on. Dr. Bessner, Baedeker in hand, mumbled to himself in German. He preferred the written word.

Tim Allerton had not joined the party. His mother was breaking the ice with the reserved Mr. Fanthorp. Andrew Pennington, his arm through Linnet Doyle's, was listening attentively, seemingly most interested in the measurements as recited by the guide.

"Sixty-five feet high, is that so? Looks a little less to me. Great fellow, this Rameses. An Egyptian live wire."

"A big business man, Uncle Andrew."

Andrew Pennington looked at her appreciatively.

"You look fine this morning, Linnet. I've been a mite worried about you lately. You've looked kind of peaky."

Chatting together, the party returned to the boat. Once more the *Karnak* glided up the river. The scenery was less stern now. There were palms, cultivation.

It was as though the change in the scenery had relieved some secret oppression that had brooded over the passengers. Tim Allerton
had got over his fit of moodiness. Rosalie looked less sulky. Linnet
seemed almost light-hearted.

Pennington said to her, "It's tactless to talk business to a bride on
her honeymoon, but there are just one or two things—"

"Why, of course, Uncle Andrew." Linnet at once became businesslike. "My marriage has made a difference, of course."

"That's just it. Some time or other I want your signature to several
documents."

"Why not now?"

Andrew Pennington glanced round. Their corner of the observation saloon was quite untenanted. Most of the people were outside on
the deck space between the observation saloon and the cabins. The
only occupants of the saloon were Mr. Ferguson—who was drinking
beer at a small table in the middle, his legs, encased in their dirty
flannel trousers, stuck out in front of him, whilst he whistled to himself in the intervals of drinking—M. Hercule Poirot, who was sitting
close up to the front glass, intent on the panorama unfolding before
him, and Miss Van Schuyler, who was sitting in a corner reading a
book on Egypt.

"That's fine," said Andrew Pennington. He left the saloon.

Linnet and Simon smiled at each other—a slow smile that took a
few minutes to come to full fruition.

"All right, sweet?" he asked.

"Yes, still all right. . . . Funny how I'm not rattled any more."

Simon said with deep conviction in his tone, "You're marvellous."

Pennington came back. He brought with him a sheaf of closely
written documents.

"Mercy!" cried Linnet. "Have I got to sign all these?"

Andrew Pennington was apologetic.

"It's tough on you, I know, but I'd just like to get your affairs put
in proper shape. First of all there's the lease of the Fifth Avenue
property . . . then there are the Western Lands Concessions . . ."

He talked on, rustling and sorting the papers. Simon yawned.

The door to the deck swung open and Mr. Fanthorp came in. He
gazed aimlessly round, then strolled forward and stood by Poirot
looking out at the pale blue water and the yellow enveloping
sands. . . .

"—you sign just there," concluded Pennington, spreading a paper
before Linnet and indicating a space.

Linnet picked up the document and glanced through it. She turned back once to the first page, then, taking up the fountain pen Pennington had laid beside her, she signed her name *Linnet Doyle*. . . .

Pennington took away the paper and spread out another.

Fanthorp wandered over in their direction. He peered out through the side window at something that seemed to interest him on the bank they were passing.

"That's just the transfer," said Pennington. "You needn't read it."

But Linnet took a brief glance through it. Pennington laid down a third paper. Again Linnet perused it carefully.

"They're all quite straightforward," said Andrew. "Nothing of interest. Only legal phraseology."

Simon yawned again.

"My dear girl, you're not going to read the whole lot through, are you? You'll be at it till lunch time and longer."

"I always read everything through," said Linnet. "Father taught me to do that. He said there might be some clerical error."

Pennington laughed rather harshly.

"You're a grand woman of business, Linnet."

"She's much more conscientious than I'd be," said Simon, laughing. "I've never read a legal document in my life. I sign where they tell me to sign on the dotted line—and that's that."

"That's frightfully slipshod," said Linnet disapprovingly.

"I've no business head," declared Simon cheerfully. "Never had. A fellow tells me to sign—I sign. It's much the simplest way."

Andrew Pennington was looking at him thoughtfully. He said drily, stroking his upper lip, "A little risky sometimes, Doyle?"

"Nonsense," replied Simon. "I'm not one of those people who believe the whole world is out to do one down. I'm a trusting kind of fellow—and it pays, you know. I've hardly ever been let down."

Suddenly, to everyone's surprise, the silent Mr. Fanthorp swung round and addressed Linnet.

"I hope I'm not butting in, but you must let me say how much I admire your businesslike capacity. In my profession—er—I am a lawyer—I find ladies sadly unbusinesslike. Never to sign a document before you read it through is admirable—altogether admirable."

He gave a little bow. Then, rather red in the face, he turned once more to contemplate the banks of the Nile.

Linnet said rather uncertainly, "Er—thank you. . . ." She bit her lip to repress a giggle. The young man had looked so preternaturally solemn.

Andrew Pennington looked seriously annoyed.

Simon Doyle looked uncertain whether to be annoyed or amused.

The backs of Mr. Fanthorp's ears were bright crimson.

"Next, please," said Linnet, smiling up at Pennington.

But Pennington was looking decidedly ruffled.

"I think perhaps some other time would be better," he said stiffly. "As—er—Doyle says, if you have to read through all these we shall be here till lunch time. We mustn't miss enjoying the scenery. Anyway those first two papers were the only urgent ones. We'll settle down to business later."

"It's frightfully hot in here," Linnet said. "Let's go outside."

The three of them passed through the swing door. Hercule Poirot turned his head. His gaze rested thoughtfully on Mr. Fanthorp's back; then it shifted to the lounging figure of Mr. Ferguson who had his head thrown back and was still whistling softly to himself.

Finally Poirot looked over at the upright figure of Miss Van Schuyler in her corner. Miss Van Schuyler was glaring at Mr. Ferguson.

The swing door on the port side opened and Cornelia Robson hurried in.

"You've been a long time," snapped the old lady. "Where've you been?"

"I'm so sorry, Cousin Marie. The wool wasn't where you said it was. It was in another case altogether—"

"My dear child, you are perfectly hopeless at finding anything! You are willing, I know, my dear, but you must try to be a little cleverer and quicker. It only needs *concentration*."

"I'm so sorry, Cousin Marie. I'm afraid I am very stupid."

"Nobody need be stupid if they *try*, my dear. I have brought you on this trip, and I expect a little attention in return."

Cornelia flushed.

"I'm very sorry, Cousin Marie."

"And where is Miss Bowers? It was time for my drops ten minutes ago. Please go and find her at once. The doctor said it was most important—"

But at this stage Miss Bowers entered, carrying a small medicine glass.

"Your drops, Miss Van Schuyler."

"I should have had them at eleven," snapped the old lady. "If there's one thing I detest it's unpunctuality."

"Quite," said Miss Bowers. She glanced at her wristwatch. "It's exactly half a minute to eleven."

"By my watch it's ten past."

"I think you'll find my watch is right. It's a perfect timekeeper. It never loses or gains." Miss Bowers was quite unperturbable.

Miss Van Schuyler swallowed the contents of the medicine glass. "I feel definitely worse," she snapped.

"I'm sorry to hear that, Miss Van Schuyler."

Miss Bowers did not sound sorry. She sounded completely uninterested. She was obviously making the correct reply mechanically.

"It's too hot in here," snapped Miss Van Schuyler. "Find me a chair on the deck, Miss Bowers. Cornelia, bring my knitting. Don't be clumsy or drop it. And then I shall want you to wind some wool."

The procession passed out.

Mr. Ferguson sighed, stirred his legs and remarked to the world at large, "Gosh, I'd like to scrag that dame."

Poirot asked interestedly, "She is a type you dislike, eh?"

"Dislike? I should say so. What good has that woman ever been to anyone or anything? She's never worked or lifted a finger. She's just battened on other people. She's a parasite—and a damned unpleasant parasite. There are a lot of people on this boat I'd say the world could do without."

"Really?"

"Yes. That girl in here just now, signing share transfers and throwing her weight about. Hundreds and thousands of wretched workers slaving for a mere pittance to keep her in silk stockings and useless luxuries. One of the richest women in England, so someone told me—and never done a hand's turn in her life."

"Who told you she was one of the richest women in England?"

Mr. Ferguson cast a belligerent eye at him.

"A man you wouldn't be seen speaking to! A man who works with his hands and isn't ashamed of it! Not one of your dressed-up, foppish good-for-nothings."

His eye rested unfavourably on the bow tie and pink shirt.

"Me, I work with my brains and am not ashamed of it," said Poirot, answering the glance.

Mr. Ferguson merely snorted.

"Ought to be shot up—the lot of them!" he asserted.

"My dear young man," said Poirot, "what a passion you have for violence!"

"Can you tell me of any good that can be done without it? You've got to break down and destroy before you can build up."

"It is certainly much easier and much noisier and much more spectacular."

"What do *you* do for a living? Nothing at all, I bet. Probably call yourself a middle man."

"I am not a middle man. I am a top man," declared Hercule Poirot with slight arrogance.

"What *are* you?"

"I am a detective," said Hercule Poirot with the modest air of one who says "I am a King."

"Good God!" The young man seemed seriously taken aback. "Do you mean that girl actually totes about a dumb dick? Is she as careful of her precious skin as *that?*"

"I have no connection whatever with Monsieur and Madame Doyle," said Poirot stiffly. "I am on a holiday."

"Enjoying a vacation—eh?"

"And you? Is it not that you are on a holiday also?"

"Holiday!" Mr. Ferguson snorted. Then he added cryptically, "I'm studying conditions."

"Very interesting," murmured Poirot and moved gently out onto the deck.

Miss Van Schuyler was established in the best corner. Cornelia knelt in front of her, her arms outstretched with a skein of grey wool upon them. Miss Bowers was sitting very upright reading the *Saturday Evening Post*.

Poirot wandered gently onward down the starboard deck. As he passed round the stern of the boat he almost ran into a woman who turned a startled face toward him—a dark, piquant, Latin face. She was neatly dressed in black and had been standing talking to a big burly man in uniform—one of the engineers, by the look of him. There was a queer expression on both their faces—guilt and alarm. Poirot wondered what they had been talking about.

He rounded the stern and continued his walk along the port side. A cabin door opened and Mrs. Otterbourne emerged and nearly fell into his arms. She was wearing a scarlet satin dressing-gown.

"So sorry," she apologized. "Dear Mr. Poirot—so very sorry. The motion—just the motion, you know. Never did have any sea legs. If the boat would only keep still . . . ." She clutched at his arm. "It's the pitching I can't stand. . . . Never really happy at sea. . . . And left all alone here hour after hour. That girl of mine—no sympathy—no understanding of her poor old mother who's done everything for her. . . ." Mrs. Otterbourne began to weep. "Slaved for her I have—worn myself to the bone—to the bone. A *grande amoureuse*—that's what I might have been—a *grande amoureuse*—sacrificed everything—

everything. . . . And nobody cares! But I'll tell everyone—I'll tell them now—how she neglects me—how hard she is—making me come on this journey—bored to death. . . . I'll go and tell them now—"

She surged forward. Poirot gently repressed the action.

"I will send her to you, Madame. Re-enter your cabin. It is best that way—"

"No. I want to tell everyone—everyone on the boat—"

"It is too dangerous, Madame. The sea is too rough. You might be swept overboard."

Mrs. Otterbourne looked at him doubtfully.

"You think so. You really think so?"

"I do."

He was successful. Mrs. Otterbourne wavered, faltered and re-entered her cabin.

Poirot's nostrils twitched once or twice. Then he nodded and walked on to where Rosalie Otterbourne was sitting between Mrs. Allerton and Tim.

"Your mother wants you, Mademoiselle."

She had been laughing quite happily. Now her face clouded over. She shot a quick suspicious look at him and hurried along the deck.

"I can't make that child out," said Mrs. Allerton. "She varies so. One day she's friendly; the next day she's positively rude."

"Thoroughly spoilt and bad-tempered," said Tim.

Mrs. Allerton shook her head.

"No. I don't think it's that. I think she's unhappy."

Tim shrugged his shoulders.

"Oh, well, I suppose we've all got our private troubles." His voice sounded hard and curt.

A booming noise was heard.

"Lunch," cried Mrs. Allerton delightedly. "I'm starving."

That evening, Poirot noticed that Mrs. Allerton was sitting talking to Miss Van Schuyler. As he passed, Mrs. Allerton closed one eye and opened it again. She was saying, "Of course at Calfries Castle—the dear Duke—"

Cornelia, released from attendance, was out on the deck. She was listening to Dr. Bessner, who was instructing her somewhat ponderously in Egyptology as culled from the pages of Baedeker. Cornelia listened with rapt attention.

Leaning over the rail Tim Allerton was saying, "Anyhow, it's a rotten world. . . ."

Rosalie Otterbourne answered, "It's unfair; some people have everything."

Poirot sighed. He was glad that he was no longer young.

CHAPTER 9

ON THE MONDAY morning various expressions of delight and appreciation were heard on the deck of the *Karnak*. The steamer was moored to the bank and a few hundred yards away, the morning sun just striking it, was a great temple carved out of the face of the rock. Four colossal figures, hewn out of the cliff, look out eternally over the Nile and face the rising sun.

Cornelia Robson said incoherently: "Oh, Monsieur Poirot, isn't it wonderful? I mean they're so big and so peaceful—and looking at them makes one feel that one's so small and—and rather like an insect—and that nothing matters very much really, does it?"

Mr. Fanthorp, who was standing near by, murmured, "Very—er—impressive."

"Grand, isn't it?" said Simon Doyle, strolling up. He went on confidentially to Poirot: "You know, I'm not much of a fellow for temples and sight-seeing and all that, but a place like this sort of gets you, if you know what I mean. Those old Pharaohs must have been wonderful fellows."

The others had drifted away. Simon lowered his voice.

"I'm no end glad we came on this trip. It's—well, it's cleared things up. Amazing why it should—but there it is. Linnet's got her nerve back. She says it's because she's actually *faced* the business at last."

"I think that is very probable," said Poirot.

"She says that when she actually saw Jackie on the boat she felt terrible—and then, suddenly, it didn't matter any more. We're both agreed that we won't try and dodge her any more. We'll just meet her on her own ground and show her that this ridiculous stunt of hers doesn't worry us a bit. It's just damned bad form—that's all. She thought she'd got us badly rattled, but now, well, we just aren't rattled any more. That ought to show her."

"Yes," said Poirot thoughtfully.

"So that's splendid, isn't it?"

"Oh, yes, yes."

Linnet came along the deck. She was dressed in a soft shade of

apricot linen. She was smiling. She greeted Poirot with no particular
enthusiasm, just gave him a cool nod and then drew her husband
away.

Poirot realized with a momentary flicker of amusement that he had
not made himself popular by his critical attitude. Linnet was used to
unqualified admiration of all she was or did. Hercule Poirot had
sinned noticeably against this creed.

Mrs. Allerton, joining him, murmured:

"What a difference in that girl! She looked worried and not very
happy at Assuan. Today she looks so happy that one might almost be
afraid she was fey."

Before Poirot could respond as he meant, the party was called to
order. The official dragoman took charge and the party was led
ashore to visit Abu Simbel.

Poirot himself fell into step with Andrew Pennington.

"It is your first visit to Egypt—yes?" he asked.

"Why, no, I was here in nineteen twenty-three. That is to say, I
was in Cairo. I've never been this trip up the Nile before."

"You came over on the *Carmanic,* I believe—at least so Madame
Doyle was telling me."

Pennington shot a shrewd glance in his direction.

"Why, yes, that is so," he admitted.

"I wondered if you had happened to come across some friends of
mine who were aboard—the Rushington Smiths."

"I can't recall anyone of that name. The boat was full and we had
bad weather. A lot of passengers hardly appeared, and in any case
the voyage is so short one doesn't get to know who is on board and
who isn't."

"Yes, that is very true. What a pleasant surprise your running into
Madame Doyle and her husband. You had no idea they were married?"

"No. Mrs. Doyle had written me, but the letter was forwarded on
and I only received it some days after our unexpected meeting in
Cairo."

"You have known her for very many years, I understand?"

"Why, I should say I have, Monsieur Poirot. I've known Linnet
Ridgeway since she was just a cute little thing so high—" He made an
illustrating gesture. "Her father and I were lifelong friends. A very
remarkable man, Melhuish Ridgeway—and a very successful one."

"His daughter comes into a considerable fortune, I understand. . . . Ah, *pardon*—perhaps it is not delicate what I say there."

Andrew Pennington seemed slightly amused.

"Oh, that's pretty common knowledge. Yes, Linnet's a wealthy woman."

"I suppose, though, that the recent slump is bound to affect any stocks, however sound they may be?"

Pennington took a moment or two to answer. He said at last: "That, of course, is true to a certain extent. The position is very difficult in these days."

Poirot murmured, "I should imagine, however, that Madame Doyle has a keen business head."

"That is so. Yes, that is so. Linnet is a clever practical girl."

They came to a halt. The guide proceeded to instruct them on the subject of the temple built by the great Rameses. The four colossi of Rameses himself, one pair on each side of the entrance, hewn out of the living rock, looked down on the little straggling party of tourists.

Signor Richetti, disdaining the remarks of the dragoman, was busy examining the reliefs of Negro and Syrian captives on the bases of the colossi on either side of the entrance.

When the party entered the temple, a sense of dimness and peace came over them. The still vividly coloured reliefs on some of the inner walls were pointed out, but the party tended to break up into groups.

Dr. Bessner read sonorously in German from a Baedeker, pausing every now and then to translate for the benefit of Cornelia, who walked in a docile manner beside him. This was not to continue, however. Miss Van Schuyler, entering on the arm of the phlegmatic Miss Bowers, uttered a commanding "Cornelia, come here," and the instruction had perforce to cease. Dr. Bessner beamed after her vaguely through his thick lenses.

"A very nice maiden, that," he announced to Poirot. "She does not look so starved as some of these young women. No, she has the nice curves. She listens too, very intelligently; it is a pleasure to instruct her."

It fleeted across Poirot's mind that it seemed to be Cornelia's fate either to be bullied or instructed. In any case she was always the listener, never the talker.

Miss Bowers, momentarily released by the peremptory summons of Cornelia, was standing in the middle of the temple, looking about her with her cool, incurious gaze. Her reaction to the wonders of the past was succinct.

"The guide says the name of one of these gods or goddesses was Mut. Can you beat it?"

There was an inner sanctuary where sat four figures eternally presiding, strangely dignified in their dim aloofness.

Before them stood Linnet and her husband. Her arm was in his,
her face lifted—a typical face of the new civilization, intelligent, curious, untouched by the past.

Simon said suddenly: "Let's get out of here. I don't like these four
fellows—especially the one in the high hat."

"That's Amon, I suppose. And that one is Rameses. Why don't
you like them? I think they're very impressive."

"They're a damned sight too impressive; there's something un-
canny about them. Come out into the sunlight."

Linnet laughed but yielded.

They came out of the temple into the sunshine with the sand yellow and warm about their feet. Linnet began to laugh. At their feet in
a row, presenting a momentarily gruesome appearance as though
sawn from their bodies, were the heads of half a dozen Nubian boys.
The eyes rolled, the heads moved rhythmically from side to side, the
lips chanted a new invocation:

"Hip, hip *hurray!* Hip, hip, *hurray!* Very good, very nice. Thank
you very much."

"How absurd! How do they do it? Are they really buried very
deep?"

Simon produced some small change.

"Very good, very nice, very expensive," he mimicked.

Two small boys in charge of the "show" picked up the coins neatly.

Linnet and Simon passed on. They had no wish to return to the
boat, and they were weary of sight-seeing. They settled themselves
with their backs to the cliff and let the warm sun bake them through.

"How lovely the sun is," thought Linnet. "How warm—how
safe. . . . How lovely it is to be happy. . . . How lovely to be me—
me . . . me . . . Linnet . . ."

Her eyes closed. She was half asleep, half awake, drifting in the
midst of thought that was like the sand drifting and blowing.

Simon's eyes were open. They too held contentment. What a fool
he'd been to be rattled that first night. . . . There was nothing to be
rattled about. . . . Everything was all right. . . . After all, one
could trust Jackie—

There was a shout—people running toward him waving their arms
—shouting. . . .

Simon stared stupidly for a moment. Then he sprang to his feet
and dragged Linnet with him.

Not a minute too soon. A big boulder hurtling down the cliff crashed pass them. If Linnet had remained where she was she would have been crushed to atoms.

White-faced they clung together. Hercule Poirot and Tim Allerton ran up to them.

"*Ma foi*, Madame, that was a near thing."

All four instinctively looked up at the cliff. There was nothing to be seen. But there was a path along the top. Poirot remembered seeing some natives walking along there when they had first come ashore.

He looked at the husband and wife. Linnet looked dazed still—bewildered. Simon, however, was inarticulate with rage.

"God damn her!" he ejaculated.

He checked himself with a quick glance at Tim Allerton.

The latter said: "Phew, that was near! Did some fool bowl that thing over, or did it get detached on its own?"

Linnet was very pale. She said with difficulty, "I think—some fool must have done it."

"Might have crushed you like an eggshell. Sure you haven't got an enemy, Linnet?"

Linnet swallowed twice and found a difficulty in answering the light-hearted raillery.

"Come back to the boat, Madame," Poirot said quickly. "You must have a restorative."

They walked there quietly, Simon still full of pent-up rage, Tim trying to talk cheerfully and distract Linnet's mind from the danger she had run, Poirot with a grave face.

And then, just as they reached the gangplank, Simon stopped dead. A look of amazement spread over his face.

Jacqueline de Bellefort was just coming ashore. Dressed in blue gingham, she looked childish this morning.

"Good God!" said Simon under his breath. "So it *was* an accident, after all."

The anger went out of his face. An overwhelming relief showed so plainly that Jacqueline noticed something amiss.

"Good-morning," she said. "I'm afraid I'm a little on the late side."

She gave them all a nod and stepped ashore and proceeded in the direction of the temple.

Simon clutched Poirot's arm. The other two had gone on.

"My God, that's a relief. I thought—I thought—"

Poirot nodded. "Yes, yes, I know what you thought." But he himself still looked grave and preoccupied. He turned his head and noted carefully what had become of the rest of the party from the ship.

Miss Van Schuyler was slowly returning on the arm of Miss Bowers.

A little further away Mrs. Allerton was standing laughing at the little Nubian row of heads. Mrs. Otterbourne was with her.

The others were nowhere in sight.

Poirot shook his head as he followed Simon slowly onto the boat.

CHAPTER 10

"WILL YOU EXPLAIN to me, Madame, the meaning of the word 'fey'?"

Mrs. Allerton looked slightly surprised. She and Poirot were toiling slowly up to the rock overlooking the Second Cataract. Most of the others had gone up on camels, but Poirot had felt that the motion of the camel was slightly reminiscent of that of a ship. Mrs. Allerton had put it on the grounds of personal dignity.

They had arrived at Wâdi Halfa the night before. This morning two launches had conveyed all the party to the Second Cataract, with the exception of Signor Richetti, who had insisted on making an excursion of his own to a remote spot called Semna, which, he explained, was of paramount interest as being the gateway of Nubia in the time of Amenemhet III, and where there was a stele recording the fact that on entering Egypt Negroes must pay custom duties. Everything had been done to discourage this example of individuality, but with no avail. Signor Richetti was determined and had waved aside each objection: (1) that the expedition was not worth making, (2) that the expedition could not be made, owing to the impossibility of getting a car there, (3) that no car could be obtained to do the trip, (4) that a car would be a prohibitive price. Having scoffed at 1, expressed incredulity at 2, offered to find a car himself to 3, and bargained fluently in Arabic for 4, Signor Richetti had at last departed—his departure being arranged in a secret and furtive manner, in case some of the other tourists should take it into their heads to stray from the appointed paths of sight-seeing.

" 'Fey'?" Mrs. Allerton put her head on one side as she considered her reply. "Well, it's a Scotch word, really. It means the kind of exalted happiness that comes before disaster. You know—it's too good to be true."

She enlarged on the theme. Poirot listened attentively.

"I thank you, Madame. I understand now. It is odd that you should have said that yesterday—when Madame Doyle was to escape death so shortly afterward."

Mrs. Allerton gave a little shiver.

"It must have been a very near escape. Do you think some of those little black wretches rolled it over for fun? It's the sort of thing boys might do all over the world—not perhaps really meaning any harm."

Poirot shrugged his shoulders.

"It may be, Madame."

He changed the subject, talking of Majorca and asking various practical questions from the point of view of a possible visit.

Mrs. Allerton had grown to like the little man very much—partly perhaps out of a contradictory spirit. Tim, she felt, was always trying to make her less friendly to Hercule Poirot, whom he summarized firmly as "the worst kind of bounder." But she herself did not call him a bounder; she supposed it was his somewhat foreign exotic clothing which roused her son's prejudices. She herself found him an intelligent and stimulating companion. He was also extremely sympathetic. She found herself suddenly confiding in him her dislike of Joanna Southwood. It eased her to talk of the matter. And after all, why not? He did not know Joanna—would probably never meet her. Why should she not ease herself of that constantly borne burden of jealous thought?

At that same moment Tim and Rosalie Otterbourne were talking of her. Tim had just been half jestingly abusing his luck. His rotten health, never bad enough to be really interesting, yet not good enough for him to have led the life he would have chosen. Very little money, no congenial occupation.

"A thoroughly lukewarm, tame existence," he finished discontentedly.

Rosalie said abruptly, "You've got something heaps of people would envy you."

"What's that?"

"Your mother."

Tim was surprised and pleased.

"Mother? Yes, of course she is quite unique. It's nice of you to see it."

"I think she's marvellous. She looks so lovely—so composed and calm—as though nothing could ever touch her, and yet—and yet somehow she's always ready to be funny about things too. . . ."

Rosalie was stammering slightly in her earnestness.

Tim felt a rising warmth toward the girl. He wished he could return the compliment, but, lamentably, Mrs. Otterbourne was his idea of the world's greatest menace. The inability to respond in kind made him embarrassed.

Miss Van Schuyler had stayed in the launch. She could not risk the ascent either on a camel or on her legs. She had said snappily:

"I'm sorry to have to ask you to stay with me, Miss Bowers. I intended you to go and Cornelia to stay, but girls are so selfish. She rushed off without a word to me. And I actually saw her talking to that very unpleasant and ill-bred young man, Ferguson. Cornelia has disappointed me sadly. She has absolutely no social sense."

Miss Bowers replied in her usual matter-of-fact fashion.

"That's quite all right, Miss Van Schuyler. It would have been a hot walk up there, and I don't fancy the look of those saddles on the camels. Fleas, as likely as not."

She adjusted her glasses, screwed up her eyes to look at the party descending the hill and remarked: "Miss Robson isn't with that young man any more. She's with Dr. Bessner."

Miss Van Schuyler grunted.

Since she had discovered that Dr. Bessner had a large clinic in Czecho-Slovakia and a European reputation as a fashionable physician, she was disposed to be gracious to him. Besides, she might need his professional services before the journey was over.

When the party returned to the *Karnak* Linnet gave a cry of surprise.

"A telegram for me."

She snatched it off the board and tore it open.

"Why—I don't understand—potatoes, beetroots—what does it mean, Simon?"

Simon was just coming to look over her shoulder when a furious voice said, "Excuse me, that telegram is for me," and Signor Richetti snatched it rudely from her hand, fixing her with a furious glare as he did so.

Linnet stared in surprise for a moment, then turned over the envelope.

"Oh, Simon, what a fool I am! It's Richetti—not Ridgeway—and anyway of course my name isn't Ridgeway now. I must apologize."

She followed the little archaeologist up to the stern of the boat.

"I am so sorry, Signor Richetti. You see my name was Ridgeway before I married, and I haven't been married very long, and so—"

She paused, her face dimpled with smiles, inviting him to smile upon a young bride's faux pas.

But Richetti was obviously "not amused." Queen Victoria at her most disapproving could not have looked more grim.

"Names should be read carefully. It is inexcusable to be careless in these matters."

Linnet bit her lip and her colour rose. She was not accustomed to have her apologies received in this fashion. She turned away and, rejoining Simon, said angrily, "These Italians are really insupportable."

"Never mind, darling; let's go and look at that big ivory crocodile you liked."

They went ashore together.

Poirot, watching them walk up the landing stage, heard a sharp indrawn breath. He turned to see Jacqueline de Bellefort at his side. Her hands were clenched on the rail. The expression on her face, as she turned it toward him, quite startled him. It was no longer gay or malicious. She looked devoured by some inner consuming fire.

"They don't care any more." The words came low and fast. "They've got beyond me. I can't reach them. . . . They don't mind if I'm here or not. . . . I can't—I can't hurt them any more. . . ."

Her hands on the rail trembled.

"Mademoiselle—"

She broke in: "Oh, it's too late now—too late for warning. . . . You were right. I ought not to have come. Not on this journey. What did you call it? A journey of the soul? I can't go back; I've got to go on. And I'm going on. They shan't be happy together; they shan't. I'd kill him sooner. . . ."

She turned abruptly away. Poirot, staring after her, felt a hand on his shoulder.

"Your girl friend seems a trifle upset, Monsieur Poirot."

Poirot turned. He stared in surprise, seeing an old acquaintance. "Colonel Race."

The tall bronzed man smiled.

"Bit of a surprise, eh?"

Hercule Poirot had come across Colonel Race a year previously in London. They had been fellow guests at a very strange dinner party— a dinner party that had ended in death for that strange man, their host.

Poirot knew that Race was a man of unadvertised goings and comings. He was usually to be found in one of the outposts of Empire where trouble was brewing.

"So you are here at Wâdi Halfa," he remarked thoughtfully.

"I am here on this boat."

"You mean?"

"That I am making the return journey with you to Shellâl."

Hercule Poirot's eyebrows rose.

"That is very interesting. Shall we, perhaps, have a little drink?"

They went into the observation saloon, now quite empty. Poirot ordered a whisky for the Colonel and a double orangeade full of sugar for himself.

"So you make the return journey with us," said Poirot as he sipped. "You would go faster, would you not, on the Government steamer, which travels by night as well as day?"

Colonel Race's face creased appreciatively.

"You're right on the spot as usual, Monsieur Poirot," he said pleasantly.

"It is, then, the passengers?"

"One of the passengers."

"Now which one, I wonder?" Hercule Poirot asked of the ornate ceiling.

"Unfortunately I don't know myself," said Race ruefully.

Poirot looked interested.

Race said: "There's no need to be mysterious to you. We've had a good deal of trouble out here—one way and another. It isn't the people who ostensibly lead the rioters that we're after. It's the men who very cleverly put the match to the gunpowder. There were three of them. One's dead. One's in prison. I want the third man—a man with five or six cold-blooded murders to his credit. He's one of the cleverest paid agitators that ever existed. . . . He's on this boat. I know that from a passage in a letter that passed through our hands. Decoded it said: 'X will be on the *Karnak* trip February seventh to thirteenth.' It didn't say under what name X would be passing."

"Have you any description of him?"

"No. American, Irish and French descent. Bit of a mongrel. That doesn't help us much. Have you got any ideas?"

"An idea—it is all very well," said Poirot meditatively.

Such was the understanding between them that Race pressed him no further. He knew that Hercule Poirot did not ever speak unless he was sure.

Poirot rubbed his nose and said unhappily, "There passes itself something on this boat that causes me much inquietude."

Race looked at him inquiringly.

"Figure to yourself," said Poirot, "a person A who has grievously wronged a person B. The person B desires the revenge. The person B makes the threats."

"A and B being both on this boat?"

Poirot nodded. "Precisely."

"And B, I gather, being a woman?"

"Exactly."

Race lit a cigarette.

"I shouldn't worry. People who go about talking of what they are going to do don't usually do it."

"And particularly is that the case with *les femmes,* you would say! Yes, that is true."

But he still did not look happy.

"Anything else?" asked Race.

"Yes, there is something. Yesterday the person A had a very near escape from death, the kind of death that might very conveniently be called an accident."

"Engineered by B?"

"No, that is just the point. B could have had nothing to do with it."

"Then it *was* an accident."

"I suppose so—but I do not like such accidents."

"You're quite sure B could have had no hand in it?"

"Absolutely."

"Oh, well, coincidences do happen. Who is A, by the way? A particularly disagreeable person?"

"On the contrary. A is a charming, rich and beautiful young lady."

Race grinned.

"Sounds quite like a novelette."

"*Peut-être.* But I tell you, I am not happy, my friend. If I am right, and after all I am constantly in the habit of being right"—Race smiled into his moustache at this typical utterance—"then there is matter for grave inquietude. And now, *you* come to add yet another complication. You tell me that there is a man on the *Karnak* who kills."

"He doesn't usually kill charming young ladies."

Poirot shook his head in a dissatisfied manner.

"I am afraid, my friend," he said. "I am afraid. . . . Today, I advised this lady, Madame Doyle, to go with her husband to Khartûm, not to return on this boat. But they would not agree. I pray to Heaven that we may arrive at Shellâl without catastrophe."

"Aren't you taking rather a gloomy view?"

Poirot shook his head.

"I am afraid," he said simply. "Yes, I, Hercule Poirot, am afraid. . . ."

CHAPTER 11

CORNELIA ROBSON stood inside the temple of Abu Simbel. It was the evening of the following day—a hot still evening. The *Karnak* was anchored once more at Abu Simbel to permit a second visit to be made to the temple, this time by artificial light. The difference this made was considerable, and Cornelia commented wonderingly on the fact to Mr. Ferguson, who was standing by her side.

"Why, you see it ever so much better now!" she exclaimed. "All those enemies having their heads cut off by the King—they just stand right out. That's a cute kind of castle there that I never noticed before. I wish Dr. Bessner was here, he'd tell me what it was."

"How you can stand that old fool beats me," said Ferguson gloomily.

"Why, he's just one of the kindest men I've ever met!"

"Pompous old bore."

"I don't think you ought to speak that way."

The young man gripped her suddenly by the arm. They were just emerging from the temple into the moonlight.

"Why do you stick being bored by fat old men—and bullied and snubbed by a vicious old harridan?"

"Why, Mr. Ferguson!"

"Haven't you got any spirit? Don't you know you're just as good as she is?"

"But I'm not!" Cornelia spoke with honest conviction.

"You're not as rich; that's all you mean."

"No, it isn't. Cousin Marie's very, very cultured, and—"

"Cultured!" The young man let go of her arm as suddenly as he had taken it. "That word makes me sick."

Cornelia looked at him in alarm.

"She doesn't like you talking to me, does she?" asked the young man.

Cornelia blushed and looked embarrassed.

"Why? Because she thinks I'm not her social equal! Pah! Doesn't that make you see red?"

Cornelia faltered out, "I wish you wouldn't get so mad about things."

"Don't you realize—and you an American—that everyone is born free and equal?"

"They're not," said Cornelia with calm certainty.

"My good girl, it's part of your constitution!"

"Cousin Marie says politicians aren't gentlemen," said Cornelia. "And of course people aren't equal. It doesn't make sense. I know I'm kind of homely looking, and I used to feel mortified about it sometimes, but I've got over that. I'd like to have been born elegant and beautiful like Mrs. Doyle, but I wasn't, so I guess it's no use worrying."

"Mrs. Doyle!" exclaimed Ferguson with deep contempt. "She's the sort of woman who ought to be shot as an example."

Cornelia looked at him anxiously.

"I believe it's your digestion," she said kindly. "I've got a special kind of pepsin that Cousin Marie tried once. Would you like to try it?"

Mr. Ferguson said, "You're impossible!"

He turned and strode away. Cornelia went on toward the boat. Just as she was crossing onto the gangway, he caught her up once more.

"You're the nicest person on the boat," he said. "And mind you remember it."

Blushing with pleasure Cornelia repaired to the observation saloon. Miss Van Schuyler was conversing with Dr. Bessner—an agreeable conversation dealing with certain royal patients of his.

Cornelia said guiltily, "I do hope I haven't been a long time, Cousin Marie."

Glancing at her watch the old lady snapped: "You haven't exactly hurried, my dear. And what have you done with my velvet stole?"

Cornelia looked round.

"Shall I see if it's in the cabin, Cousin Marie?"

"Of course it isn't! I had it just after dinner in here, and I haven't moved out of the place. It was on that chair."

Cornelia made a desultory search.

"I can't see it anywhere, Cousin Marie."

"Nonsense!" said Miss Van Schuyler. "Look about." It was an order such as one might give to a dog, and in her doglike fashion Cornelia obeyed. The quiet Mr. Fanthorp, who was sitting at a table near by, rose and assisted her. But the stole could not be found.

The day had been such an unusually hot and sultry one that most people had retired early after going ashore to view the temple. The Doyles were playing Bridge with Pennington and Race at a table in a corner. The only other occupant of the saloon was Hercule Poirot, who was yawning his head off at a small table near the door.

Miss Van Schuyler, making a Royal Progress bedward, with Cornelia and Miss Bowers in attendance, paused by his chair. He sprang politely to his feet, stifling a yawn of gargantuan dimensions.

Miss Van Schuyler said: "I have only just realized Who you are, Monsieur Poirot. I may tell you that I have heard of you from my old friend Rufus Van Aldin. You must tell me about your cases sometime."

Poirot, his eyes twinkling a little through their sleepiness, bowed in an exaggerated manner. With a kindly but condescending nod, Miss Van Schuyler passed on.

Poirot yawned once more. He felt heavy and stupid with sleep and could hardly keep his eyes open. He glanced over at the Bridge players, absorbed in their game, then at young Fanthorp, who was deep in a book. Apart from them the saloon was empty.

He passed through the swinging door out onto the deck. Jacqueline de Bellefort, coming precipitately along the deck, almost collided with him.

"Pardon, Mademoiselle."

She said, "You look sleepy, Monsieur Poirot."

He admitted it frankly.

"*Mais oui*—I am consumed with sleep. I can hardly keep my eyes open. It has been a day very close and oppressive."

"Yes." She seemed to brood over it. "It's been the sort of day when things—snap! Break! When one can't go on. . . ."

Her voice was low and charged with passion. She looked not at him, but toward the sandy shore. Her hands were clenched, rigid. . . .

Suddenly the tension relaxed. She said, "Good-night, Monsieur Poirot."

"Good-night, Mademoiselle."

Her eyes met his, just for a swift moment. Thinking it over the next day, he came to the conclusion that there had been appeal in that glance. He was to remember it afterward. . . .

Then he passed on to his cabin and she went toward the saloon.

Cornelia, having dealt with Miss Van Schuyler's many needs and fantasies, took some needlework with her back to the saloon. She herself did not feel in the least sleepy. On the contrary she felt wide awake and slightly excited.

The Bridge four were still at it. In another chair the quiet Fanthorp read a book. Cornelia sat down to her needlework.

Suddenly the door opened and Jacqueline de Bellefort came in. She stood in the doorway, her head thrown back. Then she pressed a bell and sauntered across to Cornelia and sat down.

"Been ashore?" she asked.

"Yes. I thought it was just fascinating in the moonlight."

Jacqueline nodded.

"Yes, lovely night. . . . A real honeymoon night."

Her eyes went to the Bridge table—rested a moment on Linnet Doyle.

The boy came in answer to the bell. Jacqueline ordered a double gin. As she gave the order Simon Doyle shot a quick glance at her. A faint line of anxiety showed between his eyebrows.

His wife said, "Simon, we're waiting for you to call."

Jacqueline hummed a little tune to herself. When the drink came, she picked it up, said, "Well, here's to crime," drank it off and ordered another.

Again Simon looked across from the Bridge table. His calls became slightly absent-minded. His partner, Pennington, took him to task.

Jacqueline began to hum again, at first under her breath, then louder:

"*He was her man and he did her wrong . . .*"

"Sorry," said Simon to Pennington. "Stupid of me not to return your lead. That gives 'em rubber."

Linnet rose to her feet.

"I'm sleepy. I think I'll go to bed."

"About time to turn in," said Colonel Race.

"I'm with you," agreed Pennington.

"Coming, Simon?"

Doyle said slowly: "Not just yet. I think I'll have a drink first."

Linnet nodded and went out. Race followed her. Pennington finished his drink and then followed suit.

Cornelia began to gather up her embroidery.

"Don't go to bed, Miss Robson," said Jacqueline. "Please don't. I feel like making a night of it. Don't desert me."

Cornelia sat down again.

"We girls must stick together," said Jacqueline.

She threw back her head and laughed—a shrill laugh without merriment.

The second drink came.

"Have something," said Jacqueline.

"No, thank you very much," replied Cornelia.

Jacqueline tilted back her chair. She hummed now loudly:

"He was her man and he did her wrong . . ."

Mr. Fanthorp turned a page of *Europe from Within*.

Simon Doyle picked up a magazine.

"Really, I think I'll go to bed," said Cornelia. "It's getting very late."

"You can't go to bed yet," Jacqueline declared. "I forbid you to. Tell me all about yourself."

"Well—I don't know. There isn't much to tell," Cornelia faltered. "I've just lived at home, and I haven't been around much. This is my first trip to Europe. I'm just loving every minute of it."

Jacqueline laughed.

"You're a happy sort of person, aren't you? God, I'd like to be you."

"Oh! would you? But I mean—I'm sure—"

Cornelia felt flustered. Undoubtedly Miss de Bellefort was drinking too much. That wasn't exactly a novelty to Cornelia. She had seen plenty of drunkenness during Prohibition years. But there was something else. . . . Jacqueline de Bellefort was talking to her—was looking at her—and yet, Cornelia felt, it was as though, somehow, she was talking to someone else. . . .

But there were only two other people in the room, Mr. Fanthorp and Mr. Doyle. Mr. Fanthorp seemed quite absorbed in his book. Mr. Doyle was looking rather odd—a queer sort of watchful look on his face. . . .

Jacqueline said again, "Tell me all about yourself."

Always obedient, Cornelia tried to comply. She talked, rather heavily, going into unnecessary small details about her daily life. She was so unused to being the talker. Her rôle was so constantly that of listener. And yet Miss de Bellefort seemed to want to know. When Cornelia faltered to a standstill, the other girl was quick to prompt her.

"Go on—tell me more."

And so Cornelia went on ("Of course, Mother's very delicate—some days she touches nothing but cereals—") unhappily conscious that all she said was supremely uninteresting, yet flattered by the other girl's seeming interest. But was she interested? Wasn't she, somehow, listening to something else—or, perhaps, *for* something else? She was looking at Cornelia, yes, but wasn't there really *someone else,* sitting in the room.

"And of course we get very good art classes, and last winter I had a course of—"

(How late was it? Surely very late. She had been talking and talking. If only something definite would happen—)

And immediately, as though in answer to the wish, something did happen. Only, at the moment, it seemed very natural.

Jacqueline turned her head and spoke to Simon Doyle.

"Ring the bell, Simon. I want another drink."

Simon Doyle looked up from his magazine and said quietly: "The stewards have gone to bed. It's after midnight."

"I tell you I want another drink."

Simon said, "You've had quite enough drinks, Jackie."

She swung round at him.

"What damned business is it of yours?"

He shrugged his shoulders. "None."

She watched him for a minute or two. Then she said: "What's the matter, Simon? Are you afraid?"

Simon did not answer. Rather elaborately he picked up his magazine again.

Cornelia murmured, "Oh, dear—as late as that—I must—"

She began to fumble, dropped a thimble. . . .

Jacqueline said: "Don't go to bed. I'd like another woman here—to support me." She began to laugh again. "Do you know what Simon over there is afraid of? He's afraid *I'm* going to tell you the story of *my* life."

"Oh—er—" Cornelia spluttered a little.

Jacqueline said clearly, "You see, he and I were once engaged."

"Oh, really?"

Cornelia was the prey of conflicting emotions. She was deeply embarrassed but at the same time pleasurably thrilled. How—how *black* Simon Doyle was looking.

"Yes, it's a very sad story," said Jacqueline; her soft voice was low and mocking. "He treated me rather badly, didn't you, Simon?"

Simon Doyle said brutally: "Go to bed, Jackie. You're drunk."

"If you're embarrassed, Simon dear, you'd better leave the room."

Simon Doyle looked at her. The hand that held the magazine shook a little, but he spoke bluntly.

"I'm staying," he said.

Cornelia murmured for the third time, "I really must—it's so late—"

"You're not to go," said Jacqueline. Her hand shot out and held the other girl in her chair. "You're to stay and hear what I've got to say."

"Jackie," said Simon sharply, "you're making a fool of yourself! For God's sake, go to bed."

Jacqueline sat up suddenly in her chair. Words poured from her rapidly in a soft hissing stream.

"You're afraid of a scene, aren't you? That's because you're so English—so reticent! You want me to behave 'decently,' don't you? But I don't care whether I behave decently or not! You'd better get out of here quickly—because I'm going to talk—a lot."

Jim Fanthorp carefully shut his book, yawned, glanced at his watch, got up and strolled out. It was a very British and utterly unconvincing performance.

Jacqueline swung round in her chair and glared at Simon.

"You damned fool," she said thickly, "do you think you can treat me as you have done and get away with it?"

Simon Doyle opened his lips, then shut them again. He sat quite still as though he were hoping that her outburst would exhaust itself if he said nothing to provoke her further.

Jacqueline's voice came thick and blurred. It fascinated Cornelia, totally unused to naked emotions of any kind.

"I told you," said Jacqueline, "that I'd kill you sooner than see you go to another woman. . . . You don't think I meant that? *You're wrong.* I've only been—waiting! You're *my* man! Do you hear? You belong to me. . . ."

Still Simon did not speak. Jacqueline's hand fumbled a moment or two on her lap. She leant forward.

"I told you I'd kill you, and I meant it. . . ." Her hand came up suddenly with something in it that flashed and gleamed. "I'll shoot you like a dog—like the dirty dog you are. . . ."

Now at last Simon acted. He sprang to his feet, but at the same moment she pulled the trigger. . . .

Simon half twisted—fell across a chair. . . . Cornelia screamed and rushed to the door. Jim Fanthorp was on the deck leaning over the rail. She called to him.

"Mr. Fanthorp . . . Mr. Fanthorp . . ."

He ran to her; she clutched at him incoherently. . . .

"She's shot him—Oh! she's shot him. . . ."

Simon Doyle still lay as he had fallen half into and across a chair. . . . Jacqueline stood as though paralysed. She was trembling violently, and her eyes, dilated and frightened, were staring at the crimson stain slowly soaking through Simon's trouser leg just below the knee where he held a handkerchief close against the wound. . . .

She stammered out:

"I didn't mean . . . Oh, my God, I didn't really mean . . ."

The pistol dropped from her nervous fingers with a clatter on the floor. She kicked it away with her foot. It slid under one of the settees.

Simon, his voice faint, murmured: "Fanthorp, for Heaven's sake—there's someone coming. . . . Say it's all right—an accident—something. There mustn't be a scandal over this."

Fanthorp nodded in quick comprehension. He wheeled round to the door where a startled Nubian face showed. He said: "All right—all right! Just fun!"

The black face looked doubtful, puzzled, then reassured. The teeth showed in a wide grin. The boy nodded and went off.

Fanthorp turned back.

"That's all right. Don't think anybody else heard. Only sounded like a cork, you know. Now the next thing—"

He was startled. Jacqueline suddenly began to weep hysterically.

"Oh, God, I wish I were dead. . . . I'll kill myself. I'll be better dead. . . . Oh, what have I done—what have I done?"

Cornelia hurried to her.

"Hush, dear, hush."

Simon, his brow wet, his face twisted with pain, said urgently:

"Get her away. For God's sake, get her out of here! Get her to her cabin, Fanthorp. Look here, Miss Robson, get that hospital nurse of yours." He looked appealingly from one to the other of them. "Don't leave her. Make quite sure she's safe with the nurse looking after her. Then get hold of old Bessner and bring him here. For God's sake, don't let any news of this get to my wife."

Jim Fanthorp nodded comprehendingly. The quiet young man was cool and competent in an emergency.

Between them he and Cornelia got the weeping, struggling girl out of the saloon and along the deck to her cabin. There they had more trouble with her. She fought to free herself; her sobs redoubled.

"I'll drown myself . . . I'll drown myself. . . . I'm not fit to live. . . . Oh, Simon—Simon!"

Fanthorp said to Cornelia: "Better get hold of Miss Bowers. I'll stay while you get her."

Cornelia nodded and hurried out.

As soon as she left, Jacqueline clutched Fanthorp.

"His leg—it's bleeding—broken. . . . He may bleed to death. I must go to him. . . . Oh, Simon—Simon—how could I?"

Her voice rose. Fanthorp said urgently: "Quietly—quietly. . . . He'll be all right."

She began to struggle again.

"Let me go! Let me throw myself overboard. . . . Let me kill myself!"

Fanthorp, holding her by the shoulders, forced her back onto the bed.

"You must stay here. Don't make a fuss. Pull yourself together. It's all right, I tell you."

To his relief, the distraught girl did manage to control herself a little, but he was thankful when the curtains were pushed aside and the efficient Miss Bowers, neatly dressed in a hideous kimono, entered, accompanied by Cornelia.

"Now then," said Miss Bowers briskly, "what's all this?"

She took charge without any sign of surprise and alarm.

Fanthorp thankfully left the overwrought girl in her capable hands and hurried along to the cabin occupied by Dr. Bessner. He knocked and entered on the top of the knock.

"Dr. Bessner?"

A terrific snore resolved itself, and a startled voice asked: "So? What is it?"

By this time Fanthorp had switched the light on. The doctor blinked up at him, looking rather like a large owl.

"It's Doyle. He's been shot. Miss de Bellefort shot him. He's in the saloon. Can you come?"

The stout doctor reacted promptly. He asked a few curt questions, pulled on his bedroom slippers and a dressing-gown, picked up a little case of necessaries and accompanied Fanthorp to the lounge.

Simon had managed to get the window beside him open. He was leaning his head against it, inhaling the air. His face was a ghastly colour.

Dr. Bessner came over to him.

"Ha? So? What have we here?"

A handkerchief sodden with blood lay on the carpet and on the carpet itself was a dark stain.

The doctor's examination was punctuated with Teutonic grunts and exclamations.

"Yes, it is bad this. . . . The bone is fractured. And a big loss of blood. Herr Fanthorp, you and I must get him to my cabin. So—like this. He cannot walk. We must carry him, thus."

As they lifted him Cornelia appeared in the doorway. Catching sight of her, the doctor uttered a grunt of satisfaction.

"Ach, it is you? Goot. Come with us. I have need of assistance. You will be better than my friend here. He looks a little pale already."

Fanthorp emitted a rather sickly smile.

"Shall I get Miss Bowers?" he asked.

Dr. Bessner threw a considering glance over Cornelia.

"You will do very well, young lady," he announced. "You will not faint or be foolish, hein?"

"I can do what you tell me," said Cornelia eagerly.

Bessner nodded in a satisfied fashion.

The procession passed along the deck.

The next ten minutes was purely surgical and Mr. Jim Fanthorp did not enjoy it at all. He felt secretly ashamed of the superior fortitude exhibited by Cornelia.

"So, that is the best I can do," announced Dr. Bessner at last. "You have been a hero, my friend." He patted Simon approvingly on the shoulder. Then he rolled up his sleeve and produced a hypodermic needle.

"And now I will give you something to make you sleep. Your wife, what about her?"

Simon said weakly: "She needn't know till the morning. . . ." He went on: "I—you mustn't blame Jackie. . . . It's been all my fault. I treated her disgracefully . . . poor kid—she didn't know what she was doing. . . ."

Dr. Bessner nodded comprehendingly.

"Yes, yes—I understand . . ."

"My fault—" Simon urged. His eyes went to Cornelia. "Someone—ought to—stay with her. She might—hurt herself—"

Dr. Bessner injected the needle. Cornelia said, with quiet competence: "It's all right, Mr. Doyle. Miss Bowers is going to stay with her all night. . . ."

A grateful look flashed over Simon's face. His body relaxed. His eyes closed. Suddenly he jerked them open. "Fanthorp?"

"Yes, Doyle."

"The pistol . . . ought not to leave it . . . lying about. The boys will find it in the morning. . . ."

Fanthorp nodded. "Quite right. I'll go and get hold of it now."

He went out of the cabin and along the deck. Miss Bowers appeared at the door of Jacqueline's cabin.

"She'll be all right now," she announced. "I've given her a morphine injection."

"But you'll stay with her?"

"Oh, yes. Morphia excites some people. I shall stay all night."

Fanthorp went on to the lounge.

Some three minutes later there was a tap on Bessner's cabin door.

"Dr. Bessner?"

"Yes?" The stout man appeared.

Fanthorp beckoned him out on the deck.

"Look here—I can't find that pistol. . . ."

"What is that?"

"The pistol. It dropped out of the girl's hand. She kicked it away and it went under a settee. It isn't under that settee now."

They stared at each other.

"But who can have taken it?"

Fanthorp shrugged his shoulders.

Bessner said: "It is curious, that. But I do not see what we can do about it."

Puzzled and vaguely alarmed, the two men separated.

CHAPTER 12

HERCULE POIROT was just wiping the lather from his freshly shaved face when there was a quick tap on the door, and hard on top of it Colonel Race entered unceremoniously. He closed the door behind him.

He said: "Your instinct was quite correct. It's happened."

Poirot straightened up and asked sharply: "What has happened?"

"Linnet Doyle's dead—shot through the head last night."

Poirot was silent for a minute, two memories vividly before him—a girl in a garden at Assuan saying in a hard breathless voice, "I'd like to put my dear little pistol against her head and just press the trigger," and another more recent memory, the same voice saying, "One feels one can't go on—the kind of day when something breaks"—and that strange momentary flash of appeal in her eyes. What had been the matter with him not to respond to that appeal? He had been blind, deaf, stupid with his need for sleep. . . .

Race went on: "I've got some slight official standing; they sent for me, put it in my hands. The boat's due to start in half an hour, but it will be delayed till I give the word. There's a possibility, of course, that the murderer came from the shore."

Poirot shook his head.

Race acquiesced in the gesture.

"I agree. One can pretty well rule that out. Well, man, it's up to you. This is your show."

Poirot had been attiring himself with a neat-fingered celerity. He said now, "I am at your disposal."

The two men stepped out on the deck.

Race said: "Bessner should be there by now. I sent the steward for him."

There were four cabins de luxe, with bathrooms, on the boat. Of the two on the port side one was occupied by Dr. Bessner, the other by Andrew Pennington. On the starboard side the first was occupied by Miss Van Schuyler, and the one next to it by Linnet Doyle. Her husband's dressing cabin was next door.

A white-faced steward was standing outside the door of Linnet Doyle's cabin. He opened the door for them and they passed inside. Dr. Bessner was bending over the bed. He looked up and grunted as the other two entered.

"What can you tell us, Doctor, about this business?" asked Race.

Bessner rubbed his unshaven jaw meditatively.

"Ach! She was shot—shot at close quarters. See—here, just above the ear—that is where the bullet entered. A very little bullet—I should say a twenty-two. The pistol, it was held close against her head; see, there is blackening here, the skin is scorched."

Again in a sick wave of memory Poirot thought of those words uttered at Assuan.

Bessner went on: "She was asleep; there was no struggle; the murderer crept up in the dark and shot her as she lay there."

"*Ah! non!*" Poirot cried out. His sense of psychology was outraged. Jacqueline de Bellefort creeping into a darkened cabin, pistol in hand —No, it did not "fit," that picture.

Bessner stared at him through his thick lenses.

"But that is what happened, I tell you."

"Yes, yes. I did not mean what you thought. I was not contradicting you."

Bessner gave a satisfied grunt.

Poirot came up and stood beside him. Linnet Doyle was lying on her side. Her attitude was natural and peaceful. But above the ear was a tiny hole with an incrustation of dried blood round it.

Poirot shook his head sadly.

Then his gaze fell on the white painted wall just in front of him and he drew in his breath sharply. Its white neatness was marred by a big wavering letter J scrawled in some brownish-red medium.

Poirot stared at it, then he leaned over the dead girl and very gently picked up her right hand. One finger of it was stained a brownish-red.

"*Nom d'un nom d'un nom!*" ejaculated Hercule Poirot.

"Eh? What is that?"

Dr. Bessner looked up.

"Ach! *That.*"

Race said: "Well, I'm damned. What do you make of that, Poirot?"

Poirot swayed a little on his toes.

"You ask me what I make of it. *Eh bien,* it is very simple, is it not? Madame Doyle is dying; she wishes to indicate her murderer, and so she writes with her finger, dipped in her own blood, the initial letter of her murderer's name. Oh, yes, it is astonishingly simple."

"Ach! but—"

Dr. Bessner was about to break out, but a peremptory gesture from Race silenced him.

"So it strikes you like that?" he asked slowly.

Poirot turned round on him nodding his head.

"Yes, yes. It is, as I say, of an astonishing simplicity! It is so familiar, is it not? It has been done so often, in the pages of the romance of crime! It is now, indeed, a little *vieux jeu!* It leads one to suspect that our murderer is—old-fashioned!"

Race drew a long breath.

"I see," he said. "I thought at first—" He stopped.

Poirot said with a very faint smile: "That I believed in all the old clichés of melodrama? But pardon, Dr. Bessner, you were about to say—?"

Bessner broke out gutturally: "What do I say? Pah! I say it is absurd; it is the nonsense! The poor lady she died instantaneously. To dip her finger in the blood (and as you see, there is hardly any blood) and write the letter J upon the wall— Bah—it is the nonsense— the melodramatic nonsense!"

"*C'es l'enfantillage,*" agreed Poirot.

"But it was done with a purpose," suggested Race.

"That—naturally," agreed Poirot, and his face was grave.

"What does J stand for?" asked Race.

Poirot replied promptly: "J stands for Jacqueline de Bellefort, a young lady who declared to me less than a week ago that she would like nothing better than to—" he paused and then deliberately quoted, "'to put my dear little pistol close against her head and then just press with my finger. . . .'"

"*Gott im Himmel!*" exclaimed Dr. Bessner.

There was a momentary silence. Then Race drew a deep breath and said: "Which is just what was done here?"

Bessner nodded.

"That is so, yes. It was a pistol of very small calibre—as I say probably a twenty-two. The bullet has got to be extracted, of course, before we can say definitely."

Race nodded in swift comprehension. Then he asked: "What about time of death?"

Bessner stroked his jaw again. His finger made a rasping sound.

"I would not care to be too precise. It is now eight o'clock. I will say, with due regard to the temperature last night, that she has been dead certainly six hours and probably not longer than eight."

"That puts it between midnight and two A.M."

"That is so."

There was a pause. Race looked round.

"What about her husband? I suppose he sleeps in the cabin next door."

"At the moment," said Dr. Bessner, "he is asleep in my cabin."

Both men looked very surprised.

Bessner nodded his head several times.

"Ach, so. I see you have not been told about that. Mr. Doyle was shot last night in the saloon."

"Shot? By whom?"

"By the young lady, Jacqueline de Bellefort."

Race asked sharply, "Is he badly hurt?"

"Yes, the bone was splintered. I have done all that is possible at the moment, but it is necessary, you understand, that the fracture should be X-rayed as soon as possible and proper treatment given such as is impossible on this boat."

Poirot murmured, "Jacqueline de Bellefort."

His eyes went again to the J on the wall.

Race said abruptly: "If there is nothing more we can do here for the moment, let's go below. The management has put the smoking-room at our disposal. We must get the details of what happened last night."

They left the cabin. Race locked the door and took the key with him.

S.S. KARNAK
PROMENADE DECK

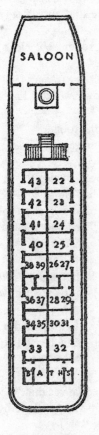

43	22 JAMES FANTHORP
42	23 TIM ALLERTON
41 CORNELIA ROBSON	24 MRS ALLERTON
40 JACQUELINE DE BELLEFORT	25 SIMON DOYLE
38 39 ANDREW PENNINGTON	26 27 LINNET DOYLE
36 37 DR BESSNER	28 29 MISS VAN SCHUYLER
34 35 MRS AND MISS OTTERBOURNE	30 31 HERCULE POIROT
33 MISS BOWERS	32 COLONEL RACE

PLAN   CABINS

"We can come back later," he said. "The first thing to do is to get all the facts clear."

They went down to the deck below, where they found the Manager of the *Karnak* waiting uneasily in the doorway of the smoking-room.

The poor man was terribly upset and worried over the whole business, and was eager to leave everything in Colonel Race's hands.

"I feel I can't do better than leave it to you, sir, seeing your official position. I'd had orders to put myself at your disposal in the—er—other matter. If you will take charge, I'll see that everything is done as you wish."

"Good man! To begin with I'd like this room kept clear for me and for Monsieur Poirot during the inquiry."

"Certainly, sir."

"That's all at present. Go on with your own work. I know where to find you."

Looking slightly relieved the Manager left the room.

Race said, "Sit down, Bessner, and let's have the whole story of what happened last night."

They listened in silence to the doctor's rumbling voice.

"Clear enough," said Race, when he had finished. "The girl worked herself up, helped by a drink or two, and finally took a pot shot at the man with a twenty-two pistol. Then she went along to Linnet Doyle's cabin and shot her as well."

But Dr. Bessner was shaking his head.

"No, no. I do not think so. I do not think that was *possible*. For one thing she would not write her own initial on the wall; it would be ridiculous, *nicht wahr?*"

"She might," Race declared, "if she were as blindly mad and jealous as she sounds; she might want to—well—sign her name to the crime, so to speak."

Poirot shook his head.

"No, no, I do not think she would be as—as *crude* as that."

"Then there's only one reason for that J. It was put there by someone else deliberately to throw suspicion on her."

Bessner nodded.

"Yes, and the criminal was unlucky, because, you see, it is not only *unlikely* that the young Fräulein did the murder; it is also I think *impossible*."

"How's that?"

Bessner explained Jacqueline's hysterics and the circumstances which had led Miss Bowers to take charge of her.

"And I think—I am sure—that Miss Bowers stayed with her all night."

Race said, "If that's so, it's going to simplify matters very much."

"Who discovered the crime?" Poirot asked.

"Mrs. Doyle's maid, Louise Bourget. She went to call her mistress as usual, found her dead, and came out and flopped into the steward's arms in a dead faint. He went to the Manager, who came to me. I got hold of Bessner and then came for you."

Poirot nodded.

Race said: "Doyle's got to know. You say he's asleep still?"

Bessner nodded. "Yes, he's still asleep in my cabin. I gave him a strong opiate last night."

Race turned to Poirot.

"Well," he said, "I don't think we need detain the doctor any longer, eh? Thank you, Doctor."

Bessner rose. "I will have my breakfast, yes. And then I will go back to my cabin and see if Mr. Doyle is ready to wake."

"Thanks."

Bessner went out. The two men looked at each other.

"Well, what about it, Poirot?" Race asked. "You're the man in charge. I'll take my orders from you. You say what's to be done."

Poirot bowed.

"*Eh bien,*" he said; "we must hold the court of inquiry. First of all, I think we must verify the story of the affair last night. That is to say, we must question Fanthorp and Miss Robson, who were the actual witnesses of what occurred. The disappearance of the pistol is very significant."

Race rang a bell and sent a message by the steward.

Poirot sighed and shook his head. "It is bad, this," he murmured. "It is bad."

"Have you any ideas?" asked Race curiously.

"My ideas conflict. They are not well arranged; they are not orderly. There is, you see, the big fact that this girl hated Linnet Doyle and wanted to kill her."

"You think she's capable of it?"

"I think so—yes." Poirot sounded doubtful.

"But not in this way? That's what's worrying you, isn't it? Not to creep into her cabin in the dark and shoot her while she was sleeping. It's the cold-bloodedness that strikes you as not ringing true?"

"In a sense, yes."

"You think that this girl, Jacqueline de Bellefort, is incapable of a premeditated cold-blooded murder?"

Poirot said slowly: "I am not sure, you see. She would have the brains—yes. But I doubt if, physically, she could bring herself to do the *act*. . . ."

Race nodded. "Yes, I see. . . . Well, according to Bessner's story, it would also have been physically impossible."

"If that is true it clears the ground considerably. Let us hope it is true." Poirot paused and then added simply: "I shall be glad if it is so, for I have for that little one much sympathy."

The door opened and Fanthorp and Cornelia came in. Bessner followed them.

Cornelia gasped out: "Isn't this just awful? Poor, poor Mrs. Doyle! And she was so lovely too. It must have been a real *fiend* who could hurt her! And poor Mr. Doyle; he'll just go half crazy when he knows! Why, even last night he was so frightfully worried lest she should hear about his accident."

"That is just what we want you to tell us about, Miss Robson," said Race. "We want to know exactly what happened last night."

Cornelia began a little confusedly, but a question or two from Poirot helped matters.

"Ah, yes, I understand. After the Bridge, Madame Doyle went to her cabin. Did she really go to her cabin, I wonder?"

"She did," said Race. "I actually saw her. I said good-night to her at the door."

"And the time?"

"Mercy, I couldn't say," replied Cornelia.

"It was twenty past eleven," said Race.

"*Bien.* Then at twenty past eleven, Madame Doyle was alive and well. At that moment there was, in the saloon, who?"

Fanthorp answered: "Doyle was there. And Miss de Bellefort. Myself and Miss Robson."

"That's so," agreed Cornelia. "Mr. Pennington had a drink and then went off to bed."

"That was how much later?"

"Oh, about three or four minutes."

"Before half past eleven, then?"

"Oh, yes."

"So that there were left in the saloon you, Mademoiselle Robson, Mademoiselle de Bellefort, Monsieur Doyle and Monsieur Fanthorp. What were you all doing?"

"Mr. Fanthorp was reading a book. I'd got some embroidery. Miss de Bellefort was—she was—"

Fanthorp came to the rescue. "She was drinking pretty heavily."

"Yes," agreed Cornelia. "She was talking to me mostly and asking me about things at home. And she kept saying things—to me mostly, but I think they were kind of meant for Mr. Doyle. He was getting kind of mad at her, but he didn't say anything. I think he thought if he kept quiet she might simmer down."

"But she didn't?"

Cornelia shook her head.

"I tried to go once or twice, but she made me stay, and I was getting very, very uncomfortable. And then Mr. Fanthorp got up and went out—"

"It was a little embarrassing," said Fanthorp. "I thought I'd make an unobtrusive exit. Miss de Bellefort was clearly working up for a scene."

"And then she pulled out the pistol," went on Cornelia, "and Mr. Doyle jumped up to try and get it away from her, and it went off and shot him through the leg; and then she began to sob and cry—and I was scared to death and ran out after Mr. Fanthorp, and he came back with me, and Mr. Doyle said not to make a fuss, and one of the Nubian boys heard the noise of the shot and came along, but Mr. Fanthorp told him it was all right; and then we got Jacqueline away to her cabin, and Mr. Fanthorp stayed with her while I got Miss Bowers."

Cornelia paused breathless.

"What time was this?" asked Race.

Cornelia said again, "Mercy, I don't know," but Fanthorp answered promptly:

"It must have been about twenty minutes past twelve. I know that it was actually half past twelve when I finally got to my cabin."

"Now let me be quite sure on one or two points," said Poirot. "After Madame Doyle left the saloon, did any of you four leave it?"

"No."

"You are quite certain Mademoiselle de Bellefort did not leave the saloon at all?"

Fanthorp answered promptly: "Positive. Neither Doyle, Miss de Bellefort, Miss Robson, nor myself left the saloon."

"Good. That establishes the fact that Mademoiselle de Bellefort could not possibly have shot Madame Doyle before—let us say—twenty past twelve. Now, Mademoiselle Robson, you went to fetch Mademoiselle Bowers. Was Mademoiselle de Bellefort alone in her cabin during that period?"

"No, Mr. Fanthorp stayed with her."

"Good! So far, Mademoiselle de Bellefort has a perfect alibi. Mademoiselle Bowers is the next person to interview, but, before I send for her, I should like to have your opinion on one or two points. Monsieur Doyle, you say, was very anxious that Mademoiselle de Bellefort should not be left alone. Was he afraid, do you think, that she was contemplating some further rash act?"

"That is my opinion," said Fanthorp.

"He was definitely afraid she might attack Madame Doyle?"

"No." Fanthorp shook his head. "I don't think that was his idea at all. I think he was afraid she might—er—do something rash to herself."

"Suicide?"

"Yes. You see, she seemed completely sobered and heartbroken at what she had done. She was full of self-reproach. She kept saying she would be better dead."

Cornelia said timidly: "I think he was rather upset about her. He spoke—quite nicely. He said it was all his fault—that he'd treated her badly. He—he was really very nice."

Hercule Poirot nodded thoughtfully.

"Now about the pistol," he went on. "What happened to that?"

"She dropped it," said Cornelia.

"And afterward?"

Fanthorp explained how he had gone back to search for it, but had not been able to find it.

"Aha!" said Poirot. "Now we begin to arrive. Let us, I pray you, be very precise. Describe to me exactly what happened."

"Miss de Bellefort let it fall. Then she kicked it away from her with her foot."

"She sort of hated it," explained Cornelia. "I know just what she felt."

"And it went under a settee, you say. Now be very careful. Mademoiselle de Bellefort did not recover that pistol before she left the saloon?"

Both Fanthorp and Cornelia were positive on that point.

"*Précisément.* I seek only to be very exact, you comprehend. Then we arrive at this point. When Mademoiselle de Bellefort leaves the saloon the pistol is under the settee, and, since Mademoiselle de Bellefort is not left alone—Monsieur Fanthorp, Mademoiselle Robson or Mademoiselle Bowers being with her—she has no opportunity to get back the pistol after she left the saloon. What time was it, Monsieur Fanthorp, when you went back to look for it?"

"It must have been just before half past twelve."

"And how long would have elapsed between the time you and Dr.

Bessner carried Monsieur Doyle out of the saloon until you returned to look for the pistol?"

"Perhaps five minutes—perhaps a little more."

"Then in that five minutes someone removes that pistol from where it lay out of sight under the settee. That someone was *not* Mademoiselle de Bellefort. Who was it? It seems highly probable that the person who removed it was the murderer of Madame Doyle. We may assume, too, that that person had overheard or seen something of the events immediately preceding."

"I don't see how you make that out," objected Fanthorp.

"Because," said Hercule Poirot, "you have just told us that the pistol was out of sight under the settee. Therefore it is hardly credible that it was discovered by *accident*. It was taken by someone who knew it was there. Therefore that someone must have assisted at the scene."

Fanthorp shook his head. "I saw no one when I went out on the deck just before the shot was fired."

"Ah, but you went out by the door on the starboard side."

"Yes. The same side as my cabin."

"Then if there had been anybody at the port door looking through the glass you would not have seen him?"

"No," admitted Fanthorp.

"Did anyone hear the shot except the Nubian boy?"

"Not as far as I know."

Fanthorp went on: "You see, the windows in here were all closed. Miss Van Schuyler felt a draught earlier in the evening. The swing doors were shut. I doubt if the shot would be at all clearly heard. It would only sound like the pop of a cork."

Race said, "As far as I know, no one seems to have heard the other shot—the shot that killed Mrs. Doyle."

"That we will inquire into presently," said Poirot. "For the moment we still concern ourselves with Mademoiselle de Bellefort. We must speak to Mademoiselle Bowers. But first, before you go"—he arrested Fanthorp and Cornelia with a gesture—"you will give me a little information about yourselves. Then it will not be necessary to call you again later. You first, Monsieur—your full name."

"James Lechdale Fanthorp."

"Address?"

"Glasmore House, Market Donnington, Northamptonshire."

"Your profession?"

"I am a lawyer."

"And your reasons for visiting this country?"

There was a pause. For the first time the impassive Mr. Fanthorp seemed taken aback. He said at last—almost mumbling the words, "Er—pleasure."

"Aha!" said Poirot. "You take the holiday; that is it, yes?"

"Er—yes."

"Very well, Monsieur Fanthorp. Will you give me a brief account of your own movements last night after the events we have just been narrating?"

"I went straight to bed."

"That was at—?"

"Just after half past twelve."

"Your cabin is number twenty-two on the starboard side—the one nearest the saloon?"

"Yes."

"I will ask you one more question. Did you hear anything—anything at all—after you went to your cabin?"

Fanthorp considered.

"I turned in very quickly. I *think* I heard a kind of splash just as I was dropping off to sleep. Nothing else."

"You heard a kind of splash? Near at hand?"

Fanthorp shook his head.

"Really, I couldn't say. I was half asleep."

"And what time would that be?"

"It might have been about one o'clock. I can't really say."

"Thank you, Monsieur Fanthorp. That is all."

Poirot turned his attention to Cornelia.

"And now, Mademoiselle Robson? Your full name?"

"Cornelia Ruth. And my address is The Red House, Bellfield, Connecticut."

"What brought you to Egypt?"

"Cousin Marie, Miss Van Schuyler, brought me along on a trip."

"Had you ever met Madame Doyle previous to this journey?"

"No, never."

"And what did you do last night?"

"I went right to bed after helping Dr. Bessner with Mr. Doyle's leg."

"Your cabin is—?"

"Forty-three on the port side—right next door to Miss de Bellefort."

"And did you hear anything?"

Cornelia shook her head.

"I didn't hear a thing."

"No splash?"

"No, but then I wouldn't, because the boat's against the bank my side."

Poirot nodded.

"Thank you, Mademoiselle Robson. Now perhaps you will be so kind as to ask Mademoiselle Bowers to come here."

Fanthorp and Cornelia went out.

"That seems clear enough," said Race. "Unless three independent witnesses are lying, Jacqueline de Bellefort couldn't have got hold of the pistol. But somebody did. And somebody overheard the scene. And somebody was B. F. enough to write a big J on the wall."

There was a tap on the door and Miss Bowers entered. The hospital nurse sat down in her usual composed, efficient manner. In answer to Poirot she gave her name, address, and qualifications, adding, "I've been looking after Miss Van Schuyler for over two years now."

"Is Mademoiselle Van Schuyler's health very bad?"

"Why, no, I wouldn't say that," replied Miss Bowers. "She's not very young, and she's nervous about herself, and she likes to have a nurse around handy. There's nothing serious the matter with her. She just likes plenty of attention, and she's willing to pay for it."

Poirot nodded comprehendingly. Then he said, "I understand that Mademoiselle Robson fetched you last night?"

"Why, yes, that's so."

"Will you tell me exactly what happened?"

"Well, Miss Robson just gave me a brief outline of what had occurred, and I came along with her. I found Miss de Bellefort in a very excited, hysterical condition."

"Did she utter any threats against Madame Doyle?"

"No, nothing of that kind. She was in a condition of morbid self-reproach. She'd taken a good deal of alcohol, I should say, and she was suffering from reaction. I didn't think she ought to be left. I gave her a shot of morphia and sat up with her."

"Now, Mademoiselle Bowers, I want you to answer this. Did Mademoiselle de Bellefort leave her cabin at all?"

"No, she did not."

"And you yourself?"

"I stayed with her until early this morning."

"You are quite sure of that."

"Absolutely sure."

"Thank you, Mademoiselle Bowers."

The nurse went out. The two men looked at each other.

Jacqueline de Bellefort was definitely cleared of the crime. Who then had shot Linnet Doyle?

CHAPTER 13

RACE SAID: "Someone pinched the pistol. It wasn't Jacqueline de Bellefort. Someone knew enough to feel that his crime would be attributed to her. But that someone did not know that a hospital nurse was going to give her morphia and sit up with her all night. Add one thing more. Someone had already attempted to kill Linnet Doyle by rolling a boulder over the cliff; that someone was *not* Jacqueline de Bellefort. Who was it?"

Poirot said: "It will be simpler to say who it could not have been. Neither Monsieur Doyle, Madame Allerton, Monsieur Tim Allerton, Mademoiselle Van Schuyler nor Mademoiselle Bowers could have had anything to do with it. They were all within my sight."

"H'm," said Race; "that leaves rather a large field. What about motive?"

"That is where I hope Monsieur Doyle may be able to help us. There have been several incidents—"

The door opened and Jacqueline de Bellefort entered. She was very pale and she stumbled a little as she walked.

"I didn't do it," she said. Her voice was that of a frightened child. "I didn't do it. Oh, please believe me. Everyone will think I did it—but I didn't—I didn't. It's—it's awful. I wish it hadn't happened. I might have killed Simon last night; I was mad, I think. But I didn't do the other. . . ."

She sat down and burst into tears.

Poirot patted her on the shoulder.

"There, there. We know that you did not kill Madame Doyle. It is proved—yes, proved, *mon enfant*. It was not you."

Jackie sat up suddenly, her wet handkerchief clasped in her hand. "But who did?"

"That," said Poirot, "is just the question we are asking ourselves. You cannot help us there, my child?"

Jacqueline shook her head.

"I don't know . . . I can't imagine. . . . No, I haven't the faintest idea." She frowned deeply. "No," she said at last. "I can't think of anyone who wanted her dead," her voice faltered a little, "except me."

Race said, "Excuse me a minute—just thought of something." He hurried out of the room.

Jacqueline de Bellefort sat with her head downcast, nervously twisting her fingers. She broke out suddenly: "Death's horrible—horrible! I—I hate the thought of it."

Poirot said: "Yes. It is not pleasant to think, is it, that now, at this very moment, someone is rejoicing at the successful carrying out of his or her plan."

"Don't—don't!" cried Jackie. "It sounds horrible, the way you put it."

Poirot shrugged his shoulders. "It is true."

Jackie said in a low voice: "I—I wanted her dead—and she *is* dead. . . . And, what is worse . . . she died—just like I said."

"Yes, Mademoiselle. She was shot through the head."

She cried out: "Then I was right, that night at the Cataract Hotel. There *was* someone listening!"

"Ah!" Poirot nodded his head. "I wondered if you would remember that. Yes, it is altogether too much of a coincidence—that Madame Doyle should be killed in just the way you described."

Jackie shuddered.

"That man that night—who can he have been?"

Poirot was silent for a minute or two, then he said in quite a different tone of voice, "You are sure it was a man, Mademoiselle?"

Jackie looked at him in surprise.

"Yes, of course. At least—"

"Well, Mademoiselle?"

She frowned, half closing her eyes in an effort to remember. She said slowly, "I *thought* it was a man. . . ."

"But now you are not so sure?"

Jackie said slowly: "No, I can't be certain. I just assumed it was a man—but it was really just a—a figure—a shadow. . . ."

She paused and then, as Poirot did not speak, she asked: "You think it must have been a woman? But surely none of the women on this boat can have wanted to kill Linnet?"

Poirot merely moved his head from side to side.

The door opened and Bessner appeared.

"Will you come and speak with Mr. Doyle, please, Monsieur Poirot. He would like to see you."

Jackie sprang up. She caught Bessner by the arm.

"How is he? Is he—all right?"

"Naturally he is not all right," replied Dr. Bessner reproachfully. "The bone is fractured, you understand."

"But he's not going to die?" cried Jackie.

"Ach, who said anything about dying? We will get him to civilization and there we will have an X-ray and proper treatment."

"Oh!" The girl's hands came together in a convulsive pressure. She sank down again on a chair.

Poirot stepped out onto the deck with the doctor and at that moment Race joined them. They went up to the promenade deck and along to Bessner's cabin.

Simon Doyle was lying propped with cushions and pillows, an improvised cage over his leg. His face was ghastly in colour, the ravages of pain with shock on top of it. But the predominant expression on his face was bewilderment—the sick bewilderment of a child.

He muttered: "Please come in. The doctor's told me—told me—about Linnet. . . . I can't believe it. I simply can't believe it's true."

"I know. It's a bad knock," said Race.

Simon stammered: "You know—Jackie didn't do it. I'm certain Jackie didn't do it! It looks black against her, I daresay, but she *didn't* do it. She—she was a bit tight last night, and all worked up, and that's why she went for me. But she wouldn't—she wouldn't do *murder* . . . not cold-blooded murder. . . ."

Poirot said gently: "Do not distress yourself, Monsieur Doyle. Whoever shot your wife, it was not Mademoiselle de Bellefort."

Simon looked at him doubtfully.

"Is that on the square?"

"But since it was not Mademoiselle de Bellefort," continued Poirot, "can you give us any idea of who it might have been?"

Simon shook his head. The look of bewilderment increased.

"It's crazy—impossible. Apart from Jackie nobody could have wanted to do her in."

"Reflect, Monsieur Doyle. Has she no enemies? Is there no one who has a grudge against her?"

Again Simon shook his head with the same hopeless gesture.

"It sounds absolutely fantastic. There's Windlesham, of course. She more or less chucked him to marry me—but I can't see a polite stick like Windlesham committing murder, and anyway he's miles away. Same thing with old Sir George Wode. He'd got a down on Linnet over the house—disliked the way she was pulling it about; but he's miles away in London, and anyway to think of murder in such a connection would be fantastic."

"Listen, Monsieur Doyle." Poirot spoke very earnestly. "On the first day we came on board the *Karnak* I was impressed by a little conversation which I had with Madame your wife. She was very upset—very distraught. She said—mark this well—that *everybody* hated her. She said she felt afraid—unsafe—as though *everyone* round her were an enemy."

"She was pretty upset at finding Jackie aboard. So was I," said Simon.

"That is true, but it does not quite explain those words. When she said she was surrounded by enemies, she was almost certainly exaggerating, but all the same she did mean more than one person."

"You may be right there," admitted Simon. "I think I can explain that. It was a name in the passenger list that upset her."

"A name in the passenger list? What name?"

"Well, you see, she didn't actually tell me. As a matter of fact I wasn't even listening very carefully. I was going over the Jacqueline business in my mind. As far as I remember, Linnet said something about doing people down in business, and that it made her uncomfortable to meet anyone who had a grudge against her family. You see, although I don't really know the family history very well, I gather that Linnet's mother was a millionaire's daughter. Her father was only just ordinary plain wealthy, but after his marriage he naturally began playing the markets or whatever you call it. And as a result of that, of course, several people got it in the neck. You know, affluence one day, the gutter the next. Well, I gather there was someone on board whose father had got up against Linnet's father and taken a pretty hard knock. I remember Linnet saying, 'It's pretty awful when people hate you without even knowing you.'"

"Yes," said Poirot thoughtfully. "That would explain what she said to me. For the first time she was feeling the burden of her inheritance and not its advantages. You are quite sure, Monsieur Doyle, that she did not mention this man's name?"

Simon shook his head ruefully.

"I didn't really pay much attention. Just said: 'Oh, nobody minds what happened to their fathers nowadays. Life goes too fast for that.' Something of that kind."

Bessner said drily: "Ach, but I can have a guess. There is certainly a young man with a grievance on board."

"You mean Ferguson?" asked Poirot.

"Yes. He spoke against Mrs. Doyle once or twice. I myself have heard him."

"What can we do to find out?" asked Simon.

Poirot replied: "Colonel Race and I must interview all the passengers. Until we have got their stories it would be unwise to form theories. Then there is the maid. We ought to interview her first of all. It would, perhaps, be as well if we did that here. Monsieur Doyle's presence might be helpful."

"Yes, that's a good idea," said Simon.

"Had she been with Mrs. Doyle long?"

"Just a couple of months, that's all."

"Only a couple of months!" exclaimed Poirot.

"Why, you don't think—"

"Had Madame any valuable jewellery?"

"There were her pearls," said Simon. "She once told me they were worth forty or fifty thousand." He shivered. "My God, do you think those damned pearls—"

"Robbery is a possible motive," said Poirot. "All the same it seems hardly credible. . . . Well, we shall see. Let us have the maid here."

Louise Bourget was that same vivacious Latin brunette whom Poirot had seen one day and noticed.

She was anything but vivacious now. She had been crying and looked frightened. Yet there was a kind of sharp cunning apparent in her face which did not prepossess the two men favourably toward her.

"You are Louise Bourget?"

"Yes, Monsieur."

"When did you last see Madame Doyle alive?"

"Last night, Monsieur. I wait in her cabin to undress her."

"What time was that?"

"It was some time after eleven, Monsieur. I cannot say exactly when. I undress Madame and put her to bed, and then I leave."

"How long did all that take?"

"Ten minutes, Monsieur. Madame was tired. She told me to put the lights out when I went."

"And when you had left her, what did you do?"

"I went to my own cabin, Monsieur, on the deck below."

"And you heard or saw nothing more that can help us?"

"How could I, Monsieur?"

"That, Mademoiselle, is for you to say, not for us," Hercule Poirot retorted.

She stole a sideways glance at him.

"But, Monsieur, I was nowhere near. . . . What could I have seen or heard? I was on the deck below. My cabin it was on the other side of the boat, even. It is impossible that I should have heard anything. Naturally, if I had been unable to sleep, if I had mounted the stairs, *then* perhaps I might have seen this assassin, this monster, enter or leave Madame's cabin, but as it is—"

She threw out her hands appealingly to Simon.

"Monsieur, I implore you—you see how it is? What can I say?"

"My good girl," said Simon harshly, "don't be a fool. Nobody thinks you saw or heard anything. You'll be quite all right. I'll look after you. Nobody's accusing you of anything."

Louise murmured, "Monsieur is very good," and dropped her eyelids modestly.

"We take it, then, that you saw and heard nothing?" asked Race impatiently.

"That is what I said, Monsieur."

"And you know of no one who had a grudge against your mistress?"

To the surprise of her listeners Louise nodded her head vigorously.

"Oh, yes. That I do know. To that question I can answer Yes most emphatically."

Poirot said, "You mean Mademoiselle de Bellefort?"

"She, certainly. But it is not of her I speak. There was someone else on this boat who disliked Madame, who was very angry because of the way Madame had injured him."

"Good Lord!" Simon exclaimed. "What's all this?"

Louise went on, still emphatically nodding her head with the utmost vigour.

"Yes, yes, yes, it is as I say! It concerns the former maid of Madame—my predecessor. There was a man, one of the engineers on this boat, who wanted her to marry him. And my predecessor, Marie her name was, she would have done so. But Madame Doyle, she made inquiries and she discovered that this Fleetwood already he had a wife—a wife of colour you understand, a wife of this country. She had gone back to her own people, but he was still married to her, you understand. And so Madame she told all this to Marie, and Marie she was very unhappy and she would not see Fleetwood any more. And this Fleetwood, he was infuriated, and when he found out that this Madame Doyle had formerly been Mademoiselle Linnet Ridgeway he tells me that he would like to kill her! Her interference ruined his life, he said."

Louise paused triumphantly.

"This is interesting," said Race.

Poirot turned to Simon.

"Had you any idea of this?"

"None whatever," Simon replied with patent sincerity. "I doubt if Linnet even knew the man was on the boat. She had probably forgotten all about the incident."

He turned sharply to the maid.

"Did you say anything to Mrs. Doyle about this?"

"No, Monsieur, of course not."

Poirot asked, "Do you know anything about your mistress's pearls?"

"Her pearls?" Louise's eyes opened very wide. "She was wearing them last night."

"You saw them when she came to bed?"

"Yes, Monsieur."

"Where did she put them?"

"On the table by the side as always."

"That is where you last saw them?"

"Yes, sir."

"Did you see them there this morning?"

A startled look came into the girl's face.

"Mon Dieu! I did not even look. I come up to the bed, I see—I see Madame; and then I cry out and rush out of the door, and I faint."

Hercule Poirot nodded his head.

"You did not look. But I, I have the eyes which notice, and there were no pearls on the table beside the bed this morning."

CHAPTER 14

HERCULE POIROT's observation had not been at fault. There were no pearls on the table by Linnet Doyle's bed.

Louise Bourget was bidden to make a search among Linnet's belongings. According to her, all was in order. Only the pearls had disappeared.

As they emerged from the cabin a steward was waiting to tell them that breakfast had been served in the smoking-room.

As they passed along the deck, Race paused to look over the rail.

"Ah! I see you have had an idea, my friend."

"Yes. It suddenly came to me, when Fanthorp mentioned thinking he had heard a splash, that I too had been awakened sometime last night by a splash. It's perfectly possible that, after the murder, the murderer threw the pistol overboard."

Poirot said slowly, "You really think that is possible, my friend?"

Race shrugged his shoulders.

"It's a suggestion. After all, the pistol wasn't anywhere in the cabin. First thing I looked for."

"All the same," said Poirot, "it is incredible that it should have been thrown overboard."

Race asked, "Where is it then?"

Poirot replied thoughtfully, "If it is not in Madame Doyle's cabin, there is, logically, only one other place where it could be."

"Where's that?"

"In Mademoiselle de Bellefort's cabin."

Race said thoughtfully: "Yes. I see—"

He stopped suddenly.

"She's out of her cabin. Shall we go and have a look now?"

Poirot shook his head.

"No, my friend, that would be precipitate. It may not yet have been put there."

"What about an immediate search of the whole boat?"

"That way we should show our hand. We must work with great care. It is very delicate, our position, at the moment. Let us discuss the situation as we eat."

Race agreed. They went into the smoking-room.

"Well," said Race as he poured himself out a cup of coffee, "we've got two definite leads. There's the disappearance of the pearls. And there's the man Fleetwood. As regards the pearls, robbery seems indicated, but—I don't know whether you'll agree with me—"

Poirot said quickly, "But it was an odd moment to choose?"

"Exactly. To steal the pearls at such a moment invites a close search of everybody on board. How then could the thief hope to get away with his booty?"

"He might have gone ashore and dumped it."

"The company always has a watchman on the bank."

"Then that is not feasible. Was the murder committed to divert attention from the robbery? No, that does not make sense; it is profoundly unsatisfactory. But supposing that Madame Doyle woke up and caught the thief in the act?"

"And therefore the thief shot her? But she was shot whilst she slept."

"So that too does not make sense. . . . You know, I have a little idea about those pearls—and yet—no—it is impossible. Because if my idea was right the pearls would not have disappeared. Tell me, what did you think of the maid?"

"I wondered," said Race slowly, "if she knew more than she said."

"Ah, you too had that impression."

"Definitely not a nice girl," said Race.

Hercule Poirot nodded. "Yes, I would not trust her, that one."

"You think she had something to do with the murder?"

"No, I would not say that."

"With the theft of the pearls, then?"

"That is more probable. She had only been with Madame Doyle a very short time. She may be a member of a gang that specializes in jewel robberies. In such a case there is often a maid with excellent references. Unfortunately we are not in a position to seek information on these points. And yet that explanation does not quite satisfy me. . . . Those pearls—ah, *sacré,* my little idea *ought* to be right. And yet nobody would be so imbecile—" He broke off.

"What about the man Fleetwood?"

"We must question him. It may be that we have there the solution. If Louise Bourget's story is true, he had a definite motive for revenge. He could have overheard the scene between Jacqueline and Monsieur Doyle, and when they have left the saloon he could have darted in and secured the gun. Yes, it is all quite possible. And that letter J scrawled in blood. That, too, would accord with a simple, rather crude nature."

"In fact, he's just the person we are looking for?"

"Yes—only—" Poirot rubbed his nose. He said with a slight grimace: "See you, I recognize my own weaknesses. It has been said of me that I like to make a case difficult. This solution that you put to me—it is too simple, too easy. I cannot feel that it really happened. And yet, that may be sheer prejudice on my part."

"Well, we'd better have the fellow here."

Race rang the bell and gave the order. Then he asked, "Any other —possibilities?"

"Plenty, my friend. There is, for example, the American trustee."

"Pennington?"

"Yes, Pennington. There was a curious little scene in here the other day." He narrated the happenings to Race. "You see—it is significant. Madame, she wanted to read all the papers before signing. So he makes the excuse of another day. And then, the husband, he makes a very significant remark."

"What was that?"

"He says—'I never read anything. I sign where I am told to sign.'

You perceive the significance of that. Pennington did. I saw it in his eye. He looked at Doyle as though an entirely new idea had come into his head. Just imagine, my friend, that you have been left trustee to the daughter of an intensely wealthy man. You use, perhaps, that money to speculate with. I know it is so in all detective novels—but you read of it too in the newspapers. It happens, my friend, *it happens*."

"I don't dispute it," said Race.

"There is, perhaps, still time to make good by speculating wildly. Your ward is not yet of age. And then—she marries! The control passes from your hands into hers at a moment's notice! A disaster! But there is still a chance. She is on a honeymoon. She will perhaps be careless about business. A casual paper, slipped in among others, signed without reading . . . But Linnet Doyle was not like that. Honeymoon or no honeymoon, she was a business woman. And then her husband makes a remark, and a new idea comes to that desperate man who is seeking a way out from ruin. If Linnet Doyle were to die, her fortune would pass to her husband—and he would be easy to deal with; he would be a child in the hands of an astute man like Andrew Pennington. *Mon cher* Colonel, I tell you I *saw* the thought pass through Andrew Pennington's head. 'If only it were *Doyle* I had got to deal with . . .' That is what he was thinking."

"Quite possible, I daresay," said Race drily, "but you've no evidence."

"Alas, no."

"Then there's young Ferguson," said Race. "He talks bitterly enough. Not that I go by talk. Still, he *might* be the fellow whose father was ruined by old Ridgeway. It's a little far-fetched but it's *possible*. People do brood over bygone wrongs sometimes."

He paused a minute and then said, "And there's my fellow."

"Yes, there is 'your fellow' as you call him."

"He's a killer," said Race. "We know that. On the other hand, I can't see any way in which he could have come up against Linnet Doyle. Their orbits don't touch."

Poirot said slowly, "Unless, accidentally, she had become possessed of evidence showing his identity."

"That's possible, but it seems highly unlikely." There was a knock at the door. "Ah, here's our would-be bigamist."

Fleetwood was a big, truculent looking man. He looked suspiciously from one to the other of them as he entered the room. Poirot recognized him as the man he had seen talking to Louise Bourget.

Fleetwood asked suspiciously, "You wanted to see me?"

"We did," said Race. "You probably know that a murder was committed on this boat last night?"

Fleetwood nodded.

"And I believe it is true that you had reason to feel anger against the woman who was killed."

A look of alarm sprang up in Fleetwood's eyes.

"Who told you that?"

"You considered that Mrs. Doyle had interfered between you and a young woman."

"I know who told you that—that lying French hussy. She's a liar through and through, that girl."

"But this particular story happens to be true."

"It's a dirty lie!"

"You say that, although you don't know what it is yet."

The shot told. The man flushed and gulped.

"It is true, is it not, that you were going to marry the girl Marie, and that she broke it off when she discovered that you were a married man already?"

"What business was it of hers?"

"You mean, what business was it of Mrs. Doyle's? Well, you know, bigamy is bigamy."

"It wasn't like that. I married one of the locals out here. It didn't answer. She went back to her people. I've not seen her for half a dozen years."

"Still you were married to her."

The man was silent. Race went on:

"Mrs. Doyle, or Miss Ridgeway as she then was, found out all this?"

"Yes, she did, curse her! Nosing about where no one ever asked her to. I'd have treated Marie right. I'd have done anything for her. And she'd never have known about the other, if it hadn't been for that meddlesome young lady of hers. Yes, I'll say it, I *did* have a grudge against the lady, and I felt bitter about it when I saw her on this boat, all dressed up in pearls and diamonds and lording it all over the place, with never a thought that she'd broken up a man's life for him! I felt bitter all right, but if you think I'm a dirty murderer—if you think I went and shot her with a gun, well, that's a damned lie! I never touched her. And that's God's truth."

He stopped. The sweat was rolling down his face.

"Where were you last night between the hours of twelve and two?"

"In my bunk asleep—and my mate will tell you so."

"We shall see," said Race. He dismissed him with a curt nod. "That'll do."

"*Eh bien?*" inquired Poirot as the door closed behind Fleetwood. Race shrugged his shoulders. "He tells quite a straight story. He's nervous, of course, but not unduly so. We'll have to investigate his alibi—though I don't suppose it will be decisive. His mate was probably asleep, and this fellow could have slipped in and out if he wanted to. It depends whether anyone else saw him."

"Yes, one must inquire as to that."

"The next thing, I think," said Race, "is whether anyone heard anything which might give us a clue to the time of the crime. Bessner places it as having occurred between twelve and two. It seems reasonable to hope that someone among the passengers may have heard the shot—even if they did not recognize it for what it was. I didn't hear anything of the kind myself. What about you?"

Poirot shook his head.

"Me, I slept absolutely like the log. I heard nothing—but nothing at all. I might have been drugged, I slept so soundly."

"A pity," said Race. "Well, let's hope we have a bit of luck with the people who have cabins on the starboard side. Fanthorp we've done. The Allertons come next. I'll send the steward to fetch them."

Mrs. Allerton came in briskly. She was wearing a soft grey striped silk dress. Her face looked distressed.

"It's too horrible," she said as she accepted the chair that Poirot placed for her. "I can hardly believe it. That lovely creature, with everything to live for—dead. I almost feel I can't believe it."

"I know how you feel, Madame," said Poirot sympathetically.

"I'm glad *you* are on board," said Mrs. Allerton simply. "You'll be able to find out who did it. I'm so glad it isn't that poor tragic girl."

"You mean Mademoiselle de Bellefort. Who told you she did not do it?"

"Cornelia Robson," replied Mrs. Allerton, with a faint smile. "You know, she's simply thrilled by it all. It's probably the only exciting thing that has ever happened to her, and probably the only exciting thing that ever will happen to her. But she's so nice that she's terribly ashamed of enjoying it. She thinks it's awful of her."

Mrs. Allerton gave a look at Poirot and then added: "But I mustn't chatter. You want to ask me questions."

"If you please. You went to bed at what time, Madame?"

"Just after half past ten."

"And you went to sleep at once?"

"Yes. I was sleepy."

"And did you hear anything—anything at all—during the night?"

Mrs. Allerton wrinkled her brows.

"Yes, I think I heard a splash and someone running—or was it the other way about? I'm rather hazy. I just had a vague idea that someone had fallen overboard at sea—a dream, you know—and then I woke up and listened, but it was all quite quiet."

"Do you know what time that was?"

"No, I'm afraid I don't. But I don't think it was very long after I went to sleep. I mean it was within the first hour or so."

"Alas, Madame, that is not very definite."

"No, I know it isn't. But it's no good my trying to guess, is it, when I haven't really the vaguest idea?"

"And that is all you can tell us, Madame?"

"I'm afraid so."

"Had you ever actually met Madame Doyle before?"

"No, Tim had met her. And I'd heard a good deal about her—through a cousin of ours, Joanna Southwood, but I'd never spoken to her till we met at Assuan."

"I have one other question, Madame, if you will pardon me for asking."

Mrs. Allerton murmured with a faint smile, "I should love to be asked an indiscreet question."

"It is this. Did you, or your family, ever suffer any financial loss through the operations of Madame Doyle's father, Melhuish Ridgeway?"

Mrs. Allerton looked thoroughly astonished.

"Oh, no! The family finances have never suffered except by dwindling . . . you know, everything paying less interest than it used to. There's never been anything melodramatic about our poverty. My husband left very little money, but what he left I still have, though it doesn't yield as much as it used to yield."

"I thank you, Madame. Perhaps you will ask your son to come to us."

Tim said lightly, when his mother came to him: "Ordeal over? My turn now! What sort of things did they ask you?"

"Only whether I heard anything last night," said Mrs. Allerton. "And unluckily I didn't hear anything at all. I can't think why not. After all, Linnet's cabin is only one away from mine. I should think I'd have been bound to hear the shot. Go along, Tim; they're waiting for you."

To Tim Allerton Poirot repeated his previous question.

Tim answered: "I went to bed early, half past ten or so. I read for a bit. Put out my light just after eleven."

"Did you hear anything after that?"

"Heard a man's voice saying good-night, I think, not far away."

"That was I saying good-night to Mrs. Doyle," said Race.

"Yes. After that I went to sleep. Then, later, I heard a kind of hullabaloo going on, somebody calling Fanthorp, I remember."

"Mademoiselle Robson when she ran out from the observation saloon."

"Yes, I suppose that was it. And then a lot of different voices. And then somebody running along the deck. And then a splash. And then I heard old Bessner booming out something about 'Careful now' and 'Not too quick.'"

"You heard a splash?"

"Well, something of that kind."

"You are sure it was not a *shot* you heard?"

"Yes, I suppose it might have been . . . I did hear a cork pop. Perhaps that was the shot. I may have imagined the splash from connecting the idea of the cork with liquid pouring into a glass. . . . I know my foggy idea was that there was some kind of party on, and I wished they'd all go to bed and shut up."

"Anything more after that?"

Tim thought.

"Only Fanthorp barging round in his cabin next door. I thought he'd never get to bed."

"And after that?"

Tim shrugged his shoulders.

"After that—oblivion."

"You heard nothing more?"

"Nothing whatever."

"Thank you, Monsieur Allerton."

Tim got up and left the cabin.

CHAPTER 15

RACE PORED thoughtfully over a plan of the promenade deck of the *Karnak*.

"Fanthorp, young Allerton, Mrs. Allerton. Then an empty cabin— Simon Doyle's. Now who's on the other side of Mrs. Doyle's? The old American dame. If anyone heard anything, she should have done. If she's up we'd better have her along."

Miss Van Schuyler entered the room. She looked even older and yellower than usual this morning. Her small dark eyes had an air of venomous displeasure in them.

Race rose and bowed.

"We're very sorry to trouble you, Miss Van Schuyler. It's very good of you. Please sit down."

Miss Van Schuyler said sharply: "I dislike being mixed up in this. I resent it very much. I do not wish to be associated in any way with this—er—very unpleasant affair."

"Quite—quite. I was just saying to Monsieur Poirot that the sooner we took your statement the better, as then you need have no further trouble."

Miss Vay Schuyler looked at Poirot with something approaching favour.

"I'm glad you both realize my feelings. I am not accustomed to anything of this kind."

Poirot said soothingly: "Precisely, Mademoiselle. That is why we wish to free you from unpleasantness as quickly as possible. Now you went to bed last night—at what time?"

"Ten o'clock is my usual time. Last night I was rather later, as Cornelia Robson, very inconsiderately, kept me waiting."

"*Très bien,* Mademoiselle. Now what did you hear after you had retired?"

Miss Van Schuyler said: "I sleep very lightly."

"*À merveille!* That is very fortunate for us."

"I was awakened by that rather flashy young woman, Mrs. Doyle's maid, who said, '*Bonne nuit, Madame*' in what I cannot but think an unnecessarily loud voice."

"And after that?"

"I went to sleep again. I woke up thinking someone was in my cabin, but I realized that it was someone in the cabin next door."

"In Madame Doyle's cabin?"

"Yes. Then I heard someone outside on the deck and then a splash."

"You have no idea what time this was?"

"I can tell you the time exactly. It was ten minutes past one."

"You are sure of that?"

"Yes. I looked at my little clock that stands by my bed."

"You did not hear a shot?"

"No, nothing of the kind."

"But it might possibly have been a shot that awakened you?"

Miss Van Schuyler considered the question, her toadlike head on one side.

"It might," she admitted rather grudgingly.

"And you have no idea what caused the splash you heard?"

"Not at all—I know perfectly."

Colonel Race sat up alertly.

"You know?"

"Certainly. I did not like this sound of prowling around. I got up and went to the door of my cabin. Miss Otterbourne was leaning over the side. She had just dropped something into the water."

"Miss Otterbourne?" Race sounded really surprised.

"Yes."

"You are quite sure it was Miss Otterbourne?"

"I saw her face distinctly."

"She did not see you?"

"I do not think so."

Poirot leaned forward.

"And what did her face look like, Mademoiselle?"

"She was in a condition of considerable emotion."

Race and Poirot exchanged a quick glance.

"And then?" Race prompted.

"Miss Otterbourne went away round the stern of the boat and I returned to bed."

There was a knock at the door and the Manager entered. He carried in his hand a dripping bundle.

"We've got it, Colonel."

Race took the package. He unwrapped fold after fold of sodden velvet. Out of it fell a coarse handkerchief, faintly stained with pink, wrapped round a small pearl-handled pistol.

Race gave Poirot a glance of slightly malicious triumph.

"You see," he said, "my idea was right. It *was* thrown overboard."

He held the pistol out on the palm of his hand.

"What do you say, Monsieur Poirot? Is this the pistol you saw at the Cataract Hotel that night?"

Poirot examined it carefully; then he said quietly: "Yes—that is it. There is the ornamental work on it—and the initials J. B. It is an *article de luxe,* a very feminine production, but it is none the less a lethal weapon."

"Twenty-two," murmured Race. He took out the clip. "Two bullets fired. Yes, there doesn't seem much doubt about it."

Miss Van Schuyler coughed significantly.

"And what about my stole?" she demanded.

"Your stole, Mademoiselle?"

"Yes, that is my velvet stole you have here."

Race picked up the dripping folds of material.

"This is yours, Miss Van Schuyler?"

"Certainly it's mine!" the old lady snapped. "I missed it last night. I was asking everyone if they'd seen it."

Poirot questioned Race with a glance, and the latter gave a slight nod of assent.

"Where did you see it last, Miss Van Schuyler?"

"I had it in the saloon yesterday evening. When I came to go to bed I could not find it anywhere."

Race said quietly, "You realize what it's been used for?" He spread it out, indicating with a finger the scorching and several small holes. "The murderer wrapped it round the pistol to deaden the noise of the shot."

"Impertinence!" snapped Miss Van Schuyler. The colour rose in her wizened cheeks.

Race said, "I shall be glad, Miss Van Schuyler, if you will tell me the extent of your previous acquaintance with Mrs. Doyle."

"There was no previous acquaintance."

"But you knew of her?"

"I knew who she was, of course."

"But your families were not acquainted?"

"As a family we have always prided ourselves on being exclusive, Colonel Race. My dear mother would never have dreamed of calling upon any of the Hartz family, who, outside their wealth, were nobodies."

"That is all you have to say, Miss Van Schuyler?"

"I have nothing to add to what I have told you. Linnet Ridgeway was brought up in England and I never saw her till I came aboard this boat."

She rose. Poirot opened the door for her and she marched out.

The eyes of the two men met.

"That's her story," said Race, "and she's going to stick to it! It may be true. I don't know. But—Rosalie Otterbourne? I hadn't expected that."

Poirot shook his head in a perplexed manner. Then he brought down his hand on the table with a sudden bang.

"But it does not make sense," he cried. *"Nom d'un nom d'un nom!* It does not make sense."

Race looked at him.

"What do you mean exactly?"

"I mean that up to a point it is all the clear sailing. Someone wished to kill Linnet Doyle. Someone overheard the scene in the saloon last night. Someone sneaked in there and retrieved the pistol—Jacqueline de Bellefort's pistol, remember. Somebody shot Linnet Doyle with that pistol and wrote the letter J on the wall. . . . All so clear, is it not? All pointing to Jacqueline de Bellefort as the murderess. And then what does the murderer do. Leave the pistol—the damning pistol—Jacqueline de Bellefort's pistol, for everyone to find? No, he—or she—throws the pistol, that particularly damning bit of evidence, overboard. Why, my friend, why?"

Race shook his head. "It's odd."

"It is more than odd—it is *impossible!*"

"Not impossible, since it happened!"

"I do not mean that. I mean that the sequence of events is impossible. Something is wrong."

CHAPTER 16

COLONEL RACE glanced curiously at his colleague. He respected—he had reason to respect—the brain of Hercule Poirot. Yet for the moment he did not follow the other's process of thought. He asked no question, however. He seldom did ask questions. He proceeded straightforwardly with the matter in hand.

"What's the next thing to be done? Question the Otterbourne girl?"

"Yes, that may advance us a little."

Rosalie Otterbourne entered ungraciously. She did not look nervous or frightened in any way—merely unwilling and sulky.

"Well," she asked, "what is it?"

Race was the spokesman.

"We're investigating Mrs. Doyle's death," he explained.

Rosalie nodded.

"Will you tell me what you did last night?"

Rosalie reflected a minute.

"Mother and I went to bed early—before eleven. We didn't hear anything in particular, except a bit of fuss outside Dr. Bessner's cabin. I heard the old man's German voice booming away. Of course I didn't know what it was all about till this morning."

"You didn't hear a shot?"

"No."

"Did you leave your cabin at all last night?"

"No."

"You are quite sure of that?"

Rosalie stared at him.

"What do you mean? Of course I'm sure of it."

"You did not, for instance, go round to the starboard side of the boat and throw something overboard?"

The colour rose in her face.

"Is there any rule against throwing things overboard?"

"No, of course not. Then you did?"

"No, I didn't. I never left my cabin, I tell you."

"Then if anyone says that they saw you—"

She interrupted him. "Who says they saw me?"

"Miss Van Schuyler."

"Miss Van Schuyler?" She sounded genuinely astonished.

"Yes. Miss Van Schuyler says she looked out of her cabin and saw you throw something over the side."

Rosalie said clearly, "That's a damned lie." Then, as though struck by a sudden thought, she asked, "What time was this?"

It was Poirot who answered.

"It was ten minutes past one, Mademoiselle."

She nodded her head thoughtfully. "Did she see anything else?"

Poirot looked at her curiously. He stroked his chin.

"See—no," he replied, "but she heard something."

"What did she hear?"

"Someone moving about in Madame Doyle's cabin."

"I see," muttered Rosalie.

She was pale now—deadly pale.

"And you persist in saying that you threw nothing overboard, Mademoiselle?"

"What on earth should I run about throwing things overboard for in the middle of the night?"

"There might be a reason—an innocent reason."

"Innocent?" repeated the girl sharply.

"That's what I said. You see, Mademoiselle, something *was* thrown overboard last night—something that was not innocent."

Race silently held out the bundle of stained velvet, opening it to display its contents.

Rosalie Otterbourne shrank back. "Was that—what—she was killed with?"

"Yes, Mademoiselle."

"And you think that I—I did it? What utter nonsense! Why on earth should I want to kill Linnet Doyle? I don't even know her!"

She laughed and stood up scornfully. "The whole thing is too ridiculous."

"Remember, Miss Otterbourne," said Race, "that Miss Van Schuyler is prepared to swear she saw your face quite clearly in the moonlight."

Rosalie laughed again. "That old cat? She's probably half blind anyway. It wasn't me she saw." She paused. "Can I go now?"

Race nodded and Rosalie Otterbourne left the room.

The eyes of the two men met. Race lighted a cigarette.

"Well, that's that. Flat contradiction. Which of 'em do we believe?"

Poirot shook his head. "I have a little idea that neither of them was being quite frank."

"That's the worst of our job," said Race despondently. "So many people keep back the truth for positively futile reasons. What's our next move? Get on with the questioning of the passengers?"

"I think so. It is always well to proceed with order and method."

Race nodded.

Mrs. Otterbourne, dressed in floating batik material, succeeded her daughter. She corroborated Rosalie's statement that they had both gone to bed before eleven o'clock. She herself had heard nothing of interest during the night. She could not say whether Rosalie had left their cabin or not. On the subject of the crime she was inclined to hold forth.

"The *crime passionnel!*" she exclaimed. "The primitive instinct—to kill! So closely allied to the sex instinct. That girl, Jacqueline, half Latin, hot-blooded, obeying the deepest instincts of her being, stealing forth, revolver in hand—"

"But Jacqueline de Bellefort did not shoot Madame Doyle. That we know for certain. It is proved," explained Poirot.

"Her husband, then," said Mrs. Otterbourne, rallying from the blow. "The blood lust and the sex instinct—a sexual crime. There are many well-known instances."

"Mr. Doyle was shot through the leg and he was quite unable to move—the bone was fractured," explained Colonel Race. "He spent the night with Dr. Bessner."

Mrs. Otterbourne was even more disappointed. She searched her mind hopefully.

"Of course!" she said. "How foolish of me! Miss Bowers!"

"Miss Bowers?"

"Yes. Naturally. It's so *clear* psychologically. Repression! The repressed virgin! Maddened by the sight of these two—a young husband and wife passionately in love with each other. Of course it was her! She's just the type—sexually unattractive, innately respectable. In my book, *The Barren Vine*—"

Colonel Race interposed tactfully: "Your suggestions have been most helpful, Mrs. Otterbourne. We must get on with our job now. Thank you so much."

He escorted her gallantly to the door and came back wiping his brow.

"What a poisonous woman! Whew! Why didn't somebody murder *her?*"

"It may yet happen," Poirot consoled him.

"There might be some sense in that. Whom have we got left? Pennington—we'll keep him for the end, I think. Richetti—Ferguson."

Signor Richetti was very voluble, very agitated.

"But what a horror, what an infamy—a woman so young and so beautiful—indeed an inhuman crime!"

Signor Richetti's hands flew expressively up in the air.

His answers were prompt. He had gone to bed early—very early. In fact immediately after dinner. He had read for a while—a very interesting pamphlet lately published—*Prähistorische Forschung in Kleinasien*—throwing an entirely new light on the painted pottery of the Anatolian foothills.

He had put out his light some time before eleven. No, he had not heard any shot. Not any sound like the pop of a cork. The only thing he had heard—but that was later, in the middle of the night—was a splash, a big splash, just near his porthole.

"Your cabin is on the lower deck, on the starboard side, is it not?"

"Yes, yes, that is so. And I hear the big splash." His arms flew up once more to describe the bigness of the splash.

"Can you tell me at all what time that was?"

Signor Richetti reflected.

"It was one, two, three hours after I go to sleep. Perhaps two hours."

"About ten minutes past one, for instance?"

"It might very well be, yes. Ah! but what a terrible crime—how inhuman. . . . So charming a woman. . . ."

Exit Signor Richetti, still gesticulating freely.

Race looked at Poirot. Poirot raised his eyebrows expressively, then shrugged his shoulders. They passed on to Mr. Ferguson.

Ferguson was difficult. He sprawled insolently in a chair.

"Grand to-do about this business!" he sneered. "What's it really matter? Lot of superfluous women in the world!"

Race said coldly, "Can we have an account of your movements last night, Mr. Ferguson?"

"Don't see why you should, but I don't mind. I mooched around a good bit. Went ashore with Miss Robson. When she went back to the boat I mooched around by myself for a while. Came back and turned in round about midnight."

"Your cabin is on the lower deck, starboard side?"

"Yes. I'm not up among the nobs."

"Did you hear a shot? It might only have sounded like the popping of a cork."

Ferguson considered. "Yes, I think I did hear something like a cork. . . . Can't remember when—before I went to sleep. But there were still a lot of people about then—commotion, running about on the deck above."

"That was probably the shot fired by Miss de Bellefort. You didn't hear another?"

Ferguson shook his head.

"Nor a splash?"

"A splash? Yes, I believe I did hear a splash. But there was so much row going on I can't be sure about it."

"Did you leave your cabin during the night?"

Ferguson grinned. "No, I didn't. And I didn't participate in the good work, worse luck."

"Come, come, Mr. Ferguson, don't behave childishly."

The young man reacted angrily.

"Why shouldn't I say what I think? I believe in violence."

"But you don't practise what you preach?" murmured Poirot. "I wonder."

He leaned forward.

"It was the man, Fleetwood, was it not, who told you that Linnet Doyle was one of the richest women in England?"

"What's Fleetwood got to do with this?"

"Fleetwood, my friend, had an excellent motive for killing Linnet Doyle. He had a special grudge against her."

Mr. Ferguson came up out of his seat like a Jack in the Box.

"So that's your dirty game, is it?" he demanded wrathfully. "Put it on to a poor devil like Fleetwood, who can't defend himself, who's got no money to hire lawyers. But I tell you this—if you try and saddle Fleetwood with this business you'll have me to deal with."

"And who exactly are you?" asked Poirot sweetly.

Mr. Ferguson got rather red.

"I can stick by my friends anyway," he said gruffly.

"Well, Mr. Ferguson, I think that's all we need for the present," said Race.

As the door closed behind Ferguson he remarked unexpectedly, "Rather a likable young cub, really."

"You don't think he is the man *you* are after?" asked Poirot.

"I hardly think so. I suppose he *is* on board. The information was very precise. Oh, well, one job at a time. Let's have a go at Pennington."

CHAPTER 17

ANDREW PENNINGTON displayed all the conventional reactions of grief and shock. He was, as usual, carefully dressed. He had changed into a black tie. His long clean-shaven face bore a bewildered expression.

"Gentlemen," he said sadly, "this business has got me right down! Little Linnet—why, I remember her as the cutest little thing you can imagine. How proud of her Melhuish Ridgeway used to be, too! Well, there's no point in going into that. Just tell me what I can do; that's all I ask."

Race said, "To begin with, Mr. Pennington, did you hear anything last night?"

"No, sir, I can't say I did. I have the cabin right next to Dr. Bessner's, number forty—forty-one, and I heard a certain commotion going on in there round about midnight or so. Of course I didn't know what it was at the time."

"You heard nothing else? No shots?"

Andrew Pennington shook his head.

"Nothing whatever of that kind."

"And you went to bed at what time?"

"Must have been some time after eleven."

He leant forward.

"I don't suppose it's news to you to know that there's plenty of rumours going about the boat. That half French girl—Jacqueline de Bellefort—there was something fishy there, you know. Linnet didn't tell me anything, but naturally I wasn't born blind and deaf. There'd been some affair between her and Simon, some time, hadn't there? *Cherchez la femme*—that's a pretty good sound rule, and I should say you wouldn't have to *cherchez* far."

"You mean that in your belief Jacqueline de Bellefort shot Madame Doyle?" Poirot asked.

"That's what it looks like to me. Of course I don't *know* anything. . . ."

"Unfortunately we *do* know something!"

"Eh?" Mr. Pennington looked startled.

"We know that it is quite impossible for Mademoiselle de Bellefort to have shot Madame Doyle."

He explained carefully the circumstances. Pennington seemed reluctant to accept them.

"I agree it looks all right on the face of it—but this hospital nurse woman, I'll bet she didn't stay awake all night. She dozed off and the girl slipped out and in again."

"Hardly likely, Monsieur Pennington. She had administered a strong opiate, remember. And anyway a nurse is in the habit of sleeping lightly and waking when her patient wakes."

"It all sounds rather fishy to me," declared Pennington.

Race said, in a gently authoritative manner: "I think you must take it from me, Mr. Pennington, that we have examined all the possibilities very carefully. The result is quite definite—Jacqueline de Bellefort did not shoot Mrs. Doyle. So we are forced to look elsewhere. That is where we hope you may be able to help us."

"I?" Pennington gave a nervous start.

"Yes. You were an intimate friend of the dead woman's. You know the circumstances of her life, in all probability, much better than her husband does, since he only made her acquaintance a few months ago. You would know, for instance, of anyone who had a grudge against her. You would know, perhaps, whether there was anyone who had a motive for desiring her death."

Andrew Pennington passed his tongue over rather dry looking lips.

"I assure you, I have no idea. . . . You see Linnet was brought up in England. I know very little of her surroundings and associations."

"And yet," mused Poirot, "there was someone on board who was interested in Madame Doyle's removal. She had a near escape before, you remember, at this very place, when that boulder crashed down— Ah! but you were not there, perhaps?"

"No. I was inside the temple at the time. I heard about it afterward, of course. A very near escape. But possibly an accident, don't you think?"

Poirot shrugged his shoulders.

"One thought so at the time. Now—one wonders."

"Yes—yes, of course." Pennington wiped his face with a fine silk handkerchief.

Colonel Race went on: "Mrs. Doyle happened to mention someone being on board who bore a grudge—not against her personally, but against her family. Do you know who that could be?"

Pennington looked genuinely astonished.

"No, I've no idea."

"She didn't mention the matter to you?"

"No."

"You were an intimate friend of her father's—you cannot remember any business operations of his that might have resulted in ruin for some business opponent?"

Pennington shook his head helplessly. "No outstanding case. Such operations were frequent, of course, but I can't recall anyone who uttered threats—nothing of that kind."

"In short, Mr. Pennington, you cannot help us?"

"It seems so. I deplore my inadequacy, gentlemen."

Race interchanged a glance with Poirot, then he said: "I'm sorry too. We'd had hopes."

He got up as a sign the interview was at an end.

Andrew Pennington said: "As Doyle's laid up, I expect he'd like me to see to things. Pardon me, Colonel, but what exactly are the arrangements?"

"When we leave here we shall make a non-stop run to Shellâl, arriving there tomorrow morning."

"And the body?"

"Will be removed to one of the cold storage chambers."

Andrew Pennington bowed his head. Then he left the room.

Poirot and Race again interchanged a glance.

"Mr. Pennington," said Race, lighting a cigarette, "was not at all comfortable."

Poirot nodded. "And," he said, "Mr. Pennington was sufficiently perturbed to tell a rather stupid lie. He was *not* in the temple of Abu Simbel when that boulder fell. I—*moi qui vous parle*—can swear to that. I had just come from there."

"A very stupid lie," said Race, "and a very revealing one."

Again Poirot nodded.

"But for the moment," he said, and smiled, "we handle him with the gloves of kid, is it not so?"

"That was the idea," agreed Race.

"My friend, you and I understand each other to a marvel."

There was a faint grinding noise, a stir beneath their feet. The *Karnak* had started on her homeward journey to Shellâl.

"The pearls," said Race. "That is the next thing to be cleared up."

"You have a plan?"

"Yes." He glanced at his watch. "It will be lunch time in half an hour. At the end of the meal I propose to make an announcement—just state the fact that the pearls have been stolen, and that I must request everyone to stay in the dining-saloon while a search is conducted."

Poirot nodded approvingly.

"It is well imagined. Whoever took the pearls still has them. By giving no warning beforehand, there will be no chance of their being thrown overboard in a panic."

Race drew some sheets of paper toward him. He murmured apologetically: "I like to make a brief précis of the facts as I go along. It keeps one's mind free of confusion."

"You do well. Method and order, they are everything," replied Poirot.

Race wrote for some minutes in his small neat script. Finally he pushed the result of his labours toward Poirot.

"Anything you don't agree with there?"

Poirot took up the sheets. They were headed:

MURDER OF MRS. LINNET DOYLE

Mrs. Doyle was last seen alive by her maid, Louise Bourget. Time: 11.30 (approx).

From 11.30-12.20 following have alibis: Cornelia Robson, James Fanthorp, Simon Doyle, Jacqueline de Bellefort—*nobody else*—but crime almost certainly committed *after* that time, since it is practically certain that pistol used was Jacqueline de Bellefort's, which was then in her handbag. That her pistol was used is not *absolutely* certain until after post mortem and expert evidence re bullet—but it may be taken as overwhelmingly probable.

Probable course of events: X (murderer) was witness of scene between Jacqueline and Simon Doyle in observation saloon and noted where pistol went under settee. After the saloon was vacant, X procured pistol—his or her idea being that Jacqueline de Bellefort would be thought guilty of crime. On this theory certain people are automatically cleared of suspicion:

Cornelia Robson, since she had no opportunity to take pistol before James Fanthorp returned to search for it.

Miss Bowers—same.

Dr. Bessner—same.

N.B. Fanthorp is not definitely excluded from suspicion, since he could actually have pocketed pistol while declaring himself unable to find it.

Any other person could have taken the pistol during that ten minutes' interval.

Possible motives for the murder:

Andrew Pennington. This is on the assumption that he has been guilty of fraudulent practices. There is a certain amount of evidence in favour of that assumption, but not enough to justify making out a case against him. If it was he who rolled down the boulder, he is a man who can seize a chance when it presents itself. The crime, clearly, was not premeditated except in a *general* way. Last night's shooting scene was an ideal opportunity.

Objections to the theory of Pennington's guilt: *Why did he throw the pistol overboard, since it constituted a valuable clue against J. B.?*

Fleetwood. Motive, revenge. Fleetwood considered himself injured by Linnet Doyle. Might have overheard scene and noted position of pistol. He may have taken pistol because it was a handy weapon, rather than with the idea of throwing guilt on Jacqueline. This would fit in with throwing it overboard. *But if that were the case, why did he write J in blood on the wall?*

N.B. Cheap handkerchief found with pistol more likely to have belonged to a man like Fleetwood than to one of the well-to-do passengers.

Rosalie Otterbourne. Are we to accept Miss Van Schuyler's evidence or Rosalie's denial? Something *was* thrown overboard at that time and that something was presumably the pistol wrapped up in the velvet stole.

Points to be noted. Had Rosalie any motive? She may have disliked Linnet Doyle and even been envious of her—but as a motive for murder that seems grossly inadequate. The evidence against her can be convincing only if we discover an adequate motive. As far as we know, there is no previous knowledge or link between Rosalie Otterbourne and Linnet Doyle.

Miss Van Schuyler. The velvet stole in which pistol was wrapped belongs to Miss Van Schuyler. According to her own statement she last saw it in the observation saloon. She drew attention to its loss during the evening, and a search was made for it without success.

How did the stole come into the possession of X? Did X purloin it some time early in the evening? But if so, why? Nobody could tell, in advance, that there was going to be a scene between Jacqueline and Simon. Did X find the stole in the saloon when he went to get the pistol from under the settee? But if so, why was it not found when the search for it was made? Did it never leave Miss Van Schuyler's possession? That is to say: Did Miss Van Schuyler murder Linnet Doyle? Is her accusation of Rosalie Otterbourne a deliberate lie? If she did murder her, what was her motive?

Other possibilities:

Robbery as a motive. Possible, since the pearls have disappeared, and Linnet Doyle was certainly wearing them last night.

Someone with a grudge against the Ridgeway family. Possibly—again no evidence.

We know that there is a dangerous man on board—a killer. Here we have a killer and a death. May not the two be connected? But we should have to show that Linnet Doyle possessed dangerous knowledge concerning this man.

Conclusions: We can group the persons on board into two classes—those who had a possible motive or against whom there is definite evidence, and those who, as far as we know, are free of suspicion.

Group I	*Group II*
Andrew Pennington	Mrs. Allerton
Fleetwood	Tim Allerton
Rosalie Otterbourne	Cornelia Robson
Miss Van Schuyler	Miss Bowers
Louise Bourget (Robbery?)	Mrs. Otterbourne
Ferguson (Political?)	James Fanthorp
	Dr. Bessner
	Signor Richetti

Poirot pushed the paper back.

"It is very just, very exact, what you have written there."

"You agree with it?"

"Yes."

"And now what is your contribution?"

Poirot drew himself up in an important manner.

"Me, I pose to myself one question: '*Why* was the pistol thrown overboard?' "

"That's all?"

"At the moment, yes. Until I can arrive at a satisfactory answer to that question, there is no sense anywhere. That is—that *must* be the starting point. You will notice, my friend, that, in your summary of where we stand, you have not attempted to answer that point."

Race shrugged his shoulders.

"Panic."

Poirot shook his head perplexedly. He picked up the sodden velvet wrap and smoothed it out, wet and limp, on the table. His finger traced the scorched marks and the burnt holes.

"Tell me, my friend," he said suddenly. "You are more conversant with firearms than I am. Would such a thing as this, wrapped round a pistol, make much difference in muffling the sound?"

"No, it wouldn't. Not like a silencer, for instance."

Poirot nodded. He went on: "A man—certainly a man who had had much handling of firearms—would know that. But a woman—a woman would *not* know."

Race looked at him curiously. "Probably not."

"No. She would have read the detective stories where they are not always very exact as to details."

Race flicked the little pearl-handled pistol with his finger.

"This little fellow wouldn't make much noise anyway," he said. "Just a pop, that's all. With any other noise around, ten to one you wouldn't notice it."

"Yes, I have reflected as to that."

Poirot picked up the handkerchief and examined it.

"A man's handkerchief—but not a gentleman's handkerchief. *Ce cher* Woolworth, I imagine. Threepence at most."

"The sort of handkerchief a man like Fleetwood would own."

"Yes. Andrew Pennington, I notice, carries a very fine silk hand-kerchief."

"Ferguson?" suggested Race.

"Possibly. As a gesture. But then it ought to be a bandana."

"Used it instead of a glove, I suppose, to hold the pistol and ob-viate fingerprints." Race added, with slight facetiousness, " 'The Clue of the Blushing Handkerchief.' "

"Ah, yes. Quite a *jeune fille* colour, is it not?" He laid it down and returned to the stole, once more examining the powder marks.

"All the same," he murmured, "it is odd . . ."

"What's that?" Poirot said gently: "*Cette pauvre Madame Doyle.* Lying there so peacefully . . . with the little hole in her head. You remember how she looked?"

Race looked at him curiously. "You know," he said, "I've got an idea you're trying to tell me something—but I haven't the faintest idea what it is."

CHAPTER 18

THERE was a tap on the door.

"Come in," Race called.

A steward entered.

"Excuse me, sir," he said to Poirot, "but Mr. Doyle is asking for you."

"I will come."

Poirot rose. He went out of the room and up the companionway to the promenade deck and along it to Dr. Bessner's cabin.

Simon, his face flushed and feverish, was propped up with pillows. He looked embarrassed.

"Awfully good of you to come along, Monsieur Poirot. Look here, there's something I want to ask you."

"Yes?"

Simon got still redder in the face.

"It's—it's about Jackie. I want to see her. Do you think—would you mind—would she mind, d'you think, if you asked her to come along here? You know I've been lying here thinking. . . . That wretched kid—she is only a kid after all—and I treated her damn badly—and—" He stammered to silence.

Poirot looked at him with interest.

"You desire to see Mademoiselle Jacqueline? I will fetch her."

"Thanks. Awfully good of you."

Poirot went on his quest. He found Jacqueline de Bellefort sitting huddled up in a corner of the observation saloon. There was an open book on her lap but she was not reading.

Poirot said gently: "Will you come with me, Mademoiselle? Monsieur Doyle wants to see you."

She started up. Her face flushed—then paled. She looked bewildered.

"Simon? He wants to see me—to see *me?*"

He found her incredulity moving.

"Will you come, Mademoiselle?"

"I—yes, of course I will."

She went with him in a docile fashion, like a child, but like a puzzled child.

Poirot passed into the cabin.

"Here is Mademoiselle."

She stepped in after him, wavered, stood still . . . standing there mute and dumb, her eyes fixed on Simon's face.

"Hullo, Jackie." He, too, was embarrassed. He went on: "Awfully good of you to come. I wanted to say—I mean—what I mean is—"

She interrupted him then. Her words came out in a rush—breathless, desperate.

"Simon—I didn't kill Linnet. You know I didn't do that. . . . I—I —was mad last night. Oh, can you ever forgive me?"

Words came more easily to him now.

"Of course. That's all right! Absolutely all right! That's what I wanted to say. Thought you might be worrying a bit, you know. . . ."

"*Worrying? A bit?* Oh! Simon!"

"That's what I wanted to see you about. It's quite all right, see, old girl? You just got a bit rattled last night—a shade tight. All perfectly natural."

"Oh, Simon! I might have killed you!"

"Not you. Not with a rotten little peashooter like that. . . ."

"And your leg! Perhaps you'll never walk again. . . ."

"Now, look here, Jackie, don't be maudlin. As soon as we get to Assuan they're going to put the X-rays to work, and dig out that tin pot bullet, and everything will be as right as rain."

Jacqueline gulped twice; then she rushed forward and knelt down by Simon's bed, burying her face and sobbing. Simon patted her awkwardly on the head. His eyes met Poirot's and, with a reluctant sigh, the latter left the cabin.

He heard broken murmurs as he went:

"How could I be such a devil? Oh, Simon! . . . I'm so dreadfully sorry. . . ."

Outside Cornelia Robson was leaning over the rail. She turned her head.

"Oh, it's you, Monsieur Poirot. It seems so awful somehow that it should be such a lovely day."

Poirot looked up at the sky.

"When the sun shines you cannot see the moon," he said. "But when the sun is gone—ah, when the sun is gone."

Cornelia's mouth fell open.

"I beg your pardon?"

"I was saying, Mademoiselle, that when the sun has gone down, we shall see the moon. That is so, is it not?"

"Why—why, yes—certainly."

She looked at him doubtfully.

Poirot laughed gently.

"I utter the imbecilities," he said. "Take no notice."

He strolled gently toward the stern of the boat. As he passed the next cabin he paused for a minute. He caught fragments of speech from within:

"Utterly ungrateful—after all I've done for you—no consideration for your wretched mother—no idea of what I suffer. . . ."

Poirot's lips stiffened as he pressed them together. He raised a hand and knocked.

There was a startled silence and Mrs. Otterbourne's voice called out, "Who's that?"

"Is Mademoiselle Rosalie there?"

Rosalie appeared in the doorway. Poirot was shocked at her appearance. There were dark circles under her eyes and drawn lines round her mouth.

"What's the matter?" she said ungraciously. "What do you want?"

"The pleasure of a few minutes' conversation with you, Mademoiselle. Will you come?"

Her mouth went sulky at once. She shot him a suspicious look.

"Why should I?"

"I entreat you, Mademoiselle."

"Oh, I suppose—"

She stepped out on the deck, closing the door behind her.

"Well?"

Poirot took her gently by the arm and drew her along the deck, still in the direction of the stern. They passed the bathrooms and round the corner. They had the stern part of the deck to themselves. The Nile flowed away behind them.

Poirot rested his elbows on the rail. Rosalie stood up straight and stiff.

"Well?" she asked again, and her voice held the same ungracious tone.

Poirot spoke slowly, choosing his words. "I could ask you certain questions, Mademoiselle, but I do not think for one moment that you would consent to answer them."

"Seems rather a waste to bring me along here then."

Poirot drew a finger slowly along the wooden rail.

"You are accustomed, Mademoiselle, to carrying your own burdens. . . . But you can do that too long. The strain becomes too great. For you, Mademoiselle, the strain is becoming too great."

"I don't know what you are talking about," said Rosalie.

"I am talking about facts, Mademoiselle—plain ugly facts. Let us call the spade the spade and say it in one little short sentence. Your mother drinks, Mademoiselle."

Rosalie did not answer. Her mouth opened; then she closed it again. For once she seemed at a loss.

"There is no need for you to talk, Mademoiselle. I will do all the talking. I was interested at Assuan in the relations existing between you. I saw at once that, in spite of your carefully studied unfilial remarks, you were in reality passionately protecting her from something. I very soon knew what that something was. I knew it long before I encountered your mother one morning in an unmistakable state of intoxication. Moreover, her case, I could see, was one of secret bouts of drinking—by far the most difficult kind of case with which to deal. You were coping with it manfully. Nevertheless, she had all the secret drunkard's cunning. She managed to get hold of a secret supply of spirits and to keep it successfully hidden from you. I should not be surprised if you discovered its hiding place only yesterday. Accordingly, last night, as soon as your mother was really soundly asleep, you stole out with the contents of the *cache,* went round to the other side of the boat (since your own side was up against the bank) and cast it overboard into the Nile."

He paused.

"I am right, am I not?"

"Yes—you're quite right." Rosalie spoke with sudden passion. "I was a fool not to say so, I suppose! But I didn't want everyone to know. It would go all over the boat. And it seemed so—so silly—I mean—that I—"

Poirot finished the sentence for her.

"So silly that you should be suspected of committing a murder?" Rosalie nodded.

Then she burst out again: "I've tried so hard to—keep everyone from knowing. . . . It isn't really her fault. She got discouraged. Her books didn't sell any more. People are tired of all that cheap sex stuff. . . . It hurt her—it hurt her dreadfully. And so she began to—to drink. For a long time I didn't know why she was so queer. Then, when I found out, I tried to—to stop it. She'd be all right for a bit, and then, suddenly, she'd start, and there would be dreadful quarrels and rows with people. It was awful." She shuddered. "I had always to be on the watch—to get her away . . .

"And then—she began to dislike me for it. She—she's turned right against me. I think she almost hates me sometimes. . . ."

"*Pauvre petite*," said Poirot.

She turned on him vehemently.

"Don't be sorry for me. Don't be kind. It's easier if you're not." She sighed—a long heartrending sigh. "I'm so tired . . . I'm so deadly, deadly tired."

"I know," said Poirot.

"People think I'm awful. Stuck-up and cross and bad-tempered. I can't help it. I've forgotten how to be—to be nice."

"That is what I said to you; you have carried your burden by yourself too long."

Rosalie said slowly: "It is a relief—to talk about it. You—you've always been kind to me, Monsieur Poirot. I'm afraid I've been rude to you often."

"*La politesse,* it is not necessary between friends."

The suspicion came back to her face suddenly.

"Are you—are you going to tell everyone? I suppose you must, because of those damned bottles I threw overboard."

"No, no, it is not necessary. Just tell me what I want to know. At what time was this? Ten minutes past one?"

"About that, I should think. I don't remember exactly."

"Now tell me, Mademoiselle. Mademoiselle Van Schuyler saw *you*, did you see *her*?"

Rosalie shook her head.

"No, I didn't."

"She says that she looked out of the door of her cabin."

"I don't think I should have seen her. I just looked along the deck and then out to the river."

Poirot nodded.

"And did you see anyone—anyone at all, when you looked down the deck?"

There was a pause—quite a long pause. Rosalie was frowning. She seemed to be thinking earnestly.

At last she shook her head quite decisively.

"No," she said. "I saw nobody."

Hercule Poirot slowly nodded his head. But his eyes were grave.

CHAPTER 19

PEOPLE CREPT into the dining-saloon by ones and twos in a very subdued manner. There seemed a general feeling that to sit down eagerly to food displayed an unfortunate heartlessness. It was with an almost apologetic air that one passenger after another came and sat down at their tables.

Tim Allerton arrived some few minutes after his mother had taken her seat. He was looking in a thoroughly bad temper.

"I wish we'd never come on this blasted trip," he growled.

Mrs. Allerton shook her head sadly.

"Oh, my dear, so do I. That beautiful girl! It all seems such a *waste*. To think that anyone could shoot her in cold blood. It seems awful to me that anyone could do such a thing. And that other poor child."

"Jacqueline?"

"Yes; my heart aches for her. She looks so dreadfully unhappy."

"Teach her not to go round loosing off toy firearms," said Tim unfeelingly as he helped himself to butter.

"I expect she was badly brought up."

"Oh, for God's sake, Mother, don't go all maternal about it."

"You're in a shocking bad temper, Tim."

"Yes, I am. Who wouldn't be?"

"I don't see what there is to be cross about. It's just frightfully sad."

Tim said crossly: "You're taking the romantic point of view! What you don't seem to realize is that it's no joke being mixed up in a murder case."

Mrs. Allerton looked a little startled.

"But surely—"

"That's just it. There's no 'But surely' about it. Everyone on this damned boat is under suspicion—you and I as well as the rest of them."

Mrs. Allerton demurred. "Technically we are, I suppose—but actually it's ridiculous!"

"There's nothing ridiculous where murder's concerned! You may sit there, darling, just exuding virtue and conscious rectitude, but a lot of unpleasant policemen at Shellâl or Assuan won't take you at your face value."

"Perhaps the truth will be known before then."

"Why should it be?"

"Monsieur Poirot may find out."

"That old mountebank? He won't find out anything. He's all talk and moustaches."

"Well, Tim," said Mrs. Allerton, "I daresay everything you say is true, but, even if it is, we've got to go through with it, so we might as well make up our minds to it and go through with it as cheerfully as we can."

But her son showed no abatement of gloom.

"There's this blasted business of the pearls being missing, too."

"Linnet's pearls?"

"Yes. It seems somebody must have pinched 'em."

"I suppose that was the motive for the crime," said Mrs. Allerton.

"Why should it be? You're mixing up two perfectly different things."

"Who told you that they were missing?"

"Ferguson. He got it from his tough friend in the engine room, who got it from the maid."

"They were lovely pearls," declared Mrs. Allerton.

Poirot sat down at the table, bowing to Mrs. Allerton.

"I am a little late," he said.

"I expect you have been busy," Mrs. Allerton replied.

"Yes, I have been much occupied."

He ordered a fresh bottle of wine from the waiter.

"We're very catholic in our tastes," said Mrs. Allerton. "You drink wine always; Tim drinks whisky and soda, and I try all the different brands of mineral water in turn."

"*Tiens!*" said Poirot. He stared at her for a moment. He murmured to himself, "It is an idea, that. . . ."

Then, with an impatient shrug of his shoulders, he dismissed the sudden preoccupation that had distracted him and began to chat lightly of other matters.

"Is Mr. Doyle badly hurt?" asked Mrs. Allerton.

"Yes, it is a fairly serious injury. Dr. Bessner is anxious to reach Assuan so that his leg can be X-rayed and the bullet removed. But he hopes that there will be no permanent lameness."

"Poor Simon," said Mrs. Allerton. "Only yesterday he looked such a happy boy, with everything in the world he wanted. And now his beautiful wife killed and he himself laid up and helpless. I do hope, though—"

"What do you hope, Madame?" asked Poirot as Mrs. Allerton paused.

"I hope he's not too angry with that poor child."

"With Mademoiselle Jacqueline? Quite the contrary. He was full of anxiety on her behalf."

He turned to Tim.

"You know, it is a pretty little problem of psychology, that. All the time that Mademoiselle Jacqueline was following them from place to place, he was absolutely furious; but now, when she has actually shot him, and wounded him dangerously—perhaps made him lame for life —all his anger seems to have evaporated. Can you understand that?"

"Yes," said Tim thoughtfully, "I think I can. The first thing made him feel a fool—"

Poirot nodded. "You are right. It offended his male dignity."

"But now—if you look at it a certain way, it's *she* who's made a fool of herself. Everyone's down on her, and so—"

"He can be generously forgiving," finished Mrs. Allerton. "What children men are!"

"A profoundly untrue statement that women always make," murmured Tim.

Poirot smiled. Then he said to Tim, "Tell me, Madame Doyle's cousin, Miss Joanna Southwood, did she resemble Madame Doyle?"

"You've got it a little wrong, Monsieur Poirot. She was our cousin and Linnet's friend."

"Ah, pardon—I was confused. She is a young lady much in the news, that. I have been interested in her for some time."

"Why?" asked Tim sharply.

Poirot half rose to bow to Jacqueline de Bellefort, who had just come in and passed their table on the way to her own. Her cheeks were flushed and her eyes bright, and her breath came a little unevenly. As he resumed his seat Poirot seemed to have forgotten Tim's question. He murmured vaguely, "I wonder if all young ladies with valuable jewels were as careless as Madame Doyle was?"

"It is true, then, that they were stolen?" asked Mrs. Allerton.

"Who told you so, Madame?"

"Ferguson said so," Tim volunteered.

Poirot nodded gravely.

"It is quite true."

"I suppose," said Mrs. Allerton nervously, "that this will mean a lot of unpleasantness for all of us. Tim says it will."

Her son scowled, but Poirot had turned to him.

"Ah! you have had previous experience, perhaps? You have been in a house where there was a robbery?"

"Never," said Tim.

"Oh, yes, darling, you were at the Portarlingtons' that time—when that awful woman's diamonds were stolen."

"You always get things hopelessly wrong, Mother. I was there when it was discovered that the diamonds she was wearing round her fat neck were only paste! The actual substitution was probably done months earlier. As a matter of fact, a lot of people said she'd had it done herself!"

"Joanna said so, I expect."

"Joanna wasn't there."

"But she knew them quite well. And it's very like her to make that kind of suggestion."

"You're always down on Joanna, Mother."

Poirot hastily changed the subject. He had it in mind to make a really big purchase at one of the Assuan shops. Some very attractive purple and gold material at one of the Indian merchants. There would, of course, be the duty to pay, but—

"They tell me that they can—how do you say?—expedite it for me. And that the charges will not be too high. How think you, will it arrive all right?"

Mrs. Allerton said that many people, so she had heard, had had things sent straight to England from the shops in question and that everything had arrived safely.

"*Bien.* Then I will do that. But the trouble one has, when one is abroad, if a parcel comes out from England! Have you had experience of that? Have you had any parcels arrive since you have been on your travels?"

"I don't think we have, have we, Tim? You get books sometimes, but of course there is never any trouble about them."

"Ah, no, books are different."

Dessert had been served. Now, without any previous warning, Colonel Race stood up and made his speech.

He touched on the circumstances of the crime and announced the theft of the pearls. A search of the boat was about to be instituted, and he would be obliged if all the passengers would remain in the saloon until this was completed. Then, after that, if the passengers agreed, as he was sure they would, they themselves would be kind enough to submit to a search.

Poirot slipped nimbly along to his side. There was a little buzz and hum all round them. Voices doubtful, indignant, excited. . . .

Poirot reached Race's side and murmured something in his ear just as the latter was about to leave the dining-saloon.

Race listened, nodded assent, and beckoned a steward. He said a few brief words to him; then, together with Poirot, he passed out onto the deck, closing the door behind him.

They stood for a minute or two by the rail. Race lit a cigarette.

"Not a bad idea of yours," he said. "We'll soon see if there's anything in it. I'll give 'em three minutes."

The door of the dining-saloon opened and the same steward to whom they had spoken came out. He saluted Race and said: "Quite right, sir. There's a lady who says it's urgent she should speak to you at once without any delay."

"Ah!" Race's face showed his satisfaction. "Who is it?"

"Miss Bowers, sir, the hospital nurse lady."

A slight shade of surprise showed on Race's face. He said: "Bring her to the smoking-room. Don't let anyone else leave."

"No, sir—the other steward will attend to that."

He went back into the dining-room. Poirot and Race went to the smoking-room.

"Bowers, eh?" murmured Race.

They had hardly got inside the smoking-room before the steward reappeared with Miss Bowers. He ushered her in and left, shutting the door behind him.

"Well, Miss Bowers?" Colonel Race looked at her inquiringly. "What's all this?"

Miss Bowers looked her usual composed, unhurried self. She displayed no particular emotion.

"You'll excuse me, Colonel Race," she said, "but under the circumstances I thought the best thing to do would be to speak to you at once"—she opened her neat black handbag—"and to return you these."

She took out a string of pearls and laid them on the table.

CHAPTER 20

IF Miss Bowers had been the kind of woman who enjoyed creating a sensation, she would have been richly repaid by the result of her action.

A look of utter astonishment passed over Colonel Race's face as he picked up the pearls from the table.

"This is most extraordinary," he said. "Will you kindly explain, Miss Bowers?"

"Of course. That's what I've come to do." Miss Bowers settled herself comfortably in a chair. "Naturally it was a little difficult for me to decide what it was best for me to do. The family would naturally be averse to scandal of any kind, and they trust my discretion, but the circumstances are so very unusual that it really leaves me no choice. Of course, when you didn't find anything in the cabins, your next move would be a search of the passengers, and if the pearls were then found in my possession it would be rather an awkward situation and the truth would come out just the same."

"And just what is the truth? Did you take these pearls from Mrs. Doyle's cabin?"

"Oh, no, Colonel Race, of course not. Miss Van Schuyler did."

"Miss Van Schuyler?"

"Yes. She can't help it, you know, but she does—er—take things. Especially jewellery. That's really why I'm always with her. It's not her health at all; it's this little idiosyncrasy. I keep on the alert, and fortunately there's never been any trouble since I've been with her. It just means being watchful, you know. And she always hides the things she takes in the same place—rolled up in a pair of stockings—so that makes it very simple. I look each morning. Of course I'm a light sleeper, and I always sleep next door to her, and with the communicating door open if it's in a hotel, so that I usually hear. Then I go after her and persuade her to go back to bed. Of course it's been rather more difficult on a boat. But she doesn't usually do it at night. It's more just picking up things that she sees left about. Of course, pearls have a great attraction for her always."

Miss Bowers ceased speaking.

Race asked, "How did you discover they had been taken?"

"They were in her stockings this morning. I knew whose they were, of course. I've often noticed them. I went along to put them back, hoping that Mrs. Doyle wasn't up yet and hadn't discovered her loss. But there was a steward standing there, and he told me about the murder and that no one could go in. So then, you see, I was in a regular quandary. But I still hoped to slip them back in the cabin later, before their absence had been noticed. I can assure you I've passed a very unpleasant morning wondering what was the best thing to do. You see the Van Schuyler family is so *very* particular and exclusive. It would never do if this got into the newspapers. But that won't be necessary, will it?"

Miss Bowers really looked worried.

"That depends on circumstances," said Colonel Race cautiously. "But we shall do our best for you, of course. What does Miss Van Schuyler say to this?"

"Oh, she'll deny it, of course. She always does. Says some wicked person has put it there. She never admits taking anything. That's why if you catch her in time she goes back to bed like a lamb. Says she just went out to look at the moon. Something like that."

"Does Miss Robson know about this—er—failing?"

"No, she doesn't. Her mother knows, but she's a very simple kind of girl and her mother thought it best she should know nothing about it. I was quite equal to dealing with Miss Van Schuyler," added the competent Miss Bowers.

"We have to thank you, Mademoiselle, for coming to us so promptly," said Poirot.

Miss Bowers stood up.

"I'm sure I hope I've acted for the best."

"Be assured that you have."

"You see, what with there being a murder as well—"

Colonel Race interrupted her. His voice was grave.

"Miss Bowers, I am going to ask you a question, and I want to impress upon you that it has got to be answered truthfully. Miss Van Schuyler is unhinged mentally to the extent of being a kleptomaniac. Has she also a tendency to homicidal mania?"

Miss Bowers' answer came immediately: "Oh, dear me, no! Nothing of that kind. You can take my word for it absolutely. The old lady wouldn't hurt a fly."

The reply came with such positive assurance that there seemed nothing more to be said. Nevertheless Poirot did interpolate one mild inquiry.

"Does Miss Van Schuyler suffer at all from deafness?"

"As a matter of fact she does, Monsieur Poirot. Not so that you'd notice it any way, not if you were speaking to her, I mean. But quite often she doesn't hear you when you come into a room. Things like that."

"Do you think she would have heard anyone moving about in Mrs. Doyle's cabin, which is next door to her own?"

"Oh, I shouldn't think so—not for a minute. You see, the bunk is the other side of the cabin, not even against the partition wall. No, I don't think she would have heard anything."

"Thank you, Miss Bowers."

Race said, "Perhaps you will now go back to the dining-saloon and wait with the others?"

He opened the door for her and watched her go down the staircase and enter the saloon. Then he shut the door and came back to the table. Poirot had picked up the pearls.

"Well," said Race grimly, "that reaction came pretty quickly. That's a very cool-headed and astute young woman—perfectly capable of holding out on us still further if she thinks it suits her book. What about Miss Marie Van Schuyler now? I don't think we can eliminate her from the possible suspects. You know, she *might* have committed murder to get hold of those jewels. We can't take the nurse's word for it. She's all out to do the best for the family."

Poirot nodded in agreement. He was very busy with the pearls, running them through his fingers, holding them up to his eyes.

He said: "We may take it, I think, that part of the old lady's story to us was true. She *did* look out of her cabin and she *did* see Rosalie Otterbourne. But I don't think she *heard* anything or anyone in Linnet Doyle's cabin. I think she was just peering out from *her* cabin preparatory to slipping along and purloining the pearls."

"The Otterbourne girl was there, then?"

"Yes. Throwing her mother's secret *cache* of drink overboard."

Colonel Race shook his head sympathetically.

"So that's it! Tough on a young un."

"Yes, her life has not been very gay, *cette pauvre petite Rosalie*."

"Well, I'm glad that's been cleared up. *She* didn't see or hear anything?"

"I asked her that. She responded—after a lapse of quite twenty seconds—that she saw nobody."

"Oh?" Race looked alert.

"Yes, it is suggestive, that."

Race said slowly: "If Linnet Doyle was shot round about ten minutes past one, or indeed any time after the boat had quieted down, it has seemed amazing to me that no one heard the shot. I grant you that a little pistol like that wouldn't make much noise, but all the same the boat would be deadly quiet, and any noise, even a gentle pop, should have been heard. But I begin to understand better now. The cabin on the forward side of hers was unoccupied—since her husband was in Dr. Bessner's cabin. The one aft was occupied by the Van Schuyler woman, who was deaf. That leaves only—"

He paused and looked expectantly at Poirot, who nodded.

"The cabin next to hers on the other side of the boat. In other words—Pennington. We always seem to come back to Pennington."

"We will come back to him presently with the kid gloves removed! Ah, yes, I am promising myself that pleasure."

"In the meantime we'd better get on with our search of the boat. The pearls still make a convenient excuse, even though they have been returned—but Miss Bowers is not likely to advertise that fact."

"Ah, these pearls!" Poirot held them up against the light once more. He stuck out his tongue and licked them; he even gingerly tried one of them between his teeth. Then, with a sigh, he threw them down on the table.

"Here are more complications, my friend," he said. "I am not an expert on precious stones, but I have had a good deal to do with them in my time and I am fairly certain of what I say. These pearls are only a clever imitation."

CHAPTER 21

COLONEL RACE swore lustily.

"This damned case gets more and more involved." He picked up the pearls. "I suppose you've not made a mistake? They look all right to me."

"They are a very good imitation—yes."

"Now where does that lead us? I suppose Linnet Doyle didn't deliberately have an imitation made and bring it aboard with her for safety. Many women do."

"I think, if that were so, her husband would know about it."

"She may not have told him."

Poirot shook his head in a dissatisfied manner.

"No, I do not think that is so. I was admiring Madame Doyle's pearls the first evening on the boat—their wonderful sheen and lustre. I am sure that she was wearing the genuine ones then."

"That brings us up against two possibilities. First, that Miss Van Schuyler only stole the imitation string after the real ones had been stolen by someone else. Second, that the whole kleptomaniac story is a fabrication. Either Miss Bowers is a thief, and quickly invented the story and allayed suspicion by handing over the false pearls, or else that whole party is in it together. That is to say, they are a gang of clever jewel thieves masquerading as an exclusive American family."

"Yes," Poirot murmured. "It is difficult to say. But I will point out to you one thing—to make a perfect and exact copy of the pearls, clasp and all, good enough to stand a chance of deceiving Madame Doyle, is a highly skilled technical performance. It could not be done in a hurry. Whoever copied those pearls must have had a good opportunity of studying the original."

Race rose to his feet.

"Useless to speculate about it any further now. Let's get on with the job. We've got to find the real pearls. And at the same time we'll keep our eyes open."

They disposed first of the cabins occupied on the lower deck.

That of Signor Richetti contained various archaeological works in different languages, a varied assortment of clothing, hair lotions of a highly scented kind and two personal letters—one from an archaeological expedition in Syria, and one from, apparently, a sister in Rome. His handkerchiefs were all of coloured silk.

They passed on to Ferguson's cabin.

There was a sprinkling of communistic literature, a good many snapshots, Samuel Butler's *Erewhon* and a cheap edition of Pepys' Diary. His personal possessions were not many. Most of what outer clothing there was was torn and dirty; the underclothing, on the other hand, was of really good quality. The handkerchiefs were expensive linen ones.

"Some interesting discrepancies," murmured Poirot.

Race nodded. "Rather odd that there are absolutely no personal papers, letters, etc."

"Yes; that gives one to think. An odd young man, Monseiur Ferguson."

He looked thoughtfully at a signet ring he held in his hand, before replacing it in the drawer where he had found it.

They went along to the cabin occupied by Louise Bourget. The maid had her meals after the other passengers, but Race had sent word that she was to be taken to join the others. A cabin steward met them.

"I'm sorry, sir," he apologized, "but I've not been able to find the young woman anywhere. I can't think where she can have got to."

Race glanced inside the cabin. It was empty.

They went up to the promenade deck and started on the starboard side. The first cabin was that occupied by James Fanthorp. Here all was in meticulous order. Mr. Fanthorp travelled light, but all that he had was of good quality.

"No letters," said Poirot thoughtfully. "He is careful, our Mr. Fanthorp, to destroy his correspondence."

They passed on to Tim Allerton's cabin, next door.

There were evidences here of an Anglo Catholic turn of mind—an exquisite little triptych, and a big rosary of intricately carved wood. Besides personal clothing, there was a half completed manuscript, a good deal annotated and scribbled over, and a good collection of books, most of them recently published. There were also a quantity of letters thrown carelessly into a drawer. Poirot, never in the least scrupulous about reading other people's correspondence, glanced through them. He noted that amongst them there were no letters from Joanna Southwood. He picked up a tube of Seccotine, fingered it absently for a minute or two, then said, "Let us pass on."

"No Woolworth handkerchiefs," reported Race, rapidly replacing the contents of a drawer.

Mrs. Allerton's cabin was the next. It was exquisitely neat, and a faint old-fashioned smell of lavender hung about it.

The two men's search was soon over. Race remarked as they left it, "Nice woman, that."

The next cabin was that which had been used as a dressing-room by Simon Doyle. His immediate necessities—pyjamas, toilet things, etc., had been moved to Bessner's cabin, but the remainder of his possessions were still there—two good-sized leather suitcases and a kit bag. There were also some clothes in the wardrobe.

"We will look carefully here, my friend," said Poirot, "for it is very possible that the thief hid the pearls here."

"You think it is likely?"

"But yes, indeed. Consider! The thief, whoever he or she may be, must know that sooner or later a search will be made, and therefore a hiding place in his or her own cabin would be injudicious in the extreme. The public rooms present other difficulties. But here is a cabin belonging to a man who cannot possibly visit it himself, so that, if the pearls are found here, it tells us nothing at all."

But the most meticulous search failed to reveal any trace of the missing necklace.

Poirot murmured "Zut!" to himself and they emerged once more on the deck.

Linnet Doyle's cabin had been locked after the body was removed, but Race had the key with him. He unlocked the door and the two men stepped inside.

Except for the removal of the girl's body, the cabin was exactly as it had been that morning.

"Poirot," said Race, "if there's anything to be found here, for

God's sake go ahead and find it. You can if anyone can—I know that."

"This time you do not mean the pearls, *mon ami?*"

"No. The murder's the main thing. There may be something I overlooked this morning."

Quietly, deftly, Poirot went about his search. He went down on his knees and scrutinized the floor inch by inch. He examined the bed. He went rapidly through the wardrobe and chest of drawers. He went through the wardrobe trunk and the two costly suitcases. He looked through the expensive gold-fitted dressingcase. Finally he turned his attention to the washstand. There were various creams, powders, face lotions. But the only thing that seemed to interest Poirot were two little bottles labelled Nailex. He picked them up at last and brought them to the dressing-table. One, which bore the inscription Nailex Rose, was empty but for a drop or two of dark red fluid at the bottom. The other, the same size, but labelled Nailex Cardinal, was nearly full. Poirot uncorked first the empty, then the full one, and sniffed them both delicately.

An odour of pear drops billowed into the room. With a slight grimace he recorked them.

"Get anything?" asked Race.

Poirot replied by a French proverb, *"On ne prend pas les mouches avec le vinaigre."* Then he said with a sigh: "My friend, we have not been fortunate. The murderer has not been obliging. He has not dropped for us the cuff link, the cigarette end, the cigar ash—or, in the case of a woman, the handkerchief, the lipstick or the hair slide."

"Only the bottle of nail polish?"

Poirot shrugged his shoulders.

"I must ask the maid. There is something—yes—a little curious there."

"I wonder where the devil the girl's got to?" said Race.

They left the cabin, locking the door behind them, and passed on to that of Miss Van Schuyler.

Here again were all the appurtenances of wealth, expensive toilet fittings, good luggage, a certain number of private letters and papers all perfectly in order.

The next cabin was the double one occupied by Poirot, and beyond it that of Race.

"Hardly likely to hide 'em in either of these," said the Colonel.

Poirot demurred. "It might be. Once, on the Orient Express, I investigated a murder. There was a little matter of a scarlet kimono. It had disappeared, and yet it must be on the train. I found it—where do you think? In my own locked suitcase! Ah! it was an impertinence, that!"

"Well, let's see if anybody has been impertinent with you or me this time."

But the thief of the pearls had not been impertinent with Hercule Poirot or with Colonel Race.

Rounding the stern they made a very careful search of Miss Bowers' cabin but could find nothing of a suspicious nature. Her handkerchiefs were of plain linen with an initial.

The Otterbournes' cabin came next. Here, again, Poirot made a very meticulous search, but with no result.

The next cabin was Bessner's. Simon Doyle lay with an untasted tray of food beside him.

"Off my feed," he said apologetically.

He was looking feverish and very much worse than earlier in the day. Poirot appreciated Bessner's anxiety to get him as swiftly as possible to hospital and skilled appliances.

The little Belgian explained what the two of them were doing, and Simon nodded approval. On learning that the pearls had been restored by Miss Bowers, but proved to be merely imitation, he expressed the most complete astonishment.

"You are quite sure, Monsieur Doyle, that your wife did not have an imitation string which she brought abroad with her instead of the real ones?"

Simon shook his head decisively.

"Oh, no. I'm quite sure of that. Linnet loved those pearls and she wore 'em everywhere. They were insured against every possible risk, so I think that made her a bit careless."

"Then we must continue our search."

He started opening drawers. Race attacked a suitcase.

Simon stared. "Look here, you surely don't suspect old Bessner pinched them?" Poirot shrugged his shoulders.

"It might be so. After all, what do we know of Dr. Bessner? Only what he himself gives out."

"But he couldn't have hidden them in here without my seeing him."

"He could not have hidden anything *today* without your having seen him. But we do not know when the substitution took place. He may have effected the exchange some days ago."

"I never thought of that."

But the search was unavailing.

The next cabin was Pennington's. The two men spent some time in their search. In particular, Poirot and Race examined carefully a case full of legal and business documents, most of them requiring Linnet's signature.

Poirot shook his head gloomily. "These seem all square and aboveboard. You agree?"

"Absolutely. Still, the man isn't a born fool. If there *had* been a compromising document there—a power of attorney or something of that kind—he'd be pretty sure to have destroyed it first thing."

"That is so, yes."

Poirot lifted a heavy Colt revolver out of the top drawer of the chest of drawers, looked at it and put it back.

"So it seems there are still some people who travel with revolvers," he murmured.

"Yes, a little suggestive, perhaps. Still, Linnet Doyle wasn't shot with a thing that size." Race paused and then said: "You know, I've thought of a possible answer to your point about the pistol being thrown overboard. Supposing that the actual murderer *did* leave it in Linnet Doyle's cabin, and that someone else—some second person— took it away and threw it into the river?"

"Yes, that is possible. I have thought of it. But it opens up a whole string of questions. Who was that second person? What interest had they in endeavouring to shield Jacqueline de Bellefort by taking away the pistol? What was that second person doing there? The only other person we know of who went into the cabin was Mademoiselle Van Schuyler. Was it conceivably Mademoiselle Van Schuyler who removed it? Why should *she* wish to shield Jacqueline de Bellefort? And yet—what other reason can there be for the removal of the pistol?"

Race suggested, "She may have recognized the stole as hers, got the wind up, and thrown the whole bag of tricks over on that account."

"The stole, perhaps, but would she have got rid of the pistol, too? Still, I agree that it is a possible solution. But it is clumsy—*bon Dieu*, it is clumsy. And you still have not appreciated one point about the stole—"

As they emerged from Pennington's cabin Poirot suggested that Race should search the remaining cabins, those occupied by Jacqueline, Cornelia and two empty ones at the end, while he himself had a few words with Simon Doyle.

Accordingly he retraced his steps along the deck and re-entered Bessner's cabin.

Simon said: "Look here, I've been thinking. I'm perfectly sure that those pearls were all right yesterday."

"Why is that, Monsieur Doyle?"

"Because, Linnet"—he winced as he uttered his wife's name—"was passing them through her hands just before dinner and talking about them. She knew something about pearls. I feel certain she'd have known if they were a fake."

"They were a very good imitation, though. Tell me, was Madame Doyle in the habit of letting those pearls out of her hands? Did she ever lend them to a friend, for instance?"

Simon flushed with slight embarrassment.

"You see, Monsieur Poirot, it's difficult for me to say. . . . I—I—well, you see, I hadn't known Linnet very long."

"Ah, no, it was a quick romance—yours."

Simon went on.

"And so—really—I shouldn't know a thing like that. But Linnet was awfully generous with her things. I should think she might have done."

"She never for instance"—Poirot's voice was very smooth—"she never, for instance, lent them to Mademoiselle de Bellefort?"

"What d'you mean?" Simon flushed brick red, tried to sit up and, wincing, fell back. "What are you getting at? That Jackie stole the pearls? She didn't. I'll swear she didn't. Jackie's as straight as a die. The mere idea of her being a thief is ridiculous—absolutely ridiculous."

Poirot looked at him with gently twinkling eyes.

"Oh, la! la! la!" he said unexpectedly. "That suggestion of mine, it has indeed stirred up the nest of hornets."

Simon repeated doggedly, unmoved by Poirot's lighter note, "Jackie's straight!"

Poirot remembered a girl's voice by the Nile in Assuan saying, "I love Simon—and he loves me. . . ."

He had wondered which of the three statements he had heard that night was the true one. It seemed to him that it had turned out to be Jacqueline who had come closest to the truth.

The door opened and Race came in.

"Nothing," he said brusquely. "Well, we didn't expect it. I see the stewards coming along with their report as to the searching of the passengers."

A steward and stewardess appeared in the doorway. The former spoke first.

"Nothing, sir."

"Any of the gentlemen make any fuss?"

"Only the Italian gentleman, sir. He carried on a good deal. Said it was a dishonour—something of that kind. He'd got a gun on him, too."

"What kind of a gun?"

"Mauser automatic twenty-five, sir."

"Italians are pretty hot-tempered," said Simon. "Richetti got in no end of a stew at Wâdi Halfa just because of a mistake over a telegram. He was darned rude to Linnet over it."

Race turned to the stewardess. She was a big handsome looking woman.

"Nothing on any of the ladies, sir. They made a good deal of fuss—except for Mrs. Allerton, who was as nice as nice could be. Not a sign of the pearls. By the way, the young lady, Miss Rosalie Otterbourne, had a little pistol in her handbag."

"What kind?"

"It was a very small one, sir, with a pearl handle. A kind of toy."

Race stared.

"Devil take this case," he muttered. "I thought we'd got *her* cleared of suspicion, and now—Does every girl on this blinking boat carry around pearl-handled toy pistols?"

He shot a question at the stewardess. "Did she show any feeling over your finding it?"

The woman shook her head. "I don't think she noticed. I had my back turned whilst I was going through the handbag."

"Still, she must have known you'd come across it. Oh, well, it beats me. What about the maid?"

"We've looked all over the boat, sir. We can't find her anywhere."

"What's this?" asked Simon.

"Mrs. Doyle's maid—Louise Bourget. She's disappeared."

"*Disappeared?*"

Race said thoughtfully: "She might have stolen the pearls. She is the one person who had ample opportunity to get a replica made."

"And then, when she found a search was being instituted, she threw herself overboard?" suggested Simon.

"Nonsense," replied Race, irritably. "A woman can't throw herself overboard in broad daylight, from a boat like this, without somebody realizing the fact. She's bound to be somewhere on board." He addressed the stewardess once more. "When was she last seen?"

"About half an hour before the bell went for lunch, sir."

"We'll have a look at her cabin anyway," said Race. "That may tell us something."

He led the way to the deck below. Poirot followed him. They unlocked the door of the cabin and passed inside.

Louise Bourget, whose trade it was to keep other people's belongings in order, had taken a holiday where her own were concerned. Odds and ends littered the top of the chest of drawers; a suitcase gaped open, with clothes hanging out of the side of it and preventing it shutting; underclothing hung limply over the sides of the chairs.

As Poirot, with swift neat fingers, opened the drawers of the dressing-chest, Race examined the suitcase.

Louise's shoes were lined along by the bed. One of them, a black patent leather, seemed to be resting at an extraordinary angle, almost unsupported. The appearance of it was so odd that it attracted Race's attention.

He closed the suitcase and bent over the line of shoes. Then he uttered a sharp exclamation.

Poirot whirled round.

"Qu'est ce qu'il y a?"

Race said grimly: "She hasn't disappeared. She's here—under the bed. . . ."

CHAPTER 22

THE BODY of a dead woman, who in life had been Louise Bourget, lay on the floor of her cabin. The two men bent over it.

Race straightened himself first.

"Been dead close on an hour, I should say. We'll get Bessner on to it. Stabbed to the heart. Death pretty well instantaneous, I should imagine. She doesn't look pretty, does she?"

"No."

Poirot shook his head with a slight shudder.

The dark feline face was convulsed, as though with surprise and fury, the lips drawn back from the teeth.

Poirot bent again gently and picked up the right hand. Something just showed within the fingers. He detached it and held it out to Race, a little sliver of flimsy paper coloured a pale mauvish pink.

"You see what it is?"

"Money," said Race.

"The corner of a thousand franc note, I fancy."

"Well, it's clear what happened," said Race. "She knew something—and she was blackmailing the murderer with her knowledge. We thought she wasn't being quite straight this morning."

Poirot cried out: "We have been idiots—fools! We should have known—then. What did she say? 'What could I have seen or heard? I was on the deck below. Naturally, if I had been unable to sleep, if I had mounted the stairs, *then* perhaps I might have seen this assassin, this monster, enter or leave Madame's cabin, but as it is—" Of course, that is what did happen! She did come up. She did see someone gliding into Linnet Doyle's cabin—or coming out of it. And, because of her greed, her insensate greed, she lies here—"

"And we are no nearer to knowing who killed her," finished Race disgustedly.

Poirot shook his head. "No, no. We know much more now. We know—we know almost everything. Only what we know seems incredible. . . . Yet it must be so. Only I do not see. Pah! what a fool I was this morning! We felt—both of us felt—that she was keeping something back, and yet we never realized the logical reason, blackmail."

"She must have demanded hush money straight away," said Race. "Demanded it with threats. The murderer was forced to accede to that request and paid her in French notes. Anything there?"

Poirot shook his head thoughtfully. "I hardly think so. Many people take a reserve of money with them when travelling—sometimes five pound notes, sometimes dollars, but very often French notes as well. Possibly the murderer paid her all he had in a mixture of currencies. Let us continue our reconstruction."

"The murderer comes to her cabin, gives her the money, and then—"

"And then," said Poirot, "she counts it. Oh, yes, I know that class. She would count the money, and while she counted it she was completely off her guard. The murderer struck. Having done so successfully, he gathered up the money and fled—not noticing that the corner of one of the notes was torn."

"We may get him that way," suggested Race doubtfully.

"I doubt it," said Poirot. "He will examine those notes, and will

probably notice the tear. Of course if he were of a parsimonious disposition he would not be able to bring himself to destroy a *mille* note
—but I fear—I very much fear that his temperament is just the opposite."

"How do you make that out?"

"Both this crime and the murder of Madame Doyle demanded certain qualities—courage, audacity, bold execution, lightning action;
those qualities do not accord with a saving, prudent disposition."

Race shook his head sadly. "I'd better get Bessner down," he said.

The stout doctor's examination did not take long. Accompanied by
a good many Ach's and So's, he went to work.

"She has been dead not more than an hour," he announced.
"Death it was very quick—at once."

"And what weapon do you think was used?"

"Ach, it is interesting, that. It was something very sharp, very thin,
very delicate. I could show you the kind of thing."

Back again in his cabin he opened a case and extracted a long, delicate, surgical knife.

"It was something like that, my friend; it was not a common table
knife."

"I suppose," suggested Race smoothly, "that none of your own
knives are—er—missing, Doctor?"

Bessner stared at him; then his face grew red with indignation.

"What is that you say? Do you think I—I, Carl Bessner—who so
well-known is all over Austria—I with my clinics, my highly born patients—I have killed a miserable little *femme de chambre?!* Ah, but it
is ridiculous—absurd, what you say! None of my knives are missing—
not one, I tell you. They are all here, correct, in their places. You can
see for yourself. And this insult to my profession I will not forget."

Dr. Bessner closed his case with a snap, flung it down and stamped
out onto the deck.

"Whew!" said Simon. "You've put the old boy's back up."

Poirot shrugged his shoulders. "It is regrettable."

"You're on the wrong tack. Old Bessner's one of the best, even
though he is a kind of Boche."

Dr. Bessner reappeared suddenly.

"Will you be so kind as to leave me now my cabin? I have to do
the dressing of my patient's leg."

Miss Bowers had entered with him and stood, brisk and professional, waiting for the others to go.

Race and Poirot crept out meekly. Race muttered something and went off. Poirot turned to his left. He heard scraps of girlish conversation, a little laugh. Jacqueline and Rosalie were together in the latter's cabin.

The door was open and the two girls were standing near it. As his shadow fell on them they looked up. He saw Rosalie Otterbourne smile at him for the first time—a shy welcoming smile—a little uncertain in its lines, as of one who does a new and unfamiliar thing.

"You talk the scandal, Mesdemoiselles?" he accused them.

"No, indeed," said Rosalie. "As a matter of fact we were just comparing lipsticks."

Poirot smiled. *"Les chiffons d'aujourd'hui,"* he murmured.

But there was something a little mechanical about his smile, and Jacqueline de Bellefort, quicker and more observant than Rosalie, saw it. She dropped the lipstick she was holding and came out upon the deck.

"Has something—what has happened now?"

"It is as you guess, Mademoiselle; something has happened."

"What?" Rosalie came out too.

"Another death," said Poirot.

Rosalie caught her breath sharply. Poirot was watching her narrowly. He saw alarm and something more—consternation—show for a minute or two in her eyes.

"Madame Doyle's maid has been killed," he told them bluntly.

"Killed?" cried Jacqueline. *"Killed,* do you say?"

"Yes, that is what I said." Though his answer was nominally to her, it was Rosalie whom he watched. It was Rosalie to whom he spoke as he went on: "You see, this maid she saw something she was not intended to see. And so—she was silenced, in case she should not hold her tongue."

"What was it she saw?"

Again it was Jacqueline who asked, and again Poirot's answer was to Rosalie. It was an odd little three-cornered scene.

"There is, I think, very little doubt what it was she saw," said Poirot. "She saw someone enter and leave Linnet Doyle's cabin on that fatal night."

His ears were quick. He heard the sharp intake of breath and saw the eyelids flicker. Rosalie Otterbourne had reacted just as he had intended she should.

"Did she say who it was she saw?" Rosalie asked.

Gently—regretfully—Poirot shook his head.

Footsteps pattered up the deck. It was Cornelia Robson, her eyes wide and startled.

"Oh, Jacqueline," she cried, "something awful has happened! Another dreadful thing!"

Jacqueline turned to her. The two moved a few steps forward. Almost unconsciously Poirot and Rosalie Otterbourne moved in the other direction.

Rosalie said sharply: "Why do you look at me? What have you got in your mind?"

"That is two questions you ask me. I will ask you only one in return. Why do you not tell me all the truth, Mademoiselle?"

"I don't know what you mean. I told you—everything—this morning."

"No, there were things you did not tell me. You did not tell me that you carry about in your handbag a small-calibre pistol with a pearl handle. You did not tell me all that you saw last night."

She flushed. Then she said sharply: "It's quite untrue. I haven't got a revolver."

"I did not say a revolver. I said a small pistol that you carry about in your handbag."

She wheeled round, darted into her cabin and out again and thrust her grey leather handbag into his hands.

"You're talking nonsense. Look for yourself if you like."

Poirot opened the bag. There was no pistol inside.

He handed the bag back to her, meeting her scornful, triumphant glance.

"No," he said pleasantly. "It is not there."

"You see. You're not always right, Monsieur Poirot. And you're wrong about that other ridiculous thing you said."

"No, I do not think so."

"You're infuriating!" She stamped an angry foot. "You get an idea into your head, and you go on and on and on about it."

"Because I want you to tell me the truth."

"What is the truth? You seem to know it better than I do."

Poirot said: "You want me to tell what it was you saw? If I am right, will you admit that I am right? I will tell you my little idea. I think that when you came round the stern of the boat you stopped involuntarily because you saw a man come out of a cabin about half way down the deck—Linnet Doyle's cabin, as you realized next day. You saw him come out, close the door behind him, and walk away from you down the deck and—perhaps—enter one of the two end cabins. Now then, am I right, Mademoiselle?"

She did not answer.

Poirot said: "Perhaps you think it wiser not to speak. Perhaps you are afraid that, if you do, you too will be killed."

For a moment he thought she had risen to the easy bait, that the accusation against her courage would succeed where more subtle arguments would have failed.

Her lips opened—trembled—then, "I saw no one," said Rosalie Otterbourne.

CHAPTER 23

MISS BOWERS came out of Dr. Bessner's cabin, smoothing her cuffs over her wrists.

Jacqueline left Cornelia abruptly and accosted the hospital nurse.

"How is he?" she demanded.

Poirot came up in time to hear the answer. Miss Bowers was looking rather worried.

"Things aren't going too badly," she said.

Jacqueline cried, "You mean, he's worse?"

"Well, I must say I shall be relieved when we get in and can get a proper X-ray done and the whole thing cleaned up under an anaesthetic. When do you think we shall get to Shellâl, Monsieur Poirot?"

"Tomorrow morning."

Miss Bowers pursed her lips and shook her head.

"It's very unfortunate. We are doing all we can, but there's always such a danger of septicaemia."

Jacqueline caught Miss Bowers' arm and shook it.

"Is he going to die? Is he going to die?"

"Dear me, no, Miss de Bellefort. That is, I hope not, I'm sure. The wound in itself isn't dangerous, but there's no doubt it ought to be X-rayed as soon as possible. And then, of course, poor Mr. Doyle ought to have been kept absolutely quiet today. He's had far too much worry and excitement. No wonder his temperature is rising. What with the shock of his wife's death, and one thing and another—"

Jacqueline relinquished her grasp of the nurse's arm and turned away. She stood leaning over the side, her back to the other two.

"What I say is, we've got to hope for the best always," said Miss Bowers. "Of course Mr. Doyle has a very strong constitution—one can see that—probably never had a day's illness in his life. So that's in his favour. But there's no denying that this rise in temperature is a nasty sign and—"

She shook her head, adjusted her cuffs once more, and moved briskly away.

Jacqueline turned and walked gropingly, blinded by tears, toward her cabin. A hand below her elbow steadied and guided her. She looked up through the tears to find Poirot by her side. She leaned on him a little and he guided her through the cabin door.

She sank down on the bed and the tears came more freely, punctuated by great shuddering sobs.

"He'll die! He'll die! I know he'll die. . . . And I shall have killed him. Yes, I shall have killed him. . . ."

Poirot shrugged his shoulders. He shook his head a little, sadly.

"Mademoiselle, what is done, is done. One cannot take back the accomplished action. It is too late to regret."

She cried out more vehemently: "I shall have killed him! And I love him so . . . I love him so."

Poirot sighed. "Too much. . . ."

It had been his thought long ago in the restaurant of M. Blondin. It was his thought again now.

He said, hesitating a little: "Do not, at all events, go by what Miss Bowers says. Hospital nurses, me, I find them always gloomy! The night nurse, always, she is astonished to find her patient alive in the evening; the day nurse, always, she is surprised to find him alive in the morning! They know too much, you see, of the possibilities that may arise. When one is motoring one might easily say to oneself, 'If a car came out from that crossroad—or if that lorry backed suddenly —or if the wheel came off the car that is approaching me—or if a dog jumped off the hedge onto my driving arm—*eh bien,* I should probably be killed!' But one assumes, and usually rightly, that none of these things *will* happen, and that one will get to one's journey's end. But if, of course, one has been in an accident, or seen one or more accidents, then one is inclined to take the opposite point of view."

Jacqueline asked, half smiling through her tears, "Are you trying to console me, Monsieur Poirot?"

"The *Bon Dieu* knows what I am trying to do! You should not have come on this journey."

"No—I wish I hadn't. It's been—so awful. But—it will be soon over now."

"*Mais oui—mais oui.*"

"And Simon will go to the hospital, and they'll give the proper treatment and everything will be all right."

"You speak like the child! 'And they lived happily ever afterward.' That is it, is it not?"

She flushed suddenly scarlet.

"Monsieur Poirot, I never meant—never—"

"It is too soon to think of such a thing! That is the proper hypocritical thing to say, is it not? But you are partly a Latin, Mademoiselle Jacqueline. You should be able to admit facts even if they do not sound very decorous. *Le roi est mort—vive le roi!* The sun has gone and the moon rises. That is so, is it not?"

"You don't understand. He's just sorry for me—awfully sorry for me, because he knows how terrible it is for me to know I've hurt him so badly."

"Ah, well," said Poirot. "The pure pity, it is a very lofty sentiment."

He looked at her half mockingly, half with some other emotion.

He murmured softly under his breath words in French:

> "*La vie est vaine.*
> *Un peu d'amour,*
> *Un peu de haine,*
> *Et puis bonjour*
>
> *La vie est brève.*
> *Un peu d'espoir,*
> *Un peu de rêve,*
> *Et puis bonsoir.*"

He went out again onto the deck. Colonel Race was striding along the deck and hailed him at once.

"Poirot. Good man! I want you. I've got an idea."

Thrusting his arm through Poirot's he walked him up the deck.

"Just a chance remark of Doyle's. I hardly noticed it at the time. Something about a telegram."

"*Tiens—c'est vrai.*"

"Nothing in it, perhaps, but one can't leave any avenue unexplored. Damn it all, man, two murders, and we're still in the dark."

Poirot shook his head. "No, not in the dark. In the light."

Race looked at him curiously. "You have an idea?"

"It is more than an idea now. *I am sure.*"

"Since—when?"

"Since the death of the maid, Louise Bourget."

"Damned if I see it!"

"My friend, it is so clear—so clear. Only there are difficulties—embarrassments—impediments! See you, around a person like Linnet Doyle there is so much—so many conflicting hates and jealousies and envies and meannesses. It is like a cloud of flies, buzzing, buzzing. . . ."

"But you think you know?" The other looked at him curiously. "You wouldn't say so unless you were sure. Can't say I've any real light, myself. I've suspicions, of course. . . ."

Poirot stopped. He laid an impressive hand on Race's arm.

"You are a great man, mon Colonel. . . . You do not say 'Tell me. What is it that you think?' You know that if I could speak now I would. But there is much to be cleared away first. But think, think for a moment along the lines that I shall indicate. There are certain points. . . . There is the statement of Mademoiselle de Bellefort that someone overheard our conversation that night in the garden at Assuan. There is the statement of Monsieur Tim Allerton as to what he heard and did on the night of the crime. There are Louise Bourget's significant answers to our questions this morning. There is the fact that Madame Allerton drinks water, that her son drinks whisky and soda and that I drink wine. Add to that the fact of two bottles of nail polish and the proverb I quoted. And finally we come to the crux of the whole business, the fact that the pistol was wrapped up in a cheap handkerchief and a velvet stole and thrown overboard. . . ."

Race was silent a minute or two then he shook his head.

"No," he said, "I don't see it. Mind, I've got a faint idea what you're driving at, but as far as I can see, it doesn't work."

"But yes—but yes. You are seeing only half the truth. And remember this—we must start again from the beginning, since our first conception was entirely wrong."

Race made a slight grimace.

"I'm used to that. It often seems to me that's all detective work is, wiping out your false starts and beginning again."

"Yes, it is very true, that. And it is just what some people will not do. They conceive a certain theory, and everything has to fit into that theory. If one little fact will not fit it, they throw it aside. But it is always the facts that will not fit in that are significant. All along I have realized the significance of that pistol being removed from the scene of the crime. I knew that it meant something, but what that something was I only realized one little half hour ago."

"And I still don't see it!"

"But you will! Only reflect along the lines I indicated. And now let us clear up this matter of a telegram. That is, if the Herr Doktor will admit us."

Dr. Bessner was still in a very bad humour. In answer to their knock he disclosed a scowling face.

"What is it? Once more you wish to see my patient? But I tell you it is not wise. He has fever. He has had more than enough excitement today."

"Just one question," said Race. "Nothing more, I assure you."

With an unwilling grunt the doctor moved aside and the two men entered the cabin. Dr. Bessner, growling to himself, pushed past them.

"I return in three minutes," he said. "And then—positively—you go!"

They heard him stumping down the deck.

Simon Doyle looked from one to the other of them inquiringly.

"Yes," he said, "What is it?"

"A very little thing," Race replied. "Just now, when the stewards were reporting to me, they mentioned that Signor Richetti had been particularly troublesome. You said that that didn't surprise you, as you knew he had a bad temper, and that he had been rude to your wife over some matter of a telegram. Now can you tell me about that incident?"

"Easily. It was at Wâdi Halfa. We'd just come back from the Second Cataract. Linnet thought she saw a telegram for her sticking up on the board. She'd forgotten, you see, that she wasn't called Ridgeway any longer, and Richetti and Ridgeway do look rather alike when written in an atrocious handwriting. So she tore it open, couldn't make head or tail of it, and was puzzling over it when this fellow Richetti came along, fairly tore it out of her hand and gibbered with rage. She went after him to apologize and he was frightfully rude to her about it."

Race drew a deep breath. "And do you know at all, Mr. Doyle, what was in that telegram?"

"Yes, Linnet read part of it out aloud. It said—"

He paused. There was a commotion outside. A high-pitched voice was rapidly approaching.

"Where are Monsieur Poirot and Colonel Race? I must see them *immediately!* It is most important. I have vital information. I— Are they with Mr. Doyle?"

Bessner had not closed the door. Only the curtain hung across the open doorway. Mrs. Otterbourne swept it to one side and entered like a tornado. Her face was suffused with colour, her gait slightly unsteady, her command of words not quite under her control.

"Mr. Doyle," she said dramatically, "I know who killed your wife!"

"What?"

Simon stared at her. So did the other two.

Mrs. Otterbourne swept all three of them with a triumphant glance. She was happy—superbly happy.

"Yes," she said. "My theories are completely vindicated. The deep, primeval, primordial urges—it may appear impossible—fantastic —but it is the truth!"

Race said sharply, "Do I understand that you have evidence in your possession to show who killed Mrs. Doyle?"

Mrs. Otterbourne sat down in a chair and leaned forward, nodding her head vigorously.

"Certainly I have. You will agree, will you not, that whoever killed Louise Bourget also killed Linnet Doyle—that the two crimes were committed by one and the same hand?"

"Yes, yes," said Simon impatiently. "Of course. That stands to reason. Go on."

"Then my assertion holds. I know who killed Louise Bourget; therefore I know who killed Linnet Doyle."

"You mean, you have a theory as to who killed Louise Bourget," suggested Race sceptically.

Mrs. Otterbourne turned on him like a tiger.

"No, I have exact knowledge. I *saw* the person with my own eyes."

Simon, fevered, shouted out: "For God's sake, start at the beginning. You know the person who killed Louise Bourget, you say."

Mrs. Otterbourne nodded.

"I will tell you exactly what occurred."

Yes, she was very happy—no doubt of it! This was her moment, her triumph! What of it if her books were failing to sell, if the stupid public that once had bought them and devoured them voraciously now turned to newer favourites? Salome Otterbourne would once again be notorious. Her name would be in all the papers. She would be principal witness for the prosecution at the trial.

She took a deep breath and opened her mouth.

"It was when I went down to lunch. I hardly felt like eating—all the horror of the recent tragedy— Well, I needn't go into that. Half way down I remember that I had—er—left something in my cabin. I told Rosalie to go on without me. She did."

Mrs. Otterbourne paused a minute.

The curtain across the door moved slightly as though lifted by the wind, but none of the three men noticed it.

"I—er—" Mrs. Otterbourne paused. Thin ice to skate over here, but it must be done somehow. "I—er—had an arrangement with one of the—er—*personnel* of the ship. He was to—er—get me something I needed, but I did not wish my daughter to know of it. She is inclined to be tiresome in certain ways—"

Not too good, this, but she could think of something that sounded better before it came to telling the story in court.

Race's eyebrows lifted as his eyes asked a question of Poirot.

Poirot gave an infinitesimal nod. His lips formed the word, "Drink."

The curtain across the door moved again. Between it and the door itself something showed with a faint steel blue gleam.

Mrs. Otterbourne continued: "The arrangement was that I should go round to the stern on the deck below this, and there I should find the man waiting for me. As I went along the deck a cabin door opened and somebody looked out. It was this girl—Louise Bourget, or whatever her name is. She seemed to be expecting someone. When she saw it was me, she looked disappointed and went abruptly inside again. I didn't think anything of it, of course. I went along just as I had said I would and got the—the stuff from the man. I paid him and —er—just had a word with him. Then I started back. Just as I came around the corner I saw someone knock on the maid's door and go into the cabin."

Race said, "And that person was—"

Bang!

The noise of the explosion filled the cabin. There was an acrid sour smell of smoke. Mrs. Otterbourne turned slowly sideways, as though in supreme inquiry, then her body slumped forward and she fell to the ground with a crash. From just behind her ear the blood flowed from a round neat hole.

There was a moment's stupefied silence. Then both the able-bodied men jumped to their feet. The woman's body hindered their movements a little. Race bent over her while Poirot made a catlike jump for the door and the deck.

The deck was empty. On the ground just in front of the sill lay a big Colt revolver.

Poirot glanced in both directions. The deck was empty. He then sprinted toward the stern. As he rounded the corner he ran into Tim Allerton, who was coming full tilt from the opposite direction.

"What the devil was that?" cried Tim breathlessly.

Poirot said sharply, "Did you meet anyone on your way here?"

"Meet anyone? No."

"Then come with me." He took the young man by the arm and retraced his steps. A little crowd had assembled by now. Rosalie, Jacqueline and Cornelia had rushed out of their cabins. More people were coming along the deck from the saloon—Ferguson, Jim Fanthorp and Mrs. Allerton.

Race stood by the revolver. Poirot turned his head and said sharply to Tim Allerton, "Got any gloves in your pocket?"

Tim fumbled.

"Yes, I have."

Poirot seized them from him, put them on, and bent to examine the revolver. Race did the same. The others watched breathlessly.

Race said: "He didn't go the other way. Fanthorp and Ferguson were sitting on this deck lounge; they'd have seen him."

Poirot responded, "And Mr. Allerton would have met him if he'd gone aft."

Race said, pointing to the revolver: "Rather fancy we've seen this not so very long ago. Must make sure, though."

He knocked on the door of Pennington's cabin. There was no answer. The cabin was empty. Race strode to the right hand drawer of the chest and jerked it open. The revolver was gone.

"Settles that," said Race. "Now then, where's Pennington himself?"

They went out again on deck. Mrs. Allerton had joined the group. Poirot moved swiftly over to her.

"Madame, take Miss Otterbourne with you and look after her. Her mother has been"—he consulted Race with an eye and Race nodded—"killed."

Dr. Bessner came bustling along.

"Gott im Himmel! What is there now?"

They made way for him. Race indicated the cabin. Bessner went inside.

"Find Pennington," said Race. "Any fingerprints on that revolver?"

"None," said Poirot.

They found Pennington on the deck below. He was sitting in the little drawing-room writing letters. He lifted a handsome, clean-shaven face.

"Anything new?" he asked.

"Didn't you hear a shot?"

"Why—now you mention it—I believe I did hear a kind of a bang. But I never dreamed— Who's been shot?"

"Mrs. Otterbourne."

"*Mrs. Otterbourne?*" Pennington sounded quite astounded. "Well, you do surprise me. Mrs. Otterbourne." He shook his head. "I can't see that at all." He lowered his voice. "Strikes me, gentlemen, we've got a homicidal maniac aboard. We ought to organize a defence system."

"Mr. Pennington," said Race, "how long have you been in this room?"

"Why, let me see." Mr. Pennington gently rubbed his chin. "I should say a matter of twenty minutes or so."

"And you haven't left it?"

"Why no—certainly not."

He looked inquiringly at the two men.

"You see, Mr. Pennington," said Race, "Mrs. Otterbourne was shot with your revolver."

CHAPTER 24

MR. PENNINGTON was shocked. Mr. Pennington could hardly believe it.

"Why, gentlemen," he said, "this is a very serious matter. Very serious indeed."

"Extremely serious for you, Mr. Pennington."

"For me?" Pennington's eyebrows rose in startled surprise. "But, my dear sir, I was sitting quietly writing in here when that shot was fired."

"You have, perhaps, a witness to prove that?"

Pennington shook his head.

"Why, no—I wouldn't say that. But it's clearly impossible that I should have gone to the deck above, shot this poor woman (and why should I shoot her anyway?) and come down again with no one seeing me. There are always plenty of people on the deck lounge this time of day."

"How do you account for your pistol being used?"

"Well—I'm afraid I may be to blame there. Quite soon after getting aboard there was a conversation in the saloon one evening, I remember, about firearms, and I mentioned then that I always carried a revolver with me when I travel."

"Who was there?"

"Well, I can't remember exactly. Most people, I think. Quite a crowd, anyway."

He shook his head gently.

"Why, yes," he said. "I am certainly to blame there."

He went on: "First Linnet, then Linnet's maid, and now Mrs. Otterbourne. There seems no reason in it all!"

"There *was* reason," said Race.

"There was?"

"Yes. Mrs. Otterbourne was on the point of telling us that she had seen a certain person go into Louise's cabin. Before she could name that person she was shot dead."

Andrew Pennington passed a fine silk handkerchief over his brow.

"All this is terrible," he murmured.

Poirot said: "Monsieur Pennington, I would like to discuss certain aspects of the case with you. Will you come to my cabin in half an hour's time?"

"I should be delighted."

Pennington did not sound delighted. He did not look delighted either. Race and Poirot exchanged glances and then abruptly left the room.

"Cunning old devil," said Race, "but he's afraid. Eh?"

Poirot nodded. "Yes, he is not happy, our Monsieur Pennington."

As they reached the promenade deck again, Mrs. Allerton came out of her cabin and, seeing Poirot, beckoned him imperiously.

"Madame?"

"That poor child! Tell me, Monsieur Poirot, is there a double cabin somewhere that I could share with her? She oughtn't to go back to the one she shared with her mother, and mine is only a single one."

"That can be arranged, Madame. It is very good of you."

"It's mere decency. Besides, I'm very fond of the girl. I've always liked her."

"Is she very upset?"

"Terribly. She seems to have been absolutely devoted to that odious woman. That is what is so pathetic about it all. Tim says he believes she drank. Is that true?"

Poirot nodded.

"Oh, well, poor woman, one mustn't judge her, I suppose; but that girl must have had a terrible life."

"She did, Madame. She is very proud and she was very loyal."

"Yes, I like that—loyalty, I mean. It's out of fashion nowadays. She's an odd character, that girl—proud, reserved, stubborn, and terribly warm-hearted underneath, I fancy."

"I see that I have given her into good hands, Madame."

"Yes, don't worry. I'll look after her. She's inclined to cling to me in the most pathetic fashion."

Mrs. Allerton went back into the cabin. Poirot returned to the scene of the tragedy.

Cornelia was still standing on the deck, her eyes wide. She said: "I don't understand, Monsieur Poirot. How did the person who shot her get away without our seeing him?"

"Yes, how?" echoed Jacqueline.

"Ah," said Poirot, "it was not quite such a disappearing trick as you think, Mademoiselle. There were three distinct ways the murderer might have gone."

Jacqueline looked puzzled. She said, "Three?"

"He might have gone to the right, or he might have gone to the left, but I don't see any other way," puzzled Cornelia.

Jacqueline too frowned. Then her brow cleared.

She said: "Of course. He could move in two directions on one plane, but he could go at right angles to that plane too. That is, he couldn't go *up* very well, but he could go *down*."

Poirot smiled. "You have brains, Mademoiselle."

Cornelia said, "I know I'm just a plain mutt, but I still don't see."

Jacqueline said, "Monsieur Poirot means, darling, that he could swing himself over the rail and down onto the deck below."

"My!" gasped Cornelia. "I never thought of that. He'd have to be mighty quick about it, though. I suppose he could just do it?"

"He could do it easily enough," said Tim Allerton. "Remember, there's always a minute of shock after a thing like this. One hears a shot and one's too paralysed to move for a second or two."

"That was your experience, Monsieur Allerton?"

"Yes, it was. I just stood like a dummy for quite five seconds. Then I fairly sprinted round the deck."

Race came out of Bessner's cabin and said authoritatively: "Would you mind all clearing off? We want to bring out the body."

Everyone moved away obediently. Poirot went with them. Cornelia said to him with sad earnestness: "I'll never forget this trip as long as I live. Three deaths. . . . It's just like living in a nightmare."

Ferguson overheard her. He said aggressively: "That's because you're overcivilized. You should look on death as the Oriental does. It's a mere incident—hardly noticeable."

"That's all very well," Cornelia said. "They're not educated, poor creatures."

"No, and a good thing too. Education has devitalized the white races. Look at America—goes in for an orgy of culture. Simply disgusting."

"I think you're talking nonsense," said Cornelia flushing. "I attend lectures every winter on Greek Art and the Renaissance, and I went to some on Famous Women of History."

Mr. Ferguson groaned in agony. "Greek Art! Renaissance! Famous Women of History! It makes me quite sick to hear you. It's the *future* that matters, woman, not the past. Three women are dead on this boat. Well, what of it? They're no loss! Linnet Doyle and her money! The French maid—a domestic parasite. Mrs. Otterbourne—a useless fool of a woman. Do you think anyone really cares whether they're dead or not? *I* don't. I think it's a damned good thing!"

"Then you're wrong!" Cornelia blazed out at him. "And it makes me sick to hear you talk and talk, as though nobody mattered but *you*. I didn't like Mrs. Otterbourne much, but her daughter was ever so fond of her, and she's all broken up over her mother's death. I don't know much about the French maid, but I expect somebody was fond of her somewhere; and as for Linnet Doyle—well, apart from everything else, she was just lovely! She was so beautiful when she came into a room that it made a lump come in your throat. I'm homely myself, and that makes me appreciate beauty a lot more. She was as beautiful—just as a woman—as anything in Greek Art. And when anything beautiful's dead, it's a loss to the world. So there!"

Mr. Ferguson stepped back a space. He caught hold of his hair with both hands and tugged at it vehemently.

"I give it up," he said. "You're unbelievable. Just haven't got a bit of natural female spite in you anywhere." He turned to Poirot. "Do you know, sir, that Cornelia's father was practically ruined by Linnet

Ridgeway's old man? But does the girl gnash her teeth when she sees the heiress sailing about in pearls and Paris models? No, she just bleats out, 'Isn't she beautiful?' like a blessed Baa Lamb. I don't believe she even felt sore at her."

Cornelia flushed. "I did—just for a minute. Poppa kind of died of discouragement, you know, because he hadn't made good."

"Felt sore for a minute! I ask you."

Cornelia flashed round on him.

"Well, didn't you say just now it was the future that mattered, not the past? All that was in the past, wasn't it? It's over."

"Got me there," said Ferguson. "Cornelia Robson, you're the only nice woman I've ever come across. Will you marry me?"

"Don't be absurd."

"It's a genuine proposal—even if it is made in the presence of Old Man Sleuth. Anyway, you're a witness, Monsieur Poirot. I've deliberately offered marriage to this female—against all my principles, because I don't believe in legal contracts between the sexes; but I don't think she'd stand for anything else, so marriage it shall be. Come on, Cornelia, say yes."

"I think you're utterly ridiculous," said Cornelia flushing.

"Why won't you marry me?"

"You're not serious," said Cornelia.

"Do you mean not serious in proposing or do you mean not serious in character?"

"Both, but I really meant character. You laugh at all sorts of serious things. Education and Culture—and—and Death. You wouldn't be *reliable*."

She broke off, flushed again, and hurried along into her cabin.

Ferguson stared after her. "Damn the girl! I believe she really means it. She wants a man to be reliable. *Reliable*—ye gods!" He paused and then said curiously: "What's the matter with you, Monsieur Poirot? You seem very deep in thought."

Poirot roused himself with a start.

"I reflect, that is all. I reflect."

"Meditation on Death. Death, the Recurring Decimal, by Hercule Poirot. One of his well-known monographs."

"Monsieur Ferguson," said Poirot, "you are a very impertinent young man."

"You must excuse me. I like attacking established institutions."

"And I am an established institution?"

"Precisely. What do you think of that girl?"

"Of Miss Robson?"

"Yes."

"I think that she has a great deal of character."

"You're right. She's got spirit. She looks meek, but she isn't. She's got guts. She's—oh, damn it, I want that girl. It mightn't be a bad move if I tackled the old lady. If I could once get her thoroughly against me, it might cut some ice with Cornelia."

He wheeled and went into the observation saloon. Miss Van Schuyler was seated in her usual corner. She looked even more arrogant than usual. She was knitting. Ferguson strode up to her. Hercule Poirot, entering unobtrusively, took a seat a discreet distance away and appeared to be absorbed in a magazine.

"Good-afternoon, Miss Van Schuyler."

Miss Van Schuyler raised her eyes for a bare second, dropped them again and murmured frigidly, "Er—good-afternoon."

"Look here, Miss Van Schuyler, I want to talk to you about something pretty important. It's just this. I want to marry your cousin."

Miss Van Schuyler's ball of wool dropped onto the ground and ran wildly across the saloon.

She said, in a venomous tone, "You must be out of your senses, young man."

"Not at all. I'm determined to marry her. I've asked her to marry me!"

Miss Van Schuyler surveyed him coldly, with the kind of speculative interest she might have accorded to an odd sort of beetle.

"Indeed? And I presume she sent you about your business."

"She refused me."

"Naturally."

"Not 'naturally' at all. I'm going to go on asking her till she agrees."

"I can assure you, sir, that I shall take steps to see that my young cousin is not subjected to any such persecution," said Miss Van Schuyler in a biting tone.

"What have you got against me?"

Miss Van Schuyler merely raised her eyebrows and gave a vehement tug to her wool, preparatory to regaining it and closing the interview.

"Come now," persisted Mr. Ferguson, "what have you got against me?"

"I should think that was quite obvious, Mr.—er—I don't know your name."

"Ferguson."

"Mr. Ferguson." Miss Van Schuyler uttered the name with definite distaste. "Any such idea is quite out of the question."

"You mean," said Ferguson, "that I'm not good enough for her?"

"I should think that would have been obvious to you."

"In what way am I not good enough?"

Miss Van Schuyler again did not answer.

"I've got two legs, two arms, good health and quite reasonable brains. What's wrong with that?"

"There is such a thing as social position, Mr. Ferguson."

"Social position is bunk!"

The door swung open and Cornelia came in. She stopped dead on seeing her redoubtable Cousin Marie in conversation with her would-be suitor.

The outrageous Mr. Ferguson turned his head, grinned broadly and called out: "Come along, Cornelia. I'm asking for your hand in marriage in the best conventional manner."

"Cornelia," said Miss Van Schuyler, and her voice was truly awful in quality, *"have you encouraged this young man?"*

"I—no, of course not—at least—not exactly—I mean—"

"What do you mean?"

"She hasn't encouraged me," said Mr. Ferguson helpfully. "I've done it all. She hasn't actually pushed me in the face, because she's got too kind a heart. Cornelia, your cousin says I'm not good enough for you. That, of course, is true, but not in the way she means it. My moral nature certainly doesn't equal yours, but her point is that I'm hopelessly below you socially."

"That, I think, is equally obvious to Cornelia," said Miss Van Schuyler.

"Is it?" Mr. Ferguson looked at her searchingly. "Is that why you won't marry me?"

"No, it isn't." Cornelia flushed. "If—if I liked you, I'd marry you no matter who you were."

"But you don't like me?"

"I—I think you're just outrageous. The way you say things . . . The *things* you say . . . I—I've never met anyone the least like you. I—"

Tears threatened to overcome her. She rushed from the room.

"On the whole," said Mr. Ferguson, "that's not too bad for a start." He leaned back in his chair, gazed at the ceiling, whistled, crossed his disreputable knees and remarked, "I'll be calling you Cousin yet."

Miss Van Schuyler trembled with rage. "Leave this room at once, sir, or I'll ring for the steward."

"I've paid for my ticket," said Mr. Ferguson. "They can't possibly turn me out of the public lounge. But I'll humour you." He sang softly, "Yo ho ho, and a bottle of rum." Rising, he sauntered nonchalantly to the door and passed out.

Choking with anger Miss Van Schuyler struggled to her feet. Poirot, discreetly emerging from retirement behind his magazine, sprang up and retrieved the ball of wool.

"Thank you, Monsieur Poirot. If you would send Miss Bowers to me—I feel quite upset—that insolent young man."

"Rather eccentric, I'm afraid," said Poirot. "Most of that family are. Spoilt, of course. Always inclined to tilt at windmills." He added carelessly, "You recognized him, I suppose?"

"Recognized him?"

"Calls himself Ferguson and won't use his title because of his advanced ideas."

"His *title?*" Miss Van Schuyler's tone was sharp.

"Yes, that's young Lord Dawlish. Rolling in money, of course, but he became a communist when he was at Oxford."

Miss Van Schuyler, her face a battleground of contradictory emotions, said, "How long have you known this, Monsieur Poirot?"

Poirot shrugged his shoulders.

"There was a picture in one of these papers—I noticed the resemblance. Then I found a signet ring with a coat of arms on it. Oh, there's no doubt about it, I assure you."

He quite enjoyed reading the conflicting expressions that succeeded each other on Miss Van Schuyler's face. Finally, with a gracious inclination of the head, she said, "I am very much obliged to you, Monsieur Poirot."

Poirot looked after her and smiled as she went out of the saloon. Then he sat down and his face grew grave once more. He was following out a train of thought in his mind. From time to time he nodded his head.

"*Mais oui,*" he said at last. "It all fits in."

CHAPTER 25

RACE FOUND him still sitting there.

"Well, Poirot, what about it? Pennington's due in ten minutes. I'm leaving this in your hands."

Poirot rose quickly to his feet. "First, get hold of young Fanthorp."

"Fanthorp?" Race looked surprised.

"Yes. Bring him to my cabin."

Race nodded and went off. Poirot went along to his cabin. Race arrived with young Fanthorp a minute or two afterward.

Poirot indicated chairs and offered cigarettes.

"Now, Monsieur Fanthorp," he said, "to our business! I perceive that you wear the same tie that my friend Hastings wears."

Jim Fanthorp looked down at his neckwear with some bewilderment.

"It's an O.E. tie," he said.

"Exactly. You must understand that, though I am a foreigner, I know something of the English point of view. I know, for instance, that there are 'things which are done' and 'things which are not done.'"

Jim Fanthorp grinned.

"We don't say that sort of thing much nowadays, sir."

"Perhaps not, but the custom, it still remains. The Old School Tie is the Old School Tie, and there are certain things (I know this from experience) that the Old School Tie does not do! One of those things, Monsieur Fanthorp, is to butt into a private conversation unasked when one does not know the people who are conducting it."

Fanthorp stared.

Poirot went on: "But the other day, Monsieur Fanthorp, that is exactly what you did do. Certain persons were quietly transacting some private business in the observation saloon. You strolled near them, obviously in order to overhear what it was that was in progress, and presently you actually turned round and congratulated a lady— Madame Simon Doyle—on the soundness of her business methods."

Jim Fanthorp's face got very red. Poirot swept on, not waiting for a comment.

"Now that, Monsieur Fanthorp, was not at all the behaviour of one who wears a tie similar to that worn by my friend Hastings! Hastings is all delicacy, would die of shame before he did such a thing! Therefore, taking that action of yours in conjunction with the fact that you are a very young man to be able to afford an expensive holiday, that you are a member of a country solicitor's firm, and therefore probably not extravagantly well off, and that you show no signs of recent illness such as might necessitate a prolonged visit abroad, I ask myself—and am now asking you—what is the reason for your presence on this boat?"

Jim Fanthorp jerked his head back.

"I decline to give you any information whatever, Monsieur Poirot. I really think you must be mad."

"I am not mad. I am very, very sane. Where is your firm? In Northampton; that is not very far from Wode Hall. What conversation did you try to overhear? One concerning legal documents. What was the object of your remark—a remark which you uttered with obvious embarrassment and *malaise?* Your object was to prevent Madame Doyle from signing any document unread."

He paused.

"On this boat we have had a murder, and following that murder two other murders in rapid succession. If I further give you the information that the weapon which killed Madame Otterbourne was a revolver owned by Monsieur Andrew Pennington, then perhaps you will realize that it is actually your duty to tell us all you can."

Jim Fanthorp was silent for some minutes. At last he said: "You have rather an odd way of going about things, Monsieur Poirot, but I appreciate the points you have made. The trouble is that I have no exact information to lay before you."

"You mean that it is a case, merely, of suspicion."

"Yes."

"And therefore you think it injudicious to speak? That may be true, legally speaking. But this is not a court of law. Colonel Race and myself are endeavouring to track down a murderer. Anything that can help us to do so may be valuable."

Again Jim Fanthorp reflected. Then he said: "Very well. What is it you want to know?"

"Why did you come on this trip?"

"My uncle, Mr. Carmichael, Mrs. Doyle's English solicitor, sent me. He handled a good many of her affairs. In this way, he was often in correspondence with Mr. Andrew Pennington, who was Mrs.

Doyle's American trustee. Several small incidents (I cannot enumerate them all) made my uncle suspicious that all was not quite as it should be."

"In plain language," said Race, "your uncle suspected that Pennington was a crook?"

Jim Fanthorp nodded, a faint smile on his face.

"You put it rather more bluntly than I should, but the main idea is correct. Various excuses made by Pennington, certain plausible explanations of the disposal of funds, aroused my uncle's distrust.

"While these suspicions of his were still nebulous, Miss Ridgeway married unexpectedly and went off on her honeymoon to Egypt. Her marriage relieved my uncle's mind, as he knew that on her return to England the estate would have to be formally settled and handed over.

"However, in a letter she wrote him from Cairo, she mentioned casually that she had unexpectedly run across Andrew Pennington. My uncle's suspicions became acute. He felt sure that Pennington, perhaps by now in a desperate position, was going to try and obtain signatures from her which would cover his own defalcations. Since my uncle had no definite evidence to lay before her, he was in a most difficult position. The only thing he could think of was to send me out here, travelling by air, with instructions to discover what was in the wind. I was to keep my eyes open and act summarily if necessary—a most unpleasant mission, I can assure you. As a matter of fact, on the occasion you mention I had to behave more or less as a cad! It was awkward, but on the whole I was satisfied with the result."

"You mean you put Madame Doyle on her guard?" asked Race.

"Not so much that, but I think I put the wind up Pennington. I felt convinced he wouldn't try any more funny business for some time, and then I hoped to have got intimate enough with Mr. and Mrs. Doyle to convey some kind of a warning. As a matter of fact I hoped to do so through Doyle. Mrs. Doyle was so attached to Mr. Pennington that it would have been a bit awkward to suggest things to her about him. It would have been easier for me to approach the husband."

Race nodded.

Poirot asked: "Will you give me a candid opinion on one point, Monsieur Fanthorp? If you were engaged in putting a swindle over, would you choose Madame Doyle or Monsieur Doyle as a victim?"

Fanthorp smiled faintly.

"Mr. Doyle, every time. Linnet Doyle was very shrewd in business matters. Her husband, I should fancy, is one of those trustful fellows who know nothing of business and are always ready to 'sign on the dotted line' as he himself put it."

"I agree," said Poirot. He looked at Race. "And there's your motive."

Jim Fanthorp said: "But this is all pure conjecture. It isn't *evidence*."

Poirot replied, easily, "Ah, bah! we will get evidence!"

"How?"

"Possibly from Mr. Pennington himself."

Fanthorp looked doubtful.

"I wonder. I very much wonder."

Race glanced at his watch. "He's about due now."

Jim Fanthorp was quick to take the hint. He left them.

Two minutes later Andrew Pennington made his appearance. His manner was all smiling urbanity. Only the taut line of his jaw and the wariness of his eyes betrayed the fact that a thoroughly experienced fighter was on his guard.

"Well, gentlemen," he said, "here I am."

He sat down and looked at them inquiringly.

"We asked you to come here, Monsieur Pennington," began Poirot, "because it is fairly obvious that you have a very special and immediate interest in the case."

Pennington raised his eyebrows slightly.

"Is that so?"

Poirot said gently: "Surely. You have known Linnet Ridgeway, I understand, since she was quite a child."

"Oh! that—" His face altered, became less alert. "I beg pardon, I didn't quite get you. Yes, as I told you this morning, I've known Linnet since she was a cute little thing in pinafores."

"You were on terms of close intimacy with her father?"

"That's so. Melhuish Ridgeway and I were close—very close."

"You were so intimately associated that on his death he appointed you business guardian to his daughter and trustee to the vast fortune she inherited."

"Why, roughly, that is so." The wariness was back again. The note was more cautious. "I was not the only trustee, naturally; others were associated with me."

"Who have since died?"

"Two of them are dead. The other, Mr. Sterndale Rockford, is alive."

"Your partner?"

"Yes."

"Mademoiselle Ridgeway, I understand, was not yet of age when she married?"

"She would have been twenty-one next July."

"And in the normal course of events she would have come into control of her fortune then?"

"Yes."

"But her marriage precipitated matters?"

Pennington's jaw hardened. He shot out his chin at them aggressively.

"You'll pardon me, gentlemen, but what exact business is all this of yours?"

"If you dislike answering the question—"

"There's no dislike about it. I don't mind what you ask me. But I don't see the relevance of all this."

"Oh, but surely, Monsieur Pennington"—Poirot leaned forward, his eyes green and catlike—"there is the question of motive. In considering that, financial considerations must always be taken into account."

Pennington said sullenly, "By Ridgeway's will, Linnet got control of her dough when she was twenty-one or when she married."

"No conditions of any kind?"

"No conditions."

"And it is a matter, I am credibly assured, of millions."

"Millions it is."

Poirot said softly, "Your responsibility, Mr. Pennington, and that of your partner, has been a very grave one."

Pennington replied curtly: "We're used to responsibility. Doesn't worry us any."

"I wonder."

Something in his tone flicked the other man on the raw. He asked angrily, "What the devil do you mean?"

Poirot replied with an air of engaging frankness: "I was wondering, Mr. Pennington, whether Linnet Ridgeway's sudden marriage caused any—consternation, in your office?"

"Consternation?"

"That was the word I used."

"What the hell are you driving at?"

"Something quite simple. Are Linnet Doyle's affairs in the perfect order they should be?"

Pennington rose to his feet.

"That's enough. I'm through." He made for the door.

"But you will answer my question first?"

Pennington snapped, "They're in perfect order."

"You were not so alarmed when the news of Linnet Ridgeway's marriage reached you that you rushed over to Europe by the first boat and staged an apparently fortuitous meeting in Egypt."

Pennington came back toward them. He had himself under control once more.

"What you are saying is absolute balderdash! I didn't even know that Linnet was married till I met her in Cairo. I was utterly astonished. Her letter must have missed me by a day in New York. It was forwarded and I got it about a week later."

"You came over by the *Carmanic,* I think you said."

"That's right."

"And the letter reached New York after the *Carmanic* sailed?"

"How many times have I got to repeat it?"

"It is strange," said Poirot.

"What's strange?"

"That on your luggage there are no labels of the *Carmanic.* The only recent labels of transatlantic sailing are the *Normandie.* The *Normandie,* I remember, sailed two days after the *Carmanic.*"

For a moment the other was at a loss. His eyes wavered.

Colonel Race weighed in with telling effect.

"Come now, Mr. Pennington," he said. "We've several reasons for believing that you came over on the *Normandie* and not by the *Carmanic,* as you said. In that case, you received Mrs. Doyle's letter before you left New York. It's no good denying it, for it's the easiest thing in the world to check up the steamship companies."

Andrew Pennington felt absent-mindedly for a chair and sat down. His face was impassive—a poker face. Behind that mask his agile brain looked ahead to the next move.

"I'll have to hand it to you, gentlemen. You've been too smart for me. But I had my reasons for acting as I did."

"No doubt." Race's tone was curt.

"If I give them to you, it must be understood I do so in confidence."

"I think you can trust us to behave fittingly. Naturally I cannot give assurances blindly."

"Well—" Pennington sighed. "I'll come clean. There was some monkey business going on in England. It worried me. I couldn't do much about it by letter. The only thing was to come over and see for myself."

"What do you mean by monkey business?"

"I'd good reason to believe that Linnet was being swindled."

"By whom?"

"Her British lawyer. Now that's not the kind of accusation you can fling around anyhow. I made up my mind to come over right away and see into matters myself."

"That does great credit to your vigilance, I am sure. But why the little deception about not having received the letter?"

"Well, I ask you—" Pennington spread out his hands. "You can't butt in on a honeymoon couple without more or less coming down to brass tacks and giving your reasons. I thought it best to make the meeting accidental. Besides, I didn't know anything about the husband. He might have been mixed up in the racket for all I knew."

"In fact all your actions were actuated by pure disinterestedness," said Colonel Race drily.

"You've said it, Colonel."

There was a pause. Race glanced at Poirot. The little man leant forward.

"Monsieur Pennington, we do not believe a word of your story."

"The hell you don't! And what the hell do you believe?"

"We believe that Linnet Ridgeway's unexpected marriage put you in a financial quandary. That you came over post haste to try and find some way out of the mess you were in—that is to say, some way of gaining time. That, with that end in view, you endeavoured to obtain Madame Doyle's signature to certain documents—and failed. That on the journey up the Nile, when walking along the cliff top at Abu Simbel, you dislodged a boulder which fell and only very narrowly missed its object—"

"You're crazy."

"We believe that the same kind of circumstances occurred on the return journey. That is to say, an opportunity presented itself of putting Madame Doyle out of the way at a moment when her death would be almost certainly ascribed to the action of another person. We not only believe, but *know,* that it was your revolver which killed a woman who was about to reveal to us the name of the person who she had reason to believe killed both Linnet Doyle and the maid Louise—"

"Hell!" The forcible ejaculation broke forth and interrupted Poirot's stream of eloquence. "What are you getting at? Are you crazy? What motive had I to kill Linnet? I wouldn't get her money; that goes to her husband. Why don't you pick on him? *He's* the one to benefit—not me."

Race said coldly: "Doyle never left the lounge on the night of the tragedy till he was shot at and wounded in the leg. The impossibility of his walking a step after that is attested to by a doctor and a nurse— both independent and reliable witnesses. Simon Doyle could not have killed his wife. He could not have killed Louise Bourget. He most definitely did not kill Mrs. Otterbourne! You know that as well as we do."

"I know he didn't kill her." Pennington sounded a little calmer. "All I say is, why pick on me when I don't benefit by her death?"

"But, my dear sir," Poirot's voice came soft as a purring cat, "that is rather a matter of opinion. Madame Doyle was a keen woman of business, fully conversant of her own affairs and very quick to spot any irregularity. As soon as she took up the control of her property, which she would have done on her return to England, her suspicions were bound to be aroused. But now that she is dead and that her husband, as you have just pointed out, inherits, the whole thing is different. Simon Doyle knows nothing whatever of his wife's affairs except that she was a rich woman. He is of a simple, trusting disposition. You will find it easy to place complicated statements before him, to involve the real issue in a net of figures, and to delay settlement with pleas of legal formalities and the recent depression. I think that it makes a very considerable difference to you whether you deal with the husband or the wife."

Pennington shrugged his shoulders.

"Your ideas are—fantastic."

"Time will show."

"What did you say?"

"I said, 'Time will show!' This is a matter of three deaths—three murders. The law will demand the most searching investigation into the condition of Madame Doyle's estate."

He saw the sudden sag in the other's shoulders and knew that he had won. Jim Fanthorp's suspicions were well founded.

Poirot went on: "You've played—and lost. Useless to go on bluffing."

"You don't understand," Pennington muttered. "It's all square enough really. It's been this damned slump—Wall Street's been crazy. But I'd staged a comeback. With luck everything will be O.K. by the middle of June."

With shaking hands he took a cigarette, tried to light it, failed.

"I suppose," mused Poirot, "that the boulder was a sudden temptation. You thought nobody saw you."

"That was an accident. I swear it was an accident!" The man leant forward, his face working, his eyes terrified. "I stumbled and fell against it. I swear it was an accident. . . ."

The two men said nothing.

Pennington suddenly pulled himself together. He was still a wreck of a man, but his fighting spirit had returned in a certain measure. He moved toward the door.

"You can't pin that on me, gentlemen. It was an accident. And it wasn't I who shot her. D'you hear? You can't pin that on me either—and you never will."

He went out.

CHAPTER 26

As THE DOOR closed behind him, Race gave a deep sigh.

"We got more than I thought we should. Admission of fraud. Admission of attempted murder. Further than that it's impossible to go. A man will confess, more or less, to attempted murder, but you won't get him to confess to the real thing."

"Sometimes it can be done," said Poirot. His eyes were dreamy—catlike.

Race looked at him curiously.

"Got a plan?"

Poirot nodded. Then he said ticking off the items on his fingers: "The garden at Assuan. Mr. Allerton's statement. The two bottles of nail polish. My bottle of wine. The velvet stole. The stained handkerchief. The pistol that was left on the scene of the crime. The death of Louise. The death of Madame Otterbourne . . . Yes, it's all there. Pennington didn't do it, Race!"

"What?" Race was startled.

"Pennington didn't do it. He had the motive, yes. He had the *will* to do it, yes. He got as far as *attempting* to do it. *Mais c'est tout*. For this crime, something was wanted that Pennington hasn't got! This is a crime that needed audacity, swift and faultless execution, courage, indifference to danger, and a resourceful, calculating brain. Pennington hasn't got those attributes. He couldn't do a crime unless he knew it to be safe. This crime wasn't safe! It hung on a razor edge. It needed boldness. Pennington isn't bold. He's only astute."

Race looked at him with the respect one able man gives to another.

"You've got it all well taped," he said.

"I think so, yes. There are one or two things—that telegram, for instance, that Linnet Doyle read. I should like to get that cleared up."

"By Jove, we forgot to ask Doyle. He was telling us when poor old Ma Otterbourne came along. We'll ask him again."

"Presently. First, I have someone else to whom I wish to speak."

"Who's that?"

"Tim Allerton."

Race raised his eyebrows.

"Allerton? Well, we'll get him here."

He pressed a bell and sent the steward with a message.

Tim Allerton entered with a questioning look.

"Steward said you wanted to see me?"

"That is right, Monsieur Allerton. Sit down."

Tim sat. His face was attentive but very slightly bored.

"Anything I can do?" His tone was polite but not enthusiastic.

Poirot said: "In a sense, perhaps. What I really require is for you to listen."

Tim's eyebrows rose in polite surprise.

"Certainly. I'm the world's best listener. Can be relied on to say 'Oo-er!' at the right moments."

"That is very satisfactory. 'Oo-er!' will be very expressive. *Eh bien,* let us commence. When I met you and your mother at Assuan, Monsieur Allerton, I was attracted to your company very strongly. To begin with, I thought your mother was one of the most charming people I had ever met—"

The weary face flickered for a moment; a shade of expression came into it.

"She is—unique," he said.

"But the second thing that interested me was your mention of a certain lady."

"Really?"

"Yes, a Mademoiselle Joanna Southwood. You see, I had recently been hearing that name."

He paused and went on: "For the last three years there have been certain jewel robberies that have been worrying Scotland Yard a good deal. They are what may be described as Society robberies. The method is usually the same—the substitution of an imitation piece of jewellery for an original. My friend, Chief Inspector Japp, came to the conclusion that the robberies were not the work of one person, but of two people working in with each other very cleverly. He was convinced, from the considerable inside knowledge displayed, that the robberies were the work of people in a good social position. And finally his attention became riveted on Mademoiselle Joanna Southwood.

"Every one of the victims had been either a friend or acquaintance of hers, and in each case she had either handled or been lent the piece of jewellery in question. Also, her style of living was far in excess of her income. On the other hand it was quite clear that the actual robbery—that is to say the substitution—had *not* been accomplished by her. In some cases she had even been out of England during the period when the jewellery must have been replaced.

"So gradually a little picture grew up in Chief Inspector Japp's mind. Mademoiselle Southwood was at one time associated with a Guild of Modern Jewellery. He suspected that she handled the jewels in question, made accurate drawings of them, got them copied by some humble but dishonest working jeweller and that the third part of the operation was the successful substitution by another person—somebody who could have been proved never to have handled the jewels and never to have had anything to do with copies or imitations of precious stones. Of the identity of this other person Japp was ignorant.

"Certain things that fell from you in conversation interested me. A ring that had disappeared when you were in Majorca, the fact that you had been in a house-party where one of these fake substitutions had occurred, your close association with Mademoiselle Southwood. There was also the fact that you obviously resented my presence and tried to get your mother to be less friendly toward me. That might, of course, have been just personal dislike, but I thought not. You were too anxious to try and hide your distaste under a genial manner.

"*Eh bien,* after the murder of Linnet Doyle, it is discovered that her pearls are missing. You comprehend, at once I think of you! But I am not quite satisfied. For if you are working, as I suspect, with Mademoiselle Southwood (who was an intimate friend of Madame Doyle's) then substitution would be the method employed—not barefaced theft. But then, the pearls quite unexpectedly are returned, and what do I discover? That they are not genuine, but imitation.

"I know then who the real thief is. It was the imitation string which was stolen and returned—an imitation which you had previously substituted for the real necklace."

He looked at the young man in front of him. Tim was white under his tan. He was not so good a fighter as Pennington; his stamina was bad. He said, with an effort to sustain his mocking manner: "Indeed? And if so, what did I do with them?"

"That I know also."

The young man's face changed—broke up.

Poirot went on slowly: "There is only one place where they can be. I have reflected, and my reason tells me that that is so. Those pearls, Monsieur Allerton, are concealed in a rosary that hangs in your cabin. The beads of it are very elaborately carved. I think you had it made specially. Those beads unscrew, though you would never think so to look at them. Inside each is a pearl, stuck with Seccotine. Most police searchers respect religious symbols, unless there is something obviously queer about them. You counted on that. I endeavoured to find out how Mademoiselle Southwood sent the imitation necklace out to you. She must have done so, since you came here from Majorca on hearing that Madame Doyle would be here for her honeymoon. My theory is that it was sent in a book—a square hole being cut out of the pages in the middle. A book goes with the ends open and is practically never opened in the post."

There was a pause—a long pause. Then Tim said quietly: "You win! It's been a good game, but it's over at last. There's nothing for it now, I suppose, but to take my medicine."

Poirot nodded gently.

"Do you realize that you were seen that night?"

"Seen?" Tim started.

"Yes, on the night that Linnet Doyle died, someone saw you leave her cabin just after one in the morning."

Tim said: "Look here—you aren't thinking . . . It wasn't I who killed her! I'll swear that! I've been in the most awful stew. To have chosen that night of all others . . . God, it's been awful!"

Poirot said: "Yes, you must have had uneasy moments. But, now that the truth has come out, you may be able to help us. Was Madame Doyle alive or dead when you stole the pearls?"

"I don't know," Tim said hoarsely. "Honest to God, Monsieur Poirot, I don't know! I'd found out where she put them at night—on the little table by the bed. I crept in, felt very softly on the table and grabbed 'em, put down the others and crept out again. I assumed, of course, that she was asleep."

"Did you hear her breathing? Surely you would have listened for that?"

Tim thought earnestly.

"It was very still—very still indeed. No, I can't remember actually hearing her breathe."

"Was there any smell of smoke lingering in the air, as there would have been if a firearm had been discharged recently?"

"I don't think so. I don't remember it."

Poirot sighed.

"Then we are no further."

Tim asked curiously, "Who was it saw me?"

"Rosalie Otterbourne. She came round from the other side of the boat and saw you leave Linnet Doyle's cabin and go to your own."

"So it was she who told you."

Poirot said gently, "Excuse me; she did not tell me."

"But then, how do you know?"

"Because I am Hercule Poirot! I do not need to be told. When I taxed her with it, do you know what she said? She said, 'I saw nobody.' And she lied."

"But why?"

Poirot said in a detached voice: "Perhaps because she thought the man she saw was the murderer. It looked like that, you know."

"That seems to me all the more reason for telling you."

Poirot shrugged his shoulders. "She did not think so, it seems."

Tim said, a queer note in his voice: "She's an extraordinary sort of a girl. She must have been through a pretty rough time with that mother of hers."

"Yes, life has not been easy for her."

"Poor kid," Tim muttered. Then he looked toward Race.

"Well, sir, where do we go from here? I admit taking the pearls from Linnet's cabin and you'll find them just where you say they are. I'm guilty all right. But as far as Miss Southwood is concerned, I'm not admitting anything. You've no evidence whatever against her. How I got hold of the fake necklace is my own business."

Poirot murmured, "A very correct attitude."

Tim said with a flash of humour, "Always the gentleman!" He added: "Perhaps you can imagine how annoying it was to me to find my mother cottoning on to you! I'm not a sufficiently hardened criminal to enjoy sitting cheek by jowl with a successful detective just before bringing off a rather risky coup! Some people might get a kick out of it. I didn't. Frankly, it gave me cold feet."

"But it did not deter you from making your attempt?"

Tim shrugged his shoulders.

"I couldn't funk it to that extent. The exchange had to be made sometime and I'd got a unique opportunity on this boat—a cabin only two doors off, and Linnet herself so preoccupied with her own troubles that she wasn't likely to detect the change."

"I wonder if that was so—"

Tim looked up sharply. "What do you mean?"

Poirot pressed the bell. "I am going to ask Miss Otterbourne if she will come here for a minute."

Tim frowned but said nothing. A steward came, received the order and went away with the message.

Rosalie came after a few minutes. Her eyes, reddened with recent weeping, widened a little at seeing Tim, but her old attitude of suspicion and defiance seemed entirely absent. She sat down and with a new docility looked from Race to Poirot.

"We're very sorry to bother you, Miss Otterbourne," said Race gently. He was slightly annoyed with Poirot.

"It doesn't matter," the girl said in a low voice.

Poirot said: "It is necessary to clear up one or two points. When I asked you whether you saw anyone on the starboard deck at one-ten this morning, your answer was that you saw nobody. Fortunately I have been able to arrive at the truth without your help. Monsieur Allerton has admitted that he was in Linnet Doyle's cabin last night."

She flashed a swift glance at Tim. Tim, his face grim and set, gave a curt nod.

"The time is correct, Monsieur Allerton?"

Allerton replied, "Quite correct."

Rosalie was staring at him. Her lips trembled—fell apart. . . .

"But you didn't—you didn't—"

He said quickly: "No, I didn't kill her. I'm a thief, not a murderer. It's all going to come out, so you might as well know. I was after her pearls."

Poirot said, "Mr. Allerton's story is that he went to her cabin last night and exchanged a string of fake pearls for the real ones."

"Did you?" asked Rosalie. Her eyes, grave, sad, childlike, questioned his.

"Yes," said Tim.

There was a pause. Colonel Race shifted restlessly.

Poirot said in a curious voice: "That, as I say, is Monsieur Allerton's story, partially confirmed by your evidence. That is to say, there is evidence that he did visit Linnet Doyle's cabin last night, but there is no evidence to show why he did so."

Tim stared at him. "But you know!"

"What do I know?"

"Well—you know I've got the pearls."

"*Mais oui—mais oui!* I know you have the pearls, but I do not know when you got them. It may have been *before* last night. . . . You said just now that Linnet Doyle would not have noticed the substitution. I am not so sure of that. Supposing she *did* notice it. . . . Supposing, even, she knew who did it. . . . Supposing that last night she threatened to expose the whole business, and that you knew she meant to do so . . . and supposing that you overheard the scene in the saloon between Jacqueline de Bellefort and Simon Doyle and, as soon as the saloon was empty, you slipped in and secured the pistol, and then, an hour later, when the boat had quieted down, you crept along to Linnet Doyle's cabin and made quite sure that no exposure would come. . . ."

"My God!" said Tim. Out of his ashen face, two tortured, agonized eyes gazed dumbly at Hercule Poirot.

The latter went on: "But somebody else saw you—the girl Louise. The next day she came to you and blackmailed you. You must pay her handsomely or she would tell what she knew. You realized that to submit to blackmail would be the beginning of the end. You pretended to agree, made an appointment to come to her cabin just before lunch with the money. Then, when she was counting the notes, you stabbed her.

"But again luck was against you. Somebody saw you go to her cabin"—he half turned to Rosalie—"your mother. Once again you had to act—dangerously, foolhardily—but it was the only chance. You had heard Pennington talk about his revolver. You rushed into his cabin, got hold of it, listened outside Dr. Bessner's cabin door and shot Madame Otterbourne before she could reveal your name."

"N-o!" cried Rosalie. "He didn't! He didn't!"

"After that, you did the only thing you could do—rushed round the stern. And when I rushed after you, you had turned and pretended to be coming in the *opposite* direction. You had handled the revolver in gloves; those gloves were in your pocket when I asked for them. . . ."

Tim said, "Before God, I swear it isn't true—not a word of it." But his voice, ill assured and trembling, failed to convince.

It was then that Rosalie Otterbourne surprised them.

"Of course it isn't true! And Monsieur Poirot knows it isn't! He's saying it for some reason of his own."

Poirot looked at her. A faint smile came to his lips. He spread out his hands in token of surrender.

"Mademoiselle is too clever. . . . But you agree—it was a good case?"

"What the devil—" Tim began with rising anger, but Poirot held up a hand.

"There is a very good case against you, Monsieur Allerton. I wanted you to realize that. Now I will tell you something more pleasant. I have not yet examined that rosary in your cabin. It may be that, when I do, I shall find nothing there. And then, since Mademoiselle Otterbourne sticks to it that she saw no one on the deck last night, *eh bien,* there is no case against you at all. The pearls were taken by a kleptomaniac who has since returned them. They are in a little box on the table by the door, if you would care to examine them with Mademoiselle."

Tim got up. He stood for a moment unable to speak. When he did, his words seemed inadequate, but it is possible that they satisfied his listeners.

"Thanks!" he said. "You won't have to give me another chance."

He held the door open for the girl; she passed out and, picking up the little cardboard box, he followed her.

Side by side they went. Tim opened the box, took out the sham string of pearls and hurled it far from him into the Nile.

"There!" he said. "That's gone. When I return the box to Poirot the real string will be in it. What a damned fool I've been!"

Rosalie said in a low voice, "Why did you come to do it in the first place?"

"How did I come to start, do you mean? Oh, I don't know. Boredom—laziness—the fun of the thing. Such a much more attractive way of earning a living than just pegging away at a job. Sounds pretty sordid to you, I expect, but you know there was an attraction about it —mainly the risk, I suppose."

"I think I understand."

"Yes, but you wouldn't ever do it."

Rosalie considered for a moment or two, her grave young head bent.

"No," she said simply. "I wouldn't."

He said: "Oh, my dear—you're so lovely . . . so utterly lovely. Why wouldn't you say you'd seen me last night?"

"I thought—they might suspect you," Rosalie said.

"Did you suspect me?"

"No. I couldn't believe that you'd kill anyone."

"No. I'm not the strong stuff murderers are made of. I'm only a miserable sneakthief."

She put out a timid hand and touched his arm.

"Don't say that. . . ."

He caught her hand in his.

"Rosalie, would you—you know what I mean? Or would you always despise me and throw it in my teeth?"

She smiled faintly. "There are things you could throw in my teeth, too. . . ."

"Rosalie—darling . . ."

But she held back a minute longer.

"This—Joanna?"

Tim gave a sudden shout.

"Joanna? You're as bad as Mother. I don't care a damn about Joanna. She's got a face like a horse and a predatory eye. A most unattractive female."

Presently Rosalie said, "Your mother need never know about you."

"I'm not sure," Tim said thoughtfully. "I think I shall tell her. Mother's got plenty of stuffing, you know. She can stand up to things. Yes, I think I shall shatter her maternal illusions about me. She'll be so relieved to know that my relations with Joanna were purely of a business nature that she'll forgive me everything else."

They had come to Mrs. Allerton's cabin and Tim knocked firmly on the door. It opened and Mrs. Allerton stood on the threshold.

"Rosalie and I—" began Tim. He paused.

"Oh, my dears," said Mrs. Allerton. She folded Rosalie in her arms. "My dear, dear child . . . I always hoped—but Tim was so tiresome—and pretended he didn't like you. But of course I saw through *that!*"

Rosalie said in a broken voice: "You've been so sweet to me—always. I used to wish—to wish—"

She broke off and sobbed happily on Mrs. Allerton's shoulder.

CHAPTER 27

As THE DOOR closed behind Tim and Rosalie, Poirot looked somewhat apologetically at Colonel Race. The Colonel was looking rather grim.

"You will consent to my little arrangement, yes?" Poirot pleaded. "It is irregular–I know it is irregular, yes–but I have a high regard for human happiness."

"You've none for mine," said Race.

"That *jeune fille,* I have a tenderness toward her, and she loves that young man. It will be an excellent match; she has the stiffening he needs; the mother likes her; everything is thoroughly suitable."

"In fact the marriage has been arranged by heaven and Hercule Poirot. All I have to do is to compound a felony."

"But, *mon ami,* I told you, it was all conjecture on my part."

Race grinned suddenly.

"It's all right by me," he said. "I'm not a damned policeman, thank God! I daresay the young fool will go straight enough now. The girl's straight all right. No, what I'm complaining of is your treatment of *me!* I'm a patient man, but there are limits to my patience! *Do* you know who committed the three murders on this boat or *don't* you?"

"I do."

"Then why all this beating about the bush?"

"You think that I am just amusing myself with side issues? And it annoys you? But it is not that. Once I went professionally to an archaeological expedition–and I learnt something there. In the course of an excavation, when something comes up out of the ground, everything is cleared away very carefully all around it. You take away the loose earth, and you scrape here and there with a knife until finally your object is there, all alone, ready to be drawn and photographed with no extraneous matter confusing it. That is what I have been seeking to do–clear away the extraneous matter so that we can see the truth–the naked shining truth."

"Good," said Race. "Let's have this naked shining truth. It wasn't Pennington. It wasn't young Allerton. I presume it wasn't Fleetwood. Let's hear who it was for a change."

"My friend, I am just about to tell you."

There was a knock on the door. Race uttered a muffled curse.

It was Dr. Bessner and Cornelia. The latter was looking upset.

"Oh, Colonel Race," she exclaimed, "Miss Bowers has just told me about Cousin Marie. It's been the most dreadful shock. She said she couldn't bear the responsibility all by herself any longer, and that I'd better know, as I was one of the family. I just couldn't believe it at first, but Dr. Bessner here has been just wonderful."

"No, no," protested the doctor modestly.

"He's been so kind, explaining it all, and how people really can't help it. He's had kleptomaniacs in his clinic. And he's explained to me how it's very often due to a deep-seated neurosis."

Cornelia repeated the words with awe.

"It's planted very deeply in the subconscious; sometimes it's just some little thing that happened when you were a child. And he's cured people by getting them to think back and remember what that little thing was."

Cornelia paused, drew a deep breath, and started off again.

"But it's worrying me dreadfully in case it all gets out. It would be too, too terrible in New York. Why, all the tabloids would have it. Cousin Marie and Mother and everybody—they'd never hold up their heads again."

Race sighed. "That's all right," he said. "This is Hush Hush House."

"I beg your pardon, Colonel Race?"

"What I was endeavouring to say was that anything short of murder is being hushed up."

"Oh!" Cornelia clasped her hands. "I'm *so* relieved. I've just been worrying and worrying."

"You have the heart too tender," said Dr. Bessner, and patted her benevolently on the shoulder. He said to the others, "She has a very sensitive and beautiful nature."

"Oh, I haven't really. You're too kind."

Poirot murmured, "Have you seen any more of Mr. Ferguson?"

Cornelia blushed.

"No—but Cousin Marie's been talking about him."

"It seems the young man is highly born," said Dr. Bessner. "I must confess he does not look it. His clothes are terrible. Not for a moment does he appear a well-bred man."

"And what do you think, Mademoiselle?"

"I think he must be just plain crazy," said Cornelia.

Poirot turned to the doctor. "How is your patient?"

"Ach, he is going on splendidly. I have just reassured the little Fräulein de Bellefort. Would you believe it, I found her in despair. Just because the fellow had a bit of a temperature this afternoon! But what could be more natural? It is amazing that he is not in a high fever now. But no, he is like some of our peasants; he has a magnificent constitution, the constitution of an ox. I have seen them with deep wounds that they hardly notice. It is the same with Mr. Doyle. His pulse is steady, his temperature only slightly above normal. I was able to pooh pooh the little lady's fears. All the same, it is ridiculous, *nicht wahr?* One minute you shoot a man; the next you are in hysterics in case he may not be doing well."

Cornelia said, "She loves him terribly, you see."

"Ach! But it is not sensible, that. If *you* loved a man, would you try and shoot him? No, you are sensible."

"I don't like things that go off with bangs anyway," said Cornelia.

"Naturally you do not. You are very feminine."

Race interrupted this scene of heavy approval. "Since Doyle is all right, there's no reason I shouldn't come along and resume our talk of this afternoon. He was just telling me about a telegram."

Dr. Bessner's bulk moved up and down appreciatively.

"Ho, ho, ho, it was very funny that! Doyle, he tells me about it. It was a telegram all about vegetables—potatoes, artichokes, leeks— Ach! pardon?"

With a stifled exclamation, Race had sat up in his chair.

"My God," he said. "So that's it! Richetti!"

He looked round on three uncomprehending faces.

"A new code—it was used in the South African rebellion. Potatoes mean machine guns, artichokes are high explosives—and so on. Richetti is no more an archaeologist than I am! He's a very dangerous agitator, a man who's killed more than once, and I'll swear that he's killed once again. Mrs. Doyle opened that telegram by mistake, you see. If she were ever to repeat what was in it before me, he knew his goose would be cooked!"

He turned to Poirot. "Am I right?" he asked. "Is Richetti the man?"

"He is *your* man," said Poirot. "I always thought there was something wrong about him! He was almost too word perfect in his rôle; he was all archaeologist, not enough human being."

He paused and then said: "But it was not Richetti who killed Linnet Doyle. For some time now I have known what I may express as the 'first half' of the murderer. Now I know the 'second half' also.

The picture is complete. But you understand that, although I know what must have happened, I have no proof that it happened. Intellectually the case is satisfying. Actually it is profoundly unsatisfactory. There is only one hope—a confession from the murderer."

Dr. Bessner raised his shoulders sceptically. "Ach! but that—it would be a miracle."

"I think not. Not under the circumstances."

Cornelia cried out: "But who is it? Aren't you going to tell us?"

Poirot's eyes ranged quietly over the three of them. Race, smiling sardonically, Bessner, still looking sceptical, Cornelia, her mouth hanging a little open gazing at him with eager eyes.

"*Mais oui,*" he said. "I like an audience, I must confess. I am vain, you see. I am puffed up with conceit. I like to say, 'See how clever is Hercule Poirot!' "

Race shifted a little in his chair.

"Well," he asked gently, "just how clever *is* Hercule Poirot?"

Shaking his head sadly from side to side Poirot said: "To begin with I was stupid—incredibly stupid. To me the stumbling block was the pistol—Jacqueline de Bellefort's pistol. Why had that pistol not been left on the scene of the crime? The idea of the murderer was quite plainly to incriminate her. Why then did the murderer take it away? I was so stupid that I thought of all sorts of fantastic reasons. The real one was very simple. The murderer took it away because he *had* to take it away—because he had no choice in the matter."

CHAPTER 28

"You and I, my friend," Poirot leaned toward Race, "started our investigation with a preconceived idea. That idea was that the crime was committed on the spur of the moment, without any preliminary planning. Somebody wished to remove Linnet Doyle and had seized their opportunity to do so at a moment when the crime would almost certainly be attributed to Jacqueline de Bellefort. It therefore followed that the person in question had overheard the scene between Jacqueline and Simon Doyle and had obtained possession of the pistol after the others had left the saloon.

"But, my friends, if that preconceived idea was wrong, the whole aspect of the case altered. And it *was* wrong! This was no spontaneous crime committed on the spur of the moment. It was, on the contrary, very carefully planned and accurately timed, with all the details meticulously worked out beforehand, even to the drugging of Hercule Poirot's bottle of wine on the night in question!

"But, yes, that is so! I was put to sleep so that there should be no possibility of my participating in the events of the night. It did just occur to me as a possibility. I drink wine; my two companions at table drink whisky and mineral water respectively. Nothing easier than to slip a dose of harmless narcotic into my bottle of wine—the bottles stand on the tables all day. But I dismissed the thought. It had been a hot day; I had been unusually tired; it was not really extraordinary that I should for once have slept heavily instead of lightly as I usually do.

"You see, I was still in the grip of the preconceived idea. If I had been drugged, that would have implied premeditation, it would mean that before seven-thirty, when dinner is served, the crime had already been decided upon; and that (always from the point of view of the preconceived idea) was absurd.

"The first blow to the preconceived idea was when the pistol was recovered from the Nile. To begin with, if we were right in our assumptions, the pistol ought never to have been thrown overboard at all. . . . And there was more to follow."

Poirot turned to Dr. Bessner.

"You, Dr. Bessner, examined Linnet Doyle's body. You will remember that the wound showed signs of scorching—that is to say, that the pistol had been placed close against the head before being fired."

Bessner nodded. "So. That is exact."

"But when the pistol was found it was wrapped in a velvet stole, and that velvet showed definite signs that a pistol had been fired through its folds, presumably under the impression that that would deaden the sound of the shot. But if the pistol had been fired through the velvet, there would have been no signs of burning on the victim's skin. Therefore, the shot fired through the stole could not have been the shot that killed Linnet Doyle. Could it have been the other shot—the one fired by Jacqueline de Bellefort at Simon Doyle? Again no, for there had been two witnesses of that shooting, and we knew all about it. It appeared, therefore, as though a *third* shot had been fired —one we knew nothing about. But only two shots had been fired from the pistol, and there was no hint or suggestion of another shot.

"Here we were face to face with a very curious unexplained circumstance. The next interesting point was the fact that in Linnet Doyle's cabin I found two bottles of coloured nail polish. Now ladies very often vary the colour of their nails, but so far Linnet Doyle's nails had always been the shade called Cardinal—a deep dark red. The other bottle was labelled Rose, which is a shade of pale pink, but the few drops remaining in the bottle were not pale pink but a bright red. I was sufficiently curious to take out the stopper and sniff. Instead of the usual strong odour of pear drops, the bottle smelt of vinegar! That is to say, it suggested that the drop or two of fluid in it was red ink. Now there is no reason why Madame Doyle should not have had a bottle of red ink, but it would have been more natural if she had had red ink in a red ink bottle and not in a nail polish bottle. It suggested a link with the faintly stained handkerchief which had been wrapped round the pistol. Red ink washes out quickly but always leaves a pale pink stain.

"I should perhaps have arrived at the truth with these slender indications, but an event occurred which rendered all doubt superfluous. Louise Bourget was killed in circumstances which pointed unmistakably to the fact that she had been blackmailing the murderer. Not only was a fragment of a *mille* franc note still clasped in her hand, but I remembered some very significant words she had used this morning.

"Listen carefully, for here is the crux of the whole matter. When I asked her if she had seen anything the previous night she gave this very curious answer: 'Naturally, if I had been unable to sleep, if I had mounted the stairs, *then* perhaps I might have seen this assassin, this monster enter or leave Madame's cabin. . . .' Now what exactly did that tell us?"

Bessner, his nose wrinkling with intellectual interest, replied promptly, "It told you that she *had* mounted the stair."

"No, no; you fail to see the point. Why should she have said that, to *us?*"

"To convey a hint."

"But why *hint* to us? If she knows who the murderer is, there are two courses open to her—to tell us the truth, or to hold her tongue and demand money for her silence from the person concerned! But she does neither. She neither says promptly: 'I saw nobody. I was asleep.' Nor does she say, 'Yes, I saw someone, and it was so and so.' Why use that significant indeterminate rigmarole of words? *Parbleu,* there can be only one reason! She is hinting to the murderer; therefore the murderer must have been present at the time. But, besides myself and Colonel Race, only two people were present—Simon Doyle and Dr. Bessner."

The doctor sprang up with a roar.

"Ach! what is that you say? You accuse me? Again? But it is ridiculous—beneath contempt."

Poirot said sharply: "Be quiet. I am telling you what I thought at the time. Let us remain impersonal."

"He doesn't mean he thinks it's you now," said Cornelia soothingly.

Poirot went on quickly: "So it lay there—between Simon Doyle and Dr. Bessner. But what reason has Bessner to kill Linnet Doyle? None, so far as I know. Simon Doyle, then? But that was impossible! There were plenty of witnesses who could swear that Doyle never left the saloon that evening until the quarrel broke out. After that he was wounded and it would then have been physically impossible for him to have done so. Had I good evidence on both those points? Yes, I had the evidence of Mademoiselle Robson, of Jim Fanthorp and of Jacqueline de Bellefort as to the first, and I had the skilled testimony of Dr. Bessner and of Mademoiselle Bowers as to the other. No doubt was possible.

"So Dr. Bessner *must* be the guilty one. In favour of this theory there was the fact that the maid had been stabbed with a surgical knife. On the other hand Bessner had deliberately called attention to this fact.

"And then, my friends, a second perfectly indisputable fact became apparent to me. Louise Bourget's hint could not have been intended for Dr. Bessner, because she could perfectly well have spoken to him in private at any time she liked. There was one person, *and one person only,* who corresponded to her necessity—Simon Doyle! Simon Doyle was wounded, was constantly attended by a doctor, was in that doctor's cabin. It was to him therefore that she risked saying those ambiguous words, in case she might not get another chance. And I remembered how she had gone on, turning to him: 'Monsieur, I implore you—you see how it is? What can I say?' And his answer, 'My good girl, don't be a fool. Nobody thinks you saw or heard anything. You'll be quite all right. I'll look after you. Nobody's accusing you of anything.' That was the assurance she wanted, and she got it!"

Bessner uttered a colossal snort.

"Ach! it is foolish, that! Do you think a man with a fractured bone and a splint on his leg could go walking about the boat and stabbing people? I tell you, it was *impossible* for Simon Doyle to leave his cabin."

Poirot said gently: "I know. That is quite true. The thing was impossible. It was impossible, but it was also true! There could be only one logical meaning behind Louise Bourget's words.

"So I returned to the beginning and reviewed the crime in the light of this new knowledge. Was it possible that in the period preceding the quarrel Simon Doyle had left the saloon and the others had forgotten or not noticed it? I could not see that that was possible. Could the skilled testimony of Dr. Bessner and Mademoiselle Bowers be disregarded? Again I felt sure it could not. But, I remembered, there was a gap between the two. Simon Doyle had been alone in the saloon for a period of five minutes, and the skilled testimony of Dr. Bessner only applied to the time after that period. For that period we had only the evidence of visual appearance, and, though apparently that was perfectly sound, it was no longer certain. What had actually been *seen*—leaving assumption out of the question?

"Mademoiselle Robson had seen Mademoiselle de Bellefort fire her pistol, had seen Simon Doyle collapse onto a chair, had seen him clasp a handkerchief to his leg and seen that handkerchief gradually soak through red. What had Monsieur Fanthorp heard and seen? He heard a shot, he found Doyle with a red-stained handkerchief clasped to his leg. What had happened then? Doyle had been very insistent that Mademoiselle de Bellefort should be got away, that she should not be left alone. After that, he suggested that Fanthorp should get hold of the doctor.

"Accordingly Mademoiselle Robson and Monsieur Fanthorp go out with Mademoiselle de Bellefort and for the next five minutes they are busy, on the port side of the deck. Mademoiselle Bowers', Dr. Bessner's and Mademoiselle de Bellefort's cabins are all on the port side. Two minutes are all that Simon Doyle needs. He picks up the pistol from under the sofa, slips out of his shoes, runs like a hare silently along the starboard deck, enters his wife's cabin, creeps up to her as she lies asleep, shoots her through the head, puts the bottle that has contained the red ink on her washstand (it mustn't be found on him) runs back, gets hold of Mademoiselle Van Schuyler's velvet stole, which he has quietly stuffed down the side of a chair in readiness, muffles it round the pistol and fires a bullet into his leg. His chair into which he falls (in genuine agony this time) is by a window. He lifts the window and throws the pistol (wrapped up with the telltale handkerchief in the velvet stole) into the Nile."

"Impossible!" said Race.

"No, my friend, not *impossible*. Remember the evidence of Tim Allerton. He heard a pop—*followed* by a splash. And he heard something else—the footsteps of a man running—a man running past his door. But nobody should have been running along the starboard side of the deck. What he heard was the stockinged feet of Simon Doyle running past his cabin."

Race said: "I still say it's impossible. No man could work out the whole caboodle like that in a flash—especially a chap like Doyle who is slow in his mental processes."

"But very quick and deft in his physical actions!"

"That, yes. But he wouldn't be capable of thinking the whole thing out."

"But he did not think it out himself, my friend. That is where we were all wrong. It looked like a crime committed on the spur of the moment, but it was *not* a crime committed on the spur of the moment. As I say it was a very cleverly planned and well thought out piece of work. It could not be *chance* that Simon Doyle had a bottle of red ink in his pocket. No, it must be *design*. It was not *chance* that he had a plain unmarked handkerchief with him. It was not *chance* that Jacqueline de Bellefort's foot kicked the pistol under the settee, where it would be out of sight and unremembered until later."

"Jacqueline?"

"Certainly. The two halves of the murderer. What gave Simon his alibi? The shot fired by Jacqueline. What gave Jacqueline *her* alibi? The insistence of Simon, which resulted in a hospital nurse remaining with her all night. There, between the two of them, you get all the qualities you require—the cool, resourceful, planning brain, Jacqueline de Bellefort's brain, and the man of action to carry it out with incredible swiftness and timing.

"Look at it the right way, and it answers every question. Simon Doyle and Jacqueline had been lovers. Realize that they are still lovers, and it is all clear. Simon does away with his rich wife, inherits her money, and in due course will marry his old love. It was all very ingenious. The persecution of Madame Doyle by Jacqueline, all part of the plan. Simon's pretended rage. . . . And yet—there were lapses. He held forth to me once about possessive women—held forth with real bitterness. It ought to have been clear to me that it was his wife he was thinking about—not Jacqueline. Then his manner to his wife in public. An ordinary, inarticulate Englishman, such as Simon Doyle, is very embarrassed at showing any affection. Simon was not a really good actor. He overdid the devoted manner. That conversation I had with Mademoiselle Jacqueline, too, when she pretended that somebody had overheard. *I* saw no one. And there *was* no one! But it was to be a useful red herring later. Then one night on this boat I thought I heard Simon and Linnet outside my cabin. He was saying, 'We've got to go through with it now.' It was Doyle all right, but it was to Jacqueline he was speaking.

"The final drama was perfectly planned and timed. There was a sleeping draught for me, in case I might put an inconvenient finger in the pie. There was the selection of Mademoiselle Robson as a witness—the working up of the scene, Mademoiselle de Bellefort's exaggerated remorse and hysterics. She made a good deal of noise, in case the shot should be heard. *En vérité,* it was an extraordinarily clever idea. Jacqueline says she has shot Doyle; Mademoiselle Robson says so; Fanthorp says so—and when Simon's leg is examined he *has* been shot. It looks unanswerable! For both of them there is a perfect alibi—at the cost, it is true, of a certain amount of pain and risk to Simon Doyle, but it is necessary that his wound should definitely disable him.

"And then the plan goes wrong. Louise Bourget has been wakeful. She has come up the stairway and she has seen Simon Doyle run along to his wife's cabin and come back. Easy enough to piece together what has happened the following day. And so she makes her greedy bid for hush money, and in so doing signs her death warrant."

"But Mr. Doyle couldn't have killed *her?*" Cornelia objected.

"No, the other partner did that murder. As soon as he can, Simon Doyle asks to see Jacqueline. He even asks me to leave them alone together. He tells her then of the new danger. They must act at once. He knows where Bessner's scalpels are kept. After the crime the scalpel is wiped and returned, and then, very late and rather out of breath, Jacqueline de Bellefort hurries in to lunch.

"And still all is not well, for Madame Otterbourne has seen Jacqueline go into Louise Bourget's cabin. And she comes hot foot to tell Simon about it. Jacqueline is the murderess. Do you remember how Simon shouted at the poor woman? Nerves, we thought. But the door was open and he was trying to convey the danger to his accomplice. She heard and she acted—acted like lightning. She remembered Pennington had talked about a revolver. She got hold of it, crept up outside the door, listened and, at the critical moment, fired. She boasted once that she was a good shot, and her boast was not an idle one.

"I remarked after that third crime that there were three ways the murderer could have gone. I meant that he could have gone aft (in which case Tim Allerton was the criminal) he could have gone over the side (very improbable) or he could have gone into a cabin. Jacqueline's cabin was just two away from Dr. Bessner's. She had only to throw down the revolver, bolt into the cabin, ruffle her hair and fling herself down on the bunk. It was risky, but it was the only possible chance."

There was a silence, then Race asked, "What happened to the first bullet fired at Doyle by the girl?"

"I think it went into the table. There is a recently made hole there. I think Doyle had time to dig it out with a penknife and fling it through the window. He had, of course, a spare cartridge, so that it would appear that only two shots had been fired."

Cornelia sighed. "They thought of everything," she said. "It's—horrible!"

Poirot was silent. But it was not a modest silence. His eyes seemed to be saying: "You are wrong. They didn't allow for Hercule Poirot."

Aloud he said, "And now, Doctor, we will go and have a word with your patient."

CHAPTER 29

IT WAS very much later that evening that Hercule Poirot came and knocked on the door of a cabin.

A voice said "Come in" and he entered.

Jacqueline de Bellefort was sitting in a chair. In another chair, close against the wall, sat the big stewardess.

Jacqueline's eyes surveyed Poirot thoughtfully. She made a gesture toward the stewardess.

"Can she go?"

Poirot nodded to the woman and she went out. Poirot drew up her chair and sat down near Jacqueline. Neither of them spoke. Poirot's face was unhappy.

In the end it was the girl who spoke first.

"Well," she said, "it is all over! You were too clever for us, Monsieur Poirot."

Poirot sighed. He spread out his hands. He seemed strangely dumb.

"All the same," said Jacqueline reflectively, "I can't really see that you had much proof. You were quite right, of course, but if we'd bluffed you out—"

"In no other way, Mademoiselle, could the thing have happened."

"That's proof enough for a logical mind, but I don't believe it would have convinced a jury. Oh, well—it can't be helped. You sprang it all on Simon, and he went down like a ninepin. He just lost his head utterly, poor lamb, and admitted everything." She shook her head. "He's a bad loser."

"But you, Mademoiselle, are a good loser."

She laughed suddenly—a queer, gay, defiant little laugh.

"Oh, yes, I'm a good loser all right." She looked at him.

She said suddenly and impulsively: "Don't mind so much, Monsieur Poirot! About me, I mean. You do mind, don't you?"

"Yes, Mademoiselle."

"But it wouldn't have occurred to you to let me off?"

Hercule Poirot said quietly, "No."

She nodded her head in quiet agreement.

"No, it's no use being sentimental. I might do it again. . . . I'm not a safe person any longer. I can feel that myself. . . ." She went on broodingly: "It's so dreadfully easy—killing people. And you begin to feel that it doesn't matter . . . that it's only *you* that matters! It's dangerous—that."

She paused, then said with a little smile: "You did your best for me, you know. That night at Assuan—you told me not to open my heart to evil. . . . Did you realize then what was in my mind?"

He shook his head.

"I only knew that what I said was true."

"It was true. I could have stopped, then, you know. I nearly did. . . . I could have told Simon that I wouldn't go on with it. . . . But then perhaps—"

She broke off. She said: "Would you like to hear about it? From the beginning?"

"If you care to tell me, Mademoiselle."

"I think I want to tell you. It was all very simple really. You see, Simon and I loved each other. . . ."

It was a matter-of-fact statement, yet, underneath the lightness of her tone, there were echoes. . . .

Poirot said simply, "And for you love would have been enough, but not for him."

"You might put it that way, perhaps. But you don't quite understand Simon. You see, he's always wanted money so dreadfully. He likes all the things you get with money—horses and yachts and sport— nice things, all of them, things a man ought to be keen about. And he'd never been able to have any of them. He's awfully simple, Simon is. He wants things just as a child wants them—you know—terribly.

"All the same he never tried to marry anybody rich and horrid. He wasn't that sort. And then we met—and—and that sort of settled things. Only we didn't see when we'd be able to marry. He'd had rather a decent job, but he'd lost it. In a way it was his own fault. He tried to do something smart over money, and got found out at once. I don't believe he really meant to be dishonest. He just thought it was the sort of thing people did in the City."

A flicker passed over her listener's face, but he guarded his tongue.

"There we were, up against it; and then I thought of Linnet and her new country house, and I rushed off to her. You know, Monsieur Poirot, I loved Linnet, really I did. She was my best friend, and I never dreamed that anything would ever come between us. I just thought how lucky it was she was rich. It might make all the difference to me and Simon if she'd give him a job. And she was aw- fully sweet about it and told me to bring Simon down to see her. It was about then you saw us that night at Chez Ma Tante. We were making whoopee, although we couldn't really afford it."

She paused, sighed, then went on: "What I'm going to say now is quite true, Monsieur Poirot. Even though Linnet is dead, it doesn't alter the truth. That's why I'm not really sorry about her, even now. She went all out to get Simon away from me. That's the absolute truth! I don't think she even hesitated for more than about a minute. I was her friend, but she didn't care. She just went baldheaded for Simon. . . .

"And Simon didn't care a damn about her! I talked a lot to you about glamour, but of course that wasn't true. He didn't want Linnet. He thought her good-looking but terribly bossy, and he hated bossy women! The whole thing embarrassed him frightfully. But he did like the thought of her money.

"Of course I saw that . . . and at last I suggested to him that it might be a good thing if he—got rid of me and married Linnet. But he scouted the idea. He said, money or no money, it would be hell to be married to her. He said his idea of having money was to have it himself—not to have a rich wife holding the purse strings. 'I'd be a kind of damned Prince Consort,' he said to me. He said, too, that he didn't want anyone but me. . . .

"I think I know when the idea came into his head. He said one day, 'If I'd any luck, I'd marry her and she'd die in about a year and leave me all the boodle.' And then a queer startled look came into his eyes. That was when he first thought of it. . . .

"He talked about it a good deal, one way and another—about how convenient it would be if Linnet died. I said it was an awful idea, and then he shut up about it. Then, one day, I found him reading up all about arsenic. I taxed him with it then, and he laughed and said: 'Nothing venture, nothing have! It's about the only time in my life I shall be near to touching a fat lot of money.'

"After a bit I saw that he'd made up his mind. And I was terrified —simply terrified. Because, you see, I realized that he'd never pull it off. He's so childishly simple. He'd have no kind of subtlety about it— and he's got no imagination. He would probably have just bunged arsenic into her and assumed the doctor would say she'd died of gastritis. He always thought things would go right.

"So I had to come into it, too, to look after him. . . ."

She said it very simply but in complete good faith. Poirot had no doubt whatever that her motive had been exactly what she said it was. She herself had not coveted Linnet Ridgeway's money, but she had loved Simon Doyle, had loved him beyond reason and beyond rectitude and beyond pity.

"I thought and I thought—trying to work out a plan. It seemed to me that the basis of the idea ought to be a kind of two-handed alibi. You know—if Simon and I could somehow or other give evidence against each other, but actually that evidence would clear us of everything. It would be easy enough for me to pretend to hate Simon. It was quite a likely thing to happpen under the circumstances. Then, if Linnet was killed, I should probably be suspected, so it would be better if I was suspected right away. We worked out details little by little. I wanted it to be so that, if anything went wrong, they'd get me and not Simon. But Simon was worried about me.

"The only thing I was glad about was that I hadn't got to do *it*. I simply couldn't have! Not go along in cold blood and kill her when she was asleep! You see, I hadn't forgiven her—I think I could have killed her face to face, but not the other way. . . .

"We worked everything out carefully. Even then, Simon went and wrote a J in blood, which was a silly melodramatic thing to do. It's just the sort of thing he *would* think of! But it went off all right."

Poirot nodded.

"Yes. It was not your fault that Louise Bourget could not sleep that night. . . . And afterward, Mademoiselle?"

She met his eyes squarely.

"Yes," she said, "it's rather horrible, isn't it? I can't believe that I—did that! I know now what you meant by opening your heart to evil. . . . You know pretty well how it happened. Louise made it clear to Simon that she knew. Simon got you to bring me to him. As soon as we were alone together he told me what had happened. He told me what I'd got to do. I wasn't even horrified. I was so afraid—so deadly afraid. . . . That's what murder does to you. Simon and I were safe—quite safe—except for this miserable blackmailing French girl. I took her all the money we could get hold of. I pretended to grovel. And then, when she was counting the money, I—did it! It was quite easy. That's what's so horribly, horribly frightening about it. . . . It's so terribly easy. . . .

"And even then we weren't safe. Mrs. Otterbourne had seen me. She came triumphantly along the deck looking for you and Colonel Race. I'd no time to think. I just acted like a flash. It was almost exciting. I knew it was touch or go that time. That seemed to make it better. . . ."

She stopped again.

"Do you remember when you came into my cabin afterward? You said you were not sure why you had come. I was so miserable—so terrified. I thought Simon was going to die. . . ."

"And I—was hoping it," said Poirot.

Jacqueline nodded.

"Yes, it would have been better for him that way."

"That was not my thought."

Jacqueline looked at the sternness of his face.

She said gently: "Don't mind so much for me, Monsieur Poirot. After all, I've lived hard always, you know. If we'd won out, I'd have been very happy and enjoyed things and probably should never have regretted anything. As it is—well, one goes through with it."

She added: "I suppose the stewardess is in attendance to see I don't hang myself or swallow a miraculous capsule of prussic acid as people always do in books. You needn't be afraid! I shan't do that. It will be easier for Simon if I'm standing by."

Poirot got up. Jacqueline rose also. She said with a sudden smile: "Do you remember when I said I must follow my star? You said it might be a false star. And I said, 'That very bad star, that star fall down.' "

He went out onto the deck with her laughter ringing in his ears.

CHAPTER 30

IT WAS early dawn when they came into Shellâl. The rocks came down grimly to the water's edge.

Poirot murmured, *"Quel pays sauvage!"*

Race stood beside him. "Well," he said, "we've done our job. I've arranged for Richetti to be taken ashore first. Glad we've got him. He's been a slippery customer, I can tell you. Given us the slip dozens of times."

He went on: "We must get hold of a stretcher for Doyle. Remarkable how he went to pieces."

"Not really," said Poirot. "That boyish type of criminal is usually intensely vain. Once prick the bubble of their self-esteem and it is finished! They go to pieces like children."

"Deserves to be hanged," said Race. "He's a cold-blooded scoundrel. I'm sorry for the girl—but there's nothing to be done about it."

Poirot shook his head.

"People say love justifies everything, but that is not true. . . . Women who care for men as Jacqueline cares for Simon Doyle are very dangerous. It is what I said when I saw her first. 'She cares too much, that little one!' It is true."

Cornelia Robson came up beside him.

"Oh," she said, "we're nearly in."

She paused a minute or two then added, "I've been with her."

"With Mademoiselle de Bellefort?"

"Yes. I felt it was kind of awful for her boxed up with that stewardess. Cousin Marie's very angry though, I'm afraid."

Miss Van Schuyler was progressing slowly down the deck toward them. Her eyes were venomous.

"Cornelia," she snapped, "you've behaved outrageously. I shall send you straight home."

Cornelia took a deep breath. "I'm sorry, Cousin Marie, but I'm not going home. I'm going to get married."

"So you've seen sense at last," snapped the old lady.

Ferguson came striding round the corner of the deck. He said: "Cornelia, what's this I hear? It's not true!"

"It's quite true," said Cornelia. "I'm going to marry Dr. Bessner. He asked me last night."

"And why are you going to marry him?" asked Ferguson furiously. "Simply because he's rich."

"No, I'm not," said Cornelia indignantly. "I like him. He's kind, and he knows a lot. And I've always been interested in sick folks and clinics, and I shall have just a wonderful life with him."

"Do you mean to say," asked Mr. Ferguson incredulously, "that you'd rather marry that disgusting old man than Me?"

"Yes, I would. You're not reliable! You wouldn't be at all a comfortable sort of person to live with. And he's *not* old. He's not fifty yet."

"He's got a stomach," said Mr. Ferguson venomously.

"Well, I've got round shoulders," retorted Cornelia. "What one looks like doesn't matter. He says I really could help him in his work, and he's going to teach me all about neuroses."

She moved away. Ferguson said to Poirot, "Do you think she really means that?"

"Certainly."

"She prefers that pompous old bore to Me?"

"Undoubtedly."

"The girl's mad," declared Ferguson.

Poirot's eyes twinkled.

"She is a woman of an original mind," he said. "It is probably the first time you have met one."

The boat drew in to the landing stage. A cordon had been drawn round the passengers. They had been asked to wait before disembarking.

Richetti, dark faced and sullen, was marched ashore by two engineers.

Then, after a certain amount of delay, a stretcher was brought. Simon Doyle was carried along the deck to the gangway.

He looked a different man—cringing, frightened, all his boyish insouciance vanished.

Jacqueline de Bellefort followed. A stewardess walked beside her. She was pale but otherwise looked much as usual. She came up to the stretcher.

"Hullo, Simon," she said.

He looked up at her quickly. The old boyish look came back to his face for a moment.

"I messed it up," he said. "Lost my head and admitted everything! Sorry, Jackie. I've let you down."

She smiled at him then.

"It's all right, Simon," she said. "A fool's game, and we've lost. That's all."

She stood aside. The bearer picked up the handles of the stretcher. Jacqueline bent down and tied the lace of her shoe. Then her hand went to her stocking top and she straightened up with something in her hand.

There was a sharp explosive "pop."

Simon Doyle gave one convulsed shudder and then lay still.

Jacqueline de Bellefort nodded. She stood for a minute, pistol in hand. She gave a fleeting smile at Poirot.

Then, as Race jumped forward, she turned the little glittering toy against her heart and pressed the trigger.

She sank down in a soft huddled heap.

Race shouted, "Where the devil did she get that pistol?"

Poirot felt a hand on his arm. Mrs. Allerton said softly, "You—knew?"

He nodded. "She had a pair of these pistols. I realized that when I heard that one had been found in Rosalie Otterbourne's handbag the day of the search. Jacqueline sat at the same table as they did. When she realized that there was going to be a search, she slipped it into the other girl's handbag. Later she went to Rosalie's cabin and got it back, after having distracted her attention with a comparison of lipsticks. As both she and her cabin had been searched yesterday, it wasn't thought necessary to do it again."

Mrs. Allerton said, "You wanted her to take that way out?"

"Yes. But she would not take it alone. That is why Simon Doyle has died an easier death than he deserved."

Mrs. Allerton shivered. "Love can be a very frightening thing."

"That is why most great love stories are tragedies."

Mrs. Allerton's eyes rested upon Tim and Rosalie, standing side by side in the sunlight, and she said suddenly and passionately, "But thank God, there is happiness in the world."

"As you say, Madame, thank God for it."

Presently the passengers went ashore.

Later the bodies of Louise Bourget and Mrs. Otterbourne were carried off the *Karnak*.

Lastly the body of Linnet Doyle was brought ashore, and all over the world wires began to hum, telling the public that Linnet Doyle, who had been Linnet Ridgeway, the famous, the beautiful, the wealthy Linnet Doyle was dead . . .

Sir George Wode read about it in his London club, and Sterndale Rockford in New York, and Joanna Southwood in Switzerland, and it was discussed in the bar of the Three Crowns in Malton-under-Wode.

And Mr. Burnaby's lean friend said, "Well, it didn't seem fair, her having everything."

And Mr. Burnaby said acutely, "Well, it doesn't seem to have done her much good, poor lass."

But after a while they stopped talking about her and discussed instead who was going to win the Grand National. For, as Mr. Ferguson was saying at that minute in Luxor, it is not the past that matters but the future.